F
GAB

Gabriel, Marius.

The mask of time.

$22.95

DATE			

THE MASK of TIME

By Marius Gabriel
from Bantam Books

THE ORIGINAL SIN
THE MASK OF TIME

MARIUS GABRIEL

THE MASK

of TIME

BANTAM BOOKS

NEW YORK · TORONTO · LONDON · SYDNEY · AUCKLAND

THE MASK OF TIME
A Bantam Book / April 1994

Book design by Donna Sinisgalli

Library of Congress Cataloging-in-Publication Data

Gabriel, Marius.
    The mask of time / Marius Gabriel.
      p.   cm.
    ISBN 0-553-08988-9
    1. World War, 1939–1945—Prisoners and prisons—Fiction.
  2. Journalists—United States—Fiction.   3. Family—United
States—Fiction.   I. Title.
    PR6057.A273M37   1994
    823'.914—dc20   93–26833
                                                          CIP

Published simultaneously in the United States and Canada

Bantam Books are published by Bantam Books, a division of Bantam
Doubleday Dell Publishing Group, Inc. Its trademark, consisting of
the words "Bantam Books" and the portrayal of a rooster, is
Registered in U.S. Patent and Trademark Office and in other
countries. Marca Registrada. Bantam Books, 1540 Broadway, New
York, New York 10036.

PRINTED IN THE UNITED STATES OF AMERICA

BVG   0   9   8   7   6   5   4   3   2   1

*F*OR
LINDA
AND
THEODORE

Acknowledgments

Once again, my thanks go to Elizabeth Murray for her invaluable help; also to Gene Young and Kate Parkin; to Vivienne Schuster and Jane Gelfman; to my beloved parents; and most of all, to Linda.

They stript Joseph out of his coat, his coat of many colours that was on him; and they took him, and cast him into a pit.

GENESIS 37:23

Prologue:

BIRTHS, DEATHS, MARRIAGES

1 9 4 5

ITALY

The labor had started the previous night. Now, as the evening of the second day closed in, the girl was exhausted and ill. She had once been extremely pretty, with sparkling brown eyes and raven hair. But now there was little vestige of that enchantment. Her hair clung limply to her wan face. Her eyes had sunk into their sockets, and her lips were cracked. As the convulsions arched her swollen body, a rasping sound was forced from her throat; she was becoming too weak to scream.

The midwife sponged her face gently. "Rest now, Candida," she advised. "Rest awhile."

Candida's eyes were blurred. "It won't . . . come," she whispered.

"Of course it will come. It has to get out, doesn't it? Don't fret. Just rest until the contractions come again."

"Drink this, *cara*." Candida's mother stooped at her other side, holding the cup to her daughter's lips. Candida tried to swallow, but managed only to moisten her lips. She closed her eyes again, and her head fell limply back on the pillows.

The birth bed had been made up in the "best" room of the rambling old farmhouse, a room that was only ever used for grand occasions like births, or marriages, or deaths. Not that this was a grand birth. It wore an air of desertion. Apart from the two women at the bedside, the only other person in the house was Teo, Candida's brother, who sat huddled by the fire in the back room and who flinched each time Candida screamed. Nobody else had come near.

The midwife looked at Candida's mother and jerked her head at the door. They went out into the passageway and conferred in low voices.

"She still isn't dilating enough. I don't know why. Maybe she's too small in the bone."

"Where's that damned doctor?"

"He's coming, Rosa. He'll be here soon." She laid her hand on the other woman's arm. "I can't hear the babe's heart anymore. I think it might be dead already."

"That would be a mercy for all of us." Rosa Cipriani's face was prematurely lined and reflected a hard strength. An expression of rage suddenly crossed it. "God has cursed the child," she said bitterly.

"Don't talk like that," the midwife whispered.

"He has cursed us all. He's already sent *them* to hell," Rosa said through clenched teeth.

A low moan came from the front room, rising to a hoarse shriek that made them hurry back in. Candida had lifted herself up on her elbows. The contractions had returned. Her head was thrown back, the veins and tendons of her throat showing stark.

"Oh my God," she gasped. "Oh my God. Help me. *Help me.*"

The Doctor Arrived at last. He came in the back door, a portly little man with a balding head. He stamped mud from his boots irritably, shoulders hunched. Teo's face lifted from his hands. His eyes met the doctor's for a moment.

"This time we'll get the little bastard out," the doctor said grimly. It was the third time he had been called to the farmhouse, and he hated the long, muddy, uphill climb. He went into the front room, slamming the door behind him.

Teo lifted his eyes to the crucifix that hung over the stove. The apocalypse had come. In the last months of the war that had just ended, great cities had been razed, populous lands had sunk in blood, horror had piled on horror millionfold. Among the devastation and death, this tiny sparrow's life seemed matterless. And yet it overwhelmed him.

"Aren't you satisfied?" he whispered to the crucifix. "Do you want her, too?"

He started as screams began again in the front room. They tore at him like a knife, terrible screams, transcending exhaustion and weakness.

The door of the front room burst open, and the midwife came hurrying through, her face tense. She wrapped her hands in cloths and lifted the copper pan of hot water that steamed on the stove.

"Is it coming?" Teo asked her urgently.

But she had no time to answer him. She carried the hot water into the front room, and the door slammed behind her.

Silence Reigned Over *Il Noce*.

Candida was no longer crying out. She had made no sound for a long while. It must be over at last. But there was no cry of a babe. Teo crushed his hands together and tried not to imagine what the little doctor might have done to Candida in there. She should have been taken to the hospital to give birth. They should not have hidden her up here in the mountains, with her shame and her grief.

He waited, dread weighing him down.

Finally, the door of the front room opened. The doctor emerged, carrying his black bag. His swollen drinker's face was weary, his eyes almost closed. Rosa Cipriani followed him. Her face looked as though it was carved out of stone, and in that moment Teo felt a single terrible pain seize his heart.

The doctor took two pieces of paper from his bag and sat at the table to write on them. When he had filled both certificates out, he pushed them across to Rosa. Rosa did not touch or look at them.

"Let the midwife clear up," the doctor said. "She knows what to do." He screwed the cap back on his pen and looked up at Rosa. "You understand?"

Rosa nodded imperceptibly.

"Better go and call the priest, then."

And with that, he snapped his black bag closed and went out of the house.

Rosa Cipriani remained where she was for a while. Teo tried to speak to his mother, but could not.

Finally, she took her old shawl from its peg by the door and went out into the night like a sleepwalker.

It took Teo a long while to get out of the chair. A Greek bullet had smashed his left femur in 1941. Now, tuberculosis had been diagnosed in the crippled bone. Soon, he would not be able to move at all, except in a wheelchair. He pushed himself to the table laboriously and looked at the two pieces of paper. Both were death certificates. The first was for Candida Cipriani. The second was for her stillborn infant, Catarina Eleonora.

LATVIA

"I am an American."

He had said the words so many times that they had started to lose meaning, even to him. He had shouted them, whispered them, spoken them like a reasonable man, screamed them like an animal.

He had used every language he knew, and many that he did not: English, Italian, German, French, Russian, Latvian, Yiddish, Polish. But no one had listened. There were so many others screaming at the same time, in such a Babel of languages, that his words had been lost. And though the guards wore Russian uniforms, they had Mongoloid faces, and God alone knew what language they spoke.

He grasped at the struggling bodies that barred his way, pulling, shoving. "I am an *American*."

And in any case, the bleak wind from the steppes swept all words away. Words had little relevance in this world. He had been in many Displaced Persons camps run by the Red Army, each one indistinguishable from the others. Each time a muddy chaos ringed by barbed wire, a huddled mass of thin bodies in gray rags, each human cipher verminous and indistinguishable from the next. Outside the barbed wire, a landscape laid waste by the retreating Nazis.

It was an abyss, this world of the refugees. A desolate and forlorn place, haunted by the displaced, the exiled, the orphaned, the fugitive. Millions of them, their lives smashed by war, swept like chaff on the whirlwinds that had raged from one end of Europe to the other for six years.

It was a world of degradation and hunger, where brutality passed for order, where inhuman indifference passed for compassion.

Yet even here there was a deeper terror. An ultimate terror:

To be taken from the camps and shipped back to Lithuania, Latvia, Estonia, Poland, Czechoslovakia, Hungary, Yugoslavia, Romania. To be sent back to the lands Stalin had wrested from Hitler. To be shut forever behind the Iron Curtain that had already been closed across half of Europe. That was a fate worse even than the refugee camps. An annihilation even more complete.

And if he missed this moment, that fate would befall him. He knew it. They all knew it.

"I am an American," he shouted, thrusting through the pack of writhing bodies. An elbow smashed into his ribs, hands clawed at his eyes. He lunged forward to the truck. A fist swung into his face, pulping his lips against his teeth. He did not waste time in defending his flesh. He had learned better than that. He did not even pause to wipe the blood that was now streaming from his mouth. His eyes were fixed on the official from Moscow who stood irresolutely on the running board of the truck, vainly trying to keep the door between his clean uniform and the pack of half-human wolves who swarmed around him.

"*I am an American,*" he screamed again, clambering on the backs of an elderly couple who had been forced to their knees by the mob. "*An American! An American!*" He felt the old man's spine crumple beneath his boots and hurled himself toward the official, his arms outstretched.

Yes, because he had something more than words. Something of infinitely more value.

He had papers.

Papers that proved that his name was Joseph, that he was an American, that he did not belong here in hell.

He was almost at the truck now, eyes glaring, every muscle in his weakened body straining with the superhuman effort. He got one hand on the handle of the door, grasped it with convulsive urgency. He dragged himself up over the writhing bodies, screaming over the dozens of other voices.

The official was looking frightened now. He had a pudgy civilian's face, a neatly cropped mustache between a round nose and a well-fed mouth. He represented sanity. Salvation. But the wolves were alarming him. His eyes caught Joseph's for a moment. *"I am an American,"* Joseph screamed at him.

The official's eyes slid away. His plump face contorted with a mixture of disgust and alarm. He swung himself abruptly back into the seat of the truck and tried to close the door.

But Joseph was clinging to the handle as though his life depended on it. The elderly couple had collapsed under the trampling feet now, and he hung there like a half-crucified Christ, one hand reaching up, clutching his papers.

The engine of the truck started up with a cough of diesel fumes. The panic intensified. The others raked at him with their nails, tried to pull his arms away. He kicked out at them wildly, waving his papers.

Then a club delivered an expert double blow to his kidneys. The guards had arrived. Only a guard could have delivered such a blow. The terrible pain crushed him, forcing the breath from his lungs. He could no longer scream. Darkness rushed in front of his eyes. But he clung to the door of the truck somehow, and with the last of his strength, threw his papers through the open window.

He threw them, knowing he was perhaps throwing away the major part of his existence, the only things that could prove his shadowy identity and rescue him from hell. He threw them knowing it was his last chance at life.

The club struck again, smashing into his neck. It was all over. He fell to the ground and crawled in the mud, knowing that if he did not move fast, the Russians' boots would break his ribs, and then he would die.

He had cast his die. Had cast and lost. He had no emotions left. He had expended them all.

"Wait."

The voice spoke in Russian, far above him.

"That man. Bring him here."

Hands grasped Joseph's arms, dragged him to his feet. He tried to lift his head, his eyes glazed.

"You. Are these your papers?"

The official from Moscow had opened the door of the truck again and was standing on the running board, the grimy bundle of papers in his hand. He jumped down in front of Joseph. The guards were driving the despairing gray mass of displaced persons back through the barbed-wire gate.

"Are these your papers?" the official repeated.

Joseph nodded, still unable to speak.

"You are an American soldier?"

He nodded again, his lean face a grimace of pain and joy. The official understood. He understood!

"Joseph Krasnowsky?"

"Yes!" he gasped.

The official thrust his plump face into Joseph's, pouchy eyes suspicious. "Say something in English," he commanded.

"I'm an American. Oh say can you see, by the dawn's early light—" He started coughing violently, doubling forward. The soldiers jerked him upright. The paroxysm of coughing had distended the veins in Joseph's face and throat. The infection had been there for weeks. He knew it was becoming pneumonia. The official drew back, wiping the spittle from his greatcoat in repugnance. He stared uncertainly from the soiled sheaf of papers to the wild-looking man before him, evidently uncertain what to do.

Joseph could not speak for coughing. There were so many things he wanted to say. But he could not speak, even though his life hung in the balance.

The official came to his decision. He thrust the papers back at Joseph.

"All right," he said to the soldiers. "Put him in the back with the others."

He clambered awkwardly back into the cab, an unwieldy civilian unsuited to military clothing or military life. An unlikely angel.

The soldiers hustled Joseph round to the back of the truck and banged impatiently on the door. It opened.

"One more."

Hands reached down and grasped the man called Joseph Krasnowsky. He was crying. Not quiet tears. Gasping, agonized sobs of relief and suffering. He clutched his precious papers in both thin hands as they dragged him upward and into the truck.

As the door closed, he caught a last glimpse of the mud and

the Quonset huts he was leaving behind, the gray figures that clung to the barbed wire, the blasted landscape. A last glimpse of hell.

Then the door crashed shut, and the truck started forward with a growl.

NORTHUMBERLAND, ENGLAND

She had been introduced to him earlier on, but he had not made any great fuss of the moment, preferring to bide his time. He'd turned away politely but dismissively and had moved on to other guests. He'd known exactly what he was doing.

He knew all about Evelyn Sandys. Indeed, he had pulled a whole succession of strings to make sure she was here today in his house. She was twenty-one years old, a distant cousin of the Churchill family. During the closing eighteen months of the war, she had been a member of the Prime Minister's personal staff, an appointment she had only just lost. And on the death of her father, Robert Sandys, she would inherit a fortune of some seven million pounds.

She stood in a remote corner of the room, talking without animation to a spindly looking young artillery officer named Freddy, whom David knew to be a crashing bore. Without seeming to take his attention away from the two young ladies who were so eagerly interrogating him about his wartime experiences, David studied the Sandys girl.

She was not unhandsome. Tall and lean, she at least carried her clothes with some style, which set her apart from most other women in the room, who did not wear their plain wartime utility garments with any sort of panache. She had an aristocratically bony face, with a thin mouth and fine gray eyes. Her eyebrows lifted in an interrogative slant that bordered, David felt, on the ironic. David Godbold was not an admirer of irony in women. However, she had beautiful hair, dark brown and glossy, and the kind of lithe body that David instinctively felt would be interesting in bed; interesting, if not voluptuous. Quality was written all over her. Like a thoroughbred filly, he thought, ungainly and self-conscious, but quality written in every line. No, she was certainly not unhandsome.

But she was frightfully wooden. She had a flat, awkward manner that almost certainly covered a deep shyness. She was not easy in company. Unusually for a girl of her class and background, she had no gift for small talk, the little soft nuances that made social intercourse—or any other kind—flow smoothly. She was a virgin, he was sure of that. A shy, superbly connected, extremely wealthy virgin.

She was perfect.

He had intended to play the field, of course. To search for as long as it took. Two or three years, if necessary. He could scarcely believe that he had already hit the jackpot. On the other hand, his every instinct was telling him that she was perfect. Telling him to strike now, at once, before some other hunter drew his bow.

The two bright young things prattled at him, each trying to outdo the other in skillful flirtation, eyelids fluttering, sticky lips pouting. He had lost weight in the POW camp, but that had only improved his looks. The slight gauntness set off his natural tendency to fleshiness, and he knew that compassion could be a powerful aphrodisiac.

He glanced across the room now and had to hide a smile. The spindly officer named Freddy was sidling off toward another group, leaving the Sandys girl where she stood. David saw the dull red flush touch her cheekbones as she looked down into her drink.

Snubbed by Freddy! Not even enough social glue to keep the attention of a world-famous bore, and seven million pounds dangling over her head! She stood there, slim and awkward and alone, staring into her glass as though the answer to some great riddle lay in there.

David waited for a while longer, interested to see whether any other young buck would stroll over. None did. He felt a little thrill of excitement prickle around his heart. Was this the moment? Was this how fortunes were made, in spotting an investment opportunity every other man had overlooked?

He took a breath and smiled at the two bright young women, showing his beautiful teeth. "Dreadfully sorry, old things," he said with a slight sigh, "but I feel a little weary. Would you excuse me for a moment?"

They followed him with melting eyes as he eased himself away from them and drifted between the chattering groups toward the corner where the Sandys girl stood staring into her glass.

"Penny for them?" he greeted her softly.

She looked up in something like fright, gray eyes widening. The light from the window gilded the delicate curve of her cheekbone, making her brown hair lustrous. For a moment she was all awkwardness and timidity. Then it was gone, and the eyebrows slanted up challengingly.

"My thoughts are overvalued at a penny, Captain Godbold."

"Please call me David."

"Very well," she said. She was blushing again. She did not blush well, partly because she did not duck her head like a schoolgirl when she did so, but continued to look him in the eye; but the dark flush was soon gone from her cheeks. "Have you come to rescue me from solitude?"

"Actually, I came to offer you my sympathy."

"Oh?" She held herself even straighter, her eyes suddenly cool. "What for?"

"What happened to the Prime Minister."

"What has happened to the Prime Minister?"

"He's lost the election," David said. "It's a damned disgrace. The guns haven't even stopped firing. After everything Winston's done for this country—and I don't just mean during the war—I can't believe the British people would have the ingratitude to kick him out." David frowned, his mouth stern, warming to his task. "It's the most shocking thing I ever heard. A national disgrace. I'd like to personally horsewhip every one of the dirty little swine who voted against him."

"You'd have a long job," Evelyn Sandys said. "Labour won by an overall majority of one hundred and forty-six seats. They polled almost twice the number of votes as the Conservatives."

"That's what I fail to understand," David said vehemently. "That's what I *completely* fail to understand."

"It's called democracy," the girl said calmly. "It's what we've been fighting about for six years."

He stared at her, slightly taken aback. He wondered whether she was mocking him. But her bony face was tranquil, her thin mouth level. "I must say, you're taking it on the chin," he said.

"What other option is there?" She drank from her glass, her eyes holding his. "And why should you want to offer your sympathy to me in particular?"

"Well," he said with a shrug, "I know how closely you were linked to Winston. It must have been a particularly severe shock to you. I mean, you even lost your job."

She nodded slowly. "Yes. But I never quite saw myself as working for Winston. I worked for the government. For the country. When they didn't want me anymore, that was that."

She was swirling the dregs in her glass. David saw that her lips were wet from her last sip, shining in the light from the window. It was far from the most erotic thing he had seen since coming back to England, but he felt desire flow smoothly into his loins, stirring his manhood. He reached for her empty glass. "Can I get you another drink?"

She gave him a brittle little smile. "All right, if you like."

He took it from her. "Fruit punch?"

"A gin and tonic, actually."

"Good," he said, turning. "Then shall we go out onto the terrace? It's a lovely afternoon for a change."

"All right," she said in exactly the same cadence, "if you like."

David smiled. He had the sudden conviction that, if he did decide to go for this girl, victory might be his very quickly. He enjoyed quick victories. "Don't go away."

ITALY

The midwife came out of the best room, drying her hands.

"Is there a drink in the house?" she asked Teo.

He was still leaning on the table, his head sunk on his chest. "In the cupboard," he whispered.

She hunted in the little dark cupboard until she found the half-bottle of grappa. She poured herself a stiff jolt and took it into the kitchen to drink it.

At last Teo found the strength to move. He heaved himself around and limped toward the front room, leaning heavily on his stick. He entered the room. It smelled of carnage.

The midwife had laid them out side by side, wrapped in the same bloodstained sheet. He reached out with a trembling hand and drew the sheet away. He looked, appalled, at the bodies of his sister and her child.

Candida's face was like marble. Her eyes were half-open and stared blindly at the ceiling. The first milk leaked from her naked breasts.

But the face of the tiny baby that was nestled up to her was infinitely piteous. It, too, was pale as marble, with the chubby cheeks of a cherub and a thatch of dark hair. The marks of the forceps were livid on the sides of the head. The eyes were closed, and the little mouth was open, as though it were no more than asleep. Teo saw that it was a girl-child, perfectly formed.

It was the scene not of a childbirth, but of a crime, an unforgivable crime.

He dropped his stick and lifted the infant into his arms. She was limp, a little warmth still clinging to the soft skin. One arm hung slack. Her head lolled on his chest.

No, he thought suddenly. *I will not permit this to happen.*

Hobbling awkwardly, his crippled leg feeling like a bough that might break at any moment, he carried the baby as quickly as he could through the house. The midwife's face blanched as she saw him.

"Are you mad?" she gasped.

"I will not permit it," he said aloud.

"You've lost your reason, Teo. It's all been too much for you." He stumbled past her with the baby, out into the yard. *"Teo!"* she screamed after him.

There was a bucket of water standing in the yard, its surface covered with a glassy film of ice. Teo crouched over the bucket, the pain tearing at his bad leg. He scooped out the thin shards of ice and plunged the baby into the achingly cold water.

Instantly, he felt the tiny body convulse in his hands.

He thought he had imagined that impossible movement, until he felt it again. He pulled the baby out, water streaming from her thatch of black hair. She choked, her face crumpled in rage. And then she began to cry, a sharp, healthy wail.

The midwife was standing in the doorway, her face blank with shock. "My God. What have you done?"

Stupefied by the miracle, Teo heaved himself to his feet, clutching the squalling infant. He hobbled back into the house with her. A pink flush was stealing across her blanched skin. Her legs were kicking, her small fists clenching and unclenching. She screamed with a ferocious lust for life.

"She's cold," he said in a strange voice. He offered the baby to the midwife, but she shook her head superstitiously.

"You brought her to life. You hold her." She ran for the baby blanket.

"Catarina Eleonora," The priest said, "do you renounce the Devil and all his works?"

"Yes," Teo answered for her.

Rosa Cipriani stared silently at the little creature in Teo's arms while the priest anointed her forehead. She did not wake.

"I baptize thee in the name of the Father and of the Son and of the Holy Spirit. Amen."

Rosa crossed herself slowly. The midwife had tears in her eyes. Teo gazed into the baby's face as though hypnotized. The child had not left his arms. No one seemed to want to take her away from him.

The priest left. The midwife remained to keep an eye on the baby. She began to whimper now, her small limbs stirring in the folds of her shawl. Teo shifted her awkwardly in his arms. "She's hungry," he said, and remembered the dead breasts leaking milk in the front room. His eyes met his mother's. She had barely spoken a word, and her face still looked as though carved from stone. She had greeted the miraculous revival of the baby with neither joy nor astonishment.

He held the baby out to her. "She's all we have left, Mama."

Rosa took the baby at last. Mechanically she folded the blanket around the tiny head. "She'd have been better off without your help, Teo," she said.

He did not know what to reply. "I had to do it," he said at last.

"Yes." Rosa had her little finger in the baby's mouth, and it had stopped whimpering. She looked up bitterly at Teo. "Well, Teo. I hope she'll grow up to thank you for it one day."

ENGLAND

They walked outside onto the terrace. The house stood at the brow of a hill, its golden stone facade staring down the long slope of the garden to the mixed moorland and woodland beyond. It was a big house, almost a manor; it had four peaked gables, and the mullioned windows on the first two floors were masterpieces of stonework. The third floor, added in the eighteenth century to accommodate servants' quarters, was plainer in style, but just as noble. Ivy crept across the front elevation, green fingers probing each chink in the gray stone.

"It's such a beautiful house," Evelyn Sandys said, looking upward.

"Yes," David replied, watching her expression. "But it's going to have to go. Or rather, I am."

She turned to him in surprise. "You're not thinking of selling?"

"I don't have any choice," he said, lifting the glass to his lips. "This war has changed things forever. You can imagine what it costs to keep up a place like Great Law. I simply don't have the money."

She was staring at him, a frown creasing her smooth, high forehead. "Can't you . . . do anything?"

"It's mortgaged to the hilt," he said with disarming frankness. "My father saw to that. He died while I was in Italy, you know."

"Yes, I know that."

"Of all the things I regret, I regret that the most," David said, tightening his jaw. "That I wasn't able to say good-bye to the old man."

That line usually brought a visible lump to the throat of most women. But the Sandys girl seemed unmoved. "I take it he didn't leave anything? Sorry to be so forthright, but it seems a terrible, terrible shame to have to part with a place like this. It's so very beautiful."

"Yes, it is beautiful. And no, my father left nothing. Only debts."

"Our house is hideous," she said matter-of-factly. She was gazing up at the barley-twist chimneys, ornate creations that rose from the dark slate roof. "It's in Yorkshire. Victorian red brick. An actual monstrosity."

He smiled. "Great Law was started in 1650. The top floor was added in the eighteenth century. There are eighteen bedrooms. It'll make a nice hotel."

"A *hotel*?" she echoed in distaste.

"Who else is going to want a great stone pile like this?" he asked.

She arched one slender eyebrow in disdain. "A hotel," she repeated. She turned away and walked along the terrace, running one hand caressingly along the stonework of the balustrade. He followed her, smiling to himself. There was a strange singing in his blood, an elation he had experienced during hunting, and sometimes during the war, when the killing had started.

They reached the parterre. She stood at the top of the steps, looking down onto the garden. He leaned on the balustrade at her side, pointing. "There's a lot of land, of course. It reaches right up to those woods along the line of the hill. Good for sheep, but not for anything else."

"And for keeping out visitors," she said.

"Oh, I'm master of all I survey," he agreed. "But all I survey are debts."

She made a little noise that sounded like "Hmmm," and stooped to pick a daisy that had sprouted between the lichen-spotted flagstones. He looked down at her. The front of her blouse swung open, and suddenly he found himself gazing at the smooth ivory swell of her breasts, loosely held by some kind of silk undergarment. Small breasts, virginal. Not like Candida's. He remembered, with a rush of conflicting emotions, the feel of Candida's breasts, buttery, heavy, warm. He felt a choking tightness in his throat.

The Sandys girl was down on one knee now, reaching for other small flowers that had appeared between the cracks, girlishly intent on her task. But her body was not that of a girl. Her breasts were firm and high, and as she moved, he caught the pink shadow of a nipple among the silk folds.

She looked up suddenly and saw his face. "Oh. Sorry." She pushed her blouse flat against her chest. "Showing off my shortcomings." She stood up, completely unembarrassed, a little posy in one hand. Now he was both aroused and intrigued. What a strange one she was! Strange and bewitching. He wanted to take her in his arms and kiss that narrow mouth, hard.

"It's only temporary, of course," he said.

"What is?"

"This Labour government. I doubt if they'll last four years without wrecking the country and collapsing. Come next election, the Conservatives will win with a landslide. Attlee and his crew will be out, and Winston will be Prime Minister again."

"Winston will be seventy-five in 1949," she said thoughtfully. "But you may be right."

"I *am* right," he said with conviction.

"Are you interested in politics?"

"Very," he said. He took a breath. "As a matter of fact, I'm thinking of standing for my constituency in 1949."

She did not move, but her face changed subtly, as though she were seeing him with new eyes, considering him seriously for the first time. "Are you, indeed," she said with a slight drawl.

"Yes. I want to be a Member of Parliament. The only thing I want more than that is to be a member of the government."

"I see."

"I have a lot of advantages," he said. "Local boy. War hero and all that." He touched the ribbon on his chest. "For what it's worth. Of course, I have disadvantages, too."

"Such as?"

"No money. No political background. No connections." He looked directly into the cool gray eyes. "No wife."

There was a very long silence. Conversation from the party inside the house filtered out onto the terrace.

The Sandys girl continued to stare at him without speaking, lips compressed. The gray eyes were extraordinarily intelligent, he thought suddenly. Disconcertingly so. He had the feeling that he was being measured as unemotionally as she might measure the material for a dress she wanted.

Had he gone too far, too quickly? Thinking back over the past few minutes, he was abruptly aware that he had rushed headlong, without pause for reflection. He had been hypnotized in some way by those gray eyes and had bared himself utterly, bared his venal soul. It had probably been a mistake. A terrible mistake.

And now it was he who felt the blood seep into his cheeks, coloring his skin.

"I say," he said, unconsciously falling into his schoolboy speech of a decade ago, "that sounded rather odd, didn't it? You'll think I'm proposing to you next!"

"Aren't you?" she asked quietly.

He thought he had misheard her. "What?"

"I said, aren't you proposing to me? Isn't that what you're doing?"

His heart was pounding now, the blood rushing in his ears. Christ! He had thought it might be quick, but not this quick! Who was the hunter here, and who the hunted? He remembered Candida, her gentleness, her complaisance. This woman was not like Candida. This woman was a very different kettle of fish altogether. His lips were dry. He cleared his throat. "You're a funny one," he said, his tone hovering uncertainly between badinage and seriousness. "We hardly know each other."

"That is easily remedied," she said. She smiled at him for the first time. It was a dazzling smile, turning her from a plain woman into a beautiful one, and it made him feel even dizzier. She took his arm, her slender fingers curving around his biceps. "Let's walk along the terrace. And you can tell me all about your political ambitions."

He felt, as he fell mechanically into step beside her, that a conquest had definitely been made. But he could not for the life of him tell who had been the conqueror, and who the conquered.

LATVIA

He detected the pattern instantly, as soon as the second officer came into the cell and laid a gentle hand on the first man's shoulder.

"Take it easy, Mikhail Mikhailovich. Maybe he's telling the truth."

"This scum? His mouth's so full of shit he can hardly speak." The first interrogator half-rose and pulled his automatic out of the holster. He racked the slide noisily and rammed the pistol against Joseph's forehead. "We've wasted enough time. I'm going to blow his brains out right here and now."

Joseph was trembling violently, his head thrust back against the wooden chair by the pistol. He felt a hot flood at his loins, and wondered if he'd wet himself.

"Come on, Mikhail. We're not Nazis. We don't shoot prisoners."

"I do," Mikhail said through clenched teeth. His face was contorted into an animal mask of rage. He had been screaming at Joseph for two hours, the sheer volume of his voice terrifying. "I've had enough lies. Stand back if you don't want this bastard's brains all over your uniform."

The second man sighed patiently. He jogged his friend's pistol arm gently. "You're tired. Go on, take a break. I'll carry on."

The muzzle ground into the skin of Joseph's forehead. Joseph waited for death, eyelids fluttering.

After an eternity, Mikhail lowered his arm. "I'll go take a

smoke. But I warn you, Alexei, if you don't get somewhere fast with this turd, I'm going to put a bullet through his skull." He ejected the unspent round and thrust it into Joseph's face. "This bullet, turd. You understand me? It's got your name on it." He made a great performance of slotting the unspent bullet back in the clip and slamming the clip back into the butt of the automatic. Through his terror, Joseph had to admire the man's expertise. He sagged in physical and emotional exhaustion as the interrogator named Volsky stamped out of the cell, his jackboots ringing on the concrete floor.

The other man sighed again as he took the chair opposite Joseph. He was much smaller than Volsky, a clerkish man with kindly, myopic eyes behind steel-rimmed spectacles. He shook a cigarette out of a pack of Luckies and offered it to Joseph.

"I don't smoke," Joseph whispered.

"My name is Major Alexei Feodorev," the clerkish man said. "I'm sorry about the way Volsky behaved just now. But you see the way he is." He leaned forward, lowering his voice a little. "I'm afraid he's a bit of a psychopath. Between you and me, he killed a prisoner last week. Beat him to death with his fists." He lit a cigarette and exhaled smoke. "He's a problem. Unfortunately, he's also my boss."

Joseph's hands were manacled together in his lap. He looked down at them, trying to get his breathing under control. He stank. He had not wet himself, he saw. But he would the next time, or the next.

"You take your time. Get your breath. Try and relax. I know what it's like." Feodorev smoked in silence for a while, apparently lost in thought. At last, he sat back in his chair. "I tell you what. Let's go over the questions again, okay? You think hard, my friend. Give me something I can show Volsky. Anything. Doesn't matter if it's a lie. You understand? A little something to calm him down. Stop him from shooting you." He laid a hand on his heart. "Personally, I don't care either way. But Volsky does. Are you listening?"

"Yes."

"Then Volsky can close his file on you. That's all he wants. To close his files. Then we can let you go. Back to your own people. See?"

The hard-guy, soft-guy routine was no less effective because it was so obvious. Joseph wanted to rest his head against this man's chest and cry like a baby. He had to remind himself that both men were equally officers of the NKVD. "Yes," he whispered.

"Good! Okay. Where did you get those papers?"

"They're my own papers," Joseph whispered.

"Speak up, son. I can't hear you."

"Those are my own papers."

"Come on," Volsky said with a forbearing smile. "They're transparent forgeries."

"No!" Joseph's bruised, exhausted face was passionate. "They're *not* forgeries, goddamn it! Can't you see they're real? Show them to anyone in the Red Cross. Show them to any British Army officer. They're authentic!"

Feodorev listened impassively. "Krasnowsky is a Russian name. You speak good Russian."

"My family emigrated from Latvia. I told you."

"You say you're an American. But you were fighting in the British Army."

"I volunteered! I told you a thousand times!"

"You volunteered. Okay. But Varga isn't a prisoner of war camp, son. It's a concentration camp. If you're who you say you are, how come you ended up in Varga?"

"I told you!"

"Tell me again."

"I was captured in North Africa. They shipped me to a POW camp in Italy. The Italians let us out on the day of the armistice. We joined the Italian Partisans and fought with them. Then the Germans recaptured us. As a punishment, they sent us to concentration camps."

Feodorev was writing laboriously in his notebook, repeating Joseph's words under his breath. He lifted the book and read what he had written. Then he laughed with genuine amusement. "It's a good story. A damned good story!"

"It's the truth!" Joseph screamed. "I am who I say I am! You can't keep me here like this! I demand to see a Red Cross official! I demand to see someone from the British Army!" He could no longer hold back the tears. They spilled down his cheeks, choking his words.

Feodorev sighed. He closed the notebook. "A pity. I thought we were getting somewhere at last."

"You'll get nowhere with him. He's an expert. A hard man." Volsky was standing in the doorway, a cigarette in his mouth, his face grim. "He needs stronger persuasion."

Feodorev took off his glasses to polish them. "Unfortunately, I think you're right," he said with a long-suffering expression. "Sorry, son. I warned you."

Volsky jerked his head.

Two soldiers bustled through the doorway. Both were squat, powerful men. Both carried thick rubber truncheons.

Adrenaline surged through Joseph's body, driving exhaustion away. He tried to rise, but his ankles had been strapped to the wooden chair, and he collapsed back down, gasping.

As the soldiers with the truncheons stepped forward, Feodorev rose to his feet and prepared to leave the room. He was taking his chair with him to give the others more space.

"Okay," he sighed with what was almost genuine regret. "I'll leave you to it."

Volsky started rolling up his sleeves, eyes squinting against the smoke from his cigarette. "Doesn't matter how hard you are," he told Joseph. He wasn't bothering to shout anymore. "This is going to break you."

ITALY

Later, Teo stared down at the baby, who was squalling lustily in her crib, her fists clenching and unclenching. The noise she made was out of all proportion to her size.

"You will," he whispered to her. "One day, you will thank me. You're a fighter. A survivor. Aren't you, Catarina?"

He reached out with his forefinger and touched her hand. The tiny fingers closed around it with a possessive strength that astonished him. He smiled, despite himself, feeling that fierce grasp on life.

She stopped crying. For a moment, her eyes opened. They were a cloudy blue, though who knew what color they would become? He noticed that she had long, dark lashes. She had a strange, a wonderful, look of Candida. She seemed to look at him, and though he told himself she could barely see, he felt awed by her gaze.

Her lids slowly drooped, and she drifted into sleep. Her fingers opened at last and released him.

He kissed her brow, rose from the cot, and went out to attend Candida Cipriani's funeral.

1

THE GOLDEN CITY

---

1 9 9 2

ST. PETERSBURG, RUSSIA

The General was a massive presence behind his steel-topped desk.

His face seemed to have been carved out of the same somber granite that had been used in this building, and in so many buildings, of the state apparatus in Russia. His eyes, though, were animal and alive, the watchful eyes of a grizzly bear, brown with yellow centers. He had been staring at her with hulking impassivity as the interpreter conveyed her carefully worded message to him, phrase by phrase.

Despite his bulk, his olive-green uniform was immaculately starched and pressed. Kate knew that he was sixty-five, and that some of the multicolored tape stitched across his left breast commemorated that terrible Stalingrad autumn of 1942, when the General had been a teenage hero.

She also knew that he had been drafted into the NKVD before the end of the war, and that the rest of those bright ribbons had been earned in the service of the KGB over fifty years, from Berlin to Kabul.

Kate had dressed that morning as conscientiously as the General, and her clothes constituted as much of a uniform as his tunic and shoulder boards. Before perestroika, he and his wife and daughters had been given automatic access to those Western delights denied to ordinary communists. Her Donna Karan suit needed no interpreting. It was an instantly recognizable emblem.

She'd also been generous with the Tiffany that morning, wanting it to drift recognizably across his desk. She wanted him to have no doubt that she was a well-connected Western woman with money and intelligence—and above all, with that most Western of traits, willingness to deal.

She had watched his brown eyes watching her, had seen them dwell on her face, her hair, her hands, her clothes, her jewelry, her legs. And always, they had come to rest on the crocodile-hide attaché case she held on her lap.

It had been a laborious trail, but she knew instinctively that she was closer to her goal than she had been since she had arrived in Moscow three weeks earlier.

Kate would always remember Moscow as a city of bread lines and protest marches, the faces of its people pinched, a feeling in the air that hung between depression and nervous tension.

She would never forget the extraordinary sights she had seen: U.S. Air Force transport planes disgorging crates of food and medical aid under the floodlights at the airport. Swastikas sprayed on the walls of the capital city of Marxism. Colonel Sanders dispensing extra-crispy fried chicken in the heart of Moscow.

She had carefully avoided the United States Embassy, preferring to work directly with Russians. She had several lines of contact: General Dmitri Volgokonov, the military historian close to President Boris Yeltsin; Lieutenant Colonel Boris Yuzhin, the ex-KGB turncoat, himself released from a gulag in February; the Ark Project, a private research team with exceptional inside knowledge of the system.

Her contacts had quickly gained her access to the rococo building in Dzerzhinsky Square where her search had begun. Going in, she had seen the Lubyanka squatting behind the graceful ocher palace, like a hideous face behind a golden mask, and had felt an unreasonable rush of fear.

Later, her heart had failed her again, for quite a different rea-

son: because she had lost hope of finding what she had traveled so far
to uncover.

She had been bewildered by the number of buildings that the
KGB occupied in Moscow, some of them Western-style office blocks,
one an immense semicircular Modernist structure on the ring road that
circumscribed the city center.

She had visited them all, and had found all of them in varying
states of confusion. Few of the administrators she had wanted so badly
to see had been available. The whole organization was convulsed in a
frantic effort to track down the tens of thousands of nuclear weapons
scattered across the sprawling, bloodied territories of what had once
been the Union of Soviet Socialist Republics. The past was suddenly
irrelevant in the face of an unimaginably awful future, and nobody was
interested in her questions.

Besides, she had been only one of an army of strangers in the
drab corridors, screaming for answers, demanding, berating. They all
wanted what she wanted, access to the secret records of the state. Each
one of them believed what she believed, that somewhere within the
labyrinth must lie the answer to a personal mystery, a personal agony.

It was a hope that could not have been more forlorn if all the
paper of the Russian state had turned back into the trackless forest that
had been hewn down to produce it.

She had spent days in the archives, exhausting the patience and
energies of a long succession of guides, to no avail. She had tasted bitter
despair. She had begun to suspect that it was all an intricate game being
played by the historians and the officials, manipulated by the new re-
gime for purposes of its own.

At the very end, she had come to the realization that the only
people who really knew the secret path through the maze were in the
KGB itself.

It was then she had changed her strategy. With the new approach, it had not taken long to secure the name of the General in St.
Petersburg. They had told her that he was the only man who might be
able to help her, but that it would prove costly. She had been prepared
for that. She had boarded the Aeroflot shuttle the next morning, knowing it was the last lead that remained to her.

The flight south had taken her to a gracious golden city in the
snow. In this imposing building on the Kirovskiy Prospekt, frowning

down on the river Neva, a semblance of order still reigned. There remained more than a whiff of that awesome power the KGB had exerted for so long. It hung especially around the General who sat opposite her, and as soon as she had tasted it, the glimmer of hope had flickered into life.

Now, as the interpreter conveyed her final sentence to him, she was taut with nerves.

There was a long silence during which the General sat motionless, continuing to watch Kate. At last he spoke. His voice was coarse, and he paused often to allow the girl to relay his words.

"*Madame,* the General wishes to inform you that this topic is already the subject of official exchanges at the very highest level. An inquiry was instigated by Mikhail Gorbachev before leaving office. President Yeltsin is currently continuing that inquiry with even greater vigor, at the personal request of President Bush."

"I know that."

"The General fails to understand why you do not pursue your researches through formal channels."

Kate's voice was low and steady. "Tell him that I prefer not to rely on formal channels. They are often slow and seldom efficient. It is also my desire to avoid publicity."

The interpreter spoke in Russian and listened to the reply. She was a rather plain, bespectacled girl, a student at Leningrad University whose shabby clothes contrasted painfully with the elegant couture of the Western woman who was hiring her. She was also evidently in profound awe of the KGB officer, despite all that had happened in these momentous past months. She turned back.

"The General wishes to inform you that he does not have the authority to help you, even if he was able to do so."

But the General's watchful eyes held another message, and she felt her nervousness increase. "Please tell him that my sources assure me he is one of the most powerful men in the Confederation."

Kate's piece of unveiled flattery seemed to please the General. "He says this is a topic of the utmost delicacy," the interpreter chanted in her flat, slightly breathless way.

"Tell him I understand that."

"He reminds you that international relations are directly affected by this matter."

"I understand that, too. Please tell him that I have nothing to do with the official inquiry. I need only one name. One name, one set of dates, one piece of information."

"The General asks, what is your interest in this one name?"

"I need to find the truth."

The translator spoke in Russian, and the General uttered a husky bark of laughter. He spoke briefly.

"*Madame,* the General says that truth is an expensive commodity in Russia."

A cold, clear chill settled on her skin. Suddenly she was very calm. She met the General's eyes and thought of the terror, the pain, the humiliation that he and his kind had inflicted on so many millions for so long. And it had come, in the end, to this. She smiled at the interpreter with a touch of grimness. "Ask the General if you can use the bathroom."

The girl blinked. "I beg your pardon, *madame?*"

"Ask him if he will excuse you while you go to the lavatory. Don't come back until you're called."

The girl hesitated, then spoke to the General. He had huge hands, one of which he waved without speaking. The girl rose and left the office, closing the door behind herself. The General clasped his thick fingers and nodded to the woman who sat opposite him, as though giving her permission to continue.

Kate lifted the crocodile-hide attaché case onto his desk and flicked open the gold clasps. She took out the square box and slid it across the steel desktop toward him.

He opened it. His eyes smoldered as he took out the watch. It was an all-gold Rolex Oyster, with diamonds marking the hours. He unclipped the steel Timex from his wrist and replaced it with the new watch, swinging in his chair to study it in the light from the window.

Despite the cold, blustery weather, the sky outside was a pure eggshell blue, with barely a wisp of cloud. She looked over his shoulder at the distant view of the Cathedral of St. Peter and St. Paul, which seemed to rise miraculously out of the river, its golden spire soaring like an arrow to pierce Heaven. She wondered whether there was any mercy in that bright blue vault.

All her life, Kate had been superstitious about omens, alert to symbols. Seventy years after the October Revolution had been won in this city, the bronze statues of Lenin were being carted to the junkyard, along with that chillingly ugly name, *Leningrad.* The city had reverted to its original name, St. Petersburg. Its true parentage had been reestablished.

She wondered whether she would be any closer to the truth when she had been answered. Whether she would be any closer to finding out who she was.

The General cleared his throat and rasped a phrase. She spoke no Russian, but she knew what he meant:

What else you do you have?

She took the other package out of the attaché case and slid it over to him. He was greedier now, his fingers tearing clumsily at the corner to reveal the stack of green bills. He buzzed their sharp corners with his thumb and asked her a question. Again, she knew what he meant:

How much?

She picked up her pen and wrote on a notepad, in figures, the sum: $50,000.

She watched his eyes. Despite her appearance, she was a working woman. That sum represented a lot of very hard work, a lot of careful saving. It was not easy just to pass it across the desk to this lout. But she had been advised that only cash, a large amount of cash, would cut any ice.

Fifty thousand American dollars, translated into the ballooning Russian ruble, represented a significant sum to a man who would soon have to survive on a grossly devalued state pension. She could see that thought going through his mind.

He rose, scratching the cropped back of his neck, evidently speculating. He walked round the desk, limping slightly, and peered into the attaché case, as if to see what other goodies were in there. She spread her hands.

"That's all I have, General."

He poked among the contents of the case with a blunt forefinger, located her passport, and took it out. He studied it, reading out her name and the date and place of her birth, the familiar words odd in his thick accent.

He tossed the passport back into the briefcase and perched one buttock on the desk in front of her. He stared down at her. Kate was in her mid-forties and remained one of the most elegant women of her generation. Part of her beauty had always been honesty, and she had not abandoned that. She had not dyed away the silver threads that now appeared in the jet-black mane of her hair. Nor had she deigned to submit to the little surgical nips and tucks that would have ironed the faint lines from her face and made her look thirty again. She was as she was, without pretenses or apologies.

She returned his gaze, her large, dark eyes calm, her full mouth slightly compressed in an expression that was neither a smile nor a scowl. Her fingers were laced in her lap, the oval nails unvarnished, wearing only a single ring, a big, sumptuously colored emerald that glowed like a lioness's eye in the pale northern light.

Then, as if it were the most natural thing in the world, he slid his hand into her jacket and cupped her left breast assessingly. She reacted sharply, knocking his hand away and rising swiftly to her feet.

"Are we going to deal?" she demanded tautly. "Or are we going to waste each other's time?"

The Russian's eyes narrowed like a Tartar's when he smiled, meshing into a web of wrinkles. He waved both palms downward, as though requesting pianissimo from an orchestra. "Posháluista. Posháluista." She sank slowly back into the chair.

He scooped the package of dollars and the steel watch into a drawer and locked it. He went back to sit in his chair and admired the Rolex on his wrist, turning it this way and that, lifting it to his ear to hear the tick. When he started talking, his accent was so strong that at first she did not register that he was speaking English, and he had to repeat himself.

"How much money you got?"

"I beg your pardon?"

"How much money you got?"

"That's everything," she said, nodding at the bundle.

"*Nyet.*" He pointed his finger at her like a revolver. "You. How much money *you* got? In bank?"

She lifted one shoulder. "I'm not rich."

He chuckled. "You very rich. Pretty soon I got no job."

"I don't think you'll be missed," she replied calmly.

"Maybe you find me job in West."

"What skills do you have?"

He tapped a little medal on his chest. "Hero of Soviet Union."

"The Soviet Union doesn't exist anymore."

"Fifty thousand dollars is not enough."

"Fifty thousand dollars is a fortune. With the Rolex, it's more like seventy-five thousand."

His smile went. He leaned forward. "You want dangerous information. These are things that did not happen. You understand, 'did not happen'?"

"I understand."

"I get information for you—maybe you make trouble between America and Soviet Union. I lose my job, lose pension."

Kate studied the rocky face. "How much do you want?"

"One hundred thousand."

"That's absurd."

"So no deal."

"I'll give you ten thousand more. When you give me the information I want."

"Twenty thousand more. When you get information."

She did not hesitate. "Very well. I agree."

His fist thumped gleefully into his other palm. Then he became brisk. "Vietnam?"

"No. World War Two."

He raised his bushy eyebrows. "Long time ago."

"Yes. A long time ago."

He drew a notepad toward him. "Okay. You give me his name."

DENVER, COLORADO

His eyes were fixed on the two girls silhouetted against the bright store window. His erection was so tight against his belly that it hurt.

The girls, still unaware of his presence, were talking, laughing under their pretty floral umbrellas. Daddy's girl came out of the store where she worked every night at this time.

The mall was upscale, with a Saks Fifth Avenue and a Lord & Taylor. The lot was brightly lit, and there were people around, but he was confident. He had it all planned. He'd managed to park the van right by her car. That would make things a whole lot easier.

The van bore the logo of a plumbing company. He himself wore a duffel coat and a wool cap that covered the cropped hair. Only the skintight jeans, cut short to display the lace-up army boots, might give the game away; but the livery had become fashionable lately among spineless imitators of the true breed.

Now the girls had separated. Daddy's girl was walking into the lot, digging in her bag for her car keys. Her thighs were tight in her cords, and her silky brown hair fluttered behind her.

He followed her with narrowed eyes, inhaling deeply on his cigarette, hearing the savage music in his head. He knew he could also rape her, if he wanted. But he also knew self-discipline would prevail.

Truck had discovered self-discipline like a religion. He had learned to love it. The long, wild storm of his adolescence had ended in a Colorado Springs courtroom, charged with six counts of rape. If they had not helped him, supplied him with the psychologist, the fancy Denver lawyer, he would have gone down for fifteen years.

It was they who had taught him discipline. It was Control who had harnessed his powers.

Control had taught him about himself.

And everything since then had been for Control. This was for Control.

As the girl neared his van, Truck climbed over the back seat and moved to the back doors. He tossed the cigarette onto the metal floor, a tiny red meteor in the gloom, and watched for her to pass by the small, sticker-plastered back window.

When he saw her, he swung the doors open fast. She was a few feet away. She stopped in shock as he got out, one hand lifting to her throat.

She laughed uncertainly. "You startled me!"

He checked around for witnesses. There were none. He rushed at her, boots thudding heavily. She only had time for a single brief scream before he caught her. One horny palm slammed over her mouth, the other knotted in her hair, dragging her forward and down. She lost her balance and fell heavily to her knees in front of him. He dragged her swiftly to the van, hauling her struggling body up into the interior. She was making strangled snuffling sounds. He slammed the doors shut and locked them.

She had opened her mouth to scream again, but he did not give her the chance.

He smashed his knee into her face, letting the power erupt from the thigh muscles. He struck seven, eight times more, gripping her shoulders. He was big and very strong. He knew how to hit. Each time he felt something crush, cartilage or bone or teeth. She would not be pretty anymore. He had taken that from her.

When he had finished, she was lying motionless on the floor of the van.

She had made no sound. Perhaps she was unconscious after the first blow. He bent over her. Saw the glint of blood in the dark, the pulped nose. Daddy would listen to reason now. He reached out and touched the blood with his fingers, carrying it to his mouth. It tasted briny, metallic. He swallowed, crouching low over his swiftly blossoming orgasm. He felt release, pleasure and pain wrapped into one orgiastic moment. Wetness and heat flooded his loins. For a moment he could not move. Then he clambered back into the front seat, his knees weak.

He drove out of the lot, hearing her inert body rolling around in the back of the van. He reached out to switch on the stereo. The savage chords of Megadeth boomed out of the heavyweight speakers.

Several streets away, in the darkness behind a deserted lot, he stopped the van again. He opened the back doors and pulled the girl out. He tossed her into the gutter, feeling, as so often on these occasions, a kind of casual tenderness for the limp body he had devastated.

As he drove away, he began to laugh, breathlessly, hysterically.

He was still giggling when he reached the trailer camp half an hour later. He parked the pickup and let himself into the mobile home. He wrinkled his nose at the stench of his own unwashed plates and unwashed clothes. The place was a pigsty, "mobile" only in the sense that it had once moved, to get to this weed-infested park. It had been twenty years since then, and it would be another twenty before it moved again. It was exactly like all the others around it, a bleakly poor, inadequately insulated box, huddled against the bitter Colorado autumn.

Unusually, this trailer had a telephone. He ripped open a can of Coors and drained it in two prolonged swallows. He belched loudly and kicked off his stained jeans, flinging them into a corner. Then he picked up the telephone and punched in the number he knew by heart, the only number he ever called.

Control's gravelly voice came on the line. "Yes?"

"It's done," he said.

"Properly?"

"Hamburger," he said, and giggled.

"You ready for more work?"

He was about to rip open a second beer, but sat up eagerly. "Yes, *sir*."

"I need to do a friend a favor. A little job that needs tact. Tomorrow, at the cabin."

Truck opened his mouth, but Control had already hung up.

Truck put the telephone down and opened his Coors. He was grinning, the old acne scars pulling tight around his jaw. "Yes, sir," he said softly. "I'm all tact."

PÉTIONVILLE, HAITI

"*Docteur* Levêque will see you in ten minutes, *mam'selle*. He invites you to take a drink while you are waiting."

"A guava juice, if that's convenient."

"*Avec plaisir, mam'selle.*"

The butler gestured toward a chair, but Anna shook her head slightly, and he melted away. She stood holding the cool, dewy glass to her lips. She had dressed with more flair tonight, a thigh-length cotton jacket with high-waisted stretch trousers, an extravagant pearl choker around her throat. Big pearl drop earrings framed her dark face. She was brown-skinned, slender, with smoky black eyes and hair. The fawn cotton and creamy pearls gave her the effect of an Indian princess, not inappropriate to this tropical night.

It was a remarkable house, a stark contemporary sonata of glass and white concrete. The man who had built it was a brilliant pediatric surgeon, specializing in transplant work, corneas and hearts and kidneys. Anna knew this house was the man's monument to himself.

André Levêque had two clinics. One was in Palm Beach, Florida, where he charged tens of thousands of dollars for his work. The other was here in Haiti, in Port-au-Prince, where he performed his work for next to nothing.

Drew McKenzie, her editor, had sent her out here to do a story on the Haitian doctor. A strange and terrible story.

"Good evening."

She turned quickly. André Levêque had now come into the room, wearing a white tropical suit, his shirt open at the throat. He studied her. "You look exquisite, Mata Hari."

"It's very kind of you to give me yet another interview," she said, sitting on the sofa he had indicated. "I promise this one will be the last."

"You are being extremely painstaking in your research."

She glanced at his face. Levêque was handsome, with the chiseled, calm features of a young Alain Delon; but his eyes were the cloudy greeny-brown of a disturbed ocean. "I like to get to the bottom of things, Dr. Levêque. Do you mind if I use the machine again?"

"Not at all."

Anna took the little Sony cassette recorder out of her bag and laid it on the coffee table between them. She folded her notebook open on her crossed legs and uncapped her pen. "Since our last conversation, one or two things have come up."

Levêque inclined his head. "Yes?"

"There was a scandal here in Port-au-Prince earlier this year. It was said that you were not giving Haitian children the same attention you were giving American children. Specifically, that you performed almost no transplants here. It was said that whenever donor organs were available in Haiti, you were smuggling them to Palm Beach in your private jet, which is equipped with a special refrigerated container, and using them for highly paid transplant work in Palm Beach. On the children of wealthy Americans."

He smiled. "Let me explain something. Transplant work is not a question of one talented surgeon. It's a question of a very large and highly skilled team, not to mention advanced facilities. It should be obvious why I do less transplant work in Haiti than in the United States."

"Oh, yes. I can see that. But there seems to be more to the rumors than at first appeared. My editor in Miami received a call from a local priest, Father Jérémie. Your clinic is in his parish."

"I know Father Jérémie."

"Father Jérémie made some rather disturbing allegations, Dr. Levêque."

He was watching her steadily. "You have come here tonight to inform me that you are going to destroy me and obliterate my life's work."

Her skin prickled. She braced herself inwardly, both afraid of his reaction and ready to face it. "Then you know what Father Jérémie told my editor."

"I have been making inquiries about you, too. You are not the innocent you had me believe, Miss Anna Kelly. You are what is called an investigative reporter, with a formidable reputation, despite your captivating smile and dewy youth. I can see the sword of justice flaming in your fair hand. But I will not spoil your pleasure. Please continue." He was speaking with an oddly flat, slurred note in his voice, and she suddenly realized that he was either drunk or on some drug. She could see the drowned look in his eyes. "What has the good priest said, Anna?"

"That some of your Haitian donors, especially of infant corneas, are not dead when you remove the organs you need. That they aren't even sick or injured. They say that you have so much work in Palm Beach, and so many stockbrokers' children awaiting your skills there, that there just aren't enough naturally occurring donor organs. So you've set up your own source of supply. You buy unwanted children from poor mothers here in Haiti, in some cases infants, and sacrifice them to get the spare parts you need for your wealthy American clients. It's a very, very profitable network, and it involves other doctors, midwives, nurses . . . " She broke off. "Dr. Levêque? Are you listening to me?"

"Of course. Why should I not be?"

"You show no emotion." Anna's voice tightened. "I'm accusing you of one of the foulest crimes I can think of, and you're just sitting there, smiling at me. No outrage? No horror?"

"I knew what you had come for when we first met, a week ago," he replied gently. "I have no outrage or horror."

"So you don't deny it?"

"What difference would it make?" He still wore that unfocused smile. In her eyes, he had violated the most fundamental ethics of humanity. He had perverted a great, God-given talent, and drowned it in evil. She still remembered what he had said to her in their first interview: *There are no ethics to transplant surgery, only practicalities.* He gestured with his fine surgeon's hands. "Down there at the other end of the Pétionville Road is a city of almost a million densely packed, desperately poor human existences, feeding on one another in misery and violence and squalor. I was born down there. I climbed my way up here to Pétionville. But part of me will always remain down there. Their blood is my blood." His narcotized green eyes met hers. "Have you ever wondered how it feels to come from Port-au-Prince to Palm Beach, and to return again?"

"Is that an apology, Dr. Levêque?"

"I make no apology." He studied her. "You are quite a phenomenon. Do you know that? Twenty-six years old, and so very beautiful. You should have taken that extraordinary face and that delectable body to Hollywood, Anna."

"The way you took your gifts to Palm Beach?"

"Your editor has sent you here to ruin me." He leaned forward. "But your readers do not know Haiti from Hawaii," he said, his voice quiet and persuasive. "Whose interests do you imagine your editor is serving?"

"The interests of your victims, for a start, I'd say."

"Some patients die. That means other patients may live."

"The murder of children is not so easily justified."

"Haiti is the poorest and most densely populated nation in the Western Hemisphere." For the first time, there was a note of anger in his voice. "One of the most wretched countries on earth. Those children are born to live in hell."

"They might have had a chance. *You* escaped. You grew up to become a great surgeon."

"Whom you plan to destroy."

"Evil must be destroyed," she replied in a low voice. "For a Haitian child to die so that an American child regains his sight is monstrous."

He seemed amused. "I wonder whether the present White House administration would agree with you, Anna? With Russia become a toothless beggar, this is the dawn of the *imperium Americanum*. Compared to what your country is doing to other vassal states, are a few transplanted corneas and kidneys so unacceptable?"

"Don't blame America for what you're doing," she said sharply. "This was your idea. And you do it for money." She gestured at the room. "To build yourself all this."

His face seemed to have sagged, his mouth drooping like a petulant child's. "Do you know what cuts deepest? The accusation that I neglected my Haitian children. What do you know of my work? Transplants! My patients here are not queuing up for *transplants*. They are dying from diarrhea and malnutrition, for want of the most basic medical care. A cornea transplant in Florida pays for four thousand courses of penicillin here in Haiti. One life for four thousand, Anna! It's a perfect symbiotic relationship. If I could show you how it all worked, you would see the pattern, the meaning . . . "

He seemed to have ground to a halt. She waited awhile longer, until the silence grew oppressive. Then she switched off her tape recorder and rose to her feet. "If you have nothing to add, Doctor, I think that's about it."

There was a red flicker in his eyes. "Sit," he said softly.

"I'm sorry, but I must be going."

He said nothing, but she saw that one of the guards was now standing in the doorway, arms folded, staring at her with baleful yellow eyes. Levêque must have touched some electronic signal without her noticing.

She was suddenly very frightened. She tried not to let it show. "I've already filed nine-tenths of my story," she said, surprised at how calm her voice sounded. "I did it this morning. Witnesses, names, dates, everything. And a copy will go to the AMA."

He smiled at her. "You are afraid of me."

"I mean it. That story will break, whatever happens. And if you try to interfere with me in any way, it will be read by five times the number of readers."

"*Hypocrites lecteurs.*" His face was suddenly eager. "Write a book about me, Anna. Tell McKenzie to finance it. I would cooperate fully. Even from a prison cell, if that is what you want."

She stared at him in stunned silence for a moment. "You're not a fit subject for a book, Dr. Levêque. I'm sorry."

Anna saw his face grow blank and cruel, like the evil masks in the case. The man was drugged, certainly ruthless, and no doubt the hulking guard would do anything he ordered. She regretted her thoughtless words. Her heart was pounding. She wondered just how spaced-out he was. She forced herself to speak. "I have to go now." She tried to make it sound firm.

"To the next kill? Come, then." He held out his arm, waiting for her. His mouth wore a loose, empty smile. Her throat dry with fear, she took his arm, wondering if it was the last thing she would ever do.

He led her outside and down into the garden. The frogs and night insects sounded in the velvety night. Beyond, the throbbing of drums.

"You hear the drums?" he asked softly.

"Yes."

"Voodoo drums. I grew up to the sound of those drums. I have seen the ceremonies those drums summon the faithful to. Ceremonies no white will ever see."

She could hear the heavy footsteps of the guard behind them. Her knees seemed to have turned to water. She was forced to cling to him, even though the touch of his flesh made her skin creep.

They walked deep into the garden, into the darkness of the jungle Levêque had created. She thought of all the things she wanted to do before she died. Fall in love. Sail a yacht. Win the Pulitzer. Get close to her mother again. She wondered whether anyone would ever find out what had happened to her.

And then Levêque was opening a gate, and she was looking at the street outside. Her rental car standing under a street lamp, a sweet chariot of salvation.

He turned to her. His eyes were unfocused, his mouth a little lopsided. "Good-bye, Anna," he said. He shook her hand formally, his palm dry and cool against hers. "See you in Purgatory."

Were they going to do it here, in the deserted street?

The gate shut slowly, closing Levêque and his guard in the jungle-garden. She heard the bolts slam shut.

Her heart racing, she went quickly to her car and got in, throwing her bag onto the seat beside her. She fitted the key into the ignition and started the Jeep. She pulled off so sharply that the tires shrieked.

St. Petersburg

They had two days to wait.

She shopped for presents, mostly things for her daughter, scarves and shawls and a little silver-mounted icon that the dealer swore was authentic. She also bought things for her staff in Vail, little tokens of affection.

To fill in the time, the interpreter acted as her guide around St. Petersburg. She was knowledgeable and articulate. The city was magnificent, but calculatedly so. It was as much the creation of one man's conceit as if he had been a child making sand castles on a beach, rather than a tsar creating a city. She was left with a taste of artificiality, of a colossal vanity without restraint.

When they paused for coffee in a bar—she was not interested in expensive restaurants—the television screen above the vodka bottles told a bloody tale of an empire crumbling. Among the chaos of the civil war in Nagorno-Karabakh, packs of wild dogs devoured corpses and attacked the living. In Moscow, soup kitchens ministered to endless lines of the starving elderly. The vast Soviet army was suddenly leaderless and torn by ethnic loyalties.

"They keep warning that there will be another coup," the girl translated, watching a shot of a nuclear-missile launcher trundling through some anonymous forest. "They say if the West does not invest, there will be another military dictatorship in Russia."

"And then men like the General will be back in charge?"

"It is possible."

But who was going to invest in this country? she thought. The economy was being run, as far as she could tell, by black marketeers and gangsters.

They continued their tour, but she had no more appetite for St. Petersburg's gilded splendors.

The girl sensed her restlessness, and on the second day took her to Petrodvorets, the yellow-and-white palace that the tsar had built outside his city, where golden statues disported among fountains and cascades. But there was no distraction here, either. She preferred to walk among the trees, away from the opulence and the vanity.

In the evening, she took pity on the transparently covetous glances the girl had been giving her and invited her up to her hotel room, where she made her a present of some of her own clothes—stockings, shoes, underthings, skirts, blouses, sweaters. The girl was overwhelmed.

"They're only clothes," Kate said gently.

"But they're such expensive clothes, *madame*!"

"You deserve them. You've worked hard to amuse me." She went to the cupboard and took out the bottle of vodka and two glasses. "And please don't call me *madame* anymore. I think we should be on first-name terms."

The girl smiled. "My friends call me Petruschka."

"Mine call me Kate." She held out the glass. *"Nasdarovye."*

"Nasdarovye."

They sat by the window, the girl holding the vodka glass in one hand, with the other wonderingly stroking the stack of clothes in her lap. She looked up rather shyly. "You have so many beautiful things. You must be very rich."

"No, I'm not rich. It's just part of my job to have beautiful things."

"What is your job?"

"I work in a hotel in America."

"Where is this hotel?"

"A place called Vail, in Colorado."

Petruschka's face lit up. "I have heard of Vail!"

"Have you?"

"It is a ski resort, yes?"

Kate nodded. "Yes."

"A beautiful place. Very glamorous. All the film stars go there."

"The film stars would probably go to Aspen," Kate said with a smile. "Vail is a little quieter. More of a family resort."

"A resort for very rich families," Petruschka said. "And your hotel must be magnificent, yes?"

"It's a fine hotel."

"Are you the manager?"

"I'm a director. One of two." She had been away a long time. It would be Thanksgiving soon, and the season had already started because of early snowfalls. She was cutting it close. She wondered whether Jennifer Prescott, her assistant, was coping in her absence. She wondered whether she would return to find she no longer worked at that fine hotel.

"Are you married?" Petruschka asked.

"No. Not anymore."

"Any children?"

"A daughter. She's a reporter. An investigative journalist. She works in Florida. Right now, she's gone to Haiti to do an interview."

"God, how lucky you both are." Vodka had emboldened Petruschka. "What wonderful lives you have!"

"Yes, I suppose so." But she did not feel that she was lucky, or that she had a wonderful life. She wondered whether Anna felt she was lucky and had a wonderful life. It was the sort of thing they no longer discussed. Happiness. Fulfillment.

Petruschka's eyes were sly. "You must have very many lovers, Kate."

"Not exactly," she said dryly.

"But there must be one special man in your life?"

"Yes. There is one special man."

Petruschka brightened. "Is he beautiful?"

"Some women would think so."

"Have you got a picture?"

"I think so, somewhere."

"Please," the girl begged.

Kate rose and searched in her suitcase until she found the leather-framed photograph of Campbell Brinkman. She passed it to Petruschka, who took it eagerly. Her face lit up. "He is very handsome! And he loves you?"

"He says he does."

"And you love him, of course?"

"I don't know."

The interpreter was awed by the calm statement. "Isn't he a good lover?"

She laughed. "He's a good lover."

"So! And you don't love him?"

The girl's open curiosity was not irritating. In some way, it was endearing. In another way, it was almost a relief, almost cathartic, to say the things she could say to no one else. She leaned back in the armchair, her slender neck relaxed, the mop of raven hair cascading. Her eyes closed. "I didn't say I don't love him. Just that I don't know."

"If you don't know whether you love him or not," Petruschka said decisively, "then you don't love him."

"It's not as rudimentary as that."

"Love isn't uncertain, Kate. When it happens, it happens!"

Kate opened her eyes slowly. "Has it happened to you like that, Petruschka?"

The girl shook her head. "No. But it will, one day."

She looked at the girl with her dark, compassionate eyes. "I hope so."

Kate would be fifty in a few years. And sometimes, in the dark hours of the night, she looked back on the decades gone by and saw them all wasted, all vanity and hollowness, like this gilded city. No more than the blundering of a child in a toy store, grasping at playthings, deceived by appearances, never penetrating the truth beyond. Riches, not reality. Treasures of the flesh, not the spirit.

She did not want to spend the rest of her life in that glittering toy store. She wanted to touch something real. She wanted the truth, the truth about herself, about her own substance. That was why she could not give Campbell Brinkman a glib answer. She could not make him into another toy. She loved him at least enough to realize that. If she was to give herself to him, she had to know what she was giving.

She wanted the truth, and she wanted it with a desperate need that Petruschka, with her youthful certainties, would never know.

Petruschka's cheeks were now flushed with the vodka. "And this other man—the one you were asking the General about—who is he?"

"I don't know."

"You don't know? Then why have you come all this way to find out what happened to him?"

Kate refilled their glasses. "I don't know that, either."

Petruschka smiled crookedly and drank. "This is Western *politesse*. You do not wish to talk about these things, so you say you do not know."

"No, I'm not being polite. It's the truth."

The girl leaned forward. "I look at you," she said, and her eyes traveled dreamily over Kate as she spoke, "and I see a woman who has everything. Everything. She has beauty, money, culture. Intelligence. Taste. Above all, freedom to enjoy what she is. I do not believe that this is a woman without certainties."

Kate smiled a little tightly. "Drink up, Petruschka. We have a long day ahead of us tomorrow."

IRON CREEK, COLORADO

Truck hated being here alone.

The place gave him the creeps. The walls were paneled in knotty pine and bristled with snarling faces: stag and wild boar, chamois and ibex, swooping eagles, beasts from foreign lands whose names he did not know. They frightened him. The horns and skulls and tusks and fangs and talons made his flesh cringe.

Worst of all was the seven-foot black bear in the corner, curved claws raking at the air. The bear terrified him. It was humiliating. He, a trained warrior, to be afraid of a stuffed animal. He deliberately avoided meeting its furious glass eyes as he waited. Tried not to imagine it was moving stealthily toward him.

Outside the windows, the dark forest stretched in all directions. He always met Control here, but usually on weekends. Through the week, it was the loneliest place on God's earth.

To console himself, he thought about last night, reliving the assault in his mind. But not even that could take away the stare of the black bear. He gave a little whimper of relief when he heard the Mercedes G-Wagon roaring up the drive.

He stayed where he was, listening to the thump of the car door, the crunch of gravel, the heavy thud of Control's boots across the floor-boards. He was already standing to attention, clutching the seams of his jeans between finger and thumb, face looking rigidly forward.

Control grunted as he put something down on the floor, went into the lavatory, urinated. A good stream for an old man, rattling loudly into the pan without interruptions.

The cistern flushed, and Control came up behind Truck.

"Not bad." He slapped Truck on the back. The blow was so powerful it made Truck rock on his feet, despite his musculature. "Not bad at all. That son of a bitch had it coming to him. You did good."

Truck flushed hotly with pleasure. "Did my best, sir."

"You did good," Control repeated. His iron fingers kneaded Truck's shoulder. "Got something else for you. No violence this time. Not yet, anyhow. A li'l intelligence work."

"Sir."

"You prefer action, huh? Maybe you'll get a li'l action, too. But not yet. Got ourselves a potential enemy here. Rich lady up in Vail. Sticking her nose into what don't concern her. My friends asked me to check her out." The fingertips bit and molded Truck's muscles, crossing and uncrossing the border of pleasure and pain until Truck wanted to cry out. "Lady's away from home right now. Gives us a good chance to take a look in her apartment. Check on what she's up to. You understand?"

"Yes, sir."

"We got a contact in Vail. Mr. Ray. He's gonna drive you up there himself. You do whatever he tells you, okay?"

"Sure."

The fingers clamped so hard he almost screamed. "You're gonna be discreet, boy. No mistakes."

"No, sir!"

"Tomorrow morning. Eleven-thirty. You be ready for Mr. Ray. Okay?"

"Yes, sir!"

Control's hand dropped at last, leaving Truck's shoulder bruised and throbbing. "Unload the car," Control ordered.

Truck jumped to it.

Control had brought twelve cases of Krug champagne in the back of the Mercedes four-wheel-drive, another five cases of bourbon. Truck carried the cases two at a time, at the double, grunting with the effort. He loaded them into the huge refrigerator.

When he had finished, he snapped back to attention, his chest heaving.

Control was smoking a cigar, his heavy features pensive. "We need to know where we are," Control said. "Then," he said softly, "maybe I'm gonna let you loose on her."

Truck's face stretched in a rictus of excitement. *Yes.*

Control patted his shoulder, unerringly finding the bruised tendons. "You're gonna like Mr. Ray," he said. "You do whatever he says."

Truck remained at attention until he could hear the roar of the G-Wagon's engine no longer. Then he slowly relaxed.

His excitement slunk back into its lair for the time. This was the worst part. He had to wait at least one hour before leaving the place, busying himself with tidying and sweeping. Alone with the black bear.

St. Petersburg

The next day, Kate was once again sitting in the office overlooking the Neva. Petruschka sat at her side, wearing one of the skirts Kate had given her with a luxurious alpaca cardigan. Perched on the edge of her chair, with her booted legs crossed, she visibly preened in the costly garments. She talked idly as they waited for the General to come in.

Kate herself was tense and silent. Would it be yet another dead end? Yet another lie? A truth more dreadful than any falsehood? The weather had changed. The sky loomed heavily over the cathedral, and the river was dark and turbulent. Snow whirled against the window-panes, big flakes that clung and slid down the glass sluggishly. She had put on a severe, almost somber Gianni Versace overcoat that morning, and she kept it on, even though the General's offices were comfortably heated.

The inner door opened and the General bustled in, carrying a folder under one arm. It was evidently twenty or more years old, a dusty sage green, printed with Cyrillic characters. He nodded curtly to the women, all business. This time he neither smiled nor dusted off his labored English. He spoke in rapid Russian, directly to the interpreter.

"The General asks, do you have the money?" From her wide eyes, the girl was surprised by what she had been asked to translate.

Kate opened the attaché case and took out the package. She tore open one corner to reveal the money inside, but did not pass the package to the Russian.

He nodded, satisfied, and spoke to the girl.

"The General says he has the information you asked for. He understands that you want no further information, and that this will conclude your transaction."

"Tell him that is correct."

"He says that since you cannot read or speak Russian, he will dictate to you the information in the file, and you will write it down."

"What about the file itself?"

"He cannot give it to you."

"How do I know this information is accurate?"

The interpreter conversed with the General. The General, for answer, lifted the file and opened it. There was a small photograph stapled to the first page. She leaned forward. It showed the haunted face of a young man with a number stamped across his chest. She had seen that face before.

She must have made some small sound, a moan perhaps, because Petruschka reached out involuntarily as if to touch her hand.

"*Madame!* Are you all right?"

"Yes," she said huskily.

"Would you like some water?"

She shook her head slightly. Her fingers trembled as she took the notepad out of the case and uncapped the gold Dupont fountain pen. There was a strange metallic taste in her mouth, a frightening turbulence in her heart. She was accustomed to hiding her emotions, but it cost her a physical pain to keep still.

"I'm ready," she said.

The General consulted the file and spoke brusquely. Petruschka was uncertain now. She stammered over the first words, which were a list of Cyrillic characters and identifying numbers. Kate copied them down.

"The prisoner was first identified in a Displaced Persons camp on the Eastern Front in the summer of 1945. At the end of the war he had been liberated from a Nazi extermination camp near Riga, in Latvia. After processing, the military authorities passed him on to the NKVD for questioning. His interrogators were named Alexei Feodorev and Mikhail Volsky."

She wrote the names down. "What did they question him about?"

"There is no record of the interrogations," the girl relayed.

"Is there any way of finding out whether these men, the interrogators, are still alive?"

"The General says, we Russians are a long-lived race."

Kate did not answer the General's smile. "Please go on."

"After initial interrogation, it was decided to prepare charges against him."

She looked up. "What charges?"

"That is not recorded."

"Why wasn't he given back to the proper authorities? Why was he turned over to the NKVD?"

"The General says the NKVD was the proper authority."

"Was he tortured?"

The translator's face took on a pinched look as she listened to the reply. "Considering that the prisoner had recently emerged from a Nazi death camp," she relayed, "a few beatings would probably have sufficed to secure a confession."

"A confession to what?"

The reply was short and calm. Petruschka did not meet Kate's eyes. "The General says, a confession to anything."

Kate sat in silence. She was not here to express her anger and pain at events that had taken place forty-seven years ago. This was not the place to protest against the monstrous injustice of the Soviet system. She controlled her face and voice. "Please continue."

"In September 1945, he was sent to a prison near Gorky. In

March 1947, he was moved to the Lubyanka Prison in Moscow, and held in a preliminary detention cell."

"Preliminary detention? But he had already been in prison for two years."

"It indicates he was still being interrogated."

"He was still being interrogated two years after his arrest?"

"Yes."

"Was he ever charged with any crime? Was he ever tried and found guilty of anything?"

"The General says there is no record."

Her patience snapped. "Goddamn it," she said explosively. "How can there be *no record*?"

It didn't need translating. The General's bushy eyebrows came down heavily. He spoke gruffly to the girl, who swallowed anxiously.

"The General says the information he has is simply a record of dates and places. He has no other information. It is of no use to question him on details which he cannot supply." The General was speaking again. Petruschka listened, then translated. "He says, you wanted the truth, without embellishments. He will give you the truth as he knows it, and then you will give him the money. That is all. If you want lies, they come extra."

Kate forced herself to control her feelings. "All right. Continue."

She did not interrupt again. The gruff voice of the KGB general and Petruschka's chanted translations became a litany.

"In 1948, he was moved to Lefortovo Prison in Moscow. He was given the number E-615.

"In 1949, he was sent to Gulag Corrective Labor Camp Number 5431 in Tambov.

"In 1952, he was sent to Gulag Corrective Labor Camp Number 2112 near Vladivostok.

"In August 1956, he was sent to a transit camp, C-56, near Tashkent.

"In December 1956, he was sent to Gulag Corrective Labor Camp Number 732 near Kiev.

"During 1957, he was moved to Gulag Corrective Labor Camp Number 9513 in Lithuania.

"In the winter of 1959, in the same camp, he was shot."

Kate lifted her head slowly. She repeated the last word, as though it were new to her.

"Shot?"

The interpreter licked her lips. "The General means he was shot dead. Executed."

Silence flooded into the room.

They were both staring at her, as though apprehensive, waiting for some reaction to the brief, brutal sentence that had curtailed the brief, brutal history she had traveled so far and paid so much to unearth. But she was no longer conscious of them. Her gaze was directed inward, at a scene in her own mind, of snow and blood and despair. There was a hot, hard lump in her throat. Tears welled in her eyes and spilled, unchecked, down her cheeks. She did not know she was crying. She was so hypnotized by her vision of the past that it was as if the present had lost its meaning to her. She was not aware that Petruschka was holding out a handkerchief to her. Only when the girl leaned forward and began to dab at her cheeks did she move and push the consoling handkerchief away.

She wiped her eyes with her wrists, an oddly childlike gesture. Her voice was choked. "Ask the General why he was shot."

The interpreter began relaying this, but the General cut her off with a rattle of Russian.

Petruschka translated: "Kate, the General says the execution was an act of mercy."

Anger rescued her from her pain. "An act of expediency, you mean. Because he could never have been freed alive, could he? He couldn't ever be released, in case he told the world what they had done to him. Isn't that so?"

Petruschka hesitated, evidently struggling with the ingrained dread of this man and what his uniform represented.

"Ask him that," Kate commanded harshly. "In those words."

The girl obeyed. The reply was curt. "The General says, exactly so. That is why the execution was an act of mercy."

"And how many other American soldiers did this happen to?"

Petruschka looked frightened as she listened to the reply. "The General says he warned you at the outset that this was a topic of the utmost delicacy and that vital international relations could be harmed. You assured him you had only a private interest. He asks, did you lie to him?"

"No. I did not lie." The woman in the beautiful Milan coat made a concentrated effort to conquer her emotions. She held up the page she had written on, with its dozen sparse lines of dates and places. "Is this all he can give me?"

The General spoke at some length. Petruschka translated: "The General says you have paid for the truth, not for an official lie. He says you were correct not to rely on formal channels. He says you now know the true fate of this man, something they would never tell you in Moscow."

The General's eyes held hers as he spoke again.

"He says, please watch him closely."

Kate watched as the General closed the file. There was a paper shredder at his side. He switched it on and began feeding the file into the hopper.

"No! *Please!*" There was such raw bereavement in Kate's voice that the General stopped instinctively. "Please," she said in a shaking voice, poised on the edge of her chair. "The photograph. Let me have the photograph."

He hesitated, uncertain.

"Please," she repeated with a terrible urgency. "I have no other picture of him."

He pulled the photograph loose and passed it to her. She clasped it between both hands, as some communicants clasp the communion wafer.

The General fed the rest of the file into the machine. There was a brief growl, and a fistful of confetti was expelled into the bag. The General switched the shredder off and dusted his hands symbolically two or three times.

The transaction was over. It was finished.

Kate put the photograph into her attaché case without looking at it again. She felt empty, dreamlike, as though she had been wrenched out of her own reality into another world.

She had to get out into the air. She rose to her feet. "Thank the General," she instructed the girl, "and tell him I appreciate his frankness."

Petruschka wiped her palms on her new skirt as she, too, rose. Her plain face was pale. The General spoke to her, a succession of guttural commands to which she nodded submissively. Kate shut the attaché case with a click, leaving the money on the desk. "Is he telling you to keep your mouth shut?"

"Yes, Kate."

"It's good advice."

"I know."

They stood together while the General picked up the telephone and issued commands to the security guards to let the women out of the building.

"Where will you go to now?" Petruschka asked Kate in a low voice.

"Back to Moscow."

"Have you found out everything you wanted to know?"

"Almost."

The General accompanied them to the door. As they were going through it, his thick fingers closed around Kate's wrist. She had a wild flash of nightmare, of things that clutched from under beds in the dark.

"This man who was shot," he said in his heavy English. "Who was he?"

Kate searched his face intently for a moment. Then she smiled bleakly into his eyes.

"He was a survivor," she said.

She pulled her wrist free from his grasp and left to continue her journey.

VAIL, COLORADO

Born and bred in Colorado, Truck had never been to Vail before.

He had never seen anything like it, except maybe on a Christmas card when he'd been a kid.

It was early evening. High above the town, the snowy peaks caught the last pink glow of the setting sun. Down in the valley below, the shadows were purple and blue. Vail was a sparkle of lights and windows, trees and houses strung with fairy lights. He saw a sign reading, WELCOME TO VAIL: FOUNDED IN 1962. The town was only six years older than he was.

They drove into a parking structure, where other cars were parked, Mercedeses and Porsches. "No cars allowed in Vail," Mr. Ray said, switching off the engine. "Parking's short. Know what this space costs me? Ten thousand dollars a year."

Truck said nothing.

Mr. Ray got out and opened the doors. Truck carried Mr. Ray's luggage along the street from the parking structure, heavy bags, pairs of skis and poles, a huge sheepskin coat that must have weighed fifty pounds.

Expensive clothes shimmered in brightly lit shop windows. Several shops specialized in furs, sleek pelts gleaming under halogen spots. Restaurants were already doing business. Snow was heaped on the sidewalks. Christmas music was coming from speakers. Mr. Ray inhaled the crisp air with a grunt of enjoyment. "Smell that? Like champagne."

Truck had never tasted champagne, but he nodded.

Mr. Ray ran into a group of acquaintances carrying skis and poles over their shoulders. Rich, happy people, having a good time. They called hellos to Mr. Ray. Mr. Ray didn't introduce Truck, but some of them glanced at Truck with amusement. He stared back, uncomprehending.

Mr. Ray led Truck to a lodge with iron-railed balconies piled high with firewood. They climbed stairs to get in. The apartment was warm, in contrast to the crisp air outside; some kind of heating system must be on all the time. It *smelled* expensive, even before you looked around.

The floor was covered with a pile carpet that ran wall to wall and was so thick you couldn't hear a footfall. There were violet lilies with green leaves in the carpet. The furniture was heavily padded, softly comfortable. There were several paintings, mostly of mountains and snow, and a big bronze statue of a cowboy on a rearing horse.

There was a lot of wood, gleaming and figured, heavy with varnish. The walls were paneled in it. So were the ceilings, which were set with recessed lights. Huge windows looked out at the ski runs that sloped down toward the town from the mountains all round.

"Bought me this place in '72," Mr. Ray said, his voice furry with pleasure. Mr. Ray was around the same age as Control. He even looked like him a bit, big and heavy, with a beaky nose and glassy, suspicious eyes. "Vail was just a village then. Modernized it last year. German kitchen, hot tub on the roof, all the woodwork." He was not interested in Truck's opinion. "Put the stuff through there."

Truck carried the luggage into a bedroom. The bed was the

biggest he had ever seen, an ocean of quilted pink satin. Hanging over the bed was a big painting, a nude. But not a woman. A muscular boy, his body contorted in a weird pose that indicated some kind of ecstasy or torment. The painting was embarrassing. Truck wondered where he was going to sleep.

When he came back, the old man had poured himself a bourbon and had spread a map on the coffee table. He stabbed at it with a thick forefinger. "She lives right there. A condo in Potato Patch. You can walk to the place from here."

"Do I have to break in?" Truck asked, staring at the map.

"Don't be an asshole. I got the key."

"How?" Truck asked.

"What's it to you?"

"Nothing."

Mr. Ray gulped at the bourbon. "Shut your yap, then. We're gonna dress you up like a sportsman, boy. Down jacket, skis over your shoulder, a ski hat. You're gonna walk down to Potato Patch and just let yourself into the apartment like you owned the place."

"Yes, sir."

"Siddown," Mr. Ray said, gesturing to the sofa. "Open your ears. I'm gonna tell you what you have to do."

His Heart Was pounding. He'd never been so nervous before. Excited, yes, but not afraid. He felt ridiculous with the goggles slung round his neck and the skis over his shoulder, the clumsy boots squeaking in the snow. He felt as though the whole world could see he didn't belong here, could no more ski than he could fly. But no one challenged him, and self-discipline prevailed on the long walk.

Getting into the woman's condo was as easy as Mr. Ray had said it would be. There were people around, but nobody looked twice at him. He just opened the door with the key Mr. Ray had given him, trying to keep his breathing nice and easy, and let himself in.

He shut the door and leaned against it. He'd committed more assaults than he could remember, had even killed for Control, twice. None of that had been as difficult as this. He was at home in city streets. He was a fish out of water here in this living Christmas card, among the laughing rich folks.

He straightened and looked around. The place was shadowy. It had a sweet smell. The smell of the woman who lived here. Now excitement was taking the place of fear. He had made it. He was inside. He wished she was home. Lying in her bed asleep.

He moved silently round the apartment, drawing down the shutters, as Mr. Ray had told him to do. When they were all shut, he finally turned on the lights.

It was different from Mr. Ray's apartment. At first sight it confused him. The colors weren't bold and flat, but subtle, delicate. It fell into place as he stared. She collected all kinds of Indian junk, proudly displayed like treasures around the place. The paintings weren't of mountains and snow, but were either dark with age, in heavy gold frames, or vague, abstract things he had no way of understanding. The furniture wasn't padded and comfortable, but old and ornate. His eye slid uneasily over inlay and carving. There were porcelain and silver bowls on a table. He had never seen anything like the porcelain before; it glowed like a soft rainbow. She liked old things. Old, but in perfect condition. He felt an instant contempt for the place, partly because he instinctively recognized it as the product of money, education, and taste.

He pushed into the bedroom. A double bed, smaller than Mr. Ray's. A wood-burning stove, enameled in pink and green, also old but in perfect condition. Didn't she have anything new? More Indian crap, more weird paintings. The sweet smell was stronger. Almost like the smell of a naked woman's skin. He felt lust rise in him, an adrenaline rush that made his vision darken.

He opened the dresser and yanked out drawers until he found her underwear, neatly arranged in piles of panties, bras, slips. These things covered her intimate body. Something inside him was twisting for release. He'd have torn the place up if he was doing this on his own, ripped the crotch out of all her panties. But he was on duty here. Mr. Ray had told him not to leave the slightest trace of his presence. He shut the cupboard reluctantly and got down to business.

He unscrewed the mouthpieces of all three telephones in the apartment and inserted the tiny electronic appliances Mr. Ray had given him. He used a jeweler's screwdriver to connect them to the red and green wires inside the telephones. His fingers were big and clumsy, but he'd done electrical work before.

Then he dialed the number Mr. Ray had made him remember. He let it ring three times, then hung up. He sat by the telephone, staring around the apartment. He was anxious to prove himself, prove that Control's trust in him was not misplaced. This assignment made him something special. Not just a dauber of paint, a smasher of windows, a killer of decrepit old men, and a beater of teenaged girls. The biggest thing that had happened to him since he had started working for Control.

Absently, he lifted his right hand to his mouth and sucked the tattoo. He'd had them done when he was seventeen, in the flaps between finger and thumb on both hands. A spider in a cobweb on the right hand, a swastika on the left. Stylish.

The telephone rang once, then stopped. It was the signal the electronic devices were working. Pleased with himself, he pulled on the glove liners and started looking for the papers Mr. Ray had told him about.

He hit lucky the first place he looked, a big inlaid cabinet. The rolltop drawer was filled with folders and papers. There were also some photo albums.

He opened one and stared at the pictures in them. A good-looking woman around forty, maybe more, standing in the snow, holding ski poles. With her, a Marlboro Man look-alike, grinning to show his white teeth against his winter tan. They were having a good time in the photographs, drinking at an outdoor table, skiing, walking arm in arm.

A couple of pages later, there was a full-face shot of the woman, a studio portrait. She was smiling faintly into the camera. Close up, she was a little older than he had guessed from the other shots. Maybe forty-five. There were faint lines around the eyes, gray in the thick, dark hair.

But she was a doll.

She was fucking beautiful.

He bet that body of hers was in juicy shape. She was a woman who took good care of herself. Excitement flared in him like wildfire. *Maybe I'm gonna let you loose on her.*

He picked up the photo album, feeling his whole body prickle. He stared at the picture greedily, dragging the image into his mind. He felt it begin, the bonding process. He could smell her skin, her hair. He could feel the softness of her skin under his fingers, hear the sounds she would make. He could taste the metallic brightness on his tongue.

He knew it was going to happen. He knew it with animal certainty. He smiled into the warm eyes of the photograph. When Control asked him to take her out, he'd do it with style. He had never killed a woman before.

Before he did, he would take the reward that had nothing to do with the money they paid him. He knew how to do it so they would never even know. It was so simple. You wore a condom. That way there were no traces. You could do it any way you wanted, and there were no traces.

"You and me, babe," he whispered to the photograph. "You and me."

He had to force himself to put it down and complete the task that his masters had set him.

VAIL

Halfway through her unpacking, Kate came upon the good-bye present Petruschka had bought her in St. Petersburg. It was a brightly painted wooden doll of the sort called *matryoshka,* little mother. You twisted the dumpy figure open, and inside was a smaller, younger woman. Inside that, a smaller, younger woman yet. And so on, opening the hollow figures, until you uncovered the smallest and youngest of all, a tiny solid baby, its painted eyes closed in wooden sleep.

She was certain Petruschka had been aware of its symbolism when she had bought it. Petruschka had recognized that this was what she was doing to herself, unpacking the past, layer by layer, searching for the solid core within.

She had begun a walk into herself that had taken her a long, long way from her starting point. She'd hardly known what she was looking for at first. What she had found had gone beyond her expectations.

The trip to Russia had opened a chasm at her feet, an abyss

whose edge was crumbling, even as she walked on it. It had exposed a possibility she had never dreamed of, vistas of shadowy questions without answers.

She sighed and put the doll on a shelf. Over the past ten years, she had become a devoted collector of Native American art, and her acquisitions were displayed against the dusky pink walls: fragments of weaving, pieces of figured pottery, some small, exquisite medicine dolls. The Russian doll came from another world, another culture. A culture less innocent, infinitely more cunning.

She finished her unpacking and showered, rinsing away the weariness of the flight. Then, bracing herself, she called Campbell.

"Where are you?" he demanded grimly before she'd even finished speaking.

"At home."

He was silent for a moment, incredulous. "Why didn't you call me from Russia, so I could meet you at Denver?"

"I thought it was better this way," she said. "Are you very angry with me?"

The line clicked dead in her ear.

She spent three-quarters of an hour wondering whether she would ever see him again. Then she heard the ominous rumble of his Porsche in the drive.

He walked into the apartment stiff with anger. Despite the fact that he came from one of Colorado's richest families, he cultivated the handsome ranch-hand look of a cigarette advertisement. He did not touch her. He spoke roughly. "How could you do this to me, Kate?"

"I'm sorry," she said helplessly. "I'm so sorry."

"I've been sick with worry. You knew what I would be going through."

"Yes, I knew."

"But you didn't care."

"I tried to call you, Campbell, so many times. It's almost impossible to call out from Russia right now. The lines are in chaos." It was at best a half-truth. But she hadn't avoided contacting him out of indifference. She'd known she wouldn't have been able to cope with his questions, his concern, his demands that she come home. On top of what she had been going through, it would have been too much.

"I've had half the diplomatic staff in Moscow out looking for you," he said grimly.

"Oh, Campbell!" she said in dismay. "You didn't!"

"I called the American ambassador and the British ambassador. They couldn't even find a trace of you."

"You should not have done that," she said tiredly. "I expressly *begged* you not to do that kind of thing."

"What was I supposed to do? Let you vanish without trace into a disintegrating wasteland?"

"That's melodramatic."

"Don't accuse *me* of melodrama," he said savagely. "How long has this charade been going on? How long will you keep it up? Until you've destroyed our relationship? Until you've destroyed yourself?"

He was angrier than she had ever seen him. She was almost afraid of his passion. "I avoided the embassies," she said, keeping her voice deliberately flat. "I wanted confidentiality. I know you were worried, but you shouldn't have done that."

He was very tense. "This was too much, Kate. Too much. I've put up with a lot from you, but I cannot believe you could treat me as badly as this."

"I've said I'm sorry, Campbell," she said quietly. "I've also been through a lot. Don't attack me just yet."

"You've been on this wild-goose chase for months now, Kate. You've changed out of all recognition. I think you're going crazy."

"Campbell, please . . . "

"Have you spoken to Connie?"

"Not yet."

"You used to have a wonderful job, Kate. She loved you. Now she's going to fire you."

"If Connie fires me, then she fires me," Kate said calmly.

"Don't you *care*?"

"Of course I care. But I have a scale of values—"

"A scale of values!" He was shouting, filling the apartment with noise. "What values? What are you looking for? Why do you have to do this to yourself, to us? Is this caprice of yours so fucking important?"

"It is not a caprice. I'm simply looking for the truth."

"Truth?" he echoed bitterly. "I don't think so. I think what you're interested in is fiction. A dream. A childish game of fantasy, played at the expense of those who love you!"

"That is not fair."

For a moment she thought he was going to hit her. He took

her arms, his fingers biting into her flesh fiercely. "Kate, I can't stand any more of this. You've got to choose between me and this obsession of yours."

"My obsession, as you call it, is no threat to you," she said quietly. "It's not your rival or your enemy. And I won't be doing any more research for the next few months, I promise you that. I'm going to be too busy at work. I can't let Connie down."

"But you can let me down," he said, staring into her eyes. "And in the spring, the whole circus starts up again, right?"

"Perhaps."

"Give it up, Kate. It's destroying our relationship."

"You don't know what you're asking me. I promise you, our relationship would be destroyed far more surely if I did *not* pursue this thing to the end."

"No. You must choose, Kate."

"Right now?" she asked, trying to make it sound light.

"Yes," he said. "Right now. Otherwise I'm going to look for someone else. A less complicated relationship. Maybe with a younger woman, someone who isn't consumed by the past."

"A younger woman?" Her smile was twisted. "You have a nice way with ultimatums, Campbell."

"I'm not speaking of a fantasy," he said brutally. "I know exactly who I'll go to."

"Jesus."

"You've been completely ruthless in your own way," he said. "Now I'm being ruthless in mine."

Her eyes blurred with tears. "I need more time, Campbell. Just a little more time."

"*No.*" His face darkened with renewed anger. "No more time. No more trips. No more mysteries. Either you give this thing up, or I'm leaving you here and now!"

"I can't give it up," she whispered.

There was a terrible silence. Then, at last, he released her and stepped back. She knew by his face that he had already made up his mind, long before coming here tonight. At some point during her absence in Russia, she had lost him. She wondered with dull incuriosity who the young woman was who was waiting for Campbell, and whether he had already made her his. "Good-bye, Kate," he said.

He did not kiss her.

She was still standing in the same position when she heard the Porsche pull away down the drive.

She Awoke Early, just as the sun was beginning to push up over the Rockies. For a moment after awakening, she was aware of the gaping hole inside her, without quite knowing what had torn it. Then she remembered, and the pain rushed into the empty place. It was an immense effort to get out of bed.

She made herself a cup of coffee and went to the window to drink it. Her condominium commanded a magnificent view of Vail Mountain. There had been a storm in the night, and the world was white. She had, at least, got back just in time for the snow. The town was filling with people. From now until Easter, there would be no rest for anyone who worked in Vail.

As the sun rose in glory, the Sno-cats were out, grooming the slopes. From this distance they looked like industrious, armored bugs. She watched them, drinking her coffee, until it was time to go in to work.

The Graf Resort was one of the biggest hotels in Vail. With seventy suites, three restaurants, a Bavarian-style *weinstube*, two spas, a conference facility, and unparalleled access to the best slopes, it represented the multifaceted future of what had started out as a small family ski hotel twenty years earlier.

The Graf Resort was equally capable of hosting a young couple on their first skiing holiday or a convention of industrialists. It could supply an uncomplicated Western breakfast for two or an elaborate European banquet for two hundred. Masseurs and physiotherapists in the spa could tone up muscles before a day on the slopes or soothe them down afterward. It had a brainstorming center, equipped with sophisticated computing and presentation equipment, where a new model of car could be launched or a new company profile planned.

The finest craftsmen had built the Graf Resort, and the finest personnel ran it. It had been proudly designed to cater to anything the most demanding guest could dream up. It was run with flair and precision.

And as a supremely successful by-product of all this effort, it generated money. With suites averaging $350 per night in the season, the Graf grossed an easy $30,000 daily, over a million dollars per month. With successful stratagems to extend the season into the summer, through conventions and conferences, the Graf had not taken less than seven million dollars in each of the past three years.

The woman who, more than anyone else, had created the Graf had a square, masculine face, a brusque manner, and a vigor of presence that belied her sixty-five years. She moved and looked like a woman twenty years younger. A recent biography, detailing Constanze Graf's thirty years in the hotel industry, had made her into an almost legendary figure. Many of her employees were afraid of her, though Kate had never heard her utter an unjust reproof or a cruel word. She thought the fear was more an awe of Connie's passionate belief in herself. Nor was she intimidated by the penetrating gray eyes that met hers as she entered the starkly uncluttered office.

They kissed briefly, cheek to cheek. Though she had come to know Connie relatively late in life, Kate considered her one of the best friends she had. Their working relationship did not alter that fact. But Connie's face had already given Kate an ample hint of what was to follow. As always, Connie smelled hauntingly of Diorissimo. "Sit," Connie said shortly, gesturing at the chair that was opposite her own across the black marble desk. Kate obeyed, crossing her hands in her lap. "Are you rested, Kate?"

"Yes, Connie."

Connie studied her. She probably already knew about Campbell—there was not much Connie did not know—but she did not comment. "You're still tired. But you'll soon recover. You have youth on your side." She spoke in staccato sentences, almost without pauses. "You spent a long time in Russia."

"It took me a long time to find the person who had the information I wanted. That is why I was away for so long. I'm sorry if there have been problems, Connie. I hope Jennifer was able to cope."

She waved abruptly. "We'll come to that later. I take it you found the information you wanted."

"I found something extraordinary."

"An answer?"

"A question."

"So it isn't over?"

"Not yet, Connie."

Connie's face became stony. "You will not rest until you have the answer?"

"I cannot rest, Connie. But I promise you, I won't let you down through the snow season. And I promise you, I'll make up for my absence these past weeks."

"But next year no doubt there will be other places to go? Other people to see?"

It was the same question Campbell had asked her. "Yes, Connie."

"How much more time do you need?"

Kate spread her hands. "I don't know."

Connie rose abruptly from her desk and went to the window of her office. The exterior of the Graf was elaborately timbered and rough-plastered, as though a dozen fourteenth-century inns had been swept up in some Wizard of Oz cyclone all the way from Bavaria to be gently put down in line here, in the foothills of the Colorado Rockies. The restaurants and guest suites followed the same lines, oozing European charm and *gemütlichkeit*. But the working areas of the hotel, from the kitchens to the offices, reflected quite another taste, stark, modern, and coldly efficient. Without turning to look at Kate, she asked, "How long have you been with us?"

"Eleven years. You know that."

"Are you happy with us?"

"Yes."

"Then why this?"

Kate hesitated, but only momentarily. "I *am* happy in my work. You know I am. But I also have a deep longing to know the truth about myself. It goes deeper than words, deeper than I can express. I can't help it, Connie. I have to find out about the past—"

"In my experience," Connie cut in, "the past is dangerous. Just as dangerous as the future."

"I'm driven, Connie. I'm not doing this willingly."

The older woman's exquisitely tailored back was very straight. "Once I was driven, too. But I was driven in the opposite direction. I was twenty-seven when I left Europe. I left my country in ruins. My husband dead on the Eastern Front. My family killed in the raids. My own child buried under a million tons of rubble. I cut free from the past, Kate. And I was never so stupid as to want to go back and dig it up again."

Kate was silent for a while, deeply moved by Connie's words. "I understand what you're saying to me, Connie."

"You've devoted a considerable amount of time, money, and energy to this obsession of yours. You admit that you're disturbed by what you are finding. Have you considered that what drives you may be an abnormally powerful fantasy? That you may need help of a psychiatric nature?"

Kate winced. Campbell had hurled the charge at her as a weapon. Connie would not have said it unless she meant it.

"I'm not unhinged, Connie."

"Would you know if you were?"

"I think so."

"I'll take your word for it." She paused for a while. "If my daughter had lived," she went on quietly, "she would have been about the same age as you. I think you know how I feel about you."

Kate nodded, her eyes moist.

But when Connie turned, her face was hard. "This hotel is my life's work. I value you highly, have done so from the start. That is why I placed so much trust in you. I depend heavily on you, Kate. As for Jennifer Prescott, she likes to think she can do your job. As you will see, I think, she feels she can step into your shoes. She cannot. She is bright and ambitious, but she cannot stand in for you. Only you can do your job. You, or someone as qualified as you."

"I know that."

"You have done exceptionally well, Kate, and I am fully aware that your contribution to the success of this hotel is considerable. By arguing for corporate customers all those years ago, you added a new dimension to this business. I made you director in charge of corporate guests, and over the years you brought in thousands of new clients who will come again and again. You are one of the reasons the Graf Resort has become what it is today. I will always be grateful to you. More grateful than I can say." She paused. "But this is a time of serious recession, in the hotel industry as everywhere else in the economy. And you know that the corporate business is the first to be hit. We cannot afford to carry anyone. Not even you. We can't be satisfied with anything less than one hundred percent of your time or attention."

"I know that, too." Kate reached into her bag and took out the sealed envelope. She laid it on the desk. "You don't have to say any more, Connie. This is my letter of resignation."

Connie was silent for a while, her eyes on Kate's face. "Does it really mean so much to you?"

Kate's voice was husky but steady. "Yes."

Connie picked up the letter and turned it in her fingers. "I won't open this yet. I'm going to take your word that you will show the utmost loyalty during this winter season. At Easter, we will talk again. I am going to hope that a season of intensive work will help restore you to your senses. If, at Easter, you can tell me that your odyssey is over, that you have got all this out of your system, and that you can once again give this hotel one hundred percent of your professional attention, then I am going to offer you a partnership, something I would have done this winter, under other circumstances. Otherwise, I am going to accept your resignation, Kate. And in doing so, I am going to recommend that you seek psychiatric help."

Kate found she was trembling slightly as she rose. "Connie, this means a lot to me."

"Come back to us, Kate." Connie walked her to the door and opened it. "Come back the way you were."

K ate's Section Was strategically placed between the central administration offices and the conference areas. It took no more than two minutes to walk down from Connie's suite to her own.

She tapped at the door of Elaine Brodie's office and walked in. Elaine, the conference coordinator she had recruited six years earlier, jumped up from behind her desk

"Kate!" Elaine hugged her tight, her slim rib cage pressed close to Kate's. Kate hugged her back. When they stepped back to look at each other, Elaine's face was flushed with pleasure, her eyes bright beneath the glossy chestnut fringe. Elaine had a model's slimness and a model's wide-cheekboned face. "You look terrific. How was Russia?"

"Interesting," Kate said wryly.

"Can't wait to hear about it."

Kate held out the small but heavy package. "Here. A small present from Moscow."

Elaine opened the wrapping paper eagerly and slid out the elegant tin. "Caviar! Beluga, too! Kate, you shouldn't have."

Alerted by their voices, Luke Milton came into the office, a bustling little man with a General Custer beard and mustache. He, too, hugged Kate robustly. It always touched and surprised her that her staff showed such genuine affection for her. Brought up in a cool English family, she was still startled by American warmth now and then.

"For you." She gave him his package. It was the same as Elaine's, and he was equally delighted. He, too, wanted to know about Russia, and she told them a few vignettes: the specter of poverty facing ordinary people, men and women sitting in the markets with only three things to sell: a can of shaving cream, a pack of cigarettes, a light bulb. The contrast with the imperial glories of St. Petersburg and Kiev. The ominous murmurs of a hard-line backlash, a military coup.

"So we're not about to build a Graf Hotel in Kiev?" Elaine said with a smile.

"They're begging for Western investment," Kate replied. "But the whole system seems hopelessly corrupt. How can any Western company go in there? You're dealing with racketeers and gangsters the whole time."

"Sure," Luke said with a shrug. "They're the only ones who have any idea how capitalism works."

"It's a very debased kind of capitalism, Luke."

"They'll learn. They'll have to. It's good to have you back, Kate," he boomed, his deep voice out of proportion to his size. "We've missed you."

"I've only been gone a couple of weeks," she protested.

"That's all it took," Elaine said with a wary glance at the door.

"What does that mean?" She followed Elaine's thumb-jerk up the corridor toward Kate's own office. "Wasn't Jennifer able to cope?"

"I'd say Jennifer copes a little too well," Luke said, making no effort to lower his tone.

"Oh?" Kate prompted uneasily.

"We've had a number of directives from along there," Elaine said enigmatically. "Jennifer feels your policies have been on the conservative side. She has ideas of her own."

"Jennifer likes to think she's God's own gift to the hotel industry," Luke said. "She's been running not only your job, but Elaine's and my job, too. Or she thinks she has."

"I see," Kate said, though she didn't. "But Jennifer has no right to give either of you direct orders."

"You tell her that," Luke advised dryly. He laid his hand on Kate's arm. "Know the fable about the man who nursed a viper in his bosom?"

"Yes. Why?"

"Just watch your back." Elaine nodded, her shiny ringlets starting their daily escape from her chignon.

Kate walked to her office, a flicker of anger and unease awakened in her. All Jennifer had had to do was carry out well-laid plans and follow well-defined instructions. It had not been her place to criticize or direct any of Kate's expert staff. Despite her distrait appearance, Elaine Brodie was brilliant at her job, which was to take all the bookings, check out exactly what each party would require, from special diets to special equipment, and make sure every relevant department of the hotel knew what was called for. For his part, Luke was a born fixer who could make a dollar do three dollar's work any day. If Jennifer had been alienating Kate's precious and talented staff, Kate would find it hard to forgive her.

She entered her own suite. Jennifer Prescott, who had been sitting behind her desk, stood up. She was a pale-skinned, blond-haired beauty of twenty-four, a summa cum laude graduate from a college hotel-management course in Colorado Springs. She was, as Constanze Graf had said, bright and ambitious. She was also, beneath a charming and efficient exterior, as cold as the December wind that brought the white riches of Vail. She greeted Kate with a kiss on the cheek, but her smile was wintry.

"Wonderful to see you back," she said, standing back to study Kate from head to toe, as though her trip to Russia might have left some visible traces. "We were beginning to think you'd decided to take up residence in Moscow."

"Not this year." Kate smiled. She looked around and immediately saw the changes.

Her desk had been moved from its place by the window and now faced the wall, a position Kate hated, but which Jennifer preferred. Her potted caladium had been replaced by an austere arrangement of dried flowers; the caladium had been pushed into a corner by the radiator, where the delicate crimson and white leaves had long since drooped and died.

Kate turned slowly to survey the room. Her photographs, pictures of Evelyn, Anna, and Campbell, had been taken off the desk and unceremoniously pushed into a corner of a shelf. In their place was a photograph of Jennifer's current boyfriend, an Italian ski instructor with a Hollywood smile. Even the geometric Navajo rug had been changed for a pastel-blue carpet. The Navajo rug was nowhere to be seen. There were too many other, smaller changes to bother looking at. The message was blatant. It was no longer her office. It was Jennifer Prescott's office.

So this was what Connie, Elaine, and Luke had meant.

Kate swung on her heel to look Jennifer in the eyes. There was a flush on the pale cheeks, but the clear green eyes were defiant, even hostile. "I made a few changes while you were away. I hope you don't mind."

"This is not your office," Kate said, keeping her voice even. "You have your own room next door."

"You were gone so long. I needed access to your files, your computer. It got tedious, coming and going. I asked Constanze whether I could set up a temporary headquarters here. She agreed it would be better."

"This isn't a temporary headquarters. It's an *Anschluss*."

"I'm sorry you choose to see it that way. It wasn't intended as such."

"Wasn't it?"

"I don't know what you were doing in Russia," Jennifer said, her flush deepening, "but someone has had to do this job. That someone was me. While you were away, I have had to carry the full burden of this job, Kate—"

"Bullshit," Kate said crisply, and saw the other woman's cold eyes widen. Jennifer's vocabulary did not include four-letter words. "You had to keep up the impetus, for a couple of weeks, of projects which I conceived and initiated. That's all. Don't kid yourself you did anything more than that." She walked up to Jennifer, trying to keep the anger out of her voice, trying to keep it clinical. "You're not capable of carrying what you call 'the burden of this job,' Jennifer. I invented this job, and I was doing it while you were still in pigtails. As for Elaine and Luke, they have probably forgotten more about this business than you will ever know. You have a great deal to learn, not just about your work, but about common human courtesy. How *dare* you tell them how to do their jobs?"

"They needed guidance."

"That's the most arrogant thing I've ever heard," Kate said sharply. "And how dare you move my personal possessions out of this office?"

"I haven't had time to straighten things out—"

"I got back yesterday. You knew that."

Jennifer could not meet Kate's dark eyes. She looked down, her red-nailed fingers tightening around the bunch of files she was now clutching to her bosom like a shield. "Please don't make an issue out of this, Kate."

"There's no issue, Jennifer. You tried to give me a little message. Now I'm giving you one in return. I'm going to the restaurant to get a cup of coffee. While I'm gone, you get hold of one of the maintenance men, and you get my office back the way it was. Move all your stuff out, and move all my stuff back in. Then I want you to go to Luke and Elaine and apologize quietly for any offense you may have caused them. I don't care what you said. I don't even want to know. I just want you to tell them you are very sorry for your rudeness." She saw the flush become an ugly red stain in each pale cheek. "You have fifteen minutes."

She took the bunch of files from Jennifer's hands, pushed past her, and walked down the corridor to the elevator. She felt somehow cleansed by anger.

Kate was one of the few members of the staff who were permitted to use the main restaurants and bars, rather than the staff facilities. She preferred the Jäger Restaurant to the others. The elk trophies and fine Victorian furniture reminded her pleasantly of Great Law. There was even the same kind of smell, of beeswax and potpourri, and of clean wood smoke from the big log fire. It was an unashamedly opulent setting and the closest thing to a genuine European ambience she had seen in Vail.

She picked a table on the outer fringes, away from the breakfast buffet area, where the guests were still coming in. Her severe wool suit and scarf marked her apart from the guests, most of whom wore unzipped ski suits, ready for a day on the slopes, bright nylon jackets slung over the backs of their chairs.

She crossed her legs and sorted through the files with practiced swiftness, checking on the status of her top projects for the coming weeks: symposiums, conventions, banquets, courses, large parties of businesspeople being rewarded with a skiing vacation for work well done by the corporations that employed them.

They were her special clients, the guests she was personally responsible for.

She had seen the possibilities of such corporate customers long ago, had seen in them not only a potentially rich field, but a means of solving the perennial problem of a ski-resort hotel. Hosting conferences was one of the only ways to keep going through eight or nine long, snowless months.

Eleven years ago, a widow fresh in grief, she'd come to Vail and had promised Constanze Graf she could find those clients. She'd hardly known what she was saying, but Connie had taken her at her word and had given her the brief.

She'd persuaded Connie to provide some initial facilities, little more than a meeting room and some presentation equipment in those days, and then, as marketing manager, she had begun the long, grueling process of selling the product, making up the rules as she went along.

The inspiration had always been there, but in the first years, going out to find the clients had been pure toil: making endless calls, organizing mailings, visiting every company within four hundred miles that had ever held a conference or run a course. She would not forget the physical exhaustion of those days, what it was like to invite a hundred shrewd businessmen to a party at the Graf, organize it more or less single-handedly, down to the catering, smile for three hours, make speeches, showcase the goods, press the flesh, project the friendly, creative, innovative image that was so important to attracting these potential customers. Then fend off the two or three that always tried to jump on her weary bones afterward—and then do it all again two nights later.

But it had paid off.

Within five years, by the mid-80s, corporate clients were bringing in a million dollars a year, and her staff had expanded to twenty-five people. Connie had appointed Kate one of the two directors directly under herself, had moved Kate up out of the hurly-burly to plan overall strategies for the sector, with a massively increased salary that reflected her importance to the hotel. They had appointed a professional marketing manager, brought in Elaine and Luke as conference coordinator and technical supremo, each with logistical and secretarial support. At around that time, Kate had persuaded Connie to sign the Graf up with a marketing consortium. Again, her instinct had proved infallible; the high initial costs of joining had been dwarfed by the huge response, not only from clients from all over the United States, but from Europe and the Pacific, too.

It had been the right move at the right time. As Vail grew from a small skiing resort to a multinational leisure axis, it had gained an unparalleled reputation as a place conducive to inspiration, where intellectuals and businessmen from all over the world could find an atmosphere uniquely suited to thinking and making decisions, where imaginations could expand and tired minds rekindle. Of late, even the religious had begun flocking to the town on large-scale annual pilgrimages, perhaps hoping to be closer to God among the snows of the Rockies. The success story of the Graf had mirrored the success story of Vail, beginning with wild scenic beauty and ending with an unrivaled professional service.

Kate had pioneered in her field, and Connie had not been exaggerating when she'd said that Kate had shaped the hotel as it now stood. During the major reconstruction work of four years earlier, millions of dollars had been spent to add facilities for the kind of delegates the Graf now attracted—suites of conference chambers, syndicate and meeting rooms, audiovisual equipment, even a separate gymnasium, indoor pool, and sauna for these clients. Kate had argued that only the most contemporary facilities could allow the Graf to compete in an ever more competitive market; the upsurge in business since then had proved her triumphantly right.

Kate had worked long and hard for Connie Graf. In return, Connie had paid her supremely well. The offer of a partnership would be the culminating link in a relationship that had matured and strengthened over more than a decade.

Kate had enriched Connie and the Graf Hotel. But Connie had been right: Corporate business was fragile. In a recession, corporations canceled or curtailed conferences. They brought their personnel home, instead of hosting them overnight. Their accountants shook their heads over entertainment budgets. They stopped holding banquets. They demanded even greater discounts in an area where discounting was already honed to a knife edge. Now, more than ever, Connie was relying on Kate's imaginative skills and inspiration to ease the Graf through the rocky patches ahead.

Kate bent her head over the papers, her mind reaching into the future, engaging with the familiar rhythms and inspirations of her work.

The first was a report from the marketing manager. For the past six years, they had employed a Denver-based advertising agency to promote the Graf as a conference center. The campaign had been successful, but was now starting to look a little uninspired, while the budget had risen to the extent that it was now a major expense. Kate was sure they weren't getting value for their money anymore. She turned the conventional options over in her head: Shake up the existing agency? Move to an even bigger, more expensive, but perhaps more talented agency? Cut the budget, maybe even cancel the contract for a year? Could they do the job better than an agency?

"Great to see you back, Miz Kelly."

She looked up as the waiter placed her cappuccino in front of her. "Oh, hi, Joey. Good to see you, too."

He put a glossy pastry tray next to her cup. "Try the almond biscuits," he said conspiratorially. "The pastry chef's latest secret weapon. Watch the guests sneak 'em into their pockets."

"Thanks, Joey," she said with a smile. "I can't afford the calories, but it looks so good."

"How did the Soviets treat you?"

"They don't like being called Soviets anymore. They've gone ethnic."

"So what else is new?" Joey shrugged. "Good to see you home, Miz Kelly." He glided away. Home? she wondered. Was this home? Yes, she decided. It was. She turned back to the files.

Jennifer had done a competent job in her absence, that much was evident. The preparations were up to date, the correspondence in order. Later, she would reward the girl with the praise she deserved. She had been harsh with her just now, but she had been angered by the insolence of Jennifer's assumption that she had earned Kate's job by a few weeks of sitting in. It was not that easy. And offending Luke and Elaine had been unforgivable. That little humiliation had been warranted.

Kate checked her watch. She would give Jennifer rather more than fifteen minutes to get the offices sorted out and make her apologies. There was a limit to how much face you could make people lose without impairing their capacity to work, and Jennifer was good at her job. Kate had been grooming her for three years, and she did not want all that training to go to waste if she could help it. The girl just had to find her place.

She sat at the table for ten minutes longer, making notes in her quick, neat script. She drank the coffee, ate enough of the pastry to please Joey, then gathered up her things.

On the way back up to her office, she thought about Campbell Brinkman. Last night he had called her completely ruthless. He had been right. There was a stony trait of ruthlessness in her that he, though they had been lovers for over three years, had never seen until now.

She, for her part, had seen traits in him she had not known about—or had not wanted to know about—until now. His selfishness, his shallowness, his inability to understand how important her search was to her; those had come as an unpleasant revelation.

It did not make her love him any the less. Nor did it take away her own grief at the chasm between them, nor the blazing jealousy she knew would replace the grief over the next weeks.

She had lost Campbell. A gaping hole in her life. An amputation that would leave her lonelier and more isolated than ever. Was it worth it, her search for the truth?

She no longer knew whether she had the courage to follow those rusted links, one by one, to their secret root.

Maybe, if she could give it up now, she could persuade Campbell to come back. Forget any of it ever happened. Resume her life. Return to normality. Get back her soul.

A wave of dizziness made her sway in the plush elevator. Could it really be that easy?

She remembered the golden rim of the sun edging up over the mountains that morning, filling the sky with luminescence. Its warmth touching her face.

No, she thought. It's not as easy as that.

She closed her eyes and thought of the little faded photograph the General had given her. In her mind's eye, she stared at the gaunt face with the hollow eyes.

It's not as easy as that.

And one thing is certain, she thought. Whoever you are now, whatever you were then, wherever in the world you are hiding, I will find you.

When she got upstairs, she pushed Elaine's door open and peered in. Elaine was talking to her secretary, but she caught Kate's eye over the secretary's shoulder. She grinned, and made a circle with her finger and thumb.

Kate walked briskly down the corridor and into her office. Everything had been restored to normal, as if by magic. The Navajo rug was back in its place, looking as though it had been carefully cleaned. Jennifer was standing submissively by the desk, waiting. Her eyes met Kate's from under the fringe of pale blond hair.

"I apologized," she said in a small voice. "I guess I owe you an apology, too."

Kate glanced around and smiled warmly. "Good. I've checked through the files, and you did a fine job. I'm pleased. Now, shall we get down to work?"

IRON CREEK

He had fitted a stereo in the pickup, and he always rode around with a dozen cassettes he had bought for it: Metallica, Def Leppard, Thin Lizzy, Megadeth. He put *Master of Puppets* into the machine now, and the shrieking, distorted guitars hammered against his ears.

He drove up the fir-lined avenue that stretched for two miles from the road to the hunting cabin. It was set high up in the woods, a remote and silent place among the snows.

He parked the pickup in front of the stone building. Heavy eyebrows of snow and ice over each window gave the place an angry, glaring look. It was Saturday, but no one else was here yet. He unlocked the heavy front door and threw open all the wood shutters. Wintry light made the skulls and teeth gleam on the walls. The bear's curved talons reached for him.

He set about building a fire. They liked a big blaze, and he piled thick crosscut logs onto the andirons, using plenty of kerosene to get the kindling going. Soon a sheet of yellow flame was roaring up the chimney.

Control did not arrive until several others were already at the lodge, sitting around the blazing fire, drinking ice-cold Krug, smoking cigars, getting their expensive weaponry ready for the morning's entertainment. Truck watched Control greeting the others, his heart pounding in anticipation. He was certain Control would give him the orders today. Control had the style of a king, despite his age and girth. He was like the black bear, a potent killer, one of the old brigade. The real thing, Truck thought. Beside him, all the others were like puppets.

He was standing up straight as a soldier, fingers grasping the seams of his jeans, face rigidly forward. Control ambled over to him, big yellow teeth gleaming in a bear's smile, his rifle slung over one arm. There were sniggers as the fat bankers and lawyers noticed Truck's pose. They thought Control's devoted soldier was a joke. They knew nothing about what was inside him. Knew nothing of the bonds, the duty, the discipline.

Control ignored them. "Truck. Sonny boy." His paw closed on Truck's shoulder.

Truck felt the fingers bite savagely into his muscles. Control's strength was awesome, not the strength of an old man; the strength of a pack leader not yet out of his prime. Excitement loosened Truck's bowels.

"We gonna have some fun today, ain't we?" Control asked jovially.

"Yes, sir," Truck replied, nodding his cropped head. The 12,000-acre private estate abounded in elk and mule deer, and there were rainbow and brown trout in the brooks; but Truck knew Control's real pleasure lay in the spring bear hunt, a savage ritual carried out with dogs and beaters. The bear hunt outraged ecologists across the state. Control laughed in their faces; the 12,000 acres were private.

Control thrust Truck along as they walked to the door. Their boots crunched on the gravel. Out of hearing of the others, Control snicked the bolt of his rifle open and peered into the breach. It was a fine weapon, German-made, the magnum slugs capable of dropping a fully grown bear with one shot. "We passed on the information, Truck. They sent back to say you did good. They know which way to move now. They know what they want." Truck's mouth was dry. Control slammed the bolt shut and looked up with his hard, glassy eyes. "The woman's back in Vail. They want action. Quick action."

Truck rubbed his mouth with his palm. His hands were shaking.

Control grinned, seeing. "I said I was gonna set you loose on her, didn't I?"

Truck nodded.

"Raring to go. Hey, Truck?"

Truck smiled, feeling the old acne scars pull tight.

"You like the sound of that?"

"Yes," he said hoarsely.

"She's a whore," Control said, his voice like gravel sliding down a chute. "An enemy whore. You're the one to execute her. Aren't you?"

"When?" Truck asked, his voice unsteady.

The old man slapped Truck's shoulder hard enough to rock him. "Soon, sonny boy. Maybe you and Mr. Ray gonna take another trip up to Vail this weekend. You liked Vail, didn't you?"

Truck nodded. He was already doing it in his mind's eye. Every detail unfolded with hallucinatory clarity.

"There may be some special instructions," Control said. "But Mr. Ray'll supply everything you need. Take it easy."

He ambled back into the lodge. Through the roaring in his ears Truck heard a guffaw rise up from the others as Control made one of his legendary witticisms.

He felt like one of the elect. Exalted.

MIAMI, FLORIDA

Gritty-eyed and somnambulistic, Anna let herself into her rented beachside cabin. She lugged her suitcase inside and locked the door. It was late afternoon, the sun slanting dustily in through the blinds, obliquely zebra-striping the walls and the neutral furnishings. Beyond the straggly, overgrown garden, the flat and lazy waters of the gulf stretched to a hazy nothing. She was tempted to walk down to the beach and loll in the warm water, but her body was too exhausted.

She got a Michelob out of the refrigerator and drank it from the can, grateful for the wintry foam in her parched gullet. Then she flopped onto the sofa and thought about André Levêque.

Why hadn't she been more duplicitous? She'd been a fool to go in there to confront him like that. It had achieved nothing, and it had risked her life.

He could have killed her if he'd wanted to. He and that thug of his could have cut her throat and dumped her in the sea somewhere for the sharks to take care of.

She found herself wishing, as she had done so many times before, that she had inherited less from her father and more from her mother. It was from her father that she had inherited her single-mindedness, her combative morality. She saw the world as he had done, in black and white; not as her mother did, in shades of gray. That was how her father had brought her up: not to see gray areas.

The manner of his death had only cemented his teaching all the more grimly in her psyche, even though she knew his stiff and unbending principles had led directly to his destruction. If she'd ever possessed her mother's virtues of compromise, of being able to see six sides to every question, they had submerged at the time of her father's death. She was uncompromising.

That was why Drew McKenzie had chosen her to be groomed as the paper's youngest investigator.

It was also one of the reasons she and her mother had grown so much apart. Anna knew in her heart that each time her mother looked at her, she saw the oily flames swirling from the gutted car, the street full of broken glass.

She and her mother were not very alike physically. Anna's coloring was darker than her mother's. Her skin was dusky, her eyes and hair were very dark; her hair, heavy and abundant, appeared black in almost all lights but direct sunlight, when it revealed a sienna gleam. Her mother's looks were serene and classical. Anna, slim and mysterious, burned like a dark flame. She had her mother's willowy grace without her height, and though she was more beautiful than her mother, it was a far more elusive beauty.

It would have been difficult for a stranger to guess her ancestry; there were shadows in her face that were sometimes Moorish, sometimes Celtic, sometimes almost Oriental. Most men found her exotic, baffling. They were enchanted by the smoky eyes and the mouth that seemed to brim with the promise of passion. The slender, flamelike body fascinated them. Most were surprised, unpleasantly, by the cool, forceful mind. Long ago, an early boyfriend had told her, "You're a houri. What every good Muslim finds waiting for him in paradise." She had realized that her face and body corresponded to some male dream-ideal, like the women on the covers of fashion magazines. That apparently innocent beauty had reminded Levêque of Hollywood and had probably led him to underestimate her. Until it was too late.

She was accustomed to being underestimated by men. But whatever else she was, she was sharp-brained, and Levêque had not been the first man to underestimate her.

It was such a long time since she had seen her mother. They had grown so much apart. Since her father's death, things had somehow disintegrated between them, as though neither woman knew how to comfort the other. It was time to try and reconstruct the relationship. Get back to being mother and daughter again. Suddenly the thought of sweet, clean Vail, where her mother now lived, was wonderfully appealing. She would make time this winter, she told herself, to go there and be with Mama.

She sank into the cushions and reached for the telephone. She punched in her mother's number in Vail. Jennifer Prescott's cool voice came on the line, and a minute later she was put through to her mother's much warmer tones.

"Darling!"

"Hi, Mama. I just got back from Haiti."

"I'm so glad you're back. How did it go?"

"Okay. No problems."

"Was he nice, this surgeon of yours?"

She grimaced. She hadn't told her mother anything substantive about the assignment. "No, he wasn't very nice. In fact, he's involved in something very ugly."

"You haven't been taking any risks, have you?" She could hear the instant worry in her mother's voice. "Haiti can be a dangerous place, Anna."

"Yeah, I know that. And I haven't been taking any risks." She crossed her fingers as she uttered the lie. "I'll send you the clippings." Her mother would hit the roof when she saw the clippings, but she would face that when it came.

"Do that. It's been a while since I had anything to put in my album."

Anna smiled. "I tried to call you a couple of days ago, but they said you were away."

"Yes. I was in Russia."

"In Russia! Mama, you're amazing. What on earth made you decide to go to *Russia*?"

She heard the gentle laugh. "Midlife madness, I suppose. I saw a special offer in a travel agent's window in Denver, and thought, what the hell. So I threw some clothes in a bag and went off for three weeks. Moscow, Kiev, and St. Petersburg."

"Good for you! How was it?"

"Mixed. Moscow was grim. St. Petersburg and Kiev were magnificent. The whole experience was an eye-opener."

"I'll bet. I'm dying to hear about it. Did you take lots of pictures?"

"Well, not too many. I brought you a couple of presents. I hope you like them."

"I will, don't worry." Anna rested the ice-cold can on her hot forehead. "Just don't talk about snow right now. It's like a sauna here. Did Campbell go with you?"

"No, Campbell didn't go."

Anna sensed, rather than heard, the change in tone. "Oh? Everything okay between you?"

"Not exactly."

"Oh, Mama. What's gone wrong?"

"I can't really discuss it right now."

"Sure." Not with that little creep Jennifer Prescott probably glued to the extension. "I'll call you again at home."

"I'll call you. I don't want you wasting your money."

"I don't count calls to you a waste of money," she said with a smile.

"I'll still call you."

"Okay. I was thinking . . . "

"What?"

"Well . . . " She cursed herself for the way her manner had become so diffident, but couldn't change it. "I've got a couple of weeks vacation coming up. I know this is your busiest time, but I thought maybe we could spend Christmas together for a change."

"Wonderful!" The joy in her mother's voice chased her shyness, making her feel warm inside. "That's the best news I've had in months. When will you come?"

"I haven't worked out the details yet. But probably just before Christmas. Around the twentieth?"

"Oh, Anna, it'll be so lovely to have Christmas together again. You're right, I am going to be busy. But you can take care of yourself during the day. The town's full of young people. I'll fix you ski passes, lift tickets, everything you need. You can use my car. And we can have the evenings together."

"Roasting chestnuts and toasting marshmallows."

Kate laughed. "Neither of us has roasted a chestnut or toasted a marshmallow in our lives."

"No reason not to start now."

"Oh, honey, this is wonderful news. I'm so excited."

"Me, too." Her mother's delight made her feel guilty. "I'm looking forward to seeing you so much."

"Me, too."

"Maybe it's fate," Kate said musingly.

"I'm sorry?"

"You coming right now. I want to talk to you."

"About what?" Anna pressed, curious.

"A bit of family history. A few things I've never told you, that I should have done."

"Sounds creepy."

She heard the warm, soft laugh. "It beats the Addams Family, I promise you." There were voices in the background. "Honey, I can't stay on the line. I have to go."

"Okay. I'll wait for you to call me."

"Okay."

There was a silence on the line. It was the silence that always came just before the end of their conversations. The pause in which each woman said silently to the other, *I love you. I'm sorry I lied to you.*

"Good-bye, darling."

" 'Bye, Mama."

Anna put the telephone down, and for some reason she could not fathom, felt like crying.

3

VAIL

The banquet hall looked magnificent, adorned with flowers and banners for the salesmen.

Like other entertaining areas in the Graf, it had been decorated in Austrian style, with a strong Germanic hunting theme. The huge fireplace was a replica of one from a famous castle in Salzburg, its stone mantel six feet high and eight feet wide. With a log fire blazing, it provided a dramatic focus to the room, which was half-paneled in oak; above the paneling, dark, glossy oil paintings of hunting themes alternated with mounted deer heads, some of them magnificent. Over the fireplace hung a 330-pointer killed ten miles from the hotel a few years earlier. In each corner stood a suit of armor, a pike gripped in the empty steel glove, while high above the paintings, in the shadowy recesses near the ceiling, ancient weapons were arranged in orderly rows.

It was easy for guests to fantasize they were Teutonic knights back from a Crusade, or hunters who had just swaggered in from slaughtering wild boar in the Black Forest. Guests who had never swatted a fly or been farther east than Topeka loved it.

Kate checked the menus, handsomely printed in black-letter Gothic script on parchment, and reflected that tonight's meal of venison and Rhine wines would encourage the fantasy still more. It was an appropriate one. The sales force being regaled by their employers tonight liked to see themselves as knights, carrying their corporate banner boldly forward. Their marketing strategy was expressed in terms of battle and conquest, of new territories to be subdued, enemies to be vanquished, honors to be won. In this case, the prize was a weekend spent skiing and feasting at Vail.

Though privately she was amused by the imagery when applied to the thirty-two men and two women who would be dining here tonight, these were good customers, and it was her task to make sure the fantasy was seamless. She felt a little sorry for the two women.

It was certainly a heroic menu, starting with cured German ham, followed by a rich *Linsensuppe;* the main courses were marinated baked venison *en croûte,* served with wild berry sauces, and ten brace of roasted woodcock with chestnut stuffing. To conclude, there was a cream-laden selection of *Schwarzwälder* chocolate gateaux and *Kirschtorte,* followed by a spectacular board of American and European cheeses.

They could, she thought, work it off on the slopes or in the gym tomorrow.

Together with sodas, cocktails, six bottles of Perrier-Jouët, twenty bottles of Piesporter Goldtröpfchen, mineral waters, and coffee, the whole banquet was going to cost $5,000, just over $150 per head. And that included service, tax, and the special decorations for the banquet hall.

Kate was proud of the keen price they had come up with, prouder still of the service they were going to provide. She ran her eye along the table, remembering the early days at the Graf, when her duties had extended to checking that the maids had laid out the silverware and the crockery correctly. She reached out and stroked the snowy damask with her fingertips, aware of an earlier memory surfacing, a much earlier memory.

Standing beside Evelyn Godbold in the dining room at Great Law, soon after David's death, listening while Evelyn explained about the knives, the forks, the water glasses and the wineglasses, the napkins and the bread plates . . .

She felt a mixture of emotions steal over her, that mixture of emotions associated with Evelyn that she had never, even after thirty years, been able to shed: awe, respect, resentment, love. In the final analysis, always love. She had not yet called Evelyn, and she reminded herself to do so soon. Evelyn's health had been poor in recent years, and Kate had an uneasy instinct, though Evelyn had said nothing lately, that it was taking another turn for the worse.

"Kate?" Elaine Brodie came through from the kitchen into the banquet hall, interrupting Kate's thoughts. She was wearing a beautiful wool suit, her chestnut hair held back with a velvet band that accentuated her model's cheekbones. She was holding a portable telephone in one hand. She smiled at Kate. "What do you think?"

"It looks stunning," Kate said.

"Your menu is *formidable,* Kate."

"They're nice people, and they recognize good value. I think they're going to have a good time."

"We'll make sure they will." Elaine proffered the telephone slightly hesitantly. "Switchboard has put through a call for you, Kate. A Mr. Philip Westward, from New York. I don't know who he is, and he won't say what it's about. Do you want me to tell him you'll call back?"

"No. I'll take the call." Kate took the telephone, nodding her thanks to Elaine. She thumbed the talk switch. "Good morning, Kate Kelly speaking."

"Mrs. Kelly, my name is Philip Westward." The voice was deep and slow, authoritative. "We haven't met yet. I run an investment consultancy called Philip Westward Associates, here in New York. Your name was passed on to me by a mutual acquaintance in Moscow. Lieutenant Colonel Boris Yuzhin."

The name swept Kate instantly back to Russia, back to the search she had just agreed to suspend until next spring. Her heart lurched violently. "Yes?" she prompted tautly.

"I don't have any specific information for you." The slight softening of his tone told her he'd intuited the mixture of hope and dread that had caught her by the throat. "Not relative to the man you're looking for, I mean. But from what Colonel Yuzhin tells me, you and

I are engaged in the same kind of search. We're looking for the same kind of people. Men who suffered the same kind of fate."

"I see."

"I was born while my father was fighting in Europe during World War Two, Mrs. Kelly. I never knew him, because he never came back. I believe he wound up in a Russian prison camp in Siberia. I believe he was alive up until the 1960s. He may still be alive. I've been looking for traces of him for a long time now."

"I see." Her pulses were racing. "How can I help you, Mr. Westward?"

"I'd like to meet you." The deep voice had a husky undertone. "I think it could be very useful. We may be able to pool information. Or at the least, a common experience."

She said nothing in reply.

"Mrs. Kelly? Are you still there?"

"Yes." She pinched the bridge of her nose hard, her eyes shut. "Yes, I'm here."

"Is this a bad time to call?"

"Yes, it is."

"Would you like to return the call later, at a better moment?"

"I mean it's a bad time in general. I don't . . . I can't . . . " She was conscious of stammering. "This is the start of the season here in Vail. I hadn't intended to do any more research this year. I've decided to shelve it until Easter, or later."

"I thought we could simply talk. Exchange impressions."

"Time is very tight," she said.

"I see. Okay, I understand. I'm sorry to have bothered you."

"No, please. Wait."

"Yes?"

"I would like . . . " Kate glanced at Elaine, who was talking busily to Hans Mosel, the chef. There was guilt in the glance. "I mean, I don't want to put you off, Mr. Westward. I'm interested to meet you."

"I'm glad."

"It's just that . . . "

"I have my own plane." He said it matter-of-factly, with no vanity in his tone. "I could fly out to Vail this weekend, snow permitting. Perhaps Sunday. Would that suit you?"

"Yes," she said without thinking, her decision made.

"Good," he said. He had a slightly flat delivery, as though he were reading lines off a piece of paper, though the voice was pleasant and masculine. "I'll give you some numbers where I can be reached in the meantime."

She took them down and agreed to his provisional suggestion of dinner together on Sunday night in Vail. When she clicked the telephone off again, her palms were damp with sweat.

Elaine came over, her forehead wrinkling. "Are you okay? You look a little spooked. Bad news?"

"Oh, no. Just someone who wants to meet me."

"For a date?"

"Well, as a matter of fact . . . "

"Oh, good," Elaine said with a grin. "He had a great voice. Like warm molasses. Bet he's a hunk."

Kate mustered a dry look and passed the telephone back to Elaine. She felt shaken.

On the way back up to her office, she thought about the name Philip Westward had greeted her with. She had met Lieutenant Colonel Yuzhin in Moscow. A fifty-year-old former KGB officer, Yuzhin had spied in California during the late 1970s, but had grown disenchanted with his employers. He had become a double agent and had worked for the FBI until the Russians had caught him. He'd been tried for treason in Moscow in 1986, and had been lucky not to receive the death penalty. He'd spent the next five years in labor camps, but history had saved him. Boris Yeltsin had released him in February 1992.

On his release, Yuzhin had founded a research team called the Ark Project, chiefly composed of former gulag inmates, to search for the Americans he claimed to have met or heard about in the camps.

Kate had visited Yuzhin's small Moscow flat on two occasions. There, cramped by shelves of research materials and constantly interrupted by a ringing telephone, Yuzhin had assured her that there were hundreds of Americans, many prisoners of war from Vietnam, Korea, and World War II, who were still buried in the icy wastes of the Soviet penal system.

Despite the fact that Yuzhin had already turned up one American, Victor Hamilton, in a KGB psychiatric hospital, Kate had not been sure how much of Yuzhin's information was accurate. In any case, he had been unable to help her. He had put her in touch with others, and she had moved on.

Now here was this stranger from New York, telling her that he, too, had been looking for a man missing since 1945, a man who might have been swallowed into the gulag archipelago. He must be around the same age as she was, must have passed through many of the same experiences. She had promised Connie that she would do no more research this winter, but this was too important a contact to pass up. She had too much in common with Philip Westward to let him drift away.

She asked Gloria, her secretary, to bring the New York telephone directories, and searched for the name Philip Westward.

It was there. Several entries, in fact. Offices called Philip Westward Associates on Park Avenue, and a private address at 870 U.N. Plaza. *I have my own plane.* Whoever he was, Mr. Westward was not hurting for money. She was more intrigued than ever to meet him.

⁂

"That's Her," Mr. Ray said in a soft, furry voice.

Truck started to lean forward excitedly, but Mr. Ray's steel fingers clamped around his shoulder, digging into the muscles so that Truck almost gasped in pain.

"Easy, boy," Mr. Ray said.

Truck watched Kate Kelly through the window of the coffee shop. She was smaller than he had expected. But beautiful. More beautiful. She had her hair free, and it fluttered like a dark flame. Her skin was tan. You would never guess she was in her forties. She looked so young.

She wore a coat and boots. Despite the covering, you could see the swell of her bosom, her pert ass. Dainty as a doe. And he the hunter.

She had stopped, was looking in the big, practical-looking bag slung over her shoulder. The bag irritated him. It ought to have been more feminine.

She found what she was after, her dark glasses. She put them on against the bright glare off the snow.

Truck felt the smile stretch the acne scars tight across his face. The dark glasses were perfect. They made her even remoter, even more unavailable. When the orders came, he hoped she would be wearing them. So he could take them off, look into her eyes as he showed her what he would do it with.

Mr. Ray's breath was hot in his ear, his whisper a piercing rasp. "You like the look of her?"

"Yes," Truck said.

"Looking forward to doing it?"

He just nodded, unable to speak.

Mr. Ray rose and paid for their coffee and doughnuts. They walked out into the street. Truck still felt self-conscious in the bright skiing gear, the hat pulled down over his cropped head. He felt he looked like an asshole. But he recognized the cover was good. Nobody even looked twice at him.

When they got back to Mr. Ray's apartment, he pulled off the jacket and stretched his shoulders with an audible series of creaks and clicks. Mr. Ray popped a can of beer. "Feeling cooped up?"

"Yes, sir," Truck admitted. "Normally I'd go work out every day or so."

"Missing your gym, hey?"

"Yes, sir."

Mr. Ray's heavy lids lowered on his glassy eyes. "Tell me about your exercise routine."

Truck was so flattered he flushed red. "Lately, I been working on my deltoids." He hunched the big slabs of flesh that ran from shoulder to neck to show the old man. "These ones."

"Uh-huh."

"They're the punching muscles," he said, looking along his own scarred cheek at the swell of hard flesh. They were the ones that made people step aside in the street, made lesser breeds back off with fear in their eyes. "The best one is a bench press with the big barbells, at least a hunnert pounds." He stopped, thinking he was talking too much.

But Mr. Ray was still watching him. "Got any stuff you can do without the weights?"

"Yes, sir," Truck said. "Push-ups, that kind of stuff."

"Go ahead."

"Huh?"

"Go right ahead," Mr. Ray said. "Do your exercises. I don't want you getting out of condition."

It was an order, not an invitation, but Truck still asked, "You don't mind?"

"No. I'll sit here and watch. Take your shirt off."

That wasn't an invitation, either. Truck pulled his T-shirt off, baring his pale-skinned, overdeveloped torso. Between his hairless pectorals, a rash of scabby acne clustered. There was more, angrier acne on his back.

"Take off your jeans, too."

Feeling weird, Truck stripped his jeans. He stood there in his underpants, hands clasped in front of his groin. Mr. Ray studied him, drinking from the can, a sip at a time. Something in Mr. Ray's eyes made Truck feel a little frightened, a little sick.

Mr. Ray sat back in the settee, stretching out his boots. "Go ahead, son. Don't mind me. I'll just watch the show."

Truck hesitated for a moment, trying to figure out what it was his master wanted. Then he crouched and started into his push-ups. He clenched his teeth and started counting under his breath.

The flow of energy into his muscles was instant, driving away self-consciousness. He felt the muscles respond gratefully to the exertion, blood flowing into their veins, pumping up the tumescent flesh. He swiftly forgot Mr. Ray was there. His mind narrowed, focused brightly on the assignment. Whatever way Mr. Ray ordered him to do it, he would take his pleasure. He promised himself that. Nobody would know. Not the cops, not Mr. Ray, not Control, nobody. He'd have at least an hour. He could do a lot to a woman in an hour.

Then he would smash her to jelly with his boots.

Sweat started to break out on his skin as he moved faster and faster, oblivious to the old man who sprawled on the settee, watching him with hooded eyes.

MIAMI

Drew McKenzie gestured, thick fingers clamped around his cigar. "Think it's too subtle?"

Anna looked at the two-page-wide headline: THE UGLIEST OF TRADES. Levêque's face beamed from the main photo, the facade of his Palm Beach clinic visible in the background. "No," she said. "I think it's perfect."

The main article beneath began with the byline, ANNA KELLY, HAITI. Down on the right-hand corner of the second page, there was a small inset photograph of herself, dark eyes looking past the camera. As she watched, the layout technician delicately pasted a square of text into the space beneath. It read simply, *Anna Kelly, Investigative Reporter.* She felt her face flush slightly.

On a neighboring table, other artists were making up the copy for the two Saturday papers, which would in part lead on to and prepare for the big impact of the Sunday spread.

"I promised you a splash." McKenzie stuck the cigar back in his face and puffed it into life, clouds of acrid smoke mingling with the chemical reek of the acetate and defying the "No Smoking" signs on the walls. He squinted at her. "You nailed this son-of-a-bitch good and proper, kid. Feel good?"

She nodded. "I hope he winds up in jail."

"He won't. There'll be a lot of yelling. He'll probably lose his U.S. visa for a while. He'll have to give up his Palm Beach practice for a couple of years, sell the waterfront mansion, mothball the yacht. But I'll bet a hundred bucks the State Department won't be interested in a prosecution. And out there?" McKenzie shrugged. "He's a national hero in Haiti. And he has a lot of money. It won't even make the local papers."

Anna shook her head. "He's a criminal. He should be made to pay."

"Robin Hood had it ass-backwards, Anna. Levêque robs eyeballs from the poor to give sight to the rich. That's the way to do it."

"You sound as if you admire the guy," she protested.

"He's a realist," McKenzie said. "You have to admire realism."

She looked disgustedly at the editor. "You call that realism?"

"What would you call it?"

"Gross cynicism."

The layout artist rolled her eyes. It was not common for young reporters, no matter how brilliant, to accuse their editor of gross cynicism to his face. But Anna was different. In his rough way, Drew McKenzie had adopted her and allowed her privileges few others were granted—including access to his vast store of wisdom.

"Same thing, goddamn it." He made swimming gestures with his meaty hands, the cigar clamped between his yellow teeth. "Life flows, Anna. Flows like a river." The big palms fluttered like fat fish in a stream. "Always flows the same way. Toward the rich. Away from the poor. Unto him that already hath shall be given, or whatever."

The layout artist looked up with a smile. " 'For whosoever hath, to him shall be given, and he shall have more abundance,' " she quoted.

" 'But whosoever hath not, from him shall be taken away even that he hath.' "

"Who said that?" Anna challenged.

"Jesus Christ," the layout artist said piously.

"See?" Drew McKenzie grunted. "From the poor son-of-a-bitch who hath nothing, even his eyeballs shall be taken away."

Anna didn't want to press the point, so she simply shrugged. "I guess that's life."

"Damn right, that's life. It's a question of fitness to live. The rich are fitter to live than the poor. The powerful are fitter to live than the weak. It's self-defining, see? Fitness to live *makes* people rich and powerful."

She glanced askance at the layout artist, who was studiously bent over her work. Talk about a gentler, kinder America. She had always wondered how McKenzie squared his private cynicism with his crusading editorial image.

McKenzie laid a palm on her shoulder and led her out of the layout studio. "There could be a follow-up on this, Anna. Don't think it stops here. I'll probably want you to go back to see Levêque again."

"Oh, no," she said in dismay. She remembered the dark terror she had experienced in Levêque's jungle garden. "Do I have to, Mr. McKenzie?"

"Why not?"

"After all that comes out?" She nodded back in the direction of the layout room. "He'll put a bomb in my car. Or feed me to the sharks."

"Why should he? He'll have nothing left to lose. It'll be all in the open by then."

"He'll want revenge?"

"The man's a surgeon, for Christ's sake."

"He *kills* people, Mr. McKenzie!"

"All surgeons kill people. But they do it in the operating theater. Guns and bombs aren't their style. And don't worry, I'll send a brawny cameraman along to be your bodyguard. Maybe Perkins. He's a karate black belt. Splits wooden boards with his dick."

She did not respond to the crudity. "What the hell can I say about him I haven't already said?"

"He'll want to talk," McKenzie said with conviction. "He'll want to give his side of the story. It's a fascinating moral issue. With all the new transplant stuff, all the genetic engineering stuff, the time is ripe for a big debate about ethics in health. Levêque's right there at the cutting edge." He grinned ferociously. "So to speak."

She recalled Levêque's offer to collaborate on a book, but didn't relay it to McKenzie. "I could call him on the telephone—"

"Nah. It's gotta be face-to-face."

"I don't like it, Mr. McKenzie—"

"But you like seeing your byline there, don't you?" he said, cunningly silencing her protests. "You're a crusader, kid. That's what I like about you. You're my secret weapon. You look so innocent. By the time they pick up on you, it's already too late." He chuckled and checked his big gold watch. "Onward Christian soldiers," he said, and set off back to his office.

They made their way through the newsroom, the busy noise enfolding them. She could never pass through the newsroom without feeling excitement flutter her nerves. It was the beating heart of a newspaper, this orderly chaos of desks, people, telephones, computer screens, and buzzing printers. Not for the first time, Anna wondered whether she had made the right decision in letting McKenzie turn her into a lone gun. There was something adrenaline-pumping about being part of a news team. Like being a worker bee in a hive. You shared everything, you were at the center of the news, at the center of action, friendships, rivalries, constant work. You were constantly driven, too, it was true, with ulcer-inducing pressures on your back from the moment you reached work. Not for nothing was alcoholism an ever-present danger for journalists. But it was, by God, exciting.

The life of an investigator could be very solitary. When McKenzie had first picked her out, she'd loved the romance of being a lone wolf. When something happened to her like the scare André Levêque had given her in Haiti, she found herself glancing around the newsroom with something like wistfulness.

The noise was only partly muffled by the closing of the glass door to McKenzie's inner sanctum. The editor slid his round frame into his oversized black-leather throne. "You're coming along, Anna," he said, rifling through papers. "I'm proud of you. Take a look." He shoved a piece of paper across the desk with stubby fingers. She read it. It was a photocopy of a check, authorized by McKenzie, that had apparently been paid into her account that morning. She blinked at the amount. It was for a thousand dollars. "A little bonus," he said. "Wait until the syndication fees come in." He gave her a nod as she thanked him. "Keep yourself free, kid. I'll call you soon. Hang loose."

She caught the elevator downstairs, signed out of the building, and walked into the balmy warmth of a Miami city street, putting on sunglasses against the white glare of light. Immediately, perspiration broke out on her skin. It was time she got out of this city, started making plans to travel up to cool, white Vail.

VAIL

She had been dreaming of a golden city in the snow.

The name of the city was Byzantium, and its streets throbbed with music. The river spread through the heart of the city, veins of lapis lazuli among the gold. She wandered along the riverbank, piecing together a steel chain, link by link. She knew the chain tied her to a hidden truth, a truth that had haunted her all her adult life. If she could find all the links, she would know the answer. She would be free of her chain, free to dance to the wild, sensual music of the city.

The rusted links stained her hands with red. She looked up; a golden mechanical bird sat on a golden bough, and the music of the city came from its throat. The exquisite beauty of its craftsmanship made her eyes fill with tears. She reached out to touch the enameled wings . . .

Kate awoke in the darkness, her skin prickling. A wind was stirring through the apartment. A window must have blown open. She swung her legs out of bed and reached for her bedside light.

Before she could switch it on, she heard the noise. A single footstep.

There were two big Persian carpets in the area that served for dining and reception. As you passed from one to the other, you sometimes stepped on the underlying parquet floor. She had done it herself a thousand times.

Suddenly her heart was pounding. She withdrew her hand from the light switch. She strained her ears, but all she could hear was the wild thudding of her own blood. A presence touched her face, perhaps the opening of a door somewhere, or a movement, making her skin crawl. There was someone in the apartment.

A moment of sheer terror took her, making her so weak she could hardly draw breath. Her breathing was ragged, and it hurt to try and control it. It seemed to roar. Her bedroom door was ajar. Everything was in darkness. Perhaps she had imagined that footfall?

Then she heard another sound. A rustle of clothing.

"Oh, God," she mouthed silently. Her stomach was hurting violently with fear now, making her want to vomit. "Oh, Jesus, oh, God."

She knew exactly what she had to do: slip out of her bedroom, down the corridor to the kitchen, out onto the service landing. She had to do it silently and swiftly, before he realized.

She had no weapon. Then she remembered the skiing gear in the corridor, Anna's skiing gear, which she had taken out of the storeroom yesterday to get ready for her arrival.

Her fingers closed around one of the poles. It was a pathetically ineffective thing, designed to weigh next to nothing and slip aerodynamically through the air, but the skis themselves were far too heavy and unwieldy.

Clutching the pole like a spear, she pushed through her bedroom door, eyes wide and staring into the pitch blackness. Her feet were almost noiseless on the thick pile carpet.

Then she was drifting down the corridor toward the glass door, like a ghost.

As she pushed the kitchen door, it creaked softly. Her head whipped round to look over her shoulder, and there was a tall figure against the dim rectangle of the window. She saw the angular head turn to stare at her.

Then, with a harsh grunt, he lunged at her. She heard his boots thudding on the wooden floor toward her.

With a choked gasp, she twisted to one side and swung the ski pole up with both hands, using all her force. She felt the point thud solidly into some part of him, face or chest, and he uttered a gasp of pain. But the violent contact made her miss her own footing, and she fell clumsily onto the floor, almost losing the ski pole.

She scrabbled wildly to get up, hearing his heavy breathing above her. Something swept past her ear with an explosion of air. His boot. He was going to kick her to a pulp.

She rolled away, the pole tangling between her thighs, tripping her up. There was not enough oxygen in her lungs, and she could not breathe. Terror seemed to have frozen her diaphragm. At any moment his heel would stamp into her soft vulnerability, crushing her.

His boots clumped on the parquet. She managed to get to her feet, crouching, the pole held in front of her body, a forlornly inadequate protection. Then there was a blaze of light. A flashlight. He had a flashlight. The halogen beam slashed across her naked legs, swept up to stab into her eyes.

She jabbed the pole again with the violence of desperation, aiming at the dark silhouette of his head. The point struck him with enough force to bend the fiber shaft. The flashlight's beam swung wildly across the ceiling. She heard him curse viciously, his voice thick with hatred.

She turned and thrust through the kitchen door and slammed it behind her. Lunging across the kitchen, her hip cannoned into the heavy table with bone-jarring force. It almost stopped her in her tracks. She hobbled in whimpering agony to the service door, fingers groping wildly for the key. It turned, but she could not move it. In her terror-stricken clumsiness, it had stuck in the lock. Without it, she was lost.

She moaned as she wrestled with it, her whole body cringing against the battering blows that would rain down on her, smashing her to the floor. The ski pole slipped out of her free arm. She rammed it against the door with her knee to stop it falling.

She heard the kitchen door open. She looked in horror over her shoulder. He came through the door fast, the flashlight probing the dark, finding her.

The key would still not budge. His boots were thudding across the kitchen floor toward her. She flinched away from the attack.

Then something erupted in her neck, sending her sprawling on her hands and knees on the checkered *terrazzo* floor. Dazed, bewildered, she scrambled for the kitchen table, trying to heave herself upright. She was only dimly aware of the intruder looming over her, of a weapon lifting above her head.

Then it smashed into her skull. Light flared, shattered into splinters. She dipped into darkness momentarily, then emerged crawling on the floor at his feet. He had her pinned in the beam of his flashlight, like a doe in a car's headlights. He wore lovingly shined, military-style boots. She could see her own reflection in the black leather as he stepped forward to kick her.

MIAMI

The telephone jerked her out of sleep. As she groped for the receiver, she registered that she had fallen asleep on the sofa in front of the television. She groped for the remote and switched down the sound.

"Yes? Hello?"

The line had the echoing quality of a long-distance connection.

"Anna Kelly?"

"Yes, I'm Anna. Who is this?"

The man's voice was deep. "My name is Philip Westward. I'm calling from Vail, Colorado."

"Yes?" she prompted uneasily.

"This is about your mother. I've just taken her to hospital. Your name and number were in her diary."

Anna's heart lurched. "Is she sick?" she demanded.

"She's had a bad accident."

There was suddenly an icy core in her warm and drowsy body. She swung her legs round and sat up. "Is she okay? Can I speak to her?"

"I'm sorry. She's in intensive care."

"What happened to her?"

The caller hesitated briefly. "It looks like she was attacked in her apartment."

Sharp physical pain surged in her heart. "Oh, Jesus, no."

"She's been badly beaten. She has multiple injuries. They're doing X-rays right now."

"Was she raped?" she asked, dry-mouthed.

"I don't know," he said flatly.

Anna tried to fight off the nightmare unreality. "Who did you say you were?"

"My name is Philip Westward. I had an appointment to see your mother today. When she didn't turn up, I went to her condominium and found the door open. I went in and found her in the kitchen. She was unconscious."

"Oh, Jesus, no," she repeated, her knuckles to her mouth.

"Is there anyone else I should call?"

"Connie," she said at once. "Constanze Graf, her employer at the Graf Hotel. And Campbell Brinkman—he's a friend. He has a house in Vail at—"

"Campbell Brinkman is being interviewed by the police right now."

Another wave of shock hit her at the flat statement. "Did *he* do it?"

"I have no idea. The police have just taken him down to Denver from the hospital. Miss Kelly, I think the important thing is that you come over to be at your mother's side right away."

"Yes," she said. "I'll come."

He must have sensed she was numbed. "Want me to find you the quickest flight to Denver?"

"Yes," she said shakily. "Yes, please—"

"I'll call you with the details as soon as I have them. I'll meet you at Stapleton and fly you up to Eagle in my plane. Okay?"

"Okay," she said, obedient as a child.

"I'll speak to you again in five minutes."

"Thank you—"

The line clicked dead in her ear, leaving her in space, starting to fall to earth, fast.

2

ADOPTIVE DAUGHTER

1959 – 60

ITALY

She awoke to the wailing of old women and knew her world had ended.

She ran downstairs, her heart pounding, almost tripping on her long nightgown. She burst into the front room and stopped dead.

The old women who were weeping over the bed looked to her like a throng of ravens. They, for their part, stared at Catarina as though she were the angel of death herself. Perhaps she looked like it. Her black hair snaked in wild disorder around her pale face, and her thin body was rigid. She saw the face of the woman who lay on the bed, her arms crossed on her breast, and screamed.

It was a scream quite unlike their formal keening, a sound so ragged, so filled with despair, that one of the old women crossed herself in shock.

The girl flung herself forward. *"Nonna,"* she screamed. *"Nonna!"* She shook her grandmother's corpse desperately. Rigor mortis had not yet set in, and the jaw fell open blankly. That brought her to her senses a little. "Oh, *Nonna,*" she said brokenly. She pressed her lips to the cool brow. She'd refused to believe that her grandmother would not get better. But the old women had known. While she slept, they had gathered, drawn by some instinct, to watch the death. She wanted to beat them away, but her grief was choking her.

She tried to close her grandmother's mouth. Withered hands intervened, pushing her aside. This was their work, not hers.

They set up their wailing again, filling the air with the shrill ritual of grief. The sound had its own rhythm, ancient and piercing. Catarina backed away. Her grandmother's face was already that of a stranger. She paused at the door, but it was too late for farewells. She was already alone in a world from which she had long since stopped expecting pity.

SOVIET UNION

Snow spiraled down from a low sky. The forest was great and dark. It brooded in a vast silence that swallowed the shuffle of boots in the snow, the moans of the prisoners, the shouted orders of the guards.

Roped to the old man behind him, prisoner E-615, who called himself Iosif Alexandreyevich—Joseph, son of Alexander—lurched along the forest track. The prisoners moved crookedly. All were shaven-headed, and all were terribly thin. Some had difficulty walking, including the old man roped behind Joseph, who had once made propaganda films exalting Stalin's five-year plans. Whenever he stumbled, the ropes jerked on Joseph's wrists. He tried desperately to ignore the pain. He tried to ignore the bitter cold that clawed through his clothes and the mounting terror that was loosening his bowels. He focused his mind on a means of escape. There must be a means of escape. Something. Anything.

The prisoners wore the ragged tunics of what was euphemistically called a Corrective Labor Camp. The chief labor of the camp was death. The ordained death was usually slow. But it seemed new orders had come from Moscow. The camp seethed like an anthill. For the past twenty-four hours, gangs of prisoners had been herded into cattle trucks headed toward Leningrad. Other, smaller groups like this one had been marched out of the camp into the forest. They had not been issued with tools for work. None had returned.

The prisoners had survived, somehow, the fathomless cruelty of their sentence. When Stalin had died and been replaced by Khrushchev, many had thought deliverance would come. It did not. Despite Nikita Sergeyevich's program of liberalization, despite the surge of releases, nobody was freed from this camp. Nor did the killing conditions change. Nothing changed. Dictators had changed, but the gulag had remained. At least the prisoners had survived until this hour. Now death was upon them.

As that conviction grew, those who could began to pray aloud. The ragged murmur rippled along the line:

Hail Mary, full of grace, the Lord is with thee . . .

He was a tall, dark man. His face, long ago, had been fine-boned. Now it was a skull-like mask. The hands that were tied behind his back had once been elegant. Now they were claws that writhed.

He had once borne himself with grace, but now he moved like an animal, feverishly hunting around him for a way out of the snare.

But no way opened. Though they were in haste, the guards allowed their prisoners no chance to stop or lag behind. Roped as he was to his comrade, Joseph knew he would not be able to run more than ten steps before he would be cut down.

Even if he could get into the ominous black haven of the forest, what then? The forest stretched unbroken for miles in all directions. They would not even bother to hunt him down, knowing he would be dead of cold in a few hours, and food for crows.

Still, his eyes flickered to left and right unceasingly, while his stumbling feet took him to the edge of oblivion.

Joseph And The others jerked to a halt at last. The guards, jabbing at them with bayonets, forced them into a ragged line, then urged them backward.

The prisoners who saw it first began to scream. Here the earth plunged down into a deep chasm, a long, deadly fall. At the crumbling edge, trees had died, their gnarled roots exposed. Some already hung out over the void, ready to fall with the weight of snow that had gathered in their branches.

The guards' faces were intent as they drove the prisoners to the brink. They were careful not to step too near the edge themselves, where the snow was trampled and stained, and where the darkness yawned.

Slowly, the babbled pleas for mercy died away. The silence of the forest prevailed. The prisoners stood or crouched along the cliff-edge, the snow whirling into their faces. Most covered their eyes with their arms, as though to ward off what was coming.

The fingers of his companion knotted around Joseph's. "Where are we?" he asked hoarsely. "What is it?"

"It's the end," Joseph said. He held the old man's hand tightly and watched the guards as they drew the canvas off the machine gun.

"But I never did anything wrong," the old man said sadly. "I loved Comrade Stalin. It was all a mistake. A mistake."

A sense of peace overcame Joseph suddenly. It was all over at last. After so many years of agony and hope, it had ended.

He listened to the murmuring voices:

Blessed art thou amongst women, and blessed is the fruit of thy womb, Jesus . . .

The machine gun began firing. It made a ponderous churning sound. Blue and yellow flame fluttered at its snout.

. . . Holy Mary, Mother of God, pray for us sinners . . .

Their bodies smashed by the bullets, the prisoners began tumbling over the edge of the ravine, still roped together. Above the sound of the machine gun, they could be heard crashing down through the rocks and trees far below.

. . . now and at the hour of our death.

The bullets ripped into the man who clung to Joseph's hand.

Joseph felt the man crumple a second before giant fists struck his own body and hurled him backward into the abyss.

Then he was whirling down, like a leaf in an autumn gale, over and over. His mouth was full of blood, but he felt no pain, and the prayer continued in his mind until the dark triumphed.

ENGLAND

The Bentley was waiting for David in New Palace Yard as he emerged from the House into the bitter cold of an autumn night. The second reading was still in progress. He'd spoken a short while earlier and had been well received. He was forty-six, below the average age for a Member of Parliament, but after nearly a decade in the House, he was, as the Chief Whip had told him recently, attaining *gravitas*. Macmillan had given a nod of approval. Even the opposition had listened attentively. He was pleased.

Fog was drifting off the Thames, making a halo around the glowing face of Big Ben, which towered over the quadrangle. As he looked up, the deep carillon of eleven-thirty boomed out from the great bells. There was a smell of ice in the air. The driver, who had been watching for him, got out to open the door.

"Nasty evening, sir."

"Yes." He climbed into the car, shivering.

The driver got in front and reached out a gloved hand to the heater controls. "Soon warm up, sir." He half-turned, expectant. David Godbold sat, drumming his fingers on his briefcase, making up his mind while the driver waited patiently. At last, he sat back in the rich leather seat and said, "Gower Mews."

"Very good, sir."

The Bentley slid forward across the courtyard and through the gateway. The barrier lifted to let them into the street outside. There was little traffic, not even along Whitehall. David turned and watched out of the rear window for a while, but the street behind was occupied only by fog.

He was a handsome man, his blond hair becoming silver at the temples. He had a commanding mouth and a strong chin with a Hollywood cleft in it. His ears were flat to his head. It was a very masculine face, a very engaging one. His eyes were a bright royal blue. They could stare with disconcerting directness, or twinkle with charm. His image reproduced well on the little black-and-white television screens of the day, and the newspapers liked to print his picture.

The journey took ten minutes. The driver stopped at the corner of Bedford Square, at the heart of Bloomsbury, a short walk from Gower Mews. David looked at his watch. "One o'clock, Wallace."

"Very good, sir."

"Great Russell Street, in front of the museum steps."

"I'll be waiting, sir."

This time, Wallace did not open the door for his master. David glanced round. One or two figures hurried along the pavement, huddled, as he was, in coats and hats. He walked round the corner, his chin buried in his greatcoat.

There was no one in the lobby. He took the elevator up to the third floor. The flat at the end of the corridor was locked, but he had his own key.

The girl was curled up in an armchair in front of the fire that glowed in the grate. She was in her early twenties, a rich blonde with a face at once childish and sinful. David hung up his hat and coat and came to her. He felt the delicious softness of her as she lifted her mouth to his.

They'd been lovers for a little over four months, and the charge of excitement mounted between them eagerly.

She began to unbutton his fly. "Did you make a good speech?"

"The House seemed to like it."

"Clever David." Her smile was mocking. "So the big boys are letting you play at last." Her hand was hot, skillful. "You're staying the night, aren't you?"

He shook his head. "Evelyn came down from the north today. I should have gone straight home. I can only stay an hour or so."

"What a *bore.*"

"I'm sorry, Monica."

"When does she go back?"

"I don't know."

"Send her away."

"Don't be silly."

"Don't call me silly." She bent over his lap, and he barked in sudden pain.

"Jesus, Monica!"

"You're not bleeding." She rose. Her smile was that of a cruel child. "Come to bed and I'll kiss it better."

Evelyn Godbold Stood motionless at the window of her husband's study. The house was half a mile from Westminster, overlooking St. James's Park. They had rented it for the first five years, to be close to the House of Commons. Then, when David had been reelected, he'd persuaded her to buy the hundred-year lease. It had been expensive. But now it belonged to them, for their lifetimes, and the lifetimes of their children. If they'd had any children.

The letter lay on the rosewood desk behind her. It had arrived in Northumberland three days ago. She'd fought her immediate instinct to rush down to London and confront David with it. She was glad, now, that she had not done so. The three days of reflection had been vital to absorb some of the anger. To dull some of the pain. To decide what came next.

It was strange to have to consider what came next when, for twelve years of marriage to David, everything had flowed with such even, and sometimes dreadful, continuity. But she had been a woman capable of decision before her marriage, and she had not lost that capacity now. There remained, of course, the question of informing David.

She turned to face the room. Her eyes drifted across the shelves of leather-bound volumes, the snug armchairs, the morocco-topped desk where the letter lay, a blue rectangle in the pool of light from the lamp. There was nothing else on the desk. It awaited responsibilities that had not yet come.

David was certain of a junior ministry in the next Cabinet. A source close to Macmillan had told her that. She had not passed the information on to her husband, even though she knew how his frustrated ambition gnawed at him. It was important that David be gnawed at by something, for his own good. And for hers. It helped her live with what gnawed at her.

He would be with his latest concubine now, the blonde he'd installed in Gower Mews.

She walked across the room to the cupboard and took out a bottle of Laphroaig. She poured a little into the crystal tumbler and glanced at her watch.

Mounted on her body in a warm room, grunting fiercely as he rutted. She drank, her eyes closing to shut out the gross image.

Evelyn Godbold's hair was dark, cut in a simple but flawless style that she had not changed since she was eighteen. Little about her, indeed, had changed since then. She was now thirty-four, and expected that little would change until she was fifty.

Her own face had not a trace of the carnal prettiness of the woman her husband was at that moment making love to. It was handsome enough, a bony face, marked by a long nose and patrician cheekbones, with fine gray eyes whose gaze was very direct. But her lips were thin, giving her face a slightly harsh expression, even in repose, and her eyebrows arched in a way that seemed to pose an ironic question. A man would need courage to find that face desirable. She'd once thought David had that courage. She no longer thought so.

That David should lust after flesh other than hers had been a grave insult. That he chose such relentlessly prosaic sluts was worse. She drained the glass. The smokiness of the malt hung on her palate. She smoothed the suit over her lean hips. It was cashmere, Balenciaga. Her frame was slender, incapable of haste or lack of elegance. Her clothes always looked exquisite on her, and she had always taken advantage of that to wear exquisite clothes. It was her only true extravagance, and one she indulged to the hilt. Nowadays, David no longer noticed. He was losing his judgment. He was losing his sense of justice. Real life had stopped intruding on his pleasures or his ambitions long ago.

She sank into the chair and lit a Balkan Sobranie. The tarry smoke stung her throat. She smoked only when she felt the need, not out of habit. She laid her fingertips on the blue envelope. But real life did not go away. Real life was in this letter. She did not open it again. She already knew every word of it by heart. She waited, motionless, for David to come home.

SOVIET UNION

It was dark, but the clouds above were ragged, and a moon shone fitfully down through the firs. In the past few hours, two more executions had taken place. Bodies were piled among the rocks.

Some had survived. Most, of course, would be dead by morning, but the piles of corpses stirred with eerie, broken movements.

One of the prisoners was sitting up. His name was Ignatieff, and he had once been a diplomat, sentenced to twenty-five years hard labor for some real or imagined disloyalty to Stalin. A little knife gleamed as he hacked weakly at his bonds. He had been shot through the stomach, and he barely had the strength to cut the ropes. He would not live long.

Joseph watched him intently.

He was still roped to the man who lay dead and stiff beside him. He felt weightless. Only one bullet had struck him, in the face. His jaw was badly broken. The splintered teeth had pierced his tongue like needles. The fall had battered his legs. He did not know whether he could walk. But he was going to try.

Ignatieff's grunts became something else. He leaned back on his elbows, his breathing shallow and rasping. Joseph had heard that shallow breathing many, many times. Suddenly frantic that someone else would get the knife, he began to crawl across to the ex-consul.

He had to drag his companion along behind him, and it was almost too much for him. But he reached the dying man at last. Gasping for breath, Joseph tried to prize Ignatieff's fingers loose from the knife. They stared into each other's eyes as they wrestled weakly in the snow.

The consul opened his mouth and seemed to try and speak. But no words came out, only a gush of blood. And then the knife was Joseph's.

The struggle had been exhausting. Reawakened pain crushed him. He fought it off as fiercely as he had fought for the knife.

Then he rolled onto his other side and began sawing at the rope that tied him to his dead companion.

ENGLAND

The fog had thickened, and he felt the pavement slippery with ice under his feet. The Bentley was waiting for him in Great Russell Street, its taillights glowing red, its exhaust adding to the fog. Wallace pushed the door open from the inside, and David Godbold climbed in gratefully.

He saw the man's eyes glance at him in the mirror, calm, uninquisitive.

"Home, Wallace."

"Very good, sir."

He exchanged no more words with Wallace, who had been his driver since 1952 and knew many things about him that the world did not. After seven years, they preserved a silence that was not so much companionable as distinguished by a politic understanding.

He could hear Big Ben chiming 1:30 A.M. as he let himself into the house. He went upstairs and saw the door of his own study ajar.

She was sitting at his desk, her chin on her clasped hands. On the leather top in front of her was a blue envelope, one ragged edge showing it had been opened. He knew at once that it meant trouble, possibly bad trouble, but he pretended he hadn't noticed it.

He stooped and kissed her temple lightly. The fine skin was thin over the bone. She smelled of some French perfume he did not recognize. "Hello, old darling," he said easily.

"Hello, David."

"Wonderful to see you. Sorry I'm late. The second reading came in for rather a rough ride. They're still at it. I knew you'd be waiting, so I came away."

"Via Gower Mews." She looked up at him. Her eyes did not waver from his. He felt a chill.

"What on earth are you talking about, darling?"

"I'm talking about a bosomy little stenographer with peroxide hair. What's her name? Moira?"

His smile faded. "Monica, if you must know. I think I'll have a drink."

Her eyes followed him as he poured himself a whiskey. "She's even more plebeian than the usual run."

He was suddenly very tired. "You're breaking all the rules, Evelyn."

She laughed abruptly. "Oh, are there *rules*? I didn't know. You must let me have a copy."

"Can't this wait until morning?" he asked wearily.

"No. It can't wait."

"Did you come down to London, hell for leather, just to row about Monica?"

"No." She pushed the letter across the desk to him. "This came to Great Law. It's addressed to you. Read it."

He wore an expression of contempt. "Is it from a whore or an amateur?"

"Read it and see."

David reached out and picked up the envelope. He frowned as he saw the foreign stamps. It had been sent from Italy. He pulled out the letter and unfolded it. His frown deepened for a moment. Then his face became completely blank. He read it quickly and laid it down without speaking or looking at his wife.

"Is it true?" she asked quietly.

He lifted the glass. "Is what true?"

"That this child is yours."

"It's possible."

"Possible?"

He drank. "Yes."

She rose abruptly and went to the window. Staring out, she said, "David, don't be evasive with me. I can stand a great deal, but not that. Not now." She drew the heavy drapes on the night and turned to face him. She looked very calm, but he felt that the icy fog of outside had entered the room. "If the child isn't yours, why have you been sending these people money all these years?"

"As a mark of my gratitude. They hid me from the Nazis during the war."

"And you repaid them by fathering a bastard on their daughter."

David's face tightened. "We're talking about things that happened a long time ago, Evelyn."

"Yes, I know that. The girl is fifteen already. Ten pounds a month." Her lip curled. "Not exactly a fortune."

"It was all I could afford in 1945."

"You're a rich man now."

"No. I'm married to a rich woman."

"Is your name on the birth certificate?"

"I believe so." He shrugged angrily at her expression. "I was in a stalag in Germany at the time. They could have done anything they chose."

"You've sent them maintenance since 1945. That's a tacit acknowledgment that you are the father of this girl."

"I've never conceded that she's my child."

"Who else could the father be?"

"Half of northern Italy, for all I know."

"What happened to the mother?"

"She died."

"How?"

"In childbirth."

"How old was she?"

"When I knew her, about eighteen."

"So she died before she was twenty. Having your child. A simple peasant girl whose family gave you shelter at risk of their own lives. And you say half of northern Italy could be the father."

For the first time that evening, for the first time in many years, David Godbold felt a hot flush fill his face. "Don't be a bitch, Evelyn."

"Should I have more respect for your finer feelings?"

"This all happened in the middle of the war," he said surlily, "long before we were married. It has nothing to do with you."

She walked slowly round the desk, smoothing the cashmere over her hips in a habitual gesture as she spoke. "I learned about your selfishness long ago, David. Your cruelty. Your duplicity. Your immorality. I didn't think you had the capacity to surprise me any longer."

He was breathing more quickly now, his face pale. He was both disconcerted and angry. He spoke with an effort. "Have you finished?"

"I haven't even started." She tapped the letter. "How long did you think this could stay hidden?"

"It was nobody's business but my own!"

She stopped in front of him. "And what will happen when Fleet Street gets hold of this story? Do you think they won't tear you to pieces because it's nobody's business but yours?"

"For Christ's sake," he snapped. "You're talking as though I'm some kind of war criminal. I had an affair with a peasant girl in 1944. She got pregnant. Do you think that didn't happen to ten thousand others?"

Evelyn shook her head slowly. "Don't be an imbecile, David. The point is not that you fathered an illegitimate child. The point is that you turned your back on her. That you fobbed her family off with ten pounds a month, infinitely less than you gamble on horses or squander on your mistresses. *That* is the point, David. That is what will destroy you when the press get hold of this."

"The press won't get hold of it."

"Oh, yes, they will. And then do you think you'll ever get that Cabinet post you want so badly?"

He was even paler now. She watched the expressions chase across his face, first fear, then anger. "That letter," he said in his House of Commons voice, "is a piece of transparent blackmail."

"Can't you face it?" she asked bitterly. "Have you less courage than I, David?"

"What have *you* had to face?"

"That I am barren." She met his eyes. "We've had no children in twelve years. I thought you were sterile. Now I know I'm the sterile one."

He avoided the pain in her eyes. He picked up the letter again and looked blankly at the laboriously typed words.

After a silence, Evelyn spoke again, her voice calm and still. "Do you understand what that letter says, David?"

"Yes."

"It says that if you don't take financial responsibility for that girl, they are going to take her out of school and put her to work."

"Naturally, I'll do something."

"What?"

"I'll send them more money. Enough to finish her education. Maybe a little more."

She sat down across the desk from him and looked him in the face. She was smiling grimly. "No, David. That is not what you're going to do."

SOVIET UNION

The day dawned with a rattle of machine-gun fire from up above.

Joseph jerked into wakefulness, his head lifting off his knees. He had dragged himself under the shelter of an overhang, his last action before exhaustion claimed him last night. It had saved his life then, because it had snowed heavily in the night, and yesterday's victims had been covered in thick, unmoving white mounds. It saved his life now, as the bodies of the freshly slain tumbled down into the ravine among a shower of rocks.

He sat without emotion, watching the bodies plummet into the snow, staining it scarlet, limbs and faces writhing in a last agony.

It was over in two minutes. The tangle moved spasmodically, but the gunners' aim had been good, and the movement died gradually away. The voices of the guards faded. Silence fell again. Up above, the leaden gleam of the sky promised more snow soon. He felt a warm lethargy take him in its arms.

A noise roused him. He turned his injured head slowly and looked to his side. Farther along the overhang, two other survivors crouched. One had been badly wounded in a leg. The other, miraculously, was unscathed.

It was he who now crawled over to Joseph. He had the hollow cheeks and sharp canines of a weasel. Joseph recognized him. He was a journalist named Voloshin, actually a Belgian citizen, though of White Russian descent. He had been arrested during a visit to his family in Moscow, years ago. His record of anticommunist writings had earned him a fifteen-year sentence. He had survived the deranged world of the gulag by treading the fine edges of insanity. Now he looked madder than ever. He peered at Joseph's shattered face.

"Very nasty," he said in a hoarse whisper. "But you'll live. If you *want* to live, looking like that. Do you want to live, looking like that?"

Joseph nodded imperceptibly.

"Then you will. Still got the knife?"

Joseph slowly opened his hand. The little blade gleamed in his palm. Voloshin reached for it, but Joseph's fingers snapped shut again.

"We've got to do it now," Voloshin said urgently. He gestured at the tangle of freshly killed bodies. "Before they freeze, like the others."

Joseph looked into his eyes and saw the spark of madness in their depths. He shook his head slightly.

"You've only been here one night, Iosif Alexandreyevich," Voloshin hissed. "I've been here two days." Joseph saw him reaching furtively behind him for a rock. He was in no condition to fight off any more attacks. He held out his hand, the fingers opening slowly.

Voloshin snatched the knife without a word and scuttled toward the pile of corpses. Joseph saw him fumble with the clothes of one of the dead and begin to hack at the exposed flesh. The man with the leg wound uttered a harsh sound and dragged himself toward the feast.

Joseph's nausea drove away the fatal lethargy that had overcome him. The grim reality of madness and death was suddenly vivid again.

He would have to make do without the knife. He pulled himself laboriously to his feet. With the first movements, pain began to flood in. But he persevered.

He emerged from the overhang and looked up, and his heart plummeted into his stomach. The chasm was so deep. The sides were precipitous, offering no toehold. He was weak with pain and hunger. For a healthy man, it would be a daunting climb. For him, it was impossible.

He did not look at the Belgian and the other man, crouched over their meal. His eyes traveled around the ravine. At the far end, the steep sides closed in, making a dark cleft. Perhaps there was a better chance over there. He began plodding toward it.

It took him an hour to hobble across the floor of the ravine, only to be crushed by despair. It had been a futile journey. The guards had chosen their killing place well. Here, at the narrow end of the great cleft in the rocks, the sides were even steeper, the climb even less possible.

It was snowing heavily, huge flakes that whirled down silently from a sky that was nearly black, though it was midmorning.

Joseph stood trembling with exhaustion, looking at the cliff edge that towered high above him. The snow was piling up in the branches of the conifers, which drooped perceptibly. He was facing the end.

The injustice. The dreadful injustice that had been done to him was suddenly overwhelming. He had kept it in the deepest dungeon of his mind for fifteen years, so that it could not do to him what hunger had done to Voloshin. Now it was like a physical structure, a vast obelisk, crushing him to the earth.

He sank to his knees, tears spilling from his eyes, and waited for death.

ITALY

Catarina stood at her grandmother's grave, the black twists of her hair blowing across her face. She had arisen early, before dawn, to come and place the flowers in the urn that was clamped with an iron ring to the marble plaque.

There was nobody else at the cemetery on this bitter morning. The wind whipped at the flowers she had brought, wild cyclamens she'd found pushing through the leaf mold in the woods. The crimson flags fluttered valiantly.

Her grandparents were buried together here. She stared at the names on the slab:

Vincenzo Cipriani. 1889–1944

Rosa Cipriani. 1892–1959

She had never known her grandfather, who had died before her birth. But Nonna had shaped her life. That formidable presence had schooled her, protected her, stood between her and harm since babyhood. When Nonna had died, she had known that she was defenseless. That nothing and no one could ever protect her in the same way again. That was partly why her grief had been so sharp.

And yet Nonna had never loved her.

She'd known that from the beginning. The earliest knowledge she'd had about herself was that she was unwanted. Not just an affliction to a grandmother already afflicted with old age, and an uncle afflicted with tuberculosis, but something more. A shadow that fell over them all.

To the remoter family, those long-faced cousins and great-uncles from Brescia, she was a focus of bitterness, even hatred. Later in her childhood, especially after Teo had gone to the lung hospital, she became an Ishmael to them, her hand against theirs, theirs against hers; and when Nonna had died, she had become their responsibility. It had been they who'd written to David Godbold.

Catarina hadn't known that they'd done it. It hadn't occurred to her that they would do it, though she knew they didn't want her, and she was prepared for the two eventualities that seemed most likely now that her grandmother was dead, a factory or an orphanage.

Of the two, she had no hesitation in preferring a factory. She accepted, without vanity, that her mind was exceptional, powerful and thrusting beyond her years. Yet earning a wage would secure the thing she wanted most in the world right now, independence. She could always educate herself later. One day, she would soar on wings, high above the darkness where she had been spawned in shame and dishonor. For now, all she wanted was to escape the cold charity of kinsfolk who despised her.

She'd been enraged when she'd learned they had written to her father. Enraged and humiliated. To beg for money from *him,* from such a man as that—a man she'd loathed since she could think. To beg from him yet again, to risk yet another insult; for it was the second time in fifteen years that her family had written to him.

Nonna herself would never discuss the events surrounding her birth. She would not even discuss Catarina's mother, and had brusquely rebuffed all of Catarina's first, puzzled questions.

There had been a well of great bitterness in the old woman, a deep and silent well that Catarina had only seen overflow once, when Teo's fragile health had finally collapsed and he'd been sent to the lung hospital; and then, her bitterness had been directed at a person who was to Catarina a remote historical figure: Benito Mussolini.

"That monstrous clown and his war," Nonna had raged. "It took everything from me—my husband, my daughter, and now my son!"

The disease, Catarina knew, had taken root in the bones of her uncle's leg, where he had been badly wounded during the war, and had spread throughout his frail body.

She'd been six years old when she'd finally learned who her father was, a question she'd tried to solve with various wild imaginings up until then. A particularly contemptuous cousin had taken relish in telling her.

Her father was a foreign soldier named David Godbold who had taken refuge in Nonna's house during the war. He had been recaptured by the Germans and taken to Germany, leaving her mother pregnant but—and this was overwhelmingly important, for it made her a bastard—not married. Her mother's death in childbirth had been, the cousin had implied, a direct consequence of her unmarried state.

So she'd learned that day that her mother's blood lay equally on the head of David Godbold, who had not married her, and on her own head, because her difficult path toward life had killed her mother.

"But I couldn't help it!" she'd wept. And in that moment, she had already begun to hate David Godbold.

Later in her childhood, she'd heard more details. That when

the war had ended, David Godbold had been set free and had returned to his own country. But that he had never come to see his child.

She'd learned that her grandmother had written to him then, in that year of 1945, to remind him that he had a daughter in Italy, and that food was scarce, money scarcer.

That his lawyers had replied in frozen terms, denying that the child was his, insisting no further contact take place, dangling a paltry bait: a stipend of ten English pounds per month in recognition of "the shelter given our client by the Cipriani family during the late war."

And this, although he was a rich man. Nothing else.

At eight or nine, that had not made her hate him any more. She could not have done so; she already hated him as much as she possibly could, for having made her an accomplice in the murder of her own mother. But it had left her profoundly wounded. The wound had grown deeper over the years, the pain sharper. And the pain had generated rage. And the rage had generated a fierce intellect, impatient of restraint, slashing out like a sword at the tangle of shame and poverty that enmeshed her.

The wind changed direction and whipped her cyclamens out of the urn. For a while she stared at the bright splashes, scattered like blood on the paving stones. Then she turned and walked slowly toward school.

SOVIET UNION

When he heard the creaking, he looked up.

One of the firs at the very rim of the gorge was sagging outward. Its roots had been exposed by erosion, and now the extra weight of snow in its branches was starting to bring it down.

He wiped his eyes and watched, his heart beginning to hammer. The tree's tall spire dipped, and the thick trunk swayed downward regally, like a standard being lowered. Slowly, steadily, it sank.

At last it was horizontal, hanging out over the ravine. The snow slid from its branches in a billowing cascade. Relieved of the weight, it stopped moving.

Fall, he screamed at it silently. *Don't stop!* But it did not move any farther.

An hour passed. He did not take his eyes off the tree. Snow began to build up in the branches again.

And then it started to move again, its knotted roots tearing out of the soil that held them. It picked up speed as it swung down, until it fell with a crash among a shower of rocks and dislodged snow. Its spire touched the floor of the ravine. But some of the roots still held to the cliff top above. It made an upside-down ladder that a grimly determined man might scale.

Joseph staggered upright. He had to move, now. The next firing squad would be here any moment. He floundered through the snow toward his ladder out of hell.

ENGLAND

David awoke with a crushing headache and a sensation of impending doom. They'd slept in separate bedrooms. "Oh, Jesus," he whispered, remembering it all.

He struggled out of bed, clutching at his temples. There was one sure way to get some sense into her. She was not a passionate woman, not in the sense that Monica was. But he'd learned one thing about women—it was impossible for them to stay angry at you after a good, energetic fuck.

He groaned as he saw what the night and the whiskey had done to his face. It took him ten minutes to wash and shave. He raked his hair back from his temples, rubbed aftershave on his cuts, pulled on his dressing gown, and went to Evelyn's bedroom. He pushed the door open without knocking.

"Darling—" She was out of bed already, standing in front of the mirror. Her nakedness startled him. He hadn't seen her completely unclothed for a long time, perhaps years. "Sorry. I didn't know you were dressing."

Her cold gray eyes met his in the mirror. "What is it, David?"

"What you proposed last night. You know it isn't possible."

"It is perfectly possible."

He licked his lips. Her frame was remarkable, not voluptuous, but exquisitely put together. He found himself staring at the neat, almost girlish triangle of dark curls at her loins. "Oh, come on, darling. I've been a naughty boy, and all that. But surely—"

"Surely what?"

"Surely you must see what this would do to my career."

"Your career is no longer of interest to me."

He was appalled. "To our lives, then. To our marriage. You still care about *that,* don't you?" She walked to her wardrobe without replying, her slim body purposeful and elegant. "Evelyn, for God's sake. It's just not on."

"It is on. I advise you to accept that as soon as possible."

"It's lunacy!"

"Go away and put some clothes on."

She began to dress, starting with her brassiere. He'd always thought of her small breasts as unripened fruit. Her allure was something he'd always recognized, though he had not felt a physical response in years. But now, for reasons he could not quite fathom, he felt a sudden sharp wave of desire for her.

"Don't get dressed," he said.

"Why not?"

He walked to her and took her shoulders. "I want you."

"You're a joke," she said with arctic contempt, and shook his hands away. "Do you really expect me to lie down submissively and open my legs?"

"Evelyn—"

"Do you think what I said last night was some kind of *game?*"

"No, but—"

"Do you have any idea how much you've hurt me since we married? Oh, I know you're not gifted with compassion. And I don't care to show you my wounds. I have my pride, after all. But you must have guessed. Something." He began to speak again, but she cut through his words. "I've had one shred of consolation to cling to for twelve years, David. The belief that you were not stupid enough to do anything truly indiscreet. But that hope was false. As were all the hopes I had of you." Her voice quietened. "I've never been so angry in my life. I've never been so insulted. This may have been the last straw. I don't know yet. Just don't lean on me any further. Now go and get dressed. We have an appointment with my lawyers at ten-thirty."

His mouth was dry. "What—what for?"

"To make arrangements about the girl, of course. I don't want to lose any time. The schools are in their second term already." She walked into her bathroom and shut the door.

David sank onto her bed and put his head in his hands. He felt like weeping.

SOVIET UNION

If he were to walk the other way, into the darkness of the forest, he would be dead by the next morning. There was only one chance, and it meant walking back toward the camp. He had to force his trembling limbs to obey, so great was his fear of the place.

He followed the track that the guards had forced them along an eternity ago. He did not walk on it, but beside it, moving among the trees like a shadow, stopping with his heart in his throat at every sound. But for the most part, the great forest was profoundly silent. Perhaps the shootings had stopped. Perhaps there was no one left. It was not, after all, a very large camp.

The trees were twisted black shapes against the mist, stylized as a Japanese ink drawing. Through the trees he saw the camp, a quarter of a mile down the valley. Lights were burning, dim yellow stars atop the spidery watchtowers set along the barbed-wire fence. There were no lights visible in the long, low barracks. Nobody moving in the compound. But a yellow bulldozer was parked by the open gate, its plough pointed at the barbed wire.

Khrushchev's mercy had finally come. The camp was being dismantled. The dirt was being swept under the carpet.

And now he stood on the outside. Badly injured, half-dead. But alive.

It was as though he felt his own being for the first time.

He lifted his face to the darkening sky. He opened his mouth, and something was torn from deep within him, perhaps a cry, perhaps no sound at all. It soared above the firs, carried on the wind. Alive at last.

He turned laboriously. The village lay beyond the camp. He would have to take a wide loop around it, adding many hours to his journey. But there was no choice. In the village was his only chance of survival.

Of accomplishing the things he had survived in order to accomplish.

His mind was starting to wander with the fatigue, the pain, the loss of blood. It was becoming a vast effort to put one foot in front of the other. You are not going to die, he instructed himself. You will not accept it.

There was now a raging pain in his shattered jaw. He did not know how badly he was disfigured. His fingers were too numb to explore the wound. With the cold, more tissue would die, making the disfigurement worse.

He was stumbling with exhaustion, his head roaring, his limbs numb. His foot hooked on something, a buried branch. He floundered in a drift and collapsed heavily. The snow felt like lead, pinning his arms and legs. Its cold struck through his thin tunic, paralyzing him. Like a fly stuck in molasses, he moved helplessly, painfully.

Then he heard the woman's voice, calling his name in Russian.

He managed to lift his face and peer blearily up. She was clambering down the drift toward him, a bulky figure, her arms flapping to keep her balance in the deep snow.

At first he did not recognize her. Then, when she squatted beside him, her red cheeks puffing out with the effort she had made, he knew who she was. Her name was Tanya, and she had come into the camp every day to work at the infirmary, where Joseph was responsible for inventorying the drugs, the job that had kept him alive. Her presence here bewildered him. She had taken hold of his arm and was trying to pull him to his feet.

"Get up, get up," she was calling hoarsely. She half-dragged, half-coaxed him to his feet. He lurched, and she sustained him with both hands on his chest. She peered into his face with piggy eyes. A mittened hand reached out to brush the bloodstained ice from his face.

"Tanya," he mumbled. "Tanya. Please. Help me."

"That's what I came for," she said. She swung his arm up and over her broad shoulders. She felt as solid as a sea lioness, and as strong. "Come," she said urgently, pushing him forward. *"Come."*

The Village Was a small, wretched place, buried in the heart of a wilderness of firs, birches, pines, and aspens, snow-bound in winter, a sea of mud in summer. The houses were squalid wooden shacks, their chimneys belching the stink of low-grade coal. A few lights glimmered dimly as evening approached.

They kept to the trees as long as they could, Joseph near the end now, clinging to the woman's shoulders. The village looked deserted. The atmosphere of a cataclysm hung over the place, as it had done over the camp. If the camp was being dismantled, then the village was under sentence of death, too. It was inextricably linked to the camp, the camp to it. The camp provided the only source of employment for the village. The village provided the only place of recreation within fifty miles. The commodities of work, food, vodka, and female flesh were exchanged in a symbiotic relationship without joy or hope.

The house lay in a street of other houses, but there was a way into the backyard through an alley. Panting like a walrus, she urged Joseph into a shambling run.

Staggering on legs that could no longer support his meager weight, he let her determination carry him along. They ploughed through the snow to the back door. She reached out to the lock and pushed hard. It was unlocked, and it shuddered open. She thrust him ahead of her, stopping to glance over her shoulder to see if they had been observed.

A blast of heat rushed into Joseph's face, rich with the smells of cabbages, alcohol, and sweat. The woman slammed the door and locked it. She pulled off her fur hat, pulled off the thick scarf she wore beneath that. Dimly, he saw that her face was swollen and red, her cheeks wet with tears of pain or exhaustion.

And then the darkness rushed upward, and he was plummeting to meet it.

ITALY

The lung hospital was in Arco, at the far end of the lake, where the air was said to be sweetest and cleanest. It was a fortified town set on the top of a hill, and it looked like Jerusalem in a medieval painting. Behind it were the Alps, ever whiter and more jagged as they rose in waves toward Trentino.

As a child, Catarina had thought that heaven must be like the hospital, with its tall palm trees, its nun-haunted corridors, its profound silence. She'd thought of her uncle as a privileged dweller in paradise, a kind of angel. Lately, she'd begun to see other sides to the life he had led here for so many years.

Teo was the only person in the world who had truly loved her, and though she'd long known his love had no power to change her fate in any way, she loved him passionately in return.

She wheeled him out of the ward into the dayroom, where a cast-iron stove was burning. Her dark head was close to his gray one, and she was whispering with fierce intensity.

"I'm not going. I'm not. I'm not. I'm *not*."

"You have no choice."

"I do have a choice. I'm not leaving you. You're all I have now!"

He raised his worn face to hers. "But you're going to a new life. Don't you understand? There's nothing for you here."

She pulled the wheelchair up by the window and sat on a bench beside him.

"Why now?" she asked in a taut voice. The dull, wintry light had cast her face into chiaroscuro. "Why now, after all these years?"

He smiled at her. "You look very much like your mother today," he said. "So beautiful. Just as she was."

She was fifteen. Whatever potential she had for beauty was well-hidden beneath the mark of poverty and neglect. She had magnificent eyes, huge, black, glittering, but they were veiled by the disheveled curls of her hair. Her mouth, too, was splendid, large and passionate, although the full lower lip was disfigured by a half-healed cut, as though she'd suffered a blow.

She wore a greasy leather flyer's jacket, liberally embroidered with patches advertising motor oil, brake fluid, and gasoline. Like the scuffed high heels, it had been a used-clothes-shop find. The laddered black stockings were hand-me-downs from a woman in the village. Nonna would never have let her wear clothes like this, but since she had gone, nobody commented on her dress anymore. She liked the dangerous look the leather jacket gave her. And her legs were satisfyingly adult in the heels and stockings.

She held herself with fierce pride these days, keenly aware that her body was maturing. Not just her legs. Her breasts thrust outward, and her hips curved beneath the skirt, and in certain clothes she already looked eighteen.

Teo's expression was rueful, as though he were aware of all that, yet confounded by it. "Have you been working at your English?" he asked.

She shrugged.

He reached out and touched her cut lip. "You have a wonderful mind, Catarina. You inherited that from him."

"I hate him," she said with a gleam in her dark eyes.

"You've never met him, so you cannot say whether you hate him or love him. Your grandmother left me *Il Noce* in her will. If it was worth anything, I'd sell it to pay for your education. But all the land was peddled off long ago, for my sake, and old farmhouses are worth nothing these days. When I die, it will go to you. So at least there will always be a roof over your head, even though it leaks like a sieve. Whatever you think of him, he's a powerful and wealthy man. Your mind is a flame, child. A flame can blaze into brilliance, or be choked out and die. He can make your flame burn bright. He can advance you further than you can imagine possible. Don't waste this chance, child. Don't squander it."

"I'm not going! I *do* have a choice, and I'm not going!"

He began to cough, not harshly, but hopelessly, with a sound like rotten sticks breaking inside him. She saw his lips grow blue, quite suddenly.

Frightened, she ran to get him a mug of water. He sipped at it in between spasms, and the attack slowly soothed. "Decay," he gasped. "Decay, poverty, drudgery. Nothing else for you here."

She showed him her hands, which were callused and broken-nailed. "I'm not afraid of work."

He took her hands in his. His touch was feather light. She'd never in her life known him to be rough or raise his voice. "But it's not your birthright, child."

"Did you know that Nonna never spent that pitiful allowance all these years?" she asked bitterly. "She saved it up for me. I only found out after she died. Fifteen hundred English pounds. That's my birthright, *Zío*."

Teo opened his eyes slowly. "I'm dying, Catarina."

"No!" she cried, so loudly that heads turned and people stared.

"Yes," he said gently. "My life is over."

"Oh, *Zío*." Her eyes filled with tears. She put her arms around his neck and pressed her face to his fragile chest. She could hear the diseased lungs laboring, like torn bellows. He stroked the dark tangle of her hair lightly. "Listen to me. It's my dying wish that you go to him."

"Don't say that!"

"For me, Catarina. Do it for my sake, if you won't do it for your own."

She huddled closer to his chest. "He doesn't want me! He rejected me when I was a baby. Why does he want me now?"

"Perhaps a miracle has happened."

"No. He wants to use me for some purpose of his own."

"Then use him in return. Listen to me, Catarina, because I know him. He is a man dominated by his emotions. He has a fine brain, but he is easily swayed by passions. Anger, fear, and desire, above all. You understand what I am saying?"

"Yes," she whispered.

"For that reason, he will always be a weak man. He has a capacity for love, though he will never love anyone the way he loves himself. If you grasp those things about your father, you will be able to understand him. Perhaps even learn to control him."

She was biting her lower lip savagely, a habit she had grown into over these past weeks, and the fresh blood seeped into her mouth. He winced as he saw the bright smear of blood on her lip. "Why must you do that to yourself? Hasn't the world hurt you enough?" He began to cough again.

A sister materialized and touched Teo's shoulder. "You've been out of bed too long," she said firmly.

"Another minute," Catarina pleaded. The nun glanced at Catarina's grimy jacket and stockinged calves with undisguised disapproval and walked away.

Teo smiled with infinite tenderness at Catarina. Their eyes met, hers bright with unshed tears, his milky with illness. "You can't refuse my dying wish, my darling girl."

"No," she said wearily. "I can't."

"You'll go?"

"Yes," she said with an effort.

He closed his eyes. "When your mother died," he said softly, "I wanted to be a father to you. But this . . . " He touched his chest. "This would not let me."

"I love you, *Zío*."

"Good-bye, my child," he said gently. "I'll pray for you."

She rose, aching with the effort, to wheel him back to the ward.

On The Bus home, a group of three adolescent boys were seated opposite her. They stared at her greedily, whispering and snickering. She ignored them, gnawing at her lip as her thoughts surged.

Catarina was too intelligent not to realize she stood at a crossroads in her life. He had summoned her. They had asked him for money, and he had offered her a home. It was past belief.

Though she would never have admitted it, deep in her soul there had always been a secret dream that one day she would hear from her father. A card, a photograph, the barest inquiry about her health or progress. It had never come. Year after year, it had never come, and adolescence had brought her the final, devastating realization that he had long since forgotten her very existence. And now this.

Catarina glanced down at her stockings. The ladder was creeping rapidly upward from the knee. She lifted her skirt to see how far it had spread. The glimpse of her thighs provoked an explosion of sniggers from the boys opposite. She looked up and stared deliberately at each in turn. Their laughter trickled away into an abashed silence.

To be stared at by boys—and men, for that matter—was becoming a familiar experience. In one sense it angered her, in another it excited her, made her heart swell with possibilities. It was a rich luxury to be admired, and yet when she studied their faces and saw the grossness there, she was repelled.

Her sexual feelings were powerful but inchoate. She dreamed of passion, vividly, and yet without a distinct shape. The dreams evaporated as soon as she woke, leaving her lying in her narrow bed with yearning loins and a galloping heart. On such mornings, her body would be filled with pangs and wild pleasures, with rage and longing, and her soul seemed to strain like a kite at its string. If only she could let the string go! But she did not know how to, not yet. Abandonment was a trick she had not yet learned.

She could not remember a time when she hadn't known she was stronger than other people. Stronger and cleverer. Cleverer than the other children at school, who taunted her and tried to hurt her with stones; cleverer than the teachers who'd tried to hurt her with those even sharper stones that leave no bruise, words; cleverer than the long-faced cousins from Brescia.

So much cleverer, in fact, that it was beyond most people's capacity to see how clever she really was. She knew that Nonna had regarded her intelligence as an upsetting aberration. Teo alone had seen partway into her mind and had recognized the treasures that were there. But by then, Teo's own life had shrunk to the iron bounds of a hospital bed, and he'd become as much an outcast as she. Yes, even more hated, because Nonna had been forced to sell off the lands that belonged to

Il Nóce to pay for Teo's treatment, and the cousins and great-uncles in Brescia had been outraged.

They had called her sullen and rebellious. Had they known what she called them, in her own mind, their long faces would have paled.

The sun was setting over the lake. She huddled into her flyer's jacket and remembered how many times she had prayed to be set free. She wondered how those prayers were now going to be answered.

ENGLAND

"You didn't tell us about this in 1949."

"No."

"We heard the thrilling tale of your escape from the Germans. We heard about your heroic activities in the Apennines, with the Italian Partisans, whom you led to dazzling exploits. Not to mention the numerous escape attempts you organized in the German prisoner-of-war camp after your recapture. But not about the bastard daughter you left behind."

David was silent. The Chief Whip had a stare that was notorious throughout the party. Tipped as a future prime minister, he had a sonorous voice and a turn of phrase that was rumored to have reduced at least one junior MP to tears. He reminded David, painfully, of a former headmaster who'd possessed similar faculties. He studied David now without expression, his lids hooded over his pale blue eyes.

It was late at night. David had spent the evening in an interminably dull committee, and he was tired. A coal fire was burning in the grate, and the Chief Whip's wood-paneled room was overwarm, but he knew better than to fidget.

There was another whip present, who had apparently been asleep in the armchair in the corner of the room. He drawled, "When does the girl arrive?"

"In a fortnight."

"Have you ever actually set eyes on . . . what was the name again?"

"Catarina."

"Soon to be plain English Kate, no doubt?"

"I've never met her."

He lit a cigarette, watching David through the smoke. "The whoring on its own was bad enough. Combined with an illegitimate daughter whom you have allowed to live in destitution, you have mixed yourself a rich cocktail, Godbold."

"I hope you'll give me credit for attempting to rectify the situation now—"

"Oh, nonsense," the Chief Whip said in a voice that made David wince. "Do you think we can't read between the lies and the self-justifications? You attempted to conceal this from Evelyn. She found out in the end, as of course she would. *She* is the force insisting you face up to your paternal duties. That much is obvious."

"The newspapers will almost certainly get wind of this," the other whip said. "This could be a serious embarrassment for the government."

"Surely it won't come to that," David said, trying to sound confident.

The Chief Whip's cold eyes met David's. "What do you intend to tell the press, Godbold?"

David cleared his throat. "The truth," he said.

"And what is the truth?"

He answered very carefully. "Catarina's mother died in childbirth. I was heartbroken when I found out, on my release from prisoner-of-war camp in 1945. I wanted to take the girl then, but her grandmother wouldn't let her leave Italy. I've paid maintenance since then—"

The other whip snorted.

"—and now that the girl's grandmother has died, I am taking responsibility for her education here in England."

The Chief Whip's long nose wrinkled as though at a rotten smell. He sat in silence for a long while.

"You have no legitimate children, do you?"

"No," David said shortly.

The Chief Whip made a conclusive gesture with his large, white, elegant hand. "Very well. There will be a considerable amount of attention focused on you from now on."

The other whip smiled thinly. "The whoring will have to stop, of course. You're a paterfamilias now. No more nonsense."

"We mean it, Godbold," the Chief Whip said. "I don't mind telling you that you were in line for a cabinet appointment next year."

He paused, and David's heart leaped in his chest painfully. "But that," he continued, "will have to wait. You are on a tightrope from now on. And there will be no safety net. Understand?"

David's mouth was bitter with the taste of disappointment and humiliation. "I understand."

"You may go."

David rose, swallowing his indignity.

"And Godbold—"

"Yes, Chief Whip?"

His face was like stone. "God knows she has been a matchless wife to you. Why don't you try making a halfway decent husband to her from now on?"

David's face reddened. Evelyn came from a family whose connections with the Conservative Party went back to Stanley Baldwin, and half of the senior members seemed to regard her as a goddaughter, a fact he'd had well to the fore of his mind when he'd married her in 1947, on the eve of his political career. "My marriage—" he began, but the Chief Whip turned to his papers.

"No, Godbold, don't. I'm not remotely interested. Get out."

S O V I E T   U N I O N

He had never grown accustomed to the suffocating, oily heat of Tanya's house.

After half a lifetime of terrible cold, some organic thermostat had broken inside him, and the warmth he had dreamed of all those years was intolerable to him now.

But he was too weak and ill to care. He lay in her bed, wrapped in her down quilt, hovering between consciousness and feverish nightmares.

He had passed through the worst agony during that first week, while she picked the shreds of splintered bone from his face with tweezers, murmuring to him comfortingly as he whimpered.

Then, with needle and thread, she had stitched the torn flesh herself, her fingers deft and steady.

"Don't worry, *zek*." She used the ugly word as an endearment. "I've darned a lot of shirts in my life. I make lovely stitches."

But afterward, he had heard her weeping in the corner.

And then the fever came, and with the fever, the dreams.

He saw places he had been, lakes and mountains and thronged cities. He saw the barbed wire, and the snow, and the dim barracks where the bodies were piled in bunks, and where, each morning, some bodies did not rise.

He saw the executions. The hangings. The torture cells. He saw the blood and the broken skin. He saw faces brutish with evil, faces hollow with suffering, the two sides of the human coin. He heard the voices, screaming orders, screaming for mercy that never came.

In his dreams, he was still in the camps. In his dreams, he would always be in the camps.

Tanya cared for him with overwhelming kindness. She called him pet names, coaxed him to eat, washed his inert body with a sponge. By day she sat for hours watching him. At night, she clambered into bed beside him.

"Don't scream so," she implored him in the night, again and again. "Don't scream, *zek*. Someone will hear."

And when the screams were too much for her to bear, she clamped her big hand over his scarred mouth, and stifled the agony, and drew him roughly, tenderly, into the warm shelter of her own body.

ENGLAND

"They said it could be a serious embarrassment to the government," David said bitterly. "I may not be perfect, but *they* are the coldest hypocrites God ever put wind in."

"I think they're the most honorable men I know." Evelyn, tall and slim against the lights, was arranging white hothouse lilies in a copper bowl by the window. She wore a new dress, black wool with wide lapels, black stockings, and glossy high-heeled shoes. The dress was tailored to fit her slim figure, a wide belt accentuating her waist. On another woman, the outfit might have seemed funereal. On Evelyn, it was exquisitely elegant. Alluring, even, in its severity. "She'll be here soon," she said absently, clearly indifferent to David's dealings with the whips.

David stared at her for a moment, his eyes narrowed. Then he turned to pour himself a drink.

"I don't like the idea of the girl wandering around unescorted. She's probably never been on a train before."

"She's made it this far without your assistance, David. I'm sure she'll manage to sit on a train from Milan to London without difficulty."

"I was thinking more of her talking to the wrong people."

"And embarrassing you?" she said dryly. "The nuns will take care of her where she has to stop."

"Ah yes, the nuns," David grunted. The girl being a Catholic was yet another wearisome detail.

Evelyn slid a lily into place. "It's better she arrives without fuss. For her sake, and everyone else's. She'll need time to adjust before she appears in the public eye."

She spoke evenly, but with no trace of warmth. Her anger had not softened in the slightest. It had merely quietened. He could feel it in her voice, see it in her gray eyes. He would need to appease her before life became bearable again. It was a daunting task.

Over the past six weeks, there had been times when she had actually frightened him. She held all the cards, and for the first time in their marriage, she did not hesitate to play them. He'd had no doubt that, had he not capitulated, she would have left him. That was the bottom line.

She had confronted him with his dependence on her. She had let him see, in pitiless detail, how it would all collapse without her— his career, his finances, his reputation.

She had inflicted on him a humiliation far worse than anything he had suffered in Edward Heath's office at Westminster that morning, and he would never forget it.

For now, he accepted it. That was something he had understood since his school years. Humiliation was essential to self-preservation. You swallowed it in large doses when necessary, to save your skin. Then you bided your time.

He did not even begin to understand her motivation. He'd accused her of doing it simply to punish him. Now that things had quietened, he doubted that interpretation. On the other hand, there was no other interpretation he could understand.

At least she had not insisted on the tedious rigmarole of a full adoption. For the time being, they were simply to offer the girl board, lodging, and schooling. In theory, anyway. He could only hope that it was a whim that would pass. That once she was faced with the reality of the girl—dirty, primitive, unable to speak a word of English—she would change her mind. With luck, the whole caprice would end within a few weeks, and the girl could be shuffled off to some distant institution where she could sink back into merciful obscurity.

As if reading his thoughts, Evelyn spoke again. "And she'll certainly have to be groomed and kitted out before she's presentable. I'll see to that, here in London. Take her to the right shops, and so forth. Then I'll take her up north with me." She carried the bowl of lilies to the grand piano. Like everything she arranged, the bowl was immaculate, graceful. She made some final adjustments and stood back to study the bowl. "There," she said. "I think that will do."

David drained the glass, feeling the whiskey slide around the hot, sore place inside him. He took a deep breath and walked up behind Evelyn. He laid a hand on her shoulder. It was the first time he'd touched her since that ghastly morning six weeks ago. She became very still.

"This morning Ted Heath reminded me how lucky I was." She said nothing. He found himself looking at the white nape of her neck, the soft, gleaming brown curls of her hair. She was wearing the same perfume as on the night she'd given him the letter, something astringent, with a haunting suggestion of jasmine. "Let's make peace, darling." He leaned forward and brushed her neck with his lips. She bent away from his kiss and turned to face him with disconcerting speed. There was a flush of color on her cheekbones, and her eyes glittered.

"And are you pawing me now because Ted instructed you to?"

"Of course not." David smiled. "I'm pawing you because you're my wife."

"Well, please don't bother. I'm not in the mood for slap and tickle."

"We have to make it up sometime," he said.

Her lean face was dangerous. "Why?"

"For one thing, because we have a daughter arriving in a fortnight. One has to preserve equanimity in front of the children." He saw the muscles knot at the corners of her jaw, and for a moment he thought she would slap his face. "Come on, Evelyn. Six weeks is enough." He reached out and brushed her cheek with his fingers. She had wonderful skin, satin-smooth and cool. He had not had a woman in six weeks, and he was badly on edge. "Are we friends, at least?" he wheedled. He lifted her hand to his lips and kissed the knuckles, then the palm. "Evelyn, I'm *sorry*. What more can I say?"

"Nothing."

"There you are, then. Is it too late for us to make a new start, darling?"

"A new start?" she repeated, as though it were a phrase in a foreign language.

Judging that the moment was right, he drew her to him and kissed her cheek, then her temple. She did not thrust him away. He kissed her mouth, concentrating on the right mixture of tenderness and force. Her narrow lips were lifeless against his, dry and cool. But he sensed her start trembling, deep inside. "You're beautiful," he whispered between kisses. "I've never stopped wanting you, no matter what happened. My darling . . . "

He pulled her close, crushing her mouth to his, grinding his loins against hers. It was not a subtle approach, but it was at least an unaffected one, and perhaps she sensed that, because he felt the rigidity of her body relax at last. She sank back against the piano.

"Oh, David," she whispered. "Oh, David . . . "

"God, I want you." Encouraged. David hoisted the black wool of her dress around her hips and groped at her stocking tops, fumbling with the garters.

"No." She tore away from him, smoothing her dress back down. They were both breathing quickly, both their faces flushed. "Keep your hands to yourself."

"Until when?" he demanded, hearing the unsteadiness in his own voice.

"Until I say so."

"It's been six weeks, Evelyn!"

"The discipline will do you good."

She walked quickly out of the room and slammed the door behind herself.

SOVIET UNION

Today he was able to sit on the edge of the bed.

There was almost no pain anymore. The wounds were pulling tight as they healed, and he was aware of his face changing shape, like the bark of an injured tree.

She had not yet let him see a mirror.

"Wait until your beard has grown, *zek*. Don't worry. You're still a pretty boy."

But he could not speak properly. His tongue felt like a wooden peg in his mouth, and the sibilants rushed through the broken teeth. It was the voice of an idiot, a simpleton. He hated to hear it, so he did not speak very much.

He stood shakily and felt his head spin. Tanya reached out to help him, but he shook his head.

"I'm all right."

She watched him in concern as he took a few shuffling steps. All his joints ached, and tiredness overwhelmed him. He leaned on the wall and stared blearily at the window. The snow was still falling, whirling against the filthy panes.

"There now," she clucked. "You've satisfied yourself. Now come back to bed."

"I want to see."

She swore to herself, rich Russian curses. "This child and its vanity. Wants to see if it's still a pretty boy. Stupid child. Forget about your face. Come back to bed."

But he pulled his arm away from her restraining hand and tramped unsteadily across the single room of the house. There was a mirror in the corner, over the washbasin. As he approached it, Joseph felt a sick fear engulf him. He groped at the basin and supported his weight on it, panting with the effort. He lifted his face, and peered into the mirror.

"Oh, Christ."

Tanya covered her eyes with her hands and uttered a sharp sob.

The face was not his. It was a mask to make children scream. The beard could not hide the savage injury. The right cheek was deeply sunken. The jaw had set to one side, twisting the mouth into a grisly sneer. His lower lip, torn by the bullet and tacked together by Tanya, would not close over his lower teeth. He opened his mouth. Most of the teeth on the right side of his jaw were missing. His lacerated tongue seemed to have no tip. That was why he could not form his words properly.

The stitches were still livid. The scars had twisted his face, so that his nose had been pulled over to one side. He was haggard, and after so many years of being shaved close to his skull, his hair had grown in a bizarre shock, gray from temples to chin.

Only his eyes, dark and haunted, were as he remembered them.

He did not speak for a long while, just stared at the grotesque mask he would have to live behind until he died.

At last, he straightened and turned to Tanya. "You were right," he said, forming the words carefully. "You make lovely stitches."

She took her hands away from her face, which was red and tear-stained. "I did my best, *zek*."

"I know, Tanya."

"You were in such a mess. And I couldn't call a doctor, or take you to the hospital—"

"I know." He reached for her and took her in his arms. "You did a wonderful job. I'm grateful."

She laughed through her tears. "Such a polite boy. I give him a face like a darned sock, and he thanks me."

"You saved my life. I can live with the face."

Her waist was thick and strong. She hugged him back. Then she thrust him away and wiped her eyes. "You're going to have to live with it, *zek*. You have no choice."

ENGLAND

Catarina sat where she had been told to sit, on the hard wooden bench next to the weighing machine in Victoria Station. She looked very much younger than her fifteen years. She was wearing her gray school tunic and blazer, the clothes the nuns had insisted she travel in. Her bare knees were cold above the grimy white socks. She had tucked the big suitcase behind her calves. The smaller suitcase was on her lap, and she clung to it as though clinging to the meager nugget of her own identity.

The noise of the station rolled around her like thunder, made up of rumbling wheels, pounding feet, clamoring voices. Until two days ago, she'd had no experience of crowds. This pandemonium would have terrified her, if she hadn't realized, at some point in her journey, that the world was not interested in her.

She sat ignored, a forgotten parcel, a mislaid umbrella. A nothing. She was a pebble in a world that thundered and jostled and babbled and hustled all around her.

She did not know how many miles she had traveled in the past two days. She only knew that she had left every familiar thing behind her.

Her relations had put her on the train at Brescia, a long time ago. She hadn't got to Milan until nightfall. Nuns had met her there, and she had spent the night in a convent dormitory in the city center, unable to sleep for the roar of traffic and the fear and anger in her.

The London train had been much bigger, and she'd shared a compartment with five strangers. She'd watched Italy, then France, hurtle past the carriage windows, an endless stream of fields and towns, fields and towns.

They had stopped at Paris for several hours. Then the rattling procession of fields and towns, fields and towns, a landscape that seemed limitlessly vast, hour after hour, mile after mile, until the purple evening had fallen, and blotted it out.

By the time they reached Dover, and she was in the country of her adoption, she was dizzy with weariness. More nuns, English ones, had been waiting for her, and had taken her to a small convent just outside the town. She'd been the center of gentle attention and curiosity. Then she had spent another night in a strange bed, with the rumble of strange traffic in her ears.

This morning, very early, they had put her on the train to London, and at seven-thirty she had rolled into the cold and clamor of Victoria Station.

There had been no nuns here. No one to meet her except a busy stationmaster, who had put her on this bench to wait, with strict instructions not to move.

And here she'd sat since then.

A group of men passed, so English they were caricatures, with their pinstriped suits, their bowler hats, and their furled umbrellas. She stared after them. Would her father be dressed like one of these?

She felt another wave of unreality pass over her. She slumped, staring at the feet that passed by unceasingly, pounding on errands, with places to go. So many feet. She stared at them in a daze for a long time, until she realized that one pair, wearing polished black leather shoes, was standing in front of her. She sat up, her heart lurching.

The man was middle-aged, with a flat, expressionless face. He wore a dark gray uniform, with a peaked cap, which he now removed in order to study her. He could not possibly be her father.

"Miss Catarina Cipriani?"

She nodded.

He held out his hand for her suitcase. "Let me take your luggage, miss."

Catarina clutched her suitcase defensively. The man looked at her uncomprehending face. "You understand English?" he asked doubtfully.

She nodded again, still silent.

"My name is Wallace. I'm Mr. Godbold's chauffeur. You must come with me," he said gently. "I'll take you home."

She Sat In the back of the car. Wallace did not speak, and neither did she. The deep leather seats swallowed her, so she had to stretch to look out of the window.

She had never been in the streets of any city in her life. She was unprepared for the scale of London, or the noise of the ocean of traffic on which they moved. She thought of the vast wealth needed to construct and possess all these towering buildings. They came within sight of the river, winding wide and gray through the heart of the city, spanned by arched bridges. The chauffeur pointed. "That's where Mr. Godbold works."

She stared in astonishment. "What is it?"

"Westminster Palace, miss. The Houses of Parliament."

She turned in her seat to watch the building go by. She remembered Teo's words to her. *Whatever you think of him, he's a powerful and wealthy man. He can make your flame burn bright.* This was an awesome manifestation of that power and wealth.

They drove past a large park, where the trees were leafless, but the grass was still green. People were riding along the pathways, singly or in pairs, wearing coats against the cold wind. The park was bordered by avenues of gracious white houses, their porticos supported by columns, ornate black railings secluding them from the pavement. She knew at once that this was a place where the very rich dwelt. Parked all along the road were limousines as grand as the one she was traveling in. She jolted as the car drew to a stop. Wallace got out and opened the door for her. "We're here, miss."

The Bentley had pulled up in front of a cream-colored, three-story house with a green door, which opened. A thickset woman in early middle age came down the stairs toward her, wearing a white apron.

"Come in, miss. Wallace will see to your bags."

Her initial impressions of the house were of height and warmth. As she followed the housekeeper, she had the feeling she was growing smaller and smaller. There were beautiful flowers everywhere: scarlet tulips on a lacquered Chinese table, a spray of white lilies on a grand piano, flame-yellow gladioli on a commode. Catarina saw them in the same dazed way she saw everything else in the house. It did not remotely occur to her that the flowers might be for her benefit.

She was led down a long corridor to a handsome room like a study. But there was no one in it. The housekeeper pointed to a sofa.

"You may sit there. Mrs. Godbold won't be long. She's riding in the Row." Catarina's look of incomprehension appeared to irritate the woman, who frowned. "Oh, never mind. Just wait. Understand? Wait here. And don't touch anything." She went out, banging the door behind herself.

Catarina sat. Her heart was fluttering like a trapped bird. She smoothed her dress and ran her fingers through her hair, knowing she must be dirty and crumpled.

There was a piano at the far end of the room, in front of a set of glass doors that led out onto a garden. It was a full-scale concert grand, with its scalloped lid propped up. A smell of roses overlay the perfume of wax. There was a large bowl of them on a table, among silver-framed photographs. The room was furnished to an unmistakably womanly taste, with rich satins and velvets. Everything was meticulously clean and orderly. She knew whose room this must be.

She closed her eyes, and snatches of her journey raced through her mind. Fields and towns, darkness and daylight, milling crowds and empty spaces. She thought of Teo's face, the last time she had seen him, in the lung hospital at Arco; the lines etched so deep, the hair so thin and white. She'd known then that she might never see him again, and now that thought brought the tears flooding to her eyes.

The sound of brisk footsteps made her jerk upright, her memories scattering. The door opened abruptly, and a woman came into the room. With a sense of shock, Catarina found herself meeting deep-set, clear gray eyes.

The woman was wearing cream jodhpurs and glossy black riding boots, the toes spattered with mud. There were also spots of mud on her tight black jacket. Above the white silk scarf at her throat, the face was angular, elegant, dominated by a long nose. The mouth was thin and unsmiling. The eyebrows were arched in a disdainful slant. She was wearing a black velvet riding helmet, which she now took off and laid on the table, beside her gloves and silver-hilted crop. She studied Catarina in complete silence for a long while.

"How much English do you speak?" she said at last.

"A little."

She walked over to Catarina. Catarina rose instinctively. They were of an equal height. Close up, the woman had exceptionally smooth skin, like porcelain. There were faint lines beneath her eyes and at the corners of her mouth. She was old enough to be her mother, but she did not look it. The smell of sweated horse overlay her expensive perfume. The gray eyes studied Catarina with concentration. Catarina felt that she was being devoured by that gaze, swallowed by it. Its intensity disturbed her.

"I didn't come to meet you. I thought it was better you arrived without fuss."

"Like a package," Catarina said quietly. "To be collected by the servants."

The other woman's eyebrows lifted fractionally. "Hardly. Do you know who I am?"

"You are Mrs. Godbold."

"You may call me Evelyn. I've been giving your name some thought. In this country, it makes you look either foreign or pretentious. I can't have that. So you'll be Catherine. Kate for short. Kate Godbold."

She was taken aback. "My name is Catarina!"

"It was your name in Italy. It is not your name anymore. You have come to a new world. A new life."

"I am still myself."

The gray eyes showed a gleam of interest. "You speak English well. The accent is a little thick, but we can deal with that." Evelyn took Catarina's hands and lifted them. The gesture was not one of tenderness. She studied them minutely, turning them over to examine the backs. "Oh, dear," she said in distaste.

Catarina was hotly aware of the calluses, the far-from-clean nails. She pulled them away quickly and hid them behind her back.

Evelyn touched the tangle of black hair. "We'll have to do

something about this. You look like a Gypsy's child." She glanced at Catarina's school uniform, by now wrinkled and travel-worn. "And we have some shopping to do. But all that comes later." She opened a cigarette box and tapped a cigarette briskly on the lid. "You've come to a new life, Kate." She lit up and exhaled a plume of aromatic smoke. "You'd better grasp that fact from the beginning. The sooner you sever yourself from what went before, the better. The pain will be less. Italy is over. Catarina Cipriani is over. You are Kate Godbold, and your home is here."

Physical and emotional exhaustion had made Catarina brittle. She did not know what greeting she had expected, but not *this*, this flat denial of her identity. Tears of mortification swelled in her eyes as she stood in the alien room, her hands tightly clutching her gray school dress. "You cannot change who I am," she choked.

"Don't be pretentious. You're only a girl."

"I am a human being!"

"Nobody says you aren't. You seem to be a little confused. You are here for your own benefit, not for anyone else's."

"Are you so sure about that?" Catarina replied.

She felt Evelyn's eyes consider her thoughtfully. "I hope we're not going to get off on the wrong foot." The phrase was unfamiliar, but the crisp, cold tone made the meaning clear. "Has something offended you?"

Everything, she wanted to blurt out, everything from that first peremptory summons in Italy to your last words. But she was silent.

"It is you who have made the change, Kate. You are in a new world now. You have to change step. You have a month or so to acclimatize, here in London. Then we will go up north, and in the early spring you will start attending school."

"Why did you bring me here?"

"What an extraordinary question!" Evelyn laughed sharply. "Your relations were going to send you to work in a factory."

"I was prepared for that."

"What, with your intelligence? To stand deafened by some machine for eight hours a day, watching it wear away your life?"

"I'm not afraid of work."

"You were not born to it. This is your father's house. Do you know your Bible, Kate? Do you know the story of Ruth?"

"Yes."

" 'For whither thou goest, I will go; and where thou lodgest, I will lodge; thy people shall be my people, and thy God my God.' That must be your philosophy from now on. Well, perhaps not as regards your God. I have no objection to your practicing your religion as you wish. I believe that is a matter for an individual's conscience. In all other things, you will have to change, whether you like it or not. I suppose you're wondering where your father is. He's at the House. The House of Commons. He'll be back this afternoon. Do you know what he looks like?"

"He never sent me a photograph."

"Come here, Kate."

"My name is *not* Kate!" she said.

Evelyn lifted a framed photograph off the table. "You can have this." She walked forward and put the photograph into Catarina's hands. It had been mounted in a heavy silver frame, a head-and-shoulders portrait of a young man in military uniform. "This is your father," she said. "It was taken a short while before he was captured. Not long before he met your mother, and fathered you. He doesn't look all that different now. You'll soon see."

Catarina looked at the image blankly.

Evelyn was silent for a moment. Then she said, "I was unaware of your existence until your relations wrote to us. It came as something of a shock to me."

"He never told you?"

"No."

Catarina felt, rather than heard, the anger behind the dry monosyllable. She looked up. "Perhaps it slipped his memory," she said.

Evelyn smiled thinly. "Your English really is very good, isn't it? Not just your vocabulary. Your inflections. You've mastered the art of saying one thing and meaning another. A considerable feat in a foreign language." She crushed the cigarette in an ashtray. "I am not going to try and defend your father's actions to you. Or to try and explain them. I doubt if I could. He is your father. If you have questions, you must put them to him."

"Did you bring me here to punish him?"

She knew her lash had landed, for she saw the color flick across the porcelain cheekbones. The effect was handsome. She thought of a phrase she had learned from a book: an English rose. This was a rose with sharp thorns. "That is an insolent and vicious remark."

"It was a question, not a remark. You brought me here, not my father. I can tell. I still don't know why."

Evelyn took a breath. "You are David's daughter all right. You have the same mind. Do you ride?"

"I don't understand."

"Can you ride a horse?"

"No."

She made a brief gesture. "Mrs. Davies will show you your room."

It was a dismissal. The housekeeper was waiting at the door.

Catarina thought of the words she had learned. The stilted little speech of gratitude and pious feeling. "There are some papers for you," she said. "In my suitcase."

"Mrs. Davies will bring them down to me later." Evelyn Godbold turned back to the piano.

The thickset housekeeper was waiting for her outside the door, her suety face inscrutable. Clutching the silver-mounted photograph of the man who was her father, Catarina let the woman lead her to her room.

SOVIET UNION

Every day had brought added strength and mobility. He was able to help her around the house, do odd chores. The movement brought life back to his limbs. He was growing into the clothes she had given him, garments of a bigger man. His mind was working again. He asked her about the camp.

"All gone," she said briefly. "Shut down. Nothing left. They even took away the barbed wire. Most of the village went with it. Only a handful of us left in this shithole now. I'd have gone, too, long ago. Except for you."

"The prisoners?"

"They say the ones the guards took away have been sent to their homes, with Nikita Khrushchev's blessing. About seventy disappeared. The night of the shootings, I was crying for them. When I could bear it no longer, I went looking, to see if any had escaped. That's how I found you, lying in the snow like a dead log, and there you were, covered in ice and blood. I thought the vodka must have rotted my brain." She was suddenly shy. "You were always my favorite. You knew that, didn't you?"

"Yes," he lied.

"It was fate that you were the only one to live. Fate."

"Yes," he agreed.

"You were always the most handsome."

"There's not much left of me, Tanya."

She took his hand. "Your eyes are very beautiful. The bullet didn't change that. Women will still desire you."

Joseph made a wry face that was the closest he could come to a smile.

The earth was in the dead grip of winter. Snow had piled to the sills. He swept the floor, washed the dishes, dug a path through the snow to the coal heap outside. Every day he emptied the clinkers out of the stove, their pulse of life, and every day brought the precious black chunks in to fill it up. She watched him work, assessing his recovery, studying his strength.

Then, one day, she stoked the stove until it glowed red and put the huge copper kettle on the lid.

"You stink, *zek*, and so do I. We're going to take a bath."

It took eight kettles to fill the galvanized iron tub, and the house billowed with steam.

Tanya undressed matter-of-factly. Her body was white as marble, blue veins branching beneath the milky skin. Her swaying breasts were tipped with the maidenly nipples of a childless woman. A thick, dark pelt grew between her heavy thighs. She had no figure to speak of, but at the sight of her nakedness, Joseph's senses swam wildly.

"You, too," she commanded as she sank into the tub. "Hot water is not for wasting."

He undressed and climbed in with her. The tub was small, the water scaldingly hot, the intimacy of their nakedness staggering. He was dreadfully dizzy. She soaped his body. Her hands explored with gentle directness. Urges he had not felt in years were suddenly rampant in him. He cried out loud at her touch.

"Ah," she said in quiet satisfaction. "You are strong again. Very good. Now you can wash me." She gave him the soap. His hands trembled as they touched her skin. Slippery, smooth, and soft, she was paradise itself. She wriggled, giggled. Beneath the years and the lard was a pretty young girl. Beneath his ugliness, a virile young man.

Afterward, scarlet with the heat, their coupling was joyous, primitive. Joseph was afraid his powers would fail him, but they did not. When they had finished, he was in a daze, she was crying. She kissed his marred mouth, again and again. "Oh, *zek,*" she whispered. "Oh, my love."

ENGLAND

"And of course you'll want a bath," Mrs. Davies said firmly.

Catarina stood in the middle of the room, listening to the sound of the taps running next door. They were afraid she might dirty this spotless place. As well they might be. She had never seen a room like it in her life. So pure, so clean, so abounding in frills, so white.

"We'll have to make do in English," Mrs. Davies said, "because I don't speak any Italian." She pronounced it "eye-talian." "Understand?"

"I can speak English."

Mrs. Davies looked suspicious. "What's that, then?" she demanded, pointing.

"A bed."

"And that?"

"A cupboard."

"And that?"

Angered by the crude test, Catarina shrugged. "A rather horrible toy animal."

"No need to be sarky, my girl. That's a teddy bear Mrs. Godbold bought for you, and very pretty, too." Catarina looked at the toy blankly. "So you speak English. Good. Now, then. Shall we unpack your things?"

"I can do that," Catarina said, but it had not been an invitation. Ignoring her, the woman opened the first suitcase. She studied each article critically as she folded it away or hung it up. "You've never had a mother, have you, dear?" she asked pointedly.

"No," Catarina replied.

"Choose all your own clothes, do you?"

Something in the housekeeper's tone made her feel hot. "What is wrong with my clothes?"

Mrs. Davies sniffed. "Not for me to say, is it?"

"But you *are* saying."

"Well, I mean." She dangled a brassiere. "Fancy a child like you wearing a thing like this. Who do you think you are? Jane Russell? Nice young girls don't wear this kind of thing."

"Why not?"

"You're far too young."

"How old do I have to be?" Catarina asked dryly.

"And what in the wide world is *this*?" The black leather dress was the most expensive thing she had ever bought herself. She'd seen it in a secondhand clothing shop in Saló and had fallen in love with it. It had a heavy zipper up the front, chrome studs on the shoulders, and tassels on the arms. The girls in Marlon Brando's *The Wild One* had worn dresses just like it, and it had seemed to her the essence of wicked glamour. It had taken her months to save up the money. Mrs. Davies was incredulous as she inspected it. "Where on earth did you get this? Where do you *wear* it?"

"To go out."

"To go out? With the motorcycle gangs? I think you've seen too many nasty American films, my girl."

"It suits me."

"It's cheap and vulgar!"

Catarina flushed. "I'll go and bathe now."

"You do that. I'll come and wash your hair in a minute."

"I do not *want* you to wash my hair," she said shortly.

Mrs. Davies grunted. "What you want and don't want ain't relevant, dear. Not yet, any rate. Get along with you."

Torrents of steaming water were pouring from the heavy brass taps into the bath, which stood on ornate clawed feet. She undressed and got into the bath. The soap was octagonal and smelled so sweet that she closed her eyes, inhaling the flowery scent. It lathered richly, covering her skin with luxury. She thought of the miseries of bathtime at home.

Her body was pale in the water. It was unmistakably a woman's body, the breasts filling, the nipples swollen like autumn berries. The curve of her hips was a lyre that framed the dark triangle of her sex, where each month proud evidence showed that the womb within was becoming capable of bearing a child.

She was still angry. What right did that fat woman have to judge her? She dressed as she pleased. She did not dress as a child because she was no longer a child. She was an adult, and in Italy there had been nobody to deny that.

You're far too young. Far too young for what? She had not been a child for many years. She had led her own life, with her own comings and goings, her own ways. She was not about to give that up now. She was at least as much of a woman as Evelyn Godbold, for all her arrogance and wealth.

Mrs. Davies came bustling in. "We're going to have a clear-out. I can't see Mrs. Godbold letting you wear any of that lot."

She did not cover herself, but looked up at the housekeeper with hot eyes. "Because I'm too young?" she asked pointedly.

The older woman glanced at her body. "I can see you're not a child. But you're not an adult, neither. There are limits. Besides, half of them have holes in them."

"But I've made the holes better!"

Mrs. Davies was filling a flowered jug at the tap, mixing hot and cold carefully. "In this house we don't wear clothes with darns in them. Mrs. Godbold says she's going to take you shopping. So it doesn't really matter, does it?" She poured the water over Catarina's hair, then picked up the shampoo. "Such beautiful hair, but *what* a tangle. And it looks like you've been cutting it yourself." Catarina felt fingers prying at the roots of her hair. "Well, at least you haven't any little guests in there. That's a mercy."

She clenched her teeth. "Did you think I had parasites?"

"Parasites? You must have swallowed a dictionary. By the look of you, I wouldn't have been surprised if you'd had a nit or two. You'll need a couple of visits to the hairdresser, but this will do for now. Shut your eyes. There. Just look at the color of that water!"

An hour later, Mrs. Davies left her lying on the bed, wearing a white bathrobe. Her hair had been pulled severely away from her face, and her skin had been scrubbed until it felt flushed all over. She was supposed to sleep, but her nerves were strung tight, and her limbs were rigid.

Mrs. Davies had put the photograph of her father on the dressing table, and she turned her head to look at it now. The man was handsome, merry. She could find no connection between those features and her own. He wore a peaked cap, and he looked directly at the viewer with insolent eyes. *You bastard,* she thought wearily.

Somehow, she drifted jerkily into sleep. Her last thought was of Evelyn Godbold's cool voice:

Catarina Cipriani is over. You are Kate Godbold, and your home is here.

She Awoke In a panic, not knowing where she was at first. She rose and went to open the frilled curtains, which Mrs. Davies had drawn. It was early evening. Across the street, the park was dark and somber looking, the sun a red disk above the trees. She was in London, in the house of wealthy strangers, a lifetime away from the crumbling *podere* on the shores of Lake Garda.

Whose room had this been? Had there been another girl here before her? It was furnished for a princess, every detail exquisite, feminine. Beside the bed was a bowl of pristine lilies-of-the-valley. Their sweet scent overlaid the smells of new linen and new wood.

Everything in the room was new. Evelyn Godbold had no children of her own. No one had ever been in this room before.

Had it been furnished for "Kate Godbold"? Had the woman with the thin mouth and the cold gray eyes ordained that this room be prepared to receive the arrival?

Catarina thought of the years of neglect, loneliness, shame. She had longed so fiercely to escape. And had it come to this? To find herself washed and combed, a living doll for a childless woman's dollhouse?

A realization shot through her like a spear. Soon she was to meet her father.

Soon she would look him in the face. She would be able to say to him the things she had burned to say since childhood.

Suddenly agitated and trembling, she turned to get dressed. Instinctively, she chose the garment Mrs. Davies had picked on, the black leather dress. In any case, it was, to her mind, the most adult thing she owned. It was shiny tight across her hips and her neat backside. She left the zipper dangling between her breasts, which, reinforced by the bra, thrust aggressively against the thin leather. Her smooth white throat was stark against the black. She pulled on stockings and high-heeled pumps and looked in the mirror.

Her own image was dark, potent. When she had worn these clothes in the summer, to go to the pictures in Saló, the boys had whistled like factory sirens. Her mouth twisted. Her father would think she looked cheap and vulgar. But there was no doubt about her woman-hood. She was no doll. No child. Let him chew on *that*.

Fiercely pleased with the effect, she pulled the band from her hair and shook it free, letting it fall in a tangle over her eyes, the way it always did. "Murderer," she whispered to herself. "You're a mur-derer!" She dug into the little bag she had carefully hidden from Mrs. Davies because it contained her scraps of makeup. No question but makeup would be considered cheap and vulgar, too.

No one had ever taught her how to apply it. She had picked up that art the way she had picked up the materials, in cast-off scraps. The stump of lipstick had belonged to a forty-year-old and Catarina relished its vivid shade. It turned her mouth into a crimson slash. She'd tried to re-vive the dried-up mascara with olive oil, and it stuck to her long lashes in clots. But she did not care. She *wanted* to affront him, to shock him. To show him that she did not belong in this virginal white room. That she might be cheap and vulgar, but that she was no doll. No child.

She walked up and down in front of the mirror, muttering to herself, spitting out the words she would say to him. She was grateful for her intelligence now, grateful for the vocabulary she had amassed in his language, a pile of jagged stones to hurl at him. Tension rose in her, tightening her nerves, filling her with a charge like electricity.

She could hear a car in the quiet street outside, and she walked to the window. The gray Bentley was idling outside the front door. She gripped the sill as she saw the door open. A man in a dark suit emerged. He said something to Wallace, who drove on. Then the man looked up at her window.

His eyes were a startling blue, the color of the fountain-pen ink she'd used at school. The face was the same as the one in the photo-graph, handsome, with a cleft in the chin. But it was older, the hair graying, and it lacked the charming smile of the photograph. The eyes met hers with an intensely seeking look that held not a trace of warmth.

Her father.

They held one another's gaze for a moment. She lifted her hands to her breast, as though to try and start the paralyzed engine of her heart. Then, with a kind of grimace, a look almost of pain, he walked through the front door and out of her sight.

She could hear his voice, at first a distant rumble, then growing slowly clearer on the stairs:

"No, I'll see her now, before dinner. Has she any English?"

"She's fluent," she heard Evelyn reply. "It's extraordinary. According to her school reports, she's been studying English for only three years. They say she excels at everything. In fact, as far as I can understand what they say, she's a brilliant child. Maybe more than that."

"By village school standards, 'brilliant' doesn't mean much."

"Wait till you see her. Oh, David!" She could hear a strange eagerness in Evelyn's voice. "Wait till you see her. She's exquisite. A Botticelli. Why didn't they want her?"

"Perhaps we're going to find out."

"There's nothing that can't be improved out of all measure. She's completely unfinished, of course. But the potential. The *potential*, David! I've spoken to—" The voices dulled into a murmur.

"All right, all right," he said impatiently, just outside her door. "That's your province. Don't involve me."

Catarina jolted at the loud rap on her door. It opened before she could get to it, and her father came into her room.

He was very tall, far taller than she had expected, and he towered over her, so that she stepped back involuntarily.

He still wore that expression of pain. It made the bold face oddly vulnerable. Nor did she feel the presence she had expected. The authority, the arrogant, confident maleness she had been sure he would exude, all that was absent. She saw only an irresolute middle-aged man whose mouth was twisted against remembered pain.

It was a moment she had thought of so many times, envisaged in so many ways. Now it was here, and her head whirled.

"Jesus," he said abruptly, staring her up and down. "You're not what I expected."

"What did you expect?" she asked breathlessly. Her heart was racing so fast she couldn't breathe properly.

"Something more . . . childlike."

"I am not a child."

"You mean you don't want to be one. Is that the way you usually dress?"

"Yes, it is."

He clenched and unclenched his fists uncertainly for a moment. "You're very like your mother. When I saw you at the window—" He broke off. "Very like her," he repeated. He examined her features intently, as though seeking his own lineaments there, as well as her mother's. She wondered whether he found them. The haunted look on his face faded slowly. His stare became a man's worldly assessment of her crimson mouth, the thrust of her breasts, the tightness of the leather around her hips. She saw his mouth relax, then turn downward in a smile. There was contempt in that smirk, and perhaps something else. Something knowing and cynical.

She had a sudden intuition that he had been searching for something to despise, and had found it quickly, and was glad of it. Was this the way he'd been hoping she would look? As though something had clicked into place, she sensed his confidence return. He put one fist on his hip. "Your mother had a lighter hand with the makeup."

She felt the first shock of the encounter subside, felt the old emotions rise to the surface. "I'm surprised you remember."

"Oh, I remember. My wife assures me that you're not a fool. Is that true?"

"I am not a fool."

"Then don't play the fool with me. Not ever." His eyes drifted back to her cleavage. This was the way he had looked at her mother, she felt, with the same arrogant superiority. "You can't dress like that here."

"Why not?"

"You look like a tart."

"A tart?"

"*Una puttana,*" he said in Italian. Her face flamed. "Did your grandmother sanction that outfit?"

She clenched her teeth. "She was too sick to know how I dressed."

"I see. You'll find the administration in this house rather more vigilant. You don't just have yourself to think of anymore. You're under my roof, and you're going to have to behave accordingly." He checked his watch, a slim gold disk nestling among the golden hairs on his wrist. "You're aware that I'm an important man in this country?"

"I know that."

"One of the thousand or so most important men in Britain."

"So what?" She shrugged, deliberately insolent.

"Important men have enemies. There are people whose aim is to drag me down."

"Why?"

He shook his head irritably. "That's the parliamentary system.

It's a game, you see. The socialists are our enemies. They'll use any means to attack me."

"I am a socialist," she retorted.

"That is rather inconvenient," he said dryly. "You'd be well advised to keep your juvenile opinions to yourself. And don't ever go out in public dressed like that."

"I will dress as I please," she said tensely.

"You will dress as you are told," he snapped. "And I don't want you to talk to strangers about me. In fact, I forbid it. No matter how nice and charming they are. Even if they offer you money or—" He searched for a word, and failing to find it, glanced around the room impatiently. "—or trinkets. Say nothing. Just tell them you're very fond of me. And I'm very fond of you. That's all. Nothing else. Above all, don't admit I'm your father. Got it?"

"What is it you are ashamed of?"

She sensed his sudden and acute discomfort. "I'm not ashamed of anything, girl."

"But you must be, or you would not forbid me to speak to people about you—even if they offer me money or trinkets."

The way she said the last words made him wince. His face grew even colder. "I don't think you've quite understood me."

She had started to tremble. "But I have. I understand that you are ashamed of having a bastard child. But I am far more ashamed of you than you could ever be of me."

She saw the blue eyes narrow in anger. "And what, precisely, do you mean by that?"

She wanted to scream into his face, scream all the things she had stored up for him. But the words caught in her throat, choking her, and she was silent.

He was watching her intently. "I warned you," he said softly, menacingly. "Don't play the fool with me. Not ever. You'll regret it." When she did not reply, he went to the door. "Evelyn!"

A moment later, Evelyn came into the room. The smile on her face faded at once as she saw Catarina. "What have you done to yourself?" she exclaimed.

"Is this your Botticelli?" David asked sardonically. "A motorcycle Mona Lisa, more like."

Evelyn stared at the black leather, the garish red mouth, the black-edged eyes. She seemed unable to believe that the drab, inhibited schoolgirl had somehow become a sluttish adolescent with a sullen face. "Oh, Kate!"

David was once again wearing that contemptuous smile. "Lovely, isn't she? Is this what you call exquisite? If she sets foot outside like that, we'll have the whole of Fleet Street camped on our doorstep. You might as well hang a red light over the door."

He walked out.

"You stupid girl," Evelyn said quietly. She took Catarina's chin in her hand and wiped off the lipstick with four ruthless strokes of her handkerchief. "Go and wash your face. You will not wear makeup until you have grown up."

"But—"

"Go."

Catarina obeyed, not knowing quite why. Her own face looked back at her from the mirror sullenly, traces of lipstick smeared garishly round her mouth. She had met her father. After fifteen years, she had looked him in the face.

She emerged from the bathroom, her face bare.

"Change out of that dress," Evelyn commanded. "You may imagine it makes you look like an adult. It does not. It makes you look like a trollop."

"I bought it! With my own money!"

"You were a fool to waste your money on such a thing. And you were a bigger fool to wear it for your first meeting with David. You want him to respect you, don't you?"

"I don't care what he thinks of me."

"Oh, but you do. You put that on to disgust him. You succeeded, and I hope you're satisfied."

Catarina remembered the shock on her father's face, the contempt in his eyes. Yes, she had wanted to provoke that. But the experience had not been as satisfying as she'd anticipated. She had been degraded by that look. Sullied. She decided abruptly she would put away the dress and never wear it again. "I don't know what you want me to wear," she replied tiredly.

Evelyn went to the closet and pulled it open. She studied the garments within briefly. "Where did you get these clothes?"

"I chose them myself, when I could. The rest were given to me. Out of charity."

"They don't seem very suitable."

"Your housekeeper has already informed me of that."

"Come with me." Evelyn took her arm and led her to her own bedroom. In the aftermath of the shock of meeting David Godbold, she felt oddly disembodied. The floor seemed to give beneath her feet, like a sponge. Why hadn't she been able to say the things she'd wanted to say?

Evelyn's room was as white and pristine as her own. Perhaps she sees herself as a doll, too, she thought. Perhaps she thinks all women are dolls, as flat-chested and sexless as herself.

Evelyn selected a wool skirt and a Fair Isle sweater from her own closet. "Wear these. And you don't need that brassiere. A vest will do for the time being. Take this one."

Evelyn watched in silence as Catarina undressed, aloof eyes surveying her body without embarrassment. Evelyn's clothes felt soft and expensive against her skin.

When Catarina had finished, Evelyn took the hairbrush and began brushing the tangled hair out of Catarina's eyes. She stood stiffly, submitting. Neatening the doll, she thought. Putting it all right. "You're well-developed for your age," Evelyn said. "But you need not advertise that fact. You get your periods every month?"

"Yes."

"Any pain?"

"Sometimes."

"Are you a virgin?"

Catarina choked. "That's none of your business!"

"You are my business from now on. Everything about you is my business." Evelyn pushed the hairband back into the dark hair, then studied her. "Do you have any jewelry?"

"My budget did not run to *jewelry*," Catarina said bitterly.

"Just as well, if your taste in clothes is any indication. Normally, I don't like to see children wear gewgaws. But you seem to have already developed a taste for adult pleasures. You may wear this."

She took the string of pearls out of the box and looped it around Catarina's neck. Catarina stared down at it blankly.

"Take care of them," Evelyn said dryly. "Pearls are fragile."

Dressed in Evelyn's clothes, wearing Evelyn's pearls, she felt as though a new identity had been pasted over her own. As though Evelyn's prediction had already begun coming true. *Catarina Cipriani is over. You are Kate Godbold, and your home is here.* She'd wanted to confront David Godbold with his own evil, accuse him of his crimes, and her courage had failed her. She felt like crying.

Evelyn took Catarina's arm and turned her to face the mirror. Despite her dark skin and Evelyn's fair skin, despite the difference in their ages, their features, and almost everything else, the clothes made them alike. "Don't slouch," Evelyn said sharply.

Catarina straightened her spine. Despair and anger sat heavy on her heart.

"You need to be shown everything, don't you?" Evelyn said. "How to stand. How to sit. How to walk. How to cut your nails. How to wear your hair. How to dress." She studied their reflected images with satisfaction. "However, that is already a considerable improvement," she said. Her eyes were almost warm.

Does she think it's that easy? Catarina thought. Does she think she can make me into her daughter by dressing me in her clothes?

"I think your father will have recovered his composure by now," Evelyn said. "Dinner is going to be ready soon. So let's go downstairs and start again. Shall we?"

SOVIET UNION

In a month they had made love countless times. She was insatiable, he was inexhaustible. Their lovemaking was a whirlwind that swept out of the desert of the empty years, carrying them on its wings.

But Joseph had farther, much farther, to go than the sweaty passion of Tanya's bed.

"I'll never forget you, Tanya."

He saw her heavy face change on the pillow. "What do you mean?"

"I can't stay with you."

She was incredulous. "And where are you going?"

"I have to go back home."

She searched his face intently. Then she smiled, sadly. He could see that she thought she understood. "Child, wherever they are, they all believe you're dead by now. She has a new husband, the children a new daddy. Leave them be. It's better that way."

"I have to go, Tanya."

"The KGB would pick you up in twenty-four hours and send you to another camp."

"There is no KGB where I'm going."

"And exactly where are you going?"

"To the West."

She laughed shortly. "You're mad."

"It's where I came from."

Her eyes opened wide in outraged disbelief. "You're a Westerner?"

"Yes."

"Not a Russian?"

"No."

"You're lying to me. You talk like a Russian."

"But I'm not. I have to go back."

Tanya rose, naked. "How could you *do* this to me?"

"I'm sorry," he said lamely.

"Sorry!" She stamped around the house, her flesh shaking. He heard her swearing, spitting out the fierce obscenities she used to comfort herself. "I love you! Who else will love you, the way you are?"

"I don't know."

She came back to him and thrust her face at his. "They'll scream their heads off when they see you," she snarled. "You're a monstrosity. Only another monstrosity could look at you without vomiting!"

When she came to him again, her rage was ebbing out of her. Her piggy eyes were bloodshot, her mouth drooped tragically. She had the bottle of vodka, and she poured them both a glass. She sat beside the bed, thighs splayed round the back of the chair. "You can't face your family like that. You know I'm right."

"Yes," he said. "I know you're right."

"Then why are you going back?" she pleaded.

"To claim what is mine."

Tanya laughed harshly. "You have a treasure waiting for you in the West?"

"It's what I stayed alive for."

She leaned forward and peered into his eyes. They were jet-black, but not shallow, as some dark eyes are shallow. Suffering had made his gaze an abyss. Deep, deep down in those depths burned a point of flame. Tanya shuddered.

"Those are a wolf's eyes, *zek*. But you are not a wolf. You are only a child." She poured another glass of vodka. "And how will you get to the West? Are you going to sprout wings and fly?"

"If necessary, I'll crawl."

"But you thought my little car would take you part of the way?"

He did not reply.

"You bastard," she said. "You never loved me. When will you go?"

"When the spring comes."

She snorted. But she looked a little happier. "Spring comes late to these parts, wolf." She came to him, and they embraced, each seeking comfort, giving it. She pushed him onto his back and straddled him, her strong thighs clamping his hips.

"We made each other young again." She rocked her loins on him, urging him to respond. He was swiftly erect, and Tanya guided his body into hers. Her eyes gleamed. "You'll never forget me."

"No. I never will."

She began to sway on him, her weight ruthless, tender. "Does that feel good?" she demanded.

"It feels wonderful," he whispered.

"We'll get our money's worth, wolf."

With the formidable strength that endured within his wiry body, he twisted, overturning her. She laughed breathlessly, then cried out as he began to thrust in her. "Yes," he whispered. "There's time to get our money's worth."

ENGLAND

The sweaters were cashmere, soft as clouds, in a range of pastel colors.

The assistants had snapped to attention at their arrival, as they did everywhere Evelyn took her. The buying had been going on for a solid ten days, amassing a wardrobe Catarina could never have imagined. She let the women attend to her, standing motionless while they fussed and straightened the hang of the garments.

Evelyn, seated opposite her, watched serenely. No prices were mentioned, but Catarina caught sight of one of the tags. More money than Nonna or Teo would have spent in months.

Eventually there was a pile of perhaps a dozen sweaters on the counter, and Evelyn seemed satisfied. "Pick three," she invited.

As a concession to her tastes, it was not momentous. Without looking, Catarina took the top three. "These."

Evelyn's face stiffened. She rose. "Can't you even be bothered to sort through them?"

"I've chosen these." Catarina shrugged, wondering what she had done wrong.

"I thought it would amuse you to make a choice."

"But they're all the same."

She hadn't intended to be rude, but Evelyn was clearly angered. Her slender fingers drummed on the counter as she waited for the sweaters to be wrapped in the green and gold paper.

Catarina had never heard of Harrods until this morning. She'd never seen anything like this vast department store, with its cascades of luxury, its avalanches of wealth, its glittering, gleaming, polished merchandise so temptingly displayed. It gave her a feeling at once sick and sinful, as if she'd glutted on chocolates. And yet she could not shake off the feeling of unreality, that none of it was substantial, that it was all a shimmering vision.

As they walked away, Evelyn's face was still frigid. At the bottom of the escalator, she stopped so suddenly that other shoppers bumped into them. She turned to Catarina. Her mouth was a thin line. "Why didn't you tell me you didn't like those jerseys?"

"I just said they were all the same."

"Not your taste," Evelyn said bitterly, "because they're not black leather with steel studs." Catarina said nothing. "You deliberately behave like a mental deficient. You stand there in utter silence, staring into space. You show no pleasure in anything you try on. You express no preferences, no dislikes. You're like a zombie."

Catarina's dark eyes were suddenly hot. "You're not interested in my opinions. You know exactly how you want me to look. There isn't any point in my saying anything."

"So you let your contempt show, instead."

"I don't feel contempt."

"You don't feel gratitude, either."

"If you want the truth," Catarina retorted, "it's difficult to feel grateful when things you don't want or need are being thrust down your throat!"

Shoppers were streaming round them, but neither noticed. They stood face-to-face, eyes locked.

The annoyance in Evelyn's face hardened. "So. None of this has given you the slightest thrill of excitement. Not the slightest moment of pleasure." ·

"I didn't say that."

"You didn't have to. Tell me something. Is there anything, anything in this whole store, that has fired your imagination? Anything that you looked at, and thought, *I want that?*"

Catarina looked around. They were standing opposite a display of crystal that, artfully lit on glass shelves, sparkled like a frozen waterfall. In the mirrored panels behind the Waterford, she caught sight of her own reflection, split in two. Catarina-Kate. Neither one thing nor the other, staring with somber black eyes that for the first time in years were free of the tangled fringe that had screened them. No longer shabby, yet ill at ease in the strange clothes that had been bought for her. No longer herself, and yet familiar, like a long-lost friend glimpsed in a crowd.

"Well? Anything at all?"

She turned slowly. "Yes."

"Show me."

She led the way in silence. The leather goods section had the most pungent, expensive smell in the shop. She pointed. "That."

"A notebook?" Evelyn picked it up. It was a handsome thing, with marbled end pages and a calf's-leather binding. "What do you want this for?"

"To write in."

"What do you want to write in it?"

"Things. Thoughts."

Evelyn opened it and stared at the blank pages, as though they were covered with runes that could explain the silent, dark girl at her side. "Have you kept notebooks before?"

"Yes."

"In Italy?"

"Yes."

"Where are they now?"

"I burned them all before I left home."

Evelyn closed the book. "And you really want this?"

"Yes."

"Then say it."

"I really want that," Catarina said.

Evelyn took it to the cash register and paid for it. Catarina watched her, a tall, slim figure among the crowds of shoppers. Her anger had subsided a little. She felt she understood Evelyn, but that Evelyn would never understand her.

Evelyn brought the notebook back to her and put it in her arms. "Here. The first thing you've wanted."

"Thank you," she said simply.

Evelyn was staring at her. "You'd improve if you learned to smile, Kate. Come on. Let's go to lunch."

They went to a little Mayfair restaurant, opulently decked out in velvet and mahogany, with old silver and fine white linen on the tables. There was the usual catechism with the menu. Catarina sat in silence as Evelyn explained what the names of the dishes meant, described how they were made, and finally made choices for them both. A bowing waiter took the order, and Evelyn leaned back in her chair and lit one of her Balkan Sobranies, a rare enough action during the daytime as to indicate that her tension had still not dissipated.

"You have been waging psychological warfare on us ever since you arrived, Kate. I'm heartily sick of it."

"I don't understand."

"I think you do. Since you came, it's as though a black cloud has settled over the house."

"I didn't ask to be brought here," Catarina said in a low voice. "They had no right to write to you."

"But they did. And you came."

"Not out of choice. And I gave no promise that I would be happy here."

"Oh, you make it painfully clear that you are *not* happy here, despite our strenuous efforts to make you happy. We're giving you a great deal. But you give us nothing in return. You spoil everything. You've spoiled this morning completely."

"I'm sorry."

"I can accept your rudeness to me. But your rudeness to your father is disgraceful."

Catarina looked away sullenly. "I've said nothing to him."

"That's what I mean," Evelyn said sharply. "You don't even *look* at him. You pretend he doesn't exist."

"He doesn't want me there. All he cares about is that the newspapers don't get to hear about me."

"That is a hateful thing to say!"

"But it's true."

"Coming from your background," Evelyn said, "I would have expected a little more appreciation."

"You mean, because I am poor I ought to be overjoyed that you're squandering money on me?"

Evelyn crushed out her half-smoked cigarette. "I am glad you've at least noticed that this is not a cheap exercise."

Catarina took a breath, trying to control her own antagonism. "At first," she said, "it was very difficult for me to understand the money you were spending on me. We never saw such sums of money in my family. It was not easy for me to accept. It upset me more than you can imagine. Eventually, I realized something. This is your game. I am a plaything, not a participant."

"What do you mean, 'a plaything'?"

"A doll."

"Is *that* what you think?"

"Isn't that what I am?" She had to raise her voice over the noise of people all around. "Since I came, you have been amusing yourself with me. You take me to the hairdresser and tell her how you want my hair cut. You take me to expensive shops and have me measured for clothes which you pick."

"Well, you looked like a savage when you arrived. And you had nothing suitable to wear."

"You take me to expensive restaurants and choose what food I should eat."

"Because you have no idea!"

"You tell me how to sit at the table, how to hold my knife and fork—"

Frustration creased Evelyn's high forehead. "For God's sake! I've been trying to *teach* you, Kate. Haven't you understood? I've been trying to *show* you."

"You're trying to make me into something I'm not, and can never be!"

The waiter arrived with their first course, and they fell silent. When he had gone, Evelyn leaned forward. "It's high time you started school," she said. "I wanted to wait until the new term, but I think now that was a mistake. That brain of yours needs work. Your body needs games. You need the company of girls your own age. Perhaps they will be better at knocking off your rough edges than I am. Next week, you and I will go up to Northumberland, and you can start at St. Anne's. It's my old school. The headmistress is my godmother. You'll enjoy it thoroughly." For a moment, there was a gleam in the gray eyes. Then it faded. "How many times must I tell you not to hold the fork like that?"

S O V I E T   U N I O N

The snow had fallen heavily, whirling down for week after week without end from a lowering sky. But the river had not frozen. It flowed, black and swift, toward the Baltic.

The river was Joseph's guide. He would follow its course as far as Riga, if he could negotiate the remote country roads that would now be treacherous with mud and slush, and if he was not stopped and asked for papers he did not have.

If he reached Riga, he would travel beyond, to one of the dreary villages that lay along that dreary coast.

If he reached the village, he had an appointment with Tanya's brother, Pyotr Nikolayevich. Pyotr Nikolayevich was acquainted with the captain of a trawler that picked up contraband off the shore of Gotland. Tanya's money would pay the captain.

The Swedes who met the trawler came heavily laden with radios and television sets, capable of picking up Swedish broadcasts, and highly prized all along the Baltic coast. They went back with a much lighter cargo, Soviet industrial diamonds.

Joseph would go with them back to Burgsvik.

And if he reached Gotland, Joseph intended to get the ferry to Oskarshamn on the Swedish mainland.

There were so many ifs that Tanya occasionally burst into laughter just thinking of it. But Joseph's wolf eyes burned with black fire, and energy trembled in his body, which had strengthened fiercely over the long winter.

"Wolf, how do you know the money will still be there?"

"Because I left it there before the war," he replied.

"In a bank? The capitalists will have stolen your money years ago!"

"Capitalists aren't all thieves. Swiss banks don't swindle their clients."

"All banks swindle their clients," she said brusquely. "And what if your family have cleared out the account?"

"Nobody knew it was there but me."

"If you don't get the money, those Swedes will cut your throat, my child."

"Swedes are pacifists."

"How much this child knows about the world," she said in mock admiration. "Knows that banks don't swindle and Swedes don't cut throats." She explored his face with her fingers. The wounds had hardened into silvery weals, partly covered by the grizzled tangle of his beard. Her lips were full and moist as they kissed his. "I want you not to go, wolf. I want you not to die."

And On The day he left, she wept as though she would never stop.

He kissed her one last time, tasting the bitter salt of her tears, bitter as the Baltic spray, where he was headed.

He did not look back as he drove away from the village. He was hunched over the wheel of the Moskvitch, concentrating on the melting snow that churned under his wheels.

And slowly, through the rhythm of the road, his thoughts focused on the life, the new life, to which he was at last traveling.

ENGLAND

Wallace arrived to pick her up in the Bentley. She had neither expected nor wanted Evelyn or David to come. While Wallace loaded her bags into the car, she went to say good-bye to Miss Marsh.

Miss Marsh was standing at the window in her study, the brightness of the blue sky beyond making her a thin silhouette.

"So, Kate," she said. "We part for the summer."

"Yes, Miss Marsh."

"Well, you needn't worry about the examinations. I've had a preliminary look at your papers. You've done brilliantly. As always, you're far ahead of your year. When you come back, I intend to speak to the headmistress about your skipping a year and moving straight up to the fifth. You'd like that, wouldn't you?"

"I find the work easy." She shrugged.

"You find the work *far* too easy, despite your late start." The house mistress wore an odd smile. "I'm not so sure about the rest of it.

School in the larger sense. Hockey and house spirit. Discipline. England. The English."

"I've survived," Kate said.

"Is that all? I was a girl at this school myself, Kate, not so very long ago. I know all about the Honourable Code of never telling on another girl. But house mistresses get to hear things, just the same. It's our duty to hear things we're not meant to hear, and see things we're not meant to see. In theory, we're supposed to relay anything that looks like serious trouble to the headmistress. However, we house mistresses have something of an Honourable Code ourselves."

She came forward and laid her hand gently on Kate's shoulder. Kate knew that Miss Marsh had in some way fallen in love with her. But she also knew that Miss Marsh's love would never take a physical form, and that it was one of the things that had enabled her to survive the past six months.

"I know something about the problems you've been having. I don't say that it's all your fault. There is viciousness in all children, not least in adolescent girls from good families. But there is too much rage in you, Kate. Too much passion. You must learn to curb it."

Kate was hanging her head now, staring blindly at the floor. "I try," she said thickly.

"Try harder. Too much passion is a poison in the blood. Too much rage burns up your energy, leaving you weak and blind."

"I hate this place," she whispered. "It's driving me mad."

"Don't fight it," Miss Marsh whispered back, her head close to Kate's. "St. Anne's could be so good for you. I think you have done more than survive, Kate. It seems to me you have gained immensely from these six months."

What of the things I have lost? she thought. What of the way you are taking my identity from me, robbing me of what I was, turning me into something I am not? But she said nothing.

"You know how a perfect rose is grown, don't you?" Miss Marsh's fingers kneaded her shoulder slowly, driving in the words. "A cultivated scion is grafted onto a vigorous rootstock. You have outstanding natural advantages. You have great beauty and great intelligence. But without refinement, those are raw things, not necessarily productive on their own. St. Anne's can transform you, if you let us. Assimilate us. Let us assimilate you." Her hand dropped away. She stepped back. "Now, go and enjoy yourself."

In the courtyard, she said good-bye to the three or four girls with whom she'd formed friendships. They kissed and hugged and exchanged promises to write daily over the long summer holiday.

The school was already half-deserted. It wore an end-of-term sleepiness, the gray buildings already shuttered, the playing fields empty. She got into the Bentley.

"How did the examinations go, Miss Kate?" Wallace asked.

"All right, thank you."

"Looking forward to the summer holidays?"

"Yes, thank you." She was to be taken to Sicily with David and Evelyn, to stay in the seaside villa of friends. She had no desire to see Sicily, not even any curiosity about the place. She had never known the Italy of the Mediterranean. Her Italy had been of the lakes and Alps, of forests and mountains. But it was a relief not to have to spend the summer at Great Law, where the only escape from an existence that seemed to center relentlessly around horses and dogs was the bleak moor, where the wind boomed like somber cannon. She had hated Great Law from the start. Its grim architecture had repelled her on her very first sight of the place, and the few weekends she had spent there had been unutterably dreary.

But as they drove out through the school gates, a feeling of intense relief, almost of joy, shot through her unexpectedly. Wallace met her eyes in the rearview mirror, as though sensing her emotion. His normally impassive face wore a faint smile.

"Good to get out, isn't it, miss?"

SWITZERLAND

"I'm afraid it is impossible."

For several reasons, the banker was acutely uncomfortable. He had a folder on the desk in front of him, and he kept his eyes busy on it, or on his hands, or anywhere except on the face of the man opposite him. "The loss of a key is a serious matter. When a key is lost, special rules come into force. The deposit is designated as frozen, and the bank cannot, without proper credentials—"

Joseph's fingers tightened like claws. "You have already explained all that to me, Herr Emmanuel."

"It is the question of identification which presents the greatest problem. This is a safe deposit which has not been opened for—" He riffled through the folder. "—almost twenty years."

Joseph was fighting to hide his desperation. He thought of Tanya. *The capitalists will have stolen your money years ago!* "Please. You must recognize that my situation is an exceptional one."

"You say that you have been in labor camps behind the Iron Curtain during this time." Emmanuel's eyes flicked as far as Joseph's chest, then dropped away again. "Something of an ordeal."

"Yes," Joseph said in his dry, husky voice. Emmanuel was a smooth-faced, plump man. His office, as befitted his status, was luxurious in the Swiss style, with treacle-colored furniture and ponderous drapes occluding the windows. "Something of an ordeal."

"I, personally, am inclined to believe that you are who you say you are. But you have entered Switzerland on travel documents which you admit are not your own—"

"They are forgeries."

"Quite," Emmanuel said with distaste. "You do not wish to approach your own consul to apply for proper documentation—"

"No."

"—nor will you allow us to contact a family member who could vouch for—"

"*No.*" Joseph's voice was harsh enough to make the Swiss blink. Joseph took a deep breath. It was vital not to lose his self-control, not to let his desperation show. That would frighten the man off completely. "Herr Emmanuel. Please. Look at my face."

The man raised his head with patent reluctance. In Sweden, Joseph had cropped short the beard Tanya made him grow. It revealed the injuries more, but at a distance was less conspicuous than all that wild hair. Emmanuel flinched involuntarily as his eyes rested on Joseph's face.

"I was hit in the face by a heavy-caliber bullet," Joseph said quietly. "They left me for dead. My jaw was not set properly. The stitching was done with household needles and thread." He saw Emmanuel's Adam's apple bob up and down. "My family must have resigned themselves to my death years ago. It would be a considerable shock if I reappeared in their lives. Even more of a shock if I reappeared looking like this."

Emmanuel licked his lips. "Who knows, with specialist surgery—"

"I need time to consider that. I need time to consider many things. What I don't need is to be thrust into a glare of publicity, or to have to face people I have not seen in two decades. I have always been a private man, Herr Emmanuel. That was one of the reasons I acquired a safe deposit in a Swiss bank, many years ago. I felt I could rely absolutely on the discretion of men like you."

Emmanuel smiled unhappily. *"Ach, so."*

"Now I need privacy more than ever. For many years, I have lived in an environment which was so far from normality that . . . " He glanced around Emmanuel's homey office. "Don't be offended if I say you couldn't possibly imagine it. I have awoken, like Rip Van Winkle, to a world I barely know. Where even the automobiles in the street look to me like science fiction." He paused to dab his lips with his handkerchief. The effort of speaking coherently tended to fleck his beard with saliva. "Escaping from Soviet Russia was not easy. I have no money of my own. I have had to borrow money from people who could not spare it, and even that has now run out. But I am not going to walk into a consulate or an embassy like this, far less into the bosom of my family. I need access to what is in that box. I must have that, before I do anything else."

"I see your problem." Emmanuel spread his plump hands. "I hope you see mine."

Joseph's strength had come to an end. He felt despair. "I have nothing else in the world," he said, his voice trembling. "That box contains everything I have."

Emmanuel's face closed. "I must repeat, I cannot let you have access to the deposit until you can bring me satisfactory proof of identity."

Joseph tried to keep his expression calm, but something in his eyes frightened the Swiss, who reached surreptitiously under his desk.

"You don't need the alarm," Joseph said tightly. He rose, and Emmanuel's wary gaze followed him, the plump hand hesitating. Joseph could only imagine what he looked like through Emmanuel's eyes, with his workman's boots and his cheap suit, the twisted jaw grotesque under the grizzled beard. A dangerous vagrant. He forced a smile to his lips. "I'll see what I can do."

"It might be wisest, in your case, to inform the police—"

"I am a client, Herr Emmanuel, whether you believe it or not. In my estimation, you are bound in exactly the same way as a priest is bound in the confessional. Perhaps even more so."

Emmanuel hesitated, then inclined his balding head in reverence to Mammon. "I shall, of course, preserve your confidentiality."

"*Gruss Gott*, Herr Emmanuel."

"*Gruss Gott.*"

Joseph walked out into the quiet Zurich street with no idea where he was headed.

S<small>WANS</small> W<small>ERE</small> M<small>ATING</small> on the silvery surface of the Limmat. Joseph wandered along the banks of the river, watching the beating white wings and arching necks. He thought of Tanya, of how the dance of love so often resembled a dance of torment.

It was summer. It had taken him almost five months to get from Riga to Zurich. And now he was free, truly free, for the first time since his youth. And yet cornered here, like a rat. To be so near, and to find the polished steel doors shut in his face! In that office he'd wanted to take Emmanuel's fat throat in his fingers and tear the smug life out of him.

It was the disfigurement that had frightened Emmanuel, he was sure of that. The disfigurement was going to be a severe handicap in one sense. In another, it was a miraculous blessing. It enabled him to choose any mask he wanted.

But he desperately needed what was in the steel box under the orderly Zurich street. If he could not reach it, he might as well slip into this quiet river and let the waters close over his head.

He paused suddenly on the bridge. A knife of remembrance twisted in his belly. There was someone. Down in the waters of the Limmat, he saw a face, shimmering up out of the memories. A woman's face. Of course. Always a woman, all his life, for the turning points. When fate wanted the big effects, she always chose a woman for Joseph.

This face must have changed over the decades, but not too much, perhaps. If he could only grasp at the name.

He stood, gripping the railings as though his talons could twist the iron. Passersby glanced covertly at the strange figure hunched over the river. What did he see with those glaring black eyes?

He rocked slightly, gritting his teeth, the machinery of his mind straining to dredge up the long-buried name. It was a heavy name, a leaden name. It would not rise out of the darkness. He closed his eyes and lifted his face, groaning in his throat like an animal. A woman shied away from him. Other pedestrians took care to walk around him.

Then, with a wrench, the name burst out of the dark waters.

Joseph was gasping with the effort. There was a pain in his chest, and he swayed a little. But the effort had been successful. He had the name now. It would lead him to the key.

He dabbed his mouth with the handkerchief. Then he turned and walked swiftly back toward the bank.

"I Have A suggestion, Herr Emmanuel."

"Please make it."

"I remember a woman who worked here at the time I acquired the deposit. Her name was Marlene Kniphoffer. She accompanied me to the vaults several times."

"No such person works at this branch now."

"Perhaps she has been transferred. She would only be my age. If she can be found, I believe she would vouch for me."

The banker's face creased dubiously. "After so long, *mein Herr* . . . and you have changed a great deal."

"Fraulein Kniphoffer had an excellent memory. Moreover, we got on well. We used to share certain jokes. She'll remember, I'm sure."

Emmanuel's expression seemed to doubt that anyone could ever have shared a joke with the man who sat opposite. Or perhaps he was expressing disapproval at the idea of any levity taking place in banking hours. He drummed his fingers, then glanced at his watch. "It is highly irregular. Highly."

"But you will look into it?"

"Perhaps you will give me a little time to consider . . . "

Joseph rose. He felt calm come over him. "I'll call in tomorrow at the same hour."

"Very well."

And after a moment's hesitation, Herr Emmanuel extended his smooth hand.

Which was more, Joseph reflected on his way back to the *hauptbahnhof,* than he had done on first acquaintance.

The Elevator Doors closed. The clerk's eyes avoided Joseph's in the cramped space. Joseph knew he must smell unclean. He had been with the Gypsies, across the river, for the past four nights, and Zurich was not an easy city for the homeless and moneyless. But Joseph had spent nights that made these look like luxury, and he would never lose the faculty of survival, not even when he had a feather cushion to lay his head on and wealth to protect his nakedness.

Well, none of that mattered now. As the elevator clanked down into the vaults, he held the key in his hand, freshly cut and sharp-edged. Marlene Kniphoffer had not hesitated to help him. Nor had her blue eyes flinched when she saw what had become of the handsome young man who flirted with her all those years ago, before war raged and youth fled.

The elevator released them in the vaults. Here, in the cold neon light, the subterranean entrails of the bank glistened. This basement had been modernized since he was last here and was impressive in its clinical severity. There were three sets of steel gates to be negotiated, and each one slammed shut with a crash behind them. The sound raised the hackles on Joseph's neck, and his skin prickled with sweat by the time they reached the anteroom to the final door, which was solid, polished steel. The small camera scanned them from the ceiling with its single red eye. They waited in silence. Then there was a loud click, and the door hissed open slowly.

Within was a gleaming chamber. The walls were lined, from steel floor to steel ceiling, with the doors of boxes, each one numbered, each bearing two keyholes. Behind these surgical facades lay wealth, secrets, crimes. The clerk went to one and inserted his key into the left-hand slot. He twisted it three times, then gave Joseph a formal bow.

"When you are ready, please call."

He went to sit in the corner.

Joseph's fingers trembled badly as he inserted the key into the right-hand slot of the safe-deposit box. His heart was pounding.

As he slid it out, its lightness told him it was almost empty.

"No!" he whispered.

Horror surged in his veins. He had never felt such despair. He managed somehow to carry it into the little cubicle and drew the curtain behind him. He put it on the table, and wrenched off the lid.

He had been holding his breath, and now he let it out in a harsh, tormented moan.

"Mein Herr?" The clerk had come anxiously to the curtain. "Are you all right, *mein Herr?"*

He steadied himself, leaning on the table, eyes closed for a moment. "Yes," he said through clenched teeth. "Leave me alone."

The world rocked around him. Slowly, he straightened and looked down.

The box was not completely empty. It contained two oilskin pouches. He opened the larger one first, and the rich sparkle greeted his eyes. First-quality blue-white diamonds, some fifteen or twenty.

A little heartened, he unfolded the second pouch with care.

A bitter smile crossed his lips.

The pistol was not quite a miniature. But it was so small that when Joseph gripped it in his hand and put his index finger through the knuckle guard, barely an inch of the blued barrel thrust forward. He gripped the weapon tightly. A handful of diamonds and a pistol. That was what they had left him.

There were no bullets for the pistol—time would have made them unpredictable in any case—but the .22-caliber ammunition was commonly used for hunting weapons. Lightweight bullets, and with such a short barrel, no accuracy to speak of, unless you held the weapon to a man's temple and squeezed the trigger with care.

He folded it back into the oilskin and put it into the bag he had brought, together with the diamonds.

For a moment he stood immobile, staring at the wall. His despair had not lasted long. He already knew what he had to do. Knew the course he had to take.

Better than nothing. Much better than nothing.

He zipped up the bag and left the cubicle. He slid the steel box back into its hole. He twisted his key three times, pocketing it. Then he nodded to the clerk and said, "I am ready."

SICILY

She came slowly out of the deep white silence. Sensations returned: the heat of the sun on her skin, the smell of the sea, the lapping of waves. She lay on her back, placid as a child. No thought moved in her mind. No speculation stirred.

How wonderful this peace was. How wonderful this faculty was that she had learned here, on this sun-baked island, of passing time without thought.

Time without thought. How sweet that was.

A breeze stirred, bringing distant male voices to her ears. She sat up. Twenty yards up the beach, a group of fishermen were bringing in their boat with the morning's catch. Kate brushed sand from her arms and clasped her shins, resting her chin on her knees to watch. They hauled their boat, a heavy wooden launch, up onto the sand. They were short, wiry men, each alike to the others. Fathers, uncles, sons, brothers. Their naked torsos had been burned almost to the color of mahogany by the sun. They chattered to each other in Sicilian. She could hardly follow the thick dialect, but it was good to listen to.

They beached the boat and spread their nets out on the sand to dry. Actions of ten thousand years, performed without haste or reflection. Time without thought.

One of the fishermen walked over to her. He was a young man, not yet twenty, but his torso was beautifully muscled, and he had the solemn face of a classical Greek god. He carried a fish in his hands, a big sea bass, the silver and yellow stripes on its fat body not yet faded in death. He smiled the shy smile of the island as he laid it down beside her. His skin glittered with salt crystals. The fish jolted and convulsed on the sand.

"Oh, what a beautiful fish. But I have no money."

He shook his head and said something in dialect.

She spread her hands helplessly. "I don't understand."

"It's a gift," he said in mainland Italian.

"But it's your morning's work. I should pay you."

"It's a gift," he repeated with another quick smile. His eyes searched hers intently. "I thought you were English."

"I'm Italian."

"From the north?"

"Yes."

"What's your name?"

She hesitated momentarily, as if unsure of her own name anymore. "Catarina," she said firmly. "And yours?"

"Santino." His eyes held hers, and she was suddenly aware of a smoky heat in them. She felt embarrassment wash over her. She ducked her head quickly to hide her blush, and studied the fish. It was still kicking. She felt a pang of sorrow for its death. It was such a beautiful thing, muscled, smooth, designed to slip through the currents with no resistance. She stroked it with her fingertip. It was hard and slippery, the muscles potent as they convulsed. The fins were delicate as flower petals. The sun glanced off it like quicksilver. She looked up to say something to the boy, but he was already walking away from her, back to his boat.

"Thank you," she called after him. He did not turn.

Evelyn had walked down the beach to fetch her. She was dressed all in white, with dark glasses and a straw hat. She smiled down at Kate. "Have you been fishing?"

"No. A man came out of the sea with it."

"Was he riding a porpoise?"

"No."

"Be careful of the local Romeos, Kate. Lunch is ready. Let's go."

Kate carried the fish carefully down to the sea. When she was knee-deep, she lowered it into the water. The smooth body lay still in her hands, and for a moment she thought it was dead. Then, with almost shocking force, it spurted from her hands, and with a quicksilver flash, was gone.

She gathered her things, and they walked up to the house.

The courtyard of the house was shaded by a pergola supporting a century-old grapevine. Clusters of grapes hung heavily among the leaves. One of the children of the family who took care of the house was standing on a chair with a pair of scissors, cutting the ripest bunches. Kate smiled at her and got that quick, bashful grin in return.

Claude and June Cotterell, their hosts, were old friends of David's. They had inherited the house from an uncle. Set in a remote fishing village on the southern coast of the island, well away from the tourist trail, its only concession to modernity was dim electric lighting. The flagged floors were wildly uneven, and the walls had been white-washed so many times that hard corners had become rounded, irregularities had smoothed into dips and mounds. The rooms were almost completely bare. The white, stark walls were empty canvases on which the daily routine was painted, as if by a brush.

They ate in the huge dining room. Like all the downstairs rooms, it was high and vaulted, and cool even in the summer heat. From the ceiling hung an old-fashioned bird cage in which a canary twittered and hopped. A shelf held an array of terra-cotta pots and jars. A rush mat covered the floor. That was all. Yet there was a tranquil beauty in it, as there was throughout the house.

She did not know how Evelyn and David had explained her to the Cotterells, but she presumed they had been told the truth, for they treated her as though she were part of the family. The Cotterells brought a collection of five children from respective previous marriages, but all were either too old or too young to have made close friendships with Kate. She sat peacefully among their horseplay and chatter, toying with her food, lost in her own thoughts.

"What did you do all morning, Kate?" June Cotterell asked her.

"Sunbathed. Swam."

"Well, I'll say this for you, you're easy enough to entertain." June smiled. "Sunbathing, swimming, and writing in your room. Innocent pleasures. Our lot claim to get bored here."

"I never get bored."

"A merman came to see her this morning," Evelyn said.

"Did he?"

"A young fisherman. He brought her a fish."

"Ah," June said significantly. "Probably amorous."

"That's what I said."

June ran her eyes over Kate's face and the swell of her breasts. "She's growing up," she said obliquely. She rang the little bell, and the woman came from the kitchen to clear away the plates. She brought a bowl of fruit, grapes and figs from the garden, apricots and oranges from the market. Kate picked up a fig and split it open. She studied the ripe flesh within, thinking about how beautiful the boy had been.

An African Breeze touched the island that week, hot from the desert, aromatic with the spices of the Barbary coast. The summer was well-advanced. Fruit had ripened and been gathered, and now the islanders started laying it out to dry. Kate came across carpets of apricots, figs, raisins, almonds, spread out in the sun. The heady smell of the fruit was everywhere as the heat baked it, leaving the sweet quintessence of summer behind.

She clambered down the rocky path, her towel slung over her

shoulder. She had fallen into the habit of taking long walks around midday, while the others dozed in the cool shade of the house. She seemed to be impervious to the sun. It could not stun her, or make her peel, like the others. It could not even coax perspiration from her fine skin. Indeed, she basked in its searing caress, reveled in the way her skin darkened a little more each day. She was so dark already that she could have been taken for a Sicilian. It was, Evelyn said, a love affair with the sun. She would take off her straw hat for the sheer pleasure of feeling her black hair bake like iron in the furnace.

The little villages had a primitive, Arab air. The houses were square, flat-roofed, with small, wary windows that peeped from almost pitch darkness within. She would meet few people in the noonday heat; perhaps a cat or a bony dog, or an old woman sitting by her door, all in black, a black fan fluttering in one hand. Only church bells broke the profound silence. The peace of Sicily was priceless. She felt as though she had been here forever.

She finished her walk, as always, at the tiny strip of beach she had come to think of as her own. Arriving on the shimmering, deserted white sand, she stripped off her dress and walked into the water naked. There was never anyone to see. It was her secret place.

The swirl of the sea around her naked body was a sweet caress. She looked down at her own body in the translucent water. Now that she was so tanned, there was less contrast between her skin and the darker disks of her nipples and the triangle at her loins. It made her body seem more like a child's again, its sexuality subdued.

As she floated in the warm shallows, she reflected that the holiday was dribbling away, like sand through an hourglass. It could not be long before they would have to go back to England. The thought of returning to St. Anne's, and the miseries of boarding-school life, was intolerable.

She walked out of the sea. She dried herself with the towel, then stood on the sand, combing her hair back with her fingers, staring out to sea. The sun dazzled off the water like gold. She put her straw hat on to shade her eyes and stood wearing nothing else, her hands clasped behind her back, thinking about David Godbold. To all intents and purposes, they coexisted by ignoring one another completely. It was rare that they exchanged a word, in company or alone. And yet she was burningly conscious of him, and she knew in her heart that he was just as burningly conscious of her. Their mutual detestation was an accepted thing. Evelyn had stopped even attempting to reconcile them.

Yet there was something else. She had seen the way he looked at her, looked at her body when she swam or lay on the sand. The look in his eyes had been disturbing, both frightening and yet fascinating. She had found herself wondering whether he had looked at her mother like that, once.

Conscious of another presence, she turned suddenly. A man was standing on the rocks, watching her. Her heart lurched. Then she recognized Santino, the boy who had brought her the fish. He walked across the sand toward her. She thought momentarily about picking up her dress and pulling it on, but the gesture would have been somehow gauche. And in any case, she did not feel shame.

As before, he was bare-chested, his torso glowing in the sunlight. He stopped a few paces away. His dark eyes were wide as he stared at her nakedness. She saw his throat move as he swallowed. She smiled at him without speaking.

"You shouldn't come here all alone," he said sternly. "With no clothes on."

She was slightly amused by his tone of authority. "Why not?" she asked.

"People," he said with an uneasy shrug.

"You mean I might offend people?"

"People might offend *you*. Hurt you."

"There are no people like that here," she said.

"There are," he said shortly. His gaze was anchored on her face now, as though he were ashamed to look at her nakedness again. "And you are very beautiful."

"So are you." She smiled. His face flamed at once. He lost his masterful poise and became an embarrassed young man. She saw the muscles of his stomach tense into relief. "But if you think I should," she went on, "I'll put my dress on."

She stooped for her dress and picked it up. He took a step forward as she straightened. His face was taut.

"What is it?" she asked.

"I love you," he blurted out.

She stood still. She wanted to smile, not because she was amused by the naive declaration, but out of compassion for his innocence. She kept her mouth still, knowing he would be wounded if she smiled.

"Thank you," she said gravely, still holding her dress against her breasts.

"I've seen you every day since you came here," he said.

"Have you been—" She was about to say *spying*, but stopped herself. "Have you been here every day?"

He nodded. "You're the most beautiful girl I ever saw. You're like a goddess."

They stared at one another. He was the same height as she was, but his body was far stronger, packed with the muscles of having worked since childhood. His hands were rough and chipped, but his face had the calm classicism of a Greek carving. He was breathing more quickly now. "Do you want to make love?" he asked.

She shook her head, slightly alarmed. "No."

"I know how," he said, reddening again.

"I'm sure you do," she said. She pulled her dress on quickly.

"Are you a virgin?" he asked.

She raised an eyebrow. "That's none of your business!"

"You are. I can tell."

She made no reply. The dress clung to her damp skin. She pulled it straight.

Now that she was clothed, his eyes devoured her body hungrily. "Are you afraid your father will beat you?"

"I'm not afraid of him." She pushed past him and walked quickly up the beach.

"I'll wait for you here," he called after her, "every day, Catarina!"

But she did not turn or answer him. She scrambled up the rocky path like a mountain goat, heading back to the villa.

It Was Missing.

She felt her heart contract. She had always locked it in her bedside table, trusting that nobody would find where she hid the key. She had been stupid in her trust. Stupid to assume they would not search her private places.

And now they had taken it, and her most secret, most intimate thoughts were exposed. A spasm of rage tightened every muscle in her body.

She ran out of her room. Which of them had taken it? Evelyn? David? One of the Cotterell children?

She thrust the door of David and Evelyn's bedroom open and went in. Her father was seated at his desk, the calfskin notebook open in front of him. He looked up at her as she came in. His eyes were empty, but his face was pinched around the nose and mouth. He turned the page and read aloud. " 'We are born in shame, we the illegitimate, the misbegotten, the bastards. Yet no shame attaches to those who fathered us. Who are the greatest sinners, we or they?' "

"How dare you read that!" she said breathlessly.

"How dare you write it?" he asked, his voice dry and rough. He read again. " 'I cannot bear to be near him. When I think of the way in which he has destroyed lives, I feel myself choking, as though I cannot breathe.' " His knuckles were white. "I take it this means me?"

"You had no right to take that book!"

"Answer me."

"I will not!"

"Answer me!" he shouted, his cheeks flaming mulberry red with anger. "Answer me, girl! Does this refer to *me?"*

She could feel his fury. His anger thrilled her in a strange, disturbing way. She wanted to laugh and cry at the same time. She wanted to scream at him, but her throat was too tight. "I wrote in English," she said, "so you could understand it one day. I did not intend you to read it yet. That book is not yet finished."

His fist crashed down onto the book. "What do you mean, I destroyed lives?"

"You ought to know," she said in a choked voice. "You're a murderer. You killed my mother."

He stared at her. For a moment she saw the network of red veins around the deep blue eyes. Then he hurled the book at her.

It was so quick she had no time to raise her arms, and the heavy leather cover smashed into her face, knocking her backward, her head exploding with sparks.

He was on his feet, bearing down on her with a terrifying face. "You killed your mother yourself!"

She had expected the accusation to crush him. This savage counterattack had astounded her. "I did not!" she gasped. "I did not!"

"*You* killed her. Not me. She bled to death because of you."

She began to sob. "It was your fault!"

"That's a lie. It was nothing to do with me. How could it be? I was in Germany, in prison camp. It was you. You had decided in the womb to kill her. You tore her body open."

She covered her ears with her palms in horror. "No! You abandoned her! You left her to die!"

"How dare you throw that vile accusation in my face? What the hell do you know about it?"

Her face had been numb. Now her cheek and temple were throbbing from the heavy blow of the book. "I know! You left her to die, and then you abandoned me!"

She thought he would hit her again. "I took care of you, you ungrateful little heathen. I have nothing on my conscience."

"Your conscience must come cheap," she threw at him tearfully, "if it can be bought off at ten pounds a month!"

He was breathing heavily, his handsome face distorted with anger. "That's rich, coming from a bastard who even had to steal her name."

"I did *not* steal my name!"

He laughed, an ugly, harsh sound. "You don't even know you're my child."

"I am your child! My mother was not a whore!"

The Cotterell children were crowded in the doorway, watching in fascination. June Cotterell pushed through them, consternation in her plump face. "What on earth is all this about?"

"I know better than you what your mother was," David snarled. "And even if she was a whore, she was a better woman than you will ever be!"

June exhaled sharply. "David, for God's sake!"

"I hate you," Kate said, hurling the words at him. "You're guilty, guilty! *I hate you.* You left her to die! You turned your back on me!" Evelyn had now come into the room. Kate swung on her, her eyes blazing. "What did you bring me to England for? Why did you take me away from Italy? I didn't want to come! I didn't want your charity! I didn't want your clothes or your money. *He* doesn't want me. He never did. It was a mistake, a terrible mistake!" She couldn't go on. She was crying wildly, the scalding tears pouring down her cheeks. She was aware of the Cotterell children's gaping mouths.

David was still breathing hard. His mouth was bitter. "I hope you're satisfied with what you've achieved, Evelyn."

"David, please—"

"Look at her. Look at her, Evelyn. Read the filth in that notebook. Then tell me that vicious little monster is my daughter."

"David!"

He turned on his heel and left the room. June, after a frightened glance at Evelyn, shepherded her own children out and shut the door, leaving them.

Kate was shaken by her sobs. They seemed to be tearing at her, and all the pent-up pain and anger was spilling out.

"I will not tolerate this," Evelyn said in a deceptively quiet voice.

"I want to go home," Kate sobbed.

"They don't want you at home. And if this is a specimen of your behavior, I'm not surprised."

Kate's knees gave way, and she sat on the bed, looking up at the older woman with spilling eyes. "He killed my mother."

"If it comes to that," Evelyn said unemotionally, "David is right. You killed her between you."

"It was not my fault! I didn't *ask* to be born!"

"Ah. That adolescent cry. Well, if it's any consolation, your father didn't ask for you to be born, either. But you were born. And your mother died bearing you. And that is all. It cannot be helped or changed. Stop crying."

Kate fought her tears, hating the older woman's calmness, recognizing its strength. She groped on the floor for her notebook. The pages had been crumpled when David had thrown it at her. She flattened them with shaking hands, then hugged the smooth leather cover to her breast. "It's my book. He had no right to read it!"

"I would not have bought it for you if I had known what you intended to write in it."

"So you've read it, too!"

"Yes. Your command of English is extraordinary. It's a pity the content is such poisonous rubbish. You had your little say just now. No doubt you've had that on your chest a long time, and now you've got it off your chest." Evelyn's face was flinty. "I cannot tell you how distasteful that scene was. I never want to see it repeated."

"It was the truth!"

"You never knew your mother. It strains credulity to suppose you have any emotional attachment to her. This is self-dramatization, not grief. And I will not put up with that."

Her rage at her father had died a little. At least he was human. His emotions were vivid and hot, like her own. They were of the same blood, he and she. But Evelyn's icy calm was an alien thing, beyond her understanding.

Evelyn walked to the window and looked out, a tall, erect figure against the deep blue Mediterranean sky. "Listen to me, Kate. I dislike misunderstandings, so let's get this clear. You are with us to stay. You will not be sent back, no matter how badly you behave. I know what has been going on at St. Anne's. The fights. The wildness. If you prove intractable at St. Anne's, I will send you to an institution which is equipped to deal with habitual misbehavior. You can have no idea how unpleasant that will be. I assure you that they will break your spirit very quickly there, and that you will not find the process enjoyable. You would be better advised to learn to curb your temperament voluntarily. It will save you a great many very bitter tears. And the end result will be far better." She turned. "Have I used language which is above your head?"

Kate looked down. "No," she said in a low voice.

"I didn't think I had. I want you to remember something. In conflicts between discipline and intelligence, discipline always wins. That is how your Roman ancestors conquered races far more civilized than their own. You probably excel in history, just as you do at languages. Be a Roman, not a Greek. You are going to apologize to your father."

Kate's cheeks flamed. "I will not take back what I have written," she hissed, hugging the book to her breast.

Evelyn's face was like stone. "You have to live with him," she said. "He has to live with you. Can't you understand that?"

"Send me to your reformatory if you want. I will not apologize to him!"

She threw the book at Evelyn's feet and ran out of the room.

AUSTRIA

"Nowadays, apart from hunting accidents, such injuries are rare. During the war, of course, they were commonplace."

Professor Schneider's chambers were handsome, the ceilings scrolled with rococo gilt, the furniture Louis XVI or excellent facsimiles. The Professor had spent the past days taking photographs, making X-rays, noting measurements. He had a talent with the pencil and had drawn several sketches to illustrate what he could do for Joseph. Joseph studied them in silence. Nothing would ever make him look as he used to, but even granted a little artistic license on Schneider's part, something could be done to make him less grotesque.

"A tailor-made face," Joseph said.

Schneider, who had heard this pun on his name many times, laughed politely. "Your last tailor was well-intentioned, but did more harm than good."

"She was trying to save my life, not preserve my beauty."

"Quite. Please rest assured, we have had a great deal of experience with this kind of work, and we have at our disposal the most modern techniques available. Those crude wartime operations are a thing of the past."

Joseph tapped the drawings. "How long?"

"Difficult to predict. Many operations. A lot of recovery time. A lot of discomfort, I am afraid. If the bone and skin grafts take well, and there is no infection, maybe not too long."

"How long before there is a significant change?"

Schneider smiled blandly. "How would you classify a significant change?"

"When my face would no longer frighten a child."

"Ah. That rather depends on the child, doesn't it?"

"Yes," Joseph said heavily.

"The first operations will make some degree of difference. If they are successful. Remember what I told you: grafts often need to be repeated."

"How much money?"

"Also difficult to predict. In the region of fifteen thousand francs." Schneider steepled his fingers and smiled benignly at Joseph. The diamonds had already changed many things about him. The cheap suit and heavy boots had been replaced by neutral-colored, good-quality Swiss clothing. He wore a silk scarf that disguised his lower face. In his gray tweed suit and wool coat, with his hair neatly cut, Joseph was no longer the wild hobo who had frightened Herr Emmanuel. He looked like a man who could afford fifteen thousand francs. Apart from the disfigurement, he seemed to be a well-heeled, bourgeois middle-European. That was what Schneider, who knew nothing of Joseph's past, and almost believed his story of a hunting accident, was prepared to take him for. It was only the wolf's eyes that were disturbing now. They still held the darkness of the forest from which he had emerged. "Fifteen thousand," Schneider repeated. "Perhaps less, perhaps a little more."

Joseph nodded. "Very well. I am prepared to go ahead."

Schneider beamed. "A wise and brave decision."

"But not just yet. I have a project to conclude first. Some loose ends to tie up. I will be ready for you in three months' time."

"Which takes us into the winter. Excellent. Summer is not the season for our work. The sun is our enemy. It discolors the scar tissue." He helped Joseph on with his coat and patted his shoulder. "It will be painful, yes, but you have nothing to fear. A fit, strong man like you is easily capable of withstanding it."

It was true that Joseph was strong. He ate voraciously, and his spare frame had filled out. His chosen form of exercise, a fast daily walk of at least four hours, was building up muscle and stamina. His hair was prematurely iron-gray, making him look ten years older than he was, but his body, with the extraordinary resilience of bodies, was once again young.

Joseph walked across the square. In 1944, an SS Panzer division had fought a bloody rearguard action through this suburb; but the pockmarks and the shell holes had long since been patched, and the square was gay and elegant once more. He went into the travel agency, whose window was bright with posters advertising Tahiti. The bell tinkled cheerily as he let himself in.

Half an hour later, having left a cash deposit, he walked out. It had been set in motion.

He had taken rooms in a small hotel, well out of the center of Vienna, almost in the country, but he did not think of a tram or cab. He set off at his fast wolf's stride, each pace stretching his tendons, pumping the hot blood through the chambers of his heart, bringing him toward the kill.

SICILY

She waited, sitting on the sand, hugging her knees. The sky had become overcast. A long smudge of darkness lay along the horizon, and there was a muttering of approaching thunder in the air. She was no longer crying. She had shed all her tears, and now there was only the emptiness inside her, the void that had always been waiting.

When she heard the boy's voice, she rose impatiently and turned to face him. He had come down the path, calling her name. He was wearing a patched shirt and jeans, a faded cap perched on his head. He stopped, his head on one side inquiringly. "What are you doing here?"

"I'm ready," she said.

Santino's dark eyes widened. "Ready for what?"

"To make love."

He looked astounded. Then he glanced up at the sky. "It's going to storm," he said.

"I don't care." She was as taut as a bow, her fists clenched at her side. "I'm ready."

"But, Catarina . . . " He looked almost afraid of her, licking his lips nervously. Her anger burst out of her.

"Was it all talk?" she shouted at him. "Aren't you a man?"

His face became expressionless. "Yes, I'm a man."

"Then come on." She turned, and without waiting to see if he was following, strode over to the place she had chosen, among the jagged rocks, so close to the water's edge that the little bed of sand was humid and smooth. There, she pulled her dress over her head, and now naked, faced him. "Take your clothes off," she commanded.

He obeyed slowly, as if reluctant, his eyes on her nakedness. In the somber light, his skin glowed like honey. There was a tangle of black hair at his loins. She looked at his manhood and thought of the fish he had brought her, virile and alive, designed to slip through the currents without resistance. She sat on her own outspread clothes and lifted her arms to him.

He began trembling as he came to her, his breathing ragged. He took her in his arms and kissed her, not on her face, but on her throat, her shoulders, the slope of her breasts, with awe and passion.

"I love you," he whispered. "I love you, Catarina. I knew you would be mine."

She felt that there was an anvil inside her, that a hammer was clubbing onto red-hot iron in her breast. The heat spread through her like a furnace. She was impatient with his attempts to arouse her. His fingers were caressing her thighs, his mouth at her nipples; but she did not want arousal, did not want tenderness. She wanted something that would chime with her rage, the ferocity of that iron hammer, beating into the heat. She dug her nails into his smooth, muscled shoulders. "Just take me," she commanded. "Don't wait. Do it now."

Still he seemed uncertain. He pressed his open mouth to the base of her throat, whispering endearments. Frustrated, she reached for his loins and grasped his penis. He was hot and erect, filling her hand. She reached up with her other hand, knotting her fingers in his thick hair, dragging his body onto her, into the harbor of her parted thighs. He groaned as she guided him to her, the way she had seen farmers guide a bull to a cow, steering the swollen head to the gateway of her own flesh. Her strength was ferocious, her determination overwhelming his attempts at niceties. When she felt him in place, she took her hand away, and looking into his eyes, commanded, "Now, push *now.*"

He thrust into her with blind force. She felt her maidenhead tear, felt the searing pain of his entry into her body, where no entry had been made before. Her back arched, and she screamed up at the lowering sky, a fierce scream of grief and triumph. For a long moment she was curved there, like a bow in his arms, her eyes staring unseeing at the darkness above. Then, shuddering, she dissolved into sobs. It was done. It was accomplished.

He did not notice she was crying, or if he did, was too intent on his own satisfaction. She was aware of him thrusting, his body driving into hers, and the dull pain flooded her lower body with no precise location. She waited for him to finish, her palms flat on the muscular back that pumped and convulsed like a dying fish. She had expected no pleasure, and received none. It had not been about pleasure.

She heard his voice calling her name, his gasps rising, becoming incoherent. His mouth was crushed to her temple, his breath hot on her skin. Then, with a spasm as if of agony, he climaxed and was discharging into her. She held him tight, feeling his body batter hers in the final throes. Then his neck drooped like a broken stem, and he was still.

The rain began to fall, in slow, heavy drops that spattered her face and rinsed the salt from her eyelids and her lips.

ENGLAND

It would have been reckless to use public transport of any kind, so he had hired a van in London and had driven it up through Birmingham to the west Midlands. The van was a prewar-vintage Morris, battered and nondescript, but it was reliable enough. It had a sturdy tailgate that could be used as a ramp, and there was ample room in the back for a mattress, on which he could sleep.

He spent four days in Bradford, engaged in reconnaissance. By day he drove out into the country, returning to the city by night and parking the van in industrial estates and factory areas, where it would not be noticed. He avoided cafés, living on fruit that he bought, or eating fish and chips from newspaper packages, brewing tea on the Primus twice a day and keeping it warm in a Thermos flask. He was not a tea drinker by nature, not even after all those years in Russia. He would have preferred coffee. But he was fitting himself as completely as he could into the role he had chosen, and assembling the tools he needed.

He had once again changed his appearance. He had left the urbane Swiss clothes in London. Now he wore a flat cap and a shabby linen coat on top of overalls and boots. He had picked up the clothes in a secondhand shop in the East End of London.

He had also picked up a pair of horn-rimmed glasses, which he put on whenever he had to deal with people. They blurred his vision, but they gave him a harmless, peering air. There was no way he could hide the scars; and yet, as soon as he entered the working-class milieu, dressed as a worker, moving among workers, it was as if he had submerged and become invisible. The working classes, he noticed with grim irony, were more used to scars and amputations. They did not stare at him as the bourgeois did. They treated him with instinctive companionship and a rough, natural compassion.

He soon realized that almost everyone assumed he had sustained the injury during the war. The scars already looked weathered under the growth of beard. At the garage where he bought the motorcycle, the owner asked him where he had served.

He hadn't wanted to engage in any form of conversation, but it would have been more conspicuous to have shrugged the man off. "North Africa, mainly," he replied shortly.

The man's face lit up. "Me, too." He proved talkative, but was mercifully uninterested in Joseph's brief replies, content to reminisce with a faraway stare in his eyes while Joseph looked over his stock. At length, he waved a dismissive hand at the assortment of motorcycles in the forecourt. "Load of shit," he said contemptuously. "Got something special round the back. Come on." He led Joseph into the workshop and pulled the tarpaulin off a big Triumph 750 with the gas tank missing and the exhaust pipes off. "That's a serious motorcycle," the man said proudly. "Not exactly new, but she'll never let you down, and she'll do a hundred without straining. Have her ready for you by five this afternoon, if you want."

"How much?"

"Seeing you're an old soldier, twenty pounds."

"Fifteen."

They settled on seventeen pounds ten shillings. He gave the man a five-pound note as deposit and walked back to the van. Earlier, he had seen a number of pawnshops in a street along a canal, and he drove there now. He found a serviceable leather jacket in one shop, a helmet, goggles, and dust mask in another. The leather dust mask was especially valuable. With the goggles, it obscured his face completely.

It was a Saturday afternoon, and the streets were full of cloth-capped men and scarfed women. Noisy groups of youths hung around the dingy pub doorways. He had been not much older than these young men when the war had begun, he reflected. Yet they were a different generation, their hair greased back in strange quiffs and duck's tails, wearing clothes he found ugly and bizarre. The youths were boisterous, affecting a dangerous air; yet they stepped aside automatically to let Joseph through, and none called after him.

He spent the afternoon sitting on the banks of the canal, drinking tea from his Thermos, watching the men fishing. He had time to kill, and he was far less conspicuous here than up there among the barren moorland. While in London, he had learned that his quarry had been away on holiday on the continent, but was due back at his home on the ninth, today. He glanced at his watch. He would be there now.

Although Joseph had already reconnoitered the property several times and had noted a number of possibilities, there was no point in making elaborate plans; he would play the final scene by ear, seizing whatever chance presented itself. That was how he had lived for fifteen years. That was how he had been schooled. There was no man alive better than he at grasping an opportunity, reacting with blind instinct to the moment's chance. And when he had done it, he would drive immediately to Humberside and get on a ferry. And it would be over. The long years of waiting would have been fulfilled. He could begin to live again.

He thought he had himself well under control. But fits of trembling seized him from time to time, shaking his whole body.

He would do it quickly, cleanly, without hesitation.

Then, a little time to meditate before he faced the surgeon's knife. And then the prize. He felt a tremor shake his heart at the very thought. He remembered the nights he had frozen in his bunk, when hate yawned like the pit below him, and the thought of his lost prize was like a distant star above.

That was all to come, the creamy dessert after the bloody main course.

At five o'clock, as the summer shadows lengthened, he parked the van in a silent, empty street at the back of a gasworks and walked to the garage, where he picked up the Triumph. He rode it back to the van, assessing the performance of the machine. The mechanic had not lied. The exhaust note was throaty and healthy, and the engine throbbed with raw energy. Riding the powerful machine was a kind of release. It stopped the trembling, made his movements fluid and instinctual again. It was the right tool.

He let down the ramp and drove the motorcycle up into the back of the van with one spurt of the accelerator. No one had observed him. He got into the cab and drove out of the narrow street.

7

Because her horse had cast a shoe, the excursion was cut mercifully short for Kate. While Evelyn and the others rode on down the lane, she dismounted and led the mare slowly back to the house, the horseshoe in her free hand.

She was still thinking about Santino, about that violent moment under the darkening sky, about the way they had gone into the sea afterward, as if to wash themselves clean in the salt water.

They had not made love again during the week that had remained to them. For her, there had been no need. She had taken from him what she wanted, and had given him what he wanted in return. He had wept on the day she'd left, making her promise to write to him; but she had known she would never see him again.

Now, under paler English skies, among greener English countryside, she remembered him with an emotion she could not define, something warm and pure. She had passed a watershed on that day. With her virginity, the Sicilian boy had taken something else from her—

an immaturity, a wildness. He had freed her to look back over the past months, perhaps even over the whole course of her short and unhappy life, and see herself as she really was.

It had been a rite of passage. A last farewell to childhood, an entry into adulthood. She had recognized how wrong she had been about so many things. Even about her father, and what he had done. Evelyn had been right. She'd had no emotional attachment to her mother. Her rage had been born of self-pity, not moral indignation. She had been selfish, self-centered, self-dramatizing.

She had wanted her father to read that notebook. She had wanted to hurt him, and she had succeeded. Now she regretted that act with sorrow. Evelyn had been right about many other things. She had to live with her father, and he with her. And she owed him more than the sullen bitterness she had been venting on him.

She did not know where to begin making things better. But she would do so. She had taken the decision somewhere on the long journey home. She would behave like an adult toward him from now on, and to Evelyn, too. She would try and become what they wanted.

She rounded the stable building and saw the gleam of the big motorcycle parked in the hedgerow. It struck her as odd, but not odd enough to investigate.

She stabled the horse and rubbed her down, lost in her own thoughts. Then she put the saddle back in the tack room and hung the horseshoe on a nail for the farrier to see when he came. She walked back to the house.

She stopped short at the strange sight of her father kneeling on the gravel beside a tall, strange man in a leather jacket who stood at his side, his fist held to her father's head. It was an odd tableau. Her mind told her it was some kind of game, even as her heart told her it was no game, and she saw that the strange man's fist held a gun.

They were no more than thirty feet away from her, and she could see her father's eyes. They were streaming with tears. His mouth was open, terrible grief etched into every line.

She wanted to scream, but her throat was paralyzed. She started toward them, moving like a person in a dream. The tall man was so intent that he seemed not to hear or see her. But she did not reach him in time to drag that accusing, sentencing arm down.

She heard the report, incongruously soft, and saw the puff of smoke around her father's head. Then, as he pitched forward, she saw the black hole in his temple, and the bright blood pump out in a jet. His fingers dug into the gravel with a quivering movement, as though trying to dig himself a shelter, or a grave.

She stopped short, and her voice awoke at last, a shriek of despair and unbearable loss.

"Daddy!"

She saw the grotesquely scarred face turn to her, met the wild black wolf's eyes of the man who had orphaned her for the second time in her life.

There was no breath in her lungs, no blood in her heart. The executioner walked swiftly toward his motorcycle. She ran at him, flung up her arms to stop him. But he thrust her aside with easy strength, gloved hands ramming her back, so that she fell onto the ground.

His motorcycle exploded into life and roared away down the drive. Its wheels scattered her with gravel as she lay near her father's body.

3

THE GHOST IN THE MACHINE

1 9 9 2 – 9 3

COLORADO, UNITED STATES

It was snowing hard in Denver.

Anna emerged from the plane's walkway into the softly lit, carpeted concourse. Inside Stapleton, the weather was perpetually balmy. A couple of uniformed attendants waited for the arriving passengers. One of them was holding a square of cardboard; she saw her own name was written on it.

She walked toward him, tense and unsmiling.

"I'm Anna Kelly."

"This way, please, ma'am." The attendant took her bag and led her over to a desk, where a formidably big, hard-looking man waited.

"Philip Westward." He took her hand in a brief, firm grasp. The soft telephone voice had not prepared her. Her first impression was of the electric contrast between his tanned skin and his Adriatic-blue eyes. He wore a beautiful fawn Burberry, beneath which she glimpsed an even more beautiful pinstripe suit, a slash of crimson silk tie vivid against his white silk shirt. His hair was very dark, looped over his brow to hide either a high forehead or a receding hairline. He towered over her by at least a foot. He was probably in his mid-forties, though his face had a battered look that made his age difficult to estimate.

"How is my mother?" she asked without preamble.

"No change. But she's holding her own." He glanced her over assessingly. "My plane's ready to take off. I can offer you coffee or a drink on board. But if you'd rather take a break on the ground—"

"I'm okay. Let's just get to Vail as soon as possible."

"Fine." He nodded to the uniformed attendant and set off through the crowd, Anna following behind his broad back.

Conscious of having been less than gracious, she caught up with him. "This is very kind of you, Mr. Westward. You didn't have to come and pick me up in your private plane."

"There's no problem," he replied, apparently unoffended by her manner. "I'm glad to be able to do something. This way."

A driver was waiting to take them to the private airplane hangar in a hulking Jeep Cherokee. He loaded her luggage in the back. She could hardly remember what she had packed. She wondered whether she'd been clearheaded enough to include some clothes suitable for winter in the Rockies.

The Cherokee trundled out toward the group of private aircraft. It was a white world. Huddled close to Philip Westward's side, she saw airport personnel blowing snow off the wings of the big jets. Her cream linen suit and tan sandals had been suitable in Miami. Her clothes had crumpled on the flight, and now seemed to be freezing to her body.

He caught her uneasy shiver. "Cold?"

"I've just come from Miami. And I'm beginning to think I've packed rather stupidly."

He took off his Burberry and slung it around her shoulders. "That'll help till you warm up."

She pulled his coat around her, trying to soak up the warmth his body had left in the material.

His plane was a white twin-engined Beechcraft, a pilot already sitting at the controls. The pilot hoisted her aboard, Westward following.

There was seating for eight passengers, which left six seats empty, giving the interior of the Beechcraft the look of a boardroom. Westward helped her to buckle herself into the seat, which was plush and comfortable. She noticed the fittings were luxuriously trimmed with walnut. He'd said, *my plane*. As he strapped himself in beside her, she saw oval gold cuff links at his wrists, the sleek gleam of a watch no doubt boasting a double-barreled Swiss name. But the suit and gold trimmings could not hide what looked to be a soldier's body, tough and lean. Wealthy Mr. Westward. Who the hell was he? She pulled the collar of his Burberry up around her cheeks defensively.

"You must be bushed," he said as the pilot started up the engines. "We have about a twenty-minute flight to Eagle. Maybe a bit longer with the snow. Would you like to catch a little sleep on the way?"

"I slept on the flight," she lied.

The plane lurched forward, wheels slipping a little in the snow. It taxied two hundred yards, turned, and paused on the takeoff runway, behind a large civil jet.

"You'd better tell me what to expect," she said.

"Yes," he agreed, "I'd better." The husky note in his voice, which she had noticed on the telephone, was quite pronounced. "Your mother is very sick. She's been badly hurt. They had to do an emergency neurosurgical operation straightaway, but she hasn't regained consciousness since the assault."

She looked away from him, at the whirling propeller on the starboard wing. Somehow she formed the words. "Is she going to die?"

"I don't know." He said it flatly, not evasively. "They seem to be taking pretty good care of her. She's in the intensive care unit. Her face isn't injured. And she wasn't raped or sexually interfered with in any way."

He'd answered two of the questions that had been haunting her all through the flight from Miami. She swallowed. "Why hasn't she woken up?"

"I'm not a doctor," he said carefully. "You'll have to speak to them. Carr Memorial is an excellent hospital. She's getting the best care available."

Anna nodded, turning her face away from him. The heavy snow meant air traffic was congested, slow moving. The jet finally took off, way down the runway, the shimmer of its engine gases reflected off the wet runway. The crackling voice of the control tower okayed them for their own takeoff.

The pilot half-turned to look at them from the cockpit. "We're off, Mr. Westward."

"Okay, Paul."

The pilot pulled the screen closed on the cockpit. The note of the engines rose until the whole plane was vibrating. Then they were accelerating down the runway. Anna's stomach felt as though it were flattening against her spine. She resisted the temptation to reach out and clutch the hand of the stranger who sat beside her.

Then, with a surge of power, the Beechcraft swept into the air and began climbing steeply. As soon as it started leveling off a little, Philip Westward unbuckled his seat belt and went forward into the cockpit. She turned her head to watch Denver pass beneath their wings, a toy city made of icing sugar. The Rockies loomed up a few miles ahead, spectacular and somehow ominous.

When Westward returned, he was carrying two cups of coffee. She took hers eagerly, cupping her palms around the hot china. The aroma of brandy lifted off the coffee. She didn't comment, just drank gratefully.

"What about Campbell?" she asked.

"As far as I know, he's still being interrogated by the police."

She shivered icily. "The whole idea is horrible. Is there any evidence against him?"

He had a habit of pausing for a few seconds before speaking, as though assessing the question, weighing his answer. "It appears he and your mother ended their relationship on bad terms a short period before the attack."

"Well, I knew that. But to do this—"

"Look, Anna. I don't know your mother, or anything about her personal life. I don't know Brinkman, either. I had never met either of them until the weekend."

She stared at him. "I thought you were an associate of my mother's."

"No. I don't work with your mother. I found myself in the middle of all this by a coincidence. I made an appointment to see her on Sunday. I kept calling her, but there was no reply. I went to her apartment and got the manager to open up. The place had been ransacked, and your mother was unconscious on the kitchen floor. I called the ambulance and the police."

"What *was* your connection with my mother then?"

"We had some interests in common."

"Such as?"

Again the pause. "Primarily, your mother's concern with American prisoners of war in Eastern Europe. We were put in touch by a research agency in Moscow."

Anna could not hide her astonishment. "American prisoners of war? Research? What research?"

Westward looked at her carefully. "She never told you about this?" he asked.

"She never said anything about it. Nor has she ever mentioned your name."

"There's no reason why she should. I told you. We had never met."

"I'm sorry if this sounds discourteous," she said grimly, "but just who the hell are you?"

He dipped into his pocket and passed her a business card. It was a handsome thing, embossed with the words PHILIP WESTWARD ASSOCIATES, and an address on Park Avenue, which went with the suit, the watch, and the private plane.

She studied it blankly. "What is it you do?"

"I'm an investment consultant."

"And the prisoner of war business?"

He was silent for a moment. Then he said, "My father was captured by the Germans in World War Two. He never came home. I believe he ended up in a prison camp behind the Iron Curtain."

She glanced at him. The battered look, she now saw, was produced by a sprinkling of small scars on his temples and around his cheeks. A shattering windshield, she speculated. The incident had not marred his looks. His dark blue eyes were beautiful, remote and watchful. He had movie-star looks to go with the money and power. "You're too young to have had a father in the war," she said.

"I was born in 1945. Conceived on his last leave."

"So you never knew him?"

"No. But I've been looking for him all my life."

The words ought to have been moving. But there was something flat in his manner, something detached, aloof. Ruthless, perhaps. Her gaze rested on his mouth, then flicked away restlessly. "I'm sorry to sound suspicious," she said awkwardly. "I'm just a little taken aback by all this." There was a mystery here that made her uneasy. She was suddenly wondering what she was doing in this stranger's plane, soaring through clouds heavy with snow. He seemed to catch her thoughts.

"I'm just helping out because I was on the spot. It's no big deal. You don't have to bother yourself with any of the background right now. We can discuss it later. You're going to need all your concentration for your mother. We're going to land shortly. Just relax until we get there, okay?"

She nodded, too tired and anxious to think any longer.

Anna Stroked Her mother's hand, feeling the occasional tremors that stirred the otherwise limp fingers. Kate lay motionless, her lungs moved by a respirator, plastic tubes running in and out of her body. Her head had been shaved and was now covered with a dressing. An oxygen tube had been taped into her mouth. What could be seen of her once-beautiful face was a white mask, the closed eyelids trembling in time with the fingers.

The room was darkened, lit by the ghostly flickering of the life-support monitors. The place had a mechanical existence of its own, the rhythmical sucking of ventilators, the chirp of monitors, the hum of generators. From behind a glass panel, nurses kept a constant check on the patient.

Her mother looked so vulnerable. Anna could not help being terrified of this place, almost hating its inhumanity. What if her mother were to wake, alone and bewildered, and see all this?

"I'm here now, Mama," she whispered. "You're going to be all right. You're going to be all right."

She repeated the litany again and again, watching her mother's face, wanting to believe the involuntary movements were signs of recognition. Love and regret threatened to overwhelm her.

The pneumatic door hissed open. Philip Westward, who had been waiting in the corridor outside, touched her shoulder.

"Anna? The doctor's here. He wants to speak to you."

She nodded and rose.

The corridor outside her mother's unit looked like a florist's shop. The staff had to pick their way through a dozen or more bouquets and floral arrangements, some of them beautiful, all bearing cards with messages of sympathy and affection. It had been deeply touching to see how much love her mother inspired.

The doctor was a small, dark-skinned man with a lilting Asiatic accent, Indian or Pakistani, she guessed. He introduced himself as Dr. Jay Ram Singh and led them to an office impressively lined with reference books. She and Westward sat behind his desk, which was neatly piled with telephones and stacks of folders.

His opening words were stark. "Your mother has been violently assaulted, Miss Kelly. The assailant was strong and extremely vicious. Most of the damage was almost certainly inflicted by repeated kicking while she was prone on the floor."

Anna closed her eyes involuntarily in shock. Then she glanced at Westward. His face was expressionless. The doctor switched on a light box and pinned several X-rays onto it.

"The most serious injuries were to the head. You can see fracture lines here, here, and here. These dark tracts indicate some hemorrhaging in the frontal and parietal lobes, and rather more severe hemorrhaging in the midbrain area."

Anna nodded, feeling sick. The eerie outline of her mother's skull looked so terribly fragile.

"Your mother's condition is particularly dangerous because intercranial pressure had risen sharply as a direct result of the injuries, and had remained high for several hours until Mr. Westward discovered her. The cerebrum and cerebellum are separated by a fold of the dura mater called the tentorium. As the pressure rose, this part of the brain, the temporal lobe, was forced through the tentorium, exerting pressure on the brainstem and the third cranial nerve. This has produced the profound unconsciousness and the breathing difficulties. You follow?"

"Yes." Anna nodded tersely.

"Immediate decompression was necessary to prevent a further rise in pressure. The neurosurgeon drilled burr holes into your mother's skull here and here, to relieve the edema. Think of them as safety valves," he said, seeing her appalled expression. "These are scans we did after the operation. They show we achieved the desired result. She is no longer in danger from the edema. Her condition has stabilized. We'll keep on monitoring her over the next days. Of course, she is continuing to be treated with mannitol and dexamethasone to make sure the pressure remains as close to normal as possible." He looked up. "I have to tell you that we have also been monitoring your mother with the electroencephalogram, and it shows that there has been no substantial overall increase in brain activity." He watched her face for a reaction.

"You mean, she hasn't started coming round?"

"I mean that she is in a coma."

The word was like a blow. "What's the outlook?"

The man hesitated. "Perhaps we should discuss the prognosis later on, when you've had time to—"

"No," she cut in brusquely. "I'm not a child, Doctor. Tell me now."

He inclined his head. "All right. The outlook is very uncertain. I would be failing in my duty if I did not emphasize that. In the first place, recovery from such a deep coma is rare."

"And in the second place?" she prompted when he stopped.

"In the second place, your mother's brain has probably suffered injuries which may affect her movement, her memory, even her personality. The prognosis is not good. In fact, it is at best poor."

Anna wiped her wet palms on her skirt. "How much physical damage is there to the brain?"

"That is almost impossible to say. A very few patients like this go on to lead full and happy lives. Far more commonly, they never emerge from profound coma."

"Oh, Jesus," she said. "Are you saying you can't help her? You can't do anything for her?"

"No, I'm saying we're doing all that is within our power."

"I want a second opinion," Anna said tautly. "I want to know where the best trauma center in America is. I want the best neurologist in the country."

She felt Westward's hand take her arm, offering her symbolic support.

"We've already had an authoritative second opinion," the surgeon said gently. "We called in David Ballantyne from Los Angeles right away. He happens to be the best neurologist around. He flew in from California two days ago to see your mother. His opinion is in no way different from our own. He'll continue to be consulted throughout your mother's treatment, of course. You can call him any time you want to. In fact, you're perfectly welcome to call in whomever you want, Miss Kelly, at your own expense. I don't think you'll get any different opinions. As for the best center for treatment, you'd have to go a long way to find a better hospital than Carr Memorial. This is America's top skiing country. We see an awful lot of head trauma cases, I assure you. An awful lot."

"I need information," Anna said. It was her first, instinctive reaction. "Is there an organization for head trauma?"

"Yes." The surgeon nodded. "I'll give you their address."

"Can you give me some literature about comas?"

He shrugged. "I could. I doubt you'd understand it."

"There's nothing wrong with my understanding," Anna said grimly. "And I want a copy of my mother's case notes."

He raised his eyebrows in distaste. "I need hardly tell you that's a completely unethical suggestion, Miss Kelly."

"I don't believe ethics come into it, Dr. Ram Singh."

He stared at her for a while, then rose. "Excuse me one moment." They sat in silence until he returned. He was carrying some papers and a blue medical textbook. He laid them on the desk in front of her. "If you read all that, you should have a much better idea of your mother's condition."

"Thank you." She nodded, taking the stuff onto her lap. It felt like taking up a heavy burden.

"We're doing all we can," the surgeon continued, still standing. "I promise you that. But as time goes by, our hopes must dwindle. The longer she remains in coma, the less her chances of recovery will be. If she does not begin to surface soon, then I am afraid we can have little hope."

"Will it help if I stay at her side, talk to her?"

"It may do," the doctor replied neutrally. "But not tonight. You have made a strenuous journey, and there is nothing you can do here now. Get some rest." He touched Anna on the shoulder. "Her condition is now stable, as I said. We do not foresee any change."

It sounded like a death sentence.

Anna walked out of the doctor's office at Westward's side. Out in the corridor, she must have stumbled, because he caught her quickly, keeping her upright as her legs gave way. Her face was a contorted wet mask of grief. She pressed it to his chest, trying not to break down. His arms came around her.

He held her gently, unassertively, letting her get her breathing under control. At length she stepped back, fumbling the books Ram Singh had given her, groping for a tissue. She had left tear stains on his exquisite pinstriped suit. "Sorry."

"She's getting the best care," he said. "Carr Memorial is as well run as any hospital in the state. And he's right. They treat an awful lot of head trauma cases."

"I know." Anna nodded, drying her eyes. Her face felt numb and swollen with the flood of pent-up grief.

"Anna!"

She turned. Campbell Brinkman had arrived, huddled in a camel-hair overcoat, spotted with melting snow. He hurried toward her, his hands outstretched. She fought down her panicky inclination to shy away from him. She let him kiss her cheek. He looked haggard. "They told me you were here. Why didn't you call me?"

"Mr. Westward kindly offered to fly me in from Stapleton," she said awkwardly. "I didn't know you were . . . free."

"I've been trying to call you in Miami all day." He did not say whether he had been cleared yet, and she had no way of asking. The moment was painfully tense. The thought that Campbell might have done this terrible thing had been haunting her. She could hardly bear to look at him. He sensed that she was shrinking away from him. "I didn't do it," he said forcefully. "You have to believe me. I loved her."

She nodded, tongue-tied, with no idea how to respond to his urgency.

"I'll explain later," he said, suddenly weary. "Have you seen your mother?"

"Yes."

"Have you spoken to the doctors?"

She nodded.

Campbell looked at Westward at last. "Thank you for picking her up," he said formally, but with unmistakable bitterness. "You're making a habit of standing in for me."

Westward nodded an acknowledgment. "I think what Anna needs right now is relaxation and sleep. Where is she going to stay?"

"With me, of course," Campbell said. "There's a bedroom ready at my house at Gypsum."

She shook her head quickly. "Thanks, but no. I'll stay at my mother's apartment here in Vail. It's where I always stay."

Campbell grimaced. "That's not a good idea."

"Why not?"

"It was ransacked, Anna. It's in chaos."

"Then I'll be able to tidy up for her."

"It's a crime scene. The police probably won't allow it."

More than anything else, she wanted to avoid having to stay in Campbell's house. "How do you know?" she said in a brittle voice.

"We can ask them," Westward suggested mildly. "I'll go call Jorgensen."

"No." Campbell made a sharp movement. "*I'll* speak to him. Please wait here."

They watched him walk to the telephones. Though she'd always thought of Campbell as an egotistical playboy, he was a vital, charismatic man. Now he was somehow shrunken, diminished.

"Who's Jorgensen?" she asked Westward in an undertone.

"The policeman in charge of your mother's case. He's a homicide detective on the Denver City force."

"Do you think they've cleared Campbell?"

"I don't know." He shrugged. "You can ask Jorgensen. He'll want to speak to you, in any case."

She had been thinking about what the little Indian doctor had told her. "If you hadn't found my mother, she'd have died."

She watched him process the question, turn it over behind those beautiful dark blue eyes. "Maybe."

"Thank you for what you did."

He moved his wide shoulders gently. "It was luck."

She looked up into his face. "Where are you staying?"

"At the Westin."

"Can I call you there tomorrow?" she asked. "I want to talk to you."

"I want to talk to you, too," he replied after one of his brief pauses. "I'll be at my hotel tomorrow afternoon." Their eyes met briefly. Hers slipped away first. "The apartment really is a mess," he warned her.

"Like I said, I'll clean it up."

He touched her arm and pointed. Campbell was leaning out of the public phone booth, beckoning her.

"The police want to speak to you." He passed her the receiver.

"Hello," she said into the mouthpiece. "This is Anna Kelly."

"My name is Detective Bill Jorgensen," the other voice crackled. "I'm in charge of the Catherine Kelly case. You're the daughter?"

"Yes."

"You plan to stay in your mother's apartment?"

"If that's okay."

"There's no problem," he told her. "We changed the locks, because it looked as though the intruder picked the front door. I'll authorize the management office to give you the new keys."

"Thank you."

"You can clean up if you wish. But please—make a list of any things you believe may be missing from the apartment. Can you do that for me?"

"Yes. I can do that."

"I need to speak to you. Tomorrow morning, if possible."

"Yes. That's okay."

"I'll be at your mother's apartment at ten-thirty."

"Okay."

"Bye." The line clicked dead.

"He says I can stay at my mother's place," she said, turning to the two men.

"I'll take you," Campbell said firmly.

This time Westward didn't intervene. "I have to get my things out of Mr. Westward's car," she said reluctantly.

"Then let's go."

"Wait a minute," she said. The two men watched as she walked back to her mother's unit. She let herself in and kissed her mother's brow. It was as smooth as a sleeping child's. Beneath the chemical smell of medicines, she caught the warm scent of her mother's skin. "I love you," she whispered. "I'll be back."

Outside in the corridor, she stopped a passing nurse. "I'm Mrs. Kelly's daughter. What will happen with these?" she asked, pointing at the mountain of flowers that had been left at her mother's door.

"They're kind of in the way right there," the nurse admitted. "Flowers aren't allowed in the ICU, and there isn't a place to keep them. They're a problem, frankly."

"Could you maybe see that they got to some of the other patients?" Anna suggested. "Maybe some of the people who don't have flowers?"

"That's an excellent idea." The nurse beamed. "I'll do it right away."

Anna knelt and picked all the cards carefully off the bouquets. She would call the well-wishers tomorrow to thank them for their kindness. She walked back to Brinkman and Westward. "I'm ready."

It had finally stopped snowing, but it was very cold. Her exhausted, nightmare feeling had intensified, and she felt she was wading through heavy oil between the two men.

When they had transferred the luggage to Campbell's Maserati, she held out her hand to Philip Westward. "You've been very kind. I don't know how to thank you."

His hand was warm and strong. "Please don't even try."

"I'm still wearing your coat," she remembered, starting to pull off the Burberry.

He shook his head. "Keep it for the time being. You can give it back to me when we next talk."

She watched him walk away into the night. She suddenly felt very lonely.

They climbed into Campbell's car. Anna let her head slide back against the seat and closed her eyes. Fatigue washed over her. "Does Grandmama know about Mama?" she asked.

"I haven't dared tell Evelyn yet."

"She has to be told. She and I are the only family my mother's got left."

"She's so frail these days. The shock might kill her."

"I'll call her as soon as there's some positive news. It'll have to be broken to her as gently as possible."

"What did that man say to you?" he asked, and she caught the tension in his voice.

"Philip Westward? Only that the police took you to Denver for questioning."

"I did not do it," he repeated. "Only an imbecile could believe I did. They treated me like a criminal. Like a monster. As if *I* could have harmed a hair on her head. They kept me there until my lawyer came down in person and got me out." His lips were trembling. "On top of the shock, that almost broke me, Anna."

She could not meet his eyes, not because she disbelieved him, just because she could deal with no new emotions right now. "I'm sorry," she said helplessly. "Campbell, Philip Westward claims he came to see my mother about some kind of research she was busy with. Would you know anything about that?"

His knuckles tightened around the wheel. "It was an illness with her."

The vehemence of his tone shocked her. "I'm sorry?"

"A mania. An obsession. She couldn't think of anything else."

Anna saw the white tension at his jaw. "But what was she so obsessed with?"

He swung the Maserati so sharply into a bend that the tires slipped in the snow, and the car lurched. "She broke my heart."

"Was that why you separated from her?"

He was silent for so long she thought he either hadn't heard the question or wasn't going to answer. Then he exhaled. "I couldn't stand losing her. It was easier to walk away."

They had reached the apartment block in Potato Patch. It was an elegant structure, hedged with thick, dark firs, its stone-clad facade prettily lit from below. It hardly looked like the scene of a vicious crime.

Someone from the management office, a portly little man with a sad basset face, was waiting with the keys. "Didn't hear a thing," he said. "Can't believe a thing like this could happen right here in Vail. She was a fine woman, your mother, a fine, fine woman." He was talking of her as though she were already dead. Anna accepted his sympathy patiently. She stood silently next to Campbell as he went through the ritual of opening the door.

She stepped into the apartment, and the shock hit her like a physical blow. She closed her eyes and took a deep breath to steady herself.

"Are you all right?" Campbell asked.

She nodded. "You needn't come in with me."

"Perhaps I should—"

"I'm fine. Really."

"This will be bad for you, Anna."

"I know. I'd rather face it on my own."

He did not insist. With a brief kiss on the cheek, he left her there. The portly man gave her the keys, and she locked the door and turned to look around her.

When Westward and Campbell had told her the apartment had been ransacked, they'd given her no idea of the savagery with which it had been done.

The contents of every cupboard and drawer had been strewn and trampled. The artworks had been thrown onto the floor. Some, intact for centuries, had been wantonly destroyed. Cushions had been slashed, sofas upturned and ripped open. Everything that had been locked had been broken into. To complete the chaos, the forensic police had dusted every smooth surface with a gauzy white powder for latent prints.

Her mother had always been so neat, so orderly in her ways. As Anna walked slowly around her mother's apartment, she was acutely aware of the others who had been there before her, looking at the debris of her mother's life strewn on the floor: the police, their technicians, and before that, the intruder. She was only the last in a long line of trespassers on her mother's privacy. She felt an irrational pang of guilt.

In the kitchen, the shape of her mother's body was still outlined on the tiles in yellow tape, among the scattered contents of the refrigerator. It was a heartrending detail.

The intruder had done his pillaging, Anna realized, after the attack. While her mother lay inert on the kitchen floor, her skull cracked like an eggshell. A cold fury filled her. The monster who had done this would be caught, she vowed. He would be caught and would pay dearly.

She forced herself to control the anger and think logically. Why had the attack taken place in the kitchen? Had he been at the refrigerator, helping himself to a midnight snack, when her mother had surprised him? It seemed unlikely.

She glanced at the kitchen door. It opened out onto a little steel landing, at the opposite end of which was the service stairwell leading down to the garage and ground floor. Short of leaping off the balcony, it was the only other way out of the apartment.

Her mother had run in here to escape. She'd wanted to get out, take the service stairs to safety. So he had pursued her into the kitchen, and here he had savagely beaten her to the floor. Anna felt cold gooseflesh run up her back.

He could have gone the other way, avoided a confrontation. But he hadn't been an ordinary sneak thief. He had assaulted a defenseless woman with every intention of causing serious injury, perhaps death.

And then he had systematically wrecked the apartment, with such violence that it astonished her the neighbors had heard nothing. What had that been done for? A gloating carnival of power? A panicky effort to find something of value when the crime had suddenly become far more serious than a simple burglary?

The whole apartment stank of spoiling milk and meat. Somehow the stink was *his,* the fetid aura of the man who had done this. She cleared all the perishable food into a plastic bag and put it outside the service door to take down in the morning.

Then she remembered the safe. She went back into her mother's bedroom. The large eighteenth-century oil painting of Rome hung in its usual place on the wall. She touched it, and it swung back on hinges to reveal the olive-green door of the built-in safe. She pulled on the steel handle, but the door did not budge. She had no idea what the combination was.

The safe looked very solid and had apparently not been disturbed. She frowned at the odd amateurism. He had ransacked the apartment, but he had not even found the safe.

She swung the painting flat and forced her exhaustion to the back of her consciousness. She could not face the prospect of waking to this tomorrow morning. It would be better to start clearing this horrible mess now, do something to counteract the shock of the past few hours.

As she worked, she suddenly saw her own face looking up at her from the wreckage. She stooped and picked up the photograph. The glass was miraculously unbroken. It was a portrait taken a couple of years back in Paris, one of her mother's favorite pictures. Her own smile was sweet, her thick dark hair tossed by the wind across the Seine. But her eyes looked warily back at the camera, and the fingers that held the lapels of her coat were tightly clenched. An uneasy love. She felt a lump in her throat as she cleaned the glass.

Why had she and Mama grown so much apart? Why had they let her father's death separate them, when it ought to have drawn them together? It was eleven years since Belfast. A decade in which they had drifted apart. And now her mother lay in a hospital room, her body kept alive by machines, her mind swallowed in unfathomable darkness.

Mama, she promised, when you're better we'll make it up. I mean it.

Anna Awoke From a dream of Haiti, of André Levêque, laughing at her in a Rousseau jungle. There had been madness in the sea-murky eyes. But she was not in Haiti. She was in Vail, and her mother lay in a coma in a local hospital. It was eight-forty-five.

She reached out for the telephone and called Carr Memorial right away. There had been no change in her mother's condition.

Anna rolled out of bed and went to the window, opening the

curtains on the panoramic view. The slopes were fatly white, the mountains above towering rocky and magnificent against a sky that hurt the eyes to look at. The red and yellow cabs of the Lionshead gondola were moving upward, spots of bright color against the stark whites and grays of the mountains.

Her waking feeling of cold melancholy increased, and although the apartment was comfortably heated, after she had showered she pulled one of her mother's lamb's-wool sweaters over her cotton blouse and jeans. The faint smell of her mother's perfume was consoling, like a gentle embrace. She poured herself a bowl of cereal and opened her mother's mail while she spooned it up. All of the letters were routine brown-envelope bills, which she sorted for payment. Then the telephone began to ring.

There were three calls in quick succession, all from friends of her mother's, to express shock and deep sympathy. The third was from Constanze Graf, inviting Anna to come and see her as soon as she had a free moment.

At precisely ten-thirty the intercom buzzed to announce Jorgensen, the detective. He was holding up his ID, and she nodded recognition. She let him into the apartment. He was a raw-boned, gaunt-faced man with an aquiline nose and a bushy black mustache. His dark eyes looked weary. He brought a strong smell of cigarettes into the apartment.

"Can I make you some coffee?"

"Thank you, ma'am."

"Come into the kitchen. There's nowhere else to sit. They wrecked all the sofas."

He glanced around but did not comment on the transformation she had worked. The apartment would not look normal for a long time, but at least it was clean and orderly. She had worked until the small hours, exorcising her horror with the physical effort, until she had dropped.

The yellow outline of her mother's body was still taped on the floor. "You can take up the tape," he said laconically. "It's not needed anymore."

She nodded. But it would seem horribly like removing the last trace of her mother's presence here. "I've made a list of things that I think are missing," she said, passing it to him. "It's some time since I was in this apartment, but those are things that definitely ought to be here, and aren't." She tried to figure out how her mother's espresso machine worked.

Jorgensen dipped his fingers in the top pocket of his leather jacket, fishing out a crumpled pack of cigarettes. He offered her one.

"I'd rather you didn't smoke," she said. "My mother hates the smell of tobacco in the apartment."

He gave her a strange look. "They didn't explain your mother's condition?"

"They explained," she said.

"She is not going to recover," he said brutally. Anna said nothing. He put the cigarettes back in his pocket with a sigh. He took a spiral-bound notebook out of his briefcase and flipped it open. "How long will you be staying in Vail?"

"As long as I'm needed."

"You're not going back to Miami?"

"And leave my mother like this?"

"In that case, you could be here a long time."

"I'm not leaving her."

He shrugged slightly. "Keep us informed of your plans, whatever you decide. When did you last see your mother, Miss Kelly?"

"The last time was about six months ago."

"Did you normally go that long without seeing each other?"

"I work in Miami these days, so it isn't easy. We normally see each other three or four times a year."

The espresso machine had made a bitter brew, far stronger than anything she was used to, though Jorgensen was drinking it without comment. He made a note, then flipped a new page. "Did you have the impression that your mother's personality had changed in any way over the last few months?"

"What do you mean?"

"Had she shown any signs of irrationality to you?"

"My mother was the most rational person I know. Did Campbell say she'd become irrational?"

"Also her employer," he said flatly.

She was taken aback. "Connie Graf said that?"

"Mrs. Graf had warned her she faced imminent dismissal for negligence."

"What?"

"Mrs. Graf attests that she had become agitated over the last six months. She was distracted in her work and personal relationships, obsessive and secretive in her private life. You didn't notice any of these traits in her?"

"None of those words describe my mother. Not as I know her. She can be withdrawn at times, but she's never obsessive or secretive. And she loves her job. She's very good at it. I can't imagine her neglecting her work for any reason."

"Let me ask you another question. Had your mother given you any indication lately that she had a lover, a lover other than Campbell Brinkman?"

"Why, no."

"Sure? Did she tell you she and Mr. Brinkman had recently broken up?"

"Yes. We spoke on the telephone a couple of weeks ago, and she told me that. But when I spoke to Campbell last night, he implied he'd left her because she was obsessed with some project he disapproved of, not because she'd found another man." He was still staring at her, as if expecting more, so she went on. "Campbell is the only close male friend she's had since my father was killed. He's wanted to marry her for some time, and although she's been putting it off, I always thought she would eventually agree."

"Did you think they were well-matched?"

She hesitated for a moment, then decided to be frank. "Campbell needed her more than she needed him. He depended on her quite heavily."

Jorgensen checked his notes. "Mr. Brinkman is a very rich man."

She nodded. "He's the son of Campbell P. Brinkman, Senior. The chairman of Brinkman Industries. They're one of the biggest aerospace constructors in Colorado. Campbell Junior is on the board, but I don't think he does much work. He's built himself a magnificent house up in Gypsum, and his life seems to revolve around skiing. When I said he depended on my mother, I meant in an emotional sense. Personally, I think he's a spoiled playboy. I don't think he has any real strength of character. In a sense, she loves him because he needs her. She's a very caring person."

"Would you say Campbell Brinkman, Junior, was a passionate man? A man of strong emotions?"

"I hate to think he'd be capable of doing this."

His eyelids drooped. "What if your mother had fallen in love with someone else?"

"That's pure conjecture," Anna retorted.

He shifted his position restlessly. She guessed he was longing for a cigarette. "Okay. This 'project.' Know anything about it?"

"She never told me a thing, Detective. The first I heard of it was yesterday."

Jorgensen leaned back in his chair, fixing her with a dark, world-weary gaze. "So you weren't really in touch with your mother's activities anymore."

"She didn't normally hide things from me," Anna said awkwardly. "I don't know why she didn't tell me about this."

"Do you know about her trip to Russia?"

"Well, yes. But I don't know what she did there."

"Know about her other trips?"

"What other trips?"

"Last autumn, she went to Israel. Before that, she made three trips to London. She may have made other trips we don't know about. These were not holidays, but connected with her research. Did you meet her during any of those trips?"

She stared at him, bewildered. "No."

"What if these mysterious trips covered a secret relationship with another man?"

"I can only say that my mother was not that sort of woman. She was always honest." Anna twisted her hands restlessly together. "Almost painfully honest at times. If she'd fallen in love with someone else, it would have been more in character for her to tell Campbell straight out. Not carry on some elaborate, clandestine affair. That would have been . . . " She searched for a word. "Bizarre. And even if it were true, it's hard to see Campbell as a killer. If he thought she was seeing someone else, he would fly into a rage, maybe smash the place up—" She faltered into silence, looking around. She had a sudden hideous flash of Campbell in a fury, striking out at her mother. After a moment, she went on. "Who would this other man be, in any case?"

"What about the man from New York, Philip Westward?"

"That's crazy!"

"Why?"

"Because he and my mother had never met, that's why. He came up to Vail on Sunday to meet her for the first time."

"Maybe," Jorgensen said, still watching her intently, "we can rearrange that sentence. Maybe he came up to meet her *in Vail* for the first time on Sunday."

"You mean they'd met elsewhere, away from Vail?"

"It's a possibility."

"Then why don't you question him?"

"We have."

"And?"

"He denies he had ever met Catherine Kelly before."

"There you are, then."

"So what's his connection with your mother?"

She told him what Westward had told her, the terse account of his missing father. "That's all I know."

Jorgensen nodded. "He told us the same thing. Any idea why this should interest your mother?"

"None. But as a matter of fact," she said grimly, "I have an appointment with Mr. Westward at his hotel this afternoon. I'll try and straighten that out. All I know for the present is that he's a rich stranger with some kind of mission."

Jorgensen flipped some pages of his notebook. "He's not just rich, Miss Kelly. He's a millionaire. He runs a very successful investment consultancy service in New York." He looked up at Anna. "Your mother had a taste for very rich men, it seems."

"I don't think that's a seemly comment," she said tersely.

"Sorry," he acknowledged. "But you'd classify Westward as an attractive man?"

"Well, sure," she said impatiently, drumming her fingertips on the table. "None of that makes him my mother's lover. And she loved Campbell Brinkman, Detective. I can't believe Campbell did this. Don't you have burglars in Vail? Don't you have drug addicts? Or is Vail too up-market for that?"

"Yes, we get addicts in Vail." Jorgensen leaned forward. "But addicts don't usually kill. This intruder wore gloves and took care not to leave traces. Not so much as a footprint. There's not a single substantive forensic clue, no witnesses. On the face of it, solving this crime is practically impossible. But there are a couple of aspects that make this case different. One is the violence of the assault. He meant to kill your mother. I have no doubt of that. He hit too hard, and too many times, to have had any other intention. He left her for dead. People generally kill for a reason. They generally kill people they know."

She felt as though some icy fluid were being released into her bloodstream. "Yes," she said quietly.

He picked up the list of missing possessions she had compiled. "This is another puzzling aspect. You list missing jewelry, some silver, some small ornaments. What interests me more is what is *not* on this list. This apartment is full of precious, easily saleable things he could have taken. Your mother's art, for example. It's valuable. He smashed some, but he stole none. He left things worth thousands of dollars which he could have easily carried away with him."

"He didn't even find the safe," Anna said.

"The safe?"

She led him to her mother's bedroom and swung the oil painting aside. Jorgensen nodded slowly. "No, he didn't find it. We didn't notice it either. Maybe because hiding a safe behind a painting is a very old-fashioned idea. You don't see it much anymore." He tried the steel handle. "It's locked. Do you know the combination?"

"No. I thought it might be in my mother's diary, but I can't find it."

He spun the dial. "A specialist could open it. Do you want us to send someone, or will you arrange it?"

"I'll arrange it," she said.

"Let me know what you find inside it."

"I will."

Jorgensen held out his hand. In his palm, her mother's emerald ring glowed with a fierce green fire. "He didn't take this, either. It was on her finger when he attacked her." She stared at the ring. "It's valued at twenty thousand dollars. He left it. And yet he destroyed the apartment." He put the emerald ring in her hand. His eyes met hers as her fingers closed around it. "That suggests one of two explanations to me. Either he meant to commit murder and dress it up as burglary, or he was looking for something other than trinkets. Something he didn't find."

Just As She was leaving to go to the hospital, the telephone began to ring again.

It was Drew McKenzie in Miami.

"Seen the papers?"

"Not yet. I haven't had a chance."

"The phones still haven't stopped ringing. You've stirred up a hornet's nest. I knew it would happen. You gotta get back to Miami in the next couple of days, Anna. I want you to go back to Haiti to see Levêque again. He wants to give us an exclusive. Are you there?"

It was characteristic of the man that he had made no inquiry about her mother's condition.

"I'm sorry, Drew," she said flatly. "My mother is in a coma."

"An *exclusive,* Anna."

"No. There are things to be taken care of here."

"Can't you deputize?" he rasped.

"She's my mother, Drew. I can't abandon her."

"Listen, this is the hottest story you'll ever handle. You did well, Anna, very well. Right now I got calls from every news agency, every TV station from here to New York. The tabloids are picking up the crumbs, running with bullshit versions, 'The Voodoo Doctor,' that kind of crap. Levêque is holed up in Pétionville, won't talk to anyone but 'the beautiful Irish girl.' The local DA's office wants to speak to him, but he's refusing to answer questions. There are three separate inquiries going on here, including one by the AMA. He won't say a word. You're the only one with the real inside track."

"You've got my file on him. Give it to someone else."

"Anna. He says he'll only talk to you."

"He'll talk to anyone who flatters him. He's a psychopath."

"You're not listening." He spelled it out, as though to an idiot. "He—will—only—talk—to—*you*. In person. Face-to-face."

"There are American patients willing to talk, Drew. And some of the nursing staff at the Palm Beach clinic must have known what was happening. There's a lot to work on. It's in my file."

There was an ominous silence. "Exactly how long are you gonna stay out there?"

"As long as it takes."

"People stay in comas for months. Years."

"I know," she said quietly.

"You're telling me you're giving up on the biggest story of your career right now, to nurse your comatose mother? Just as you've made it to the top of the tree?" The incredulity in his voice scraped on her raw nerves. She had to remind herself that McKenzie's group had a total circulation of 2.5 million, and that to McKenzie himself, the group was more than mother, father, brothers, and sisters combined.

"I'm telling you I can't abandon her, Drew."

"No matter how long it takes?"

"No matter how long it takes."

"You'll never get another story like this again," he said, his voice like a steel file. When she did not reply, he made it even clearer. "That's not an opinion, Kelly. It's a prediction. You let me down, and I won't forget it."

"I'm sorry" was all she could say.

"Maybe he'll talk to you on the telephone. He said he wouldn't, but maybe he will."

"Drew," she said sharply, "I just can't handle it right now. Not on the phone, nohow."

"Your salary is suspended as of *now*!"

"Yes, of course."

He was silent. She could hear him breathing through his nose, like a bull about to charge. At last he said abruptly, "Okay, I respect your feelings." But the disgust in his voice was like bubbling acid. "I'll call you back in a couple days." He slammed the phone down.

She stood with folded arms, feeling Drew's barbs snagging in her flesh. He knew how to hurt. Was she abandoning the crucial story of her career at a critical moment? Might she never get another break like Levêque again? Drew was quite capable of starving her of stories in punishment. It was the way he worked. She could sit for years, watching the flow of information go around her. That thought hurt like hell.

Then her thoughts cleared. To hell with Drew, and Levêque. Her mother came first, before anything else. The story meant damnall. She'd made her decision. There was no point in stewing over it. She had to get on with it.

Something caught her eye, something she had seen but not registered up until now. It was on a shelf, clashing with everything else in the apartment. A gaudy Russian doll, the sort of thing tourists brought back as souvenirs.

She walked over to it and picked up the doll. She twisted it open. There was a smaller doll inside it, and there would be a yet smaller one inside that.

She opened them all out and stood them in a line on the table, little Russian peasant women with pink cheeks and bold black eyes. The red lips smiled at her enigmatically. The smallest of all was a baby in swaddling clothes.

Her mother must have brought it back from Russia. Was her mother like this doll? A woman who contained other personalities hidden inside? Personalities not even her daughter knew about?

She thought of Philip Westward. He'd said he had no more than a common interest with her mother. But he was the most powerfully magnetic man she had seen in a very long time, and if they had ever met in the past, doubtless her mother would have felt that magnetism. Was it possible he had come between Campbell and her mother? There had been tension between the two men last night. Enough to justify a suspicion they were rivals?

She put the doll back on its shelf and left for Carr Memorial.

Anna Opened The packages and took out the portable cassette player she had bought that morning. She'd also bought a dozen long-play tapes, concentrating on the music she knew her mother loved. She'd chosen the ghetto-blaster for its excellent speakers and the fact that it had two decks with auto-reverse. She loaded it with a two-cassette recording of *The Magic Flute;* it would play the whole opera right through. She would ask the nurses to make sure music was always playing at her mother's bedside. At the very least, it would cover the eerie noises of the machines.

The music swelled into the silence. She sat holding her mother's hand, intently watching the flickering tremors on the still face, praying there would be a response to the Mozart. Once or twice she thought there was something like an embryonic smile, and she felt her heart twist with hope. She sat talking gently, softly to her mother.

After an hour, the door opened and Campbell Brinkman came into the ICU. He greeted Anna wearily, but she saw that he did not look at Kate. He did not sit down.

"What are you doing?"

"It's one of her favorite operas. I thought it would help to bring her back."

He made no comment, but his expression showed his indifference. "Your mother's legal advisers want to speak to you urgently.

They'll arrange for you to obtain legal control over your mother's affairs. It means declaring your mother incompetent."

Anna flinched. She rose and went over to him. "Was it necessary to say that in her presence?" she asked with quiet anger.

"She is not present."

"She's right there, Campbell."

He dug his fingers into his eyes. "You'll have to manage things from now on. You're her next of kin, not me. There are bills to be paid, decisions to be made. Even her admission to the hospital needs to be formalized." He took a business card out of his wallet and passed it to her. "This is the address of your mother's lawyers in Denver. Please call them as soon as you can."

"All right."

"Something else. Your mother's insurance claims adjuster wants to meet you. He's in Vail today. Have you got time for him?"

"Yes. I'll be at the apartment around four."

"I'll pass that on." Campbell looked even worse than he had before, dark brown smudges under his eyes, his usually imperious mouth bitter. He seemed unable to bring himself to look at the woman on the bed. It was obvious he hated coming here.

"I've been watching her face," she told him. "I'm sure she smiled just now."

"It's just a facial tic. She does it from time to time."

"She's not dead," Anna said. "She will get better."

"She will not get better." He almost screamed the words, and she flinched. His breath was rank. There were tears in his eyes now. "I loved her," he said hoarsely. "I loved her so much."

Anna glanced uneasily at him. Was it possible Jorgensen's suspicions had any foundation? Could Campbell have done this? A furious quarrel that got completely out of hand? He was a man of strong passions and little inner discipline. "I could do with something to eat," she said neutrally. "There's a cafeteria on the next floor. Will you come with me?"

They walked down to the cafeteria, which was crowded with visitors. She was hungry enough to pick up a piece of chicken pie and a bowl of salad, but Campbell took only a large, strong black coffee. Just the thing for his nerves. No wonder he hovered on the edge of hysteria.

But by the time they found themselves a place at one of the long tables, he had swallowed his tears.

"Where are you staying, Campbell?" she asked him.

"Up in Gypsum."

"Alone?"

He nodded, staring into his coffee. She forked up the chicken pie in silence for a while, thinking of him brooding up there in the mountains. Gypsum was well over thirty miles west of Vail, way up past Eagle, a beautiful but also a wild and lonely place. Campbell had rented out his house in Vail when it got too crowded for his patrician tastes, and had built himself a magnificent stone ranch among the cottonwoods of Gypsum Mountain, overlooking Eagle River. It had several acres of land, stunning views, an indoor heated pool, and every other luxury imaginable. In happier times, Anna had been to the ranch several times. Buzzing with a house party of beautiful people, it was a delightful place. Empty, it would be about as cheerful as Wuthering Heights. "You shouldn't be all alone up there, Campbell. Why not come back down to Vail? For a start, you wouldn't have an eighty-mile round trip to come and see Mama."

"Can't stand the tourists," he grunted.

"But the roads must be bad at this time of year—"

"I don't mind," he said shortly.

She left it at that. "This research of Mama's, Campbell. What was it all about? What was she looking for?"

"She wouldn't tell me."

"But she must have given you some inkling. It's not like her to be obsessive about anything."

He made a bitter face. "I told you. She didn't confer the distinction of confidence on me."

"If it's any consolation," she offered gently, "she didn't confide in me, either. This is the first I've heard of it."

"You hardly spoke to her anymore," he retorted. "Why should she confide in you?"

She flushed. Only her compassion for his grief stopped her from snapping. She picked up her fork and addressed the pie again. "I'm her daughter," she said controlledly. "She didn't normally keep secrets from me."

He was growing visibly tenser. "At first it was a little private joke that she was going to tell me when she was ready. Then, almost at once, she turned from me. She found something better than me."

"By 'something better,' " she said carefully, "do you mean another man?"

He swung on her aggressively. She drew back a little. He saw that and laughed bitterly. "Is that what the police told you? That she was having an affair?"

"Not in so many words."

"I thought she had a lover. For a while. She didn't. She had an illness, Anna. It made her neglect everything. Her life. Her work. Me. She couldn't share the things that were important to me. My life meant nothing to her anymore." He gulped down the last of his coffee and rose. "Please don't forget to speak to your mother's lawyers as soon as you can."

"I won't. See you soon, Campbell."

She watched him walk out. A rich man's son, he had been spoiled from childhood. He had been overindulged, overeducated, never denied anything except responsibility, the one thing that might have made him whole. His father had never trusted him to take over the reins of the family business. That had fallen to his younger brother, a more ruthless and less hedonistic personality. Campbell had drifted into the life of a playboy, making a few routine appearances at board meetings, effectively excluded from decision making. His relationship with Kate Kelly had almost saved him. Now, Anna thought, he had become a stranger with whom she no longer had anything in common.

When he had gone, she finished the salad and went back up to the ICU. She stared down at her mother's oval face for a while, the lawyers' card in her hands. "You've been a very good mother to me," she said at last. "I'm supposed to go and have you declared incompetent. I hope you're going to be able to forgive me, Mama."

Westward's hotel was designed to cater to the very richest clientele. The reception area was thickly carpeted, softly lit. The woman behind the desk, who had evidently just stepped off the cover of *Vogue,* called Philip Westward's room.

"If you care to wait through there, ma'am," she relayed, putting down the receiver, "Mr. Westward will be down in a few minutes."

She walked into a large and graceful room, well-stocked with nineteenth-century European furnishings. Philip Westward had a taste for luxury, she reflected. She took off her dark glasses and stood at the window, looking out on Gore Creek, upon which a little afternoon sun now glimmered.

She had come to Vail with her mother as a teenager, soon after her father's death, over a decade ago. She had spent the last couple of years of her schooling here, at Vail Mountain School, before leaving to go to college in Boston. Since then, although her mother had made her home here, Anna had spent only a few weeks of each year in Vail. Her mother had needed the intimacy, the secluded tranquility of this beautiful valley; Anna had been driven to seek the anonymity and wider confines of a big city. But she was fond of the town. Vail had that combination of scenic beauty and moneyed denizens that distinguished other famous resorts—Palm Springs or Lake Tahoe—but without the vulgarity or the snobbishness. The town was prosperous, charming. Shop windows glowed with costly objects of desire, buildings deliberately echoed the European Alps, the streets, barred to cars, were tranquil and pretty.

But violence lurked even here. Somewhere in this handsome little town, she thought, is a man who tried to kick my mother to death.

She felt a touch on her arm and spun quickly. Westward's deep blue eyes smiled into hers. "I didn't mean to startle you."

"Sorry. I was lost in some rather dark thoughts."

He gestured toward an armchair. "Sit down. Will you have some coffee?"

She nodded yes and sank into the overstuffed upholstery. He ordered coffee from a waiter and sat opposite her.

She had slipped on her Ray Bans again so she could study him unobtrusively. He was dressed in dark slacks and a gray cashmere turtleneck, highly polished but well-used oxfords on his feet. Instinctively she knew that he bought all his clothes himself; there was no feeling of a woman's touch in the clothes he wore, rather of a very wealthy, very masculine, very conservative bachelorhood.

"How is your mother?" he asked.

"No change."

"I'm sorry."

"I've read all that stuff Ram Singh gave me. And I sent off to the head trauma organization for some literature. About the only thing anybody can do for coma patients, it seems, is try and stimulate their memories. Try and bring them back. So I bought a tape deck this morning and put it at her bedside. I'm going to play some of her favorite music to her. She loves Mozart."

"Excellent."

"Her lawyers want me to have her declared incompetent, so I can manage her affairs."

"That's normal procedure."

"You can't imagine how distasteful that is to me," she said. "But it's not your concern, is it?"

"I'm concerned about your mother."

"Are you?" The feeling that he was sexually unattached was undeniably appealing. As a woman, it intrigued her. If she had to dress such a physically magnificent man, she'd have chosen more flamboyant clothes. Designer clothes, not the dark hues and sober cuts of a London club.

She wondered whether she might be wrong, whether he was married. Whether he had ever been married. It seemed unlikely a man like that would reach his forties without a tangle of matrimonial history.

"Mr. Westward, I have a lot of questions to ask you. I'd be grateful for anything you can tell me."

"Go ahead."

"All right. Why exactly did you contact her in the first place?"

He ran his fingers through his dark hair. As she had suspected, beneath the loop of hair was a high, broad forehead. There were streaks of silver at the temples, but nowhere else. "I wanted to trade information about the subject that concerned us both. The subject of missing American servicemen."

"What information specifically did you want to trade?"

"Nothing *specifically*. More a general inquiry. I was given your mother's name by a man called Boris Yuzhin in Moscow. He's a researcher who hunts for Americans who may be still held in labor camps in the former Soviet Union. Your mother had applied to him for information about a specific American soldier she believed had been imprisoned in the Soviet Union after the war."

"What was his name?"

"Yuzhin didn't tell me," he said gently, "and of course I didn't ask. That would have been a breach of confidentiality. What Yuzhin did tell me was that she had been making inquiries for some time and that she had a mass of information, some of which was new even to him. He described her as a very remarkable woman. He said she had an extraordinary brain, an extraordinary persistence. That she was resourceful and determined to a degree that impressed him greatly."

"Please don't talk about her in the past tense," Anna said. "She's not dead."

He inclined his head. "You're right. I'm sorry."

"What sort of information did this man say she had?"

"As an example, she had come across a group of Georgian nationalist dissidents who were now living in France, but who had been in the gulags in the 1950s. They told her there had been American and British servicemen in the camp with them, being kept under very brutal conditions. These were soldiers who had been liberated by the Russians from Nazi camps in 1945, but they'd never been sent home. They were still registered as missing. These were the kind of contacts I was hoping she could supply me with."

"So you could continue trying to trace your own father?"

"Yes."

"If that's true, about the Americans being kept in Russia, it's shocking."

He nodded. "Yuzhin said your mother had a mass of circumstantial evidence of this kind. I was extremely interested, because that testimony coincided with what I had suspected for a long time. I wanted to see her badly. That's why I came to Vail."

"All right, but hold on. Why would Americans have been imprisoned in Russia after the war? Who were these people, and why should my mother have been so interested in them?"

"It's a long story."

"I have time," she said calmly.

He studied her face for a moment. "Since Boris Yeltsin took control in Moscow in August 1991, the KGB has been under increasing pressure. Yeltsin is eager to do anything to weaken their power. That includes revealing all the KGB's anti-American activities over the years, showing them up for the monsters we all believed them to be during the Cold War. Yeltsin is throwing open the KGB's secret files. As you can imagine, the CIA and every other Western intelligence organization is having a field day. It's going to take years to sift through all the information that has come to light. But the information that interested me, and presumably your mother, as well, was contained in Archive Twelve of the Special Archives Department of the Russian Defense Ministry. These documents are still top secret, but Yeltsin and his aides are making sure the information leaks out."

"What information?"

"Archive Twelve contains evidence that at least fourteen hundred British servicemen, who were liberated by the Red Army from German prisoner of war camps in 1945, were transported to corrective labor camps in Siberia and Kazakhstan by the NKVD, the old name for the KGB. We still don't know how many Americans. Maybe thousands more. None of them were ever heard of again."

The waiter arrived with their coffee, and Westward poured two cups.

She was watching him intently. "And you believe your father was among them?"

"Yes."

"I can understand *your* interest. But why was my mother concerned with these people? Who could this man be?"

"I told you. I have no idea. All she told me was that he was an American serviceman, and that she believed he had been in a Nazi extermination camp in Latvia called Varga when the Russians had liberated him. I had the impression this man was a member of your mother's family."

Anna shook her head. "The only member of her family who was captured by the Nazis was my mother's father, but he was sent back home in 1945. And I've never even heard of this camp—what's it called?"

"Varga. It's fifteen miles outside Riga. Up to eighty-seven thousand people were exterminated at Varga between 1941 and 1945. They arrived in cattle trucks, were stripped, herded into pits in the forest, and machine-gunned." He sipped his coffee. "The clothes were sent back to Germany. Nobody else apart from her father? An uncle, a brother?"

"Her uncle died in the 1960s. She had no brothers or sisters. My mother was a war-child." She made a little gesture. "That's a euphemism."

"For illegitimate."

"Yes. Her father was an English soldier who was with the Partisans around the lake of Garda during the war. An Italian family sheltered him from the Nazis. He fell in love with the daughter. That was my grandmother. She got pregnant, but he was recaptured by the Germans, and she died in childbirth."

"And the British soldier?"

"He went back to England and married another woman. Evelyn, my grandmother. They never had any children. They decided to adopt his little war-child when she was about fifteen. She was called Catarina, but they changed that to Kate. They brought her up in England from about 1960 on. My mother hardly talked about her Italian background. She didn't talk about her childhood very much at all. I don't think it was very happy."

He was watching her over the rim of his cup. "What was her father's name?"

"David Godbold."

"Is he alive?"

"No, he died years ago. Before I was born. Some kind of shooting accident, I think. Grandmama is still alive." Anna winced. "But she's very frail. I haven't told her about Mama being in a coma yet. I'll have to find some way of breaking the news to her."

"I'm sorry," he said gently.

She lifted her chin. "This is all a little hard to swallow."

Westward's eyes held an ironic amusement. "Why?"

"She kept all this from me, and I resent that like hell. I thought I knew her. I'm just beginning to discover how little about her I knew. I mean *really* knew."

"She must be an unusual woman," Westward said gently. He looked as though Anna's mixture of anger and wonder entertained him.

At first she had not taken to the flat manner and the pauses for thought that broke conversation up into carefully thought-out bites. Now she had grown used to it. He made her prickle, in different ways, in different places.

The oblique light picked out the little scars on his cheeks, emphasized the long black eyelashes that helped make his gaze so disturbing. He was really extraordinarily handsome. Almost perfect. Could any man be that handsome and not be a bastard?

He offered the coffee pot, but she shook her head, already conscious of a caffeine buzz in her veins. "Did you come across any of her records while you were clearing up?" he asked casually. "Any paperwork?"

She shook her head. "No. I've found nothing relating to this subject in the apartment."

"It's missing?"

"Not necessarily. There's a safe in the apartment. The intruder didn't find it. But it's locked, and I don't have the combination. She may have kept her research material in there. It's quite a big safe."

"If you do find anything, I'd be very grateful if you'd let me glance at it," he said.

His too-casual tone pricked her nerves. "Is that why you're

hanging around, Mr. Westward? To get your hands on my mother's papers?"

"Her papers may contain valuable information," he said.

"So that's why you've been so kind. Why you picked me up at the airport."

"My search for information about my father may strike you as irrelevant," he said with quiet force, "but I assure you it is of the profoundest importance to me. Successive American governments have done little or nothing to find those men. They have been discarded and then forgotten. I do not intend to give up until I have an answer." There was something steely, almost frightening, beneath the urbane manner for a moment. Then he went on easily, "Considering your skills, you might be interested in following up your mother's inquiries yourself."

"I don't even know what it was she was looking for."

"I could help you find out."

"There seem to be rather too many obsessions around here, Mr. Westward," she replied coolly. She looked at her watch. "My mother's insurance assessor is coming to see the apartment in half an hour." They both rose. She took off the Ray Bans and looked at him with smoky eyes. "Detective Jorgensen thinks you were my mother's lover, and that Campbell Brinkman killed her in a fit of jealous rage."

His face did not change expression. "I know."

"Were you my mother's lover?"

"No. The first time I set eyes on her, she was unconscious in her apartment."

"Bang goes Jorgensen's theory. But you don't have any problem making women fall in love with you, do you?"

He looked down at her. There was an animal directness to his gaze, something that pierced the smooth demeanor like the stare of a wolf. "I never knew your mother."

She weighed the question for a moment. "Are you married, Mr. Westward?"

His gaze changed subtly, just enough to let her know he found her intriguing, that he was aware of the implication of the question. "No," he said. "I'm not married."

She held his gaze a moment longer, feeling the nervous tingle slide through her middle, knowing it had nothing to do with the strong coffee. "How long will you be here?"

"I have no immediate plans to go back."

"That's convenient."

The pause lengthened, took on a new meaning. "Perhaps we should have dinner together," he said.

She felt a twist of satisfaction, excitement. "Yes. Perhaps we should."

"What about tomorrow night?"

Anna nodded. "I'm free."

"I'll pick you up at eight."

He walked her outside and summoned a taxi. Their parting was formal, brief. As she walked away from the hotel, she glanced back and saw him standing on the steps, a tall, dark figure. She waved.

I don't trust you an inch, she thought. But I could fall for you. I could fall a long way.

The Insurance Claims adjuster was waiting in the lobby of the apartment building when she arrived. He was obviously close to retirement, a white-haired portly man who smelled of the eucalyptus sweets he constantly sucked. She apologized for keeping him waiting and took him up to the apartment.

"Before anything else," she said, "I need to know about my mother's hospital bills."

"Not my department," he said. "The appropriate person will get in touch soon. But don't worry. The bills are all being taken care of."

She conducted him around the wreckage. He had a Polaroid and took several photographs. He also made copious notes, but he showed no emotion. His constant mouth-noises were not sympathetic clucks, just serene enjoyment of his sweet; after a lifetime of surveying trashed apartments, he had no feelings left to be shocked.

When he was done, he showed her the policy her mother had taken. "We divide the items into three categories—the art, the jewelry, and the furnishings. The jewelry seems to be largely untouched. Assessing the value of the art will take a couple of weeks longer. I may have to call in a colleague—I'm not an expert. But in the meantime, I've assessed the damage to the apartment itself as follows." He showed her the figure he had written down.

"Fifteen thousand dollars?" she queried.

He nodded. "If it looks as though it is going to cost much more than that, let me know. Agreed?"

"Thank you." Though she had an idea how expensive replacement furniture would be, it seemed an adequate settlement. By the time her mother was out of the hospital, she would have the apartment better than new. She would start right away.

"One final thing. In addition to property and health insurance, your mother also has a life-insurance policy with us. It's a little early to bring this up, but you ought to know. In the case of permanent serious disablement, the payment would be about four million dollars. A permanent coma would qualify as such a disablement. In the case of death, the figure goes up to six million dollars." He unwrapped another eucalyptus sweet, his pouchy eyes watching her. "You, of course, are the sole beneficiary of the policy, Miss Kelly."

She was slightly shaken. "I see. Thank you for telling me. But I'm convinced my mother will soon start recovering."

"We all surely hope so," he said blandly. "At a certain point, however, it will be necessary to decide whether to keep paying your mother's medical costs, or to make the lump-sum payment." He patted her shoulder with a pudgy hand. "Don't worry your head about it now. It's all being taken care of."

She saw the man to the door. When she was alone, she steeled herself to call Evelyn Godbold in northern England.

As a child, she'd thought of her mother's stepmother as a kind of Olympian figure, an austere, kindly goddess in her silver years. She and Kate were close, in a way that Anna had never quite understood; as a child it had seemed almost eerie to her how silences spoke as much as words between them.

Later on, age and sickness had made Evelyn seem even more remote to Anna. She had been fighting cancer for several years, and now seldom left her home in Northumberland. She had a profound dignity, which had only increased as her illness ate away at her strength and independence. It was hard to think of anyone, apart from her mother, whom Anna respected more.

Evelyn's harsh cry of grief on hearing the news was all the harder to bear.

Anna gritted her teeth. "I'm so sorry, Grandmama. She's getting superb care. Carr Memorial is a fine hospital."

"But she's gone," Evelyn said, with such hopelessness in her voice that Anna was on the point of tears.

"No, Grandmama. She'll get better. I know she will."

"Do the doctors have hope?"

"They're monitoring her constantly," Anna replied evasively. "It's a very good hospital."

"If only I could be there!"

"You mustn't even think of coming," Anna said urgently. "It's just a matter of time before she starts coming round, I'm sure of it."

"I feel so despicably useless." There was genuine rage in the patrician voice. "This wretched body of mine. How I *loathe* it. I couldn't come even if I wanted to, Anna. I can do nothing to help. I must go into hospital myself in two days."

"Oh, shit," Anna said under her breath. "What for?"

"To have more bits cut out," Evelyn said shortly.

"Another operation!"

"I didn't tell your mother. I didn't want her to worry."

Anna closed her eyes. What abysmal timing. She would never have called if she'd known. Now Evelyn would have to go into the operating room with her mind clouded by added terrors. "Oh, God, I'm so sorry."

"Don't apologize, for heaven's sake. None of it is your fault, child."

"Is it the bowel again?"

"Oh, it's nothing." The rage had abruptly given way to weariness. "Nothing to worry about."

"Perhaps Mama will be conscious again by the time you get out."

"Yes," she replied with no trace of hope in her voice. "Perhaps she will."

"Which hospital are you going to?"

"Newcastle General. Female surgical ward. I'll get you the number, Anna. Please wait."

Anna wondered just how sick she was; *nothing to worry about* was transparently untrue. This would be Evelyn's third operation in five years.

Evelyn gave her the number, and she wrote it down. "When should I call?"

"Call on Friday morning. Even if they won't let me speak on the telephone, they'll pass on a message."

"Grandmama, please, *please* try not to worry. You have enough on your mind."

"So have you, my child," the old lady said with exhaustion apparent in her voice.

After she'd said good-bye, Anna sat by the telephone, feeling an almost physical sense of responsibility beginning to weigh her down. Her own life in America had been so free: rented apartments, rental cars, few possessions, a life lived out of suitcases and paid for by credit cards. A few, transient lovers, never any commitment on either side. The adrenaline of work and yet more work to drive her on. It occurred to Anna that her mother's coma meant she herself would have to face some very fast growing up.

Two White-Uniformed nurses were tending to her mother as she came in. Over their shoulders, she saw with a start that her mother's face was naked. It took a second to register that the oxygen tube was no longer taped into her mouth, though the white dressing still covered her scalp. Suddenly she looked more human, but even more terribly vulnerable.

The two nurses had just finished a sponge bath. Anna sat quietly by the bed while they aspirated her mother's nose and mouth, dropped liquid into the unflinching eyes, drained the catheter bag. When they began massaging her legs and arms, Anna stood up.

"I can do that," she offered.

They showed her what to do and left her. Alone, she kissed her mother's brow, then gently started massaging her limbs. The skin was smooth, the muscle tone excellent. How long would it stay that way? How long before she began to waste away?

"What the hell have you been up to, Mama?" Anna asked. "What were you looking for?" She searched her mother's motionless face. "I thought I understood you. Knew you. You've pulled a fast one on me, Mama. Why didn't you trust me with your secrets?"

She pushed a cassette into the ghetto-blaster and tilted it to face her mother. A bright Vivaldi violin concerto sparkled in the air.

"I could have helped you with it. I'm a journalist. It's my job.

I'm your daughter. Who was this mysterious man the Russians put away? How did he end up in a Nazi extermination camp? How did such a terrible thing happen to him? We'll find him, Mama. When you're better, we'll get to know each other all over again. We'll keep on looking for whatever it was you were so interested in. But together this time. Was that a smile?"

She took her mother's inert hand. "I'm going to go shopping. Replacing all the broken things in the apartment. The insurance man was very nice. He's given me a good budget to work on. I saw some lovely sofas today."

For a while, she crooned along with the Vivaldi, stroking her mother's brow.

"Philip Westward is taking me to dinner," she said at last. "I hope you don't mind. I know he's interested in me. I can see it in his eyes. I'm interested in him, Mama. He's the most attractive man I've met in a long time. Maybe in my whole life. I want to find out all about him. I don't know if he is what he says he is. Is he a devil or an angel?"

She stared at her mother's face, wanting to believe she was being heard, somewhere down there in the deep, still, dark water.

Selfishly wanting to believe there was still a human being in this inert body who loved her and cared about her.

She Arrived At the Graf Hotel intending to slip quietly up to her mother's office, and then to see Connie. It proved impossible. At least a dozen staff members spotted her on her way through the lobby, and all wanted to speak to her, to express their shock and sympathy. She was touched at the amount of genuine affection there was for her mother, even though she found it grueling rather than consoling.

It was half an hour before she got up to her mother's floor, and there she was met by Elaine Brodie and Luke Milton, her mother's immediate colleagues.

Both hugged her affectionately. Anna saw the bright shimmer of tears in Elaine's eyes and held up her hand.

"Please," she begged, "don't cry. It'll set me off, and I just managed to stop in the elevator."

Elaine gulped. "It's so terrible. I don't know how a thing like this could happen in Vail."

"Anything we can do," Luke said huskily. "Anything at all, Anna."

Anna nodded. They had both called several times to offer help, but there was little or nothing they could do.

Jennifer Prescott, looking like a blond ghost, came out of her office to offer her own, more muted commiseration. If she was pleased at having been thrown into Kate's place by the trauma, she showed no sign of it; in fact, Anna thought she looked depressed and rather overwhelmed by it all.

She stood talking to them in the subdued tones of a wake or a funeral for another half-hour, then made her way up to Connie Graf's suite.

Connie Graf had not only been her mother's employer for the past eleven years, she had also been one of her mother's few trusted friends. Anna had never been quite at ease in her presence; Connie reminded her a little of Evelyn Godbold; and a little, despite the immaculate grooming and the inevitable couture suit, of some fierce old bird of prey.

The spare office looked out onto the snow-heavy slopes. "I just feel so helpless," Anna said in answer to Connie's inquiries. "The doctors are telling me she'll never get up off that bed. I can't believe it. But there's nothing I can do to help her. Nothing!"

Connie's rather formidable manner did not soften. "You can pray for her."

"Jorgensen thinks Campbell might have done it."

She'd been expecting a rebuttal, but Connie moved her hands slightly on the desk. "It is possible. He was very disturbed by the change that had come over her. As was I, of course. I felt it was a disloyalty to her work. He felt it more personally—a disloyalty to their love."

"That's why I came here. To ask you if you could tell me anything about this . . . change."

"I can tell you what I know, Anna, in two ways. I can tell you what little Kate told me. And I can tell what my own opinion was."

"What did she tell you?"

Connie had ordered coffee for Anna, a glass of some herbal infusion for herself. It stood in front of her, glowing pale amber in the watery light from the huge window. She turned it slowly in the silver holder, without lifting it to her lips. "It began with the diary."

"What diary?"

"You know nothing about the diary?"

"I don't seem to know anything about my mother's life," Anna said bitterly. "She kept all this a secret from me. She excluded me!"

Connie Graf smiled bleakly. "Now you know how I felt, how Campbell felt. Excluded. Your mother was born in a farmhouse on the shores of Lake Garda, east of Milan, in Italy. You've been there, I think?"

"She took me there once, a few years ago. It was just a ruin. But very picturesque."

Connie nodded. "She had allowed it to fall into disrepair. I don't think she had any great attachment to the place. It had bad memories for her. But of course the site was very valuable. Garda is a popular Italian holiday resort, as you know. Some time last year, a local builder talked her into selling him the house so he could restore it and put it on the market. She told me that while they were pulling down the ruined part, the workmen discovered an old book hidden under a tile. The new owner sent it to her. It was a wartime diary, belonging to a woman named Candida Cipriani."

Anna looked up quickly. "That was her mother's name."

"Yes. Kate believed that it had been written by her mother between 1943 and 1945. The final years of her life."

" 'Believed'?" Anna echoed.

"I never saw the document," Connie said obliquely. "That is what she told me. She was very excited by it. At the same time, she was very moved. She was not a temperamental woman, as you know. I had never seen her so affected. She told me it gave her a deep insight into her background. From that point on, she began to change. After a lifetime of turning her back on her family, her history, she now began to be fascinated by it. It was already interfering with her work, even at that stage, though it still seemed a hobby. Something which absorbed her time harmlessly. Then, quite suddenly, she seemed to lose touch with reality."

"How do you mean?"

"She no longer controlled it; it controlled her. Her manner changed. It was obvious she had become fixated by her search. It was obvious she could think of little else. At that point she began to travel abroad. She went to London three times, to Tel Aviv twice, for quite long periods. She overstayed the amount of time I had allowed her. She missed important conferences. Her work had to be deputized. I recognized how important what she was doing was to her, emotionally. I gave her a lot of leeway. Looking back, too much leeway. It was a mistake."

"Jorgensen says you were going to fire her."

"She promised me she would abandon this search over the winter, Anna. But I warned her that if she started up again, I would have no option but to terminate her contract."

"And you thought she would start up again."

"Yes. I'm sure she would have."

The infusion had stopped steaming now, and Connie raised the glass to her lips and sipped slowly for a while. Anna waited. Connie's office was completely silent. No busy clatter percolated through here. The only decoration was a row of large black-and-white prints of the valley in the early 1960s, when Vail had begun.

"She was looking for a man, Connie. Did she learn about him from the diary?"

Connie lowered the glass. "Yes. Before you ask, I have no idea who or what he was. She never told me. A figure she had been led to through the diary. A figure from that period. That was all I knew."

Anna rubbed her face. "Why didn't she ask me? I'm an investigative reporter. I could have helped her with whatever it was. I could have shared it. I can't associate any of this with my mother, Connie. This is the last thing I would expect from her—secretiveness, mysteries, obsessions. It's just not her."

"No. As though she had suffered a personality change. A pathological change."

Anna felt cold. "What do you mean by that?"

"I've told you what your mother told me. Now I will tell you my own opinion, Anna." Connie laid her hands flat on the desk. Her fingers were ringless, dry, the nails short and unvarnished. "Everything about your mother altered quite dramatically. Even the look in her eyes and the expression on her face. She became a different person. As I watched this change, a terrible sadness came over me, because it was not new to me. I had seen it happen before."

"To her?"

"No. To a very beloved elder sister, when I was a young woman. The process was the same. The same quite sudden falling into deep waters. The secretiveness, the restlessness, the obsession. The same look in the eyes, Anna, the same loss of reality. The same inability to be

reached. We knew she was sick long before the doctors gave a name to
the sickness. The sickness was schizophrenia."

"No!" Anna said sharply. "My mother was not mad."

"You can ask Campbell what he thinks."

"I know what he thinks. I still don't believe it."

Connie looked up at her in silence for a long while, her gaunt,
masculine face showing no emotion. Then she rose, terminating the
interview. "You are an intelligent young woman, Anna. You will draw
your own conclusions. If I can do anything to help you, please let me
know."

Connie walked her to the door. There she turned. "There is
something, Connie. I haven't come across any papers relating to my
mother's researches. You'd think there would be a folder, a dossier, a
scrapbook—something. You've no idea where she would have kept it?"

"None. I'm sorry. She was very secretive."

"And this diary my mother found—where is it now?"

"I don't know."

"It definitely isn't at the apartment. I'd have found it. I'd very
much like to see it."

"I don't think you will ever see it," Connie said with surprising
gentleness. "I don't think it ever existed."

When She Got back to Potato Patch, she picked up her mother's car
keys, which she had found on the bedroom floor, and walked down to
the garage. The air down here was moist and cool, and a mesh of droplets had condensed on the gleaming blue skin of the Saab, which stood
in her mother's parking space. It looked tough and competent, a good
vehicle in which to face severe winter conditions. Anna fiddled with the
little plastic gizmo on the keyring that was supposed to open the car by
remote control, not sure how it worked. Then, with a clunk, the doors
unlocked. She climbed into the car. Despite the heavy-duty looks, it was
smart inside, with a rich scent of leather and newness.

She opened the glove compartment, but there were no personal
possessions in the car, just the vehicle's papers and a Hermès umbrella
on the back seat. Her mother had taken delivery of the car four months
ago, but the odometer still read less than two hundred miles. Leafing
through the papers, she saw that her mother hadn't even taken the car

for its first service yet. The search had dominated her time, dominated her life.

Were Campbell and Connie right? Had her mother been afflicted by an illness, an obsession? She looked at the black dash with its sleek controls, an emblem of European certainty.

No, her mother had not been irrational. Nor mentally ill. Anna did not believe that. She had been driven not by fantasy, but by pain, by an intense yearning that Philip Westward had described as commitment.

She needed to know what that commitment had been to. What had caused the pain. What hidden truth her mother had been striving after.

She started the Saab, feeling the smooth purr of the motor. She put the car in gear and drove up the ramp into the light. She felt confident about driving this vehicle all the way to Denver. She was going to set about getting new furniture for the apartment right away.

3

She drank the first glass of wine quickly, to overcome her nervousness, taking the chance it would make her head spin. It did not, and she toyed with the second glass, staring at the amber glow in the cut glass to stop her eyes from drifting to Philip Westward. In jacket and tie, he was almost painfully beautiful.

She had not expected the nervousness, but it had come on with disconcerting force as soon as she had got into the Mercedes, her stockinged legs sliding over the dark leather. It had made her tongue-tied and awkward all through the drive from Vail up into the mountains. She'd been angry with herself for being so gauche, but confidence had refused obstinately to return. She only hoped he had taken her gawkiness for cool reserve so far.

She lifted her eyes to his and found he was watching her. There was warmth in the deep blue eyes.

"Why are you looking at me like that?" she asked.

"When I first met you, I thought you were very young. Tonight you look older."

"Maybe it's the clothes. They're my mother's." The Gucci jacket was lovely, though she would never have bought it for herself. It was perfect for her mother's style, with its dramatic black, silver, and gold pattern and faux tiger-skin trimming. Underneath she wore a severe black turtleneck and a short black skirt that showed off her legs, whose elegant lines made up for any deficiency in the bust. "My mother was very good at choosing clothes. She has wonderful taste. Much better than me. I've been refurnishing the apartment with the insurance money, and it's rather daunting. My mother is not an easy act to follow. Anyway, I wanted to dress up for tonight. I'm glad I did now."

He had obviously intended to impress her, or he would not have driven her so far, and to such a manifestly exorbitant restaurant. It was an Italian restaurant, an intensely chic place, pink table lamps glowing on white linen, the waiters wearing dinner jackets almost as good as the guests'. The arched windows would have shown a stunning view over the mountains by day. The lights of Vail sparkled like distant diamonds in the dark.

"That's your mother's, too, isn't it?"

She moved her hand so the big emerald glittered like green fire. "She always wore it. She was wearing it when she was attacked. He didn't bother stealing it. Don't you think that's strange?"

"Yes. Very strange."

"I never wear things like this normally. I don't have any jewelry of my own at all."

"Not even one tiny ruby?" he asked solemnly.

"Not even one tiny diamond." She laughed.

"Your lovers have been unforgivably parsimonious."

"My lovers were usually paying alimony and maintenance," she said wryly. "I guess I could have bought myself jewels, but that seemed a rather spinsterish thing to do. Like admitting defeat. Besides, jewels don't suit me."

"On the contrary, jewels suit you magnificently." He touched the emerald with his fingertip. "A beautiful woman is naked without jewels."

"Oh, come on."

"Your mother's apartment, her clothes, her rings. You have stepped into her life."

She didn't like that phrase. "Not quite, Mr. Westward."

"You're much darker than your mother. Your father must have been a Gypsy."

She laughed. "He was an Irishman. What they call a black Irishman. Black hair, blue eyes. But his skin was very fair. I don't know where my complexion came from. A family mystery."

"When did he die?"

"Oh, more than ten years ago. When I was sixteen." She gave him a brittle smile. "He was blown up."

She saw his eyes change. He said nothing, did not press her for more information.

She had asked him to order for her, and the waiters now arrived with the first course, whose heady fragrance swelled intoxicatingly out of the iron pan it arrived in.

"Truffles?" she murmured. "I asked you not to order anything extravagant."

"This is one of the best restaurants in Colorado. It would be a waste not to ask for the best they offer."

"Is that your philosophy of life?" There were several varieties of sautéed wild mushrooms in the pan, but it was the flaked truffles that dominated, a piercing fragrance that was at once earthy and sophisticated. He watched her face as she tasted the first mouthful. "My God," she said in awe, "that is wonderful."

"I was beginning to think you had no time for the pleasures of the flesh," he said, picking up his fork.

She looked up. "Do I give that impression?"

"There's something a little unearthly about you." He nodded. "All air and fire. Not much water or earth."

"I assure you, I'm very earthly. Especially when it comes to food." She savored the delectably loamy mixture of flavors. "Italian food must be in my blood. It has the most intense flavors I know. Truffles, Parma ham, clams in sauce . . ."

"Parmesan cheese."

"Parmesan cheese," she agreed reverently. "Salami, anchovies, *cannoli, pastareale* . . ." Their eyes met and she laughed softly. "I told you."

He was not answering her smile. His eyes held hers, serious, with no flirtation in them. And yet her heart turned over inside her, and she felt the color rush into her cheeks, as though she had exposed herself in some embarrassing way. She dropped her gaze and ate in silence for a while, feeling her heart beat unsteadily and fast inside her. When the heat had faded from her cheeks, she said, "I've been trying to think who this man may have been. The one my mother was looking for. I can't. But Connie Graf told me something interesting. This whole search began with a diary. A diary that was written by my grandmother, the one I told you about. It turned up last year in the farmhouse on Lake Garda, where my mother was born." She explained what Connie had told her. "Did my mother mention this diary to you?"

"No."

"Connie said the man was mentioned in the diary. That's where he starts. There's a pattern starting to form, Philip. This man was in a POW camp near Lake Garda. He's mentioned in Candida's diary. He must have been imprisoned with David Godbold. They may have escaped together. Maybe they were friends."

"Or enemies," Philip put in quietly.

"It's so tantalizing. I can see dozens of shadowy possibilities, but it still doesn't make sense. Grandmama might know something, but she's in the hospital."

"Did Constanze Graf ever see the diary?"

"Connie doesn't believe the diary exists. She thinks my mother was losing her reason and imagined it all—the diary, the man, everything."

Philip drank reflectively. "Oh, it existed. I am sure of that. And it's important."

"Yes. But I've looked, and the diary is nowhere in the apartment. Unless it's in the safe."

He put his glass down. "You must open that safe," he said, and there was an unexpectedly steely command in his voice.

"I know. But I don't want to have it dynamited, or whatever it is safecrackers do. I've arranged to see my mother's lawyers tomorrow. She'll almost certainly have left the combination with them. If they haven't got it, I'll ask a professional locksmith to do it." The wine had a resinous sweetness that went perfectly with the mushrooms. She turned the glass by its stem, watching the golden highlights dance on the white linen tablecloth. "I've looked again and again, and I've found no other papers, either. My mother would have kept records of her research. She has that sort of mind, meticulous, methodical. Apart from the safe, the likeliest place would have been an inlaid walnut bureau in her study, but that was empty when I arrived at the apartment. The drawers were scattered around the floor. If there was anything in it, the intruder must have taken it. The rest . . . "

"The rest is in your mother's head," he finished for her. "Swimming in silence."

She shivered unexpectedly. A man at the next table was smiling at her with unmistakable covetousness, his eyes hungry. Then she noticed his female companion was staring at Philip Westward in the same way. How did they see her and Philip? Clandestine lovers? An older man conquering a younger woman with expensive meals and soft lighting?

He had chosen the next course perfectly, mountain trout, simply grilled, served with a plain lemon butter sauce. After the richness of the mushroom dish, it was as refreshing as an Alpine stream.

"All those men the Russians kept," she went on. "I've been thinking about them, too. It's ghastly. To have been in a Nazi camp, to have been liberated by the Russians, only to be sent to another prison camp for the rest of your life . . . " She shook her head. "I've been trying to work out why the Russians wanted to keep those people. Maybe they wanted to interrogate men who had special information about Western military subjects? Maybe they were trawling for people they could use in the future as intelligence agents against their own countries?"

His eyes were darker now. "Good reasoning. But they were also just plain inefficient. They made terrible mistakes."

She nodded. "I guess it was a time of chaos, anyway. The whole of Europe was in turmoil. We'll probably never know what happened to any of those men, will we? I've read *The Gulag Archipelago*. Conditions in the Siberian gulags were very harsh."

He paused before answering. "Some may have survived."

"You haven't done that for a long time." She smiled.

"Done what?"

"Thought out your answer. You do that a lot. I ask you something, and I can see you thinking it over before you answer. Kind of like a computer processing a command."

"I don't want to give you a wrong answer," he replied seriously. Then he smiled at her. It was the first time she had seen him smile, and the effect was dazzling. She caught her breath involuntarily. She felt as though he had melted her heart inside her.

He laced his fingers. His hands were tanned and strong. "You have an investigative journalist's mind, all right. What does your work involve?"

"Mainly scams. Frauds or deceptions on a large scale."

"A consumer watchdog?"

"Nothing as organized as that. I simply have a nose for people who're ripping off the public in some way."

"Serious crime?"

She thought of André Levêque. To date, he had been her most dramatic project, and the one she hoped was going to get her byline noticed; but for various reasons, it was a topic too raw to mention at this beautiful table. "I've done some work on the Florida crime families. Before the trial, a couple of years ago, I did a big piece on John Gotti's Miami connections. That was pretty serious."

"I'd like to see some of your work sometime."

"Can I ask you something?"

"Go ahead."

"Have you ever been in the military?"

He nodded slightly. "Yes."

"I thought so. Did you serve in Vietnam?"

"No. I was a peacetime soldier. I quit in 1977."

"What outfit were you with?"

"The Rangers."

"The Rangers!" She raised her eyebrows. "I don't know why that should surprise me. The first time I saw you, at the Denver airport, I thought you looked like a soldier. The way you stand, the way you move." She glanced at the way his shoulder muscles strained the fine material of his tuxedo ever so slightly. She lowered her voice and leaned forward conspiratorially. "You're a wolf in lamb's wool, Mr. Westward. All the other men in this room are little powdered doggies. But you're a wolf. I can tell. A big, bad wolf." She was conscious suddenly that the wine had crept up on her at last, that her head was spinning dangerously, that her tongue was wagging like a tipsy girl's. She straightened in embarrassment. "I guess I've had too much wine. It makes me silly. I'm sorry, I can't finish my fish."

"You're not being silly," he said easily. "And you are perfectly correct. I'm a big, bad wolf. I advise you to be very cautious around me."

She laughed, her discomfort gone. " 'You are perfectly correct,' " she repeated. "Your accent fascinates me. It's ambiguous. Are you a New Englander?"

"I was born just north of here. In Wyoming."

She raised her eyebrows, slender question marks. "Men from Wyoming don't say, 'You are perfectly correct,' Philip. They say, 'You're darn tootin', pardner.' "

"The chef makes wonderful ice cream here," he said as the waiters materialized to clear away.

"I couldn't eat another thing. Thank you."

"Coffee, then?"

"Yes, please."

He ordered coffee for them both and turned a little in his chair, crossing his legs. "Have you been to Wyoming?"

"Mama and I once drove along the highway from Cheyenne and Laramie to Rock Springs. Next you'll tell me you come from hardscrabble farming stock."

"Grassland, not hardscrabble. But poor, yes. Very poor."

"Where were you born?"

"In Casper."

"You've come a long way from Casper, Wyoming," she said softly. "Now you have your own private airplane and eat truffles."

"And entertain exquisite women who look like Gypsies and talk like fortune-tellers," he said. "Yes. I've come a long way."

Her head had not stopped spinning. She felt high, floaty, yet she did not feel drunk. She felt in command of herself. She reached across the table and put her hand on his. His hand did not move under hers. "Do you believe your father is still alive?" she asked him.

"I don't know," he said. "Hope is a disease, Anna. I managed to survive hope. My mother did not. It killed her. She shriveled up, year by year, and one day she just blew away."

"Do you look like your father?"

"Yes."

"If you don't have hope, what do you have, Philip?"

"I have a hollow place." His eyes had darkened again. "An area of myself I'll never understand. My mother never remarried. I never had a father. I grew up staring at his pictures in three albums."

"Did it ever occur to you he may have gone willingly to the Russians? That he may have defected?"

He pulled his hand out from under hers. "He was not a traitor,"

Philip said sharply. "He was going to be a great man, and they threw him away like a piece of garbage."

Anna had never seen emotion in him until now, and suddenly she felt it throb like a big engine starting. "They betrayed him."

"Yes," he said with force. "He was betrayed by those he trusted most. By his country, by his government, by his officers. By everyone who had authority. Their governments chewed them up and threw them away. Left them to rot for reasons of political expedience. Forgot them forever." His eyes were narrowed and his mouth was a hard line. It almost shocked her to feel the power in him, and it excited her strangely, too. She felt she had suddenly seen into the workings of this complex mechanism. "The people who had authority sat by in silence while the crime was completed, and then they tried to stop justice being done. Justice must be done. I'm sure your mother understood that."

She sat in silence, meeting his eyes. She could see past the beautiful facade now. Could see, with diamond clarity, a hard and quite brutal determination in him. A commitment more profound, more unshakable, than anything she had known in her own life. She had a vision, just a flash, of what it had taken to turn a poor farm boy into the man who sat opposite her, his eyes like sapphires in the lamplight. She lowered her gaze, almost ashamed of her own inner softness, her innate squeamishness.

"What do you mean by 'justice'?"

"Finding these men, first of all. Even if there is only one alive, he must be found. And then, those who were responsible must be punished." His voice was disturbingly cold.

"You mean the Russians?"

"The guilty ones."

"That's impossible," she said forthrightly. "Believe me, I know about justice. You can't really believe that the guilty ones will be punished after all these years."

"I believe in judgment," he said quietly. "I believe in the day of reckoning."

She shivered. "Please don't look like that. It frightens me."

"Why should you be frightened?" But there was an icy cold in him now. He sat tense and bleak-eyed. So cold, she thought, so dark and lonely. What have I done? He looked at his watch. "It's getting late. I'd better take you back to Vail."

She did not argue. Maybe he regretted opening himself up to

her like that. She sat in silence while he paid the bill. Eyes followed them as they made their way through the tables. Though he had said it was late, it was a long way from midnight, and people were still arriving to eat.

The parking lot was cold and misty. They walked past Ferraris, Porsches, Rolls-Royces, without speaking. As he held the car door open for her, she turned to him, looking up into his shadowed face. "I'm sorry," she said quickly, low. "I don't know what I did or said, but I'm really terribly sorry. It was the wine."

His eyes were in darkness. "No. It wasn't the wine. It was me. I'm sorry." His hand had been resting on the door, holding it open so she could climb into the dark interior of the car. It lifted to touch her face. His knuckles were warm. She moved her head so that it was she who was caressing him with the soft skin of her cheek. She heard him make a small sound in his throat.

Then she lifted her arms to him and drew him to her and kissed him on the mouth. She felt the lean, muscular body against hers as though she had known it all her life. As though she had been waiting for this agelessly, aching for it, never knowing. She melted to him, pressing her softness to him.

He kissed her with great seriousness, with an intensity no man had ever offered her. She felt her heart soar like an eagle, opening its wings in a new heat, a new sun.

He drew back just as her lips parted, opening her moistness to him. He stared at her, but she could not see the expression in his eyes. She whispered his name, but he shook his head without speaking and drew back.

She was trembling. She did not want him to see that. She got in the car and pressed herself back into the soft leather.

He hardly spoke during the drive back to Potato Patch. At one point she said she was cold and asked him to turn up the heat. The tension between them was palpable. She was almost grateful for the silence.

He drove her to her mother's apartment and stopped outside. He turned to her to say something, but she did not let him. She reached for him instinctively, and suddenly they were kissing again.

There were no words, just the caress of hungry mouths, giving, taking, exploring, gentle mouths that tasted the other's swelling desire.

He took her face in his hands and kissed her yielding lips, her temples, the slim column of her throat. She urged toward him, her body arched in an unmistakable offering. "Are you coming in?" she whispered huskily.

"No."

She slid back in the seat, feeling the trembling come on again. "Then why are you doing this to me?"

"I don't know." A car slid past them, its headlights cutting across his face like a saber. She saw his eyes, knew he was feeling the same unbearable charge, the same drugged sensuality. This time, it was she who reached for him.

Kissing was a fever, a sickness. She could suddenly see what had been hidden in her emotions for so long, the vast expanses that opened under shadowy wings. She did not want the smooth exterior of the well-dressed wealthy man. She wanted to touch the brutal inner power, the lonely soldier, the hungry farm boy. She needed to crush her lips against his white teeth, taste his tongue on her palate, be wounded by his need.

He pushed her away.

"You coldhearted bastard," she said tautly. "I know you're using me. I just don't know what for yet."

"I'll walk you to the door."

"No." She laid her palm against his chest, pressing the heel of her hand against the hard muscles until she could feel the throb of his heart, hard and fast. "At least I've raised your pulses," she said brusquely.

"Yes. You've done that. I have to go to New York tomorrow."

Her heart twisted. "When will you be back?"

"In a couple of days. You've got my numbers there. You can call me."

"I might." She pushed the door open and got out.

She watched the red taillights slide down the street, shimmering in the vapor from his exhaust. She lifted both hands to her temples, feeling the giddiness swell and darken. She wondered if she were going to faint and felt a panicky need to get into bed before she did. Clothed, if necessary. Huddled in her solitude.

She dropped her hands and suddenly became aware of a face staring at her from the window of a car parked on the opposite side of the street. Blue lamplight pierced the dark window. The car was a new-looking, metallic red Chrysler LeBaron. The face, by contrast, was young and coarse, scarred with acne, the scalp bearing the ugly boot-camp hairstyle of a skinhead.

She felt a flash of unease. The man's stare was hard and hostile. As her eyes met his, the car pulled forward abruptly, its headlights still off. It sped past her. Over a leather-clad shoulder, she saw a profile like a skull, the jaw clenched tight.

At the end of the street, she saw the lights come on, and the Chrysler turned swiftly round a corner.

A bitter wind off the snow rustled in the firs, making her shiver. She turned and hurried into the apartment.

She Was Torn from a deep sleep by the ringing of the telephone beside her. It was somewhere around 4:00 A.M., and she cursed muzzily as she groped in the dark for the receiver.

"Yes?"

"Anna. I trust I did not disturb you."

"Who is this?"

"I wished to present my condolences. I was informed of your mother's tragic injury only yesterday."

The cultured, faintly accented tones made a sudden cold chill run through her. She sat up in the dark. "Dr. Levêque?"

"Please. Call me André."

"How did you get hold of this number?" she demanded, trying to shake off the nightmarish confusion. Was this happening, or was it another bad dream?

"As a doctor, I wanted to give you some advice."

"How did you get this number, goddamn it?"

"Constant stimulus, Anna. Constant stimulus is the key. Do not allow her to be abandoned. Recovered coma patients often report having heard conversations around them. Talk to her. Stimulate her. Have her favorite music playing at her bedside."

"I do all that already," Anna said brusquely. "What do you want?"

"Think of your mother's mind as a child, Anna. A lost child

who needs to be led out of the darkness, back into the light. Be patient. To those who are patient, all things come."

"I appreciate the advice," she said tersely. Was it her imagination, or could she hear the voodoo drums pulsing behind the atmospheric hiss on the line? "Now please—what do you want?"

"Do you remember that night in my garden, Anna?"

"Vividly."

He laughed softly. "You have made me famous. I am besieged with people wanting my *story*. Trying to get at the heart of me. But none of them are like you, Anna. They send me cynical adventurers, inane young trollops, people with neither sensitivity nor understanding."

"Dr. Levêque—"

"Have you seen the obscene rubbish they have already written about me?"

"No," she said wearily, "but I can imagine it."

"The truth needs to be told. The truth *must* be told. There are fascinating dimensions to my story. Souls like mine are born only once in a very great while. How can I open myself to such rabble? To you I could talk, Anna. I could unlock my soul."

"Can't you understand that I have no time for you?"

"I mean it. I will talk only to you. To no one else. I have told your superiors that already."

"Drew McKenzie," she guessed with a sudden hot anger. "He gave you this number, didn't he?"

"He is anxious that the truth be told."

"I'll bet he is," she snapped.

"He told me of your mother's tragedy. He knew I would want to help."

"The bastard," she muttered under her breath. "The unscrupulous *bastard*."

"And I can help, Anna. I have experience of many coma cases. It is a subject which has always fascinated me—"

"I don't think of you as a doctor," she cut through icily. "Please don't call me again."

Her hand was shaking as she hung up. As an afterthought, she pulled the plug out of the wall and curled up in the darkness in a fetal position, disturbed and wretched. Drew! How could he be such an unprincipled bastard? She imagined him crouched behind piles of copy,

coffee-stoked bile ducts squeezing out a poison virulent enough to jolt
her back to work. The unethical bastard. Hearing Levêque even mention him had given Anna acute nausea.

Drew's religion was that 2.5 million circulation, and his Nirvana
was getting it to three. Life was about people clawing to get their own
way, she thought. Everyone for himself, and devil take the hindmost.

Was that what Philip Westward was doing to her? Using her
flesh to claw his way to whatever it was he wanted?

She got out of bed to make herself a cup of coffee. Sleep would
not come for a long time now.

4

Her mother's legal firm, Morgan and Katz, was a large one, in impressive offices near the Civic Center Park in Denver. It had views of the sprawling park, the gold-domed State Capitol building, and of the mountains to the west. She waited in an airy, plant-filled atrium for twenty minutes, watching secretaries click busily to and fro with arms full of files.

Her mind was filled with turbulent thoughts of Philip Westward. She was more than attracted to him; she was hooked, like a salmon that had bitten on a hook. It had entered her flesh.

If she thought of those kisses too long, heat flooded her loins. *All air and fire. Not much earth and water.* She had desired him last night as she had seldom desired physical love.

But there was no equality. She was vulnerable, he was not. He was the hunter, she the quarry.

He had his imperatives. He wanted her mother's papers, so he could fulfill some burning private mission of his own. She should not have told him about the diary. She had seen the cold fire in his eyes when she'd mentioned it.

And yet, her treacherous heart had planned the whole thing. She'd brought up the diary deliberately, knowing he would be interested. Wanting to use it to hold him here. Wanting to stop him from getting into his private airplane and flying back to New York. *Oh, it existed. I am sure of that. And it's important.*

Of course the diary was important. And not just because it would identify the mystery man her mother had been hunting.

If, as Connie had said, it covered the last year of Candida Cipriani's life, it was easy to see why its discovery had electrified her mother. That had been the fateful year when Candida and David Godbold had met, in the midst of war. To Kate, who had never known her mother, and who had spent most of her childhood as an orphan, it must have been a touching, highly emotive document.

The diary would almost certainly have described the emotions, the passions, the terrors of the love affair between Candida Cipriani and David Godbold. It might have contained a doomed young woman's hopes and dreams for the child whom she would never see. It would have had a deep impact on Kate.

And whatever it said had triggered a search into her past so obsessive that her best friend had thought she was losing her reason, and her lover had grown distraught.

It might lead Philip Westward to vital information about his own Holy Grail, his missing father. It might teach her the truth about her mother's last few months.

"Anna?"

A bearded young man in a gray silk suit had arrived. She rose to shake his hand. He was looking at her closely. "Don't you remember me?"

Suddenly she recognized the face beneath the beard. "Nathan Morgan!"

He nodded. "In person. Good to see you, even though the circumstances could be happier ones."

"You've changed, Nate."

"So have you," he said, making it an unmistakable compliment.

They shook hands warmly. Nate Morgan had been a year ahead of her at Vail Mountain School in the valley. Because she'd spent such a short time there, no more than the last two and half years of her schooling, Anna had made few long-term friends at Vail Mountain. But she remembered Nate Morgan as a bright, friendly boy, an excellent skier who had helped the school win several state meets. "Morgan and Katz," she said. "Of course. I didn't register the Morgan, but I should have done."

He smiled. "My father. He's one of the senior partners. After Vail Mountain, I went to Boulder and then law school here in Denver. When I qualified a couple of years ago, my father brought me in. I don't normally deal with your mother's affairs; my father does that. But he's away right now, so you've got me. Come on in." He ushered her courteously into his office. "Coffee? Tea?"

"I'm fine, thanks."

He studied her. "How is your mother?"

"Much the same."

He spread his hands in sympathy or apology for the brutality of life, she was not sure which. "Such a terrible thing to happen. It still seems incredible. Somehow you never associate violent crime with Vail."

She nodded. "That's what everybody says. But it happened."

"The place must be buzzing like an ant's nest. Do the police have any leads?"

"Nothing concrete. The detective in charge of the case says it will be almost impossible to find the attacker."

"Well, that's frank, but very discouraging. How are you coping?"

"All right. I've spoken to the insurance people, and they're being very cooperative. The apartment is almost back to normal. I go in to see my mother every day, but . . . " She tailed off.

"You're planning on staying here in Vail, I understand?"

"Yes. I can't leave my mother, Nate."

"Not everybody would see it like that. We hear you're a hotshot journalist these days. A high flyer."

"Not exactly," she replied wryly.

"Come on." He smiled. "Don't be modest. You were always different. A fireball. Nobody expected you to do anything ordinary with your life. At least you've got excitement. Challenges. Freedom."

"Would you trade me for all this?" she said, glancing around the clubby, comfortable office.

"I might like to. Fact is, I couldn't." He reached out and turned a photograph on his desk to face her. It showed a broad-faced, smiling young woman with two small children on her lap. "Martha, my wife. James, three, and Melissa, fourteen months."

"Congratulations, Nate. You have a beautiful family."

"Never felt the urge to settle down yourself, raise some kids?" he asked her wistfully.

She shook her head. "Just as well. A family would be awfully difficult in the present circumstances."

"Yes." He leaned forward. "You have a lot on your mind, Anna. Your mother's legal affairs will need administering while she's—ah—incapacitated. You're ready for that?"

"Yes, of course."

He nodded. "We can, of course, handle a lot of stuff on her behalf, but it would be expensive. And frankly, it's better you get to grips with your mother's estate yourself."

"Her *estate*?" Anna repeated, not liking the word.

He pushed a piece of paper in front of her. "Take a look at this."

It was a medical certificate signed by Dr. Jay Ram Singh and others, attesting that Catherine Kelly was incapable of managing her affairs. It did not escape Anna's attention that the incapacity was described as "long-term."

The idea of declaring her mother incompetent to manage her affairs was deeply repugnant to her. Mama, of all people, who had always had her life so much under control . . .

"You understand what this means?" Nate Morgan asked.

"Yes," she said sadly.

"Good. I've already presented this to the judge. I'll make an appointment for us to see him in the next few days. He may want to ask you a few questions, and then the legal formalities will be over. He'll give you legal power to operate your mother's bank accounts, which is fundamental. All the rest follows logically." He hesitated. "Naturally, we'll try and hold off the IRS as long as we can."

Anna looked up from the medical certificate. "What does the IRS have to do with this?"

"The tax code is very complicated in this area," he said, looking uncomfortable. "If your mother were actually—ah—deceased, it would be a whole lot easier. I'm no expert on estate law, Anna, but it's clear that a more or less full transfer of the estate is going to have to take

place. Eventually, I mean. The IRS will want to monitor this very carefully. It's hard to predict how they will see it. They may even hit you
with a major tax demand before the full transfer takes place."

"Oh, Jesus," she sighed.

He held up his pink palms. "Don't worry about it right now.
When my father gets back from vacation, he'll check it out thoroughly.
We have a very good tax consultancy who handles this kind of stuff for
us. They'll probably want to set up a trust fund to hold the IRS off for
the time being. But like I said, you don't have to concern yourself with
any of that right now."

"I need to concentrate on my mother, Nate."

"Sure you do," he said soothingly. "Look, perhaps you could
give me your passport, and if you have it, your birth certificate?"

The bearded young lawyer checked over the paperwork, then
picked up the telephone. After a brief conversation, he replaced the
receiver. "The judge will see us next Monday in his chambers. Ten A.M.
Does that suit you?"

"Yes."

"One last thing. Your position as your mother's representative
will entitle you to legally draw a reasonable salary from the estate. The
judge will approve that. In this case, a thousand dollars per month
would be considered adequate. Is that okay?"

"I don't want a salary."

Nate raised his eyebrows. "You've given up your own job,
Anna."

"She's my mother. I'm not going to take her money."

"There will be purely private expenses, not to mention burdens
on your time," he warned. "This is not a moment for diffidence."

"I'm not being diffident. I don't want it."

He shrugged, obviously puzzled. "It's your decision. Any questions before we go?"

"Yes. There's a safe in my mother's apartment, which is locked.
Did she leave the combination with you?"

"I'll check," he said, and left the room. He returned a little
while later with a handsome crocodile-skin attaché case in his arms.
"This is all your mother left in our vault. There's no information about
the safe." He laid the attaché case on the desk in front of her. "I am
afraid your mother didn't give us the keys."

"They might be at the apartment," she said, picking it up. It was disappointingly light. If it contained any of the mysteries that had been obsessing her mother for so long, they were not very weighty ones.

She said good-bye to Nathan Morgan and left the offices.

Back At The apartment in Potato Patch, she looked for keys to the crocodile-skin case. There were several unlabeled keys in the walnut bureau, but none of them fitted the delicate golden locks. In the end, with reluctance, she got a screwdriver out of the kitchen drawer and prized it open. She carried the opened case to the dining-room table and lifted the lid.

Inside were two manila envelopes. She opened the bulkier envelope first. It contained a thick wad of crisp, new hundred-dollar bills. In all, $20,000. She stared at the money, slightly shocked. Why so much cash? The next envelope contained her mother's last will and testament. It was short and to the point. Catherine Kelly, formerly Catherine Godbold, née Catarina Cipriani, left all her worldly goods and possessions to "my beloved daughter, Anna." There were no bequests, no legacies to anyone else. The last paragraph requested a Catholic burial, according to her beliefs.

Anna put it back in the envelope, her eyes blurred with tears. There was a hot lump in her throat. She felt as if her mother's hand had reached out and caressed her face. It was so typical of her mother to give her love so irrevocably and unreservedly. That was how she had always loved.

Anna had never really considered her mother's death until now. With Kate in her healthy middle forties, it had seemed a remote eventuality. A man with a club had changed that.

For the first time, she was confronting the idea that her mother would never make a recovery, that everything Anna had thought of as her mother had fled that motionless body forever. That Kate would never inhabit it again.

And today, in northern England, Evelyn Godbold would go under the surgeon's knife. Poor Evelyn! Had she, too, spent the last few hours debating the mysteries of life and death?

There was a button-down compartment in the case. Anna opened it and drew out a small sheaf of papers. An Aeroflot airline ticket to Moscow issued in Denver, an Aeroflot cabin luggage label, a menu in Cyrillic from a Moscow restaurant. There were two other items. The first was a sheet of notepaper with a brief series of jottings in her mother's handwriting:

Joseph Krasnowsky.

Varga concentration camp, Latvia

APRIL 1945,   DP camp Eastern Front.

MAY 1945,   NKVD questioning. Interrogators were Alexei Feodorev & Mikhail Volsky.

SEPTEMBER 1945,   Gorky.

MARCH 1947,   Lubyanka, Moscow, preliminary detention.

1948, Lefortovo Prison, Moscow.

1949, Gulag 5431, Tambov.

1952, Gulag 2112, Vladivostok.

1956, Transit camp C-56, Tashkent.

1956, Gulag 732, Kiev.

1957, Gulag 9513, Lithuania.

1959 ?

She stared at it for a long while, feeling her skin crawl, before turning to the second. It was a piece of cheap hotel notepaper. At the top was printed, "ODESSA HOTEL, MOSCOW" with an address and telephone number. Two words were handwritten beneath it, the first in Cyrillic characters, the second in Roman:

Quecksilber

Neither word meant anything to Anna. The writing was not her mother's. It looked like it was written in an old-fashioned, shaky hand, the Cyrillic characters more confidently scrawled than the Roman.

She picked up the telephone and called Philip's office number in New York. Philip's voice came on the line.

"Anna?"

"Hi. The man my mother was looking for. I know his name now."

"How?"

"I found some of her papers. They were at her lawyer's office, in a briefcase she took to Russia. Just a few scraps. His name was Joseph Krasnowsky. Does that mean anything to you?" she asked hopefully.

"Not in itself. But it's significant that the name is Slavic. A lot of the missing men had ethnic Soviet origins, though they were American citizens. Balts, Belorussians, Lithuanians, Latvians. That may have been the initial pretext to detain them."

"I see. There's a list, too. It looks like the dates and names of Russian labor camps he was sent to. It ends with a question mark, in 1959. There are a few other things, jottings that don't seem to make any sense. What do you think?"

There was a silence. "I have contacts at the American Council for Human Rights in Washington. I could call them and ask them to run that name through their computers. If it's in there, the flags will go up. They'll tap into the government information banks. In a day we could know everything there is to be known about Joseph Krasnowsky. And maybe then you'll learn why your mother was so interested in him."

Her heart jumped. "You really think so?"

"Really."

"That's wonderful!"

"Read me everything that's on the pieces of paper you found," he commanded. "Don't leave anything out."

Slowly, she read out everything that was written on the papers, spelling out the Russian word as best she could. As she did so, she was aware that these were the vestiges of her mother's odyssey, possibly the only remnants of eight months of intensive research. "It's important, isn't it?" she concluded. "Proof that she wasn't having delusions, or anything like that."

"I never thought she was having delusions."

"Other people did. What about 'Quecksilber'? Does that mean anything to you?"

"It's German for 'quicksilver.' I don't know what the Russian word means. But I can check that out. Well done, Anna. You now have two pieces of the jigsaw."

"But all the other pieces are missing," she said. "And I don't even know what the picture is."

"Don't sound so sad," he said. "That name is pure gold. Leave it with me."

"I've arranged for a locksmith to come and open the safe. There might be some more papers in there."

"Good."

She hesitated. "When—when are you coming back?"

"Tomorrow night."

Her heart jumped. "I'll make you a meal," she suggested diffidently. "Here at my mother's apartment."

"Fine," he agreed. "Take care, Anna." He hung up.

When She Arrived at the hospital, Campbell Brinkman was waiting for her. He stood in front of the door to the ICU, as though barring her way in.

"Ram Singh has something to say to you," he informed her.

"She's improving?" she asked with a flash of painful hope.

"No," he said heavily. "She is not improving. Come."

The smooth-faced Indian doctor was waiting for them in his office, a stethoscope neatly looped round his neck. He rose to shake Anna's hand.

"How is my mother?" she asked.

"The physical signs are stabilizing well. However, the mental signs are unaltered." Ram Singh showed her a roll of paper, marked with a wavering line. "This is your mother's latest electroencephalogram. You can compare it to the previous readings. There's no substantive change." She studied the graph blankly. He cleared his throat. "She's ready to leave the intensive care unit. We'd like your permission to transfer her to another hospital."

"Which hospital?"

"Holy Cross. They're better equipped for the care your mother will need. It has a beautiful setting, up near Aspen."

"Is it a brain hospital?"

"Not exactly. It's a general hospital, but it has a large long-term neurological wing."

"Other patients in comas?"

"Yes."

"Aren't there other facilities to care for her in this hospital? Special rooms?"

"Yes," he said, "we have special rooms. But the care here would be very much more expensive than at Holy Cross. They are experts at long-term management."

"Meaning that the care here is very much better?"

"That doesn't necessarily follow."

"Surely my mother's insurance will cover those costs?"

"Up to a point," he said. "Keeping a patient like your mother is very expensive. There comes a time when the insurance company will want to consider the utility, how shall I put it, the appropriateness, of the treatment."

"What the hell does that mean, *the appropriateness of the treatment?*"

Campbell sighed heavily. "Anna, please."

"The question is valid," Ram Singh said, unperturbed by the rising anger in Anna's voice. "By appropriateness I mean expectation of recovery. In this case I would now say that expectation is negligible."

"I don't believe that," she said sharply. "Anyway, it's too soon to tell."

"I have seen coma patients who resemble astronauts strapped into a space shuttle. Millions of dollars spent to keep alive a person who is no longer there. There are far simpler and, if I may say so, more humane ways of treating such patients."

In the fluorescent light, Anna's dark eyes were suddenly bleak. "I know exactly what 'humane' means. It means letting her die."

Campbell laid a hand on her arm. "Anna, calm yourself."

"There's no question of that yet," Ram Singh said. "Letting the patient die with dignity is a final option, when all hope of recovery has drained away."

"Holy Cross is a hospice, isn't it? A nice, quiet place where she can start running down. Then, in a few months, when she's shriveled up like a leaf and doesn't even look human anymore, they can talk me into pulling the plug!"

"This has been a shock to you," the doctor said, his bland face unmoved, the schoolmaster deliberately not showing irritation with the obtuse child. "You need rest before you can make proper judgments."

She turned to Campbell. "Can they transfer her to this place without my permission?"

"Anna, don't be hysterical."

"I am her next of kin. It's my decision, isn't it?" She turned back to the doctor. "My mother is not a vegetable. She's a human being, a brilliant, wonderful woman who needs your help. She's not some anonymous carcass to be hauled away. Do you hear me?"

"I hear you." Ram Singh sighed.

"I will *not* give you permission to transfer her out of this hospital. She stays here until she recovers."

"And what if she does not recover?" the doctor asked.

Anna rose to her feet. "She is going to recover," she said grimly, looking down at him. "I don't intend to consider any other possibility."

"Very well. But I can tell you that the insurance company will soon want to stop paying our bills. They will make a lump payment and absolve themselves of any further responsibility. And then you will have to manage that sum on your own, Miss Kelly. A couple of million dollars sounds like a lot of money. But at this level of care, I can tell you it amounts to only a couple of years of hospital bills."

So *that* was what the insurance man had been talking about! They would far rather pay out four million dollars now than have to pay her mother's fees for the next ten years. Her face tightened. "I see."

She was still taut with anger as they walked into the corridor.

"Can you *believe* that man?"

Campbell was angry, too; but not with the doctors, with her. "It's no use attacking the medical staff for what has happened to your mother," he snapped. "They're doing their best."

"Maybe they need motivating to make sure it stays that way."

"Holy Cross is the best place for her. She would be at peace there."

" 'At peace' as in junkyard?"

He huddled into his astrakhan. "Don't be childish. You will have to face the fact that she will never recover." She could hear the despair in his voice. "She will never come back."

"She will," Anna said. "She will come back."

"Never," he repeated. "Never, Anna. She is dead."

"No," Anna said quietly but fiercely. "She's going to get better. Don't give up hope. She needs us to have hope, Campbell."

Campbell's face, hollow-eyed and dark with stubble, was tragic. "How can we have hope?"

"If you were lying there with holes drilled in your skull, wouldn't you want her to have hope for you?"

He gave her a twisted smile. "You're very young," he said, as though that were an answer. "Like all children, you believe in miracles."

"For Christ's sake." She grasped his arm, swinging him round to look at her. Her face was flinty. "I'm not asking for miracles. Just for a little hope, a little perseverance. Even that medical pharisee admitted there was some hope."

"Almost none."

"Coma patients do recover. It could happen! But it's not going to happen if we give up hope!"

"Don't lecture me," he snarled. "Just who the hell do you think you are, Anna? You come rushing in here like a domineering nanny, insulting Ram Singh, taking over, telling us all what we should be doing. If it was a question of money, do you think I would allow your mother to have anything but the best treatment?"

"No," she replied more gently, "I guess not. But you think of her as dead, Campbell. To me she is alive. Why are you so keen for her to go to Holy Cross? So you don't have to think of her as living and suffering any longer? So you can stop the pain of visiting her?"

He pulled his arm out of her grasp. For a moment she thought he would strike her, but he controlled himself. "It's better we don't meet for a while," he said grimly. "You've taken charge. So be it."

Anna watched him walk down the corridor, his hands thrust in his pockets. She had been cruel to him. But she was not remorseful. *Whoever is not with me is against me.* To hell with his feelings. His feelings were not of primary importance. Kate's recovery was, and Anna loathed the thought of any negative current around her mother's bed.

She went back into the ward and looked down at her mother's unmoving face. "I'm not going to let you die, Mama," she said, her voice tight in her throat. "I'm not going to let you lie there for the next twenty years, either. You've got a life to live. Things to do. You can't hide down there in the dark forever. I won't let you. So you might as well start waking up."

To Her Considerable pleasure, the new sofas she had chosen arrived the next afternoon, in advance of her dinner with Philip.

Her mother's old furniture had been covered in a muted ocher velvet, which toned unobtrusively with the dusky pink of the walls. Anna had decided not to attempt to emulate her mother's taste. She had used her own discretion. As soon as the deliverymen carried the new furniture into the apartment, she knew she had chosen perfectly. The pale lemon yellow of the material was as fresh as the scent of a citrus orchard. The color positively sang against the pink walls. She told them where to arrange the furniture and signed the invoice. They carried the ruined stuff away with them, as she'd arranged.

When they had gone, she walked around her new purchases, trailing her fingers along the heavy linen. Her mother would approve, she was sure of that. After an initial shock, perhaps. But she would approve. The change was long overdue. The new armchairs and sofas were not only far more contemporary in design, simple yet classical, they were infinitely more comfortable than the old things.

Glancing at the remaining furnishings in the old color—the weighty drapes, the dining chairs, and some footstools—Anna decided she would have them replaced with the new yellow material, too. If the insurance money didn't stretch to that, she'd pay for the work herself. There was, as always, the nagging pain of guilt that she was usurping her mother's place. To put things in perspective, she had imagined throughout that her mother had been at her side, that she had been doing this at her mother's request.

It was a profound relief to have the old furniture, with its gaping wounds, out of the place. And the fresh lemon color was a tonic. An antidote to the vicious desecration.

She felt tension slide out of her in a quiet laugh. She stretched out her arms as if to embrace the place. After days of hard work, the apartment looked, for the first time since she had arrived, normal again. Not just restored. Improved. Brightened. Cheered. A fit place for Mama to come back to. Anna was delighted with it, and herself. She wondered how Philip would react.

Offering to make him a meal had perhaps been unwise. There was far more intimacy in the apartment than at any restaurant. On the other hand, she was no cook. She had never learned how to turn out the spectacular meals that her mother excelled at. Evelyn had taught Kate to be a classical hostess in the grand style. From the age of sixteen, her stepmother had trained Kate relentlessly, as though putting her through the ultimate finishing school. The right clothes, the right accessories, the infinite shades of difference between what was stylish and what was vulgar, what was amusing and what shocking, what correct and what hopelessly wrong. It had been a long and arduous apprenticeship, but Kate had never deliberately passed on any of that vast armory of lore to Anna.

"I was forced into a mold," Kate had once told Anna. "I'm not going to force you into anything. If you want to learn, ask."

Anna used to ask. But since her father's death, she had never asked again. She had gone her own way and had developed her own style. She knew it could not match her mother's, but it was her own— modern and as simple and astringent as the lemon yellow of that beautiful linen.

Right now she wished she had the knowledge and confidence to produce the kind of occasion that would impress Philip Westward: candles flanking an exquisite floral display, an effortless succession of mouth-watering courses that matched and contrasted one another perfectly, the right wines with each course, the right cutlery in the right places, a selection of brandies and cigars to conclude.

That was beyond her. So she had settled for the candles and a simple pasta dish, followed by a grilled steak. There was a stock of wine in the pantry, and rather than make some foolish error, she would let him choose what he wanted.

She set the table for two. There was a pair of lovely silver candelabra on the sideboard, but she used only one, fitting pink candles into the five sockets. She'd bought a salmon to make a sauce for the pasta, and now she poached it and separated the flesh from the bones, forking it into small flakes, which she dressed with fresh basil, salt, and freshly ground pepper. Mixed with *taglieríni,* it would make a simple but delicious starter. Steaks, at least, she was sure about. Her mother had an electric broiler fitted in the kitchen that was more or less foolproof.

Soaping her naked body in the shower, she thought about Philip Westward.

She did not believe he was a Don Juan, despite the sex appeal. He was simply a man who had no room in his life for long-term relationships. A man with a cause, a man driven. A man as committed to his beliefs as a priest.

Maybe that was part of his appeal for her. Like the kind of woman she'd known of in Ireland, the kind who found an irresistible pleasure in spoiling a handsome priest. The dark, intoxicating appeal of trying to turn all that drive, all that commitment, all that power, onto one's self.

She had never played in this league before. Philip Westward was not the kind of man she had loved in the past. She considered herself very experienced, despite her years. She'd had affairs with three men. Two professional men in Ireland, both older than she, one married, with children, the other divorced. The third had been a fellow journalist in Miami with whom she had smoked dope and made love on moonlit beaches, shedding her responsibilities and repressions for a dizzy season until he'd up and left one day and taken a job as an editor on a California daily.

Compared to Philip, her men had been gentle, peaceable. They had been partners, not opponents. She was not an innocent child, nor the kind of woman who had needed men to make her life have meaning. But her instincts told her that if she tried to meet Philip on his own terms, he would wound her more deeply than she could handle.

And yet, all that only strengthened the currents that seemed to be drawing her to him, pulling her into his whirlpool.

She emerged from the shower and dried herself in front of the mirror. Her mother had been driven, too. She had found a cause she felt strongly enough to the point of an illness. Like Philip. Beside Philip, how ephemeral Campbell Brinkman seemed—Campbell, whose only preoccupations had ever been where the skiing was best, what new sports car to buy each year. *She could no longer share the things that were important to me. My life meant nothing to her anymore.* It was as though her mother had discovered reality for the first time in years. Anna sensed that. She had touched something real, something that hurt, but something that held meaning for her.

Anna studied her body in the mirror. The cinnamon skin went with dark nipples and a triangle of black hair at the base of her belly. The lithe, dark body of a Gypsy girl, the delicacy deceptive, strength tangible beneath the taut curves.

Was she beautiful? She stared into her own eyes. All her men had called her that. They had loved to look at her, trail their fingers across her face. There was mystery, at least, in the plush mouth and the dark eyes. But could she compete with the women *he* had known? Was there anything in her special enough to distinguish her from the others who must have tried to dig in their claws, to have and hold Philip?

She lifted her heavy black hair away from her face, watching in the mirror as her slender throat arched, her small, round breasts tilted upward, the nipples suddenly hardening like immature acorns. She turned away abruptly from her own image and started pulling open drawers.

Last time she had worn her mother's clothes. This time she dressed in her own style, her own red lace underwear and a red silk dress with a cutaway back. She put on the big artificial pearls she liked so much, a choker, and earrings. The emerald ring was too expensive, too old for her. She put it away. She brushed her hair back from her face but did not tie it. She'd brought no perfume of her own from Florida, so she borrowed a squirt of Kenzo from her mother's dressing table. She instantly regretted the too-sweet flower fragrance. She tried to wipe it off quickly, but the slick at the base of her throat was already drying.

Fluttering with nerves already, she checked herself in the mirror one last time. A dark girl in a red dress, no anxiety showing in the smoky eyes. She nodded briskly to herself and went to find some music to put on the stereo.

It Was Almost nine, and she was starting to get worried, when Philip finally called up from the lobby. When she opened the door, he was in his Burberry, carrying a briefcase in one hand, a sheaf of newspapers under the other arm.

"You just got back from the airport," she guessed.

He nodded. "The flights were all delayed this evening. Bad weather. I'm sorry."

"Don't worry, nothing's spoiling." She reached up and touched his cheek with her lips. His face had fallen into the mask of a traveler, showing nothing. "Come in. You look tired."

She took his coat. Beneath it he wore a charcoal suit with the faintest of chalk stripes. He looked around the apartment slowly. "You've changed the sofas."

"Do you like them?"

"They're beautiful. The color is perfect."

She glowed. "I hope my mother feels the same way when she gets back."

"I'm sure she will. How is she?"

Her mouth hardened. "They want to move her. To another hospital. A place for incurables, up in the mountains. A place where the fees are a lot lower."

He shook his head. "Her chances of any sort of recovery would be zero in a place like that."

"I know. I'm fighting them tooth and nail. They won't win, I can promise you. I don't want to talk about it right now. Maybe later." She forced a smile. "Can I get you a drink?"

"Scotch on the rocks."

She found the Jameson's in the liquor cabinet and poured it onto some ice cubes. She gave him the drink.

"I've got a couple of other things for you," he said.

"What?" she asked.

"This, for a start." He held out an envelope. "Your Mr. Krasnowsky. He was an interesting man."

Anna took the envelope eagerly and opened it. There were two sheets of computer paper inside, containing terse printed notes. She sat down to read them. The heading was the logo of something called the American Council for Human Rights:

Joseph Abraham Krasnowsky (also Krasnowski, Kraznowski), listed Missing In Action Sept. 1943.

Born in Latvia, December 1916. Son of Alexander Krasnowsky, born Latvia, 1884, and Justine Rapoport 1897.

1934   Foreign/war correspondent for *New York Times,* covering European affairs, with special reference to German aggression leading to the Second World War (several articles on microfiche file—ref KRAS 564/B).

1935–1936   Foreign correspondent for *New York Times* in Europe. Covered Spanish Civil War; also contributed articles on

Fascist Italy and Nazi Germany. Articles described as "libertarian, democratic, acerbic, brilliantly written." Fiercely anti-Nazi in tone.

1937   Political monograph, *The Shadow of Fascism,* published in New York. Extract in microfiche file—ref KRAS 565/B.

1938–1939   Visited Austria, annexed by Hitler in March; reported on anti-Semitic atrocities. Expelled by Nazis after invasion of Czechoslovakia. Returned to United States briefly, then volunteered to join British Army when Chamberlain declared war on Germany after invasion of Poland.

1940   With the British Eighth Army. Promoted lieutenant (rank next below captain in British Army).

1941–1942   Saw action in the Western Desert.

1942 JUNE 20–21:   Joseph Krasnowsky captured at Tobruk; sent to internment camp 307 at Brescia, Lombardy, Northern Italy (see refs), commandant Colonel Pierluigi Rovigo (see refs). Red Cross records exist until July 1943.

1943   Italian Armistice declared Sept 8. 307 Brescia opened by Italian officers. 74 British POWs escaped. 37 recaptured within 4 days. Col. Rovigo subsequently sent to Auschwitz, shot there.

JANUARY 1945   Alexander and Justine Krasnowsky, Joseph's parents, killed in an automobile accident in New Jersey. No surviving family members known.

1945   Unsubstantiated accounts from survivors that "Joseph Kraznowski," an American soldier, had been held for a while at Varga concentration camp, near Riga, Latvia (see refs). This camp liberated by Red Army but Russian authorities consistently deny all knowledge of Krasnowsky.

There was one more note, handwritten underneath:

РТУТЬ is the Russian for "quicksilver."

She looked up. "This is an extraordinary story!"

Philip nodded. "Yes. It is. So. Your Joseph Krasnowsky was a journalist, just like you."

"I know! I can hardly believe the coincidence! He must have been an incredibly brave man."

"An authentic hero." Philip smiled rather sadly. "It didn't do him much good. He was a Jew, a committed anti-Nazi who had attacked Hitler in the American newspapers. Plus he had volunteered to fight with the British before America joined the war. Plus he had escaped from an Italian POW camp. It's no wonder they sent him to Varga when they caught him again. He was lucky not to have been shot out of hand."

"I'd love to read these articles he wrote for *The New York Times*."

"I can try to get extracts, if you like."

"But why was my mother so interested in this man, Philip? Just because he was a hero?"

"There must have been more to it than that. She went to Russia to get information about him, and from what she told me on the telephone, she was successful."

"So he's alive?"

"He may be," Philip said carefully.

"But if she was going to keep looking for him next year, surely she must have been given some hope? Some reliable information that this man, whoever he was, was still alive somewhere?"

"Perhaps."

"It's so damned frustrating," she exclaimed. "If I just had *some* idea who this man was, some inkling . . . "

He held one of his newspapers out to her. "This is today's London *Times*. Take a look."

The article was right on the front page, a single-column piece, headlined BRITONS HELD IN COLD WAR LABOUR CAMPS, with a Moscow correspondent's byline. She read it out aloud.

> The first scraps of evidence are coming to light about one of the most shadowy chapters of the Cold War: the alleged deten-

tion of tens of thousands of Americans, and possibly some Britons, in the gulag labour camps of Siberia.

General Dmitri Volkogonov, the liberal military historian, told the business weekly *Commersant* that he had un-
earthed four KGB files referring to American prisoners detained
in Russia after the second world war. He had also received
"sensational" but as yet unverified reports that Americans had
been held captive at Kolyma in Siberia and at Tambov in Russia.

General Volkogonov was entrusted by Boris Yeltsin,
the Russian leader, to investigate the fate of missing Americans
after a request from President Bush. An American lobby group
called the National Alliance of Families has offered up to $2.4
million (£1.3 million) for information on the fate of missing
Americans in the former Soviet Union.

She looked up at Philip, who was reclining in one of the new
armchairs with his whisky.

"Yeltsin needs help from America," he said, "a lot of help.
Billions of dollars' worth of aid. He has very little to offer in return.
This is something he can use. He's a clever tactician. He'll play this card
to the hilt. He'll feed the information out as effectively as he can for
another year or two, until it runs its course. He did it with the Bush
Administration, and he'll do it with the Clinton Administration. Clinton
made a public statement recently promising, 'a full and final accounting
of the POW/MIA issue.' "

She nodded. "I read that. It seems influential people in Congress are opposing aid to the Russians purely on the MIA issue. Yeltsin
will hope to defuse their opposition with this."

"Exactly." She was standing by the window, her arms folded,
and his eyes were on her. "You look good in that dress," he said softly,
and she blushed, not so much at the laconic compliment as at the look
in his eyes.

"Come and choose a couple of bottles of wine, or maybe three."

He lit the candles. She switched off the other room lights, and
the rose glow of the candles filled the darkness appealingly.

He praised her salmon pasta just enough to let her know he
meant it, and left nothing on his plate. They discussed the computer
printout on Joseph Krasnowsky, going into every angle. But she could

still not imagine a single reason why her mother should have become so fascinated by this man.

Except one.

"Brescia is not far from Garda, where my mother was born," she said. "There may be a connection there."

"When you get that safe opened, maybe you'll know more."

While she broiled the steaks, he waited in the kitchen with her, leaning against the door frame.

"Not very elaborate, I know," she apologized. "My mother would have made you a meal to remember."

"I'll remember this one," he said gently. "Don't keep apologizing for yourself, Anna. You have nothing to be ashamed of."

"It just strikes me that your tastes are probably closer to my mother's than to mine."

"Why do you say that?"

"Well, look at the way you dress, for a start," she said with a smile. "That suit is Savile Row, isn't it?"

"Yes."

"If I chose a suit for you, if I let you wear a suit at all, it would be Italian. Maybe Versace. And not such a sober tie, either. Sky-blue, perhaps. Or pink."

"A Versace suit and a pink tie?" he repeated dryly. "I'd lose half my clients at one go. Don't you like my clothes?"

"They're beautiful. Just so formal." She felt herself blush suddenly. "You must think I'm being very rude. I was just regretting that I don't know how to make elaborate French sauces like my mother. I've always felt inadequate beside my mother," she confessed. "Mama never played power games with me, but she was just so good at everything. She decorated beautifully, she was a terrific hostess, she always knew what to wear and say and do. I just tagged along after her until I was sixteen years old, lost in awe."

"That was when your father died," he said.

"Yes."

"Do you want to talk about it?" he asked unemphatically.

She turned the steaks. "It's a familiar story in Northern Ireland," she said, trying to make it sound light.

"Belfast?"

She nodded. "Belfast. It has a horrible ring to it now, doesn't it? Depressing, grim. The funny thing is that it's such a lovely city. And

I never thought of it like that until I was sixteen. I was born there. I grew up there, and thought it a lovely place. I haven't been back in ten years."

When the steaks were ready, she carried them in, and he opened the bottle of velvety California burgundy he'd chosen. They toasted each other silently and started eating. He did not speak. She could sense that he was waiting, and after a while she laughed shortly. "Come on. Do you really want to hear about it?"

"Yes," he said seriously. "I really do."

"Okay. I'll keep it short. My father was a lawyer when he and my mother met. His name was Patrick O'Connell Kelly. The scion of a wealthy Northern Irish family. Protestants and Loyalists to the core, of course. They're a funny mixture, proud of their Irish heritage, yet fiercely pro-British. They think a united Ireland would be the end of civilization as they know it. Their culture submerged in hordes of wild barbarian Celts from south of the border, that kind of thing. You know what I mean?"

"I know what you mean." He was listening intently.

"My father's family had a lot of influence in Irish jurisprudence. My father was upright, very clever. Rather solemn. When he met my mother, he was a fine young lawyer with a brilliant career ahead of him. He was captivated by my mother's strangeness, I think. She being half-Italian, I mean, and so different from him physically. Of course, she was very beautiful, maybe a little mysterious."

"Like you."

She glanced at him quickly. "Well, very much more poised and classical than me. My father wasn't exactly a romantic man, but I think my mother loved him for his intellect and integrity. He was the kind of man who would always tell the truth. To a painful degree. He had no capacity to bend or fudge what he thought was the truth. That probably seemed admirable when they were young. And my mother was very young, just twenty-one. His family wasn't exactly delighted, my mother being a left-footer."

"Left-footer?"

"A Catholic. Being an Italian Catholic, it wasn't quite so bad. But they still didn't like him making a mixed marriage." She grimaced. "In Belfast, a mixed marriage is when a Protestant marries a Catholic. Well, they married in 1965. I was born in 1966. That tells you how old I am."

"I know how old you are."

"I know how old you are, too."

"A painful topic. We were discussing your parents' marriage."

She smiled. "It was never a particularly happy marriage, I don't think. My father probably couldn't make my mother respond to him physically, though I don't like to get into all that. All my life, I knew there was a reserve between them, a coolness. For her, the marriage may have been a disappointing ordeal. Nevertheless, they respected each other, and I never heard them quarrel or snap. Not once. They set up home in Belfast. My father bought a Georgian house in an old crescent, a really lovely old place. They restored it together.

"Ireland bewitched my mother. The Irish, especially the southern Irish, aren't unlike Italians. She had an instinctive sympathy with the Republican cause. Nothing political. She's never been a political person, though maybe being a Catholic had something to do with it. She understood them better than the Protestant Irish. It was just a kind of dream-vision of how Ireland ought to be. I don't know if you've ever been to Northern Ireland, but it can be a very sad country."

"All partitioned countries are sad," he said quietly.

"Yes. Well, my father became a public prosecutor. He started this kind of crusade against the IRA, which was getting to be more active then. The Troubles were restarting. You know about the Troubles?"

"I know what I've read." Philip nodded. He had stopped eating, and so had she. There was a painful knot in her stomach now, and she was starting to lose her appetite rapidly.

"In 1972, the government brought in Home Rule. That was when it all began again. The hatred, the violence. The marches. The bombings and killings." She shuddered. "You learn about hate in Belfast. You can see it on their faces. They go on marches, beating drums, playing the songs that send the other side crazy. Men, women, children. Everybody. The women beat on garbage-can lids. The children throw stones. The men just hang around in little knots, with their hands in their pockets, waiting. Then the police try and break it up, and suddenly bricks are flying. Then come the baton charges. Then the broken heads and the bleeding noses, and the people just lying there in the road with their faces in the gutter. The next night it's gas bombs and rubber bullets, and more bleeding faces. Then barricades in the street, and soldiers firing live rounds, and people die."

She glanced at Philip. He was staring into the candle flames. The orange flicker was reflected in his pupils. His gaze was haunted, as though he could see the cars burning in the stark streets of Belfast.

"It all dies down suddenly," she said. "Then come the burials. Huge funerals, endless lines of people dressed in black, and the helicopters droning over the city, and they paint the gable-ends of the houses with the names of the martyrs."

"Take it easy," he said gently, touching her arm.

"I'm all right."

"You're shaking."

"I always shake when I talk about it," she said. "You shouldn't have asked if you didn't want to see me shake."

"All right," he said, withdrawing his hand. "But you don't have to tell me what Belfast is like. I've been in similar places."

She nodded. "Then you know what it does to the women. My mother was frightened and depressed by the violence. She couldn't stand the hatred. She couldn't bear the tragedy that was overwhelming that beautiful province. She wanted to take me away, but my father couldn't or wouldn't leave. He was very courageous. He handed out the heaviest sentences he could, not in vengeance, but because he really believed it was the right thing to do. They say he connived at the torture of suspects, but I can't believe that. Maybe it's true. I don't want to know. He was suddenly a public figure. He spoke out against the Republicans, in court, in the press, on television, from whatever public platforms he could find. That attracted a lot of attention to him. Some people thought he was a saint. The others called him a devil. He became controversial. One day I suddenly realized he was part of it, part of the hate and the violence. I realized that people loathed him. They threw rocks through the windows of our house, spray-painted MURDERER on the door. Sometimes, coming home from school, the Catholic kids would chase me. If they caught me, they'd beat me up. They knocked two of my teeth out once." She lifted her lip and showed him her upper left canine. "That's bridgework. After that I had to be driven to school and back every day."

He held his hand out to her again, and this time she took it, her fingers knotting around his convulsively. She had spoken of this before, but never so intimately, with such feeling.

"Poor Mama got it worse, of course. They spat at her, jostled her. Once in a supermarket, a gang of Catholic women surrounded her,

screaming *whore* and *murderess*. The fact that Mama and I were Cath-
olics just made them hate us worse. And everywhere Daddy went, there
was a plainclothes policeman in attendance, or a Special Branch man
driving the car. You had to learn to live with police surveillance. The
marriage just withered and died. With the other tensions between them,
it couldn't survive all that. My mother was terribly unhappy, and looking
back, I know she felt she had made a fatally bad decision in marrying
my father. Well, it all ended. My father got into his car one morning,
and a bomb blew him up. The neighbors said they saw him look under
the car, but they'd just started using the new explosives, and the bomb
was small enough to be effectively hidden." Her nails bit into Philip's
hand in a spasm. She knew she was hurting him, but couldn't stop. "I
ran out into the street," she said in a shaking voice, "and saw the car
burning. Every window in the street was broken. I ran to the car. I
wanted to get my father out of there. But he wasn't in it. He was a
hundred yards down the street, in somebody else's garden. We left Ireland that year and came to Vail. My mother met Connie Graf and
started working for her. I went to Vail Mountain School until I grad-
uated. Then I broke free."

The silence stretched out. Philip offered no sympathy, no con-
dolence, just sat there, looking at her. Slowly, she controlled the shaking.
She pulled her fingers out of his and saw the red half-moons her nails
had cut in his knuckles. She lifted his hand to her mouth and kissed
the marks. "I've hurt you. I'm sorry."

"Don't be."

A little wine spilled onto the table as she tried to drink. She sat
up very straight, meeting his eyes. "There. That's effectively spoiled the
party."

"More or less terminally, I'd say." He smiled slightly. "You
have survived extraordinarily well, Anna."

"It's all behind me now. It just comes back now and then. I'm
not very good at dealing with violence. All this—" She gestured at the
apartment around them, meaning her mother's attack, everything. "It
makes me sick to my stomach. I can't deal with it."

"You've dealt with it magnificently," Philip said gently. "You're
dealing with it right now."

"I've lost my appetite. I'm sure you've lost yours."

He put his napkin down, and rose. "I bought you something

in New York." He opened his briefcase and took out a slim velvet case.
He held it out to her.

She rose to her feet. "What's this?"

"A gift."

She took the case hesitantly and opened the lid. In the soft
candlelight, she saw three stars glittering on black velvet. Astonished,
she lifted them out. A simple platinum chain, with three fiery white
stones at the throat. "They *are* zircons, aren't they?" she asked numbly.

"They're diamonds."

"Oh, Philip." The diamonds dripped from her outstretched fingers, their facets throwing out rosy fire. They seemed to shed, rather
than refract, the light. She felt as though she had stepped off a high
place and was falling silently, swiftly. "What on earth . . . "

He touched her lips with his fingertip to silence her and stepped
close to her, reaching behind her neck to unfasten the fake pearls. "A
beautiful woman is naked without jewels. And dark women should always wear diamonds." He fastened the diamond chain around her neck
and adjusted the lie of the stones against her throat, where the pulse
beat fast. Then he turned her to face the gilt-framed mirror that hung
over the sideboard. She stared at her own image. The three stars blazed
against the cinnamon of her skin. "Jesus," she said softly.

"Better than artificial pearls, I think."

She turned to him, still astounded and touched. "What the hell
did you do this for? Is this supposed to get me straight into bed?"

He studied her for a moment. "I had to consider carefully. If
I gave you the diamonds first, you might think I was suborning you. If
I gave you them afterwards, it might look like payment."

Anna's hands were shaking. "Boy," she said softly, "you know
how to choose your moments, don't you? You know what this is? This
is emotional karate."

His eyes glittered. "I'd give you diamonds every day if they
would make you look at me like that."

She moved to him, and he took her in his arms with a sudden
husky groan. Her lips were already parted as his mouth closed on hers.
His tongue tasted of wine, a hungry invasion. He crushed her to him
so tightly that the breath rasped in her throat.

Heat saturated her, as though a furnace door had been thrown
open, and the roaring blaze had enveloped her flesh. His desire was the

furnace, and Anna stretched to it, letting it encompass her, more potent and important than anything else in her life.

Her head was swimming. She felt herself soar in the fire, lifted on the wings of its heat.

His arms and shoulders were hard with muscle under her clinging fingers, and as she pressed her body to him, she could feel his arousal against her belly. With the languid eroticism of a panther, she rubbed herself against him and heard the rough growl of response in his throat.

He pushed her. She lost her footing and almost fell. He lowered her back onto her brand-new lemon-yellow sofa, pushing apart her knees. Her red silk dress rode up inelegantly around her thighs as they lifted. He buried his face in the triangle of red lace at her crotch with a shocking, animal hunger that set her alight. Desire flooded her veins like flame leaping along spilled gasoline.

"Wait," she whispered, wanting to restore decorum, wanting to impose her own will on this conflagration. *"Wait."*

He did not seem to hear her. There was no hesitation, no consultation. He knew exactly what he wanted to do to her, and all she could do was let him do it. He pulled the straps of her dress down, unceremoniously pushed up her red lace brassiere to expose her taut breasts. Thrusting his hands under her hips, he lifted her with ease, pulling her pants down brusquely, the lace rustling against her thighs. She arched back as he took her in his mouth again, naked this time, his tongue thrusting deep into her. His hands cupped her breasts greedily, fingers pinching her nipples, tugging, twisting.

"Philip!" she gasped, in a kind of terror. The pleasure he was releasing in her was like the rush of some wonderful, terrible drug. She had never dreamed sex could be like this. She had never dreamed it could be this violent assault, this ruthless attack, this cannibal love.

He sucked the petals of her secret flesh into his hot mouth, his tongue licking between them, flickering across the swollen bud. Her left thigh lifted to give him better access, her calf sliding across his back, pulling him in.

God, God, he was devouring her alive. Or was it a kind of worship? Her face was burning. She lifted one arm to cover her face, as if to hide her abandon from invisible watchers.

Biting, sucking, licking, he was driving her to an inevitable climax. There were no more thoughts of pain or grief, no thoughts of anything beyond the flesh. Only Philip mattered. She called out his name, her voice husky, lifting to a cry. Tension drained out of her in a long shudder of ecstasy. Her orgasm rippled up from the depths of a dark sea, exploding around her.

She slid off the sofa onto the floor beside him.

"Philip . . ."

She took him in her arms, kissing his lips with fierce tenderness, with adoration. She could taste her own salt on his lips, could smell her own scent on his face. She felt there could be no going back, not ever again.

She rose unsteadily, taking his hand, pulling him to his feet.

"Come," she commanded. She led him to her bedroom.

She lay back on the bed, her hair spread like a pool of ink, her dress a scarlet flag around her middle, her breasts and loins naked. One of her thighs was lifted to expose the dark triangle of hair. She left it like that, wanting her abandon to excite him.

His eyes never left her as he undressed. His body was beautiful, dark-skinned like her own, but massively strong, with sinews that rippled and tightened as he moved. He was beautifully made, muscles developed and hardened by exercise, black hair at his chest, armpits, and loins.

Anna knew she would never forget this moment. Watching him take off his clothes, watching the way he moved, she knew she would never know a man like this in her life again.

He laid his clothes on the chair and turned to her, naked and unashamed. His sex thrust up out of his loins in a hot curve.

He came to her, his mouth serious, his eyes smiling. She reached for him urgently. His muscles were hot and tight under her palms, his whole body taut with anticipation.

She reached to his loins and took him in her hand, squeezing the thick column of rigid flesh, her other hand cupping the heavy weight of his balls, holding all his manhood in her two hands, possessing him. She saw his face change. He arched back with pleasure, muscles swelling. "When you touch me like that I could die," he whispered roughly. His eyes were dark slits, his mouth half-open so she could see the gleam of his teeth.

He kissed her as he had done in the car, his warm lips brushing her eyelids, her throat, the arching wings of her collarbones, the scented valley between her breasts where she had tried to wipe off the Kenzo. She caught the faint sweet smell of the perfume now, mingling with the hot scents of their own bodies.

She had wanted to have him like this for so long, to possess the beautiful nudity of his body. He was exactly as she had known he would be, infinitely beautiful, infinitely male. She ran her palms over the powerful muscles of his deep chest, feeling his nipples tight as bronze under her touch.

She pressed her face against Philip's as his hands caressed her breasts, teasing the swollen nipples back into erection, sliding down her belly to her loins, where she was already wet and tender.

His caress was expert, exquisite. There was nothing tentative, nothing exploratory. His fingers understood everything about her, knew her every secret wish, gratified it as soon as it was formed.

"You're so lovely," he said huskily, staring at her face, her body. "Lovely as a goddess."

She moved to him, pulling him into her mouth. He was big and hard and deeply exciting. She had already learned from him. Until now, oral sex had been a delicate thing for her, of flickering tongues and caressing lips. Now she used her mouth as he had done, biting, sucking.

His response was electrifying. She heard him gasp her name as she had gasped his a few minutes earlier. She could taste the slippery salt emission of extreme male arousal on her palate, and it thrilled her.

She lifted her head to look into his face. "I wanted you the moment I saw you," she said. She was panting. "I've never wanted a man—the way—I want you."

He laughed huskily, lifting his hips so his cock touched her velvety lips again. "I've never wanted a woman the way I want you. You are exquisite."

"And you are magnificent."

He knotted his fingers in her dark hair and drew her face to his, his mouth hungry for hers. He kissed her with that extraordinary mixture of brutality and tenderness, pulling her body against his, so that she fitted within him, wrapped in the strength and power of his enfolding embrace.

He was murmuring to her softly now, gently. She could barely understand the words, but she knew what they meant, the painful pleasure he was feeling, the twofold urge to protect and dominate. It began again, gentler than before; drops of honey that fell on hot skin, touches, kisses, caresses. A slow and lingering discovery of one another's bodies, a pressing together of secret, tender places.

She felt his finger slide into her, entering the secret place of her body, where she was wet and swollen and tight. He stroked her delicately inside, finding the tenderest places, finding the sudden wild apex of desire, where the nerves were stretched to their tightest.

"Beautiful Anna," he whispered. "Beautiful, beautiful Anna . . ."

She felt the muscles of her stomach jump and quiver uncontrollably. Her lower body seemed to be melting, her thighs and loins becoming hot syrup that had no form, no shape, only an unbearable pleasure.

He touched his forehead to hers, eyes staring into hers, as though drinking in her pleasure, his breath warm on her lips.

"I love you," she said.

Then his fingers touched a place inside her that turned the world inside out, upside down. She could endure it no longer.

"Now," she said in hoarse command.

She rolled onto her back, spreading her legs in an unmistakable invitation. He mounted her, his belly hot against hers. He entered her with possessive force, making her arch and cry out. His face was intent, his eyes staring deep into hers.

"You knew this would happen," she said. "Right from the start."

"No. Only today, when I saw the diamonds in New York."

He moved in her with increasing urgency, flooding her with a swelling pleasure that grew and spread, until she was galloping across a vast red plain on a black stallion, the world become speed and heat and excitement.

She began to float, felt her orgasm begin again, deeper than before, more powerful. She had a dizzy moment of fear that it would come too soon, that she would not synchronize with him; but as she arched helplessly in the first throes of climax, she felt her inner muscles clench around him with extraordinary power, gripping him within her body so tightly that he stopped moving at once.

Then, deep inside her body, at the entrance of her womb, she felt the scalding flood of his seed. She heard his voice call her name, felt his arms crush her, his body convulsing savagely.

For a dislocated moment time ceased. The world no longer

turned. The planets were stilled for them. There was no sound, no movement, no sensation, just the knowledge of unity.

Slowly, the drugged ecstasy of gratification filled her veins, relaxing every inch of her, setting the universe in motion again. This time there were no tears. She had shed her tears. This time there was only wonder, fulfillment, and joy.

She was whispering his name long afterward, as he drew the covers over their naked bodies and took her in his arms. She sank into him, into the dark harlequin antics of her first dreams.

She Dragged Herself from a profound sleep, already aware that she was alone in the bed. She groped for her watch and saw with dismay that it was almost eleven A.M.

Philip had slipped from her arms, dressed and left the apartment without waking her, probably hours ago. Bereft, she got up, pulled on her dressing gown, and hunted for traces of him.

There was the briefest of notes on the kitchen table:

Have to go back to New York today. Will call. Philip.

"Damn," she whispered, feeling like crying. Was that all he'd found to say? The first day of their affair, and already things had slipped out of her control.

She touched the note with her fingertips. Well, she wondered acidly, what had she expected? A single perfect rose? She had wanted him to make love to her, and he had obliged. All that and heaven, too?

There was a vivid, throbbing tenderness in her loins, as though he were still there, inside her. At the memory of last night, her inner muscles spasmed again, the beginnings of another orgasm. She crouched quickly, hugging herself in a kind of panic, not wanting it to happen. The feeling swelled, spread through her body. She gasped, her skin suddenly flushed all over, astounded at the tricks her own body was playing on her. The memory of his face, the feel of his body, rose in her mind with hallucinogenic intensity.

When it had faded, she leaned weakly against the wall, arms wrapped around her own slim shoulders. What in God's name had happened to her?

Was this just sex? Was it something else?

There had been nothing like last night. Not ever. Sex had been wonderful before, gentle sex, sex on pot, illicit sex in stolen moments. But not like Philip. Not like that waterfall of fire.

Her thoughts about him came into sharp relief while she breakfasted on a pear and a chunk of cheese. She remembered that moment up in the mountains, recalled the fierce resolution in Philip's eyes, that cold loneliness. It was at that moment that she had realized just how stupid it would be to allow herself to become infatuated with him. He was not a man who needed women the way women would need him. Anna knew that instinctively. On a physical level, the level of dazzling entertainments, sublime sex, lavish gifts, he would be an incomparable lover. But no relationship would descend to any deeper level than that. Emotionally, he would give little of himself, expect less in return.

He would not want impediments. He would desire no emotional baggage that might hold him up on the road to wherever it was he was going so determinedly. He would take his pleasure, and expect his women to take theirs in return, with no possibility of permanent commitment on either side.

She had wondered what it would feel like to have his intensity turned on her, and now she wondered whether she could handle it. A too-fast car, a too-powerful drug, too-strong seas; she was already embarked upon something that could no longer be stopped and returned to its starting place.

Maybe he wouldn't give her the chance to handle. Maybe he had already taken what he wanted and had left at first light, satisfied. With no intention of returning.

That thought hurt enough to make her want to throw up her meager breakfast.

She washed the plates, then called the hospital in Newcastle-upon-Tyne where Evelyn had undergone surgery. The Northern accent that answered was cool and sweet.

"Ward sister, can I help you?"

"It's Anna Kelly, calling from the United States. It's about my grandmother, Evelyn Godbold. Can you tell me how the operation went?"

"Mr. Weir, the surgeon, is on the ward right now. I'm going to see if I can pass you on to him. He'll be able to explain better than I can. Please hold the line."

A Short While later, a man's voice came on the line. "Miss Kelly? I'm Clayton Weir. I operated on your grandmother on Tuesday. I'm afraid the operation didn't go as well as expected."

Anna's fingers tightened around the receiver. "Why not?"

"We performed an exploratory and decided not to remove any tissue."

A sick foreknowledge settled on Anna. "You mean the cancer had spread too far to be operable?"

"You know that your grandmother has suffered from cancer for some years. We've been able to control the tumors with surgery, radiation, and drugs up until now. It hasn't been pleasant for your grandmother, but it has almost certainly prolonged her life. On Tuesday, I was prepared to remove diseased parts of the bowel, but I am sorry to say the cancer had spread far too widely for that to be feasible. The liver is involved. There was no point in continuing with the operation."

Anna felt sick. "Isn't there anything that can be done?" she asked.

"In theory, we could proceed with more radiotherapy, more drugs. However, we've discussed this with your grandmother, and she is very firm that, in her words, enough is enough. We are letting her go home as soon as we can, to live out as much of her life as possible in a normal way."

She'd known in her heart that this was what she would hear. All she could ask was, "How long?"

"Very hard to say. The condition is invariably fatal."

"Will she be in pain?"

"We'll control it, of course. She has a private nurse at home, who will administer morphine when necessary. In the terminal stages, we will arrange for her to be readmitted here, or perhaps to a hospice."

Anna was silent for a while, but there was nothing she could say. "Thank you for being so frank. Can I speak to her?"

"She's sleeping right now. Perhaps later."

"Then could you give her a message for me? She knows that my mother is in a coma, and she's very upset about it. Please could you tell her there have been definite signs of improvement?"

"Of course."

"Tell her everyone here is very hopeful about my mother."

"I will."

"And give her my love."

Sickness and death, she thought, replacing the receiver. The shadow images of vitality and life. While she was in the full flood of life, head over heels in love, others were in the shadows.

She'd had no idea Evelyn was so very sick. The old lady had hidden it, even from Kate, and now Kate might never know. Anna remembered the embroidered cushions at Evelyn's Northumbrian manor house. They carried mottoes like *Never Complain, Never Explain,* and *Shun Advice at Any Price.* Evelyn had embroidered those taut aphorisms herself and had lived her life by them.

That was where Kate had learned her own self-sufficiency, her own quiet courage. Anna thought of those eloquent silences between her mother and Evelyn, that wordless communication she had never been able to understand. She could not bear the thought of Evelyn dying all alone while Kate lay in a coma. Her eyes were full of stinging tears for Evelyn Godbold and Catherine Kelly.

She gathered herself to go to Carr Memorial.

Her Mother Had already been moved from the intensive care unit to her new room, two floors down. A friendly nurse showed her the way, explaining that her mother was now in a special unit for coma patients.

Anna's first sight of the room was a severe jolt.

The bed was a huge, motorized contraption. The steel frame supported a mesh on which her mother lay. It revolved slowly, constantly, clicking a degree at a time. Both the movement and the netting were designed to reduce pressure sores, the nurse explained. Her mother lay with limbs outstretched, wearing a clinical green hospital gown. Several wires and tubes ran from her body into machines around her. A bank of monitors suspended from the ceiling over the bed showed quivering green lines or pulsing graphs.

Anna tried to hide her shock from the nurse, thanking her. The woman left her there, and she walked slowly round the bed. At first sight, the motorized bed was inhuman and frightening. It seemed one more step in the medical process that was steadily dehumanizing her mother. But the equipment was obviously brilliantly designed for patients like her mother. There was a window, and despite the machinery, the room was a more cheerful place than the overwrought darkness of intensive care.

There was a small notice on the wall, next to the oxygen tank, a warning not to discuss the patient's condition within the room, in case the patient was aware of what was being said. That cheered her more than anything.

They had brought the ghetto-blaster down, and she put one of the tapes in, the Brahms piano concerto. She sat beside her mother and took the limp hand in her own. "We've found out about Joseph Krasnowsky. He was a newspaperman, just like me! I just don't know why he was so important to you. The pieces of the jigsaw are coming together. I'm going to come in every day and tell you how we're getting on. That will give you something to live for, won't it? There are things to do, Mama. Things to find out. You can't abandon it. You've come so far. It can't end here. You must wake up, you *must*."

She thought of André Levêque's words. *A lost child who needs to be led out of the darkness, back into the light.*

"There's something else. Philip and I are lovers," she said. "Look."

She took the diamonds from her throat and touched them to her mother's cheek. In the clear light, the stones blazed. She was no expert, but she didn't have to be an expert to know that the diamonds were pure, perfectly cut, and very expensive.

"Diamonds, Mama. It happened. I knew it would. Oh, Mama . . . " She sighed, fastening the necklace round her own throat again. "I want him so much. I want him to be my lover forever." She bit her lip hard enough to hurt herself. "Isn't that the most selfish thing you ever heard? You lie here, and I fall in love. But I can't help it. It's not that I don't care about you, Mama. But I've never been in love before. I love him."

She watched the motionless face for a while, listening to the slow, steady breathing, the measured click of the revolving bed. The dressing had come off now, revealing the neat stitching where the surgeon's drill had gone in. The dark hair was starting to grow back in slowly.

Her throat was suddenly choked. She got up and went to the window, staring out. "It's hard to bear, Mama," she said tightly. The mountains were dim and blue over the rooftops. She turned back to the huge contraption. "Life's a bitch. You in here, Evelyn dying all alone in England. And I'm in love with the most wonderful man I've ever known. And I'm so happy, so sad, so confused." She shook her tears away angrily. "It's horrible. It shouldn't have happened like this."

The door opened, and Ram Singh came in, his face smooth and bland as a crème caramel. "They told me you were here. What do you think of the unit?"

"Very impressive," she acknowledged, biting down her feelings.

"How does she seem to you today?"

"A little better," Anna said defiantly.

He smiled. "Good. The music is an excellent idea, by the way. One of my favorite piano pieces."

"Hers, too."

"Did the nurse explain how all this works? These sensors attached to her chest will sound an alarm if there are any respiratory irregularities. Her blood is monitored automatically. Any irregular levels are compensated for at once. High-technology monitoring."

"Have you come to try and talk me into transferring her again?" Anna challenged.

"No. For the time being, I'm happy for her to stay here." He checked her mother's eyes with his light. "There was never any attempt to put pressure on you, you know," he said gently.

"Wasn't there?"

He carefully checked the clipboard of graphs and records that hung beside the bed; demonstrating, she thought grimly, his dedication to the patient. When he had finished, he turned to her with a pleasant expression. "Those are beautiful diamonds you are wearing."

"They were a gift."

"From a good giver. They are rare stones." He lifted his eyes from the stones to her face. "When I came in, I heard you talking to your mother."

"Yes."

"You think she is somewhere in there, don't you? You think she can hear you, even though her brain, to all intents and purposes, has stopped working?"

"Yes, I do." She met his eyes. "Tell me, Dr. Ram Singh, are you interested in the concept of mind-brain dualism?"

"In an abstract way," he replied cautiously. "Why?"

"I've been doing a lot of reading on coma patients. It led me to the subject. It's a fascinating philosophical area. Is the mind a separate thing from the electrochemical activity of the brain? Does it cease to exist forever when the brain stops working? Or is it something apart from those endlessly firing neurons, a soul, someone in charge, a ghost in the machine?"

"I find that kind of question rather abstruse," Ram Singh said. "I prefer to restrict myself to the purely medical questions of correct treatment."

"And yet it's the most fascinating question of all. If your brain is just a machine with no ghost in it, then there really is no you, Dr. Ram Singh. No self, no soul, no personality. Nothing more than nerve endings."

"As I said, it strikes me as abstruse. I have no opinions."

"But I do," she said quietly. "I have very definite opinions. I believe in the soul. I believe my mother's soul is still in her body. I believe that is infinitely more important than what has happened to the machinery of her body."

She had spoken quietly, but with great force. He stared at her for a moment, then smiled. "You fill me with respect, Miss Kelly." He reached out for the door handle.

The door swished shut behind him. Anna went slowly back toward the bed. She stood there, arms folded, biting her lower lip. "He thinks you're just a broken machine. He wants to send you to the human junkyard to die peacefully." She touched her mother's brow. "But you ain't gonna die, not peacefully, not any other way."

In The Afternoon, the locksmiths arrived from Denver.

There were two of them, pleasant-faced men in green overalls, carrying businesslike tool kits. She led them into her mother's bedroom. They studied the safe, conferring in professional shorthand for a while. Then they pulled back the carpet under the safe, spreading a canvas cloth on the floor in its place. One started unscrewing the oil painting from its hinges while the other unpacked an array of formidable-looking electric drills.

She'd had visions of a furtive little man with a stethoscope, deftly twirling the combination wheel. "Can't you work out the combination?"

The senior of the two locksmiths was a balding man with a grizzled beard. He smiled and shook his head. "If we could do that, we'd be on the other side of the business. This is a good safe. We're going to have to drill the lock out."

"Is that going to be difficult?"

"Just a little noisy. The steel is tempered, and probably an inch thick around the lock. Don't worry about the safe. When we've finished, we'll put in another lock and combination. It'll be better than new."

They made careful marks on the smooth olive-green enamel of the safe, then donned goggles, masks, and ear protectors. She backed out hastily before they started drilling, shutting the door.

The noise was dreadful, a grinding shriek horribly reminiscent of the dentist's. It made the whole apartment vibrate, even the parquet under her feet. She retreated to the kitchen with some of her mother's paperwork, hoping to hell they wouldn't be long about it.

She barely heard the telephone ring over the hellish symphony. She picked it up, blocking her free ear with her palm. "Anna Kelly— can you shout, please?"

She had no difficulty in hearing the rasping voice. "Drew McKenzie."

"Oh, Mr. McKenzie! Hello."

"Got a bit of news for you about André Levêque."

"Yes?" she said coolly.

"He came back to Miami last week. He's been arrested. The preliminary charge is some visa violation—he entered the country ille- gally—but the cops are preparing a list of charges as long as your arm."

"I see," she said, feeling an odd chill trickle down her spine. So Levêque was going to pay, after all.

"They might want to speak to you."

"I see," she said again. She pressed her palm to her ear to try and blot out the screaming counterpoint of the two drills. "What did he come back for?"

"To pick up some loot he'd hidden in Palm Beach, apparently. He was stupid enough to come in person and use a faked passport." McKenzie sighed heavily. "That's the end of the story, kid. I've been informed the whole case is sub judice from now on."

"I'm sorry, Mr. McKenzie," she said apologetically.

"You got your man, Anna. How does it feel?"

"Not too good," she said unhappily.

"Yeah? How so?"

"Well . . . I guess I feel responsible."

"Sure you're responsible. Maybe you'll get a medal. How's your mother?"

If anything made it clear McKenzie's call was a peace offering, that was it. "Much the same," she replied.

"When can we expect to see you back at work?"

"Maybe not for months, Mr. McKenzie. She's not making any progress. I'm sorry."

"Yeah." She could hear him chewing on his cigar. "Well, don't worry about your job, know what I mean? There's always a place for you here."

He hung up without letting her reply.

By The Time the drilling finally came to an end, she had a pounding headache behind her eyes. The senior man came to call her.

"It's open, ma'am."

He led her to the bedroom, where the green door now hung ajar. There were several holes around the lock, and a pile of steel filings on the floor, which the other man was now carefully sucking into a small vacuum cleaner. She could see packages and boxes in the safe.

"That's wonderful," she said in delight. For some reason, she'd had a suppressed fear they would find the safe empty.

"We'll take the lock back to the workshop with us," the bearded man said. "Tracking down one to match will probably take a week or so." He gestured at the safe. "You might want to put this stuff in the bank in the meantime."

She nodded. "You're right."

"Get a security firm to come pick it up," he advised. "Don't carry it around. You never know these days."

She waited, concealing her impatience while they cleared up and left. When they had finally gone, she opened the safe fully and unpacked the contents onto her mother's bed.

There were several items. She sorted through the envelopes first. Stock certificates and other financial documents, a spare set of keys for the apartment and the car, the deeds to the apartment, the original copies of all the insurance policies, her mother's birth and marriage certificates, her British and Italian passports. None of it was what Anna was looking for.

There were a dozen velvet boxes. She prized them open, disclosing a string of pearls, emerald earrings to match the ring, a diamond clip, other valuable things. She'd listed some of these jewels as missing to Jorgensen, and now she would have to call him and tell him they were here, after all. Her mother had also collected a lot of jewelry Anna hadn't known about or had long forgotten.

And then, in a padded envelope, she found a small book with black leather covers, the size of a Catholic missal. She opened the first page and read the handwritten inscription:

Diario di Candida Cipriani

1944

Nell' quinto anno della Guerra Mondiale

She stared at the words, feeling ice-cold gooseflesh steal over her skin. *The diary of Candida Cipriani, 1944, in the fifth year of the World War.*

When she had recovered her composure a little, she sat in the chair and started to leaf through the diary.

It was so small and light. So frail, to hold so many secrets. The pages were thin and fragile, densely covered with writing. The ink was brown with age, the script small and neat. She was moved to see how similar Candida's writing had been to her mother's, though they had never known one another. Kate would have seen that, too.

Without quite knowing why, Anna lifted the diary to her lips and kissed it. It smelled musty, of time long past. Not of anything human. My grandmother, she thought with a wave of sadness. She did not even possess a photograph of Candida Cipriani. She doubted whether one existed.

1944. Candida must have been around eighteen when she'd begun this diary, much younger than Anna herself was now.

A year and a half after writing that oddly impressive little commencement, she had died in childbirth. Anna could only imagine how her mother must have felt, reading those words. She herself was filled with emotion.

Anna looked through the diary with infinite care. It was almost full; the entries broke off a few pages before the end. There was no postscript. It was tragically symbolic of the young life that had ended so abruptly.

Somehow, they were all tied together in a fatal knot. Candida Cipriani, who had died in 1945, bringing her child to life. Evelyn, dying of cancer in Northumberland. Her mother, stretched out on a steel rack, a machine without a ghost.

Two generations of women, all of whose lives had closed with tragedy.

And she herself, the third of the generations, hampered by ignorance and youth, left to pick up the fragmented pieces.

She began reading, struggling to decipher the faded script. She spoke only a few words of Italian and could make out only what seemed to be references to a pig that was being fattened for slaughter. There were other, more intelligent references to the progress of the war, but her Italian was not up to deciphering them properly. She would have to take the diary to a translator and get it rendered into English.

She picked up the telephone and dialed Philip's office number in New York. The secretary who answered was reluctant to put her through to the lord and master, but Anna pleaded.

She heard a series of clicks, then Philip came on the line.

"Anna?"

"Philip, it's me."

"Sorry I had to leave you like that." He had lowered his voice, and she guessed he was with people.

"When are you coming back?" she asked.

"I can't make it until Friday."

"That's three *days* away!"

"I know. I'm sorry. Is everything all right?"

"I had the locksmiths here this afternoon. They opened the safe."

"Yes?"

"I found it, Philip. I found my grandmother's diary."

Anna Stood At her mother's bedside.

She had just returned from Denver, where she had been to the judge's chambers with Nate Morgan. It had been a brief and uncomplicated ceremony that had effectively put her in control of her mother's life. She had left the judge's chambers close to tears. It had been a strange moment, filled with sadness and a sense of burden.

She had also taken the diary to a firm of professional translators. It was not a very long document, and they had promised to turn it into plain English in two days. Then perhaps she would have some insights into her mother's mysteries.

She watched the still face. Ram Singh had asked her to consider the possibility that her mother's life might already be over. She'd answered him with a fine-sounding argument about mind-brain dualism. But if the woman who lay there had a soul, where was it now? Had it already moved to some higher plane? Or was her spirit trapped in there, imprisoned in a broken machine that she, out of misplaced compassion, would not allow to run down?

If I was the most primitive savage in the remotest jungle, Anna thought wryly, I'd know the answers to those questions. But I'm a highly educated, enlightened twentieth-century woman, and so I know precisely fuck-all. All I know is that I am in love with a man I do not understand, and that without him I would be lost.

Her mother's beauty had already started to fade. There were gaunt hollows under her cheekbones and at her temples. Anna could almost see the flesh melting away, the stark shape of the skull showing through. It broke her heart.

"Jesus, Mama," she said fiercely, "you can't just lie there and die! You must start waking up! *You must!*" Anger and tears choked any further words.

At first she thought one of the machines had made the noise. Then it came again. She looked closely at her mother, her scalp prickling, the hairs on her arms standing on end. It came again, on the outbreath, the faintest of sighs.

Transfixed, she listened to it happen three more times. Then it stopped, and the breathing became a whisper again.

"Mama?" she said, hearing her own voice shake.

Then her mother's lips moved, and a whisper emerged.

Her heart racing, Anna tore open the door and flew out into the corridor. She could not wait for the elevator. She took the stairs three at a time, almost colliding with medical staff coming the other way. She was panting by the time she got to the door of Ram Singh's room. She thrust it open without knocking, mouth open to speak.

Ram Singh was talking to an elderly couple seated across his desk. The wife was crying quietly into a handkerchief. All three turned to look at her.

"Sorry," she gasped. "Sorry. Forgive me."

She backed out, closed the door, and sagged against the wall, trying to get her breath back. She had not imagined the whisper. She had heard it. It had happened.

Ram Singh emerged, ushering the elderly couple to the elevator. The old woman's shoulders were bowed in defeat, the old man was upright with dignity. When they had gone, Ram Singh walked back to her, a frown on his bland face.

"I apologize unreservedly," she said hastily. "That was unforgivable of me. I was just so excited. I was with my mother just now, and she made a noise!"

He looked at her consideringly. For a moment she thought he was going to rebuke her, but all he said was, "Let's go and see her."

He checked all the monitors and examined Kate in detail, then stood at the bedside, arms folded, while she explained all over again.

"It was as she breathed out, like a sigh or a moan. Very quiet, but it was definitely there. She did it five or six times and then whispered something."

"Did she move her lips?" he asked.

"Yes!"

"But did she actually speak words? Did she *say* something? Not just a moan?"

"Yes!"

"What did she say?"

"I couldn't hear." She looked at him pleadingly. "It means she's waking up—doesn't it? *Doesn't it?*"

"She may make noises from time to time," he said in his gentle way. "She may groan or sigh. Even open her eyes and move her body. Curl up into the fetal position, or extend one of her limbs. She breathes, her heart beats, her body metabolizes glucose. The machinery moves. It doesn't mean she's waking up."

"Oh, *shit*." She turned away, her eyes flooding with tears. "I *knew* you'd say that."

"I'll run all the tests again this afternoon," he said. "I'll let you know the results as soon as we have them."

She nodded silently.

"I admire you," he said. "I admire your attitude. I do not want to take your hope away from you. But hope is sometimes more painful than acceptance."

"That's what Philip said."

"I'm sorry?"

"It doesn't matter."

"Miss Kelly, you will have to—"

He stopped. There was an odd expression on his face.

"What is it?" she asked.

And then they both heard it. The whisper of breath from the woman on the bed. Anna ran to her mother and crouched over her. The lids were flickering, the mouth had opened slackly.

As Anna stared at her mother's face, transfixed, the lids lifted, and her mother's eyes were looking into her own.

The dry lips moved. There was just a sigh of breath, but Anna knew what her mother's lips were saying.

They were saying, "Anna."

Anna sat in her mother's apartment, the English translation of the diary open in her lap, staring into space.

It had happened. The miracle she was waiting for.

Ram Singh had moved her mother to yet another unit, for special observation this time, and had called in a top neurologist to assess the treatment. The little Indian doctor told her not to get her hopes up too high.

But she knew her mother was going to recover now. Those eyes had opened and had recognized her. Her mother had spoken her name. She was going to be all right. She believed it in a way she had never been able to believe it before that tiny whisper.

The telephone started ringing, jolting her out of her reverie. She lifted the receiver.

"Miz Kelly?"

"Yes?" she replied, not recognizing the harsh male voice.

"This is Bob Christy of the Vail Police Department."

"Yes, Mr. Christy?"

"I'm calling from Mr. Campbell Brinkman's home in Gypsum. There's been an accident. I wonder if you could come on over?"

Her heart sank. "What kind of accident?"

"A shooting accident, ma'am."

She gasped. "Is Campbell okay?"

"He's a little shaken up, ma'am. Looks like he tried to do something silly. It didn't work out, which was just as well, if you take my meaning."

"You mean he tried to kill himself?" she gasped.

"I'd rather not comment on that, ma'am."

"But I don't understand!"

"Put it this way. Nobody got hurt, but we're all a little worried."

"Can I speak to him?"

"The doctor gave him a shot, and he's a little drowsy. I don't want to disturb him for a while. See, we're up here with him and the fact is, we don't like the idea of leaving him alone in a house full of guns. We asked him if there was anyone who could come sit with him a spell, and he gave us your name."

She winced. "Look, maybe it would be better if you could bring him down to Vail, Officer."

"No, ma'am. He says he won't budge from this house. We don't want to have to use force."

"I know he has a psychiatrist in Denver. I could try and get her number for you."

"Yeah?" the policeman said, sounding unenthusiastic. "That could take hours, even if she's prepared to come."

"I'm not sure what I can do," she said helplessly, ashamed of not sounding more enthusiastic, but definitely not relishing the thought of going up to Gypsum to face a suicidal Campbell Brinkman in a house full of guns.

"He sure would like to talk to you, ma'am. If you could just set him at his ease, so to speak, I'm sure he'll consent to come down to Vail with us. Then maybe we can get him back to his folks in Denver."

A sudden pang of guilt struck her. Her mother had shown the first signs of recovery today, and it hadn't even occurred to her to call

Campbell with the good news. If she had done so, she might have prevented Campbell from trying to take his own life.

"Okay, I'll come, Officer. I'll leave right away." She checked her watch. "I'll be there at around four. Could you give Campbell a message from me in the meantime? Tell him I'm bringing him some good news about my mother. Some *very* good news."

"I'm real glad to hear that. I'll pass it on. And ma'am?"

"Yes?"

"We'd appreciate it if you didn't mention to anyone where you're going, or why. It's a delicate subject, and there's no need to get the gossip going, okay?"

"I understand."

She hung up and went to find her jacket and boots. It was nice, she thought wryly, to feel wanted.

I-70 Heading West had been cleared by machines that had left huge, dirty banks of snow piled up on either side of the highway. But the weather was bad. Snow was drifting down in sizable flakes, and the heavy sky above looked as though it held plenty more.

She was not enjoying either the drive or the prospect of what lay at the end of it. Campbell was a difficult enough man in the best of times. Suicidal, probably drunk, probably determined to make some kind of dramatic display, he was going to be very difficult to handle. Too big a job for her. She'd try and lift his spirits with the news of her mother's first signs of recovery; then, with the help of the police, she'd try and talk him into heading back to Denver, to his family, and most important of all, to his shrink. She just hoped he'd have his head together enough to listen to her and to believe that her mother was starting to recover.

She passed through Wolcott at three-forty-five, aware that the heavy clouds were making the short winter's day even shorter. There were ten miles to the Gypsum interchange, but the going was slow. If conditions didn't improve, she would not be at Gypsum much before dark.

She drove with great care, knowing how treacherous the road could be, even when it looked clear. There was always the chance of black ice, invisible but deadly.

The interstate was far from crowded going in this direction; cars were few and far between, most traveling at well below the legal limit.

Anna had gained a lot of respect for the Saab. It was powerful and responded to her wishes smoothly. The ride was comfortable. She touched the controls of the cassette player, still not sure how it worked. Eventually she succeeded, and the vibrant strains of a Mozart string quartet filled the car. Difficult music, but music with a profound certainty. It reminded her of her mother.

The mountains towered around her, stark and white above the tree line. This, to her, was the heart of Colorado, containing some of the most beautiful passages of landscape in the whole of America. It was grim in the winter, but it was easy to understand the impulse that had led Campbell to want to build a retreat up here. She wondered whether he had ever really looked at the scenery—or whether it had always just been a backdrop for his lifestyle, a setting for his parties. A rich man's playground.

She sighed with relief when she reached the Gypsum interchange at four-thirty, and left the interstate to start the climb up to the tiny town. Snow was still falling, and as the temperature rapidly dropped, the road was starting to be covered by it. It was getting more difficult, with gathering darkness, to find her way, and she felt a deep unease about the road back. It looked as though she would be spending the night with Campbell Brinkman after all.

Not a welcoming prospect.

The turn-off to the Brinkman property was marked only by a small wooden sign marked "Running Elk," the name Campbell had given to the ranch. She almost missed it, and braking too hard, felt the Saab slither on the icy road. It stopped without doing any damage. She backed up, gnawing her lip, peering anxiously over her shoulder. Despite her confidence in the car, she was no expert at snow driving.

There were the rutted tracks of several vehicles along the private road to Running Elk ranch. The road cut in a long, straight line through the cottonwoods that flourished in the alkaline soil of the area. In summer, the cottonwoods were a glory of flickering silver as the breezes twisted the leaves to show the white undersides. When the female catkins were ripe, they exploded into little puffs of silky "cotton." Now they were stark and bare as witches' brooms. Campbell's land was almost pure gypsum in places, and Anna could see how the chemical in the soil had contorted the trunks and branches of the cottonwoods, making weird patterns against the stark glare of the snow.

She felt the roar, rather than heard it, and looked ahead, registering, too fast to feel emotion, that something was rushing toward her from the left.

There was a track that cut into the road at right angles. A dark-colored vehicle was charging along it on a collision course with the Saab. Its steel-shod prow was aimed directly at her door.

"Jesus!"

She stamped on her own brake pedal fiercely, the emotions rushing in: terror, rage at the unknown driver's recklessness, outrage against the unjustness of it.

Her harsh braking made the Saab fishtail wildly in the snow, but did not slow down its onward progress. She locked her elbows, bracing herself on the steering wheel, the ABS system vibrating through the drum-hard brake pedal under her foot. She knew the other car was going to hit her, hard.

The steel crash-bars of the other vehicle slammed into the Saab immediately in front of her door. Violent shock and noise erupted around her. The windshield exploded into a brilliant waterfall, and her body was catapulted sideways. She felt the seat belt bite into her shoulder and abdomen, jerking her back. A huge white mushroom exploded in her face, smothering her, blinding her. Then, immediately, it began to deflate.

The Saab slithered sideways a long way, propelled by the violent impact. Then it hit something and stopped. There was silence and stasis. I survived, she thought incredulously. I am alive.

She fought her way clear of the collapsing airbag and the seat belt.

The door was jammed, but she managed to climb out of the passenger side. She was terribly shaken. Her hair was full of broken glass, and she felt bruised all over. She floundered numbly in the snow, registering that the Saab had slid into a clump of cottonwoods. The front half of the Saab was horribly mangled by the impact. The steel bars on the front of the other vehicle, a Nissan Pathfinder, were designed to fend off elk or deer on the road. They had smashed into the Saab like great hammers, lethal in effect. The hood was sticking straight up in the air, the entrails of the engine exposed and hissing violently.

A couple of feet farther back, and her own body would have been smashed to a pulp by those steel tusks. The image was horrific.

She turned. The Nissan had careered onward, ending up way off the track. She watched numbly as the driver got out of his cab, already yelling at her in anger.

"It was your fault," she shouted back shakily. "You rammed me! You could have killed me!"

Her words were lost in a mounting roar as the radiator of the Saab suddenly gouted a fountain of boiling greenish water, making her duck and cover her face. She staggered away, wiping off the droplets that were burning fiercely on her skin.

"Jesus," she gasped, wondering if her skin had been scalded.

When she looked up, the other driver was coming toward her, taking high steps through the deep snow. He was a powerful-looking man in his twenties, wearing dark clothes and a red cap with flapping earmuffs.

He was not coming to help her.

She registered, with disbelief, the tire iron in his hands. He lifted it sideways like a baseball bat as he reached her, and swung it violently at Anna.

She lifted her arm instinctively to ward off the blow. It would have broken her arm like a matchstick had she not slipped in the snow at the same time. The steel bar struck her shoulder with shocking force, jarring her whole body, flipping her forward.

"Hey!" she screamed in pain and terror. "It wasn't my *fault*!"

But even as she uttered the words, she knew they were meaningless. In a lightning burst of understanding, she knew this was no accident.

The iron buzzed through the air again, and she threw herself forward, her whole body flinching against the crushing impact. This time the blow was glancing, raking her thigh instead of landing solidly. But the steel claw at the tip of the iron ripped open her pants, and blood spurted. She saw the red dots sprinkle the snow and felt disbelief.

The attacker's cap had fallen off with the blow. She saw the gaunt face, scarred with acne, contorted with hatred, the shaven skull.

She knew who he was. The skinhead whose face she had seen in the blue glare of the streetlight.

He was wading forward through the snow, hefting the tire iron over his shoulder, narrowed eyes measuring the distance he needed to strike. His breath hissed through his teeth, white saliva on his lips.

Knowing she was looking at her own death, she twisted and ran.

Instinctively, she was heading back to the main road. Without thinking about it, she knew there would be no police up in the big house among the cottonwoods. Nor would Campbell Brinkman be there.

She had been lured here for a single purpose. So she could be killed, the way they had tried to kill her mother.

The snow was at least two feet deep, much deeper in places, and her boots sank in with nightmare slowness. She floundered, lurching, the whole balance of her body thrust forward in a frantic attempt to keep moving, even if she lost her footing.

She could hear him behind her, his boots crunching in the snow, his breath hissing. "You *bitch*," he called. "Come here, you *bitch*."

Anna ran into an empty white world. There were no houses nearby, only the white waste of snow and the gaunt skeletons of the cottonwoods. The little town was three miles or more up the road.

There was nobody to scream for.

There was nowhere to run to.

But she kept going, her heart feeling as though it would burst in her chest, taking one plunging step after another, arms outstretched to steady herself. Like a man on a high wire, if she stopped or slipped, she would die.

"*Bitch!*" he screamed. "You're fuckin' *dead!*"

His voice sounded barely a yard behind her. She could sense the tire iron swinging at her head. With the wild instinct of a deer, she jerked to the side, changing direction. He would only need to strike her once. With his strength, the steel bar would cave in her skull like a melon.

She threw a desperate look over her shoulder with staring eyes. He was ten feet behind her, moving more cumbersomely than she. His greater weight made him sink deeper into the snow, slowing him down.

If she could outdistance him, get among the shelter of the conifers—

He let loose an inarticulate scream like a wild animal's and hurled the tire iron at her. It whirled through the air much too fast for her to dodge. It slammed into her back with violent force, jarring the breath from her lungs in a gasp of agony. The pain was so intense that she actually stumbled to a halt for a moment and sank to her knees, wanting only to crumple into the snow and wait for death.

Then something rose up in her, some feral strength that made her get off her knees and break into a run again. Every step she took drove lightning bolts of pain through her back and shoulder. The snow was treacherous, hiding the bumps and dips in the terrain, so that she stumbled with bone-jarring force from time to time.

She reached a clump of dark conifers, gasping violently for breath. She risked another glance back.

The man was stooping at the place where she had fallen, pawing through the snow, his shaven head bent. He was hunting for the tire iron. He looked up. His eyes were black slits of hate. *"Bitch,"* he screamed at her.

"Oh, God," she gasped, and blundered into the trees.

The branches of the firs had kept snow from getting to the ground here, and the going was suddenly easier. She broke into a run, knowing that the going would be easier for him, too.

Her whole body hurt, not just with the blows from the tire iron, but with fear. She had her arms thrust forward to ward off low-hanging branches. Her gloves were in the Saab. She had taken them off to drive. Jagged branches raked her palms. She was aware of the skin tearing. A bough slashed across her face, the needles stabbing at her eyes like knives.

She had nowhere to run. There was no path, only a murky labyrinth of black trunks. The evening was closing in. It was dark in the thicket, but he would be able to track her footsteps in the fresh snow, like a hunter following a deer.

The maze opened out for a moment, and she was floundering in deep snow, almost up to her waist. She could not get out of it. The more she struggled, the deeper she sank. The fluffy embrace of the powder swiftly became a heavy, icy wetness. Her limbs thrashed without result.

She heard a loud crash behind her, not far away. A big body thrusting through the trees.

Whimpering, Anna clawed at the snow. Her nails raked on something, a dead branch buried in the white. She clawed at it, her naked fingers already numb with cold, grasped hold, dragged herself forward. She got her knee on the trunk. As she pushed up, she felt an agonizing stab of pain from the slash in her thigh.

Then she was clambering out of the drift, exhaustion pounding in her ears like a drumbeat. She did not look back. There was no point. She ran on, hobbling, her breath searing her throat.

Between the trees ahead, a darker shadow among the shadows. A thicket of some shrub like dogwood, bare stems growing densely together.

Like an animal finding its lair, Anna plunged into the thicket, head ducked to protect her face.

Her hair snagged instantly, ripped piercingly, making her moan with pain. She wrapped her arms around her head and she kept going, pushing herself blindly through the leafless stems.

Now she had a fragile chance of eluding him. He would not be able to follow her tracks at least.

She heard the crashing of his movements again, but farther back now. Her heart lurched in hope. She uncovered her face and tried to move more silently, twisting her body around the clumps of naked stems. Her eye caught the dark spots in the snow, and she turned.

"No!"

Her leg had been bleeding. Leaving a trail of blood all the way.

She grabbed a handful of snow and rubbed it furiously on the wound in her thigh. There was no pain now. Between cold and terror, she was starting to go numb from the waist down. Keeping the handful of gritty snow packed to the gash to stop it from bleeding anymore, she moved on, straining to hear sounds of pursuit.

Another crash and a hoarse shout. Even more distant now, though the acoustics of the thicket made it impossible to tell whether he was still behind her, or over to the left or right.

By some miracle, she had outdistanced him.

All her movements had been instinctual until now. She'd re-acted and behaved as an animal, without thought. Her mind had been cowering in some frozen place within, not needed while her body ran on blood and adrenaline.

Now, for the first time, she felt herself return to her body, her personality and mind come alive.

Through her terror, the logic slammed home. The ramming had been meant to kill her. He'd miscalculated, or the skidding of the Saab had thrown his aim off. Now he would need to batter her to death with the tire iron, drag her body back into the Saab. And it was another accident, one of the dozens that happened every winter.

She was alone in a forest with a maniac intent on killing her. No other reality. Only night and snow.

Why? Who had lured her up here with such deadly intent?

Anna's chest was heaving with the effort to breathe, and her stomach felt as though she would throw up any moment. She could not keep running like this. She needed time to rest, to think, to reason.

She slowed to a limping walk, still pressing the handful of snow to her thigh. She'd long since lost her sense of direction, and it was growing darker and darker. Only the almost phosphorescent glow of the snow picked out the terrain.

The ground fell away, revealing a bank knotted with trees. She was out of the thicket and among the cottonwoods again, trunks and roots writhing in the gypsum-rich soil.

If her instincts were right, she was still heading down the slope toward the road. If she reached the road, she might be able to stop a passing car.

Or she could head back into the thicket. If she could bury herself deeply enough, maybe she could find some burrow to hide in until darkness fell completely. Then, maybe, she could creep up toward Gypsum.

On her hands and knees, if necessary.

She hesitated, torn between the two options.

Then she heard the crashing footsteps coming toward her and had no more choices.

Anna dropped to a crouch, hunching like a rabbit. With stealthy movements, she scuttled to the twisting trunk of a cottonwood and huddled against it, molding her body to the shape of the tree.

She could hear his body rustling in the thicket. As he got closer, she heard his harsh panting, too. She squeezed her eyes shut and pressed her face to the rough gray bark of the cottonwood, broken nails digging into the wood.

She could hear him muttering raggedly, but could not catch the words. His movements were uncertain. She could sense his rage, the urgency in him to find her and kill her.

He could be no more than ten yards away now. Her body cringed, every nerve stretched taut. Her heart felt like a hammer pounding against her sternum. She crushed her lips to the bark, trying to breathe silently through her nose. The blows would be dreadful, the pain terrible. Death would be a release.

He stopped moving. In the silence, his words rasped in his throat, garbled, only the malevolence in them comprehensible.

There was the vicious *thunk* of the tire iron hitting a trunk, and she flinched in panic. She heard him curse.

Then she could hear the snow crunching as he slithered down the bank, away from her.

She waited until she guessed he was fifty yards away. Then she rose slowly to her feet, still hugging close to the tree. Her body felt as though it had been hanging on a hook in a butcher's freezer, stiff as death and half-frozen. She had to force herself back into motion, taking a course at right angles to his, still heading toward the road to Gypsum.

She slithered down the bank, banging numbly against roots in the semidarkness. She could just make out that the cottonwoods were thinning out. Somewhere down there in the gloom must lie the road to Gypsum. Praying she was heading in the right direction, she set off at a fast trudge.

Her feet were like blocks of ice. Her pants, soaked earlier on, were now starting to freeze, stiff as boards. She had begun to shiver violently, a shuddering that started deep inside and rippled out through her muscles in great waves, so that her breath quavered in her throat. She felt empty and terribly vulnerable.

Though her face was numb, she could feel that the wind was up and that flakes of snow were starting to whirl down. They burned in her eyes, caught like points of flame in her open mouth.

She moved as quickly and silently as she could, sometimes slipping into deep patches of snow, sometimes kicking against buried obstacles.

Suddenly she saw the twin stars of a car's headlights, only a hundred yards up ahead.

The road.

She heard the rush of the car's tires on the road, saw the beams sweep around the curve, reach across the snow toward her. For a moment she was illuminated in the dazzle.

Without thinking, she lifted her arms and screamed, *"Help!"*

It was a terrible mistake. The car kept right on going, shifting gear to take the steep climb. And at the same moment she heard the hoarse shout of the attacker over to her right. She stopped dead. Over the wind she heard his footsteps thudding toward her. He had seen her in the car headlights and was making straight for her.

Desperate, she ran toward the road, her legs pounding, arms flailing in an effort to propel herself faster.

He was screaming at her, his voice breaking with fury. With nightmare slowness, she ploughed on toward her only hope of life.

In the darkness, another pair of headlights, this time moving more slowly. They rounded the bend with the roar of a diesel engine. She shouted again, arms frantically waving to catch the driver's attention as his headlights picked her out.

She was so close now, so close to salvation.

The headlights dazzled, filling her darkness with radiance. The flakes of snow shimmered like a million stars between her and the road. Her arms were held up high, her hair whipping in the wind.

She saw the dark bulk of the car slow down, heard the engine quiet to a rumble.

"Oh, God," she was gasping, aware of tears spilling icily down her cheeks, "oh, God, thank you!"

She stumbled to the car. It was stopped in the road, its engine idling. She could smell the diesel and hot metal.

She reached it, gasping for oxygen, and grasped the handle of the door.

It was locked.

She thrust her face to the glass, tugging the handle so hard the whole vehicle rocked slightly. "He's trying to kill me," she screamed. "Help me!"

In the dimly lit interior she made out a bulky figure. It leaned forward to peer at her.

The light from the dashboard illuminated him for a moment. An old man with a jowly face, a beaky nose thrusting from under heavy brows.

"Somebody's trying to *kill* me!" she screamed. "Please! Open up!"

He just sat there, staring at her. She saw his gloved hand reach out to hit the center of the steering wheel. The car's horn blared out in a succession of harsh cries.

Suddenly, she sensed that he had no intention of helping her. Instead, she sensed a wave of malevolence, of pure evil. He was summoning the other man. Telling him where she was.

She let go of the handle and ran along the road, her flesh creeping, her mind whirling. It was now completely dark. Her boots slithered on the road, which was covered with a thin layer of powdery snow. She fell once, crashing down on one hip, but clawed herself to her feet immediately and kept going.

She heard the hoarse voice of the man with the tire iron, heard his pounding feet.

He, too, was on the road now, chasing her.

She looked over her shoulder and saw his bulky figure jogging against the twin red taillights of the car. She could clearly make out the steel bar in his hand.

She got a hundred yards down the road before she started to flag, exhausted, despairing. She no longer had the strength to run, no longer had any shelter to seek. She was going to be beaten to death, right here on this lonely road.

He was gaining on her so fast that she could already hear his panting, catch the vicious words he was throwing at her.

Her muscles were failing her. She could feel herself slowing, her body unable to respond to her mind's wild commands for more speed.

"Bitch," he grunted, almost behind her now. "Come here, *bitch*."

Something tore at the back of her jacket, his fingers or the steel tip of the iron, she was not sure which.

She uttered a moan of horror.

The night ignited again, headlights blazing directly in front of her, two suns that dazzled her eyes into pain. The roar of a big engine was drowned by the bellow of air brakes.

She hurled herself to one side, her legs collapsing beneath her. She rolled once, twice, came to rest sitting on her backside in the snow.

She saw that the shaven-headed man had also slipped. He was caught in the white glare, arms upraised. She saw him try to rise. Saw him slip and fall, his body writhing on the road.

The huge lights ignited to an even more blinding intensity. The air brakes continued to blare. Anna could hear the squeal of the truck's locked tires as the driver tried to swerve and brake at the same time.

The shaven-headed man was on his knees now, trying to get to his feet, one hand outstretched as though he could ward off the behemoth that was bearing down on him.

His body seemed to incandesce like burning magnesium in the headlights.

She could not look away, not even when the steel girder swept into him, knocking him down like a rag doll. Not even while the monster devoured his body, huge wheels trampling the flailing limbs, crushing the stuffing from the rag doll's whirling torso.

The truck kept sliding for the length of a city block, air brakes still raging like an animal's howl, before it finally shuddered to a halt.

The night became silent. Only the rush of the wind, the whisper of falling snow.

Anna rose to her feet slowly. She lifted her hands to her face. Her hair was tangled, snagged with twigs and dead leaves. She walked, as if locked in some slow nightmare, toward the truck. She could see long, dark streaks in the snow, marks of the wheels, and of something else, something that lay in a ragged bundle twenty yards behind the truck. She did not look at it as she passed it, keeping her head stiffly turned away.

She heard the cab door open. The driver jumped to the ground, a woman with long hair spilling from under a wool hat.

"Oh my *Lord*," she was saying in a voice tight with shock. "I couldn't *stop*. It warn't my *fault*."

"Please," Anna said shakily, reaching out her arms.

"It warn't my *fault*," the woman repeated in a wail. "Where is he?"

Anna stumbled to her and grasped her arms. "He's dead," she said. The two women clung to one another. Way up ahead, Anna heard the sound of a diesel engine fire up and saw the two red eyes of taillights disappearing in the night.

"Are you okay?" The truck driver was peering at Anna with a panicky expression. "You look in bad shape. Oh Lord! I didn't hit you, too, did I?"

"No," she said wearily. "You saved my life."

6

Jorgensen was accompanied by two other policemen this time, middle-aged men with silver stars pinned to their leather jackets. "We got an ID on the assailant," he greeted her.

She led them into the sitting room, where she had been huddled by the fire with a mug of cocoa. It was the third interview she'd had with Jorgensen in thirty-six hours. The first had been in Denver, around midnight of that terrible evening. She had not yet managed to sleep much, despite the pills they'd given her at the hospital. She was wearing sweatpants and a bulky Arran sweater of her mother's. Her hair was tied back in a bob. She looked terrible, and she knew it, but the loose clothes were all she could bear on her bruised and aching body.

Jorgensen introduced the two other men as police detectives from Denver, but she did not catch the names, or even bother to try. Her mind felt numbed, unable to take in new information, just as her body still felt cold, as though the ice inside had not yet melted. She got right up close to the fire and invited the three men to sit.

"Sorry to subject you to any more stress," Jorgensen said. "But this may be important."

"I'm ready."

One of the leather-jacketed detectives was carrying a bulky folder, which he opened. "That's the same man, right?" He passed her a photograph. She took it. It was a police mug shot, a serial number dangling round the thick neck. She studied the angular features. The face was younger than when she had last seen it, but it was the same man, the same mean, stony stare.

She nodded and gave it back. Sick, panicky memories were flickering through her mind. "That's him."

"I've got the autopsy report right here." He pulled out a sheaf of papers that had photographs clipped to them. She caught a glimpse of something purple and red in the photographs before she hid her face.

"She doesn't want to hear about the autopsy report, George," Jorgensen growled.

"Yeah, sorry," the detective said lamely. He cleared his throat. "It was practically instantaneous, ma'am," he said, as though trying to console her. "He didn't feel a thing. That woman who ran him down? She's in bad shock. Still not out of the hospital—"

Jorgensen cut in again. "Miss Kelly doesn't want to hear about that, either, George."

There was a silence until Anna lifted her head. She was very pale. "I'm sorry. Go on."

Looking contrite, the detective went on. "You never saw him before he rammed your car?"

"Apart from the time in Vail, no. I never saw him before. Who was he?"

"He was a known criminal. A very dangerous man." The detective took the picture back and consulted his notes. "His name was Carl Rudolf Beck, also known as 'Truck.' Mean anything to you, ma'am?"

"No."

"Kind of sad, that. Guy named Truck being run down by a truck."

"Poetic justice," Jorgensen muttered.

"Twenty-four years old. Born in Colorado Springs in 1968. His father was a sergeant at one of the Air Force bases there. Name unknown.

Mother was named Carla Beck, a known prostitute and drug user. She OD'd in 1990." He glanced up at Anna again, but she shook her head.

"None of that means anything to me. I've never been to Colorado Springs."

"Truck's rap sheet starts at age fourteen. Several grand theft/ autos and two lewd behaviors, but pretty soon he settled down to his main preference—crimes against women. Mainly sexual assault and rape. He was arrested on suspicion plenty of times, but nothing ever stuck. In 1987, he was arraigned in Colorado Springs on six counts of rape with violence. He came up with a fancy lawyer and a heavy-duty psychiatric evaluation. He was just under eighteen. He wound up with community service and a suspended sentence. That was five years ago. Since then, no arrests. He came up to the Denver area and got involved in ethics instead. Took up a couple of causes." The man smiled grimly. "Joined the Aryan Warriors, the Defenders of the Blood, and the White Knights of America. Do you know what those outfits are?"

"They sound like Nazis."

He nodded. "That's right. Neo-fascist organizations. Burn the Jews, lynch the niggers, kill the Pope. They're crazies, but you'd be surprised how many members they get. The White Knights actually gave Beck a job. They do a lot of hunting, mainly bear and elk. They go in for manly stuff of all kinds. Beck was employed to take care of things on their hunting estate, further west of Vail. He was a kind of game-keeper. Maybe he learned to take his blood-lust out on deer instead of defenseless women. We've spoken to the man who paid his salary, Richard Hoffman. He says he hasn't seen Beck for a month or more. Very sad, sorry, and surprised to hear about this. Says he thought, quote, the bonds of discipline had reformed poor Carl." The detective cocked his grizzled head at her. "Any connections you can see in all this?"

"None," she said.

"We don't see any connection between the Nazi stuff and the attack on you, either. There may well be one—we just can't identify it. In fact, Beck seems to have benefited from joining the White Knights. They're mostly a bunch of fat businessmen who like to get together and drink and badmouth the rest of America. Then they go out and ease their feelings by slaughtering a bunch of animals. But Hoffman has a reputation as a disciplinarian, though he's an old man now. He was an American Nazi Party leader during the war, up in Chicago. He was in jail from 1944 to 1945. He reckons to have been a father figure to Carl Beck. He may have been able to keep Beck on the rails, for all we know. Or Beck may have been carrying on as before, and just have evaded justice until now."

"He was a psychopath," Jorgensen put in heavily. "Psychopaths are notoriously unpredictable. They can also be very cunning. This man was what police psychologists call a trapper. He lured women to remote places where he could rape them undisturbed. Sometimes he was very ingenious about it. It fits with the job he took as gamekeeper. He'd have enjoyed the work. Been good at it. But it wasn't enough. He needed a human quarry. We figure Carl Beck lured you up to Gypsum to rape you there.

"The vehicle was stolen in Denver last week, just thirty-six hours before the attack. It belongs to a bank clerk. It's a Nissan Pathfinder V6, a very powerful vehicle. Perfect for ramming somebody else. He'd changed the plates, of course. We're still doing forensic work on the Nissan, but so far no traces of anyone except Beck. His prints are all over it. He must have stolen it to do the job."

"But why me?" she asked, dark rings under her eyes as she looked from one to another of the police. "How did he know enough about Campbell Brinkman to be able to spin such a convincing story?"

"Ma'am, the whole of Vail knows about you, your mother, and Campbell Brinkman," Jorgensen said gently. "None of it is any secret. This is a very small town."

"I still can't think why he chose me."

"You're a very attractive woman," said the third man, who had not spoken until now.

She saw the other man wince. "It wouldn't just be that. You said you saw him watching you here in Vail." She nodded. "He may have built up a fixation about you. That was his pattern. One of his victims in Colorado? He raped her three times over a seven-month period. Kept coming back for more."

She shuddered. "Could he be the one who attacked my mother?"

"It's possible," Jorgensen said. "We're still working on it. When your mother gets back on her feet, she may be able to help us with that."

One of the other detectives grunted. "Unlikely she'll remember a thing about it. Any case, I think it's more likely that Beck just heard about what happened to your mother and that it excited him. Stimulated him to come take a look at you."

"Oh, Jesus," she said, disgusted.

"We're dealing with a sick personality here," Jorgensen reminded her quietly.

"What about the other man at the ranch?" Anna asked. "The older man who sounded his horn?"

"No luck there," Jorgensen replied. "We're still looking. Whoever he was, he may not have been involved. May have been just a passerby who got scared."

Anna wrapped her arms around herself, comforting the two places she hurt most, the gash on her thigh, now closed up with fifteen stitches, and the bruise on her shoulder, already an ugly purple. He hadn't fractured the bone with the tire iron, but he had come close. Talking about it was making her physically ill. She closed her eyes in pain.

One of the detectives coughed awkwardly. "We won't disturb you any further, ma'am. Just wanted to see if you'd ever come across Beck some time in the past."

She rose and forced herself to smile as they left.

Jorgensen stayed behind for a moment.

He took a pack of cigarettes out of his top pocket, not bothering to ask her permission this time. He lit up, then wandered around the apartment, studying odd things, blowing the smoke out of his beaky nose. He came to a halt in front of the fire.

"I'm concerned about you, Miss Kelly."

"Thanks," she said with a touch of irony.

"I mean it. I've asked the Vail Police Department to keep this condominium under observation."

"You mean they'll drive by once a night? That makes me feel wonderfully safe."

"They'll do more than that. I can't promise a man at the door, but the local people will keep a close eye on the place."

"Sorry," she apologized. "I appreciate it."

"Have you contacted Philip Westward yet?"

"No. He's not in his office and he's not at his apartment. His secretary says he's doing lots of meetings."

"Meetings," Jorgensen repeated. "Yeah, I know about those. I have 'em all the time. You're seeing a lot of him lately."

She looked at him wryly. "No secrets in Vail. You were right."

He nodded. "Take care. I'll be in touch."

When he left, a wave of intense loneliness washed over her. She went for the painkillers.

Anna Awoke Aching in every limb. The painkillers had worn off, and now she was throbbingly aware of the gash in her thigh, the bruised places on her back, ligaments she had wrenched in the thicket. The memory of Gypsum was a sickening fist that pushed up inside her stomach. She lay there for a while, wondering whether sleep would return, knowing it wouldn't.

Groaning, she swung her legs out of bed. It was midafternoon. She had not eaten today, but she had no hunger. A wave of dizziness swept over her. Her head felt like a balloon straining at its moorings. Visions of Carl Beck's face, sensations of violent motion, rocked her with nightmarish intensity. She rose unsteadily to her feet and went to the telephone. She had tried to call Philip a dozen times since the attack up at Gypsum, but he had been neither at his apartment nor at his office. She felt an unreasonable fury toward him. How could he not be there for her, when she needed him so desperately?

She reached for the telephone for the thirteenth time and dialed his apartment. She heard his husky voice answer at last.

"Philip, you bastard! Where have you *been*?"

"Is everything all right?" he asked, his voice tightening abruptly.

"No," she said, "everything is *not* all right. Somebody tried to kill me."

"What?" he said, his voice urgent now. "What happened?"

She told him in short, shaky sentences what had happened. "The truck just crushed him, Philip. If she hadn't have come along, I'd be dead now . . . " She broke off.

"Are you badly hurt?" he cut in harshly.

"No." She controlled herself with an effort. "No, I'm all right. Just some cuts and bruises, that's all. But I'm frightened, Philip."

"Anna, listen to me." She could hear the strain in his voice. "Where are you?"

"At my mother's place."

"Don't stay there. Pack a bag. Go to my suite at the Westin. I'll call reception and tell them to let you into my room. Lock yourself in and wait for me."

"Oh, Jesus," she said with a shaky laugh. "It's not that bad. The police are keeping an eye on the apartment."

"Do as I say," he said curtly. "Right now, Anna. I'm flying straight up to Eagle."

"All right, I'll go, if it makes you happy. When will you get here?"

"Tonight. Around midnight."

"It's been horrible," she said unevenly. "Philip, I need you."

"Around midnight," he promised. "Go now. Quickly."

She packed her bag, then called a taxi. She was aching all over. The shock seemed to have numbed her. She felt she was wading through heavy oil, the way she had felt when she'd first arrived in Vail.

She walked into the Westin half an hour later, lugging her bag. She could not stop herself from looking over her shoulder, eyes searching for a figure following her, hard eyes watching her. The anxiety was worse than she could ever have imagined.

By the time she reached Philip's room, following the bellman who was carrying her bag, she was trembling and soaked in sweat. She walked into the room and locked the door.

Then she stretched out on the bed and tried to relax.

Anna Had Been lying on his bed, the translation of the diary on the pillow beside her, staring with absent eyes into the fire the maids had lit in the grate.

She had read no more than a third of the diary yet, but she already knew everything. She knew the extraordinary truth that her mother had stumbled across. She knew who Joseph Krasnowsky was, the man who had been a journalist, just like her.

The knowledge drove away her aches and pains. Quiet triumph drove away her fear.

She knew why her mother had been searching so obsessively for information about the man named Joseph Krasnowsky.

She thought of the Russian doll her mother had brought back from Moscow. One woman packed into another, another woman inside that. Infinite personalities telescoped into one persona. A mystery. A mystery all women shared, perhaps. Perhaps we're all like that, she thought. Many people living in the same skin. Coexisting somehow. Showing our different faces to the different people who need us. Mother, daughter, lover, friend. Without understanding how we do it.

Without even understanding ourselves. We hardly know who is inside us until someone opens us up, starts unpacking the layers, pulling out the others who live within us.

The others who live within us.

It had taken her so long to get here, to assemble the jigsaw of her mother's life. But she had done it.

She remembered arriving in Denver, Philip meeting her at the airport, the first sight of her mother lying in the intensive care unit, her first struggle with despair and bewilderment. It all made sense now.

The key clicked in the lock. As the door swung open, she heard Philip's voice.

"It's me."

She jumped to her feet and ran to him.

His arms swept around her with possessive force, crushing her to him. He held her like that for a long time, his face buried in her hair, his hard, powerful body close against hers. He was hurting all her bruised places, but she did not care. The pain was heaven. She clung to him in silent bliss, her eyes closed.

At last he released her and looked down at her, his dark blue eyes burning like cobalt.

"Are you all right?"

"I'll survive," she said with a bruised smile. She took his hands and lifted them to her bosom, spreading his fingers over the soft swell of her breasts. "Oh, God, it's good to see you. I've missed you. I missed you so much."

He kissed her mouth the way that always made her senses swim, with that tender ruthlessness. She felt all her pleasure centers come to life, stars appearing in a summer night.

"I've got so much to tell you, Philip."

"I want to know what happened to you."

"No. Not about *him*. I don't want to face that yet. About my mother. She's started speaking, Philip."

She saw his eyes widen. "Are you serious?"

"Yes. She's going to get well, Philip. I know she is. And I've had the diary translated. I know everything now. I know why Mama was driven to find Joseph Krasnowsky. I know why I'm going to have to find him, too. Let me tell you."

4

THE WALNUT TREE

1 9 4 3 – 4 4

December 1943
ITALY

They huddled among the rocks with their faces down, as much for cover against the icy December wind as to avoid detection. It was very early, just before dawn, and bitter cold.

There were seven of them: Francesco, Lodovico, the Tinker, the Hungarian, little Paolo the deserter, David, and Joseph. It was Joseph who held the detonator wires in his frozen hands. He lay behind a boulder, thinking about the well-trained soldiers in the gray uniforms.

The German truck would contain anything up to thirty soldiers, which meant that they were violating one of the most fundamental rules of warfare, attacking a force that outnumbered them four to one. And when he considered that of the seven Partisans, only he, David, and little Paolo the deserter had ever faced the Germans before, the odds looked even crazier.

On their side was the momentum of attack and the five kilograms of industrial dynamite Francesco had looted from a quarry; that, and the bleak Lombardy mountains behind them, into whose remote wilderness they could retreat if things went sour. Poor odds, and yet his skin was flushed, defying the icy wind, and he felt the sweet thrill of life in his veins.

The information about the truck was by no means reliable. It sounded too good to be true. The Germans were no longer in the habit of sending trucks full of soldiers unescorted around these hills. If it appeared with an armored car, or even a motorcycle-sidecar combination with a machine gun, they were just going to have to sit there and watch it go by. Seven of them and their dynamite were no match for a Spandau.

He heard a shrill whistle and lifted his head cautiously. A hundred yards farther up the hill, he saw David sitting up in the pale light. He gestured emphatically toward the bend, indicating he had heard something. The others were all peering over their rocks toward the road. They did not, of course, have a radio. They were relying on David Godbold's keen ears to hear the truck's engine as it labored up the hill to the bend in the road where they had planned their ambush. David held up three fingers, to indicate they had three minutes to wait. Joseph nodded, his heartbeat accelerating, and huddled closer to the boulder.

The wind whistled across the scree, bringing the smell of snow from the Alps, whose white peaks were exquisite against a pale dawn sky. There were few clouds, perfect weather for spotter planes. Bad luck, that. Getting away with this was not going to be easy.

Then he, too, heard it above the wind: the labored roar of a diesel engine. Only one engine, as far as he could tell. Suddenly he felt undilutedly optimistic about the ambush. It was going to go well. He eased away the safety catch that locked the handle of the detonator and began breathing deeply, charging his blood with oxygen. If he did his part well, the feebleness of their firepower would barely matter.

It seemed a long time before the truck appeared. It breasted the hill, swaying, moving with excruciating slowness. It was alone. Just one Opel truck. Not even a motorcycle outrider. The information had been accurate. An undefended, canvas-sided truck. A perfect target for their tiny group!

The engine sounded as though it was about to burst. And as the truck finally cleared the rise, it ground to a halt, a long way from where he had concealed the explosives.

"Shit!" Joseph felt a flash of panic. Had the Germans spotted an unwary Partisan in the growing light? Was this a trap? He kept low, peering over the boulder, his knuckles white around the handle of the detonator. The engine died with a rattle of overheated pipes, and the driver and his front-seat companion got out. The driver lifted the hood of the truck, while the other man, his machine gun slung at the ready, peered around at the grim mountainsides. There was no sound but the whistle of the wind. Then a distant word in German and a hissing sound. Joseph saw steam billowing from under the hood.

"Shit," he said again, and slid back down behind the boulder. But he felt better. The truck had a radiator problem. They would let it cool off before continuing. He lay there, listening to the hiss of escaping steam. He could smell the hot metal intermittently on the wind. The sun was starting to rise, shedding gold on the mountainside. It felt colder than ever.

There were more voices now. He inched himself up to peer down at the road. At least a dozen soldiers had emerged from the truck to urinate in the road. All had Schmeissers slung over their shoulders. He heard coughing, laughter. They kept bunched up, showing no inclination to explore, helmeted heads turning constantly to survey their surroundings. They were nervous, even here in the middle of nowhere. They were in hostile country, despite the farce of Mussolini's reinstatement in Saló.

Praying that the other six would keep their heads down, Joseph settled back to wait, whistling soundlessly through his teeth, an old good-luck charm that had started in his childhood. Enjoy it, he thought grimly. You're all going to die before the next one.

The Pig Was well-grown for a wartime pig, stout and pink. He looked, so Teo said, rather like Luchetti, the notary in Saló. Candida had helped scrub him clean yesterday, and he had groaned with pleasure in such human tones that she had felt sorrier than ever for him.

"Come on, darling!"

"Come on, my lovely. They won't hurt you."

"There, little one." Candida patted his fat flank gently. "It's all right."

He was nervous now as they led him into the courtyard, grunting suspiciously, his head down and his pouchy eyes rolling. His ears were pricked, his tail twitching spasmodically. At the sight of the butcher, all his worst suspicions seemed to be confirmed. Perhaps he smelled what was on the leather apron, or perhaps it was the sight of the bright blades hanging on the belt.

He uttered a decisive grunt, swung on his axis with great agility, and launched himself back at the gate.

He was around nine months old, weighed almost 300 pounds, and had the strength of two men. To make things worse, there was a rime of ice on the cobbles. Candida, who had been gripping the rope with her father, slipped and sprawled on the ground, a human anchor clinging grimly to the hemp.

"Teo!" she gasped, her eyes shut tight. "Don't let him tread on me!"

But her brother Teo, crippled as he was, had himself collapsed on one knee, cursing violently. The screaming animal twisted and bucked, fouling himself in his terror. It was their father's brute strength that won the day. Vincenzo hauled the pig's head steadily around until it was twisted over his shoulder. Then, deftly, he reached beneath the pig's belly and jerked one of his legs out from under him. The pig crashed onto the ground with a grunt of expelled breath. Candida scrambled out of the way of the flailing trotters. Then the butcher and his son had straddled the pig, and the end had come.

Rosa had been waiting with the galvanized iron tub clutched to her ample bosom. She thrust it under the pig's head and patted him comfortingly on the forehead.

"Don't worry, little one, they won't hurt you," she soothed.

The butcher slit the pig's throat, and blood gouted into the iron tub with a ringing note like a church bell.

The first few moments were dreadful. But it did not take long before the large pink body stopped struggling, and the screams dwindled. It was not an unmerciful death.

Candida rose to her feet, aware of bruises and scraped knees. More serious was the tear in her dress, which ran from her knee to her waist, revealing the smooth white line of her thigh. Clothes were not easy to come by in wartime. Teo was still sitting on the cobbles, rubbing his bad leg, rather pale-faced.

"All right?" she asked him. He nodded without replying. She knew the butchering was almost unbearable to him now, but he was needed and would do his part.

Their mother, holding the tub with one hand, continued stroking the pig's forehead with the other, murmuring consolation long after it was dead. Peace settled on the courtyard. The dawn sky was lovely, but the wind was icy.

The butcher ignited his blowtorch with a pop. He lit his cigarette nonchalantly at the rippling yellow flame, then started expertly searing the bristles off the corpse. Candida, rubbing knuckles that ached with the cold, envied him the warmth of that job. She hated to see any creature die and was glad that this had been swift and clean. The tub was now three-quarters full of dark, greasy-looking blood. This, the first and most urgent yield of the slaughter, needed to be processed immediately, before it clotted and became useless. Candida took the other handle and helped her mother haul the tub into the kitchen. A fire was blazing in the big open hearth. In winter, the fire burned night and day, and the acrid smell of burning oak wood and olive root impregnated everything.

They lifted the tub onto the huge oak table with an effort. They had boiled barley, rice, and whatever other cereals they could gather the night before, and the glutinous white mass was ready to be mixed with the blood to make *sanguinaccio,* black pudding to be eaten sliced on bread or to enrich a winter stew.

"Too much barley," her mother said sadly, tipping the porridge into the tub. "Everything has to be stretched too thin. Only one pig, and too much barley."

They'd started the year with three pigs. One had been requisitioned by the Fascists in the summer, a second stolen by German soldiers hunting escaped prisoners of war in the autumn.

"We were lucky to be left with him," Candida said.

She plunged her arms into the hot and syrupy blood and started kneading in the barley. The mixture squelched between her fingers thickly. It took away the ache of the cold. But her hands would smell of blood for days.

It Was Twenty minutes before Joseph heard the hood slam shut.

He lifted his head. The last of the soldiers was climbing into the back of the truck. The engine started up again, revving confidently. Joseph was ready now. His lean face was expressionless, dark eyes narrowed in concentration. He had left a lichen-covered rock next to the sticks of dynamite as a marker, and he kept his eye on it as the truck began to move.

It roared forward, changed gear, changed gear again. It was doing perhaps thirty kilometers an hour as it reached his marker. The cab passed the rock, then the billowing canvas-sided body. With no conscious thought, Joseph rammed the plunger home.

A demon's yellow eye flickered. Joseph felt the brutal thump deep in his chest. He ducked his head as a torrent of debris rained down. The dynamite seemed to have lifted half of Italy into the air. When the downpour stopped, he swung the Sten gun up from his side and half rose. His ears were ringing.

A billowing cloud still hid the truck, which had stopped in its tracks. A wheel was rolling back down the road. The wind swept the smoke aside, and he saw the devastation. The truck had taken the full force of the blast. Rags of burning canvas flapped on the crazed skeleton. He thought, None of them will have survived that.

David Godbold's war cry rose shrill across the rocks, like a rooster crowing. Then they were all running down the hillside, screaming with the blind red rage of battle. Joseph had a strange flash of memory: himself, ten years old, running and screaming in just the same way, with a wooden gun in Central Park.

When he was close enough to use the Sten, he crouched and fired a long burst into the cab, seeing the pockmarks riddle the already blistered door. As he reached the cutting, he stopped again, emptied the magazine into the vehicle, reloaded, then ran on. There was no return fire.

He was the first to jump down onto the road, the first to reach the crippled truck. Heedless of his safety, he leaped onto the tailgate, his weapon at the ready. A wreckage of humanity lay strewn among the twisted struts. It had been a victory more complete than they could have dreamed of. Three of the Germans had been blown right out of the truck and lay dead on the other side of the road. The ten or twelve others had been dismembered by the blast.

The others joined him, climbing onto the bed of the truck. Little Paolo the deserter ran round the front of the truck, and hopped onto the running board. He peered through the broken glass, then reached in. They heard the muffled barking of Paolo's pistol. Then he hopped down, grinning.

"Tutti morti."

"Fucking wonderful," David Godbold said, his voice throaty. He kicked at what had been a man a minute earlier, his face white and joyful.

There was no time for self-congratulation. It might only be a matter of minutes before more Germans arrived. "Let's get the fuck out of here," Joseph commanded.

"The weapons, the weapons," Francesco shouted. "They have Lugers!"

He was already plundering the dead. The Germans' Luger pistols were prized both as weapons and as tradeable commodities with a high market value. Lodovico, Paolo, and the Tinker joined him, and Joseph knew it was useless to try and stop them. David leaped off the truck and ran down the road to the bend to keep watch.

Joseph checked his Sten. The smells of explosives and dreadful death were choking. He felt nausea rise in his throat. Above all else he loathed having to stare at the men he had killed. Once he had killed he wanted to get out, fast, before he could reflect on what he had done, what he had become.

And there would be reprisals against the civilian population for this morning's work. The Germans had herded thousands of Italians into concentration camps; they had arrested, tortured, and shot thousands more, had burned barns, houses, whole villages to the ground. When that had not quelled resistance, the SS had taken large numbers of civilian hostages, whom they murdered in savage public executions at any fresh Partisan attack.

It was something they had not discussed, because there was nothing to say about it. They had all agreed that it was better innocent Italians died than that the Nazis went unchallenged in the country they had occupied. He hoped they would feel the same way tomorrow.

He saw several stick grenades hanging at the belt of a man whom the blast had broken like a doll. Swallowing his gorge, Joseph forced himself to move forward. Even if the detonators had been damaged, the grenades were a useful prize because of the high explosive they contained, and there might be more in the man's pack.

He squatted and tore at the fastenings, his fingers growing slippery and red, stuffing the booty into the leather sack slung at his back.

He tried to pull the dead grenadier over and was appalled as he saw the man's head move. The blood-spattered face turned to his, blue eyes focusing blearily. Somehow, impossibly, the man was alive. A few minutes ago, Joseph would have killed the German without thought. Now he was frozen, unable to react. The man had his pistol in his hand. It lifted waveringly to point at Joseph. Joseph threw himself back.

He felt a numbing blow like a heavy kick. For a split second he thought one of the others had kicked him out of the way. Then liquid fire poured into his belly, and he knew he had been shot.

He heard the Sten guns rattle, more than one of them, but could not move. He lay huddled among the German dead, hugging his wound.

The Italians were screaming at him, trying to roll him over.

"No" was all he could whisper. "No."

Then David Godbold's voice was at his ear. "Joe. Joe! Let me see."

They pulled him over, and someone began unbuttoning his shirt. He felt as though his body were on fire from the chest down. David mopped at blood, his face expressionless.

"Is it bad?" he whispered to David.

"Might be," David said shortly. "Can't tell here."

"Where is it?"

"Under the ribs. Might have gone through a lung, low down. You'll have to be carried. Does it hurt?"

"Terrible," he whispered.

"Going to give you a shot of morphine. All right?"

Joseph nodded.

The Tinker carried their sparse medical supplies. Joseph saw him break open the ampoule and fill the syringe. He did not feel the needle go into his arm.

He tried to lift his head to see the wound. Someone pushed him gently down. Everything was blurring. His mind suddenly swam, and he felt as though he was being drowned in a swift, hot river. The pain did not go away; it just went somewhere else. He fought desperately to keep his head above the roaring black waters, but the flood rose and blotted him out.

It Had Taken two hours to make and season the *sanguinaccio* mixture and stuff it into a variety of sausage skins, which now festooned the old kitchen, hanging in fat loops and whorls from the ancient oak rafters.

By that time the pig had been expertly dismembered, and the

butcher had left. Every scrap of the carcass was being used. The prime cuts from loin and ribs had been carefully packed to be sold on the black market, where they would command high prices. The haunches and shoulders were already salted and hanging from rafters to cure, minus the trotters, which Rosa would bone and stuff to make *zampone*. The liver was going to provide a festive lunch for the family today, together with white beans and turnips. Everything else was going into sausages. Vincenzo and Teo were painstakingly paring every scrap of remaining flesh from the bones and chopping them up with the organs to go into the hand-cranked mincer. Stuffed into the cleaned intestines, they would produce a small mountain of sausages, salami, mortadella, and other *salumi,* each with its own shape, flavor, and texture. The work would go on all day.

The pig was going to provide scores of nourishing meals for many families through a hard winter; warmth in the blood, energy for the young to grow, the fit to work, the old to survive. What had seemed a violent and bloody ritual before dawn had now taken on an overwhelming logic of its own; slaughtering the pig was the most productive event of the year, a saturnalia of reward and survival.

Candida was wearied and blood-spattered. The smell of blood was cloying in her nostrils.

"Go up and wash," Rosa told her, pushing her gently away from the table. "You've done enough for now."

She nodded, poured herself a jug of hot water from the copper kettle that hung over the kitchen fire, and carried it upstairs.

Her small bedroom window looked out over the lake, a view that might have graced a picture postcard. The heavy mist of dawn had lifted, and the great sheet of water, winding its way between steep mountainsides, was like polished steel. There was a drone of aircraft engines in the sky. She opened the window. Two German planes were heading purposefully along the lakeshore. Their reflections sped below them in the water. They wore gray winter camouflage paint, and she could see the black-and-white crosses on their fuselage. After three years of war, she knew every model in the Luftwaffe, and she recognized these as Fieseler Storchs, spotter planes with little or no armament. They would probably be combing the mountains for Partisans.

The dirge of their engines changed note as they climbed to gain altitude over Saló. They separated, one dipping out of sight over Tormini, the other turning south toward Desenzano. Soon she could not hear either of them any longer.

Silence settled. She closed the shutters and poured the hot water into a basin to wash herself.

She unfastened her dress, watching herself in the little tarnished oval mirror. Candida Cipriani was nineteen. She had a dark beauty that was focused in her eyes. They were large and rather heavy-lidded. They glowed with both intelligence and innocence, the eyes of a woman of natural cleverness and little education. Her nose was straight, with flaring Latin nostrils. Her mouth was soft, with the blurred corners of a Mona Lisa, seeming to hover between sadness and smiles. Even when she compressed her lips, as she did when she was thoughtful, it seemed too large for her face. Her cloudy black hair sprang from her high forehead in waves that were impossible to manage.

The sun of the summer gone by had tanned her face and throat down to the line of her top button. Her breasts were creamy and smooth. She cupped them, assessing their soft weight, but avoided touching the sienna-brown nipples. Touching herself there produced feelings that were disturbing, both pleasurable and sinful.

Had she been a village girl, she would long since have been courted and married. But the admiration of male eyes was a luxury she'd had all too little of. The farm called *Il Noce* was remote, buried among oak woods, high above the lakeside towns. When she had left the village school at fourteen, she had entered her adulthood world of silence, toil, and loneliness as if entering a convent. The communal life of the nearest village was an hour away by horse and cart, two hours on foot. Neither she nor her brother left the property for months on end, not even to go as far as Salò. Meeting other young people was a rare pleasure, dances and parties rarer pleasures still.

When she had washed off the pig's blood, she put on a fresh gingham skirt and a khaki shirt that Teo had given her, pulling on a thick and plentifully darned woollen jersey. She took the slim black diary from the drawer at her bedside. She turned a fresh page and wrote the date at the top: 20 December, 1943. Her handwriting was neat and regular.

"This morning early," she wrote, "we slaughtered the pig. He weighed one hundred and thirty kilos. He died quickly." She paused, lifting her eyes to her own reflection in the mirror. She was going to miss the pig. His grunting presence in the barn had been comforting, friendly. She was lonely enough to have taken pleasure in saving table scraps for him and feeding them to him in the warm dark of his den.

"Many explosions in the night," she went on, "and much noise of traffic on the *autovia,* going south. Everyone says the invasion is going well for the Allies, and that the Germans will be driven out by the summer."

In September the Italian armies had finally collapsed. Mussolini had been arrested, all the Allied prisoners of war had been set free, and for one trembling moment it had seemed that Italy was out of the war.

But the Nazis had counterattacked with decisive swiftness. They had declared a new Fascist "Republic," quartered only a few miles from this very farmhouse, in the exquisite lakeside resort of Saló.

They had reinstated the now exhausted and listless Mussolini as their puppet and had begun a reign of terror over their former ally to ensure cooperation. And Italy had been plunged into the bloody chaos of a civil war between those who still believed in Fascism (or at least believed that the Nazis were going to win the war) and those who believed in neither.

"The war seems to have no ending," she wrote on. "We are not even at peace with ourselves." Candida hesitated, then wrote one more sentence, one that was repeated time and again through the pages of her diary: "May God help us all."

Candida had been fifteen when Mussolini had delivered Italy into Hitler's war. It was said that the huge crowd who had cheered so frenziedly in Piazza Navona that day had afterward slunk home, silent and perturbed, no man meeting his neighbor's eye. Had they foreseen, that blazing summer afternoon, the shame and ruin that the war would bring to Italy?

She herself was as old as Fascist rule. She had been born in its outset; had grown up whilst it brought Italy empire, prosperity, glory; had reached adulthood under the shadow of its final catastrophe.

Since that day in Piazza Navona, three years of slaughter and destruction had brought Italy to her knees. It had scarred their own family indelibly. Her beloved elder brother Teo had been sent to Greece, where a sniper's bullet had smashed his thigh and turned him from a loveable comedian into a melancholy, limping stranger.

She closed the diary and put it away. Then she turned to the mirror again and brushed her thick hair back from her face. Though it looked as soft as a cloud, it was stubborn and snagged in the bristles obstinately. Brushing it made it gleam, but could not truly impose order, so she tied it back firmly with a scrap of velvet ribbon. Her face in the mirror was now revealed as oval, with a pointed chin and fine bones beneath the youthful skin. Her expression was relaxed, languid.

She had dreamed vividly in the night. As so often, she could not remember the precise shape of her dreams, but they had been of love. The pictures evaporated as soon as she woke, but not the feelings, leaving her lying there with a galloping heart. On such mornings, her body would be filled with pangs and wild pleasures, and her soul seemed to fly like a kite. If only she could let the string go! But she did not know how to, not yet. Abandonment was a trick she had not yet learned. She rose and went back downstairs.

Lunch Was A festive occasion, something they had looked forward to for months. All four of them would spend the afternoon at the laborious task of sausage making out in the freezing courtyard, but for now the labors and sorrows of the year were forgotten.

Rosa had fried the liver in some of the pig's own lard. Mixed with succulent white beans and turnips in a *casseruòla,* it made the kind of meal they had only been able to dream of since the war had begun. The wonderful smell filled the house.

The rows of copper pans in the kitchen glimmered in the fire-light. The kitchen table was the hub of the household. It stood in front of the fire, a massive and authoritative presence, black as iron with age, and almost as hard, its scarred oak top a solid foot thick. It was almost certainly as old as the house, which dated back to the 1750s. Rosa was decking it out with treasures in glass bottles from the pantry, the harvest of the summer gone by, preserved in the farm's own thick greenish olive oil: plum tomatoes with whole cloves of garlic, sweet red peppers glowing like flames, porcino mushrooms, olives, fierce white goat's cheese, cucumbers pickled in eye-watering vinegar. The bread, made last week but still good, was like a river boulder. Teo sawed at it, hacking off triangular slabs that would be used to mop up the olive oil. Candida fetched a demijohn of wine in a wicker basket from the cellar. It, too, had been made on the farm and still sizzled with youth. Finally, Rosa brought the heavy stoneware *casseruòla* from the oven, and the family sat in the warmth of the fire to eat.

Vincenzo and Rosa Cipriani were a handsome couple. Vincenzo

was a stout, noble-looking man with a heavy jaw, a beaky Lombard nose, and fine black eyes, which he had passed to both his children. He had no bank account, but he was comparatively wealthy. Apart from the fieldstone farmhouse with its pan-tiled roof and big enclosed court-yard, he owned olive groves and vineyards, a flock of sheep high up in the mountains, and several acres of oak forest where wild boar had once flourished, until the Fascists had shot them all. He was a kindly man; he had never been brutal to an animal or a human being in his life, and he had always treated his family with great gentleness.

So his wife, Rosa, had not been subjected to the hard physical labor and repeated childbearing that destroyed the beauty of so many mountain women. She had kept her straight back and firm bust, and her aquiline, rather Nordic good looks. She was from Piemonte, and though Italian was her native language, she spoke it with a guttural Germanic rasp, as did all her kinsfolk, and was sometimes mistaken for a German. In many ways she was far tougher than her husband. She was respected, almost feared, for miles around.

The Ciprianis were farming people to the core, rooted in the land and its rhythms. They had raised Teo and Candida to be the same. It was Mussolini who had changed things. Had it not been for Fascism, Teo would not have gone to Greece, and the war might barely have touched the Cipriani family.

Being country people, they had never actually gone hungry, as people in the cities had done since 1940; but their diet had become very plain over the past years, and the thought of extravagant peacetime meals had become, with Candida at least, something of an obsession. They prayed briefly and started eating. The food was wonderful, a ban-quet of intense tastes and rich textures. They did not talk much: the business of eating was too important.

The pounding at the door startled them all halfway through the meal. For a moment, nobody moved. Their instinctive common thought was that German soldiers, having scented the slaughter somehow, had come to requisition the meat. Candida's heart sank.

The pounding started again, together with a muffled voice shouting, "Vincenzo! *Vincenzo!*"

Vincenzo rose to his feet, wiping his mouth with the heel of his hand. "Who's that?" he called.

"It's me! Paolo!"

"Paolo?" he hissed inquiringly at his wife.

"It's Paolo the deserter," Teo said suddenly. He had recognized the voice.

Vincenzo's eyebrows rose. Paolo was a cousin of the family who had fought in Greece with Teo. Like thousands of other Italians who had refused to continue fighting for the Nazis after the Armistice, he had been classified a deserter and had disappeared into the mountains. It was rumored he had joined the Partisans, though nobody had seen him for months.

"Don't answer," Rosa commanded Vincenzo.

"How can I not answer?" Vincenzo asked patiently. He unlatched the door and opened it a foot. Paolo's head thrust itself in. His face was white, the features no more than dirty smudges, with furtive eyes that darted urgently around the kitchen. Then he hissed, "Come," to Vincenzo, and withdrew his head.

With an apologetic shrug to his wife, Vincenzo followed him, closing the door as he went. A chill remained in the kitchen behind him.

Rosa's face was bleak. "This means only trouble," she said shortly. Candida thought of the German planes over the lake that morning. The food in her own stomach suddenly felt heavy, and she could eat no more. They sat in silence for a while, until Vincenzo came back in. He looked thoughtful, his heavy lids half-lowered over his eyes.

"What does he want?" Rosa demanded.

"They've got a wounded comrade."

" 'They'? Who are 'they'?"

"The Partisans." He was pinching his full lower lip, a habit when thinking hard. "They blew up a German truck on the pass. One of them was shot. An American. He's losing a lot of blood."

"Mother of God," Rosa said grimly. "They're not thinking of bringing him *here*?"

"He's here already," Vincenzo said calmly. "He's in the barn."

Rosa stood up, her face implacable. "Vincenzo, if the Germans find a dead Partisan in our barn they will hang the lot of us. They must take him away."

"They can't. He needs help, or he'll bleed to death."

"No!"

"I can't turn them away," Vincenzo said gently. "They're fighting for all of us."

"They're fighting for Stalin!"

"They need a doctor. There's only one man who can be trusted. I'll take the trap down to fetch him."

Rosa's eyes locked with his. She shook her head slightly, her taut expression saying what words could not. But Vincenzo only spread his hands. "I cannot turn a dying man away, Rosa," he said. "Teo, come with me."

Teo rose silently and followed his father out. Since Greece, his nerves had been stretched taut, liable to snap at any extra pressure. It was not cowardice, Candida knew, but an illness of the mind.

Candida's heart was pounding. "I'm going to help," she said. It was a statement, but it was also a question. She glanced at her mother, waiting for the whiplash countermand. But Rosa's face was now gray and weary. "Do as you please," she said quietly. "I want nothing to do with it."

Candida knew her mother meant that quite literally. She took a fresh bar of carbolic soap from the pantry, together with an old sheet. She filled a bowl with hot water from the kettle. She glanced at her mother, who sat silent and unmoving in her place. She looked old. Candida touched her mother's shoulder and carried her burden out.

The barn stood two hundred yards away from the house. The upper floor was a hayloft, one side open to let in the drying wind. The lower floor served as a storeroom for farm implements and a winter pen for animals; if the weather got really bad, Vincenzo's sheep would come down from the mountain pastures and huddle in here, munching hay. There was also a little ancient Fiat tractor in the barn, which had not run for years and was rusting quietly away to oblivion. The Partisans had huddled behind the tractor, as if behind a barricade.

Apart from Paolo, there were two others, one of whom Candida recognized at once as Giacometti the Tinker. She wondered in surprise whether this was the stuff Partisans were made of—little Paolo the deserter and Giacometti the half-Gypsy pan mender and horse doctor? The third man was more impressive, tall and well-made, with bright blue eyes set in a tanned face. He watched her as she slipped in with the hot water and the sheet, a British Sten gun cradled in his arms.

"Who are you?" he demanded.

"She's Candida Cipriani," Paolo said, "Vincenzo's daughter."

The wounded man lay on a makeshift stretcher in the soiled hay. He was moaning quietly, his eyes half-closed and filmy. As she sank to her knees beside him, a smell of male sweat and fresh blood filled her nostrils.

"Is he conscious?" she asked.

"He's had morphine," Giacometti told her. "Don't touch him. The doctor's coming."

"The doctor won't be here for hours. And he'll have to be cleaned up before the doctor can do anything." The injured man's face was dark and hawk-nosed, his sunken cheeks covered in bristle. His faded check shirt and corduroy jacket were soaked black. The day seemed to have been made of blood. But this was something very different from a wounded animal. She began carefully unfastening the chipped bone buttons. Nobody else tried to stop her.

The man's naked torso was lean and muscular. His belly and chest were covered in black hair, now matted with his own jellied blood. The wound looked terrible. Blood was welling out with a steadiness that made her heart lurch. It looked mortal. For a moment she was paralyzed.

"Hail Mary, full of grace, blessed art thou among women." The words rustled on her lips, unbidden. His eyes half opened and rested on her face. "And blessed is the fruit of thy womb, Jesus." She touched his brow, then his cheek. His skin was feverishly hot.

The prayer seemed to give her strength. She tore a strip from the sheet. She dipped it into the steaming water, soaped it with carbolic, and began sponging the flesh around the wound. She was as gentle as she could be, but the wounded man moved convulsively, his moans becoming gasps of pain. "I'm sorry," she told him shakily. "I'm trying not to hurt you." He seemed to nod. His eyes, full of pain, did not leave her face.

Cleaned up, the wound looked better in front, worse behind. The bullet had torn straight through his body. The entrance wound was neat, though there was a lot of burning. Where it had emerged from his back, gobbets of flesh and what looked like bone had been exploded outward, like the petals of a flower. It seemed to her that both the stomach and the left lung must have been pierced, and she was certain that some of the ribs were shattered. She felt a sickening conviction that this man was going to die. Despite her ministrations, the flow of blood was unchecked.

"You're bleeding," she told him. "A lot. Too much. If I tie up the wound, you might not bleed so much. But it might hurt you."

She thought he nodded again. The blue-eyed man with the Sten gun said curtly, "Do it."

She made pads and pressed them to both wounds. She tore off

several long strips to pass around his waist. "Lift him a little," she commanded. Paolo and the blue-eyed man stooped to obey. She looped the bandage around his lean ribs, pulling as tight as she dared, and trussed her homemade pads in place. The wounded man moaned hoarsely while she worked, but when they laid him down again, he seemed to lie easier.

Candida was drained, as though she had run a marathon. She lifted the wounded man's head and cradled it in her lap, stroking his face. It was wet with sweat, the bristle on his cheeks harsh beneath her fingertips. Pity welled in her, together with a sense of helplessness. "That's all I can do," she told him. His lips moved slightly, though whether he was trying to smile or to say something, she could not tell. Already, red stars were blossoming on her homemade dressing. An icy wind blew through the barn. "He'll freeze," she said.

Paolo took off his greatcoat, and she laid it over him against the cold.

"You've done well," the blue-eyed man said. He was offering her a cigarette.

She shook her head tiredly. "I don't smoke."

He lit one himself and blew a pungent cloud upward. "He'll be all right. He's as tough as a wolf, that one."

"How did he get this wound?" she asked.

He glanced at her. His expression was laconic, but she could sense his pride. "We had a little skirmish with some Germans."

She had been concentrating on his accent and knew now what he must be. "You're not an Italian," she said. "You're an escaped prisoner of war, aren't you?"

"Not escaped. Released. Him, too. We were both released on the day of the armistice. We joined the Partisans straightaway."

"Are you British?"

"To the backbone," he drawled. He nodded at the injured man, whose head lay quietly in Candida's lap. "He's an American."

"You speak good Italian."

"We've had plenty of time to learn," he said. "Two years in an Italian prison camp and then five months with the Partisans."

The Englishman's hands were large and powerful, the knuckles glinting with golden hair. But he held his cigarette elegantly poised between his fingers like a gentleman, not cupped in his palm the way most soldiers did. "Are you an officer?" she asked.

He threw her a snappy salute. "Yes, ma'am," he said crisply. She did not know whether he was mocking her. Little Paolo sniggered.

"You don't seem very concerned about your friend," she said reprovingly.

"I can see he's in good hands," he replied. "Joseph always lands with his arse in the butter." Paolo sniggered again.

"Joseph?" She looked down at the face in her lap. She had been stroking his brow mechanically, smoothing the dank hair back. The injured American's eyes were closed, but somehow she knew he was conscious. She wondered whether he knew he was dying. "What are you going to do with him? He can't go anywhere like this."

"He can stay here for a few days, can't he?"

"If the animals were in here, maybe. Without them, he'll freeze."

"We'll think of something," the Englishman said with a shrug. "What did you say your name was?"

"Candida."

"As in Voltaire?"

She shrugged, not knowing who Voltaire was. "And yours?"

"David." He was watching her with a speculative expression. "Paolo says your family is trustworthy. Is that true?"

"None of us asked you to come here," she replied, stung by the question. "You decided to trust us. It's your problem."

He seemed amused. "We didn't have much choice, Candida." He dropped his cigarette butt and ground it out with his heel, speaking casually. "There's a reward for turning in Partisans."

"I know," she said pointedly. "Two thousand lire each."

"If the Germans take us, they'll kill us. But then our friends will kill you six weeks later."

She looked at him steadily. His hair was fair, thickly curly. He had a square chin with an engaging cleft, like an athlete's buttocks, and level, dark-blue eyes. Washed of dust and earth he would be a very handsome man. The American who lay in her lap seemed gaunter, less substantial, though that was perhaps because of his wounded state. "You don't need to threaten us," she said in a quiet voice.

"She's right," Paolo said. "They're good people. Even Rosa, despite everything."

A thought was forming in Candida's mind. "Where did you have this skirmish with the Germans?"

"What's it to you?"

"They could track you to this barn."

"They won't," he said confidently.

"How do you know?"

"Believe me, I know."

"There were spotter planes in the air this morning."

"Yes. That's why we're all safer under a roof until nightfall," he replied.

The injured man's eyes opened, and he whispered a single word. She bent her head over his. "Shhh. Don't try to talk."

His eyes were dark, their gaze intense. "Dogs," he whispered. "They use dogs."

She looked up at the Englishman fearfully. "He says the Germans use dogs."

"Sometimes." He shrugged. "Maybe not today."

"That's all very well for you," she said sharply. He only smiled at her. She was angered. "You talk of us betraying you! You can run back into the woods. We live here! What if the Germans search the area, house by house? They've done it before. If they find him here, they'll hang us."

"Then you'd better hide him where they won't find him." He rubbed his stomach. "Christ, I'm starving. Will the woman feed us?"

Paolo looked uneasy. "She's a bit of a dragon," he muttered.

"There's half a pig out there in the yard. And I can smell something good on the stove. Let's go and slay the dragon."

He dropped one eyelid at Candida and left, followed less certainly by Paolo and Giacometti, both of whom had experience of Rosa Cipriani's rough tongue.

Silence fell. Candida sat cradling the wounded man's head in her arms. She was thinking about the German dogs, red tongues lolling as they strained at their handlers' leashes.

It was two hours before Vincenzo and Teo arrived with the doctor. He was a small man with the sodden face of a drinker, a big belly hanging untidily over his belt. He was known as a butcher, but was surly enough to be thought of as close-mouthed in an already secretive community.

He waddled into the barn and glared down at the wounded American. "Nice. Full of shrapnel, I suppose."

"Just one bullet, Doctor. Right through him."

He grunted. "Has he had anything to eat or drink?"

"Not since last night."

"Who put that bandage on?"

"She did," Giacometti volunteered, jerking his thumb at Candida.

The doctor stared at her with bloodshot, pouchy eyes that reminded her of the pig's. "Get it off. The rest of you get out."

The men trooped out, leaving her with the doctor. She began unwinding the bandages as best she could. The doctor thrust a pair of scissors at her.

"Here. Cut them."

"We'll need them later."

"Cut them, stupid child."

She swallowed the lump in her throat and cut carefully through the bandages. The wounds were still bleeding heavily.

The doctor looked wearily at the wounds, an unlit cigarette in his mouth. "What the hell am I meant to do with this? Eh?"

"Is he going to die?" she whispered in dread.

"I'm not the archangel Gabriel. I'm not a medical genius, either. How do you expect me to put this man back together?"

"You must be able to do something!"

For a moment she thought he would close his bag and walk out of the barn, leaving the American to die. Then he groaned wearily and took out a bottle of some pungent orange liquid and started swabbing the man's skin liberally. "If he doesn't bleed to death, and if you haven't already given him septicemia, and if the bullet hasn't gone through his spleen or his pancreas or his duodenum, I presume he has a slim chance." He filled a syringe and injected the man's arm. The American's eyes were closed again. The doctor peeled back an eyelid and peered in. "That may not take the pain away completely, sonny, so brace yourself. Do you hear me?" There was no response. The doctor rose with a grunt. "I'm going to wash my hands."

The American's eyes opened blearily and searched for Candida's face, the way a baby's eyes search for its mother's face. She stroked his cheek. "You'll be all right," she told him. "He's a good doctor. He'll do his best. And I'll pray for you."

The doctor returned, sleeves rolled up, hands dripping. "All right, child. Put him on his side and hold his head."

She took up her old position, propping his head in her lap. The doctor opened a leather instrument case and took out a large scalpel. With no ceremony, he slashed diagonally, deeply, across the entrance wound.

The American arched in agony, a hiss rasping from his throat, ghastlier than a scream. His eyes had rolled back whitely. Candida clung to him, her vision darkening. "For God's sake! He's still conscious!"

"I've only got morphine, not ether," the doctor said. He belched sour fumes of wine. "I'm a village doctor, not a field surgeon. He can have some more afterward. If he lives." He was widening the incision deftly, clamping steel instruments to the edges of the wound and pulling them back. Somehow she was managing not to faint. The American was gasping shallowly, his face white and sweating heavily. She cradled his head in her arms, pressing her cheek to his. She could think of nothing else to say but the Hail Mary, which she whispered into his ear, her own eyes shut tight. She could feel his body quivering and tensing like a galloping greyhound as the doctor worked. His pain was unimaginable, but he made no more sounds. Perhaps he was incapable, or perhaps he had passed into some merciful twilight.

After a while the doctor grunted. "Don't get your hair in the wound, child."

She looked up. The American's body had been opened like a gladstone bag. There was much less blood than she had anticipated. In the gaping aperture, smooth organic surfaces glistened. It was such an astonishing sight that her feeling of sick faintness receded.

"Is it bad?" she asked in an awed whisper.

"Could be worse," he said irritably, the still-unlit cigarette waggling between his lips. In a dreamlike way, she was fascinated. The doctor was probing with the back of the scalpel, his movements precise. He made it look so matter-of-fact, so simple. You just cut a man open, and there his inward workings were. She had a hysterical desire to laugh at the simplicity of it all. He glanced up at her suddenly. "You going to faint, child?"

"No."

"I see you killed a pig this morning. Been a morning for butchery, hasn't it?"

She nodded.

He sniffed inside the wound, the wings of his porous nose

twitching. "Missed the spleen of course, or he'd be dead already. No arteries cut. A lot of muscle damage. Broken ribs. Those bits of bowel will need sewing up. Small-caliber bullet, was it?"

"I don't know."

"Two-two, I'd guess. This little piggy's been lucky. He's going to have a bellyache, but he might live."

Her eyes filled with tears. "Thank God."

The doctor smiled at her bosom, his teeth yellow as a dog's. "This hero your lover?"

"No. I don't know him."

"You know him inside out now. You've seen more of him than his mother ever did. Is he conscious?"

She glanced at the American's face, which was now blurred and vacant. "I don't think so."

"So much the better. Now shut up and keep out of my damned way."

For ten or twenty minutes, the doctor sliced and stitched. He was quick and crude, but his work was effective. Halfway through the primitive operation, Candida felt a timid presence behind her and looked up. It was Teo. He laid his hand on her shoulder, watching the doctor in silence. She wondered whether it had been like this for him in the Greek mountains. The American moved spasmodically from time to time but was largely inert. Teo's hand stayed on her shoulder.

At last the doctor began the process of sewing up the wounds, layer by layer. When he was done, the scribble of stitching ran around the man's body as though he were a doll that had been freshly stuffed with sawdust.

He dressed the wound and gave Candida two spare dressings. "Keep these in a clean place."

"Yes, Doctor."

Teo silently held out a bottle to the doctor. It was homemade grappa, fierce and raw. The doctor gulped greedily at the bottle, exhaling a fiery gust of pleasure, like a carnival fire-eater. He checked the bottle, which was three-quarters full, then put it in his bag. "And I'll have a ham," he said calmly, at last lighting his soggy cigarette.

"A ham?" Teo said, raising his eyebrows.

"My fee. You don't think that ragtag crew of so-called Partisans can afford anything?"

"He's not our responsibility," Teo said awkwardly.

"He is now." The piggy eyes were implacable.

Teo sighed. "My mother will go mad. Those three have their shirts stuffed full of sausages already. I guess we could let you have a couple of kilos of pork ribs."

The injured man was moaning brokenly now. "You said you'd give him some more morphine afterward," she pleaded.

"He needs more than morphine." The doctor produced two ampoules and some glassine envelopes filled with powder. "These two are morphine. The powder is sulfanilamide. Watch, child." He showed Candida how to tap the powder into the wound, then how to fill the syringe and inject the morphine into the blue vein that swelled in the crook of the elbow. "Tomorrow, clean the wound and cover it with sulfanilamide again. If the pain is unbearable, give him half of the morphine. The other half later on. Bring the syringe back to my house tomorrow night. I might have found some more sulfanilamide by then. Cost you a kilo of sausage, mind."

"Can he eat?"

"Nothing tonight. Liquids only for the next two days. Then eggs beaten in milk, that kind of thing, until his system's working again." He rose to his feet, not even looking at the man whose life he had just saved. "Now give me my ribs and take me back home before the Nazis get here."

The Englishman had come into the barn. He glanced at his friend. "When can we move him?"

"Move him?" The doctor shrugged. "When he's recovered."

"How long?"

"Weeks."

"He can't stay here for weeks," Teo said sharply.

"He'll have to. Unless you want him dying in your potato patch."

They went out, arguing. Candida sat with the American, watching his face as the voices faded out. She was already thinking of places where he could be hidden. He looked serene now. The drug was ironing the lines of pain out of his face. He was young, not much older than she herself. He did not look like her preconception of an American. His face was unusual, dark and narrow. It looked to her like the mask of some ancient warrior. His mouth was half-open, showing teeth that were white and slightly crooked. His dark hair lay wetly across a high, bony forehead.

Two of the cats that lived upstairs in the hayloft had come down to watch, green eyes fixed on the wounded man, as though they would like to lick the bright blood that had been shed. He seemed completely at peace now, so she covered him with Paolo's greatcoat, shooed away the cats, and left him for a moment.

In the kitchen, a furious argument was raging.

She heard her mother's voice saying fiercely, "Anyone sheltering Partisans is subject to martial law, Vincenzo. You know what that means!"

"He'll die if he doesn't have rest," Vincenzo said. "There's no choice."

"There is a choice! Look at them, walking around as if they owned the place, helping themselves to our food. They can take him away with them!"

The three Partisans leaned against the wall, unshaven and shabby-looking. They did not join in the argument, just followed it with their eyes.

"We could hide him in the cellar," Candida volunteered.

Rosa wheeled on her daughter. "Hold your tongue."

"She's right, Mama," Teo said. "We could make him a bed in there. Just for a few days. The Germans would never think of looking in there."

"The Germans are not as stupid as you are," Rosa spat. Her blond hair was disarrayed and her face was red, signs she was losing control.

"I know about the Germans," Teo said quietly. "If nobody betrays us, he'll be safe here."

"Nobody would say a word," Candida agreed. The outlying community was close-knit and united in its contempt for fascism.

"You can hide him up in the mountains, with one of those half-witted shepherds of yours!"

Vincenzo raised his thick eyebrows. "Up there? In December?"

"Let him take his chances. Why put all our lives at risk?"

"He has to stay here," her husband said patiently.

"He must go!" She looked as though she was in a towering rage, but Candida knew it was largely fear.

Vincenzo shook his head. "He stays."

"They'll burn us alive in our own house!"

Candida glanced around the roughly plastered walls, so thick and solid, keeping out the cold in winter and the heat in summer. *Il Nóce* meant "The Walnut Tree." A huge walnut had once grown in the yard, though a storm had blown it down while she'd been a child. To her the house was a rock, unshaken by wars or tempests, proof even against Nazis.

Vincenzo spoke quietly, but his words carried authority. "This house was my father's, and his father's before him, Rosa. It's my decision."

Rosa was shaking with emotion. Her eyes were despairing. She controlled herself with an effort. "He can stay the night. Tomorrow he must go."

Vincenzo shrugged on his sheepskin coat. "I'm not sending that boy out to die in the woods like a dog. I couldn't live with myself if I did. He can go in the cellar. Candida, make it comfortable for him. Teo, you stay with the American." He jerked his head at the doctor. "Come, Doctor. I'll take you home."

Rosa went out of the kitchen without another word. Candida knew she was crying, silently and bitterly. There was a lump in her own throat—she had never been able to witness her mother's tears unaffected—but she agreed unequivocally with her father. They had to take care of the wounded man. It was a duty they could not duck. She turned to the Partisans. "I'll need help."

David, the Englishman, rose. "You two get moving," he commanded the Italians. "I'll meet you at the bridge in an hour."

Paolo and Giacometti slunk out. She could see that Teo had been right; both men's shirts bulged with sausages they had either pilfered or been given by Vincenzo. No doubt that had added to her mother's passion.

The entrance to the cellar was under the stairs, an unobtrusive little door. She lit a lantern and led the Englishman down into the darkness.

The cellar was a meandering, low-ceilinged place, full of alcoves and recesses. It was piled with all kinds of ancient rubbish, so they had to pick their way cautiously, hunched over to avoid banging their heads. The piercing cold and damp of winter were less noticeable here. It was always more or less the same temperature down here in the bowels of the earth, a degree or so higher in summer, a degree or so lower in winter.

At the far end, in the darkest and farthest cranny, was a hollow place beneath the level of the cellar itself. It was a small chamber, lined with wood. It had once been a grain store, and it was clean and dry. As children, Candida and Teo had been able to stand upright in it, but now they had to stoop. Unless you knew it was there, it was very hard to find. There was a hatch that could be pulled over it. She showed it to David.

"Our grandfather used to tell us how Piemontese soldiers hid down here from the Austrians a hundred years ago."

The Englishman's face was eerie in the lantern light as he peered in. "Perfect."

"We could put a mattress down there, and some blankets. When we pull the hatch over him and put some rubbish on top, nobody will ever guess he's there."

"Let's do it."

They lined the hole with straw and some old blankets. It would be pitch-black down there when the light was out, but it was a secure refuge. And, she comforted herself, the American would probably not even notice his surroundings for two or three days.

"Don't worry about him." David laughed. "I told you, he's as tough as a wolf."

David used his ingenuity, piling rubbish around the hatch, empty wine vats, cracked oil jars, and broken furniture, to discourage investigation. After half an hour of hot work, she was pleased with the result. "He'll be safe down here."

The American called Joseph was limp and motionless as she, David, and Teo carried him into the house and down into the cellar. Only when they started easing him into the cramped confines of the grain store did he begin moaning, making feeble warding-off gestures with his good arm. The other arm seemed immobile and hung limp.

It was awkward work, lit by the smoky flame of the lantern. She prayed they would not split the doctor's stitches or injure him further internally. She tried not to think of what it would be like for him when he woke.

At last he was lying in the straw, huddled under blankets. He looked infinitely pathetic. It tore at her heart to pull the hatch over him and leave him entombed there in the close darkness, wounded and alone, but she knew it was the only way.

David and Teo pulled an empty barrel onto the hatch, and they picked their way out into the kitchen. All three were smeared with dust and filth. David stretched his broad shoulders. "What a day," he said, yawning.

"Are you sure he'll be all right down there?" Teo asked doubtfully.

"As soon as he's stronger we'll get him out of here," David assured them. "We'll organize a party to hike up through the Val d'Aosta, and carry him into Switzerland. Or maybe our own chaps will be close enough by then, and we can get him through the front line." He slapped Teo's shoulder. "You've both been wonderful. Where did you get that leg, by the way?"

"Greece," Teo said briefly.

"Bad mistake of Il Duce's." David nodded, not really interested. "Thanks for everything." Teo nodded briefly.

Candida followed David out into the yard. "Did you kill any Germans this morning?" she asked him.

His face took on an odd expression, as of a pleasure slyly remembered. "Would you be impressed if I said yes?"

"No. My brother says killing is too easy."

He touched his lips with the tip of a pink tongue like a cat's. "It's easy if you're good at it."

Under the arch of the gate, Candida hung back. "Where will you go now?" she asked.

"Back up into the hills. I'll come back tomorrow. Unless the Nazis catch me."

"You must take care!"

"Oh, I'd risk a lot to see a girl as beautiful as you, Candida." He scrambled up the slope into the woods, his tall figure fading in the twilight. At the edge of the trees he turned and waved.

"Be careful!" she called again. Then he was gone.

She went to check on the man called Joseph for the last time before turning in at eleven. His eyes were closed, but his face flinched as the lantern light crossed it. She laid her hand on his brow. She had wrapped him in blankets, but his skin felt cold to her touch. She did not know whether that was a good sign or a bad one.

"You're safe," she told him. "We've hidden you down in the cellar. It's cramped and dark, but the Nazis can't find you here. Are you in pain?"

He did not respond.

"I'll come to you early tomorrow. At dawn. I've got sulfanilamide. And some more morphine, if you need it."

Still he did not move or speak. The light cast hollows in his
cheeks and under his brows, and she wondered with a pang whether
he really would live, or whether she would come down in the morning
to find him stiff and cold in this coffin. She bent and touched her lips
to his temple. "Sleep well," she whispered.

The house was silent. It occurred to her that the day, with all
its blood and horror, had been the greatest adventure of her young life.
She would have so much to tell her diary. But dared she write such
things?

She looked out of her window into the cold night sky, where
stars already glittered like diamonds on dark-blue silk, and felt that
her life had changed in some important, but not yet definable way,
forever.

As He Had promised, the Englishman came back to *Il Noce* the next
day at twilight. She led him down to see the American, who was sleeping
fitfully and did not wake as they peered at him by the flickering light
of the kerosene lantern.

"He doesn't look too bad," David said.

"I'm so afraid for him," she confessed. "I think he might die."

"Nonsense." The Englishman smiled. "He'll survive."

Back in the kitchen, he turned to Candida. "Before I go, can
you cut my hair?"

"Cut your hair?" she asked in astonishment.

"It's like a flag," he said, running his fingers through his blond
curls. "Might as well have the Union Jack tied round my head. See it a
mile off when it's too long. Paolo says you can cut hair."

"Yes, but—"

"Quickly, then." He unbuttoned his shirt and pulled it off. His
torso was muscular and smooth, the skin milk-white, the only bodily
hair a tawny tuft in each armpit. He pulled a chair up in front of the
fire and grinned at her. "Short back and sides, please, miss."

Teo gave her a dry look. "I'll go and finish the sausages." He
went out.

She took the scissors from the drawer and studied David's tousled mop. "I'll make a mess," she warned.

"Just do it." He issued his commands effortlessly, as though he really had been an officer. He was certainly, she thought, a gentleman. There was no furtiveness in his movements about him, as there was about Paolo's and Giacometti's. He seemed unafraid of being caught by the Nazis.

There was something instantly likable about him, a quick charm. Teo had been like that once, before Mussolini's disastrous adventure in Greece had crippled him in body and spirit. And he was very handsome. She tried to avoid looking at his body but could not help noticing his skin, fine and smooth as a girl's, despite the hard muscles. She started cutting.

"Why do you keep saying your friend is so tough?" she asked. "Aren't you worried about him?"

"He's a survivor." The Englishman smiled.

"He looks so . . . pitiful."

"He'll make it. Krasnowsky always does."

"Is that his name?"

David laughed. "Just call him Joseph, or Joe, like I do. He's a Latvian or a Pole, or something. They all have names like that. In the next generation it'll become Crawford or Crabtree."

She chopped at his hair. "Your wife won't know you when you get back to London."

"I don't live in London," he replied. "And I'm not married." He squinted up at her. "What made you think I was?"

"Nothing. It's better, anyway. If you had a wife, she'd be worried to death about you, poor thing. I suppose you have lots of girlfriends."

"I did have, before the war. But none of them will be concerned about me, I assure you. They've all forgotten me by now."

"Didn't they write to you in the camp?"

"No," he said. "Only my mother. You've got beautiful hands, Candida."

She was surprised. "Have I?"

"I always look at hands. They tell a lot about a person. Yours are very fine, with long, tapering fingers."

"And what does that tell you about me?"

"You have a virtuous and spiritual nature," he said solemnly, "but with a deep sensual undercurrent."

"What nonsense!" His fine, thick hair twined richly around her fingers, and she was suddenly tempted to yank hard, just for the pleasure of hearing him yell. "Tilt your head up."

He lifted his face to look at her. His eyes were a deep, almost royal blue. They met hers with amusement, and something else, something she was not too unworldly to interpret. She felt her treacherous nipples tighten pleasurably, and a hot flush crept up her throat into her face. "Are you really an officer?" she asked, concentrating on her task.

"A junior one. A captain. What makes you ask?"

"Paolo and Giacometti seem to jump to everything you say."

"That's the natural authority of the Anglo-Saxon race over lesser breeds." He grinned.

"You sound like the Nazis."

Rosa came into the kitchen, her mouth set, tying an apron around her waist. She had been crying, but her eyes were now hard as stones. "What's this?" she asked harshly.

The Englishman smiled disarmingly. "Presuming even further on your hospitality. Sorry."

"He needed his hair cut, Mama," Candida said shyly.

"One gets so ragged-looking. Somewhere along the line we all lost our soap and razors. We've been sleeping in abandoned shepherd's huts up in the mountains for a month, and they aren't exactly luxurious."

"Can't you hear the airplanes?" Rosa asked him grimly. "They're hunting you like vermin, and you sit here with my daughter cutting your hair."

"As soon as your charming daughter has finished, I'll melt back into the scenery, madam." His gaze dropped to the swell of Candida's breasts against the jersey. She knew the peaks of her nipples were showing and tried to cover them with her arms. "I don't know how we can repay you for your kindness. You've all been wonderful. Your husband is a great man."

Rosa slammed a wooden bowl down on the table, and began churning polenta, wielding the wooden spoon like a weapon. "My husband is a fool," she said bitterly. "His kind heart will be the death of us all."

"When the Allies win the war," David said cheerfully, "Churchill will see you all get a reward."

Rosa laughed harshly. He did not know it, but that was perilously close to the rough joke that German soldiers made nowadays whenever they smashed, stole, or looted: *"Alles gut, Churchill bezahlt das."* Candida cut his hair in silence while her mother beat the polenta, muttering to herself, her face red, her eyes hot.

At last Candida stood back and surveyed her handiwork.

"Well?" he asked.

"Well, it looks different."

"Better or worse?" he asked.

She studied him critically. "At least you don't look like a brigand now. And you speak Italian very well. If you met a German and told him you were from Piemonte, he might believe you."

She passed him the mirror. He studied his reflection, rasping a thumb across his stubbled cheek. "There wouldn't be a razor around the house, would there?"

Rosa looked at him incredulously. Candida hurried to fetch her father's shaving kit before her mother could object. The Englishman sighed with pleasure as he lathered his face with Vincenzo's brush, careless with the precious soap. He shaved with quick, deft strokes, shaking the froth into the sink, then rinsed his face, rubbing it vigorously. He dried himself on the towel, buttoned up his shirt, and lit a cigarette with a flourish. "Christ, that feels better."

The result was startling. Cutting his hair had emphasized his good looks, and his shave had added polish. As he lounged against the sink, smoking a cigarette, he was extraordinarily handsome. His blue eyes seemed to blaze even brighter than before. Even Rosa was rather awestruck. She looked at him from the tails of her eyes, apparently forgetting to be angry.

"I'd better make tracks," he said, consulting his watch. "My merry men will be waiting for me." He flashed his smile at the two women. "Thanks again. You're angels."

At the gate, the Englishman leaned forward and kissed Candida's cheek. "I want to see you again," he said in a low voice. "I'll send a message."

He was gone before she could reply. She stayed where she was, feeling the warmth linger on her cheek. Flirting with a desirable young man was a diversion she'd known all too seldom in her life, and her heart was fluttering pleasurably.

She went slowly back to the kitchen, not sure whether she had woken from a dream into real life, or stepped from real life into a dream. David's shaving lather was spattered all over the stone sink, gold stubble glinting brightly among the froth.

She Was Awakened before dawn with her heart pounding in her chest. But it was not one of her vivid dreams. What had torn her out of her sleep was a tumult of shouting and rumbling engines outside.

She threw open her shutters. The dense predawn mist glared like a thundercloud lit by lightning. The yard was filled with German soldiers, their gray-green uniforms lit by the headlights of the vehicles they had come in.

She was unprepared for how much terror hurt. It was like the bullets of the firing squad already tearing into her heart, her lungs.

The pounding on the door shook the house. The commands were in German, but their meaning was clear. They would smash the door down if it were not opened. She stumbled down the stairs, whispering Hail Marys.

Her parents and Teo were already in the kitchen. They stared at one another for a moment. Her mother was white, with bloodless lips. Teo looked dazed, his jaw hanging. Vincenzo unbolted the door, grave and silent. The soldiers marched in with a crash of boots on the ancient tiles. There were eight of them, bringing a smell of weapons, diesel, male sweat. They carried crowbars, and they wore the faces that all German soldiers seemed to wear, with vigilant eyes and hard mouths.

The officer who followed wore a black uniform. He surveyed them all with cold gray eyes, staring at each one carefully. As if in a terrible dream, Candida saw the insignia that glittered on his collar. If anything could have brought more dread into the room, it was those two little lightning flashes that meant SS.

"The whole family is present?"

"Yes," Vincenzo replied in a hoarse voice.

"You have no one else?"

"No."

"We will search the house now."

He turned and issued a command in German. The soldiers' boots thumped up the stairs.

The officer stayed behind. The fear of the whole family was like a physical presence in the room, sickening, choking. He studied them as though tasting the fear, analyzing it with a professional's palate. He was young, but his face was already harshly lined with responsibility. His eyes were pitiless. They had looked upon hangings and shootings, upon torture in blood-spattered rooms. He swung on his heel and stared at the sideboard, where Teo's medal was displayed in a little frame.

"Whose is this?"

Candida heard herself speak, dry-mouthed. "That's my brother's. He won it in Greece."

The officer looked at Teo, who stood like an idiot, his face the color of cheese. "A war hero."

"A patriotic Italian," Vincenzo said.

The officer's face did not change. "No Italian can be trusted," he said calmly. "The world has seen the proof of that." Thumps and crashes came from upstairs as the soldiers emptied a cupboard. Candida's hands were trembling like leaves. She hid them behind her back so those clear gray eyes would not see. But they were all trembling, all three of them. She could hear her mother's shallow, jerky breathing, could see her brother's lips quivering. What had they done? She remembered the unthinking cheerfulness with which she had taken charge of the wounded man two days ago. Unthinking and blind. Hiding an American soldier was bad enough. Wounded as he was, they would know he was a Partisan and had taken part in the fighting two days earlier.

She thought of what the Germans would do to him if they found him. Of what they would do to the whole family. Had some informer sold them for two thousand lire? Was that what their lives had been worth?

The officer checked his watch. "I would like a cup of coffee."

There was a silence. To admit to having real coffee was to admit being a black marketeer. "We make our own out of acorns," Vincenzo said. "It's not very—"

"Make it." He glanced up at the ceiling, where they had hung the sausages. "All this material is confiscated," he added. "Take it down."

They creaked into movement, Rosa to make coffee, Candida and Teo to take down the precious sausages. They were like store-window dummies coming to life, she thought numbly. They moved in the jerky way dummies would move. But if he were interested in coffee and sausages, perhaps this was a routine search, not a purposeful, informed hunt. It was a tiny glimmer of hope.

The boots of the soldiers thudded around the old farmhouse. Now and then the beams creaked overhead, and once there was a crash of something breaking that made Rosa gasp in shock. The officer drank his acorn coffee in silence, his eyes never leaving their faces.

At last the soldiers came down to make their report. The officer studied the Ciprianis. Then he pointed to the cellar door. "What is that?"

"The cellar," Vincenzo croaked.

"Open it."

Vincenzo obeyed, white-faced. The officer looked in and sniffed the air sharply, like a dog. The action was so sinister that Candida panicked.

"There's nothing in there," she blurted out. "Just a lot of old rubbish."

She knew at once that she'd made a terrible mistake. Her voice had betrayed everything.

The officer unbuttoned the holster at his hip and took out his pistol. He slid the breech back with a click. "You will show me. Not you, old man," he said as Vincenzo started forward. "You. The girl. Take the lantern."

Candida picked up the lantern with trembling fingers and led the way in. Please God, she was praying, please Holy Virgin, please save all our lives.

The officer picked his way down the stairs after her, kicking out with distaste at a mouse that ran across his boots. He surveyed the flickering shadows. "How can you live in such filth?" he snapped at Candida. "Why don't you Italians ever keep your houses clean?"

She kept her eyes down. She was still praying ceaselessly.

He turned and called two of his men. They came in and began smashing a path through the clutter with their crowbars. The wood splintered. Holding his pistol at the ready, the officer picked his way through the wreckage. They began methodically investigating any place that might conceal a man. Candida stood at the bottom of the steps, the lantern rattling in her hands. What if Joseph, semiconscious, let out a moan? What if he cried out for water?

Then one of the soldiers walked right over the hatch of the store. She heard the thud of his boots on the wood. He stopped and stamped hard, cocking his ear to the hollow sound.

Terror crushed her heart, cramping her bowels. This could not be how it was going to end for her, for all of them. She heard a roaring in her ears, felt sickness fill her mind. Her knees buckled and she slid down the wall, the lantern crashing onto the ground.

In the darkness, the Germans' guttural voices were like the barking of savage dogs.

She was dragged roughly to her feet. "What is the matter with you?" the officer shouted. "Why did you throw down the lantern?"

"I—I fainted," she stammered.

An open hand smashed into her cheek, making her cry out. "Why?"

"I can't breathe," she gasped. "I can't bear confined places."

He cursed at her in German. Then she was being thrust back up the stairs into the kitchen. The officer, his cap now streaked with cobwebs, was no longer calm, but coldly angry.

"No German farmer would keep a cellar like that," he spat at Vincenzo. "You people are filthy animals." He shouted commands at his men.

Beating dust from their uniforms, the soldiers filed out of the cellar. Her head felt swollen and numbed from the blow. She could not believe that they had failed to notice the hatch. But, miraculously, the soldier who had stamped seemed to have been distracted by her collapse.

The SS officer was like a frustrated dog, sensing his quarry nearby, unable to track it down. He stalked around the kitchen, dusting himself down. His voice was harsh and strained. "You know what has happened. German soldiers have been murdered in cold blood. The murderers will be caught. You all know the penalties. You know what we will do to them. Yes or no?"

"Yes," Vincenzo said quickly.

"Each act of treachery will be paid for in full. In blood. In the blood of the traitors. In the blood of their mothers and fathers. Of their wives and children. Of the scum who hide them." The officer turned on Teo, who flinched. "You, hero. You think we've lost the war because you Italians have betrayed us, not so?"

Teo stood in silence, looking down.

"Answer!"

He looked up, very pale. "Italy never wanted your war," he said quietly. "We don't want it now." The officer's eyes widened for a moment. Then he snapped a command in German. Without hesitation, two of the men moved forward, swinging their crowbars.

"*No,*" Candida screamed, lunging to put herself between Teo and the Germans. Her mother grasped her shoulders and pulled her back. She saw Teo cowering, his arms covering his head. The heavy iron bars thudded into him pitilessly. They battered him to the ground, and he curled into a ball, trying to cover his head.

Rosa crushed Candida's face to her breast, trying to shut out the terrible sight. But nothing could shut out the thud of the soldiers' boots, or Teo's gasps of agony.

At last the SS officer gave the command to cease, and silence fell. Candida clung to her mother like a child, crying desolately.

"*Hinaus! Raus!*"

The boots thudded out of the kitchen, and their engines erupted like thunder outside.

The Dawn Was gray and cold.

Rosa wept over her son. But Teo, bloodied and bruised, would not let them call the doctor. "Nothing broken," he said, tight-lipped against the pain. "Thank God, we were lucky." Refusing help, he dragged himself up to bed.

Candida's hands had stopped shaking, but there was an inner trembling that would not stop, a trembling of the muscles deep in her body, close to the bones. *Lucky.* She wondered how lucky they had been. Their house violated, Teo beaten, their precious winter supplies plundered. And down in the cellar, the American remained, a ticking human bomb who could yet destroy them all. She felt a moment of resentment against him that was so intense it bordered on hatred.

She had to force herself to go down to him, carrying water in a stoppered flask. When she pulled the hatch open, she saw his face crumple in the lantern light and knew he was conscious. His hovel stank acridly; she'd left him a clay pot for a lavatory, and he'd used it. At least his bowels were working.

"It's only me," Candida said, kneeling beside him. "Are you all right?" He was shivering. She helped him raise his head and held the flask to his lips. He drank in painful little sips. She laid her hand on his forehead and felt the skin no longer cold, but dry and hot. Perhaps he was running a fever. She lifted the lid off the clay pot, checking his wastes for any blood. There was no sign. "Are you in pain?" she asked.

"Burns. Like fire."

"I've got some more morphine."

"I heard the Germans," he said in a hoarse whisper. "What happened?"

"They were walking right over the hatch. I fainted and dropped the lantern. They got angry with me and came out."

His dark, Slavic eyes met hers. "That was clever of you."

"I didn't do it deliberately."

"Were they *Feldgendarmen?*"

"SS." Candida saw the fear in his eyes. "Here. Drink this." She watched his face as he drank some more. He was even more drawn than yesterday, and his high cheekbones pushed through the skin. His lips looked cracked and dry. She felt ashamed of her earlier resentment.

Joseph's head fell back. "I heard screaming."

"They beat my brother." She had to gulp back the lump in her throat. "For nothing. They hit him with iron bars, and kicked him like a dog . . ."

He reached out and grasped her hand. His fingers were sinewy, restless. "I'm sorry. I'm sorry. This isn't right. I must leave."

"Don't be stupid. You can't go anywhere like that."

"Tonight. I'll go tonight."

"You're sick, you don't know what you're saying." She wiped her wet eyelids. "Anyway, they've been and gone now. They won't come back." She tried to smile at him. "It's not your fault."

"If they find me, they'll kill you all. They should never have brought me here."

"Should they have left you to die in the woods like a dog?"

"That would have been better than this."

He seemed to be serious. "Well, it's done now, and it can't be helped." She drew the blanket aside and looked at the bandages. There had been some bleeding in the night; she could see the dark stains. But it seemed to have stopped, and there was no bad smell, though he flinched at her touch. Another bout of shivering shook his body. "I'm going to dress your wound. Do you want the morphine first?" she asked.

He nodded. His eyes followed Candida's movements as she drew the morphine into the syringe. She extracted the air, as the doctor had showed her, and lifted his arm, looking for the blue vein. Conscious of her clumsiness, she slid the needle under the skin and pushed the plunger slowly home.

"There. You'll feel better now."

She watched his face. Within a few seconds, the harsh lines around his mouth smoothed, the look of pain faded. She cleaned the wound and tapped in one of the glassine envelopes of sulfanilamide. He did not stir. But he was still shivering. "Are you cold?" she asked.

"Bitter cold," he murmured.

"Your skin is hot. I think you're getting a fever." She glanced round the tiny wooden room. "We'll have to move you. But I'm going to call the doctor first."

"No!" He plucked at her sleeve. "Don't go yet. Don't leave me."

"I must. I won't be long."

"Don't go," he begged. "A little longer. It's not time yet." He whispered something in English. His gaze was unfocused now, the pupils dilated and glassy. He seemed not to know where he was anymore.

She pulled the blankets around him, preparing to go. But as she tried to rise, he grasped her wrist, fingers biting into her flesh. "Kiss me," he commanded urgently. "Kiss me before you go."

Perhaps he thought she was someone else. A lover. She felt the hot flush fill her face. But she leaned forward all the same and kissed his brow gently. He seemed content with the chaste caress and lay back with a sigh. "Thank you."

She replaced the used clay pot with the fresh one she'd brought. "The water's next to you. I won't shut you in this time."

His eyes followed her as she picked her way through the dark.

The Doctor Was astonished.

"You mean he's still alive?"

It had taken Candida three hours to walk down from *Il Noce,* and she faced an even longer uphill walk back again. She was already footsore. "Of course he's still alive. Why shouldn't he be alive?"

"Shock, blood loss, septicemia, gangrene. That's why he shouldn't be alive, child." He sat in his untidy surgery with a glass of wine in one hand, the inevitable cigarette clamped between his lips. "A pigsty isn't the ideal place to lug out a man's bowels. Where have you hidden him?"

"In the cellar."

He grunted. "Better and better. I hope it's cold, dark, and damp. Ideal postoperative conditions."

Candida stared at him, realizing, as if for the first time, how heavily the odds were stacked against the wounded American. Without hygiene, without proper medical care, hunted by the Nazis, he was a man condemned to death. She remembered the fierce grip of his hot fingers, the gleam of his eyes in the lantern light. "He's surviving," she said. "And there's nowhere else to put him."

He squinted at her through the smoke. "I heard the Germans came to your place last night."

She was not surprised. News traveled with astonishing speed, despite the remoteness of the area. "They searched everybody's house, not just ours. And they didn't find anything." She held out the package of meat. "They took most of the pork. There's only *sanguinàccio* left." He made no move to take the package. "You said you'd find some more drugs," she said urgently.

"They're still in the district. Still looking. They have fourteen soldiers dead." He crushed the cigarette out with a nicotine-brown forefinger. "If they find your American, no doubt you'll blurt my name out, so they can hang me, too."

"We won't say anything."

"Oh, brave child," he said with heavy irony. "They'll start with you, of course. Then your mother. Do you know what they do to pretty young girls like you? Shall I tell you?"

"No," she said quickly.

"And they'll make your father and brother watch. You'll talk, all right."

She swallowed. "So you won't help?"

He considered her for a while. "I hate them," he said at last. "Not for any political reason. I just hate them." He heaved himself to his feet and took a handful of glassine envelopes from a locked cupboard. "This is all the sulfanilamide I've got. Our beloved authorities ration it out, in their infinite wisdom. Give him one every two days."

"And some morphine," she begged. "He's in pain!"

"Suddenly you're a nurse," he snapped. But he gave her three more ampoules. "These are addictive, child. Only give them to him if he really needs them. And give him less each time. You understand?"

"Yes," she said, delighted. "Thank you!"

"Is the dressing dirty?"

"Yes."

"Change it. Hygiene, hygiene, hygiene. Boil the needle. Wash everything. Wash yourself before you touch him. Wash *him*. Wash him thoroughly. No maidenly modesty. Use carbolic soap. I'll come to see your American in a few days and take out the stitches. In the meantime, don't come here again."

He thrust her to the door, pushed her out into the street, and slammed the door behind her. He had not even bothered to take the blood sausage she had brought him.

Sheltering in the doorway, she lifted her skirt and thrust the ampoules into her underpants, the only safe hiding place she could think of, and set off on the long uphill walk back to *Il Noce*.

She wondered when David Godbold would come back to the farmhouse. She remembered the way he had looked into her eyes, the kiss at twilight. He was so very handsome. Just thinking about him set her heart fluttering like a caged dove. He was beautiful, somehow larger than life.

Joseph was different. It was difficult to explain it to herself, because her feelings were confused; Joseph was so ill that he made her heart flutter, too, though for different reasons—reasons of pity and fear. But his dark, narrow face was not her ideal of male beauty. It was too disturbing. There was something alien about him.

Perhaps that was it. When she looked at David, she had the feeling that a dream had been fulfilled, something wonderful and yet familiar. When she looked at Joseph, she felt something else. The presence of something strange and unfamiliar. Something that almost frightened her.

How had he and David, such opposite types, come to be companions?

Perhaps it was only his wounded state that made her feel these things. Pain and illness gave him—to her, at least—a wolflike look.

Those burning eyes haunted her. Their gaze seemed to her to be full of urgency, an animal tenacity on life. She remembered his wiry body, the curly black hair on his belly. David's body was perfect, with the milky skin of a girl and the muscles of a plough horse. She had longed to reach out and touch him, lay her palm against that fine skin . . .

The glass ampoules had slid down into her crotch. They jostled slyly between her thighs, probing, nudging. She was in the woods by now, on the lonely path. Looking around quickly, she retrieved the ampoules from their hiding place and slipped them into her pocket. She had been walking so quickly that she was out of breath, and her face was flushed despite the wintry air. She rested for a few moments and then set off again.

When she got back, little Paolo the deserter had arrived at *Il Nóce*. He was sitting rather sullenly in the courtyard, nursing a glass of red wine in the cold.

"I only came to see how he was," he said defensively. "And to bring his things."

He had evidently been getting the rough edge of Rosa's tongue. Joseph's "things" were contained in a shabby rucksack lying at Paolo's feet. "Didn't David come with you?" she asked.

"He sends his love." Paolo's features were like sooty thumb marks, two smudges for eyes, a smear of a mustache, a vague blotch for a mouth. "He's taken quite a shine to you. He wants to see you again."

She hid her almost-painful contraction of pleasure. "When?"

"The day after tomorrow. You know the old stone *capanna* up on the hill?"

"Yes."

"There. About four o'clock."

"I'll try," she said. He smirked. She felt the color rise to her cheeks. "What's so funny?"

"Nothing. How's the American?"

"Surviving. I got some sulfa from the doctor," she told Paolo. "And he says he'll come and see Joseph in a few days."

"I'll tell David." He drained his glass and rose. "So long."

"Are you going already?"

"Your mother won't have me in the house. I only stayed because David said I had to see you."

"Is he—is he somewhere safe?"

"Nowhere's safe." Paolo shrugged. "We're disbanding."

"Disbanding?"

"Demobilizing. Breaking up the group. Everybody's going their separate ways to get away from the Nazis."

"David, too?" she asked in alarm.

"Maybe. I don't know. You'll have to ask him. Give the American his things. They'll keep him happy. He's crazy."

She was still carrying the package of *sanguinàccio*. She gave it to Paolo. "Here. For David."

He leered at her. "Any message?"

"Just tell him to take care. All of you, take care."

Paolo slunk out. His movements were so furtive that if she'd been a German, Candida thought she'd have arrested him on sight. But she had a tryst with David! She didn't care if it was immoral to be so happy. She took the rucksack into the kitchen, where her mother was working, stony-faced.

"Has that good-for-nothing left yet?"

"Yes, Mama."

"You've been gone half the day," Rosa said accusingly.

"I had to get the drugs, you know that. How is he?"

"You think I have time to go and take care of that so-called Partisan?" Rosa snapped. "With you not here to help?" Then she shrugged. "He seems all right. He's asking for you. Suddenly the house is full of worthless men, asking for my daughter."

Curious to see what was in Joseph's rucksack, Candida opened it on the table. There were a few spare clothes, a little money, less than a thousand lire, and five books. How extraordinary, she thought, that Joseph would bother to haul books around the mountains in the middle of a war. She opened one and found it to be so full of scribbled annotations in pencil that the text would have been almost indecipherable even if it hadn't been in English. She opened another, which turned out to be in Italian—*La Divina Commedia*. She shook her head. "Paolo said he was crazy."

"What is it?" Rosa asked, peering over her shoulder.

"Look. Dante." Candida put the books back in the rucksack. "He won't be able to read down there, but I'll take it to him anyway. Paolo said it would keep him happy."

She went down to the cellar to see her patient. She tapped on the hatch and pulled it aside. In the light of her lantern she saw that

Joseph was on his side, huddled in one corner. She propped the lantern on the sill above his head and clambered down beside him.

"How are you feeling?"

He tried to shield his eyes from the dim light. "What's happening? What's going on up there?"

"Nothing's going on. Everything's fine."

His dark eyes, sunk even deeper now, searched hers feverishly. He still looked confused. "I thought I was dead. Dead and in my coffin."

"You're alive. And as soon as it's safe, we'll put you somewhere better." She touched his forehead. His skin was still hot and papery. In the confines of the wooden box, his body smelled like an animal's. "I've got to change the dressing. I'll give you some morphine first. Do you think you're strong enough?"

"Did the Germans come back?" he asked.

"Don't worry about the Germans. Just lie still. I need to get some things."

She went back into the kitchen and prepared carefully, washing herself and boiling the needle, as the doctor had instructed. She filled a basin with hot water and unwrapped a fresh bar of carbolic soap, which had become a precious commodity lately.

Her mother noticed these preparations. "What are you doing now?" she asked sharply.

"The doctor says I have to change his dressing."

Rosa's face darkened. "Bathing a strange man is not a job for a girl, Candida!"

"I'm not a girl anymore, Mama," Candida said gently. "And he's not in any position to take advantage of me."

"*I'll* do it."

"You've got enough to do. I'm grown-up, Mama." She met her mother's eyes. "I'll do it."

Her mother turned away. "As you please," she said heavily. "My wishes count for nothing in this house anymore, anyway."

Since the arrival of the wounded American, it was as though Candida had felt her own personality come alive. Her adulthood had asserted itself. She could not remember contradicting her mother in years. Now it seemed she was doing it all the time, and her mother seemed helpless to argue. The feeling that she was able to make her own decisions both frightened and excited Candida.

"That's not true. We love you, Mama. You know that. I'm going to give him some of these clean clothes."

With care, she carried everything down into the cellar and lowered it into the little wooden chamber.

She gave him the injections. "The doctor says I have to give you less morphine every time, in case you get addicted."

"I won't get addicted."

"I'm giving you less anyway."

Undressing him was not easy. In the end, she cut his shirt off with scissors. Removing the dressing was worse. Despite the morphine, he gasped with pain at every movement, and she found herself in a hot sweat of sympathy for his suffering, and alarm at her own incompetence. Did she really know what she was doing? What if he started bleeding? "I'm sorry," she said unsteadily. "I'm trying not to hurt."

"For Christ's sake stop apologizing," he said through clenched teeth. She held her tongue from then on. She soaked the dressing in warm water, and at last, to her profound relief, it peeled away.

She studied the wound carefully. It was crusted with black but there was neither pus nor a bad smell. The magic sulfa must be doing its trick. She felt a profound relief. If he were to get really ill, she knew she'd be able to do nothing for him. She soaped the area as gently as she could. "You're healing beautifully. It's wonderful."

He had started shivering with the cold. "Where's David?" he asked.

"He's safe. Don't worry about him."

"I must speak to David. He has to take me away from here. This should never have happened. He had no right to risk all your lives."

"Keep still. The Germans have come and gone now."

"And if they come back?"

"They won't."

"They will." Despite his weakness, the man's tension radiated out of him like a physical force. "I can't stay here."

"You're my patient," she said. "*I'll* decide when to discharge you."

His eyes met hers. "You should not be in this situation."

"I'm old enough to make my own decisions."

"I doubt that."

"I'm eighteen. And you?"

"Twenty-two," he muttered.

"There. We're almost the same age." She soaped the sponge. He was more impressive naked than with his shirt on. His body was not as muscled as David Godbold's, but it had its own power and elegance. He was sinewy and lean, black hair massed on his chest and stomach.

"Little Paolo brought your rucksack," she said, trying to put him at his ease. "You've scribbled all over your books. When I was at school, the teachers used to hit us on our knuckles if we wrote in books. I've never read any poetry myself. Perhaps you can teach me about Dante?"

"I'm not a teacher," he said to the wall.

"Then you won't hit me on the knuckles. Maybe I'll learn something for a change." She washed him carefully. She had very little experience of men's bodies. Helpless and wounded as he was, he was nevertheless a man, and this contact was a strangely intimate one. You could not wash another human being's naked body without intimacy, even tenderness. "I loved school," she went on. "Beatings and all. I wish I could have stayed. But they took me out to work on the farm when I was fourteen. You're lucky to be so scholarly."

When she started unfastening his belt, he stopped her.

"No."

"I've got to wash you properly," she said gently. "You can't stay filthy."

"No!" She wrestled with him for a moment. She was surprised at his vehemence. A ferocious Partisan who read poetry and was shy of his body.

"Just relax!"

"No. I'll wash myself."

"In that condition?"

"I'll do it. Give me the sponge."

She should have given him more morphine. Recognizing the strength of his will, she passed him the sponge. "At least let me help."

"No. Turn around," he commanded fiercely.

She was deeply insulted. "Do you think I'm some kind of harpy who wants to prey on you, Joseph?"

"Turn around."

"You wouldn't behave like this in a hospital, with nurses."

"This is not a hospital, and you aren't a nurse. Turn around. Please."

She obeyed and sat facing the wall, her back stiff with affront.

She listened to the awkward sounds of the American undressing himself, his grunts of pain. "You are a rude, infuriating man," she said tersely. "I'm only trying to help you."

He said nothing in reply. She heard him struggling to wash his body single-handed, gasping.

"I feel sorry for you," she said. "You must have a very low opinion of women if this is how you behave."

The sounds continued for a while. Candida was burning with indignation at the insult. At last he moaned in pain. She turned. His loins and thighs were streaked with soap. A runnel of dark blood had emerged from the wound.

"You fool," she said, really angry now. "You've torn the stitches. Lie back."

She thrust him unceremoniously back and took the soap from his fingers. She finished washing him, not trying to spare his feelings. "I don't know what's wrong with you," she said briskly. "I've got a brother, you know. You don't have anything he hasn't got."

She recovered her equanimity as she washed him, and dressed him in clean clothes. Perhaps where he came from people were more ashamed of their bodies, and he could not help the way he was.

She tapped an envelope of sulfa into the wound. "There," she said in a cheerful voice. "That's done. I'll leave you in peace now."

His face was expressionless, his eyes not meeting hers. "Thank you. Thank you for everything."

She gathered her things together and prepared to go.

She was not sure what deviltry prompted her to say it; perhaps, in some way, she had been flattered by his response to her womanhood. "Aren't you going to ask me to kiss you before I go?"

He glanced at her. Then he smiled. For a moment it changed his face completely, from dark and grim to something almost boyish.

"Kiss me before you go."

Candida felt a little melting heat inside her. A blob of sealing wax falling on the heart. She stooped and kissed him quickly, not on the cheek, but on the mouth. "You are very brave," she whispered.

She pulled herself out of the little wooden room and left him there in the darkness.

Her father had arrived back from pruning the vines. He stood by the fire, warming his large, knotted hands, his lips and cheeks still purple with the cold. His face was somber. "How is the American, child?"

"Getting better, I think," she said in a small voice, sensing something wrong.

"I'll go down to see him. I want to talk to him."

"Tell her," Rosa said grimly.

"Tell me what?" Candida asked.

"What your wonderful Partisans have achieved. Tell her, Vincenzo."

Her father turned to her wearily. "It was the SS. In reprisal for the German soldiers who were killed in the ambush."

Candida felt sick with dread. "What did they do?"

"They went to San Vito yesterday and executed twenty people."

"All the men," Rosa said. "Every man in the village. From teen-agers to grandfathers. They built a scaffold in the town square and strung them up in front of their womenfolk. Nobody was allowed to leave until the last one stopped kicking."

Candida sank into a chair, weak and dizzy. San Vito was a tiny village up near the pass where the ambush had taken place, a wretchedly poor and primitive place. Even by the standards of the SS, it was a terrible act. "But why?" she whispered.

"You know why," Rosa said bitterly. "Tell your American friend down there. Tell him how many Italians are widows and orphans tonight because of his brave exploits."

"Rosa," Vincenzo said gently. "You cannot blame the Partisans for what the SS does."

"I blame them all," she said, turning back to her work. "Teo was right. We did not want this war in 1940, and we don't want it now. Let them wage it somewhere else."

"There's nowhere else to wage it," Vincenzo said, walking to the cellar door. "We let Mussolini pull our wagon for twenty years. Now we cannot unharness him. So we must follow, Rosa. We must follow."

She Had Been sitting shivering in the stone shepherd's hut for half an hour before she heard David's footsteps across the rocks.

The doorway darkened as he entered, stooping under the low lintel. He peered in, eyes adjusting to the gloom.

"You're early. That's not very ladylike."

"Why? Should I have been late?" she asked in confusion. She had told nobody of her appointment with David Godbold in the *capanna*. It was the first time in her life that a man had asked her to meet him anywhere. Her first tryst, an event of overwhelming importance. She had no access to makeup or perfume, but she had prepared with great care nevertheless, brushing her unruly black hair until it gleamed like jet and tying it back with a red velvet ribbon. Nor had it occurred to her to dawdle on the way. She had little coquettishness in her nature.

David hunkered down in front of her. He had not shaved since she'd seen him last, and his jaw was covered in glittering golden stubble. He grinned at her. "A lady must always be late for an appointment, Candida. To let the man know he's not the only one."

"But you *are* the only one. I mean," she added in stammering embarrassment, "I got ready especially. I didn't want to be late."

"Well, I'm very flattered," he said. "I can't stay long. Just a few minutes. I'm taking a hell of a risk coming down here to see you."

Her heart was beating hard. "Are you all right? The Germans have been combing the area."

"They haven't caught me yet."

"Paolo says you're splitting up."

He nodded. "We've stirred up too much of a hornet's nest. Giacometti has gone back to his people in Veneto. We've heard of some other English trekking up through the Val d'Aosta into Switzerland. The others have gone up into the Dolomites, where the Germans don't bother looking."

"And you?"

"I don't fancy freezing to death in the mountains. Or spending the war interned in some dreary Swiss hotel."

"But you're all alone!"

"I'm going to join another Partisan *banda*. As soon as I find one. In the meantime, some people are helping me up near Chiese. Charcoal burners. Communists. They give me food and shelter. It's a comfortable billet."

"Are you sure you shouldn't go?" she asked anxiously.

He stretched his strong body. "I know what I'm doing," he said lazily. "Don't worry about me."

"Did you hear—" She hesitated. "Did you hear what happened at San Vito?"

"Yes." He nodded. "It was to be expected." His face was closed, his eyes hard.

"I've been so worried about you. About where you're sleeping, whether you're getting anything to eat." She gave him the parcel she had smuggled out of the house. "I brought you this."

He opened it. "Bread, sausage, cheese," he said approvingly. "Good girl. I'm starving." He started laying the food out on the floor. "How's Joseph?"

"Getting better. The doctor came to see him this morning. He says it's a miracle he's survived."

"Paolo says you've been caring for him like a trained nurse."

She smiled with pleasure. "I've had to learn. I've been terrified."

"Don't get too fond of him, that's all."

"Why not?"

"Women always fall in love with men they nurse."

She was amused at the notion. "I won't fall in love with Joseph. He wants to see you. He keeps saying you've got to take him away."

He searched her face. "You don't mind looking after him? It's a risk, I know. We heard about the Germans searching the house. They knocked your brother around, didn't they?"

She nodded, her smile fading. "He's covered in bruises. They could have killed him."

"If they'd wanted to kill him, they would have done." He started eating, evidently hungry. She watched his deft movements, feeling a glow of pleasure that he was slaking his hunger with food she had prepared.

"What's England like?" she asked.

"A green and pleasant land, mostly," he said. "Our part is rather bleaker."

"What part is that?"

"Northumberland. The last place your ancestors got to before the barbarians stopped them."

"My ancestors?"

"The Romans."

"Oh."

"The Emperor Hadrian built a wall across Northumberland," he explained, chopping at the cheese. "That's where civilization ended. The boundary of the Empire. Anyway, that's where the Godbolds have their family seat."

"Is it a castle?"

"Not exactly. It's a biggish estate, though. Plenty of hunting, shooting, and fishing."

Images swam into her mind of tweed-clad gentlemen with guns under their arms, of ladies in big hats, of gleaming limousines, a world that she had only known through magazine photographs.

"Are you very rich?" she asked shyly.

"Not anymore." He bit into a sausage. "Well-connected, though."

"Well-connected?"

"All the top people used to come up to shoot. Including the old Prince of Wales."

Candida's eyes widened. "The one who gave up his throne for love?" she asked breathlessly.

"Yes. That Prince of Wales."

At first she scarcely believed him, but his calm assurance was convincing. "And did you meet Mrs. Simpson?" she asked in awe.

"Oh, many times. In England, and later in France, after the abdication." David wrapped up the rest of the food and put it in his rucksack. He lit a cigarette. "Lots of people dropped the Windsors after the abdication. We didn't."

She was enraptured. "Is she really as plain as she looks in her photographs?"

He exhaled a plume of smoke into the air. "Well, she's a very elegant woman. She spends a fortune on clothes. Chanel, Balmain, Schiaparelli, and so on. She's no beauty. But she has great charm. She bewitches people."

"How does she do that?"

He lowered one eyelid in the parody of a wink. "She's got sex appeal. They say she knows all sorts of tricks. Lived in the Far East, you know. This is her third marriage, too." Candida was dying to ask what sort of tricks, but it was a highly indelicate subject. David was watching her through a haze of smoke, his blue eyes bright. "Are you impressed?" he asked.

"If it's all true, I am."

"Why would I lie to you?" David smiled at her. "It used to be a glamorous old world. But nothing will ever be the same after this war."

"Of course it will."

"The Godbolds used to be rich. When I was a boy. My grandfather invested in rubber and teak and so forth, out in the colonies. Made a fortune in the Great War. Since then the rest of us have been busily spending it all." He drew on his cigarette, his eyes absent. "When my father made it into the Prince's circle, we all thought we were made. He wanted a baronetcy, my father did. Set his heart on it. At whatever price, and amusing David and Wallis didn't come cheap, I can tell you. Glittering parties. The best hunting and shooting. Expensive little trinkets from Asprey's. High society costs money." His face twisted into a sour smile, unlike his usual bright smile. "But all the time my father was backing the wrong horse. The silly fool abdicated, and that was the end of that."

"But your father didn't desert the Prince?"

"No, he clung loyally to his falling star." He stubbed out his cigarette. "I was twenty-two when David abdicated. I'll never forget it. I knew it was all over then. We should have cut the connection, like the others did. For one thing, we didn't have the money to keep it up when they went into exile. Yachts on the Riviera and villas in Portugal are a different proposition from entertaining at home. But my father decided to spend his last thousands on putting up a loyal show, as he saw it." He shrugged. "So I went along for the ride. It didn't last long. Hitler and company saw to that. Now it's all gone. The Windsors off to the Bahamas, France full of Nazis, my father dying alone and penniless in Northumberland. The war came along just in time, as it happened. Rescued me from boredom and penury."

She was enraptured. "It's like a film!"

He rose, dusting himself. "Yes, a bad comedy. Only one way to recoup the family fortunes now."

"How's that?"

He grinned at Candida. "Marry a rich woman."

"Oh, no," she said in dismay, rising to face him, "you mustn't do that! You must only marry for love!"

"Love?" He looked at her for a moment, his lids lowered. She suddenly knew he was going to kiss her. Her heart seemed to turn over inside her, as though she'd fallen, and was continuing to fall, without being able to stop. He took her face in his hands and pressed his lips hungrily to hers.

David's mouth was firm and masterful, and his palms were warm against her cheeks. She nestled to him with a little whimper, her eyes tightly closed.

His hand slid down her neck and cupped her breast. His thumb rubbed deliberately across her nipple, sending an electric jolt into her.

She was staggered at the intimacy of the caress, the daring of it. She drew back, gasping. He followed, bending to kiss her again, and a flood of sweet, wild panic took her senses.

At that moment, a distant burst of machine-gun fire echoed across the valley, followed by single shots. David stopped, his face changing. "Shit."

"What is it?" she asked in fear.

"I don't know, but I'd better clear off."

"When will I see you again?" she asked in anguish.

"Three days' time." He was shouldering his knapsack. "Here, at four. All right?"

She nodded. She was aching to throw her arms around him, cover his face with kisses, beg him to take care with his precious life. But she dared not detain him. "Wait here for an hour before you leave," he commanded. "Understand?"

She nodded.

He stooped quickly under the lintel and was gone.

Candida sank back onto her haunches, her head whirling. "Sweet Virgin, Blessed Virgin, please protect him," she whispered. The wild sweetness of that brief kiss was still in her blood, like wine. She wanted to laugh and cry at the same time. She was bursting with happiness and sick with fear. She had never been so torn with emotions. She had never been so close to abandonment.

JANUARY 1944

"Joseph's recovery is beginning at last," she wrote in her diary. "He is stronger now, and I no longer fear that he may die. He is growing very restless and unhappy. It cannot be pleasant to be shut in down there in the dark, even though it keeps him safe. We may soon have to think of another place for him."

Aware of the potentially deadly content of her diary, despite her cautious circumlocutions, she had taken to hiding it in a special place, under a loose floor tile under her bed. If anyone ever searched the house thoroughly enough to find it there, she reasoned, Joseph would already have been discovered. Against that dreadful eventuality, she took scrupulous care not to mention the names of any other people involved in helping the American—the doctor, for example, who had come that morning to take out the stitches. He had warned that Joseph still needed several weeks of rest.

"It has been days since I saw David," she wrote on. "I have such deep fears for his safety. I pray to the Virgin that she will keep him safe. I have faith that she will. He means so much to me."

Hiding her diary meant that she could confide in it as never before; and there were many things to confide.

In a few short weeks, something extraordinary had happened to her, something much more than an adventure, a secret just as important as the secret of hiding a wounded American from the Germans. She was falling in love.

She had met David three times more since that afternoon in the *capanna*. Each time, the meeting had been painfully brief, but each time he had kissed her on parting, with increasing tenderness. She had no romantic vocabulary to describe her feelings about him to her diary. But they were increasingly powerful.

Having drifted placidly through sleepy meadows since childhood, Candida's life was now tumbling down bright rapids. She had never felt or looked so well. When she looked in the mirror these mornings, her eyes sparkled back at her joyously. Every moment was filled with excitement. Even her terror when she saw a German uniform or heard distant gunfire was tinged with sweetness because it was connected to David.

Life at *Il Noce* was continuing around Joseph's presence like a river flowing around a boulder that had rolled into its stream, unaltered, yet dividing around the new arrival. Teo had recovered slowly from his injuries and was able to get out of bed a week later and get back to work. The beating he'd been given by the SS seemed, inexplicably, to have improved his spirits. His chronic depression had lifted for a while, and his long, melancholy face wore a gentle smile that was a distant echo of the joyous young man he had once been. Candida's mother resolutely refused to have anything to do with feeding or caring for the wounded man, as though by ignoring his presence she could exorcise the danger he brought. Her father, calm and kindly as always, visited Joseph at least once each day, and if he was eager that Joseph should recover soon and leave, and take his family out of jeopardy, he said nothing to give Joseph that impression.

None of them knew she was seeing David Godbold in secret.

None of them knew of her feelings, because she told no one, only her diary.

When the time came that she could no longer keep her feelings to herself, the person she chose to confide in was not a member of her family, but the American, Joseph.

"I've been seeing your friend," she told him while she was changing his dressing in the claustrophobic confines of the little wooden chamber.

"David?"

"Yes. We meet in an old shepherd's hut on the hillside."

"What for?" he asked sharply.

She was rather taken aback at his reaction. Over the past days, he had become increasingly aware of his surroundings, and increasingly tense and nervous. She knew that his confinement was becoming a torture to him. "Don't shout. Just to see each other. To talk. I take him food and wine."

"You're risking your life, Candida! Don't you realize that?"

"Yes, but—"

"How many times have you seen him?"

"Four or five times now."

"Do your parents know about this?"

"Of course not," she said, sponging at the wound gently. "They would never permit it. It's a secret." She smiled at his shadowed face. "You look so serious. Don't you approve, either?"

"Don't go to him again," he said, his voice low and intense.

"What do you mean?"

"You're just an amusement for him."

A lump rose in her throat, and her cheeks started to burn. "You talk as though he's taken advantage of me."

"Hasn't he?"

"Of course not."

"He hasn't—"

She met his eyes, her mouth set. "Hasn't what?"

He reached out and took her wrist. She remembered the feverish grasp of his fingers when he'd been delirious. "Be careful of David. You have no experience of men like him."

"Oh? Is he some kind of Don Juan?"

"I didn't mean that."

"What did you mean?"

"I mean that he comes from a different world, Candida."

"So far above me?" she asked ironically.

"He'll use you," Joseph said bluntly. "And then he'll discard you."

She pulled her hand brusquely out of his grasp and continued cleaning the wound in silence for a while, the lump in her throat swelling painfully. She was thankful she had not had time to expose her intimate feelings about David. "I wish I'd never said anything to you," she said. "You're so offensive."

"I don't want you to be hurt," he replied, more quietly. "That's all."

"Well you have hurt me," she said. She put the new dressing on the wound and rose. "You have no right to tell me what to do. I'll see him as and when I please."

"Candida—"

She climbed out of the little wooden room and slammed the hatch shut over it.

"I've Met Some Partisans," David told her excitedly when they next met in the *capanna*. "I've spoken to Antonio *il rósso*."

"Who's he?"

"He's the leader of one of the *bande*. He fought in Spain, on the Republican side, as a volunteer. He's a red-hot communist. That's why they call him *il rósso*." They were lying in the straw, David tearing pieces off the loaf she had brought him. "He's a real soldier, a hero."

"Does he want you to join him?" she asked, trying to hide her fear.

"He'll let me know." David's eyes blazed. "It's wonderful news. I could be back in action soon!"

She tried to look pleased, for his sake. "I'm glad, David."

He grinned. "What shall we talk about today?"

David's stories fascinated her. He had an eye for the details of women's fashion and jewelry that made him, from her point of view, an excellent raconteur. Wallis Simpson, the woman who had stolen England's king, was her favorite topic.

"Tell me about before the war," she begged, glad not to have to think about David leaving. "Tell me about the Duchess's jewels."

"Oh, they were fabulous. I saw her at a ball in 1938, in the south of France, where they had a villa. She was wearing some rubies that he'd given her for their first wedding anniversary. The biggest rubies I've ever seen, two of them, set in a platinum bangle. Someone said they weighed eighteen carats each. You could have put them in your mouth and sucked them, like fruit drops. Red as blood."

"And emeralds?"

"She has marvelous emeralds, too. A bracelet, I think, with three or four set in diamonds. And definitely a ring with a single huge emerald, a beautiful, rich, clear green."

"And diamonds?"

"Oh yes, diamonds. Plenty of diamonds. Enough to dazzle you."

"And to think she was born a commoner!"

"Ah, but I told you—she had sex appeal."

"Can any woman learn sex appeal?" she asked him.

"No, you have to be born with it."

"Oh."

David reached over and tickled her mouth with a straw. "Don't worry, Candida. You've got more than your fair share of sex appeal."

"But I don't know any tricks."

"You don't need any tricks. Only women of Mrs. Simpson's age need to know tricks."

"Why do women of Mrs. Simpson's age need to know tricks?"

He rolled over so that his face was very close to hers. "Because they're not fresh and sweet," he said softly, "like you."

She took fright at his proximity and drew back a little, her heart racing. "I have to get back," she said in a small voice.

He sat up, hugging his knees. There was an expression in his eyes that made her heart turn over inside her. "Fly away, then, little bird," he said softly.

She rose, brushing the straw from her dress. "When will I see you again?"

"Maybe next week. I'll try and come on Wednesday afternoon, around four."

"I'll be here," she promised.

This time, when he kissed her good-bye, he took her in his arms and drew her close, pressing his mouth to hers. His body was strong and warm against hers. She felt his tongue probing her lips, forcing its way in. She wriggled away, panting and flushed.

"Good-bye," she called as she fled. "Take care!"

Two Nights Later, for the first time, they brought Joseph out of the cellar, securely bolting the doors and shutters against prying eyes. The idea was Vincenzo's.

"He's been down in that coffin for too long," he said. "Buried alive. He can breathe a little fresh air and eat with us, like a human being, for a change."

Even Rosa, grimly opposed as she was to Joseph's presence here, could not find it in her heart to contest the idea.

Teo and Candida helped Joseph up the stairs into the kitchen, his weak legs stumbling at every step. He sat at the table, very pale and drawn, his arm huddled to his bad side. His jaw was now dark with stubble; soon it would be a full-grown beard. They all stared at him covertly. It was the first time he had come among them like a man, rather than a secret presence under their feet. With his sunken eyes and haunted face, he looked, Candida thought, lupine, not quite human and certainly not reassuring. One could almost be afraid of such a man as that.

"He can tell us what the BBC is saying," Teo said suddenly. "There might be important news."

"Good idea." Vincenzo fetched down their ancient shortwave radio, officially a prohibited item, which picked up the BBC intermittently. Candida and her mother prepared the meal while Vincenzo fiddled with the knobs until the crackling and sputtering turned into something intelligible, a symphony concert.

They started the meal, a simple dish of polenta enriched with a few slices of the remaining *sanguinàccio.* Candida found herself staring at Joseph, half-expecting him to gulp down his food like a beast, but of course he ate slowly and sparingly, keeping his eyes down on his plate. There was an air of tension around the table that none of them had expected.

He was a strangely powerful figure, she thought suddenly. Weak as he was, he had a presence, a disconcerting aura. She found herself wondering whether he or David had been the real leader of the little Partisan group.

Halfway through the meal, the chimes of Big Ben sounded from the radio, and Vincenzo reached over to turn it up.

"There," Vincenzo said. "What are they saying?"

Joseph listened to the faint English voice that filtered into the room. "They say that the German counterattacks are slowing down. The British Eighth Army is fighting its way up toward Rome, driving the Nazis out." He listened again. "Church bells are ringing for joy in liberated Italy. They say the war will end next year."

"Next year?" Candida echoed. It seemed as though the war had been going on forever. She had thought about its ending often, at first. Then she had stopped even believing that it could ever end.

"The war against the Japanese is also going well—"

Joseph stopped. A rush of static had drowned out the distant voice. For a while there was only crackling. Then another, much stronger voice flooded the set, speaking Italian with a harsh Germanic accent.

"The civilian population is reminded of the penalties for aiding Partisan forces." They knew that voice. It was the commander of the SS in Brescia, his voice rasping with menace. The broadcast was coming from the provincial radio station, which had been taken over by the Fascist militia after Mussolini's reinstatement.

"Any Italian feeding or protecting deserters, escaped prisoners of war, or persons guilty of acts of sabotage, is subject to martial law. There will be no mercy. A curfew is imposed on the civilian population during the hours of darkness. It will be rigorously enforced. Reprisals will be instantly undertaken against any Italian—"

Vincenzo switched off the ugly voice with a grunt. "Bastards."

Rosa's face was set and pale. She put her knife and fork down beside her plate, her breathing unsteady. Everyone knew they chose a wave band that coincided with the BBC, but there was something spine-chilling about the way the announcement had reached into their kitchen at that moment.

Joseph leaned forward, speaking to her directly. "By next week I'll be strong enough to walk," he said. His voice was naturally quiet and rather husky. "I'll leave then."

"Nonsense," Vincenzo said. "Of course you won't be strong enough to go."

Joseph shook his head. "If the Germans caught me, there's a chance the Geneva Convention would protect me. But you—" He leveled a finger at Vincenzo like a pistol, his dark eyes intent. "They would kill you all."

"Like they killed the men of San Vito," Rosa said.

Vincenzo hushed her, but Joseph turned, his eyes wary. "What happened to the men of San Vito?" There was a silence. "Tell me," he commanded.

"The SS rounded them up and executed them." It was Teo who told him. "In reprisal for what you and your friends did up on the pass."

They all saw his face change, become more haggard than ever. "How many?" he asked.

"Twenty."

He sat in silence, dark eyes staring into nothing. "My fault," he said at last.

"No," Vincenzo said, patting his shoulder. "You cannot blame yourself for what those devils do."

"I pushed the plunger. I laid the charge. I knew what would happen. We all did."

"It's war," Teo said sympathetically. "They did the same in Greece and Yugoslavia. It's their way."

"We had no right to do it. We were playing at war. We achieved nothing. Killing a dozen Germans didn't achieve a thing. I have no right to be here. I'll leave next week."

"But where are you going to go, eh?" Vincenzo asked. He rose from the table, a stout, robust figure, and opened the kitchen window. From far down in the valley, they could hear a continuous rumble across the lake. It was military traffic streaming on the road to Brescia. The sound was ominous and made Candida shudder.

Vincenzo shut the window again. "It's been like that every night since the Armistice. The valley is full of Germans."

"With no one to help you," Teo put in, "wounded as you are, you'd be picked up in a matter of hours."

"Then let them pick him up," Rosa said harshly.

"Mama, no!" Candida exclaimed.

"We've given him shelter for two weeks. But for the love of God, you don't want us all to die for his sake, do you?" Her high color was mounting higher. She pointed to Joseph. "*He* doesn't, at any rate. *He* has some decent feelings."

"Rosa, be quiet," Vincenzo said.

"I will *not* be quiet," she hissed. "Look at your children, Vincenzo. They are your responsibility, not a stranger!"

"Joseph is somebody's son, too, Mama," Teo said.

"But not mine!" Rosa's eyes were bright with tears. "The Germans will catch him anyway, Vincenzo. Don't let him be caught in our house!"

"She's right," Joseph said in his husky voice. "The stitches are out. I'll go."

Vincenzo held up a callused hand.

"Your friends are scattered. You have nowhere to go. Let me look for a safe place for you. Maybe up in the hills, with a shepherd I can trust. As soon as we find a better place, someone will take you there. But until then, you'll stay here and recover your strength."

"No," Joseph said decisively.

Vincenzo grasped the American's lean shoulder and shook him gently. "You have to abide by the majority decision, my friend. No striking out on your own. Or you'll get caught, and they will torture you, and then we *will* all be hanged."

The next day, it was Teo who came up with the solution to the problem of lodging Joseph.

"He can stay in the Hunter's Tower."

Candida looked up quickly. A mile or so to the north of *Il Noce* lay a great hunting estate, the property of a noble Milanese family. There had once been a house on the property, but it had burned down in the last century, and all that now remained, buried deep in the oak forest, was a solitary tower, known locally as *la tórre del cacciatóre,* the Hunter's Tower. It was a remote, secret place, most unlikely ever to be reached by Germans. There was a stream nearby where Joseph could get fresh water, and with a sufficient supply of provisions, he could stay there safely for months without much fear of discovery.

"But it's the loneliest place on God's earth," she said doubtfully.

Rosa's eyes were sharp. "He won't mind loneliness, that one. He's not sociable. It's a good idea, Teo. If the Germans take him, he can say he just wandered there of his own accord. Go tell your father."

Vincenzo took some convincing, but at last he began to be persuaded. "It's not such a bad idea. He can make a fire without worrying that some German will see the smoke."

"We could give him an old shotgun," Teo suggested, "and he might be able to kill a rabbit or two, even a pheasant or a partridge. Anyone who comes across him will think he's some kind of crazy hermit."

"Especially with that beard," Candida said.

"And he'll be a damned sight more comfortable than down in that coffin." Vincenzo nodded slowly. "It's not a bad notion at all."

It was given to Candida to break the idea to Joseph.

"You'll be very lonely, of course," she warned, crouching in the close darkness of the grain store. "But at least you'll have light to read your beloved books."

"Excellent." His beard gave him the look of a Byzantine Christ. "When can I go?" he demanded, his eyes glowing in the lantern light.

Candida felt an unexpectedly sharp pang at his eagerness to leave. Infuriating and offensive though he could be, looking after him had been deeply satisfying, a challenge she had enjoyed more than almost anything else in her life. "Why are you so keen to go?" she asked him.

"For your sake, Candida. Not for mine. I don't want you to die. The world would be a poorer place."

"None of us is going to die," she said brusquely. "You're too gloomy."

"I'm a realist."

"I thought Americans were all optimists."

"I was born in Latvia," he said.

Candida studied his face in the dim light. His features had a Slavic cast, with those high cheekbones and dark eyes that slanted slightly at the corners. "I'm going to miss you," she sighed. She saw his face change. "Don't flatter yourself," she said dryly. "I even missed the pig when he died. I just like looking after things. So you want to go?"

"Yes. The sooner the better. How far away is it?"

"A couple of kilometers."

"That's not far enough."

"Believe me, it is. The place is buried in the woods. Hardly anybody knows about it except local people, and most of them will have forgotten. You'll be like Robinson Crusoe. Or some enchanted prince in a fairy tale. That ought to suit you."

"What do you mean?"

"Well, you don't really like people, do you?" She did not bother waiting for an answer to the rhetorical question. "You'll need provisions. Do you know how to set traps?"

He shook his head. "I'm a city boy."

"It doesn't matter. Papa's going to give you a shotgun. You

might even meet a wild boar or two." Candida rose. "I'll go and tell them you're eager to go."

"Are you still seeing David?" he asked.

"That's none of your business," she replied sharply. "The sooner you get out of the house the better. Then you can stop worrying about me."

The First Great winter storm was gathering.

Thunder muttered restlessly among the mountains, and under the lowering sky, the great lake was almost black, with white streaks where the wind raked it. The landscape she loved was becoming ominous and brooding. The little lakeside towns, with their church steeples rising above the tiled rooftops, seemed to huddle against the shore for shelter. A fine white layer of snow already covered everything.

The gathering storm carried the breath of the high Alps, the smell of ice and winter. Candida gloried in the wild, romantic beauty of it.

Reaching the peak of the ridge, she put her basket down and spread her legs and arms to the gale like a lover. Its embrace was eager. It lifted her skirt, sweeping between her bare thighs, flattening her jersey against the thrusting peaks of her breasts. She felt the icy blast with a sensual pleasure that made her shudder. The flakes of snow danced into her face, and there was a rumble of thunder. Candida closed her eyes in rapture, arching her throat to the sky.

Since David Godbold had come into her life, she'd felt a yearning for something beyond her reach, something that had once been no more than a will-o'-the-wisp, and was now a pillar of fire. Her soul had been reaching out, as she reached out now, to the heart of the storm.

The storm came on swift wings, catching her long before she could get to the *capanna*. Lightning flared across the sky, and a shattering thunderclap followed. Snow was whirling down now, numbing her naked face and hands. Candida hugged the basket to her breast and tried to run.

It had grown very dark. She could hardly see the path at her feet. Her shoes slithered on the wet pebbles, and before long, she was sprawling on her face. She picked herself up, cursing, and made her way more cautiously up the long slope, eyes squinting against the beating snow.

"Candida! *Candida!*"

She recognized the voice instantly and gave a little sob of laughter. She did not answer him, just kept scrambling up the slope until she saw his tall figure looming out of the falling snow. She flung herself into his arms.

David was caught unawares and almost fell. She felt his strong arms tighten around her. His deep voice was close to her ear.

"You little fool. What are you doing out in this weather?"

"What about you?"

"You're mad." He grasped her hand in his and led her at a run toward the little stone shepherd's hut. They thrust the door open and scrambled into its dark shelter. The wind and snow were howling through the tiny window. "We can't stay here," he said. "You'd better run back home before the snow starts drifting."

"It might not last long." The thought of parting with him so quickly was too painful to bear. "We could wait until it eased off a little."

David glanced at her and smiled slightly. "All right. If that's what you want." He pulled off his jersey, an old castoff of Vincenzo's, and used it to plug the draft. "We'll have to make a fire if we're not going to freeze."

The *capanna* had been built against the mountainside, and one wall was bare rock. A fireplace had been chiseled into it, with a blackened iron pipe rising up through the roof to let the smoke out. There was a bundle of firewood in one corner, but no matches, only a flint and steel. Candida put a handful of straw in the fireplace and patiently struck sparks into the kindling. After a few minutes' work, a little flame leaped in the hearth.

David laid sticks carefully over the flickering yellow tongue. The fire caught and crackled, eager in the updraft caused by the high wind that boomed across the roof. "Funny how consoling a fire is," David mused. "A little bit of comfort in a world gone mad."

"Yes," she agreed. She stretched her palms out to the flame. The storm was increasing in fury. Snow was pouring down now, and it was almost as dark as night. But the little stone hut offered shelter, and the soft light of the rising fire lit the interior of the *capanna,* touching their faces with gold.

"We're moving Joseph out of the house," she told David.

"Where to?"

"There's an old tower buried in the woods behind the house. He can stay there safely. It's very isolated, but I don't think he'll mind that. Poor Joseph. He's going to be very lonely there."

"Never mind Joseph. He'll be a damned sight better off than I am. At least he'll have a roof over his head."

The tone of his voice made her look up in concern. "But so have you—haven't you?"

"For as long as my hosts put up with me. My *reluctant* hosts."

"Oh, David!" she said in dismay. "It never occurred to me you'd want to stay somewhere like the Hunter's Tower."

"Why not?"

"It's such a lonely place. You need people—Joseph doesn't. You said so yourself. He's a lone wolf. You aren't. But you could still go there if you wanted! It's big enough for the two of you to share!"

"No thanks," he answered with a grimace. "We'd be like two badgers in one den."

"I thought you and Joseph were friends!"

David glanced at their soaked clothing. "We're starting to steam." He pulled his shirt off, wrung it out, and propped it up on some sticks to dry in front of the fire. The atmosphere in the *capanna* had changed. His nakedness, firm-muscled and white-skinned, had made the air vibrate disturbingly.

"What's the matter, Candida?"

"Well . . . if someone were to come . . . "

"Who's going to come, darling?" He had never called her darling before. He produced his cigarettes, but they had got soaked. He laid them out carefully by the fire to dry. "What shall we talk about? Shall I tell you about Mrs. Simpson?"

"Oh, yes, please."

"Then stop being a silly little fool and come and sit beside me."

She obeyed. "You're icy cold," he murmured. He put his arm around her and drew her close to him. His naked body was close against her. "That's better, isn't it?" he asked softly. His skin smelled like freshly baked bread. She huddled awkwardly against him, longing to embrace him in turn, yet afraid. He stroked her wet hair away from her eyes. "There, now. What do you want to know about Wallis?"

"Tell me what she looked like," she said in a small voice.

"Oh, slim. Slim arms, slim waist, slim legs. No hips to speak of. She always said nobody could ever be too rich or too thin. She wound herself around the prince like some clinging plant. Like this." He took her arms and pulled them around his naked waist, pressing her cheek to his breast. "Ah, yes. Like that."

Her nerves were trembling. She had never been so close to him, so close to losing her possession. There was something in his face, something in his voice, that both terrified and thrilled her.

"He loved the way she clung to him. He loved to feel her slim arms around him. He would kiss her here, and here . . . "

She felt David's lips touch her temple, then her wrists.

"She would smile and know that he was hers, utterly hers. She would stretch like a cat and purr. He loved to hear her purr. That's why he loaded her with jewels. He could never spend too much on her. Wallis was like an ocean liner at night, blazing with lights. He absolutely adored her, you see." Her face was turned into his throat. His mouth was touching her temple. She could feel his breath warm in her hair, and his voice was a hypnotic rumble. His lips brushed her skin, but whether accidentally or in a kiss, she did not know. "Imagine if you had trinkets like that, Candida. You'd be a goddess."

He took her chin between finger and thumb and lifted her face to his. In the firelight, his eyes were pools of shadow. The storm raged impotently around the *capanna;* within, there seemed to be an ocean of silence. "I'd cover you in jewels," he said softly. "I'd put two star sapphires here, and here." He touched each of her earlobes in turn. "They'd match your eyes. And I'd put a string of diamonds here." He stroked her throat with his fingertips, making her shiver. She was terrified, even as her heart was yearning for him. This wild contradiction of pleasure and alarm, of wanting and not wanting, was an agony. He bent to kiss her, and she had to steel herself not to squirm out of his arms and flee into the storm. His mouth brushed hers with velvety gentleness. "This is perfect," he said after a while. "Isn't this perfect?"

"Yes," she whispered.

"Nobody else. Just you and me."

She felt him touch her breasts, smoothing their curves with his palms. "David, don't!"

He seemed not to hear her protest. "You smell so wonderful," he whispered. "You don't need perfume, Candida. Your skin is like a flower. You don't need jewels or rouge or anything . . . "

His palm slipped inside her shirt, found her naked breast. It was as though he had taken her heart in his hand. Her head swam. She knew David was going to make love to her. Her ethereal dream was about to take a physical shape. She prayed he would be gentle and not shatter the delicate crystal thing she held inside. "Don't hurt me," she begged.

"I won't," he said. His mouth closed on hers hungrily.

Candida Got Back to the farm hours later, when the storm had dwindled to a steady downpour. She was drenched, but she was in a dreamy trance with the wonderful secret she held inside. She came into the kitchen to find that Joseph was out of the cellar, huddled in front of the fireplace in a blanket. He looked feverish.

Rosa clucked over Candida irately. "Your father was out looking for you! What happened to you?"

"I got caught in the storm, Mama. I had to take shelter in a *capanna.*"

"You young fool. You're going to catch your death of cold! Dry your hair, child, and sit by the fire while I get a hot bath ready."

She wrapped the towel round her head and sat opposite Joseph by the fire's warmth. He looked up at her.

And suddenly she knew that he knew. She could see it in his eyes. The shock made her dizzy. How did he guess?

He spoke in a whisper that she had to strain to hear. "Why did you do it?"

Her face flamed. It was stupid to deny that she knew what he meant, not in the face of that somber certainty. "I love him," she whispered back fiercely.

"And does he love you?"

"Yes!" she hissed.

His face seemed made of hollows, a mask of sorrowful shadows. "Oh, Candida," he grated. "You fool!"

She was choking back tears. "How dare you! He loves me!"

"Men like him don't love women like you."

"Who else will I find?" she demanded. They were both talking in ferocious whispers, so as not to be overheard. "Who else, Joseph?"

"Don't you know?"

The question rocked her. *"You?"*

His eyes held hers, his dark compulsion riveting her. "I care about you more than David Godbold ever will."

Candida felt as though she were at the edge of a precipice, the ground crumbling beneath her feet, the void opening. "I don't believe you," she stammered. "I never gave you the slightest encouragement, Joseph. Not so much as a word."

"That does not stop me loving you."

"Don't say that!" The words were unbearable to her, making her want to rise from the fireside and flee back into the storm. "You have no right!"

"He'll destroy you." Candida turned away, but Joseph's fingers bit painfully into the soft flesh of her arm, jerking her to face him again. His husky voice took on an urgent, almost pleading note. "He is not for you. He may imagine he cares for you, but he can't. He'll leave you broken, maybe with a baby in your belly—"

"You're mad," she said, close to tears. Her own panic made her cruel. "He's twice the man you are. That's what you can't bear, isn't it?"

"I cannot bear to see him destroy you."

"Do you think I can't see through your jealousy?"

"Call it what you like."

She tried to wrench her arm free, but his grip was too strong. "It *is* jealousy. All you want is to be in his place! You're the one who wants to use me! *You're* the false one!"

"Don't throw my feelings in my face," he said quietly. "I love you, Candida."

"Don't ever say that again." She choked on the words. "Not ever!"

His eyes held hers for a moment. Then their gaze became abstract, inward. He released her arm without a further word, and his head sank slowly onto his breast.

She fled the kitchen, trying not to sob out loud. How dare he! How *dare* he! He had poisoned everything. He had defiled the most sacred feelings of her life.

Later, Candida sat in the galvanized iron tub, her mood now melancholy and faraway. She could no longer recapture her joy. Joseph had seen to that.

How had Joseph known? Was he some kind of sorcerer? Had

he sent some familiar spirit to sit outside that hut in the storm, spying on what was going on inside? His eyes had been filled with a bleak pain, but she did not want to accept the meaning.

How could he love her? Just because she had nursed him? Did he think that gave him some right over her affections?

As she soaped her body, the places David had touched, she was reminded of what had happened in the *capanna*. It was a woman's body now, no longer a girl's. There was a bruise on one of her breasts where he had bitten her in that last paroxysm, while he had groaned words in English she could not understand. She touched herself under the water and winced as she felt how he had torn the skin of her maidenhead. She'd often wondered how much it would hurt. Now she knew. She remembered the searing that had ended her innocence, the scalding of his body plunging into hers, coursing between her thighs.

After the elusive delicacy of her idyll, it had been a consummation of astonishing animality. Though it was all new, she had recognized the sounds and movements. She had seen and heard them before, made by animals. David's harsh grunting, the sound of his body thudding against hers, his final hoarse cry, as if in agony.

But David had not said he loved her, not even afterward, as they lay in each other's arms by the fire, with the thunder pealing overhead and the smoke from his cigarette curling around them.

That thought brought a sharp, deep disquiet. She recognized its source. The source of the poison. She thought again of Joseph's dark eyes. A hardness closed her heart. He was dangerous. Venomous.

The sooner he was out of the house, the better.

Candida Had Not been to *la torre del cacciatóre* in years, not since her childhood. As the pony pushed his way through the wall of dead bracken into the clearing, she had the strange sensation of entering the world of a childhood dream, even, as she had said to Joseph, of a fairy tale.

The *torre* itself was a square eighteenth-century tower some forty feet high, with a sharply raked slate roof upon which stood a rusty iron weather vane. It was more dilapidated than Candida had remembered. Where the walls were not covered with shaggy green creepers, the rendering had started to fall away, revealing the stonework beneath.

Some loose slates hung perilously over the gutters, disturbed by the snow. The wooden shutters sagged outward from the narrow windows, but the stout oak door looked sturdy enough.

Vincenzo reined the pony in, and the trap creaked to a halt in the little clearing. The thick carpet of snow had deadened the horse's hoof falls, lending an eerie quiet to their journey. Now the silence was absolute. Overhead, the sky was slate gray, and there was a smell of further snow in the air.

Candida jumped down and reached up to help Joseph. As she might have expected, he refused her proffered assistance, lowering him self painfully from the buckboard. He turned to stare at the tower.

"Your new home," Vincenzo said. "Come and take a look around."

The lock on the door had rusted or been broken years ago. It creaked open heavily as Vincenzo put his weight to it. Joseph followed, his arm pressed to his bad side.

The interior was stark and empty. The walls were roughly dressed stone, and a plain stone fireplace had been built against one wall. A narrow stairway led up to the room above. In fact, there were only three rooms, one above the other. The floors, of knotty oak board, were largely sound. Candida ran up the stairs to the next floor, which was equally empty, then up to the third. She pushed open the rickety shutters and stared out. She had hoped to be able to see over the tree-tops, but the tower was not tall enough. All the better, she thought. The smoke from the chimney would not be noticed so easily.

She came down again to find that Joseph had hauled himself up to the first floor. He was looking around him with a strange expression. She had treated him with icy aloofness since the night of the storm. Now she spoke to him brusquely.

"Well?" she asked. "Is this acceptable?"

"It's perfect."

"I told you you'd be lonely."

"I don't mind loneliness."

She brushed at the thick cobwebs, then beat her hands together. "You could fix the doors and windows. But maybe it would be better to keep the place looking abandoned. At least there's a fireplace on each floor, and there's all the firewood you could want right outside your front door."

"It's perfect," he repeated.

She turned away from him without further speech.

They unloaded the trap. Apart from his bedding, they had given Joseph bags of rice, beans, and lentils, and some iron pots to cook with. Vincenzo had supplied him with an axe and a shotgun and some basic tools. While the two men carried these things into the tower, Candida gathered armfuls of dead wood from around the clearing and heaped them just inside the door, so he would have a supply of fuel for a few days.

"Which floor are you going to sleep on?" she asked.

"The first, I think," Joseph decided.

She carried an armful of wood up to the fireplace there, which looked as though no fire had burned in it for a century or more. Hoping no storks had built their nests in the chimney, she lit the kindling and stood back as the yellow flames licked hungrily at the wood. The chimney seemed clear, and within a few minutes there was a warm blaze in the hearth. She went to help the men get the last of Joseph's things into the tower.

Within half an hour they had set up a simple household, with lentils cooking on the fire, a bed on the floor, a store cupboard neatly assembled under a cloth.

"The Hermit of Lake Garda." Vincenzo smiled, rubbing his hands by the fire. "Good thing this chimney draws well. It'll snow again before the day is out. We'll look in on you in a day or two, Joseph. Make a list of anything you find you need, and we'll bring it to you."

"No." He shook his head. "You've done far more for me than you ever needed to, Vincenzo. You've risked your life, and your family's, to help a complete stranger. I'll never forget your kindness. Never."

The words were simple, but the quiet, husky voice carried such force that Vincenzo's cheeks reddened. "Anyone would have done the same, boy," he said gruffly.

"I don't think so," Joseph replied. "Please don't take any more risks. You'd better get back to *Il Noce* before more snow comes."

Vincenzo nodded. He shook Joseph's hand firmly. "Good luck, Joseph. Come on, child."

He went down the stairs, leaving Candida with Joseph. She took a deep breath before facing him. She shook her unruly hair back from her face. "You will be all right here—won't you?" she asked in a voice that was not quite steady.

He reached out both hands to her. Not quite knowing what he wanted, she put her own hands in his. He drew her to him, his bearded face looking down at her intently. "You saved my life," he said.

"Well, what could I do?" She tried to smile. "Let you die in the barn?"

"There are angels on earth, as there are in heaven," he said gently, his eyes never leaving hers. "And you are one. You will always be in my heart, Candida."

Tears were perilously close, glistening on her lids. "Hush," she whispered. "Don't talk so foolishly."

He bent his head and kissed her on the lips. Not as David had done, with that eager pressure, with the probing tongue, but with a deep, quiet gentleness. For a moment she felt everything inside herself stand still, as though some profound peace had poured into her. Then Joseph drew back. "Your father's waiting for you," he whispered.

She did not move, just stood staring up at him as though she had never seen him before. He was watching her as though those dark eyes could pierce her heart.

"Go," he said, touching her shoulder.

She emerged from the spell slowly, nodded, and turned to go. On the way back through the forest, jolting in the pony-trap, she suddenly burst into tears. Her father stared at her.

"What's the matter?"

"Nothing."

"You got fond of him, eh? It's natural. He'll be all right."

She nodded. Perhaps David had been right. Perhaps you did fall a little in love with a man you nursed.

"What did he say to you just now?" he asked.

"He said—he said I was an angel. It sounds ridiculous, but I really think he meant it."

Vincenzo laughed softly. "We should be the ones to be careful that *he* is not an angel."

"What do you mean?"

" 'Be not forgetful to entertain strangers: for thereby some have entertained angels unawares.' " Vincenzo rapped the pony lightly with the reins to speed him up; the first flakes of snow were already drifting down from a darkening sky.

FEBRUARY 1944

The first week of February brought bitterly cold winds and lowering skies that seemed they would never clear.

Vincenzo and Teo returned from their work with chapped and bleeding hands, their cheeks reddened with capillaries burst by the cold. Candida and her mother settled into the dank household drudgery of midwinter. Candida felt strangely comfortless. Her love affair with David, which had begun so thrillingly, had given her far less fulfillment than she had anticipated. "Love affair," she recognized, was a grandiose term for a relationship that consisted of irregular meetings in a stone hut for the purpose of fornication. But she had expected something more, all the same: She had expected an idyll. Her thoughts kept returning to Joseph in his solitary tower. Her diary entries, which grew long and rambling, referred to him every day. There was some reassurance in that her father, who had visited Joseph twice since the move, said the American was settling in well. Thoughts of him haunted her. Increasingly, she felt powerless, as though her life was happening to someone else, and she had no way of influencing it.

She was due to meet David in the *capanna* on February 6th; but as she scrambled up the slope, there was a shock in store.

A large flock of dirty brown sheep was milling around the stone hut. Smoke fluttered from the chimney, together with a smell of cooking and coarse tobacco. A shepherd had moved into the *capanna* for the winter.

She stood there, stunned, until she heard a low whistle. David was crouching under the brow of the hill, beckoning to her. She went to him and clung to his arm miserably.

"What are we going to do, David?"

"We'll have to find somewhere else."

"Where else is there?"

"The barn is the only place."

"Oh, David," she said doubtfully. The barn, where the doctor had operated on Joseph, was no more than two hundred yards from *Il Noce*. "It's too close to the house."

"We'll go up in the hayloft."

"Someone will see us there. My father, or Teo."

"So what?" he said brusquely.

"You don't understand! My father would kill me!"

He stared at her. His face was unshaven, and his hair, normally bright as gold, was dark and matted. "You're a grown woman."

"That's not the point. He'd be terribly upset ... "

"We can't do it in the bushes," David said sharply. He huddled himself into his greatcoat, glancing over his shoulder at the hut they had lost. "And Christ knows I need a little warmth. It's a bloody long way down from Chiese. It's like Siberia up there. Snow and ice and blizzards. Terrible. Make your mind up."

"All right," she said, her heart heavy. "We'll try it out. But go carefully, David, *please*."

They made their way cautiously back toward *Il Noce*. Nobody saw them. They slipped into the barn. David scrambled up the ladder into the loft, which was piled high with the summer's hay. One wall was open to the wind and framed a view of the snow-clad Alps. She followed him, and he hauled her up the last step.

He sprawled in the hay without a word, drawing her down beside him.

There was no question of undressing. The world outside was white, and a bitter wind swept through the poorly sheltered loft. She pressed her mouth to his, silently begging kisses, but he was rough and hurried, as he so often was these days. He mounted her, their heavy clothes absurdly bulky. It was an undignified and uncomfortable performance.

She lay silent as he fumbled to enter her, her whole body hurting with the fear of discovery. If her father were to come up here for some purpose and discover them, his anger did not bear thinking of. Anxiety made her tense. She concentrated on her surroundings: on the snow-white Alps in the distance, on the lean cats that sat on the bales of straw watching them, on the ancient timbers of the barn. She remembered the way the cats had watched while the doctor had operated on Joseph. She noticed, with a vague sadness, that the hay had already lost its sweet summer fragrance. It had begun to ferment and gave off a rank smell of decay.

She shut her eyes as he made love to her. There was no stirring of excitement. She tried hard not to feel disgust—with herself, with the war that forced them into this demeaning parody of love, with David for his blind, insensitive sexual energy. Today was one of the worst days, more brutish than normal. Her head banged painfully against one of the roof trusses, but he did not notice. "Is that good?" he grunted.

"Yes," Candida whispered. At last it ended. He arched back, shuddering. Words were dragged from deep in his chest, but they were in his own language, and she could not understand them. She hoped— prayed—they were words of love. He had never said he loved her in Italian.

He sprawled beside her, his face gleaming with sweat, panting. "You'll catch pneumonia," she whispered, pulling the collar of his great- coat up around his face. She curled up beside him and wondered, as she had done so many times before, what was wrong with her. Didn't she love him enough? That first time, in the *capanna,* had been the best time. Every time since then had fallen short, sometimes sickeningly— for her, at any rate. She wondered whether David truly enjoyed it, either.

Her thoughts wandered. The sharp depression she so often felt after making love faded to a dreamy melancholy.

"Joseph knew about us from the start," she said at last, when her thoughts had come full circle.

David stirred. "How did he know?"

"He just knew, right from the start."

He gave a grunt. "Must have smelled it on you. What was he doing, sniffing round you? Did he take a fancy to you?"

Her face flushed hotly. "No, of course not. He was shut down there in the dark, but he saw everything. He frightened me sometimes."

"Well, he's gone now. Not your responsibility anymore." He lit a cigarette. "This fucking snow," he spat suddenly. "Christ, I'm sick of Italy!"

"You do still care for me," she asked timidly. "Don't you?"

He exhaled a cloud of blue smoke. "Don't be stupid. Of course I do."

But she was frightened for him. He was changing. The winter was changing him. Antonio *il rósso* had rejected him. He had tried to join other bands of Partisans, but had been snubbed. She did not know why he had been rejected, only that it had hurt his pride severely. For her sake, she was deeply glad that he was out of that dangerous, wild life, but the effect on him had been destructive.

She knew little about the elderly couple who sheltered him in Chiese, but they clearly did not want him hanging around their house during the day. The long walk down from Chiese to see her was his only activity, and it was fraught with dangers. The combination of inertia and danger was telling on his nerves. His morale was sinking very low.

He no longer spoke about the Duchess of Windsor, or about his life in England. Increasingly, he was irritable with her, especially after they had made love. He was like a caged animal, fretting, losing condition visibly. The black dirt of the charcoal-burners' house seemed to be ingrained in his pores. He was always unshaven and smelled rank, as though he had stopped washing.

"You felt very dry," he said idly. "I suppose that's because of what you're using."

"Using?"

He stared at her. "Aren't you using anything? Haven't you been taking precautions all these weeks? I thought you were taking care of all that!"

"I don't know what to do, David," she said in a small voice.

"Jesus Christ, didn't your mother tell you?"

She looked away. "My mother thinks I'm a virgin."

"Well, you don't want to present her with an immaculate conception, do you?"

"No," she said quietly. "What should I do?"

He looked weary. "For God's sake. Shove a sponge up there, or a piece of cloth, or something. Wash yourself afterward. Understand?"

"Yes, David," she said quietly. But she felt that yet another delicate thing had been torn.

"I should never have stayed," he said grimly. "I should have gone up into the mountains with the others."

He had spoken like this before, but it always sent a chill through her soul. "Don't talk like that, my love."

"I should have gone up to Switzerland before the bad weather settled in. Or made my way down south. Now I'm trapped here." He jerked his head in the direction of Saló. "I couldn't have picked a worse place to hole up. Twenty miles from Mussolini himself."

She reached for him, trying to comfort him. "The war news is so good, David. Your people will soon be in Rome. It can't last forever."

"Can't it? This is like being in hell, Candida. Sneaking and hiding all day. The same mountains, the same faces. Sleeping like a mouse in a cat's ear, never knowing if I'll wake up with a jackboot in my face. Never knowing who's going to betray me. And Christ knows, I'm so sick of polenta, I could vomit."

She bit her lip. The thought of losing him now was dreadful. His big hands were shaking as he reached for another cigarette. She clung to his neck, pressing her mouth to his, drawing him to her, trying to obliterate her fear and his with the clumsy coupling that seemed to be the only thing they had in common anymore.

Two Days Later, while Candida and her mother were preparing the midday meal for Vincenzo and Teo's return, they heard a truck rumble into the yard, followed by the clatter of boots and volleys of shouted orders.

They stared at one another in dread, frozen where they stood.

This time they were Italians, members of the fascist *milízia*. They marched into the kitchen in their black uniforms, their boots crashing on the tiles, machine guns at the ready.

The leader sauntered in after them, flipping his hand in the fascist salute. Candida recognized him at once: a brutal drunkard named Giusterini, who had put all his ill humor into the fascist cause years ago, and now commanded his own group of militiamen. They filled Candida with the same terror as the Germans, but with another emotion, too, a hot anger.

"What do you want?" Rosa demanded.

Giusterini studied her, his eyes puffy slits on either side of a swollen drinker's nose. "I want a full list of the persons staying in this house."

"My husband, my two children, me."

One of Giusterini's men scrawled the names laboriously in a notebook.

"Where are the men?"

"Out in the fields."

"They'll be back any minute," Candida added significantly.

Giusterini walked slowly round the women, eyeing them up and down with his ragged buttonholes of eyes. "You're the woman from Valtellina, aren't you?" he said to Rosa. "And this is your pretty little daughter."

The men moved in a tighter circle around Candida and Rosa.

Suddenly Candida felt a sharp cramp of fear. She could see by their eyes that these men were capable of raping her and her mother in their own kitchen. She turned and pulled open the drawer behind her. She took out the ponderous razor-edged knife that they used for butchering work and began steadily chopping a big, fibrous winter turnip. One or two of the *miliziàni* backed away, eyeing the weapon with respect.

Giusterini did not move. "We must search the house."

"Wait until my husband gets back," Rosa said.

"We have no time to sit around waiting for yokels," Giusterini said. "Do it."

The men scattered with alacrity. With a sense of déjà vu, Candida heard their boots thudding around the house, the crash of cupboards being emptied. With a little cry, Rosa ran out of the kitchen. Candida wanted to shout after her; it was far safer that they stayed together, and what were a few stolen or broken possessions? But she dared not show any fear in front of Giusterini, who had remained behind.

He moved beside Candida, so close that she could smell the sour reek of alcohol on his breath. "And where is your blond boyfriend?"

She felt as though he had kicked her in the stomach. There was no breath in her lungs. Somehow she found words. "I don't know what you're talking about."

He smiled, showing brown teeth. "The one you fuck in the *capanna*. The blond one. That's who I'm talking about."

Her heart was pounding wildly. The handle of the knife was slippery in her palm. Someone must have spied on them. Someone must have seen something. But what? "That's a lie."

"Careful who you call a liar," he said. "They say he's a foreigner. Is he a prisoner of war? One of the so-called Partisans who murdered those Germans up on the pass? Is that who he is?"

Courage came from somewhere. "You're mad," she snapped. "We wouldn't associate with people like that. We value our lives too much."

"Then who is he?"

Candida set her teeth against the copper taste of fear in her mouth. "There are always occasional laborers in the district. Last month it was two Calabrians. The month before, a deaf and dumb Yugoslav. They're migrant workers. They come and they go."

"And you fuck them all?"

She bit her lip. "I don't know any blond man."

"If you're so keen for a fuck, you can fuck me." He unfastened his belt. "At least I'm an Italian."

She backed away. "Don't come near me," she said quietly.

"I wouldn't want to have to share you, girl. We could all have you, and your mother, too, if we wanted. You couldn't stop us."

She gripped the handle of the knife tightly. "Stay away from me."

He pulled his belt out and looped it round his fist, grinning. "We can do it the hard way, if you like. I'd enjoy giving you the thrashing you deserve, you little whore."

"I'll kill you," she said, her voice shaky.

He stopped, watching the blade.

She said nothing, just stood tense as a spring, the knife pointed at his midriff. Desperation and fear had armed her. If he came a step closer, she would drive the blade into his belly. He could see that in her eyes.

A moment passed in silence. Then his eyes slid away from hers. His face reddened. He unlooped the belt and started sliding it back around his waist. "I hate traitors," he said, his voice wet and soft. "I'd hang them all. If I catch you alone, whore, I'll cut your womb out. And if I catch *him,* I'll feed you his balls."

A splintering of glass came from upstairs, together with a cry of distress from her mother. *"Mama!"* she called urgently, not taking her eyes from Giusterini.

A man ran down the stairs, his arms filled with clothing. There was a scratch on his cheek. "I had to give the old bitch a knock," he said to Giusterini. "There's nothing here. Let's go."

"You're nothing more than criminals," she said tightly. "You defile the name of Italy."

"Go fuck yourself," Giusterini said, lifting his arm to threaten a backhanded blow. She edged away, holding the knife at the ready. The men were hurrying out of the house now, laden with booty. Each one had grabbed whatever he could carry. One even had a chest of drawers on his back. They had plundered the house.

One of them stuck his head round the door. "Capo! Let's go!"

Giusterini glanced round the kitchen. A keg of wine stood on trestle legs in one corner. He lifted it with a grunt and walked heavily to the door. There he looked back over his shoulder, his eyes burning. "Remember what I said."

He left. The truck rumbled out of the yard. She ran upstairs to find her mother, sick with fear.

Rosa was sitting at the top of the steps, crying desolately. Candida threw her arms around her.

"Mama! Are you all right? What did they do to you?"

Her mother lifted her tear-stained face. There was blood on her lip. "Nothing," she said drearily. "But the house . . . "

Candida looked around. She was stunned. They had taken every piece of furniture they could lift, everything pretty, everything that had the slightest value. They had pillaged the house like locusts, and they had deliberately damaged what they could not lift. The heavy oak chest of drawers in her parents' room was scarred. The cupboard in her brother's room had been splintered with a kick.

Their real target had been her own room. They had cracked her dressing-table mirror and broken the dainty china bowl she washed in each morning. They had pulled the drawers out and ransacked them. Her underclothes, plain and simple things that they were, had been torn to pieces. A brassiere hung in tatters from the light. Her single pair of silk stockings was spread-eagled on the bed. Too cowardly to attack her in person, they had violated her this way.

In the soft plaster of the wall, someone had carved, with the point of a bayonet, the word WHORE.

That Italians could do this numbed her. Why? What had she ever done to them? She stood there, nauseated, feeling as though they had torn the skin from her back. She would never spend a peaceful night in this desecrated room again.

Vincenzo and Teo came back while the two women were trying to tidy. Vincenzo, white-faced, cursed quietly.

"Who was it?"

"Giusterini and his men."

"That piece of filth. They didn't touch you?"

"No."

"I'll settle with that bastard."

"Leave it be, Vincenzo," Rosa said wearily. "It's done, now."

Teo came into Candida's room. He stood beside her, his eyes slowly taking in the details. His mouth turned down bitterly. He said nothing, but she felt his hand reach for hers. His fingers twined around hers, gripped hard.

"This doesn't matter," he said quietly. "They didn't hurt you."

"I can't wear any of my clothes again," she said in a choked voice.

"You can. You just need new underwear. Don't let them win, Candida. Don't give up the fight. It's nearly won."

The word carved in the plaster accused her hideously. "I'm seeing the Englishman," she said without looking at Teo.

"I know," he replied quietly.

"He's my lover."

"Yes, I know."

"Does Papa know? Mama?"

"No, I don't think so."

"I don't know what to do, Teo."

He was silent for a while. Then he said, "Be careful, Candida. For God's sake, be careful."

She was trembling violently. Something swelled in her throat. She ached to turn to Teo and bury her face against his chest, as she had done when they'd been children and some hurt had threatened her world. But she seemed rooted to the spot.

"Who could have betrayed us?" she whispered.

"Perhaps nobody. Perhaps even one of the Partisans. The human heart is a mystery, my sister. You know that. People will do anything to earn two thousand lire these days."

Candida felt a great weight settle on her soul. She had risked all their lives. The situation was growing worse daily. Men like Giusterini had come into their own, using the chaotic situation and their own brutality to do whatever they wanted.

If Giusterini and his thugs caught David, there would be a bloody ending to her tarnished idyll. At least they seemed to know nothing of Joseph. If they knew she had nursed a wounded Partisan, they would burn the house down.

Teo released her hand, stooped, and began picking up her underclothes. "I'll take these out and burn them."

"Thank you, Teo," she said. He had guessed she could not bear the thought of touching the things. He carried the tattered armful downstairs.

She drew a deep breath and began picking up the pieces.

David Listened To her in silence, his back half-turned. His cigarette burned idly away in his fingers. She told him everything, including the attempt to rape her and Giusterini's threats against David.

"It's not safe anymore, David," she finished at last, her voice low. "They could come back at any time. The worse the war goes for them, the more vicious they get."

He tossed the butt of his cigarette at one of the cats that was always there, watching them. He turned to her, his eyes cold. "This is all your fault," he grated.

Candida felt a cold chill settle around her heart. "What do you mean?"

"You kept me here."

"I never asked you to stay!"

He did not seem to hear her.

"David," she said in a strained voice, "I didn't ask you to stay. I would never be so selfish! I thought you stayed because you didn't want to go up into the mountains or risk internment in Switzerland. You never said you were staying for my sake!"

"Well, I did," he said sullenly. "Now look where it's got me."

She could find nothing to say. She felt sick. After a long silence, he lit another cigarette. She reached for his hand. "When the weather improves," she said, her voice barely audible, "you could go up into the hills and find the others."

"Perhaps," he agreed. He lay back, his face weary. He had stopped talking about joining the Partisans, had even stopped complaining about Antonio *il rósso,* but Candida knew how desperate he felt.

"I could try and get in touch with Paolo, if you like. He could lead you to some safer place."

"Paolo's a little pimp," he said shortly. "Maybe I could get down to Rome, and wait for the Eighth Army there," he speculated.

"It's too dangerous, David!"

"I could pass as an itinerant laborer."

"No! You'd never make it."

"You took care of Joseph, all right," he said bitterly. "You fixed him up fine."

"Joseph is no better off than you are, David. He's living like a hermit in the woods. He must be lonelier than anyone could imagine."

He drew on his cigarette, the coal glowing brightly. "I made a mistake," he said.

She was thinking. "Why don't you join up with him again?" she said. "The two of you together would have a better chance. You could make your way to the Swiss border together."

"No," he said shortly.

"Why not? He's your friend."

"Joseph was never my friend."

She was startled. "But you fought together."

"That doesn't make him my friend. He never liked me. I never liked him. He took command. He assumed everyone would follow him." He flicked his cigarette butt away from him. One of the cats, prepared this time, chased after it, batting it with its paws. "He's an arrogant American Jew."

"A Jew?"

He gave her a dry look. "Jesus. I thought you'd have guessed by now."

"Well, I did notice that—" She stopped in confusion.

"You noticed what?"

"Nothing."

"You noticed he was circumcised," David guessed, his eyes narrowing. "You little trollop. I didn't realize you'd been quite that intimate with him."

"I had to wash him while he was so sick," she said awkwardly, her face now flushed with embarrassment. "I thought he was dying, David. I didn't pay too much attention to *that*, I can assure you."

"Liar," David said softly. "You had a damned good look."

"I did not," she retorted hotly.

"Then how do you know he's been snipped?"

"He was—different. But I never guessed he was a Jew."

"Do you think they've got horns and a tail? His family were refugees. Rich refugees. Bankers." David's face twisted in a cruel smile. "He's shitting himself worse than I am right now. It wouldn't be very funny if the Nazis caught him. The Italians were all right, but you know what Hitler's like about Jews. That's partly why he joined the Partisans when we were released."

Candida stared at the distant white peaks. Perhaps that was why Joseph always seemed so dark and strange to her. Perhaps that accounted for some of his mystery. She wished she had known before. Perhaps she could have got closer to him if she had known . . .

"Poor Joseph," she whispered.

"Don't waste your sympathy," David snapped. "That's one area where Hitler had the right idea."

"David!" she exclaimed, shocked. "You don't mean that!"

"I don't like them," he said flatly. "Nobody of my class does. We used to have to put up with one or two Jews at High Force before the war. My father couldn't stand them, but they were friends of friends. Financiers, mostly. They had a smell about them, like dirty money. Fistfuls of dirty money."

She turned to face him. She had never met a Jew before, not knowingly, but she had never been taught to hate them. No Italian had. She, like everyone else, knew the tragic fate of the Italian Jews, drawn inexorably into the maw of Hitler's huge persecution machine. She found David's instinctive anti-Semitism inexplicable. "What have they ever done to hurt you?"

"They're usurers." His mouth was ugly. "Bloodsuckers. Venal, vulgar parasites."

"Joseph's not like that! I thought you were friends," she repeated.

"We were thrown together. It would never have happened before the war. The war turned everything upside down." He thumped himself on the shoulders and chest to warm up, puffing clouds of vapor out of his mouth like a dragon. "Jesus, it's cold." He paused. "I might as well be in a prisoner-of-war camp as rotting here."

Something in his voice made her heart lurch.

"What do you mean?"

There was a strange look in his eyes. "At least I'd be warm. At least I'd be with civilized people."

"David, for God's sake," she said urgently. "Don't even think of it."

"What?"

"Giving yourself up to the Germans."

"Why not?"

"They'd shoot you like a dog!"

He rubbed his hands together and blew between them. "I've heard otherwise."

"You mean those pamphlets they give out? That's just propaganda. They'd kill you."

His expression was sly. "Not if I did it properly. Not if I went about it the right way."

"There is no right way!" Panic fluttered in her heart. She'd known his talk of getting to Switzerland or Rome had been blowing smoke, dreaming aloud. But his voice had changed now. She knew him well enough to tell that he had been thinking over this option and that it was real to him. "You still think they go by the Geneva Convention? David, you're not a fool! You know what they're like."

His face was set. "I could sit out the war in some stalag. Safe. Warm. It's all going to be over in a few months, anyway. Then I'll be sent back home."

"You're a soldier!"

He met her eyes, and she could see the desperation in them. "I'm a fox, and the hounds are after me. POW camp would be better than creeping around these fucking mountains, waiting for some *fascista* to cut my balls off with a carving knife."

"Oh, David!" She put her arms around him, feeling, for the first time since she had known him, the real weakness of the man, the real vulnerability beneath the outward strength.

They made love, David rutting ferociously at her, like an animal.

Plodding back through the thick snow, she felt her womb aching, whether because of the cold, or because he'd been so rough, she did not know. His talk of giving himself up had put her in a profound depression. It seemed so futile. So utterly senseless.

The Germans had been distributing pamphlets for months, urging escaped Allied POWs to give themselves up, promising fair treatment under the Geneva Convention if they did so, warning of dire consequences if they did not. She could not believe that David could be taken in by such crude messages.

She was shaken to the heart. But a quiet inner voice asked her what she had really wanted out of this affair. Being honest with herself, had she really expected he would marry her? Did men like David Godbold marry women like her? If he survived, wouldn't he go back to Northumberland and marry some titled, snow-white virgin and never even remember the *capanna* and the hayloft? The thought of losing David hung over her like a sentence of death.

Candida wept in her room. She turned to her diary for comfort. What will I have left, she wrote, when David goes? The tears that blotted the page gave her the only answer.

That Night, Candida was silent and desolate at the dinner table. Rosa watched her anxiously.

"She's sickening for something," she said. "Drink some more wine, child."

"I don't want any."

"*Buòn vino fa buòn sàngue.* Good wine makes good blood." She glanced at Teo. "You both could do with a little feeding. Look at my daughter, Teo. Look how much weight she's lost. Is that what an eighteen-year-old girl should look like?"

"She's tired, Mama."

"She was so beautiful last summer. Now she's lost all her looks."

"Mama, please," Candida said.

"Hasn't she lost all her looks, Teo?" Rosa challenged.

"No," Teo said gently, "she's still very beautiful."

Rosa sniffed dubiously. "She used to be radiant. She used to have a proper figure. Now she's a skeleton."

Candida's nerves were stretched taut. "Mama, stop nagging me, please!"

She slept badly and kept waking with terrible dreams of David in danger. At one point she dreamed he was dead, and she was standing at his graveside. Joseph was there, trying to comfort her. He stroked her hair. She looked into his eyes. They were fathomless, black, yearning. She found herself sitting up in bed, staring into the darkness.

In her heart was an almost painful longing to go and see Joseph at the Hunter's Tower. The dream memory of his yearning eyes haunted her until dawn and would not let her sleep again.

The Walk To the Hunter's Tower was wet underfoot. The sun had emerged for the first time in days, and the snow was turning quickly to slush. The leaves on the oak trees had died but not fallen, and in the dappled light, they gave an illusion of summer greenery. As she walked, she caught a faint perfume of clover above the chalky smell of melting snow. It was like a promise of new life. She lifted her face to the sky and felt the sun touch her skin. She felt tranquil, almost detached, as though the night's evil dreams had purged her of emotions.

She caught the smell of wood smoke as she approached the hidden tower. She pushed her way through the bracken into the clearing. The tower stood with its mantle of greenery, snow melting on the slate roof. He had fixed the broken shutters. Smoke curled from the chimney. Though she was weary and wet from the long walk, she made no effort to walk into the clearing. She stood staring at the tower, a strange, dreamlike feeling washing over her. Such an eerie aura sat upon this place, of folk-myth and enchantment. She half-expected to see elves and fairies dancing around it.

Then she saw the door open, and Joseph's figure stood in the doorway, watching her. She walked forward.

He was more erect than she remembered, perhaps because his wound had healed and he could stand upright. He looked less gaunt, too, younger, no longer the sick man she had known. His beard was full and black. He gave her the faintest of smiles as she reached him, and took her hand.

"I told you not to come," he said in his husky voice.

"I was worried about you. I wanted to see how you were." She held out the basket she had lugged from *Il Noce*. "I brought you some food and wine."

"Thank you, Candida. Come in."

The inside of the tower was scrupulously clean and orderly. He led her upstairs. A small fire was burning in the hearth. His bed was made in the middle of the room, stark as a prisoner's pallet. She saw that he had made two crude chairs out of trunks and stood them on either side of the hearth. She smiled.

"Two chairs? Do you get many visitors here?"

"Sometimes the spirits of the woods come and dine with me," he said solemnly. She almost believed him. He laid more wood on the fire and stoked up the blaze. Then he made her take off her shoes and sit by the fire, warming her frozen feet.

"You've made this place beautiful," she said, gazing around.

"Hardly. But it's clean."

"Are you all right here?" she asked awkwardly. "I meant to come and see you earlier, but the snow . . ."

"It's a long walk. And you should not have taken the risk." He had started preparing some food on the fire. She watched his movements. He was deft and graceful, his lean body moving without constraint now. He looked strong, hard.

"Is there no more pain?"

"From the bullet wound? None. You healed me."

She saw that he was making wild mushrooms. "Are you sure you know the right ones to pick?" she asked pointedly. "Some of them are deadly."

"I've been eating them for weeks, and I'm not dead yet," he said. He had a grave, mocking way of talking to her. "You look very pale, Candida. And you've lost weight. It doesn't suit you."

"Whereas you seem to be flourishing," she said dryly, eyeing the glow of his skin. "Life as a hermit clearly suits you."

"How are your father and mother? And Teo?"

She told him, gazing around her. He had made other pieces of simple furniture out of roughly hewn wood. His little library of books stood on a shelf. By his bed lay Dante's *Divina Commedia*. She tried to imagine his life here. Silence, tranquility, loneliness. The daily tasks of his stark household. The company of his few books. It filled her with both pity and a kind of envy. At least he knew peace. She did not. She had not known peace for a long time.

"And David?" he asked without inflection. "How is he?"

She took a deep breath. "I'm worried about him. He's so depressed. So bad-tempered."

"Does he treat you badly?" Joseph asked, intent on the pot of mushrooms.

"No, of course not," she replied quickly. "But his morale is so low. It's getting him down, the running and hiding. He keeps saying he ought to have gone to Switzerland." She hesitated. "He even talks about giving himself up to the Germans."

Joseph turned and looked her full in the eyes. "You cannot allow that, Candida."

She shrugged tiredly. "He doesn't listen to me."

"The Germans would want to know everything he had done

since the Armistice. He's been a Partisan. Any interrogation would reveal that. They would want to know where he has been hiding. There would be no amnesty for those who had sheltered him, Candida. They would shoot you all."

"David would never betray us," she said indignantly.

"Grow up," he said shortly, turning back to the fire.

She was already wishing she had not come. Why did he have that effect on her? "He won't do it, anyway," she said. "It's just talk."

Joseph said nothing further. He got the meal ready in silence. Candida watched him, a spare, strange man in a spare, strange room. She'd never seen him move around freely before. There was something fascinating about his fluidity. He was catlike, velvety. She found herself comparing him to David's blunt strength and thinking of the contemptuous way David had talked of him.

He served the food in two bowls. She was hungry and ate with relish. The mushrooms had a wild, musky flavor she did not recognize. Elf-food, she thought. "There are some mushrooms that send you crazy," she told him. "If you eat them, you see visions and dance naked in the forest like a witch."

"I told you that you were only an amusement for David," he said. "You are now learning that it's the truth."

"No! I believe in David. I trust him."

"Then you're a fool," he said shortly.

"I hate you," she said passionately. "I only came here to help you!"

"And I only want to help you," he said calmly. He leaned forward. "You're an intelligent woman," he said, speaking clearly and quietly, "but you have no experience of life. You've thrown yourself away on David Godbold because you were in love with your own dreams."

"Stop now, Joseph," she warned.

"Now is the time for you to face the truth, because David is going to leave you very soon. And if you don't face the truth, you're going to waste the best years of your life waiting for him to come back."

"He will come back!"

"He'll never come back," he said relentlessly. "He's taken advantage of you while it suited him, and he'll forget you within a day of leaving *Il Noce*."

She was so angry that she snatched up her plate and made as if to throw it in his face. Something in his eyes stopped her. She threw the food onto the fire instead, and it hissed on the coals.

"Bravo," he said ironically. "Candida makes an adult gesture."

"Why do you say these things, Joseph?"

"You know why."

"Because you think you love me? Which of us is the dreamer, Joseph?"

He cleared up the remains of the meal. She looked around the stone walls. Knowing she was in a tower lent the room a strange feeling. There were no more rooms beyond the four blank stone walls, no more people, things; just air, and the forest beyond.

"How much do you know about love, Joseph?" she asked at last. "Did you leave a woman in America?"

"Yes."

Something in his tone made her glance at him quickly. "What was her name?"

"Marian."

"Did you love her?"

"We were engaged to be married."

The information jolted her. " 'Were'? Not anymore?"

"No. She wrote to me in the prisoner-of-war camp to say that she had married someone else."

"That was a wicked, cruel thing to do!" Candida exclaimed indignantly.

He grinned, showing his uneven white teeth. "At least it was honest."

"Was she pretty?"

"Very."

Candida compressed her full mouth thoughtfully. "Is that why you're so cynical? Because she broke your heart?"

"She didn't exactly break my heart," he said dryly. "It was a blow to my pride, but I'd long since realized that I didn't really love her. If I'd really loved Marian, I wouldn't have volunteered to come to Europe. And in the end, of course, I fell in love with someone else."

"Who did you fall in love with?" she asked. The question had been quite artless. It was only when he did not reply that she flushed. "And was she the only woman you were ever . . . with?"

He looked up at last. His lips curved slightly in that smile that was half-tender, half-mocking. "The only one, Candida. Why does that surprise you?"

"Oh, I thought that men . . . "

"That men . . . what?"

"Well, David has much more experience than that," she said awkwardly.

She thought he was going to snub her until he said quietly, after a while, "David has been with a hundred whores he didn't care a cent for. I've made love to one woman I cared a great deal for. There's a difference."

She had the feeling that her world was crumbling, that everything that had been solid and real had vanished, leaving her falling, a long, terrible fall. "And I'm just the latest of David's whores?"

He straightened. "You've been here too long already. I'll walk you back now."

"You don't have to."

"I want to. Come."

The sky had darkened again, and the pace going back was slow. She walked beside Joseph, melancholy and silent. Her unhappiness was a jagged lump of bitterness she could not swallow. It pressed against her heart, choking her.

They turned into the dappled silence of the woods. As they trudged along the muddy lane, there was a loud crashing among the undergrowth that made them both start.

"What is it?" she asked fearfully.

"I don't know." He stood still and watchful, his eyes fixed on the direction the noise had come from.

There was a succession of wild crashes that made her scream and clutch Joseph's arm in both hands. And then, from out of the thicket, a big buck deer leaped. He was a magnificent animal, mature and stately, his dark coat glowing, his ears spread. On his forehead, the antlers of the coming spring were already starting to grow, covered in velvet. He stood staring at them with wild, innocent eyes, for a long moment. And then he sprang across the lane in a gleaming arc and bounded away among the trees, the thud of his hooves like the pounding of a frantic heart.

Candida stared after him, her breath pent up in her lungs. Slowly, she realized she was still clinging to Joseph's arm. His muscles were tight and sinewy under her fingers. He turned to look at her. She stared into his face and realized, as if for the first time, how beautiful he was. He was dark and male and comely, like the stag who had crossed their path. Only her blindness had prevented her from seeing that until now.

Her heart was thudding in rhythm with the stag's hoofbeats. She was dizzy. She felt some dark, barbaric power overcome her, though whether it was Joseph's, or something in the woods, or something in her own soul, she could not tell.

She swayed forward. It was a tiny movement, but it seemed to her as though she had leaped into a vast space, an abyss that had always been between them.

Then she felt his arms take her and draw her to him. "Oh, Joseph," she said shakily. "Oh, Joseph."

She clung to him, the abyss still yawning under her feet. He held her tight, stroking her hair gently. The terror faded a little. She looked up into his face. He was smiling.

"Come on," he said. "It's a long way home."

MARCH 1944

Despite everything, they continued to meet in the barn over the next days.

Fear that her parents would find out, and the knowledge that David's presence was no longer a secret, made the meetings wretched for Candida. The atmosphere between them was becoming increasingly strained and unhappy. Sex forced them into one another's company, she felt, nothing else. She no longer enjoyed the act in any physical sense, but she recognized that it was the final link that bound David Godbold to her.

David continued to talk about leaving the lake, formulating reckless plans for crossing the Alps, or walking down Italy to where the Allied armies were now fighting, hoping to reach the front line. But there seemed no conviction in his words; and March had brought forbidding weather, with more snow and black skies, making escape remoter than ever.

Sex seemed unable to lift his spirits. Now, afterward, he seemed more sullen than ever. He barely kissed her these days. All he wanted was to thrust himself as deep and as hard into her body as he could. Sometimes she felt like meat on a butcher's slab. She submitted, but with increasing resentment.

He had no right. He had no right to take his frustrations out in their lovemaking.

She no longer made any pretence of enjoyment. She simply held on to him while he pummeled her with his body, grunting words that she now no longer imagined were words of love.

At first she had felt guilty about her frigidity. Why could she not enjoy David's body the way he enjoyed hers? She'd felt that her inability to respond was a betrayal. Increasingly, however, she began to realize that the fault lay with David, not with her.

"Prison would be better than this," he said, groping for his cigarettes. "Jesus. Anything would be better than this."

It was his constant theme. Candida knew better than to argue with him now. She could only pray that, like his talk of crossing the Alps, it was a mood that would pass.

Her visit to Joseph, and his words to her, stayed in her mind.

"David," she asked quietly, "have you made love to many women?"

"Oh, dozens." He gave her a sly look. "Are you jealous?"

"No."

"Wondering if any of them were better than you?"

"No," she said, ignoring the jibe. "I just wondered what sort of women they were."

"All sorts." He shrugged. "Blondes, brunettes, redheads, you name it. Big tits, small tits, tight fannies, slack fannies."

"Were they your girlfriends? Girls you took to balls and parties?"

"You're joking," he said contemptuously. "You'd have a better chance of screwing a marble statue. Apart from one or two notable exceptions."

A cat lay along one of the knotty wooden beams, one paw dangling, green slits of eyes watching them idly. "So who were they, then, the women you made love to?" she asked.

"They were mostly whores." He said it with deliberate emphasis. She turned to look him in the face. There was a smirk on his mouth, a cruel, mocking smile.

Joseph had been right. "Is it expensive?" she asked in a brittle voice.

"It's better if you can get it for free." He spat a shred of tobacco off his tongue. "The clever ones want you to pay in advance. They give the money to the pimp, so you can't get it back off them afterwards. But the stupid ones, the inexperienced ones, they're not so sharp. They still enjoy doing it, you see. They let you have the goods first." His smile widened. "You never pay those ones."

"Like me?" she asked.

"There you go. You were too keen for it. You should have got the money in advance."

Something salty and scalding was in her throat. She rose.

"Candida—" He tossed away his cigarette and tried to take her hand, but she shook him off. "Candida, I was joking!" he called after her.

She stumbled down the ladder. He did not try and follow.

As the icy air hit her, she felt a realization dawn on her, that although she had given him everything she had, she meant nothing to him. He would never marry her. Whatever happened, the war would take him away from her, and he would never return.

She did not look back at the barn. She felt something happen inside her. Between the hard stones of her self-disgust and her sense of having been used, something soft and delicate had slowly been crushed, and now it was dead. She felt herself diminished. Older. Harder.

She found herself thinking thoughts she had never had before: about death, about the uncertainty of life, about its bleak lack of meaning. She tried to shake off the dismal mood, but it clung to her. Joseph had been right about so many things, and she had not wanted to listen. Her wise man of the woods. Her hermit in the tower. He had told her he loved her, and the words had meant nothing to her. She had not even considered them, because she had been so infatuated with David Godbold.

Like the moon at midday, Joseph had been invisible for David's brilliance. And now, as in some eclipse, Joseph was stealing over the face of her sun, and she was starting to see his shape.

Yet she knew nothing about him. Nothing at all. Only that he was a Jew and an American. She did not know from what part of that vast land he came. She did not know why he, an American, had volunteered to fight for the British. She only knew his strange surname because she had written it down in her diary.

She felt a longing to see him again, stronger than ever before; a longing to be in his quiet company, in that tower buried in the silent woods. To look into his dark eyes and learn about him, and about herself.

Dinner that night was a somber affair. Anti-aircraft fire thudded in the distance, and they could hear the drone of bombers in the sky. Allied planes now reached deep into Italy every night, striking at the great cities of the north, Milan, Bologna, Turin. And there was news of yet another SS atrocity: In a village a few miles away, the SS had publicly hanged ten suspected members of the Resistance. They had hauled them, kicking and twisting, up the scaffold with ropes tied to the backs of trucks. The mayor had been mutilated by the torturers, then shot in the town square.

In the silence, they heard explosions begin, much closer than ever before. Vincenzo blew out the kerosene lamp and opened the shutters. Across the lake there was a flickering of light in the darkness.

"My God," Rosa exclaimed. "They're bombing the factories!"

Candida clung to her mother, watching with horror as the terrible fireworks unfolded. Wavering fingers of searchlights probed the dark sky for the invisible bombers, high above the broken cloud. They could hear the drone of their engines and the wail of the sirens, borne on the wind. Then they saw the glimmer of bombs exploding. Thunder rolled across the lake.

"Yes," Vincenzo said. "They're hitting the factories between Saló and Brescia."

A red glare was born. Soon, the searchlights were illuminating a towering pillar of smoke. The droning engines faded and swelled. The sirens moaned a requiem into the night. The red glow spread like a creeping worm in the dark. It blurred in Candida's sight as tears filled her eyes. She hid her face against her mother's breast like a child. Did this terrible destruction have any meaning? Was there any meaning to anything that happened in this war?

Sleep brought Candida strange dreams of fire and Joseph.

She dreamed she was standing irresolute before a blazing pyre. The orange flames poured upward into the darkening sky. The heat baked her face, seared the tears on her eyelids. She found herself standing next to Joseph, who was watching the fire with folded arms, his head sunk on his chest.

She turned to him, her mouth forming the words, *What shall we do?*

He smiled, that white, mysterious smile, and stretched his hand out to her. *Come.*

She stared at his outstretched hand, then at the fire that was blazing high. *No!*

He grasped her hand. His fingers were extraordinarily strong.

He pulled her off her feet. She had no choice. And then they were running madly toward the roaring flames, their feet pounding. It was jump or fall into the fire. She heard Joseph shout, *Jump, Candida,* and she obeyed in terror.

She seemed to soar over the flames, her hand in Joseph's. She felt her bare legs sear in the heat, smelled her hair singe. They fell toward the dark earth.

She awoke, knowing the snow had started falling again. Perhaps it would quench the devouring flames. She lay in her bed, swollen-eyed from crying, and listened to its whisper on her windowpane.

The next day, a huge shroud of smoke had spread across the sky. It hung over the lake, motionless in the still air. Everything stank of burning. To Candida, it was like the end of the world. Had her dream been an omen? Was there a cool dark sanctuary on the other side of the flames? Could Joseph lead her there?

She went to her father. "Papa, I want to go to Joseph. Can I take the cart?"

"Yes, but be careful." He glanced over his shoulder. "You can take him another bag of rice, child. But don't let your mother know."

He harnessed the pony for her. She kissed him gratefully, clambered onto the buckboard, and set off into the forest.

With The Pony it took only an hour to reach the Hunter's Tower, despite the fresh, soft snow. Joseph had heard the muted beat of the pony's hooves and met her in the clearing, helping her to dismount. For a moment she floated in his strong arms, as she had done in her dream.

He led her into the tower. "Will you eat with me?" he asked. "It's only soup, but it's hot, and you are frozen."

"Thank you."

"Sit," he said, pulling the chairs in front of the fire. She watched him wash his lean brown hands in a bowl of water before he prepared the food.

He ladled the minestrone into their bowls, and they ate together, the fire hissing in the hearth between them. She felt painfully self-conscious. Joseph had always spoken little. It had never mattered, because she had not listened to him in any case; but now that she had come to listen, the silence of the old tower was strange, at once tranquil and unnerving.

She swallowed hard. "Joseph, I want to talk to you."

He considered her gravely. "Go on."

"I dreamed of you last night."

"Is that all?" he asked gently.

Her eyes were swimming, and Joseph dissolved in a dark blur. "No, that's not all," she whispered. "Oh, Joseph, I'm so confused . . ."

He rose and came to her. She reached for him blindly, and felt him lift her up into his arms. "Hush," he said softly. "Don't cry."

"But I feel so desperate. I don't know what's happened to my life. I don't know anything anymore."

"There's nothing to know. Just be yourself."

"I don't know who I am! Oh, God, I never thought I could be such a fool. But I can't remember who I am anymore. Why?"

"Because you let someone else give you meaning," he said gently. "It's the curse of being a woman."

Her fingers bit into his arms. "Don't go," she pleaded. "Even if David goes, stay here."

He kissed her on the lips, and she felt his immense strength in the kiss. His body was so different from David's: leaner, harder, yet more supple; and the way he kissed her was so different too, with a searching tenderness that made her senses swim. She held him, the softness of her body melting against his strength.

"We may only have today," she whispered against his mouth.

"Then let's take today," he whispered back.

Candida drew away from him. Her decision had been made somewhere deep inside, and she did not question it. The tower was so silent. She led him to the bed on the floor.

"Do you want me to undress?" she asked, in a voice that shook very slightly.

"Yes," he said huskily.

Candida began to unfasten her shirt. "I never undress for him," she said.

"Hush. Don't think about him."

She took off her clothes in silence. David had always made her feel an obscure shame about her body. He had only ever exposed the parts he wanted to use. But as she stepped out of her clothes and stood naked before Joseph, she felt a sudden confidence in her body, a knowledge that she was ready, womanly. A certainty that he would find her beautiful.

She reached up to unfasten her hair and saw his eyes follow the way her breasts lifted, the dusky nipples jutting haughtily. Since the summer, her body had changed subtly. She was thinner, less soft. She had emerged from the puppy fat of girlhood into a slim womanhood. She unfastened the ribbon and shook the unruly mass of her hair free. It fell around her face and shoulders.

Joseph touched the dark, tangled glory with his fingertips. "Like you," he said. "Willful and lovely." He touched the velvet of her lips, her chin, traced the curve of her throat. He exuded none of the urgency David always had, none of the hurry. He was poised, gentle. And yet she knew that he wanted her with a burning intensity. He touched her nipples with the tips of his fingers. They tightened instantly.

She shuddered. "Am I as beautiful as Marian?"

"God never made anything more beautiful than you," he said softly.

He undressed, laying his clothes neatly next to hers. She thought of the buck in the thicket. Joseph had the same dark, lustrous beauty. He moved with the same grace. His body was muscular, dark-skinned, so lean that she could see every muscle gleam as he moved.

He was erect. There, too, he was unlike David; where David's sex thrust bluntly outward, Joseph's curved in a taut, eager arc against his belly. She wanted to reach out and touch him, but she was timid. As if guessing her thought, he came to her and took both her hands in his, drawing them to his loins.

"You're so hot," she whispered, holding him. "Hot and hard and beautiful . . . like that stag."

He kissed her lips, and she felt his desire quiver in the rigid flesh between her palms. He took her in his arms, and their naked bodies joined. Candida felt the awakening of a languorous hunger. "I used to think you were ugly," she said. "It took me months to see how beautiful you are."

His hands caressed her back, drifting across the tight curve of her buttocks. His kiss was slow, with a sweet, searching tenderness. She felt her own lips grow slack and dreamy, parting under the pressure of his.

"Lie down," he murmured. "Let me love you, Candida."

She lay on the hard, simple bed with an abandon she had never shown David, letting him take what he wanted. But he did not take; he only gave, perusing her body with a pagan delight in finding the sources of pure pleasure. It was all so wonderful, so new; hands that caressed but never grasped, a mouth that adored but did not devour, a body that was absolute in its strength, and yet never crushed her.

Candida had never known how much joy lay in her body un-awakened. Because David had never awakened her, she had never learned that her skin could burn with pleasure, that her blood could thicken like warm honey in her veins. She was launched on the sea of a new experience.

"You are perfect," he said huskily. "Every inch of you. The most beautiful woman I've ever known." Her body was open to him. There was no shame. His gentle touch made her shudder and gasp with pleasure. "I used to dream of you like this," he said. "I dreamed of you so often. Of how I would touch you, and kiss you, and taste you . . . "

She felt him kiss the melting place, as he had kissed her mouth, gently exploring the shyly folded petals with his tongue, caressing the secret stamen that had only ever been half-awake. Her soul responded with wings. If there had been pleasure before, now there was ecstasy. It filled her, astonishing her with its force, making her cry out in a breathless voice.

"Joseph, what are you doing to me?"

His fingers twined around hers tightly. The waves had become so intense that she felt she could not bear it any longer, that something must give, something must burst. A great pressure filled her heart and stopped her breathing for a terrible moment.

And then the breach, as though something had torn open inside her, but not with pain, with a gush of sweetness. It was blindingly intense. It flooded her, relief and exultation and achievement. She gave a long whimper and curled around Joseph, drawing up her knees, cradling his head against her belly.

It took a long time before the bliss faded, and she drifted out of the bright haze and opened her dewy eyes to look at him. He was smiling at her. She kissed him and tasted her own musk on his lips.

"I love you, Candida," he said.

"No," she said, covering his mouth with her palm. "Please don't say that, Joseph. Please. Aren't you going to make love to me?"

"When you ask me to."

"Oh, what a gentleman!" She pulled the tangled hair away from her heavy lids and turned to his loins. He was still hard and eager. He was made for her, made to fill her, unite with her. It was the first time she'd ever known a physical hunger to have a man within her. Perhaps it had come with that wonderful rush of joy.

Without thinking, she took him gently in her mouth. She had never done such a thing before, never dreamed of it. Yet it seemed so natural. She was suddenly aware that what she was doing was deeply exciting to her—even more exciting than what he had done to her. She heard him cry out her name and felt his lean body arch.

"Enough," he said roughly, pulling her away at last. "I want you, darling, now!"

She could feel a pulse deep inside her, could feel that her inward body had become heavy and swollen, ready for him. "Come to me," she begged.

She drew him to her with trembling eagerness, her thighs parting so he could mount her. He took her with a wonderful assurance, holding her tight in his strong arms as he slid deep into her body. There was no resistance, none of the pain she had felt before. Instead, she felt a miraculous sense of completion, that a missing piece of her nature had slotted home, making her whole.

"Candida," he whispered, "oh, my love . . ."

And as he began to move within her, the emotion intensified, as though he were touching something beyond her womb, deeper than that.

"My soul," she whispered in a trance. "Your soul is touching mine, Joseph."

"I love you," he said. "I love you, love you, love you . . ."

She silenced him with her lips and lifted her hips to have him deeper within her. His strong buttocks pulsed under her hands. The intensity of his lovemaking touched her within, without, erotic and yet spiritual; it was the most beautiful thing she had ever known.

Fulfillment came, with a convulsive suddenness that was close to pain. They were leaping over the bonfire together, fingers entwined. The flames roared around them, the heat seared her skin. She heard Joseph call her name, with a strange, lost sound. The flood of his seed inside her was a benediction, a release. She closed her eyes and felt it slake the heat within her.

She was floating on a sense of completion, an almost over-whelming relief, as if she had fulfilled some purpose that had been set down for her long ago; like the salmon she had heard about, impelled to fight upriver to the pool where they were born, and there mate, and die.

Slowly, almost painfully, their limbs untangled, their fingers un-twined. Joseph held her in his arms, and she rested her head against his chest and felt a vast peace overcome her.

"Everything you do is a poem," she murmured, her tongue thick. Sleep was welling up in her, claiming her with dark arms. She remembered a fantasy of her childhood, that the house was a great ship that set sail every night and drifted on an endless sea. "Everything you do, Joseph . . . "

She awoke later in the afternoon, alone on the pallet. She arose in a panic and dressed. She ran down the stairs and out into the snow.

Joseph was standing in the clearing looking at the ground. As if in a dream, she went to him. "It was horrible to wake without you," she said to him. "Don't ever do that to me again."

He took her in his arms and kissed her. Then he touched her brow with his palm. "You're feverish," he said. "You ought to be in bed. You're not well."

"Is this a dream?" she asked.

He smiled as he kissed her again. "No, this is not a dream."

"Good," she said. "I'm glad. What were you looking at?"

He pointed. Alongside the track of her cart, where the snow had melted, there was a scattering of rose-pink on the ground.

"They're cyclamens," she said.

He picked one. "Does this mean spring is here?"

"No," she said, "I'm afraid not. They flower in winter. But they're beautiful, aren't they?"

"Yes, they are." He brushed her lips with the flower. "Very beautiful. And erotic."

"Erotic?" she said in wonder.

"Look." He stroked the pink petals with a lean finger. "It's like a woman's sex."

The image made her smile. "I never thought of that."

"You need never wake without me again, if you want," he said. He looked into her eyes. "I love you," he said gently. "Will you marry me?"

⁂

Driving The Pony back toward *Il Noce* in the gathering twilight, she felt that she had known joy for the first time in her life.

She carried it inside her like a bright burning light, illuminating the darkness that in these past months had filled her life.

Did she love him? She could not tell. Her emotions were too tangled for easy answers yet. But he loved her. And that was of overwhelming importance. It lit the road ahead and filled her with joy instead of despair.

When she heard the crashing in the bracken, she thought at first it was the stag again and looked up, half in fear, half expectantly. But it was not the stag. It was David.

He clambered out of the undergrowth, his greatcoat flapping, and spread his arms to stop her. Astounded, she reined in. He looked like some wild being of the woods, his blond hair tangled, his clothes bedraggled, his blue eyes wild and angry.

"David! What on earth are you doing here?"

He climbed onto the trap, his teeth bared. She knew it was not a smile. His palm crashed across her mouth so hard that her head snapped back. She was stunned.

"David!" she said numbly.

"You fucked him," he grated.

"David, no!"

"I heard you."

She saw the second slap coming just in time and managed to lift her arm. The force still knocked her sideways. *"David!"*

"You treacherous little bitch." He knotted his fingers in her hair and shook her savagely. The pain brought a scream to her throat. "How long? How *long?*"

The pony was trying to shy, but the traces held him firm. David stamped on the brake to stop the cart from moving. He dragged Candida off into the snow. "I wasn't enough for you, was I? As soon as my back is turned, you jump into bed with that dirty Jew."

She was crying. "We're going to get married, David. He wants me. You don't . . . "

He hit her again, knocking her to the ground. He stood over her, unfastening his belt.

"David," she said in panic, "don't hurt me. David!"

He crouched over her. He grinned, but there was no humor in it. "Marry you? A gentile whore?"

He grasped her thighs and thrust his body between them. She felt the icy snow soaking into her back. "David, for God's sake!"

She realized he was going to rape her. She began to fight him, with a blind, wild passion. She managed to claw his face and half-topple him. But he was too strong, too heavy.

And then he hit her, with terrible force, in the stomach. The pain was so gigantic she thought she would die. She could not breathe. Her lungs had closed, her eyes were dark. A roaring was in her ears. All her energy was focused on the agony of trying to force oxygen into her chest.

She felt him enter her. He could not be much more brutal than when they made love normally, even though she knew he was trying to hurt her as much as possible.

He hammered at her with concentrated venom, grunting with each stroke, administering punishment. Panicking from lack of breath, she felt death clutching at her soul. She arched her throat back desperately, and at last a thin, icy trickle of air entered her lungs. She started to gasp and choke.

He took hold of her breasts in his fingers and clawed at the soft flesh. The vicious pain accumulated on her other agonies. He was shouting now, in Italian. Candida could hardly hear the words above the roaring in her ears, but she knew they were curses, obscenities. She tried to fill her tortured lungs.

He grew rapidly more violent, his fingers crushing her breasts, his hips pounding her, his face swollen and distorted. He faded in her sight, blackness making a halo around his head, then shutting him out, shutting everything out.

Much later, she drifted back into cold and pain. David's body was no longer battering at hers. She lifted herself up on her elbows, her eyes blurred, her lung burning like fire. The whole center of her body was a huge pain, from her sex to her breasts. She felt that her breathing was a precarious thing that could stop at any sudden movement.

David was standing over her, watching her with dead eyes. He was smoking a cigarette.

"I thought you were dead," he said. There was no emotion in his voice. Only utter indifference.

She became aware that she was sprawled on the snow with her naked thighs splayed, her hair tangled over her face. To the pain of what David had already done to her came something unbearable—shame.

"Go away," she sobbed, trying to pull her skirt down. A torn nail was bleeding. *"Go away!"*

David laughed, a single, hard bark. "Don't worry. You'll never see me again. You can tell that bastard which of us is the better man."

He walked back into the woods.

She felt torn to the core. Somehow she managed to get to her feet, her legs were trembling. She told herself, *It doesn't matter. It doesn't matter. I still have Joseph.*

Aching in every inch, moving like an old, old woman, she groped toward the pony trap.

She Awoke To the sound of shouting.

She rose with a bleary feeling that she was someone else, that another person was inhabiting not only her flesh but her emotions, too. Perhaps that was as well. The gray blur in her head was disturbing, but at least it did not hurt.

She heard a scream. Slowly, the knowledge that something terrible was happening sank into her mind.

She pulled on clothes and still disheveled, ran downstairs. A German soldier met her on the stairs. He grasped her arm without speaking and dragged her down to the kitchen. The house was full of soldiers, led by the same young SS man who had come in October, with the stone face and the pitiless gray eyes.

"They're all here," the soldier said, thrusting Candida forward.

The SS officer jerked his head. "Outside."

The Germans lined them all up in the courtyard of the house. The soldiers stood stolidly, their machine guns at the ready. Giuliano Giusterini, wearing his black shirt and cap, stood with his arms akimbo behind the Germans, his slit eyes fixed on Candida.

The officer walked slowly around them, his hands behind his back. He stared into each face in turn, his thin mouth moving silently, as though reading the story each face told and savoring it. He came to Candida last and stopped in front of her.

"So," he said at last. "There was a rat in the cellar, after all. That was why you threw down the lantern."

Candida could hear her mother weeping. She herself felt a blank, a dreadful hollow where her terror and grief should have been. She stared at his face and saw only a field of ice.

"The Englishman has turned himself in," he said. Snow was drifting down from a dark sky, and the world was silent. "He accuses you all of sheltering a Partisan."

Candida swayed. Then she stooped quickly and was sick on the ground.

The officer watched her calmly. "Did you think it was clever to hide the rats from the rat catcher?" he asked.

"He was wounded," she whispered.

The SS officer nodded. "Yes. I know that. He was wounded while murdering German soldiers. Your English friend told us that, too. Where is he now?"

"Tell him!" Rosa screamed.

Candida shook her head very slightly. There was no hope of protecting Joseph, but she would not be the one to betray him.

The officer smiled suddenly. "It doesn't matter. We know. The Englishman told us. The Hunter's Tower. My men are picking him up now." He turned to Giusterini. "Well, my patriotic friend. What are we going to do with these traitors?"

"Shoot them all," Giuliano said. "I'll do it for you."

"Shoot them?" the German echoed. "My friend, we're not bar-barians. American bombers slaughter our families nightly, but we do not wage war on women and children." He turned back to his prisoners, pinching his lower lip thoughtfully. "The men are a different case." He stood in silence, contemplating them, his eyes drifting from one to the next. "We'll spare the war hero," he said. "He's been shot already. Take the old man."

"*No!*" Rosa lunged forward with a bereaved animal sound. She fell to her knees and clutched the polished boots of the German officer. "Please, please, please, please, please." Her voice broke with grief, and the terrible sound made Candida suddenly realize that the indifferent words the German had uttered were a sentence of death. Suddenly she was alive, alive and being torn apart.

Two soldiers were already dragging Rosa to her feet and thrusting her forcefully away, so that she stumbled, and fell brokenly on the tiles.

Everyone was screaming now. She could hear Teo's voice, in broken German, shouting, *"Das kännen Sie auf keinen vall tuhn!"* Her mother's dreadful sobs rose above the chaos in unbearable grief.

The soldiers clubbed at Vincenzo, driving him away from the others. He stumbled, shielding his head.

Candida ran to her father and clung to him frantically. "You can't!" she screamed. "You can't!"

The steel butt of a machine gun slammed into her face, knocking her to the ground. She could not rise at first, and when she did, she looked stupidly at her palms, which were welling blood.

The officer nodded to his men. "Carry on."

"Rosa," Vincenzo cried in a loud, hoarse voice as the soldiers thrust him against the wall. "Rosa, I love you."

Candida covered her eyes with her hands.

"I love you, my children!" Vincenzo called. "Pray for me!"

And then his voice was drowned by the soldiers' guns.

She Felt As though she had been walking forever through a world with no light. Her legs ached and her mind swam. She clung to herself, her fingers biting into her own flesh.

She pushed through the bracken and stared at the tower. It stood in its clearing, solitary, remote, a dark finger pointing to a dark sky.

The snow was rutted with the tracks of vehicles, churned into wet, black pools in places. She picked her way slowly to the door. Her shoes were soaked, and her body trembled constantly, though she was not aware of cold as a physical sensation, more as something internal, something within her brain.

The tower was empty and cold. His possessions and clothes were strewn across the floor. Lying in the fireplace, half-charred, was the book he had been reading, Dante's *Divina Commedia*. She picked it out and stared at it vacantly, as though its blackened pages contained the key to some essential mystery. Then she let it drop.

Night was falling slowly over the forest. She went outside again and searched the snow, her eyes intent on the checkered field of black and white.

She had come to bury him, but he was not here. They had taken him away.

Even when that realization had settled into her numbed mind, she could not tear herself away from the place, but circled the tower slowly, searching, searching.

5

THE HUNTER'S TOWER

1 9 9 2 – 9 3

NORTHUMBERLAND, ENGLAND

The white-clad figure moved slowly among the bare lines of an English country garden in winter. It was Christmas Day. The sky was a cold, pale blue, dead leaves carpeting the paths, along the edges of which dark red hellebores nodded grimly.

The voluminous veil, draped over a wide-brimmed hat, gave the woman the air of a priestess busy with the mysteries of her vocation. The hives were octagonal, made of oak boards, as finely constructed as pieces of Victorian furniture, which in fact was what they were. She held the smoke kettle in one heavily gloved hand, patiently puffing white clouds into the hive. There was no outrage among the bees, only an increasingly drowsy upsurge of humming. The swarm lifted above the hive, recoiling from the smoke. She lifted the lid of the hive and reached in with her free hand, carefully withdrawing a wooden frame, heavy with a black, clinging mass of bees. She shook the insects off gently and held it close to her veiled face, studying it intently for a while. Then she turned, and limping a little, brought it to the lawn where Anna and Philip Westward stood watching.

"I thought so," Evelyn Godbold said. She held out the frame for them to see. "Don't worry. They won't sting."

The golden-brown honeycomb had been invaded by grayish, rotten-looking sections. "What is it, Grandmama?"

"Wax moth," Evelyn said. She poked a gloved finger through the rotten sections, which fell to pieces. "It gets into the hive with the other bees. It lays its eggs in the combs. They hatch and feed on the honey and take over the hive. Filthy parasite. I hate it. I'll have to burn the infected combs and fumigate the hive right away."

"Should you be doing this?" Anna asked doubtfully. "You're only just starting to recover from your operation."

"I'll stop for tea in half an hour. Don't stay out in the cold. There's a fire in the drawing room. Wallace! Over here!"

The elderly chauffeur joined her as she walked back to the hives. Philip and Anna watched the two veiled figures as they busied themselves taking the parasitized frames out, breaking them up and tossing them onto a heap to be burned.

"She's astonishing, isn't she?" Anna said in an undertone.

Philip nodded. "Yes, she is. She's not going gently into that good night," he said. "She's going to fight every inch of the way. I like her a lot."

They walked back to the house, stooping under the low-slung limbs of the majestic Lebanon cedars. The house stood proud and erect at the brow of the hill, its golden stone facade gazing down on the gardens. It was a beautiful structure, with mullioned windows on the first two floors and four peaked gables clad in ivy. From the dark slate roof, groups of barley-twist chimneys rose against the winter sky.

They entered the sitting room. Its smell, as always, swept Anna back to her childhood: that smell of woodsmoke overlaid with potpourri and beeswax-polished furniture.

"This house has always smelled like this," she said dreamily. "Since I was a child. It's probably smelled the same way since 1650." She winced in pain as she lowered herself into the sofa. "Ouch!"

"All right?"

"Just my back." Truck's tire iron had left a dull blue welt across her shoulder blade that throbbed painfully with the cold. The sofas were unchanged since her childhood, just as lumpy and not very comfortable for a body bruised all over.

The stone fireplace had been decorated with holly wreaths, bunches of mistletoe and other winter berries, and loops of scarlet ribbon. It looked beautiful.

Philip picked up a cushion, embroidered with the motto, *One today is worth two tomorrows.* "It must have been something of a shock for your mother to come from a farmhouse on Lake Garda to this."

"You mean because it's so grand?"

"So different in every way."

Anna nodded. "I don't think she ever got used to English weather. I think you have to be born here to like the weather." She saw he was looking at another cushion, embroidered *Tempus Fugit.* "Grand-mama embroidered those. She has a somber streak."

"Serious, I'd say, rather than somber. My mother loved mottoes, too."

"Did she?" Anna was interested. He hardly ever spoke of his mother. "Such as?"

" 'You can't make an omelette without breaking eggs.' That was one of her favorites. 'Shrouds have no pockets.' She'd probably have struck you as somber, too."

"Tell me about her."

"Later."

"Always later."

He smiled. "Your grandmother's finished reading the diary."

"I know. I saw her bookmark before lunch. I feel so taut inside, Philip. So nervous."

"Why?" he asked softly.

"Her reaction. What she'll say. Why hasn't she said anything yet?"

He leaned forward, reached out, and touched her cheek with his knuckles. "Be calm. She'll speak when she's ready."

The decision to come to Europe for Christmas had been a complex one. The knowledge that Evelyn was dying had been part of it. The English doctors had told Anna it might be only a matter of a few months before her health failed completely. She had wanted to see her grandmother before that happened. Though she intended to be with her at the end, if she could, she wanted to see Evelyn in what might be the last period of normal life left to her.

Her mother, emerging from her coma at Carr Memorial, would probably not be aware that Christmas had even arrived. Evelyn, facing death, would. Anna had made a hard decision.

She had also decided that Evelyn should know about the diary. She knew the diary would shock Evelyn deeply. It did not simply challenge David Godbold's fatherhood of Kate, it also shed a merciless light on the fact that David had betrayed Joseph Krasnowsky and the Cipriani family in 1944.

But Anna felt that Evelyn had a right to know the truth about both things. The diary affected them all as a family. Evelyn, as the most senior member of the family, could not be kept from knowing.

Indeed, Evelyn might well have further information on the mysteries. Anna was hungry for knowledge, hungry for any scraps that her grandmother might be able to give her. The quest to find Joseph Krasnowsky had started to obsess her, just as it had obsessed her mother.

What had finally made her mind up had been Philip's offer to come with her. She'd been surprised and touched and had accepted eagerly, before he could think better and change his mind.

They had decided to stay in Europe for a fortnight, spending Christmas in Northumberland with Evelyn and going to Italy after the New Year. It had been years since Anna had been to Garda. She wanted to see it again from the perspective of her new knowledge. She wanted to stand where her mother and grandmother had stood. She wanted, if possible, to see the places where Joseph Krasnowsky had hidden from the Nazis during that savage winter of 1943/1944. In the absence of other information about the man she believed was her grandfather, she needed something to hold on to.

The trip had been made easier by knowing that her mother was finally getting better. She knew that Jay Ram Singh and his team were working hard to help her mother now and that it was only a matter of time before Kate was able to take control of her own life again. She was already talking and moving, and although there seemed to be a large gap in her memory, starting long before the discovery of the diary, she was coming out of the darkness. She could chew and swallow food, could sit up unassisted, could communicate her wishes by word or gesture. After so long, Anna had felt she could finally take a break from her mother's bedside.

Evelyn came into the room, dusting her hands. She was very

pale, but the exertion had brought a disk of color into each cheek. They both rose to greet her.

"I'm glad that's done." She wore an expression of grim satisfaction. "I knew there was something wrong. I could feel it in my bones. Please, do sit, both of you. Sally will bring in the tea presently. Put some more logs on the fire, child."

It was hard to believe the shadow of death hung over Evelyn. The aristocratic cheekbones were still handsome, the eyebrows still slanted their ironic challenge at the world, and she was erect as ever, her green tweed suit immaculate, her legs elegant in dark stockings.

Anna obeyed, arranging the oak logs that were cut on the estate and left to dry for five years before being burned.

Evelyn settled herself into an armchair. It took her a long time to lower herself down. They both knew she was in considerable pain, but there was no trace of it on her lean face. Only when she was settled at last did she give a little sign. "Bees can communicate, you know. They can tell you when something is wrong inside the hive. They tell you quite clearly that you'd better damned well do something about it. I wish one's own body were as well run. One could wrench out the infected parts in time and throw them on the bonfire." Neither Philip nor Anna spoke. Through the window, they could see a smudge of gray smoke rising from the bonfire where Wallace was burning the blighted frames. "I hate parasites," Evelyn went on forcefully. "Things that feed on the lifeblood of others. Things that seem to be benign, but are not what they seem to be." She turned to Philip with a sharp glance. "Don't you, Philip?"

Philip moved his shoulders slightly. "The world is made up of such creatures, Evelyn. Things that feed on the lifeblood of others. Things that are not what they seem to be."

She considered him, her gray eyes very level. The silence went on for just long enough to make Anna feel uncomfortable. Evelyn looked down at last, rubbing her long-fingered hands together. She still wore the engagement and wedding rings that David Godbold had given her in 1946. "Are you interested in beekeeping, Philip?"

"I've never seen it close up before," he said gravely.

"And what did you think?"

"It's a fascinating craft. The technicalities are very pretty. Those beautiful hives, the combs, the white veil. It gives you the look of a bride."

"Indeed. And we all know who the bridegroom will be, do we not?" She asked the question lightly, with no self-pity. "We always have our own honey for tea. You will be able to taste the fruits of the craft."

On cue, a middle-aged woman brought in a laden trolley containing mince pies, farmhouse bread, and a huge, dark Christmas cake on the bottom. Anna helped her lay out the things. The bone-china teapot and cups, with their hand-painted roses and tulips, were part of the Coalport service that had been in everyday use at Great Law since the nineteenth century, its lack of cracks and chips testifying to generations of careful service.

The Great Law honey was very clear and light, with a faint taste of the heather that stretched across miles of moorland all around the estate. It, too, took Anna back to her childhood, to those summer holidays spent in this great house, to that atmosphere of awe she had never quite been able to shake off. All the baking had been done by Sally in the kitchen, and was excellent. She knew the feudal appearance of the place would have surprised Philip, though he was far too controlled to show it. Later, she would have to try and explain that the relationships were not what they seemed, that long ties of friendship and mutual respect linked Evelyn Godbold to the people who ran the estate for her—that they were as much members of a family as if they had been related by blood.

Though Evelyn took a scone and slowly crumbled it on her plate, Anna saw that she ate none of it, only drinking a little black tea to wash down the half-dozen assorted pills that had been laid on her plate. She and Philip ate in silence for a while, watching as the pale fire spread a curtain around the logs, then began to flap peacefully in the grate, reflections gleaming in the dark leaves of the holly wreaths.

"I finished the diary this morning," Evelyn said at last, and Anna felt her heart miss a beat. "I'm sorry it took me so long." She put down her teacup and her crumbled, uneaten scone. "Thank you for bringing it to me. It's a fascinating document. I have spent half my life wondering what sort of person Candida Cipriani was. At last I think I have a true idea. I feel as though I have met her at last."

She lapsed into silence for so long that Anna sat up, unable to contain her impatience. "And the events she describes, Grandmama? The things that happened?"

Evelyn emerged from her reverie, tilting her head to one side so that the sunlight caught her graying hair, making it shimmer. "Yes.

That is what strikes *you,* of course. The things that happened. I suppose I always knew that something like that must have happened."

"You *knew?*"

"I knew David's character. I was married to him for twelve years. And he was not a particularly good liar. It was never difficult for me to read between the lines."

"Do you think he knew Mama was not his daughter?"

"Perhaps they both knew that in different ways. Your mother never accepted David as a father. They had absolutely nothing in common. When I first brought her to England, she was a wounded animal, snapping at the hands that tried to help her. She had learned to hate David, long before meeting him. When she came to England, she was at his throat from the first moment, and he at hers. I did my best to reconcile them, but there was a lot of hatred in your mother. A lot of turbulence. And of course, David died only a few months later, which intensified the wound. So finding that diary would have had a powerful impact on your mother." Evelyn touched one hand to her breast, as though the effort of talking was tiring her, or causing her pain. "It was an explanation she'd been waiting for all her life."

"It doesn't reflect very well on David," Anna said hesitantly. "I'm sorry if it was a shock."

Evelyn smiled a little grimly. "I have reached a time of life where what people are like inside is more important to me than the things they do. It comes first, you see. Spirit is father to deed. Nature is mother to action."

"You're talking in riddles, Grandmama."

Evelyn turned to Philip. "Am I talking in riddles, Philip?"

"I think your grandmother means that to understand all is to forgive all," Philip said gently.

"Yes. I mean something like that. Most of life is inexplicable unless we understand what people are like inside. I'm no philosopher, and God knows I'm no psychologist, but to me that diary is not an explanation of history, but one of character. It is the insight into character that has provided me with a little illumination. Sent a ray of light into my own life, as it were, just as I am on the point of going into the dark."

Anna glanced at the silver-framed photographs. "David was blond, with blue eyes, wasn't he? And Joseph was dark, with dark eyes. Like Mama. Like me."

"Yes, like you." Evelyn's expression still held that slant of irony, as though she could see the turmoil that seethed in Anna's heart, and was somehow amused by it. "So you believe this Joseph Krasnowsky was your grandfather, child?"

"I believe that's how my mother interpreted it," Anna answered carefully, glancing at Philip, who was sitting silent and motionless, watching the two women with inscrutable eyes. "She believed that there was at least a fifty-percent chance that Joseph was her father. She somehow came to the conclusion that Joseph was still alive—how, I still have no idea—and she was haunted with the idea of finding him. I mean it was *her,* Grandmama." She leaned forward urgently. "It defined her. Her identity. It wasn't some dusty old story in a dusty old book. It was her essence. Once the question had been posed, she *had* to find out the truth."

"There we differ." Evelyn's calm voice was in direct contrast to Anna's taut urgency. "I believe that your mother's essence has very little to do with the biological accident of her ancestry. But I see you have taken up the mantle. You're determined to continue the search for Mr. Krasnowsky. Determined to plumb the dark shades of history."

"It defines Anna's identity, too," Philip said quietly. "It's her search, too."

"And that is why you are assisting her with this quest?" Evelyn asked, cocking her head at him. "Because you are eager for her to learn all about herself?"

"Partly, yes." Philip smiled. "But I have my own selfish motives, too. As you know, I've been involved with a similar search all my life."

"Indeed. But what does your search have to do with Anna's search?"

"It's essentially the same search," he said easily. "My inquiries about my father had reached a dead end. It's temporary, I hope, but I didn't have anywhere else to go. That was why I got in touch with Kate Kelly in the first place. I'm helping Anna because she's on a fresh trail. I'm hoping that trail will bring me closer to my father. Our best information is that all the Allied prisoners of war went through the same handful of gulag camps. If we find Joseph Krasnowsky, he may be able to give me priceless information about my father. He may even have known him, been in the same places. If my father is dead, Joseph may be able to tell me. If he's alive, Joseph may be able to help me track down where he is today."

"You see?" Anna said. "We're the same. It's extraordinary. It's brought us together. Since I read that diary, I feel like I'm on fire, Grandmama. I can't stop thinking about it. I know exactly how Philip has felt all his life. How Mama felt."

"Does it really make that much difference to you?"

"Who my grandfather was? Yes, of course it makes a difference!"

"It won't change the way you are now, Anna. You're a grown woman. What do you expect to find?"

She shrugged restlessly. "It's impossible to explain, until it happens to you. You're sure of your background, Grandmama. You knew who your parents were, who your grandparents were, your great-grandparents. The line goes back. Continuity. Mama isn't like that. Nor is Philip. Nor am I. Mama was an orphan. She never knew her mother. There weren't even photos of her. You brought her to England when she was sixteen. You said she hated David on sight. That can't have been easy. She grew up in a strange country, cut off from her roots. She once told me she felt she was forced into a mold." She saw the gray eyes wince slightly. "I'm sorry, Grandmama, but it's true. She must have spent her whole life wondering just who the hell she really was! Looking back, I probably sensed Mama's own problems, right from my early childhood. Her feeling that she didn't really know who she was, I mean. She couldn't give me any guidance, because she was lost herself."

"We're all lost," Evelyn said quietly.

"Not that badly lost, Grandmama!" She looked up into the impassive face, her dark eyes importunate. "It's as though I never knew how lost I was until I read that diary. I'd thought I was so together. Good job, balanced personality, a sheaf of credit cards—I thought I had it all!"

"And you didn't?"

"If that diary hadn't turned up, I'd probably never have known. But when I read it, it was as though the ground opened up under my feet. I suddenly saw how much of me was missing. I saw that . . . " She hunted for a phrase. "I saw that I was a woman without roots. Oh, Grandmama, I'm sorry if this hurts you. But that's the way I feel. And I know Mama felt exactly the same way, too!"

"I'm not hurt. I'm just wondering whether you're not taking this whole thing more seriously than is good for you."

"Speaking from my own experience," Philip said gently, "I'd

compare it to an adopted child wanting to find out who her true parents were. It doesn't mean she doesn't love her adoptive parents, or that she isn't grateful to them for all they've done. But there's an urge, a *drive,* that makes you want to know who your real parents were. It comes from deep inside. You want to meet them, hear their voices, look into their faces, look for something of yourself. Without that you aren't complete, Evelyn. I've known a lot of adopted children, and most made some attempt at some stage to find their biological parents. They couldn't help it. If you don't make that effort, you'll never really know who you are."

"Yes," Anna said emphatically. "So if Joseph Krasnowsky survived the gulags, and if he's still alive, I want to talk to him. Hell, yes, I want to talk to him!"

"And what if Joseph Krasnowsky does not want to be found?"

"I don't understand."

"He has not come forward in all these years, Anna."

"But he probably doesn't even know that Mama has been looking for him."

"*Somebody* knows," Evelyn said sharply.

"What do you mean?"

"Somebody knew that Kate was looking for him," Evelyn repeated grimly. "Somebody who was evidently quite determined that she should *not* find him. Somebody who broke into her apartment in Vail and tried to murder her and stole all her research papers. Somebody who lured you into the mountains and tried to murder *you,* child."

Anna felt an icy chill settle around her heart. "We don't know that there was any connection."

"Maybe you don't know it," Evelyn retorted, "but I know it. And so does your urbane Mr. Westward, who sits there like a leopard, silently licking his paws." The glance she gave Philip was like gray ice. "I only trust that, since he is leading you into the forests of the night, he is capable of defending you against the tiger."

Philip said nothing, his face betraying no emotion, but Anna was taken aback and murmured, "Oh, Grandmama."

"Well, Philip? Is there or is there not danger?"

"There may be," he replied calmly.

"From whom?"

"I don't know. If there is, I will protect Anna."

"I sincerely hope so. But perhaps the best thing is that Mr.

Krasnowsky stays hidden, don't you think?" Evelyn put her hands on the arms of the chair and began levering herself painfully upright. Philip rose to assist her. She held herself erect, her fingers biting into Philip's forearm. Her eyes met Anna's. "As for why Kate believed Joseph Krasnowsky was still alive, there is an explanation. A conclusion, at least, that your mother would have leaped to."

"What is it?" Anna demanded eagerly.

"Give me time to settle my thoughts, child." She had her balance now, and she released her hold of Philip's arm. "I must go and see how Wallace is getting on with the hives. Then I have correspondence to deal with. I'm going to leave you two to your own devices for the rest of the afternoon. We'll speak after dinner."

She walked back out into the garden, her back very erect despite her limp. Anna made a face of frustration at Philip, who shrugged slightly.

"She's infuriating!" Anna said.

"No. She just wants to think."

"What do you think she knows?"

"She'll tell us in her own time," Philip replied. "Don't sweat it."

"All very well for you to say don't sweat it. I'm so nervous, Philip."

"A word of advice about your grandmother," he said, touching her hand. "Don't push her. She knows something, and she'll tell you in her own good time. But try and hurry her up, and she'll probably clam up tighter than an oyster."

She laughed ruefully. "Yes, you're right. Okay, I'll play it cool."

"Come on, let's go for a walk."

***

The Skies Above Great Law always seemed particularly vast because the estate was set along the ridge of the highest hills for miles around. From here, the countryside rolled into valleys all around, stretching across acres of fertile farmland and forest before rising again to the horizon. Across the middle of the valley, the river Tyne snaked its track toward the distant sea, and over to the southeast, a gray smudge on the horizon marked Newcastle-upon-Tyne.

The wind buffeted them, sweeping across the brown grass like a giant broom. Evelyn's dogs galloped ahead of them, overjoyed to be out, ears and tails streaming.

She held Philip's hand as they tramped down the slope, her heart lifting with the mare's-tails of white cloud, fanned out five miles above them.

"Do you think he can possibly be still alive?" she asked him.

He knew who she was talking about. It was a topic they had discussed before. "He was born in 1917. That makes him seventy-five this year. A lot of men are still fit and active at that age. Yes, of course he could be still alive."

"Know what haunts me?" she asked. Anna had to raise her voice above the wind. "It's crazy, I know, but I can't get it out of my mind."

He turned to her, his dark hair swept away from his high forehead, his eyes squinting against the wind. "What?"

"The thought that he might be in a hospital somewhere, dying, not knowing we're looking for him."

"Don't be morbid." He smiled.

"I just hope we turn up something new soon," she said. "I'm starting to think we'll never find him."

"I've got every resource I can think of working on the case, Anna."

Anna was out of breath as they clambered over a stile at the bottom of the field. He let her down in his strong arms. "Evelyn doesn't want me to keep looking for Joseph."

"I know."

She leaned against the stile, thrusting her hands into the pockets of her Barbour. "She thinks of herself as Mama's mother and she thinks of David as Mama's father. She doesn't want those relationships changed, not now, after all these years."

"Can't you sympathize with that?" he asked.

"Of course I can sympathize with that. But the biological fact is that she is *not* Mama's mother, and another biological fact is that David Godbold probably wasn't Mama's father, either!"

The dogs were seething around them impatiently, wanting to know what the holdup was. Philip picked up a stick and flung it far across the field into a thicket. They arrowed off after it, baying. "You don't know that for sure, Anna."

"Oh, come on! You saw all those cherished, silver-framed pictures of the treacherous old bastard! He was blond, blue-eyed, with a square, English face. Mama is completely different, dark hair and eyes, sallow skin, like a Gypsy. I'm even more different. In that diary, Candida describes Joseph as dark and Slavic-looking. You can't tell me it makes no difference to know whether your father was a blond, blue-eyed, Englishman or a dark-eyed Russian Jew! You can't tell me it's irrelevant whether your father was a traitor or a martyr!"

This time the smile reached his eyes. "Calm down. You're not going for the Pulitzer, here. I know exactly how you feel."

The dogs, barking madly, came galloping back from the thicket. Anna stooped to retrieve the stick, then recoiled in horror.

"Oh, no! Philip, do something! *Please!*"

The rabbit was still kicking and jerking in the retriever's slavering jaws, its eyes rolling wildly. She could not bear to see any creature suffer, and she turned away, squeezing her eyes shut and covering her ears with her hands as Philip moved quickly to the dog.

When she opened her eyes again, he was standing with the rabbit limp in his hands. Its head lolled, the sunlight glowing ruby through the long ears.

"They'd mauled it," he said apologetically. "I had to break its neck."

The dogs were around his knees, clamoring for the corpse. "Don't let them have it," she pleaded, still distressed.

"What am I going to do? Bury it with my hands?" But he took the dead rabbit back into the thicket, while she kept the frantic dogs with her. He returned a while later, empty-handed. "A fox or a weasel will get it before nightfall. Jolly old afternoon tea," he said, mimicking a plummy English voice, making her smile.

"Do you think Grandmama's right?" she asked him, her voice uncertain now. "Do you think someone was trying to stop Mama from finding Joseph Krasnowsky? Do you think that's why they attacked her and ransacked the apartment?"

"Perhaps," he said neutrally.

"Then it may have been the same people who set Carl Beck to kill me. But who? *Why?*"

"I don't know," he said gently. "But remember that Beck was crazy, a psychopath. He didn't need any reason to kill. He enjoyed it."

"Maybe. But I can't stop thinking that maybe there's something big and dark and evil behind this. Something that doesn't want anyone to find Joseph Krasnowsky. It scares the hell out of me. I just can't think who or why. Who would be prepared to do such a terrible thing to an innocent woman, just to stop her from finding out where her father is?"

He took her hand. "I'm here to protect you, Anna. If there is some bogeyman out there, I swear he won't get to you again."

She felt a little laugh rise in her. "I believe you." He was so possessive. So protective. She felt a safety with him that she had never felt before, a sense of something new, and yet profoundly familiar, like a feeling she'd searched for in dreams. Her love for him was turning into a powerful passion, and she prayed it would be reciprocated, if not now, then sometime soon. "Sometimes," she whispered, "I wonder whether I'm so drawn to you because you give me this safe feeling. Because I see you as a father figure."

"I hope not," he said. He drew her close to him.

She reached up with her fingertips and delicately traced the deep curve of his lips. "Your mouth looks hard, but it's soft. Soft and warm." She recalled his kiss with a sudden twist of electric desire.

He was still in command. And she was still afraid of him. Shy of him. He was her lover, yet he was somehow remote. Since the diary, she had discovered how alike they were in so many ways, sharing the same quest, the same obsession. And yet she felt shut out.

Their lovemaking never ceased to be transcendent for her, but so often she'd felt that he was not really with her. That somewhere deep inside the consummate lover was a secret place from which Philip Westward commanded his body, alone and untouched.

She drew her hand guiltily away from his mouth. "Sorry."

He pulled her close to him and pressed his mouth to her temple, crushing the smell of her hair deep into his lungs.

"You always smell wonderful," he muttered.

"Oh, Philip . . . " She shut her eyes as he kissed her lids, feeling herself start to tremble. His mouth stole down the curve of her jaw to the edge of her lips, where the skin became satiny and yielding. She turned her face to meet the sweet torment of his mouth.

She had not known so much eroticism in a kiss since her adolescent years, when kisses were all she knew. Philip kissed her as though it were the act of love itself, as though he were drinking something from her lips, some female essence of her, her soul. His tongue was slippery and firm, a taut organ of desire that slid along the melting sexual pathways of her mouth. The heat in her arteries was choking, her pulses throbbing like primitive music.

She arched to him, helpless in her arousal. His hands thrust under her jacket, under her jumper and cotton shirt, finding the warm skin of her flanks. She wore no bra, and she shuddered as she felt his hands sliding upward to encounter the firm curves of her breasts. Her nipples were hardening unbearably even before his fingers found them in a hungry caress. She whimpered, burrowing close to him, her whole body alive with need.

The dogs were agitated, barking impatiently. Anna could feel one scratching at her thighs, another bumping its nose urgently against her calves. She drew back. "This isn't very romantic," she whispered shakily.

"The hell it isn't," he growled, his eyes deep cobalt, the pupils huge and black. He snapped a command at the dogs, who scattered at once, tails between their legs. Then he pulled her back to him, his mouth claiming hers avidly.

She cupped her palm over his loins, thrilling to feel his arousal thrusting hotly against the crotch of his jeans. His desire always made her exult; it delighted her wildly that she could make him respond to her so easily, that he was erect as soon as he touched or kissed her. She unzipped him and pushed her hand through, grasping him tightly.

"Jesus, you're so big and hard," she said huskily. "I can't get enough of you." She had both hands on him now, and she saw his eyes grow stormy. "I'm falling in love with you, Philip," she whispered. "You know that, don't you?" She knelt quickly before him and took him in her mouth. He tried to stop her, but she wrapped her arms around his thighs, holding him tight, her mouth filled with the thrust of his manhood. She molded the taut, salt curve of him against her palate, worshipping him in a long moment of pagan abandonment. The powerful muscles of his thighs trembled in her arms, and she felt his fingers knot in the tumble of her hair. Then he withdrew himself and crouched beside her, his breathing ragged. "Not here. Not now."

"When?" she demanded, her face passionate, animal.

"Tonight. I'll come to your room."

"No." She kissed his mouth hard. "I'll come to yours. You might get lost. And I don't think I can wait an hour longer than I have to."

They Ate In the dining room, an imposing room that Anna had always found slightly claustrophobic because it was windowless and paneled all round in seventeenth-century linenfold paneling. Someone had evidently been employed in the kitchen all afternoon, for the best silver was out, gleaming in the candlelight among the sparkling crystal and the Royal Doulton. There was a beautiful centerpiece on the Christmas table, a basket in which Evelyn had arranged holly, mistletoe, pinecones, and red candles in a festive display.

There was one other person to dinner, an elderly, white-haired man with the face of a Roman senator, whom Evelyn introduced as Roderick Keane, a friend of many years' standing. Keane was a Harley Street neurosurgeon, and it was evident that Evelyn had invited him in order to hear his opinions on Kate's condition.

As tradition demanded at Great Law, the Christmas turkey was served for dinner, not lunch. The turkey was perfectly prepared and presented, its skin golden and glistening. It came with winter vegetables, roast potatoes, and stuffing.

Despite Keane's age, Evelyn had put Philip at the head of the dining table and made him carve the turkey. He did it well, slicing wafer-thin rounds, and though he was not in a dinner jacket, as Roderick Keane was, he at least conveyed the aura that he was. Anna was both pleased and embarrassed by the compliment of putting Philip at the head of the table. The implication, which Philip might or might not have missed, was that she and Philip were engaged, making Philip a member of the family, not just a guest.

Evelyn ate only tiny portions and barely moistened her lips with the dark burgundy that was served with the meal.

Anna was all in black; a simple black polo-neck top with long sleeves and a short skirt with black stockings, her hair loose around her shoulders. She wore the platinum chain Philip had given her in Vail, the three diamonds blazing fiercely against the black tricot of her shirt. She felt she looked good, and Philip's eyes drifted to her regularly, watching her with an inscrutable, disturbing intensity.

Roderick Keane asked Anna a series of searching questions about Kate's condition; how much mobility she had, how and when she spoke.

"It's still only a whisper," she told him, "but every day she says more words. Not just yes and no. She asks for things—music, or water, or to be moved. When she sees me, she says my name and smiles." Anna had to swallow a lump in her throat.

"I can only generalize on Kate's condition, of course," Keane said. He had a fine, oratorical voice to go with the Ciceronian profile. "The fact that she has started to speak is a wonderful sign."

"The first time she said my name . . . I can't tell you how I felt."

Keane smiled. "To watch a patient emerging from a profound coma is sometimes a miracle as great as birth."

"Perhaps greater," Philip said quietly. "It's a return from the grave, Mr. Keane."

Keane nodded. "Indeed." He drank, then patted his mouth dry with the linen napkin. "There is no doubt in my mind that Anna's attitude had a great deal to do with the outcome," he said. "She behaved with exceptional courage and determination. I am not saying the authorities in Colorado were wrong: given those conditions in a patient with such a severe injury, I myself would have held out no hope to the family. But by continuous stimulation, by not letting Kate be moved to a hospice, and above all by refusing to accept that all hope was lost, Anna has probably brought her mother out of the darkness. She has probably saved her mother's life in the full sense of that phrase."

"And the outlook?" Evelyn asked in her calm voice.

"The outlook is very promising," Keane replied. "Again, this is a pure generalization, but on the Glasgow Coma Scale, Kate would now be classified a hopeful case. The outcome would be expected to be slow, of course, but within one year, perhaps eighteen months, she would be expected to be approaching normality."

"When we get back to Vail, I'm going to really concentrate on Mama," Anna said. "I've decided to take at least a year off work, so I can be with her. Nobody else could give her the attention I can. As soon as they discharge her, I'll bring her back to the apartment and look after her. The important thing is to engage her mind. And the best way I can think of doing that is going ahead with her inquiries." She toyed with her glass. "I've already told her that's what I'm doing, but I don't know if she understands yet. When she does, it'll give her a new lease on life, I know it will."

"Are you so sure?" Evelyn asked dryly. "Considering that it almost took her life from her in the first place, the cure seems a trifle drastic to me."

"Don't sound so gloomy, Grandmama!"

"Take her away from Vail, Anna. Take her to Miami, to the sun. Or to California, somewhere warm and safe. Forget the past. The past is a nest of horrors."

"Yes, I was thinking of taking her somewhere warmer. Maybe at the end of the summer. Summer in Vail is so beautiful. Mama always loved it. When the cold weather comes, maybe we'll go somewhere sunny. Maybe down to the Keys."

The meal had come to an end. "There is a fire burning in the sitting room," Evelyn said. "Shall we take our coffee there?"

The Evening Ended early. Despite her grim willpower, Evelyn's strength was running out visibly by ten P.M., and Roderick Keane gracefully excused himself and left then.

The three of them remained sitting silently round the fire for a while. Evelyn spoke at last. "You wanted to know why your mother thought Joseph Krasnowsky was still alive."

Anna looked up. It was characteristic of Evelyn to bring the subject up so abruptly.

"Yes. And you said you knew why."

"I *think* I know why," Evelyn corrected. "I am making an assumption about your mother's line of thought. But I think I am correct. I believe that Kate thought the scarred man was Joseph Krasnowsky."

"The scarred man?"

"This goes back to events about which you have never been told, child. To the events surrounding David's death. You don't know this, Anna, but your grandfather was murdered."

"Murdered!" She sat up in shock. "I thought he died in a shooting accident!"

"No." Evelyn leaned back in her chair, looking tired. Philip was watching Evelyn with intense concentration. "No. He was murdered. Your mother witnessed it. We had gone for a hack that afternoon, and your mother's horse cast a shoe. She went back to the stables alone, leading the horse. We were never quite sure what she saw there, because she was hysterical for several days afterward. She was only sixteen at the time. But about some things she was certain. She saw a motorcycle parked in the hedgerow along the drive. She saw a man with a badly scarred face hold a gun to her father's head and shoot him dead."

"Jesus," Anna exclaimed involuntarily.

"She described the man as tall, dark, wearing a leather jacket. He wore a beard, but it did not hide a very bad scar, almost a mutilation, to the jaw. She said he had black wolf's eyes. The police hunted the whole of England, but they never found the man." She looked at Anna's shocked, pale face. "We never told you. It seemed unnecessary to burden you with it."

Anna stared at Philip, her mind dealing with the shocking images. "That was 1960," she said slowly. "The information from the KGB general ends in 1959 with a question mark. What if Joseph was released—or escaped somehow? What if he came to England to find David, because David had betrayed him during the war?" She was trembling, her heart pounding in her throat. She looked at Evelyn. "It was him! He came to punish David for that betrayal!"

"Anna, take it easy," Philip said gently.

"Who else could it have been?" she demanded. "He came to get justice. He didn't know Mama had been adopted, didn't know she was here. And in the moment of killing David, he looked up and recognized her at once, because she looked so much like Candida. And she'd seen him commit the murder. So in that moment, he knew he could never come to her again and tell her he was her father. He knew she'd always think of him as a murderer!" She twisted in her chair to look at Evelyn, who was sitting motionless, listening with her eyes hooded. "That's why he never came forward, Grandmama! Because if she'd ever seen him again, she'd have screamed her head off. So he could never tell her the truth about what happened in 1944. He had to let her keep believing that David was her father. My God!" She covered her face with both hands for a moment, then looked up. "There's no other explanation. That has to be it!"

"Well." Evelyn folded her thin fingers, the faintest of ironic smiles on her mouth. "There you are, child. Your thoughts have evidently followed your mother's perfectly."

"But it's the truth. I feel it in my bones, the way you felt that the wax moth was in the hives. Don't you feel it, too?"

Evelyn Godbold exhaled slowly. Her expression of irony changed to one almost of compassion. "Perhaps, child. It seems possible. Likely, even. But I prefer to remain an agnostic."

"I'm sorry, Grandmama." Anna reached out and covered Evelyn's hands with her own. "This must be horrible for you. I couldn't understand why you were so averse to my trying to find Joseph. I do now. If Joseph was the scarred man, then he murdered your husband. But isn't it more important than ever to try and find Joseph, try and bring about some kind of reconciliation?"

"I am reconciled," Evelyn replied with a cool lift of her eyebrows. "I was reconciled long ago. If your Mr. Krasnowsky killed my husband, I bear him no ill will now."

"You are extraordinary, Grandmama," Anna said in bewilderment. "I've never understood you, and I don't think I ever will."

"If you have no ill will toward Joseph Krasnowsky," Philip asked quietly, "then why don't you want Anna to follow through her mother's quest?"

"Because I can see no good coming out of it," Evelyn said promptly.

"Except the satisfaction of a burning need to know the truth."

"Which is another way of saying to satisfy a curiosity. There is a proverb about curiosity, Philip."

"So there is." Philip smiled. "And I see you are fond of proverbs, Evelyn."

"A proverb is much matter decocted into few words. I don't like any of it. Ancient crimes, ancient blood. An ancient book which tells us we are not who we think we are. A search for a man who vanished long ago. A psychopath who enjoys killing women, in the employ of men who do not want Joseph Krasnowsky found. No, Philip, I don't like it. I would advise Anna to take her mother away from Vail, away from this ill-starred search, and run to some safe, warm, happy place where they can put their lives back together again. Somewhere the shadows of the past do not reach."

Anna shivered, rubbing the gooseflesh that had rippled up her arms. "You sound like a witch."

"I have been called worse things." She pushed her chair back, preparatory to rising. Philip came round behind her to help her up. He kissed Evelyn's hand before going up to his room, a gesture Anna found touching and oddly European. Their eyes met briefly as he left, and she felt her stomach turn over inside her.

Anna helped her grandmother upstairs to her bedroom, where

the night nurse was waiting. Evelyn's bedroom had not changed much since Anna's childhood. It was a comfortable but simple room, a fire burning in the grate, the only touch of luxury the velvet-swagged four-poster bed that was an heirloom of the house. As the nurse began to assist Evelyn in undressing, Anna turned to leave, but Evelyn stopped her.

"Don't go yet, child. Stay awhile. I so enjoy having you here."

Anna felt a lump in her throat. Evelyn's words of affection were very few and far between. She sat on the bed, watching the nurse unzip Evelyn's evening dress.

"Thank you for telling me about the scarred man. I can only imagine what a terrible shock that was for you, Grandmama."

"You never knew your grandfather." Evelyn withdrew her arms from the close-fitting sleeves. She wore a beige silk camisole beneath. Her shoulders were youthful, the skin fine as ivory. "Perhaps I should no longer call him your grandfather."

"Of course you should."

"I would hate you to think David had no redeeming qualities."

"I don't. You loved him. So did Candida, whatever happened. He must have been a very charming man."

"He was all of that." She sighed. "He was so very handsome. Beautiful, even. So tall, so strong. He could turn any woman's head. He looked like a Crusader knight when he was young. You would never guess at his weaknesses . . ." The nurse, silent and discreet, slipped the blood pressure cuff around Evelyn's slim arm and began to inflate it, her fingers on Evelyn's pulse. Anna could see the delicate blue vein pulsing in Evelyn's neck and thought of a time when she must have been beautiful and have turned men's heads. "Your Philip," she said, looking across the room at Anna. "He's an extraordinarily handsome man, too. He has great magnetism. I can see why you are so in love with him."

Anna felt the blood rise to her cheeks. "Does it show that much?"

"I've known you since you were a baby. But it would be hard to imagine any woman of your age in such a man's company and not infatuated with him."

" 'Infatuated'? I hope I'm not as silly as that."

"Did he buy you those diamonds?"

"Yes," Anna said, touching the platinum chain at her neck.

"A princely gift. Platinum and diamonds. He deliberately chose two of the most precious, enduring materials on earth."

That had not escaped her, either. "But I don't know if he loves me, Grandmama. I don't know if he ever will."

"That is not what worries me about him."

"Then what worries you about him?"

"I don't know."

The nurse deflated the cuff slowly, checking the pulse, then removed the equipment. "Your blood pressure is up a little, Mrs. Godbold. I think you've overexerted yourself today. You will have to be more careful." She made a note, then administered the evening round of pills, which Evelyn swallowed, grimacing. She helped Evelyn on with her nightclothes and gown. Anna plumped the pillows comfortably for her grandmother, who lay back with a sigh of weariness, her eyes closing. Anna smoothed the bedclothes around the slim body. The nurse retreated to her armchair by the fire, put on her glasses, and picked up the book she was reading.

Anna watched her grandmother's lean face for a while, holding her hand. "Whatever happens," she said in a low voice. "I will always think of you as my grandmother."

A slight smile crossed Evelyn's mouth, and her fingers pressed Anna's for a moment. Her eyes opened dreamily. "If he does not love you, why has he come to Europe with you? Why is he so eager for you to find Joseph Krasnowsky?"

"He has his own agenda, Grandmama. He's very committed to finding out what happened to his father. He feels terribly strongly about it."

"A man he never knew."

"But his father, Grandmama. It haunts him. Exactly the way it haunted Mama." She hesitated before adding, "The way it haunts me."

Evelyn reached out and touched the diamonds at Anna's throat with her fingertips. "Exquisite stones," she murmured. Her lids drooped again and Anna could see she was on the brink of sleep. "I hope he gets what he wants," she whispered. "I hope you get what you want, child. But be careful. Be careful."

When her grandmother was asleep, Anna kissed her brow and rose. She whispered good night to the nurse and let herself silently out of Evelyn's bedroom. The old house was dark, and the corridors were drafty. Winter in Northumberland was not a season of warm nights. Neither the lighting nor the heating at Great Law were really up to twentieth-century standards, despite the costly revisions Evelyn had undertaken to her husband's house in the 1950s. The bedrooms, at least, were always warm, with wood fires burning in the grates to eke out the feeble warmth of the radiators, which were fed by a solid-fuel boiler. She could hear the sounds of someone locking up downstairs, the faint murmur of servants' voices.

She went to Philip's room and tapped on the door with her fingertips before letting herself in. It took a moment for her eyes to adjust to the darkness. The only light came from the flickering flames in the hearth. Then she saw Philip, silhouetted against the window. He was looking out into the night.

Anna locked the door, walked across the room, and joined him at the window. "What are you looking at?" she whispered.

"The dark," he replied.

"What's to see in the dark?"

"Absence of light. Nights in Wyoming were like this. I've lived in the city so long that I've forgotten how nights should look."

She pressed up beside him and felt his arm come around her shoulders, drawing her into his warm strength. He had undressed and was wearing his silk gown. "You're right," she said. "The dark is beautiful."

"You've had quite an evening."

"Yes." She nodded. "That was a shock, wasn't it? I had no idea about David. They never told me. But it all falls into place now. My mother must have carried the horror of that shooting with her, always. And when she read the diary, it suddenly all made sense. She knew who the scarred man was, and why he killed David. She had to find him, not just because he was her father, but to offer him . . . "

"Forgiveness?" Philip said when her voice tailed off. "Absolution?"

"Yes. Maybe."

"But he killed David Godbold. Blew his brains out."

"Hmmm. That probably explains why he went into hiding."

He looked at her curiously. "Doesn't it change the way you feel about him?"

"Yes," she said, nodding slowly. "Yes, it does."

"If Joseph did kill David, then it wasn't done in some rush of passion, Anna. It was a cold-blooded execution, fifteen years after the war."

"Fifteen years for *David*," she said restlessly. "Joseph had just got out of Russia, remember. Maybe his blood wasn't so cold."

"But doesn't the whole thing shock you?"

"It shocks me terribly," she admitted. "I don't want to talk about it yet, Philip. I need time to try and understand."

"All right." His hand touched her hair. "You looked so beautiful tonight, Anna. Like a Gypsy child. Those candles seemed to glow in your eyes. You certainly didn't look English."

"I'm probably a quarter-Jewish. My mother is probably half-Jewish. Don't you think that's a strange thing for a Catholic girl to discover about herself? I mean, with everything else I've had to accept, that's just the finishing touch!"

"Does it make you feel different?" he asked quietly.

She thought. "Yes. Yes, it does. Very different."

"How?"

"You'll laugh at me."

"Try me."

"Well . . . " She laid her head on his shoulder, her hair cascading across his breast. "It's as though I've found different roots. Different origins. I majored in European History at Boston, and I became a journalist. I always knew about the terrible things that happened. Like everyone else. I saw the bits of film, the books, the records. But it didn't involve me. It wasn't anything to do with me. Not a part of me. Do you know what I'm saying?" She looked up at him, groping for words. "The Jews were different. Not because I was prejudiced. They were just a mystery to me. I couldn't really identify. Now it's all suddenly touched my life. The Holocaust. The horror. It might be part of me, and I never knew it. Suddenly I want to know more, and yet I'm terrified of what I'll feel."

"Discovering a Jewish grandparent doesn't mean you have to change your whole self-image, Anna."

"I know that. It's just that knowing I have some Jewish blood—"

" 'Jewish blood'?" he cut in. "You're starting to talk like Dr. Goebbels. You're an Irish Catholic, kid. You always will be. You've looked in the closet and found a skeleton. You're horrified and delighted in the depths of your Catholic soul. You want to run around and tell everyone to come look at your skeleton. And then you tell me you're not prejudiced."

She laughed ruefully. "That's cruel, Philip. Okay. Maybe you're right. But I'm sincere. I want to know more. A lot more."

He was silent for a moment. "Varga concentration camp is a memorial center now," he said neutrally. "It's not far from Riga. There are flights to Riga from Stockholm, and flights to Stockholm from London." He paused again. "Until you come face-to-face with Joseph Krasnowsky, that's the closest you're going to come to his origins. To his life."

He said nothing more, but Anna's heart was suddenly pounding. She lifted her head. "Yes," she said passionately. "*Yes.* I want to go. Let's go, Philip!"

"Are you sure?" he asked gently. "You've never been to one of those places, have you?"

"No. But I want to see. I must see." She gripped his arm. "Please. There's time to spend two days there before we go to Italy. Please!"

She saw him nod in the dark. "Very well. If that's what you want. And seeing a bit of Eastern Europe will be a salutary experience for a spoiled little rich girl like you."

"I am not a spoiled little rich girl," she said indignantly.

"Oh, come on," he replied mockingly. "Look at the way this place is run. Butlers and gardeners. Hot and cold running chambermaids in every room. It's positively medieval."

"This is Evelyn's house, not mine. I can promise you, Mama and I never lived like this!"

"But you've been used to privilege and wealth since you were born."

She knew he was teasing her, but she could not help rising to the bait. "And you? Private planes and limousines? You're hardly on welfare."

"I earned every penny."

"I've worked damned hard, too," she retorted. "And I never took any handouts from Mama *or* Grandmama. Everything I've got now's my own!"

He put a hand on her waist and swung her easily round, pushing her toward the bed. "Pampered," he said. "Imperious and overindulged."

Despite herself, she felt the flicker of anger in her belly. "That isn't true."

"Spoiled little brat," he said remorselessly. The bed caught her behind her knees, and she fell back onto the counterpane. She kicked off her shoes, hearing them land somewhere in the dark.

"Pig."

He pushed her hair back from her face. The firelight flickered red in his dark eyes. "You're a rich kid," he whispered. "You act like a rich kid, talk like a rich kid. You even screw like a rich kid."

"Jesus, that's the last straw!" Half laughing, half in anger, she pounded her fists against his muscular chest until he caught her wrists and immobilized them. "What the hell does that mean, I screw like a rich kid? How do rich kids screw?"

"Like they were playing tennis down at the country club." He put on a wicked imitation of her English accent. "Serve, volley, lob. Oh, good shot. Well played, dahling. Shall we have cocktails now? Or the hot tub?"

"You bastard!" Part of the sting came from the fact that sex with him had been so extraordinary for her. "I never went in a hot tub in my life. What the hell do you expect from me? The Kama Sutra?"

He cupped the mounds of her breasts, soft and unconfined beneath the tricot. "You wouldn't know the Kama Sutra from the Kentucky Derby."

"So what do you want? Want me to get really down and dirty?"

He laughed. "And how would you do that?"

She squirmed as his thumbs brushed over her tightening nipples. "I don't know," she said in a small voice. "I guess I'm not very experienced. You could teach me to get down and dirty."

His lips brushed hers, warm and velvety. "I kind of like you the way you are."

"Then what are you complaining about?"

"I wasn't complaining. I merely remarked that you screwed like a rich kid."

"Meaning I let you do all the work?" She pushed herself up on her elbows, her face close to his. "I don't know how else to behave. You scare the hell out of me. Don't you know that?"

He was silent for a moment. Then he took the hem of her top

and pulled it up. She lifted her arms so he could pull the tricot over her head, then shook her tresses free, her naked breasts tiny peaked volcanoes in the firelight. He kissed each of her nipples gently. "I love the smell of your skin," he murmured. "You smell of the sun. Like a peach."

She was filled with desire. "Oh, Philip. I'm sorry if I disappoint you in bed."

"You don't disappoint me in bed. You drive me crazy." He unfastened the buckle of her belt and unzipped her skirt, pulling it down over the flare of her hips. "You're shaped like a classical Greek vase," he said. "The curve of your pelvis is so perfect. Full, but so delicate. Like some master potter shaped you on a wheel..." He broke off. Under the skirt, in place of her normal pantyhose, she wore a black garter belt to hold up her black stockings. Her lace briefs were tiny, just covering the triangle of curls where her slim thighs joined.

"I dressed for you," she whispered.

"For me?"

"Your Christmas present." She could not read his expression in the dark. Suddenly she was shy. "Don't you like it? All men love stockings, don't they?"

"Mmm-hmm." He bent and kissed the scar on her thigh where the tire iron had gashed her flesh. It was still angry-looking, but the doctors had said it would fade with time. Like the memories of that terrible evening in Gypsum.

"In my experience they do, at least," she said, lifting one knee so the stockings whispered together.

"Oh, yeah?" She caught the glint of his teeth. He unfastened the catch on a stocking. "How many lovers have you had?"

"Lots."

"Lots?"

"Yes!"

His fingers caressed her skin as he slowly rolled the silk down her thigh. "How many?"

"Three," she said defiantly.

"Tell me about them," he commanded, drawing the stocking through his fingers.

"What do you want to know?"

"Tell me about the first one. The one who took your virginity."

"What is this, twenty questions?"

"More like the Grand Inquisition." He looped the stocking around her wrist and tied it in a bow. Then he leaned over and tied the other end to the bedpost behind her.

"What are you doing?" she whispered.

"I love a four-poster bed, don't you? Tell me about him. What was his name?"

"Dan. Daniel." She felt strange lying there in the dark, one arm tied over her head. He was unfastening the second stocking now, fingertips caressing the top of her thigh as if by accident. "He was in the movie business in Belfast. A film editor. Married, with two children."

"How old were you?"

"Eighteen."

"Who seduced who?"

"Oh, he seduced me. I was very innocent. He didn't even tell me he was married until much later."

"And how was it for you, that first time?"

"Pretty good," she said. She giggled nervously. "This is weird, Philip. Confessing to you in the dark—"

"Did you have an orgasm?"

"I don't remember." The caress of his hands on her leg was maddening. Her mouth and throat were starting to dry out.

"You must remember."

"I guess I didn't. I was very nervous. So was he. And the whole guilt trip."

"Guilt?" He looped the second stocking around her free wrist. "Why guilt?"

"In a way it made the whole thing more exciting, but it also killed something for me. Especially that first time."

He tied the bow and pulled her arm out so he could fasten the other end around the other bedpost. "But later. Later you had orgasms."

"I'm a healthy woman. You know that." She was spread-eagled on the bed, her arms outstretched, naked but for her underpants. "Philip, this is kinky."

"Are you upset?"

"I feel a little panicky."

"No, you don't," he said quietly. "You feel sexy as hell." He touched her lips with his fingers. "I've tied you with bows. One good yank and you could get free. You know that."

"Oh." She moved her right arm, testing the silken bonds.

"But you don't want to get free, do you?"

She laughed again, her throat husky. "I kind of want to see what happens next."

He rose and slid off his gown. Anna heard it rustle to the floor. She knew he was naked in the dark, but she could not see his body. He settled down beside her.

"You were telling me how guilty you felt about screwing a married man."

"I did feel guilty. At first it was exciting, but then he fell in love with me. I mean, he got really crazy about me. He started talking about leaving his wife and kids. Then it hit me what I was doing. My little adventure was going to destroy another woman's happiness, break up a family. It hit me hard."

"So you ran."

"Yes." He was stroking the silky ripples of her rib cage, tracing the outline of her stomach muscles, making her belly jump with nerves. "I ran. And I stayed away from married men from then on."

"Tell me about number two."

"William."

"William. Was he also older than you?"

"Yes. He was separated from his wife. No kids. He was more . . . proficient."

"Proficient." He ran his palms over her body, stroking her gently, appreciatively, cupping her breasts. "What does that mean?"

"He treated me like a woman. Dan babied me. Liked to call me his little girl." She closed her eyes as he stroked the curves of her bosom, tautened by her upraised arms. "Bill was more . . ." She sighed as she felt her mouth close over her nipple, warm and possessive.

"Go on," he commanded, his breath hot against her skin.

"I can't think when you do that to me."

"Yes, you can." His teeth closed around her nipple and she arched, gasping. "Tell me about Bill, who treated you like a woman. Did he make you come?"

"Yes," she whispered.

"Always?"

"Sometimes. Not like you. Is that what you want to hear?"

"I want to hear the truth."

She slid her calf along his naked flank, then across his back. "There's never been anybody like you. That first time, in Vail . . . it was more than all the rest put together. I suppose that's what you wanted me to tell you."

"No." He kissed her throat, the flat plane between her breasts, his tongue sliding across her skin. "You don't have to tell me that. I knew that."

She smiled. "Arrogant bastard. I love you, Philip." She'd vowed never to say it, and today she had said it twice. Ashamed of her weakness, she pulled on the bonds, but they held fast. "You said I could get free if I wanted."

"You'll have to pull harder than that." He slid down between her thighs and kissed the soft skin at the edge of her panties. "Tell me about number three. What was his name?"

"Kurt. He worked with me on the newspaper in Miami. Actually, he was my boss." Her voice was dreamy. She could feel his tongue tracing the line of her underpants, running across the base of her belly, down inside her thighs, down to where her flesh was hot and slippery-wet beneath the lace.

"How long were you his lover?"

"Just a season. Last summer. We used to go down to the beach at night. He'd bring a bottle of wine, and we'd make love under the stars. Sometimes he'd bring a joint. He taught me to smoke grass."

"Did you like smoking grass?"

"Sometimes it just made me sick. Other times it was very sensual."

"It's a great aid to mediocre lovers."

"Untie me."

"I told you. You have to pull free."

He slid his thumbs beneath the elastic of her panties and pulled them down over her thighs. She arched her spine so he could get them off. "I can't pull free," she said languidly. "I want to touch you . . ."

He kissed her naked loins, then slid his tongue deep into her, the way he had done that first time, a caress shocking in its intimacy, dizzying in its tenderness. Panting, she wrestled with her bonds. His tongue withdrew, entered her again, slipped upward through the wet petals of her sex, rubbing wantonly across the pinnacle of her desire.

Anna lifted her thighs, crossing her ankles on his back, lifting herself to make the pleasure longer, stronger, more open to him.

The silk of her stockings was chafing her wrists almost painfully. Made desperate by desire, she jerked hard, oblivious to the pain. The knot gave at last, and her right hand was free. She reached over and untied her other hand. Then she reached down and clamped her fingers in his hair, yanking hard. "Come here," she sighed in a voice that was not like her own.

He was laughing. "I told you you could get free if you wanted."

She rolled to him and kissed his mouth passionately. "Don't patronize me," she said fiercely. "And don't ever tie me up again!"

"Didn't you enjoy it?"

"You're a sick man, Philip Westward." He rolled on his back, and she propped herself up on his chest, studying his face in the orange glow of the firelight. Her heart was pounding like a steam hammer. She felt as though she were on fire. "You really like to kiss me there, don't you?"

He smiled. "Mmm-hmm."

"Why?"

"For one thing, it arouses you like hell. For another, it arouses me like hell. It's where you're most feminine."

She slid her thigh over his loins, feeling the stark thrust of his erect penis. "I always thought oral sex was kind of kinky until now. Does that make me hopelessly bourgeois?"

"It makes you an Irish Catholic." He ran his fingers through her hair pulling the heavy silk tangles away from her eyes. "You're so beautiful, Anna. You're the most beautiful woman I've ever known."

"Oh, come on," she said, but there was a catch in her voice.

He twisted beneath her, his arms wrapping around her waist, pulling her around and onto his body, so they were facing opposite directions. She knew what he wanted. "Oh, God," she whispered. She straddled his face, sliding down to his loins. A blitz of butterflies was loose in her belly. She took his erection between her palms and melted her mouth over him. At the same time she relaxed her belly and thighs so that the hot center of her need touched his mouth. He clasped her slender waist so she could not escape again.

She was unbearably shaky, deep inside. Her mind was whirling, torn between the two erotic centers of her body, his tongue exploring her own secret flesh, his manhood throbbing against the roof of her own mouth. There was no sound but the fluttering of the flames in the grate and the pounding of blood in her own ears. She was paralyzed for a moment. She did not know what to do. His mouth was hungry, expert. Pleasure peaked between her thighs, an intensity of sexual gratification she had never known was there. Her hips moved involuntarily, swaying into a rhythm that brought her perilously close to the edge. Then the two centers were no longer two, but one. She felt her whole body flush with heat, become light and weightless. There was a sense of unity with him that transfigured everything else in her life. Nothing was important any longer. There was no other world than this. They were all that mattered, and this strange, wonderful dance of love.

He was deep in her palate as she came, so her orgasm was almost silent. His tongue did not stop moving, driving the flood of pleasure deep into her soul until she could bear it no longer and tore herself away from him.

"Please," she gasped. "Come to me."

He mounted her fast, his weight crushing her breathlessly. He was no longer calm and mocking, but panting and imperative, and she felt the sheen of sweat on his skin, his muscles pumped up with urgency.

He entered her in one endless thrust, and she felt the completion she had always known she wanted, and had never achieved until Philip. A fulfillment so intense it lay on the borderline of pain, a tearing of her preconceptions as sharp as losing her virginity a second time.

She was as deep as he was huge, her body opening to him so that he reached to her core, a great ship coming home to his berth within her body. She felt him reach to her womb, her soul.

"Please, Philip," she begged. "Now."

He made love to her with a power and intensity that he had not given her before now. This time she knew he was with her. Not in his lonely, secret place, but in her arms, inside her body, sharing the marvelous fire of their union. She gasped his name again and again as they rocked together, a rhythmical, sweet intensity rising in her, until fulfillment was not just where he entered her, but flooding her body, filling her spirit.

There was no art to this, no skill or technique. It was a union brutal in its simplicity, pure and raw. His final thrusts were deep, deep, a transfiguration. Fire spilled into her from him, and then came the thunder. It rolled in her belly, arching her like a leaping salmon. Then the clenching spasm relaxed, and she slid back down, limp and spent.

He was kissing her soaked eyelids, whispering her name. "My darling, Anna, my darling . . . "

She stroked the wet expanse of his back, tasting the salt of tears and sweat on her lips. He was gasping for air. His sex was still hard inside her, pressed to the gates of her womb.

"You were with me that time," she whispered against his throat.

"Yes. I was with you."

"You gave yourself to me. You didn't hold back."

"No."

"Don't ever hold back from me again, Philip. I couldn't bear it."

He was silent, kissing her lips for answer, crushing the bruised flesh of her mouth.

It was as though her climax had never stopped, and so wonderful to feel him still inside her, pervading her soul, prolonging the ecstasy. He began to move again, thrusting with slow, gentle strokes.

"Oh, God, aren't you satisfied?" she said on an unsteady laugh.

"No," he said. "I'll never get enough of you."

"It's too soon," she said, impaled on a sensation too intense to cope with.

"No. It's not too soon."

She arched helplessly, commanded by him, utterly in his power.

They Had Found him. They had found Joseph.

She dreamed she was running down a white corridor, her heart pounding in her throat. She was in a hospital that was a little like Carr Memorial, but bigger, brighter, with thousands of doors. He was here, somewhere, in one of these rooms, behind one of these doors.

Excitement and terror chased her heels. She rounded corners, ran down staircases, calling out loud, but the faces of the white-coated people she met were blank. They shrugged indifferently to her importunate inquiries, passed on. But he was here. She knew it.

And then she saw the white door with his name written on it. JOSEPH KRASNOWSKY. She had found him at last!

She thrust the door open and ran into the room. It was a big room, bright and airy. There was a window that stood open, the curtain flapping gauzily in the breeze. Her heart contracted suddenly. She knew what the open window meant.

In slow motion, she turned to the bed. The figure of an old man lay upon it, hands folded peacefully on his breast.

Joseph! she screamed. But it was a silent scream, a scream of the mind.

There were people standing by the bed, medical people in white coats. Their faces expressed polite regret. They shook their heads gently.

He can't! she screamed again. *He can't be dead yet!*

A nurse turned slowly and pointed to the monitor that stood by the bed. On the black screen, a thin green line showed that the heart had stopped beating. The soul had slipped through the gauzy window and into eternity.

"No," she moaned in despair. "No! Philip!"

He was there, big and strong, his arms sliding possessively around her. She opened her eyes and stared over his shoulder in the dim blue light, not knowing quite where she was. She blinked at the flowered wallpaper, the high, molded ceiling, the serpentine mantelpiece. "Philip!" she whispered, remembering. "I had a nightmare . . . "

He comforted her in his arms for a while. "Time to get up," he murmured. "It's nearly seven-thirty already."

"Who gives a damn about the time? You're not going anywhere."

"I know. This is my room. You're the one who's leaving."

"Philip!" she said in dismay. "You're not kicking me out?"

"The hot and cold running chambermaids will be bringing morning tea soon. You don't want them to find the young mistress in bed with the house guest." He pulled the warm covers off her naked body. "Go."

"Damn!" The fire had died to ashes in the night, and the air was icy on her flushed skin. She rolled out of bed hastily and found his gown on the floor, picking it up and putting it on. "You're a heartless sort of person," she muttered, shivering. She groped for her discarded clothes, bundling them to her breast. "I'd forgotten how bloody *cold* this place is."

Philip watched her, propped up on one elbow. In the pale dawn light, he was beautiful, dark smile mocking, dark eyes amused. "Don't forget your garter belt. I want no scandal below stairs."

When she'd gathered everything, she knelt on the bed and kissed his mouth hard. "I've never known anything like this in my life, Philip," she said with quiet intensity. "And you?"

He shook his head slightly. "Never."

She searched his eyes, pain twisting in her heart. "God, I wish I could believe you."

"You can."

At the door she turned and blew him a kiss. He just smiled at her. She unlatched the door and let herself out into the cold, drafty corridor.

They Left Great Law on the second of January. No parting from Evelyn had ever been so painful for Anna. She knew it was not just because she might not see Evelyn alive again. It was because, over the past week, she had come to know Evelyn as if for the first time. Anna had been able to see her grandmother as a woman, a vibrant, living woman, not as a remote figure of awe. And for the first time, Evelyn had treated her like an adult, had shown her some of the love she kept inside.

She was tearful, trying to control it, not doing a very good job. "I'll keep in touch every week, Grandmama," she promised. "I'll tell you how Mama is doing. And the moment she's well enough to make the journey, I'll bring her to England to see you."

"Yes," Evelyn said. "Bring her to me before I go." She spoke as if contemplating a trip to the village. "Good-bye, child."

Anna was too upset to speak. She held her grandmother's frail body, feeling the slender arms around her own shoulders.

Evelyn drew back, her fine gray eyes shining with unshed tears. "Go, Anna. Leave the past behind you. Go somewhere the shadows don't reach."

"There's nowhere the shadows don't reach," she choked.

"Yes there is. The sunlit uplands, child. The sunlit uplands of the future. Go there. Take your mother, and your wonderful man, and go there."

They got into the aging Bentley. Wallace, the chauffeur, got in front, adjusting his peaked cap squarely on his gray head. "Ready, Miss Anna?"

She nodded.

The limousine slid forward down the graveled drive. Anna waved to the slender figure on the steps of the house until it was out of sight. Then she buried her face on Philip's chest, letting him comfort her.

It was a long while before she felt composed enough to sit up. She opened her bag and groped for a mirror to repair her tearstained face. "God, I feel so sad for her," she said. "She's so brave." She applied fresh lipstick and blotted the mascara that had run under her eyes. "What did she mean, 'the sunlit uplands'? "

"I think it was a phrase of Winston Churchill's," Philip said. "Wasn't it, Wallace?"

Wallace half-turned his head. "Yes, sir, it was. During the war, when Mr. Churchill used to broadcast to the people, trying to give us all heart, he spoke of the sunlit uplands ahead. Meaning after the war, sir. Whereabouts exactly the sunlit uplands were, I never quite knew. It was a good phrase, though. Don't cry, Miss Anna."

Anna smiled tiredly. "I don't know if I'm ever going to see Grandmama again, Wallace."

"You'll see her, Miss Anna. Like you said, you'll bring your mother to her. Soon."

She nodded. "Yes. You're right."

"We're all very glad to hear your mother's on the mend now. It was a terrible blow to hear of her accident. Terrible."

"Thank you for saying that."

"I used to drive Miss Kate to school when she was a girl, in this very car," Wallace said after a pause. "She had a lot of spirit. A lot of fight. There was a lot of her father in her."

Anna glanced at Philip wryly. "I'll tell her you were asking after her, Wallace. She'll be pleased."

"And don't worry about Mrs. Godbold too much, either. We'll take good care of her. She's down but she's not out. Long way to go before she's out."

They arrived at Newcastle Airport forty minutes later, got their tickets, and checked in their luggage. She gave Wallace a hug, which brought a flush to the man's cheeks for a moment. "Take care of your ma, now," he said briskly. "Good-bye, Miss Anna. Good-bye, sir."

They watched him get back into the Bentley, straight-backed in his uniform, and drive off sedately past the terminal building.

The airport was busy, crowded with vacationers fleeing the approaching winter for a last dose of ultraviolet in sunnier climates. She wandered a little aimlessly by Philip's side. They bought newspapers at W. H. Smith and had coffee in the lounge.

She told herself it was not the last time she would see Evelyn. There would be other times. Lots of other times. Happier times, when this darkness was over.

Slowly, she felt her sorrow clear away, her spirits lift. She watched Philip read his newspaper, his dark brows frowning a little in concentration. He was so beautiful. So authoritative, so reassuring. She knew every woman who glanced their way would be envying her. Envying her, and speculating about the stunning man with the deep blue eyes.

A flicker of electricity jolted her heart muscles as she remembered the night before. The intimate throbbing in her loins told her of his possession, the hunger that could not be slaked, no matter how many times he entered her body and worshipped there.

She was suddenly short of breath and had to draw the air deep into her lungs to control her dizziness. She wanted to throw back her head and laugh, right there among the cigarette smoke and the squalling children and the anxious parents. It was a sensation that filled her soul, that could hardly be described. A feeling of being more alive, more beautiful, more a woman, than ever in her life. As though she were filled with light and warmth and power. That her life had changed forever, had become an enterprise of limitless wonderful prospects.

That she was a woman in love.

She reached out and laid her hand over his. He looked up.

"What is it?" he asked.

"Just you."

Philip smiled into her eyes. She felt her throat close. There was a sharp catch in her heart, a missing of a beat. "And you," he said softly.

She bit her soft lower lip, shaking her head slightly. "Thank you," she said.

"What for?"

"For everything."

"Don't be silly." He looked out of the plate-glass window. "I hope our flight isn't going to be delayed."

She followed his gaze. She had not noticed that the weather had changed. Rain was sweeping across the tarmac in long, drenching gusts. The sky ahead was lowering, dark as night.

RIGA, LATVIA

The train was heavily crowded going out of Riga, groups of students standing in the aisles, shouting to be heard over the clatter of steel wheels on steel tracks. The older people jammed into the shabby seats were grimmer-looking, staring ahead with unseeing eyes, or glumly reading newspapers. Two young Soviet soldiers sat opposite Anna and Philip, bundled into ill-fitting gray uniforms and fur hats. Both had boyish faces, cheeks reddened by the cold. They looked terribly young. She thought of Joseph Krasnowsky and David Godbold.

It was only marginally less cold inside the carriage than out in the street. The heating system, if there was one, was apparently not working. The carriage was hazy with cigarette smoke, the windows fogged and smeared, so the city outside was no more than a blurred impression of handsome nineteenth-century facades and leafless trees.

She had found Riga to be a surprisingly splendid city, its center relatively unmarked by high-rise developments, the step-gabled houses and baroque mansions reminiscent of Stockholm, its neighbor across the Baltic.

Despite the old-world graciousness of the city, many of the shop fronts had scars where lettering had been hastily removed and the plaster had not yet been repaired: the hammer and sickle, the red star, anything in the Russian language, all had been ripped away, as if in one blissful orgy of rebellion.

In some of the squares, empty plinths marked where statues of Lenin or busts of Marx had stood. Philip had shown her the palace where the KGB had until recently had its headquarters, now boarded up and abandoned. With elaborate humor, someone had painted a huge arrow on the pavement in front of the building, pointing east, neat lettering proclaiming KREMLIN, 800 KILOMETERS. Latvia was shaking off the Soviet yoke.

The city gave an impression of nervous energy, bustling with automobiles, the streets crisscrossed by tramlines upon which clattered red-and-yellow streetcars. Signs of Western entrepreneurship were sprouting up between the stately facades, the familiar neon gospel of American fast food, Japanese electronics, Korean automobiles.

But beneath the energy, Anna had sensed a dreary feeling of hopelessness. Their hotel's affectation of luxury was undercut by shoddy service and a stark menu. Philip, trying to call his investment company in New York, had had endless problems with the telephone system. Though waiters dispensed Big Macs, butcher's windows were empty. Though you could buy an IBM computer, bread was in short supply. And though the pavements were crowded, Anna had soon recognized that people on the street fell into three patterns: full-bodied women, made obese by heavy-duty coats, standing in line for scarce commodities; teenagers in imitation-leather jackets and cheap denims wandering aimlessly; men in parkas and fur caps, just standing around in groups, smoking but not talking.

There were darker undercurrents, too. Of fear. Of suspicion, and betrayal, and hopelessness. Of the past.

Perestroika and Latvian independence notwithstanding, a large proportion of the population were still ethnic Russians. The Kremlin was in no hurry to withdraw its vast armies. The two young soldiers opposite were members of what was in effect an occupying force. A few hundred kilometers to the east, fifty thousand battle tanks pointed this way. The arctic sea was filled with nuclear submarines whose missiles were trained on the Baltic republics. The future looked turbulent and cloudy. She wondered how long it would take for Riga to pick up the self-confident gloss of any other European capital. Philip had been right. The atmosphere of Eastern Europe did not take long to settle into your soul.

The train rattled across an iron bridge over the Daugava. Through the blurry window, the river was a leaden saber, curving between dark buildings. There was the feeling of a long, deep winter that had only just begun. The sky was heavily overcast. It had been raining a lot since they had arrived, and today it looked as though it might snow. Not a good day to visit a Nazi extermination camp. She shifted closer to Philip, her hand thrusting under his arm.

"Cold?" he asked.

"Freezing."

"Come here."

He pulled her close, and she huddled gratefully into his warm strength. The two Russian soldiers stared and whispered to each other, their eyes never leaving her. Whether they were impressed by her looks, or her general foreignness, she was not sure.

Yesterday Philip had taken her to the Riga ghetto. To what was left of the Riga ghetto. As they walked around, he gave her a terse account of what had happened here. It was a relatively small community until the war, amounting to some forty-three thousand people. Here the Nazis had found them in 1941, conveniently walled up in their forbidden city, ripe for the scythe.

By the end of the war, a bare hundred and fifty Jews had been left in the ghetto. Forty-three thousand had died.

Much of the ghetto had been razed. A few streets were left, antiquated houses with crumbling walls, barred doors and windows, deserted pavements, an indelible horror in the very cobblestones. The only people they had seen had been ancient, hobbling silently with bowed heads, uninterested in the strangers. Rain and wind had driven between the decaying buildings. Anna had seemed to hear the crying of children on the wind.

She had been overcome by depression. Seeing how distressed she was, Philip had taken her away, physically dragging her when she was reluctant to leave.

"Are you sure you want to go to Varga tomorrow?" he had asked. "It might be worse than today."

She had nodded. "Yes. It's what we came to Latvia for. I must go on with this."

Today she was glad of the decision, despite the tightening of nerves in her stomach.

She rested her head on Philip's shoulder, her dark hair spilling out of her wool cap across his chest, and looked around the carriage. It had emptied a little after the last stop. The students had all got out, and there was little conversation now. The two soldiers had rolled cigarettes that smelled like burning dung. On the other side, a peasant couple with seamed faces and hands shared a newspaper, both apparently reading with difficulty, thick lips moving silently, eyes squinting. A young girl with a pinched face was knitting something blue, studying Anna's American suede gloves and boots with frank envy. Anna would have traded for the girl's fur hat. Beside her, a fat, official-looking man ate nuts from a paper bag, crunching noisily, staring blankly through the smeared window. Nobody, she reflected, looked animated or even happy. Only the young smiled in Riga. Or was it the same everywhere?

The train was deafeningly noisy, a cacophony of squeaks and creaks and rattles and crashes overlaying the deep incessant thump of the wheels. Each time the connecting door opened, the noise redoubled, and an arctic blast hurled cigarette stubs and bits of paper around the carriage. The official leaned over the thin girl and spat a mouthful of shells into the aisle.

"I could easily get to hate this country," Anna said to Philip. He smiled.

They were out of the city now, running into a bleak landscape of firs and pines. She reached out to rub the fogged window with her handkerchief, but it was filthy on the outside, too, and she could make out little more than a blur of mud and trees, the occasional stretch of gray water. It was a flat country, covered with stretches of forest. Patches of mist were starting to sweep past the train.

Philip wore a down-filled gray ski jacket zipped up to the throat, faded denims, and practical hiking boots. He had not shaved that morning, and his lean cheeks were dark with stubble. She was so used to seeing him dressed as if for a business conference. It was a revelation to see him so casually, almost roughly dressed. If anything, he was even more attractive in the functional clothes, the lithe strength of his body emphasized, the aura of danger a little rawer.

She tried to imagine him twenty years younger, the lines of

experience missing from his face, a bright innocence in his eyes. He would have had an eager look at eighteen, she thought. Hard and eager. Ready to do whatever his country asked him. "The Army must have changed you a lot," she said.

"I guess," he replied neutrally.

"Will you tell me about it? One day?"

"After all these years I've pretty well forgotten," he said, smiling. But she did not believe him.

The Train Pulled into Varga twenty minutes later. They were the only passengers who got off. The platform was almost deserted; a little old woman was sweeping up cigarette butts with a birch broom. The mist was thick now.

There seemed to be a small village on the other side of the tracks. Beyond the station buildings, huge and shadowy trees lurked in the fog. The train clattered off, as if anxious to get away from the place. Through the smeared glass, she saw the two Soviet soldiers staring at her. They had risen off their seats to get a better look, but their faces stayed expressionless as the carriage swept down the line. The train vanished into the mist. Anna found herself staring at the slick steel tracks, wondering if this was the same line that had brought in the cattle trucks loaded with the doomed. Whether they had disembarked right here, at some place buried just beneath the modern concrete platform.

It was bitterly cold, and the fog was raw in her lungs. "Which way?" she asked, shivering.

"No sign." Philip was staring around. There were no indications, no signposts pointing to the death camp site. Philip walked across to the old woman and spoke to her in German. She peered up at him, her walnut face wrinkled with incomprehension under her scarf. Then, understanding, her mouth tightened in some violent expression, anger or revulsion. She gestured brusquely to the left, turned her back on Philip, and resumed her sweeping with sudden vehemence. As they walked past her, she hawked and spat directly at Anna's boots, an ugly sound that made the hairs prickle on Anna's neck.

Anna had to sidestep the clot of phlegm. She glared at the old woman. "What's eating her?"

"Maybe they don't like visitors here."

"They sure don't. There's not even a sign to the camp."

"Can't be easy having a Holocaust memorial on the doorstep," Philip said with a shrug. "These people weren't eager to accept any guilt anyway, and considering the memorial was forced on them by the Russians, they probably feel a little sore about it."

"Well, fuck them," Anna said briefly. "They cooperated with the Nazis, didn't they?"

They had still not seen any signpost to the camp. Perhaps signposts had once existed but had been torn down by the locals. However, they were now on a concrete-flagged path that led into the woods. The trees were immensely tall. Huge firs drooped inky arms across the path, birches towered stark and leafless, their trunks mottled black and white. The fog hung heavily in the woods, creating an uncanny silence. She clung to Philip's arm, keeping pace with him. It was a forest straight out of her childhood nightmares, ominous and haunted.

"I'm glad you're here," she said in a small voice. She had her camera slung over one hip, but she doubted she would be taking any photographs today.

The path rounded a corner and widened onto a large stone-flagged square. They could see a low, plain building hulking in the mist and some kind of monument set in the center of a roughly turfed lawn.

"Looks like we've arrived," Philip commented. There were no signs, no notices. Just an air of total desertion.

"I wonder how many people ever come here on pilgrimage. Or just to see."

They walked across the lawn to the monument. It was a group of bronze figures, agonized bodies set on a tall, green-stained concrete plinth.

"Look," she said, pointing. "A sign."

The arrow pointed along a grassy path into the woods. There were inscriptions in Russian and Latvian that she could not decipher. "What do you want to do?" he asked. "Follow the arrow or go to the building?"

"Follow the arrow," she decided. She was shivering constantly now, a cold, sick feeling gripping her heart.

They walked along the grassy track without speaking, Anna holding on to Philip tightly. The trees loomed overhead, forming a gloomy tunnel. Some had thrust limbs across the path as if to bar their way forward.

After five minutes, the path descended steeply into another clearing, much bigger than the first. It stretched, dreary and treeless, into the motionless fog. Beneath the turf, the ground here was weirdly lumpy, heaped up in places, rippled as if by the work of ancient builders. At first she could not identify the place. Then she saw Philip's face. It was bleak and stony, his mouth hard.

"The mass graves," he said.

"Here?" She stared at the endless humps of earth in horror. Quite suddenly, it had become real to her. She was standing in the place where tens of thousands of human lives had been extinguished.

"We've just walked along the path they used," Philip said, his voice quiet. "They stripped them naked back at the camp, then drove them along that path, between lines of Gestapo and Latvian guards. The soldiers were waiting here with the machine guns."

A vast sorrow, too deep to express, gripped her. She dropped her hold on his arm and wandered forward alone. "Philip. Look."

There were tiny, pathetic memorials set in the turf.

A gravestone, bearing a family name: ROZENBERG.

A little enameled picture of a child, spiked into the ground, with a single word: RACHEL.

A bunch of plastic flowers.

More enameled ovals. Black-and-white faces of the dead. Adults, children, the elderly.

A faded picture of a man with spectacles and a beard, enameled on a metal plaque: RABBI ABRAM WILENSKY. Beyond, a photograph of a beautiful young woman, her sad eyes already foreseeing death.

Another gravestone, but by now her eyes were too blurred to read the names, the handful out of the six million.

The terrible sorrow gripped her by the throat. No rhetoric, no mausoleum could be more infinitely moving than these little memorials to the vanished, left here by those who had survived, who had crept out after the firestorm had passed, somehow alive, somehow never to live again.

She took a shuddering breath, wiping her wet cheeks with her palms. "I don't know what to do, Philip. I want to pray. I only know Christian prayers. Would that be a desecration?"

"I don't think so," he said gently. "Go ahead and pray, if you want."

Walking Back Along the path with Philip, she felt drained. "I expected horror," she said in a low voice. "I didn't expect the grief. The sadness."

He nodded, holding her close. "There may be ugly things inside the memorial."

"I know."

The memorial was a small, square building, faced in some kind of dark granite. The door was open and lights had been left on, but there was no sign of an attendant or curator. She was starting to find the deserted aspect of the place very eerie. "Somebody must come from the village to open and shut the place," Philip said. "They obviously don't hang around."

Their footsteps echoed down a dark corridor. The granite gave way to rough-cast concrete walls and a tiled floor. The museum itself was simple and somehow unimpressive, completely lacking any of the profound emotion that had hung around the mass graves. Whoever had set the place up had evidently had little material to work with. There were several large-scale paintings depicting the arrival of the Jews at Varga, the steps of undressing and sorting the clothes, the march to the pits.

Behind a plate-glass window there was an array of blurred photographs, evidently taken by some German soldier, showing scenes of the mass murders. In one, a group of prisoners dug with picks and spades. A prisoner's bearded face looked over his shoulder into the camera lens. In another, the uniformed backs of SS soldiers leveled rifles at huddled, indistinct masses of naked bodies. Others showed the dead tumbled haphazardly in the pits, limbs tangled like pale roots.

This was where Joseph Krasnowsky had been sent after his capture in Italy. Here he had lived for almost a year. Doing what? Digging graves? She stared back at the photograph of the prisoners with shovels. One of them might be Joseph. Maybe even the bearded man, whose dark and haunted eyes stared so disturbingly back at her. Could that be Joseph? Her mother's father? Her grandfather, still living somewhere in the world?

She felt gooseflesh ripple up her back and onto her scalp. She stepped closer to the glass and stared at the face. But the closer she got, the less sense the picture made. It became no more than a black-

and-white blotch, like the bark of a birch tree. She stepped back again, and the ghostly face materialized again. She lifted her camera on its strap and focused on the display. Praying the flash would not dazzle too much off the glass, she took several pictures.

Another display case contained a scale model of how the camp had been arranged, marking the main killing grounds, which lay all round the central building. There were diagrams of the train lines out of Riga.

Also behind glass, a thick book in which the names of the victims had been listed.

She turned and saw Philip standing motionless in front of a display. She went to join him, her footsteps echoing in the bunkerlike room.

It was an arrangement of photographs, all of SS officers. There were brief typewritten notes under each name, and arrows indicating lines of command.

"The administrators of extermination," Philip said in a tight voice. His face was flinty and merciless, as it had been out at the graves. He tapped the top picture with his forefinger. "Jeckeln. Chief of SS and Police, Northern Russia. The man in overall charge."

Anna stared at the brutal, soldierly face without comment.

Philip's finger moved down. "His deputy at the camp, Klaus von Jena." His finger moved along a row of faces lower down. "The men in charge of arrest, transportation, confiscation of Jewish goods. The men in charge of the physical business of murdering tens of thousands of civilians. Their deputies. The unit commanders."

His hand dropped. Anna stared at the faces. Most had been photographed wearing the black peaked cap of the SS, oak leaves at their collars. They wore stern and somewhat self-righteous expressions, as though they had expected to be in this memorial some day and wanted to let the world know they had done their duty well. She looked from one face to the other. All were hard, disciplined faces, with compressed lips and steady eyes. No face seemed to her to be particularly marked by evil. None looked like a monster. But for the hats and the death's-head insignia, they might have been lawyers or bankers.

"They look so ordinary," she said at last. "So normal."

His voice was a rasp. "Yes. But they weren't."

She moved to the next display, which contained dozens of photographs of a trial in progress. Russian uniforms filled the seats, German uniforms the dock. She recognized some of the faces in the dock, including Jeckeln's, from the previous display, looking a lot more haggard and less self-righteous. Shots of the judges, grim-faced men who had looked on the ultimate horror of the thousand-year reich.

The Red Army had not delayed long before giving the administrators of extermination a swift trial. And in the next row of pictures, the execution of sentence. Blurry shots of German officers being driven to the gallows in trucks, held upright by Russian pickets. A group shot of the hanging in progress, a dozen figures dangling from ropes, the Russian executioners busy. Individual shots of each man, neck awry in the noose, hands cuffed behind him, booted legs swinging. She looked at the executed men and felt nothing, no vindication, no compassion, just a sure knowledge that it had been right to slay these slayers.

Anna turned to draw Philip's attention to the photographs. But he was still standing in front of the SS portraits, staring at them fixedly.

She touched his arm, felt the sinews rigid. The muscles along his jaw were bunched tight. She could sense some deep emotion in him. "Let's go, Philip. I don't think I can take anymore today."

He stood staring at the group of faces for a long while before turning to her. She was almost frightened by the look in his eyes. "What's made you so angry?" she asked.

"Those bastards," he grated. "Masquerading as soldiers."

"I know." She hugged his arm. Now it was he who seemed upset, she who was offering comfort. The atmosphere of the place was choking her. She cast one last look at the photograph of the bearded prisoner with the shovel. His gaze seemed to go deep into her eyes, accusing, pleading. "Come," she begged.

They followed a sign pointing to the exit and emerged through double doors onto a deserted country road that headed back to the railway station. On the sidewalk was a placard declaring the site of the Varga memorial. They had come in the back way. The old woman had evidently pointed them to a shortcut through the woods, rather than the long way round on the road.

She was surprised to see the sign was marked by graffiti, relatively uncommon in Latvia. She turned and gasped in shock.

The granite facade of the memorial building had been defaced by a barbed-wire tangle of savagely scrawled graffiti. There was so much of it that the words would have been difficult to decipher, even if she had understood Latvian. But there was no mistaking the swastikas.

"I don't believe it," she burst out, turning to Philip. He was looking at the graffiti with a strange expression, eyebrows lifted, something like an ironic smile on his lips.

"Well, well," he said softly.

Her eyes traveled over the hate-filled sentences, the grinning skulls, the crooked crosses. Several of the granite tiles were cracked by blows, and a window had been smashed, the safety glass sagging inward.

She was more sickened by this than anything she had seen inside the building. That, at least, had been buried in the past. This was viciously alive. "I don't believe it," she said again. "Who could do such a thing?"

"More ordinary, normal people."

"Mad dogs, you mean." There were more swastikas sprayed on the placard, together with a phrase in German—*JUDEN RAUS*. Her skin was creeping with gooseflesh. "Do you think the people who wrote this stuff have ever been inside the memorial, Philip?"

"Sure," he said calmly. "They went inside to laugh."

"This place gives me the creeps," she said, turning away abruptly. She bunched the chest of his ski jacket in her fists and shook him to and fro, her teeth gritted. "Get me out of here, Philip. I want to go home."

When they got back to the hotel, he made her eat a lunch she did not want, some kind of spicy stew with large, stodgy dumplings. She almost gagged on the heavy food, but he would brook no resistance. He also made her drink two glasses of sweet Georgian wine. The morning had shaken her. She was in a state of something like shock. They were due to fly to Milan the next day. She was very glad to be going.

When she had got down as much as she could, he took her upstairs to their room and made her get into bed. He tucked her in, smiling gently in answer to her protests. She lay there, fully dressed, shivering violently for a long while, images whirling through her mind.

The humped, anonymous graves.

The photographs of the SS men, oak leaves and sober faces.

The shadowy eyes of the bearded prisoner, staring at her over his shoulder.

The graffiti jaggedly defacing the granite.

And over everything else, the endless rattle of the train.

Sleep came to her as suddenly as stepping off a cliff, a swift slide into blackness.

She Awoke Gradually to the sounds of Riga: streetcars clattering on iron rails, cars honking impatiently, rain on the windowpane. Her shock had dissipated, but she was aware, long before she woke fully, that she was deeply troubled. Dark shadows had formed in her mind, haunting her thoughts.

It was dark; evening had fallen. She groped for the bedside light and switched it on. She was alone in the room. Philip had left a note on her night table in his clear, neat script: "Gone for a walk. Back at 7:00." She checked her watch blearily. It was 6:45. She got up and opened the curtains. It was snowing hard, though it had not started to stick yet. The wet pavement shimmered with reflections. A dimly lit streetcar sprayed water off the tracks as it rattled down the street. Where the hell had he found to walk to in this god-awful weather?

She took off her clothes and got in the shower. There was no pressure behind the water, but at least it was hot and showed no signs of diminishing as she stood under the feeble spray and washed her hair. She emerged ten minutes later, groping for the towels, which hung on a heated rail, one of the few concessions to luxury in the hotel. At the same time, she heard Philip come into the room. She went out of the bathroom to meet him.

He was pulling off a plain raincoat, which had not protected him much from the snow: His denims and boots were soaked, as though he had been walking for miles on wet streets, and his dark hair was dripping, revealing the high forehead that was usually covered by his fringe. He looked weary.

"Where on earth have you been?" she demanded, reaching up to kiss him. His face was wet and icy cold, stubble prickling her lips.

"Just walking."

"In *this*?"

"I wanted to clear my head."

"You're crazy. Come on," she said firmly, unzipping his jacket. "There's plenty of hot water. You're going in the shower before you catch your death."

She made him undress, disturbed at how cold his body was. While he showered, she called room service and managed to make herself understood as to hot coffee and a large brandy.

The coffee had just arrived when he came out of the bathroom naked and steaming, rubbing himself dry with a towel. She watched the ripple of wet brown muscle against the fluffy white folds, reflecting that he was certainly the most beautiful man she had ever seen in her life. Magnificent was the only word that really described him. Neither of them had seen much sun lately, and she now knew his coloring was naturally dark, his skin the color of newly poured bronze, black hair covering his broad chest and lean rib cage, curling over the supple muscles of his stomach and streaking his long, lean thighs. The hot shower had eased some of the tension in his face, but had not taken away the weariness, which sat around his eyes in fine lines.

He wrapped himself in his gown and took the cup she passed him, sitting beside her on the sofa. She curled up against him, sliding her hand under his gown to lay her palm on his chest. "At least you're warm now. You must be mad, walking around Riga on a night like this."

He smiled tiredly. "You sound like a wife."

"Is that such a bad thing?" she answered before she could stop herself. He made no response to the overcrude sally. "I can't stop thinking about Varga," she said, changing the subject. "Seeing that graffiti gave me a terrible shock."

"After what the Nazis did, are you shocked at a little spray paint?"

"Not at the paint. At the viciousness, Philip. The people who sprayed those slogans also vandalize Jewish cemeteries. Not to mention synagogues."

"Nowadays?" he asked incredulously.

She gave him a dry look. "Don't you know what's happening in Europe today?"

"If you're talking about those teenage hooligans, then of course I know what's happening in Europe today."

"No. I'm talking about something much more than teenage hooligans, Philip. I'm talking about the largest rise in neo-fascist politics since the 1930s."

"A couple of thousand skinheads in Nazi regalia?"

"Millions of plain folks who no longer think Adolf Hitler was such a bad guy. Plausible politicians who get airtime on national TV and seats in parliaments."

He was staring at her. "Are you serious?"

"Never more so. There are extreme right-wing parties in every

European country. Germany, France, Italy, Holland, Spain, even Britain. All quite respectable. Discreet, even. More of them every day. More members, more publicity, more power."

"But what makes people want to join parties like that?"

"There's a vacuum. Communism has vanished overnight, leaving a huge political vacuum. It's sucking all kinds of whirlwinds out of the wilderness. The collapse of the Soviet empire is the biggest political event since the collapse of the Austro-Hungarian Empire at the beginning of this century—and that precipitated two world wars."

He made a skeptical face. "The European Economic Community was meant to prevent all that."

"As long as prosperity holds out, it will," Anna said. "But prosperity's in short supply lately. I did some research on this a while back. There's a very severe recession on its way. Currencies are devaluing fast. Living standards are falling just as fast, even in the most prosperous countries. Unemployment is on the rise, there are housing shortages, there's an apparently unstoppable influx of refugees and other foreigners from the east. If these problems aren't solved quickly, and there sure as hell doesn't seem to be a quick solution, then support for neo-fascists will escalate dramatically. A degraded environment is one in which violently right-wing policies take on increasing appeal and meaning."

He lifted the brandy glass to his lips, then offered it to her. She took it. "And that applies most of all right here, in what used to be the Soviet Union. The biggest opposition to Boris Yeltsin isn't coming from communists, but from the far right. Yeltsin has been warning about a fascist counterrevolution for months, and nobody is taking him seriously. But it's as serious as hell. The old guard are determined to get back into power. They've got the muscle to do it. Except this time they may come back with a swastika on their flag instead of the hammer and sickle."

"Fascist totalitarianism is not that different from Marxist totalitarianism." He nodded.

"It's the same evil. Only the rhetoric changes. There used to be a taboo about belonging to the far right. Those taboos are breaking down. Xenophobia is the flavor of the month. It's fashionable to be a fascist."

Philip rose and went to the window, pulling the drapes aside. Snow was whirling against the window glass, already starting to settle on the lintels in white ridges. "How do you know all this?"

"I'm a journalist," she said. "And European history was my first love. Neo-Nazis are throwing gas bombs at refugee shelters night after night, and the local police seem unable—or unwilling—to control it. You talked about skinheads in Nazi regalia. But the ones throwing the Molotov cocktails are clean-cut local boys. And their mamas and papas are screaming encouragement from the balconies."

"Okay," he said. "But all that is happening in *eastern* Germany, Anna. Those kids grew up under East German communism. They have at best a limited understanding of the way a modern democracy works. They'll calm down."

"The problem isn't confined to eastern Germany. Unification is costing the country infinitely more than Helmut Kohl told them it would. Taxes are going up. Labor costs are soaring. There's not much sign of economic recovery in those East German Länder. I was listening to a man called Michael Swierczek recently. He's one of the leaders of a neo-Nazi outfit called the *Nationale Offensive*. A nice-looking guy in a suit. He said, 'Germans hate chaos and uncertainty; they must have order. And in a crisis, they always turn to the right.' He's looking forward to signing up a lot of new voters." She got up restlessly and went to join him at the window. Riga was starting to go white. The sidewalks were already empty, snow slowly piling on the roofs.

"You don't really believe that history can repeat itself?" he asked her, taking her arm.

"History does nothing but repeat itself," she said.

"Yeah, but the first time as tragedy and the second time as farce. These days, the Germans are a damned sight more civilized than the rest of us. God knows they're richer. They aren't about to throw the past fifty years away and invade Poland."

"Of course not. But look at the Yugoslav catastrophe closely. The whole of Europe looked like that in 1940. And it will look like that again if the whirlwinds keep blowing."

He drew her close so that her body molded against his lean strength. "You have a good brain, Miss Kelly."

"I wasn't born yesterday, Mr. Westward." She touched his lips, her desire for him swirling in the darkness of her uncertainty and fear. "Are you really an investment analyst, Philip? Is that what you do all day in New York? Look at a screen and add up numbers?"

"It's a living."

She ran her hands up the iron-hard muscles of his arms. "You wouldn't bullshit me, Philip? Because you'd break my heart if you did."

His eyes were dark, staring into hers. He pressed his loins to her, a relentless thrust that made the nerves in her belly tighten with desire. "I wouldn't bullshit you," he whispered, pushing her back toward the bed. "Let's make love."

LAKE GARDA, ITALY

They landed at Linate Airport, just outside Milan, an hour late because of weather delays. The passengers had sat tense and silent as the 757 circled in a holding pattern imposed by air traffic control. When at last they landed and emerged from the aircraft, it was into freezing fog. A white, unreal world, where everything solid had been reduced to a dim gray shadow. It reminded her of the world of the nightmare she'd had in Northumberland.

It was intensely cold. They hired a car at Linate, a large Lancia that seemed extravagant to Anna, and drove out on the *autostrada* toward the lakes and the Swiss border. The road to the lake was not inspiring, lined with factories and grim-looking towns that loomed forebodingly out of the fog.

But when they reached Saló, she remembered how beautiful Garda was. In the warmer air of the valley, the fog had lifted, and the great lake stretched silver-blue between wooded mountainsides, a majestic and tranquil spectacle.

They drove down hairpin bends to the lakeshore. The stark branches of leafless trees were at once beautiful and sad. They booked into the Hotel Majestic, just outside Saló. It was one of the few hotels Anna had stayed in that lived up to its name, a splendid *fin-de-siècle* palace in the opulent wedding-cake style typical of the Italian and Swiss lakes. They entered it through splendid wrought-iron gates. Its grounds stretched down to the water, richly lawned and set with exotic trees, especially palms, whose tall growth testified to the benign, almost windless climate around the lake.

Far across the glassy water, veiled in wreaths of mist, the opposite shore glimmered like a fairy kingdom. *Il Nóce* lay on that shore, but they had decided to stay in Saló and get the ferry across the lake to do their exploring.

Anna checked her watch. "It's midmorning in Colorado. I'm going to call the hospital."

She went to the telephone and dialed the number. A short while later, a telephonist put her through to Jay Ram Singh.

"Dr. Ram Singh, it's Anna Kelly. How is my mother?"

"Still making excellent progress," the lilting voice replied. "This week there's been much more flexor response."

"What does that mean?"

"She can move her arms and legs more strongly. We believe she'll begin recovering mobility in the foreseeable future."

"That's wonderful! What about her mind? Does she know where she is? Does she know what's happened to her?"

"She'll be confused for a long time yet," the doctor said, "and we shouldn't expect too much. We're taking this one day at a time."

"Sure." She forbore to remind him that a few short weeks ago he had been discussing the option of switching off the life-support system.

"But the signs are very good that there won't be permanent damage. Our consultant neuropathologist has compared her to a stroke victim. There may be problems relearning some motor skills, but her mind and personality should hopefully remain unchanged."

"I'm very grateful to you for all you're doing, Dr. Ram Singh," she said warmly. "Give her my love."

"I will do."

"I'll be back in Vail next week."

She hung up and turned to Philip, her eyes bright. "Did you hear?"

"I heard."

"Isn't it wonderful?"

He smiled. "It's a miracle." He kissed her. The kiss smoldered, then ignited. He drew her to the bed and they lay on it. He slid onto her, his mouth covering hers. She parted her thighs, desire flaring instantly, melting her bones. "Oh, Philip . . ."

They were both fully dressed, but too impatient to do more than unzip. He entered her, pushing deep. Her whole body responded instantly, hunger becoming unbearable.

Philip cupped her hips in his palms, raising her to accommodate the driving thrust of his lovemaking. She clung to him, transfigured. There had never been anything like this before. No desire had been a mansion like this one, with so many chambers, so many windows with so many dazzling vistas. She moaned softly, moving with him, the heat rising, white heat pervading her womb, her heart, her soul.

The rhythm intensified, became unbearably intense. "Now," she commanded blindly, "please, Philip—now!"

He gasped her name, moving into her with that deep, deep plunge she had come to know so well. The glorious pleasure erupted between them, sweet and strong.

He held her for a long while as she relaxed, her limbs sliding open in the abandonment of satiation. As always, he remained hard inside her, prolonging the pleasure exquisitely.

She smiled up dreamily at the dark face above her and moved herself around him, caressing him with her inner flesh. "That's a very clever trick of yours, Mr. Westward. I don't know how you keep it up."

"A purely physiological reaction to very intense desire, Miss Kelly. No matter how many times I make love to you, I can't get enough of you."

"A satyr," she murmured. "A beautiful satyr. Just what I've always wanted." She adjusted the knot of his silk tie. "And so well-dressed."

He laughed huskily, and she felt his erection move in her. She pressed her palms to his hard buttocks, urging him deeper into her. "Again," she commanded softly.

They Pushed Through the bracken. Thorny ropes of dead brambles were threaded through it like snares, snagging painfully round their legs. It was heavy going.

"Mind your face," Philip warned.

Anna peered through the tangled undergrowth. "We can't be far away now. It's got to be here somewhere."

They had walked up from *Il Noce,* directed by one of the brick-layers who were restoring the old farmhouse for its new owner. There had been little to see at *Il Noce.* Little, that was, of what the place had once been.

The interior of the house had been gutted. The rotten beams and window frames had been torn out and everywhere raw gray concrete surfaces awaited tiles or paint. The cellar where Joseph had hidden was piled with lumber. They'd been unable to get into the grain store; the hatch had long since been nailed shut.

Candida's room had ceased to exist; a new staircase now thrust through from the ground floor where it had been. The old kitchen had been modernized, the old fireplace was no more. Rows of expensive designer units were being installed by the carpenters. Even the court-yard, where the pig had been slaughtered, had been bulldozed and now formed the foundations for a glass conservatory.

The barn where Joseph had been brought after the ambush on the truck, and where Candida and David had made love, still stood. But it was now used for storing timber, sacks of cement, and other building materials. If there were ghosts there, they had not made their presence felt to Anna.

Il Noce itself no longer seemed to have a presence. It was in the middle of change, awaiting a new identity as a weekend retreat for a rich Milan businessman and his family. Anna had felt no vibrations from the ancient walls. Perhaps the new layers of fresh cement had sealed all the old vibrations in.

None of the younger workmen had even heard of the Hunter's Tower. Eventually they had called the oldest man there, a bricklayer, and he had nodded.

"If it's still standing," he'd said, pointing with his trowel, "it's up that path, in the middle of the woods. You used to be able to see the roof over the treetops, but maybe it's collapsed by now."

It had been a steep climb. For the past twenty minutes they'd been catching tantalizing glimpses of a pointed slate roof, just visible above the treetops. The trees had evidently grown taller in forty years, and the path was almost obliterated in places by the undergrowth.

She heard a distant sound like a scream of pain and stopped apprehensively. "What was that?" she called to Philip.

"A bird, that's all."

Slightly reluctantly, she followed his broad back through the woods. They had met no one on the long walk. Anna remembered a phrase from the diary: *The loneliest place on God's earth.*

She heard Philip exclaim up ahead and pushed through the dead bracken after him. They had come into a clearing. In the center of the clearing stood a stone tower with a peaked slate roof.

"This must be the place," Philip said.

"Yes," she agreed quietly. "There it is. Still standing. It's exactly as I imagined it. Like something out of the Brothers Grimm."

"Child Roland to the dark tower came," Philip said.

Square and dark, the tower thrust like a giant's finger at the sky. She took Philip's hand in her own and stared at the tower in silence. It had once been covered with ivy, but the ivy had died for some reason, and only a dry brown tracery remained, like skeletal hands keeping the crumbling stonework in place. The windows gaped like empty eye sockets. So did the doorway; the stout oak door Candida had described had long since rotted or been taken away.

But on the point of the roof, the weathervane still stood, a rusty iron arrow pointing to the distant Alps.

They walked across the clearing. The tower was ominous, silent. They reached the empty doorway, and Anna was the first to step into the dim interior.

As she did so, something erupted in her face with a wild scream. Recoiling, she threw her arms up to protect her face. Great wings buffeted the air for a moment. A white shape exploded past her and swooped away across the clearing, into the forest.

She was in Philip's arms, shuddering.

"A barn owl," he said, smiling.

"God, I almost died," she said, shamefacedly touching her pounding heart. "You go first from now on."

She followed him inside the tower.

It was stark and bare, the wooden floor rotten in places. There was a huge fireplace, blackened with ash and littered with the debris of hunters who had warmed themselves or cooked a meal here. They made their way cautiously up to the next floor, which was in much the same condition, and then up to the next.

"Yuck," she exclaimed in disgust. The barn owl had evidently made this room his banqueting hall; it stank sharply of death. The floor was thick with the bones of countless small creatures.

She pressed her handkerchief to her face to keep out the nauseating smell and went to the window for air, tiny skeletons crunching underfoot. Philip had gone to the fireplace and was brushing at the soot-caked mantelpiece with his fingers.

"Look," he called.

She picked her way through the litter of corpses to join him. Carved into the center of the stone lintel were the letters JK.

"My God!" she exclaimed. She reached out and traced the letters with her fingertips. Gooseflesh was creeping all over her body. "His initials."

Philip nodded. He was staring at the stone with an odd, sad expression. "He must have carved them there before the Nazis came for him."

"I wish I could take this stone with me." It was the first tangible proof that Joseph had ever been here. A sign. She unslung her camera and took two photographs of the initials. "Let's get out of here. The smell is choking me."

They made their way down from the owl's slaughterhouse, Anna trying to rub her fingers clean; touching the mantelpiece had smeared them with a greasy black soot that proved difficult to get off.

They wandered round the tower for a while longer, searching for any other traces of Joseph's tenure that might be left. But they found none. In over forty years the tower had played host to too many other guests, including the owl, who had obliterated old traces and left their own.

And yet the place had a powerful atmosphere, a presence, that the old farmhouse had lacked. It had not changed in any substantial way since 1944, and Anna decided perhaps that was it. Prickles kept running across her skin, down her back, and along her arms, and she kept remembering passages from the diary.

"I can feel it in the air," she said to Philip, standing in the doorway.

"What?"

"Tragedy. Disaster."

"That's just the owl's dinners," he said with a smile.

"No. I can feel *him*. Joseph, I mean. I can feel his presence here, like I never felt it before. We're close to him in this place. I know we are."

He walked over to her, hands thrust in the pockets of his jacket. "And what sort of presence does he have?"

"Tell the truth, a little ominous," she said with an uneasy laugh. "I keep asking myself what sort of person could bear to stay in such a lonely place as this."

"He didn't have much option," Philip reminded her. "What else do your witch's instincts tell you about him?"

"I don't know." She turned restlessly. "Something hard to define." She found a word. "*Power*. He has power, Philip."

"He *had* power," Philip corrected her.

"No. He's still alive. I can feel it. I knew it when you found those initials upstairs. He's still alive somewhere in the world."

He studied her for a while in silence, dark blue eyes unfathomable. At last he said, "If your suppositions are right, then Joseph Krasnowsky is a killer, Anna. He murdered David Godbold in cold blood. If you're expecting some kind of tender family reunion at the end of all this, then you may be in for a disappointment."

"You mean Grandmama is right, and he doesn't want to be found?"

"I mean he may be a dangerous man."

She felt another wave of prickles down her spine. "Yes. I've considered that. But he's an old man now, Philip. Seventy-four years old. And the way Candida writes about him in the diary, he was a man of compassion and understanding. He couldn't have changed so much, no matter what they did to him in the camps."

"Couldn't he?"

"Whatever happened between him and David, I still feel more pity than anything else for him, Philip. I've been struggling to understand." Her face was tight, frowning. "David didn't just betray him. David destroyed everything he had. His woman, his life, even his child.

Because of David he was sent to a Nazi death camp, and then to a Russian gulag. He spent half his life in prisons because of David's treachery. Can you imagine how he suffered all those years? He must have been kept alive by a single burning ambition—justice. Getting even with the man who'd done all those terrible things to him. Philip, can you be so sure you wouldn't have done the same things yourself? If you'd been in that position, wouldn't you have wanted to kill David?"

"There would have been other ways of getting my revenge," Philip said.

"How? Trying to expose him? After all those years, with no proof? I've been thinking about him so much, Philip. Thinking about what he suffered. He was in a living hell for half his life. And it didn't end when he killed David. That just started a second lifetime of suffering, because he could never come near his daughter again. Can you imagine it? Knowing you had a child by a woman you loved, but knowing she could never see you as anything but a monster? How terrible! How terrible for him, Philip!"

"None of that changes the fact that he may be a killer. It makes finding him more complicated than ever, Anna. He may not welcome your digging up all this family history. He may see it as a kind of . . . accusation."

"I don't believe that. I believe he'll be eager for reconciliation."

"You're crediting him with finer feelings which he may not have," Philip said.

"I'm crediting him with the same feelings I've got," she retorted. "And I'm his granddaughter!"

"So you've forgiven him for murdering David?"

"It's not as simple as that!" she said restlessly. "I don't try and judge him, that's all. And you shouldn't, either!"

He stared at her for a moment longer. "Come on," he said at last, brusquely. "We've got a long trek back, and it'll be getting dark soon."

She took several more photographs of the tower from the clearing and then they set off down the track they had followed. As they reached the trees, Philip pointed.

"There's the incumbent, waiting for us trespassers to leave."

She looked up and saw the white shape of the owl perched high up in some branches. It turned its flat white face to them, huge round eye sockets staring blindly. "Mama always said owls were bad luck," Anna said. She turned to get a last look at the Hunter's Tower.

It stood in its clearing, ancient and yet formidable. She remembered Candida's feeling that it was a fairy-tale place. If so, it belonged to a world before Disney, when fairy tales were also tales of blood and darkness.

She felt Philip's strong hands pushing at her back. "Come on," he growled. "Let's go."

They Did Not get back to Saló until darkfall. They were both cold and hungry. They walked along the glittering *lúngolàgo* among the crowds of elegantly dressed people doing the evening promenade. Pleasure boats at mooring bobbed gently on the dark water of the lake. The icy evening air smelled of good food, and music spilled out of café doorways. Saló reminded Anna of Vail, with its designer boutiques and fur shops, its general air of rich people at play. They bought slabs of pizza, redolent of oregano and somehow very different from the American version, and ate them as they walked toward the Majestic. As always, she was half-amused, half-impressed by the pains Italians took to dress up for an evening stroll, the women's gleaming hair vying with their glossy furs, the men in sweeping coats slung over their shoulders, smoking cigars.

"They've got to be the most elegant people in Europe," she said to Philip.

"You only think that because you're a quarter-Italian." He smiled.

"I'm a quarter-Latvian, too," she reminded him, thinking of those infinitely shabbier and poorer-looking crowds in Riga.

"And half-Irish," he said with a groan. "Oy vey. What a mixture."

"Irish hot pot," she said contentedly, licking sauce from her fingers. "I'm proud of myself."

They walked into the foyer of their hotel, arm in arm, laughing. The clerk leaned over the mahogany counter.

"Signor Westward? There has come a fax for you, sir."

Philip took the sheet of paper and read it as they walked to the elevator. Assuming it was business, Anna showed little interest.

Then she saw that his face had changed. All the expression had gone out of it, and he was suddenly pale.

"What is it?" she asked in alarm. "Bad news?"

"It's from my lawyers in New York," he said. "They think they're on the track of Joseph Krasnowsky."

NEW YORK

The streets of New York were still gay with Christmas decorations, although the sidewalks were filthy with trash and the shops were already holding their New Year sales. It was cold and windy, the temperature hovering around freezing, gusts blowing litter and lifting skirts.

The lawyers' offices were on Lexington and 50th, not far from Philip's apartment, and they had elected to walk. Anna was silent and tense, oblivious to the roar of traffic and the endless honking of horns. Philip, too, seemed preoccupied, and said little on the way.

The building, between Third and Lexington, was in the process of renovation, clad in scaffolding and protective nets. Large red warning signs advised caution and disclaimed responsibility for accidents. They took the elevator up to the fourteenth floor. The muffled groan of drills and rattle of machinery percolated through into the old-style elegance of the lawyers' offices.

The secretary who greeted them at the reception desk apologized for the state of the building. "We're trying to work through the renovations," she said. "It's not easy. Please excuse the mess and noise." She pointed them through to a waiting room.

Anna sat holding on to Philip's hand, taking in nothing of her surroundings. She had seldom felt so taut in her life. The end of their search might be in sight. The answer to the mysteries.

After a few minutes, the secretary came in with a smile.

"Mr. Lefkowitz is ready for you now."

"Come in, come in," he greeted them at the doorway of his sanctum. They had already met Lefkowitz briefly, two days earlier, at a preliminary meeting arranged at Philip's lawyers' offices. He was in his mid-fifties, a short, tubby man in a dark suit with a watch chain stretched across his ample paunch. His face was kindly, with stick-out pink ears and intelligent eyes glinting behind gold-rimmed spectacles. He exuded, and probably cultivated, an aura of old-fashioned dependability.

It was emphasized now by the Dickensian atmosphere of his office. The furniture was upholstered in red leather, the walls lined from floor to ceiling with law books. He saw Anna glancing at the impressive collection of tomes.

"Those books represent over seventy years of law practice, Miss Kelly. My grandfather started this firm in 1917. My own son graduates from Harvard Law School next year. He'll be joining us then." While he was talking, he was studying Anna with minute attention, the clever eyes darting across her face, her hands, her figure. He had studied her in the same way at their first meeting. "Can I offer you coffee? No? Then we'll get down to business. Sit, sit. Be comfortable."

They sank into the red leather, which was uncomfortably hard and slippery, while Lefkowitz gathered a folder from his desk. He came to sit opposite them, spreading the folder on the limited space of his lap.

"I read the diary. It's fascinating. Extremely fascinating. A unique document."

Anna nodded. At their first meeting, they had given him the translation of Candida's diary. "That represents the only credentials we have, Mr. Lefkowitz. I'm relieved to see that you're impressed by it."

"Oh, I'm extremely impressed, I assure you. It partly solves a mystery I've been wondering about for thirty years. And don't worry about your credentials. I've had time to check you both out pretty thoroughly." He smiled innocently at them. "First thing I've got to say is that I can't violate any of our clients' confidentialities, past or present. You understand that, I'm sure?"

They both nodded.

"However, I'm pleased to cooperate fully with your inquiry insofar as I can. By which I mean freely disclosing information which is public in any case, but which would cost *your* lawyers a lot of time, and *you* a lot of money to dig up. That kind of information I am happy to give you. There are various reasons for that. The diary is one. I will come to some others later on." He smiled. "Are either of you familiar with the laws governing inheritance in the state of New York? No? Okay. Don't worry. I just won't bother going into the technicalities of everything that happened. I'll stick to the plain facts."

"That suits us fine, Mr. Lefkowitz," Anna said.

"Good." His eyes made another intent inventory of her, bright as a fox's behind the gold-rimmed glasses. "I knew the Krasnowskys. I was just a boy at the time, but I remember. Oh, yes. I remember Justine and Alexander well. They were clients of my father's. They attended the same *shul*. As a matter of fact, it's the same *shul* I go to now, the Temple Emanu-El, on Fifth Avenue. My father had been their lawyer since they arrived in America with their son in 1917, the same year he founded this firm. They were wealthy people. They managed to get some of their money out with them. Not all, but enough to be comfortably off. They came to my father for two reasons. One, he was a Jew, and two, he spoke fluent Russian. None of those wealthy Jews from Latvia or Lithuania spoke Yiddish, you know. It was always Russian. Russian or French. That's how they got those names, Justine and Alexander. French and Russian, you see." He smiled, and Anna nodded. "They were descendants of Moshe Krasnowsky, a famous Riga rabbi, did you know that?"

"No," Anna said.

"You ought to check it out. It's interesting. His name's in the *Encyclopaedia Judaica*. A great Talmudic scholar. The Krasnowskys were a very interesting family all round. Alexander was a partner in the Krasnowsky bank. That was a family-run, private merchant bank which had extensive dealings with imperial Germany up until World War I. Alexander emigrated to America partly because of the Bolshevik Revolution, partly to get away from anti-Semitic persecution. It was a good move. Most of the other members of the Krasnowsky family died in the

Holocaust." Lefkowitz gave a little dry cough behind his hand. "My father and I checked that out ourselves after the war. When he got here in 1917, Alexander established connections with some New York banks, principally private Jewish foundations. Not in any active capacity, you understand. As an investor. Joseph, the son, was born just before they left Latvia. They brought him to America as a baby. You know anything about him apart from what's in the diary?"

"We know about his career as a journalist," Anna said. "He was a correspondent for *The New York Times*."

"That's correct. He was a socialist." He smiled at her surprise. "It was quite fashionable to be a little pink in the forties. Joseph just took it a trifle further than most young men. To the extent of volunteering to go fight the Nazis long before Pearl Harbor. I only met him a couple of times, but he made quite an impression. He wasn't what you would call handsome in any conventional way. He was dark, very intense, with quite a presence. He got that from his mother, of course." He paused, his eyes on Anna. "You've never seen any pictures of the Krasnowskys?"

"Nothing at all," Anna said.

"I think maybe you should." He delved into the folder. "I brought this. It's from my father's photograph albums."

The old black-and-white photograph showed a group of some twenty people, apparently at a picnic among trees. They wore the fashions of the 1930s, the women in long skirts, the men in hats and waist-coats. Lefkowitz's forefinger traced the figures. "My mother and father. The little girl is my elder sister. I wasn't born yet. The man with the beard is Alexander Krasnowsky. The boy next to him is Joseph."

Anna leaned forward intently. The father was a burly bear of a man, a dark beard covering half his face. The boy next to him, who looked around sixteen, was a slighter figure. He stood awkwardly next to his father, his weight thrown on one leg, his face turned away from the camera, showing an angular, adolescent profile. She stared hungrily at the bony line of the cheek and jaw. "It doesn't show him properly," she complained.

Lefkowitz nodded in sympathy. "It's the only picture I could find which showed any of the Krasnowskys. I'm sorry." His finger moved on. "This is Justine."

The women were all grouped together, sitting on a bank with their stockinged calves neatly crossed. The woman Lefkowitz pointed to was the only one not wearing a hat; it lay on her lap, and she was smiling full-face into the camera. Anna studied the dark eyes and hair for a moment before it started to sink in.

"She looks a bit like my mother," she said hesitantly.

"She looks extraordinarily like *you*," Philip said, his voice strange. "May I?" He took the photograph from the lawyer and studied it closely. "My God," he said after a moment. "It's exactly you!"

She studied it in her turn and felt her skin crawl. The face was tiny, but the quality of the old photograph was needle sharp. And Philip was right. Although there were strong elements of her mother's face, there were even stronger traces of her own. That woman sitting there in the warmth of a sixty-year-old summer could be her. Her abundant hair, her dark Gypsy eyes, her full mouth. It was like a tiny, dark mirror.

She looked up to see Philip staring at her. A strange smile was playing on his lips. "Well, well," he said softly. His eyes looked deep into hers. "It seems you're a Krasnowsky, after all."

Lefkowitz was watching them both with his bright eyes. "Interesting, isn't it? It struck me the moment I met Miss Kelly. That's one of the reasons I'm talking to you now. When I saw you the other day, I thought I was looking at a ghost. You have to understand, Justine Krasnowsky was a lovely woman. A truly lovely woman. I was only a boy when I knew her, but I have never forgotten that face. You even have something of her in your voice. She was very quiet-spoken. But she smiled a lot."

Her skin still prickling, a lump in her throat, Anna held the photograph out to him. He shook his head. "Take it to a photographer. Get it copied and enlarged. Then give it back to me."

"Thank you," she said huskily.

"I can't give you a date for that picture," he apologized. "I'd guess around 1935. If you like, I can try and get the names of some of the other people in that group. My aunts might remember. Shall I continue?"

"Please."

He laced his fingers across his ample stomach. "Joseph was around fifteen or sixteen then. He was already starting to break away. Alexander wanted him to go to college, take up a profession. But Joseph wanted to be a writer. He wanted to change the world. Not an uncommon ambition in young men, but in his case, you almost believed he could accomplish it. He was a strong character. A remarkable boy. He did go to college, but only for a couple of years. He was too interested in the outside world for academe. He wasn't your typical rich kid." Lefkowitz smiled. "He became what used to be called a Bohemian. He associated with writers, artists, revolutionaries. Relations with his father were not optimal. He spent more time editing the college magazine than sitting in lectures. Even that wasn't enough. The world was about to go up in flames, and Joseph wanted to be there with his typewriter. He managed to talk *The New York Times*'s foreign editor into accrediting him as a foreign correspondent. Then he took off for Europe. Alexander was furious, Justine was worried sick, but Joseph was not the sort of boy you could hold back." He looked up at Anna's engrossed face. "You interested in literature, Miss Kelly?"

"To an extent."

"On his trips to Europe, Joseph apparently met some of the most prominent writers of the time—James Joyce in Switzerland, Ezra Pound in Italy, Ernest Hemingway in Spain, and T. S. Eliot in London. Those names familiar to you?"

"Of course."

"By that stage, Joseph knew what the Nazis were planning for the Jews of Europe. He tried to convince other people, but nobody would believe him. Well, it was incredible, wasn't it? Persecution was one thing. Jews were used to that. Mass extermination was another. The articles Joseph wrote just seemed too fanciful, too much like horror comics. Is this long story getting wearisome?"

"I couldn't be more interested," Anna said. "It's fascinating, Mr. Lefkowitz. Please don't stop."

"Matter of fact, there isn't much more to tell. Not from that period, anyhow. Joseph volunteered to go fight in Europe with the British, as you know. He was captured in Africa and sent to Italy. He escaped from prisoner-of-war camp there in 1943. And then he effectively vanished off the face of the earth." He tapped the translation they'd given him. "This diary explains in part what happened to him then. The information your mother brought back from Russia hints at the rest of it. I'm very grateful to you for bringing this material to me. It means a lot." He gave his little dry cough again. "Let's go back to 1943. When Joseph disappeared, Justine and Alexander were sick with grief. They spent the rest of the war trying to get information about their son. They never got any." He glanced out of the window at the flapping sheet of canvas pinned to the scaffolding. "Alexander and Justine both died in an accident in New Jersey shortly before VE Day. Their car hit a chemical tanker, which exploded. They were both incinerated. They're buried in a beautiful plot in Jersey City. You can see the Statue of Liberty from their grave." His eyes returned to them. "That's incidental now. What's important, from the legal point of view, is that before he died, Alexander tied up his estate in a number of trust funds in his son's name. Waiting, you see, for Joseph to come home from Europe."

"But Joseph never came home," Philip said quietly.

"Oh, yes," Lefkowitz said with an odd smile. "Joseph came home. It took some time. But he came home in the end."

Anna sat up with a jolt. "Joseph came back to *America?*"

"Yes." He studied them both, apparently taking some dry amusement from their expressions.

"In what year?" Anna demanded.

"In 1960."

"Did you meet him?" Philip asked sharply.

"No. I was away at college, studying for my final law exams. Joseph came to see my father, here in this office. My father was the chief administrator of the trusts Alexander had set up in 1943 and 1944."

"And Joseph came to claim his inheritance?" Philip asked in the same brusque tone.

Lefkowitz inclined his head. "Yes. He was the sole beneficiary of the trusts."

"So the estate was passed over to Joseph?"

"That's correct. It amounted to quite a considerable sum by then. Enough to make the boy a millionaire."

"The *boy?*" Anna echoed.

"I'm sorry. I always think of Joseph as a boy. But you're right. He was a man in his forties by then. And he had suffered greatly. He was badly scarred in the face, although he'd had plastic surgery, and he was no longer the fiery young Bohemian."

"But it *was* Joseph?" Philip put in.

"My father had no doubt about it. Joseph had some papers to prove his identity, but I think my father was able to recognize him at once, despite the changes."

"Would it be possible to speak to your father?" Philip asked.

Lefkowitz shook his head. "Unfortunately, my father died that same year. Just a few months after Joseph got back. A heart attack."

Philip nodded, his eyes never leaving the lawyer's face. "What explanation did Joseph give for his long absence, Mr. Lefkowitz?"

"That I don't know. But the information you have given me makes that clear. As I told you, I wasn't in the office at the time, and all I know of the situation, apart from this—" He patted the folder. "—comes from a couple of conversations I had with my father before he died. I remember him telling me about the transmission of the estate, the problems he'd had with taxes and so forth. He was very moved by Joseph's return. Very moved. It overwhelmed him. After all, he'd given Joseph up for dead years ago. And Joseph had returned from the dead." He glanced from Philip's face to Anna's. "Interesting story, isn't it?"

"Mr. Lefkowitz," Anna said urgently, "please—where is Joseph Krasnowsky now?"

Lefkowitz shook his head. "That's the kind of client confidentiality I am unable to violate, Miss Kelly."

"But that's why we came to you!" she exclaimed.

"I'm sorry," he repeated. "That is where I am going to stop. My story ends right there."

"At least tell us—is he still alive?" she pressed.

"This firm stopped representing the Krasnowsky family in 1960. I can't give you any more information than I've already given you." Polite but firm, he resisted any further attempts at interrogation.

Her mind whirling, her nerves taut with frustration, Anna stood, clutching the old photograph he had given her. "Mr. Lefkowitz," she said, her voice shaking, "this leaves us exactly where we were!"

"Not exactly," he said with a small, secret smile. "The records of the Krasnowsky trust funds are accessible to scrutiny. There's a trail, Miss Kelly. There's a trail." He passed a folder over to Philip, who took it with a nod of thanks.

She looked at Philip. Hope began to dawn in her heart. "You mean—" she began, but the lawyer was already walking away. Philip reached for her hand. Trusting him, she took it.

Lefkowitz's office had two doors, so that clients need never meet in the waiting rooms. He escorted them to the second door, which opened onto a small lobby. It, too, was lined from floor to ceiling with myriads of books. The lawyer paused for a moment.

"This is my private library. Material about the Holocaust."

Anna stared at the hundreds of book spines. "You've made quite a study."

"It's a unique topic. Not just from a humanitarian point of view. From a legal point of view, it was one of the greatest crimes in the history of humanity. The biggest, most savage robbery ever committed. Ten million persons systematically despoiled and massacred by a hundred thousand killer-robbers, producing loot of incalculable proportions: trillions of dollars in today's terms. Cash, shares, art, precious stones, and metals. Not to mention the huge amounts of real estate, factories, shops, and businesses that were confiscated." He smiled bleakly. "As a Jew, I am haunted. As a lawyer, I'm engaged. Not even one percent of all that was stolen was ever paid back, you know."

"There was nobody to claim it," Philip said.

"Exactly. The victims and their families, whole cities of people, had been murdered in the death camps. Gassed, poisoned, suffocated, shot, starved, crushed, frozen, tortured, hanged, worked to death. There were a pitiful few who came forward after the war, but they met insurmountable obstacles of callousness and bureaucracy. The overwhelming majority of the loot remained in the hands of the plunderers. In Swiss bank accounts, where nobody could touch it, not even the concerted might of the United States."

"Does that explain the Holocaust?" Anna asked in a low voice. "Murder for gain?"

"Nothing fully explains the Holocaust," he replied gently. "But gain? Yes. There was plenty of that. From Auschwitz and Lublin concentration camps alone, the Reich's main security agency, the RHSA, received some two hundred and fifty billion Reichsmarks in currency, precious stones, and metals, the personal property of Jews who passed through on their way to death. I leave it to you to imagine how much was confiscated before it came to that."

He ushered them to the door, a portly little man with twinkling eyes and a razor mind. At the door he shook them both by the hand.

"I do hope you find him," he said. "After all, you know, it was a breathtaking achievement."

"What achievement?" Anna asked.

"Joseph Krasnowsky's return from the dead," he said. "Breathtaking."

"Are You Sure that'll be enough to track him down?" she asked Philip restlessly. "After all, it was more than thirty years ago."

"All we can do is hope." Philip shrugged. "My lawyers will do their best to see if there really is a trail, as Lefkowitz says. Possess your soul in patience for a while."

"I feel I'm so close to him. So close." She was standing at the window, staring at the spectacular view over the U.N. gardens and the sweep of the East River.

Philip's apartment was severely elegant, the orderly domain of an orderly mind. The furniture was a mixture of antique and modern. The paintings, set against cream walls, were all abstracts, many in sober tones of gray. It was a beautiful apartment, filled with light from the huge windows that took full advantage of the fifteenth-floor views; but there was also something taut about the apartment, something strict. It had a definite feel of one side of Philip, masculine and uncompromising. But it did not reflect the other sides she had come to know, the tenderness and sensuality of her dark lover.

She went on. "That photograph Lefkowitz gave me—I can't tell you how that makes me feel. Like there's a whole side of me waiting to be discovered." Her eyes were not taking in the beautiful view, but were fixed on an internal landscape, a family she had never known.

"Anna," he said quietly, "keep a tight grip on your emotions. We're nearly there. Don't let this get out of hand."

"How can I keep a grip?" She turned fretfully to face him. "This thing is driving me crazy. It never leaves my thoughts. I dream about it, Philip." She reached for him. "You're the only thing that keeps me sane."

He took her in his arms, and she held on to his rocklike strength.

She needed him so much. She was so much in his power. Since she'd found the diary in her mother's safe in Vail, it was Philip who had been running the investigation. He had taken over, and she had somehow slipped into second place, too absorbed in her own emotions to make the running anymore. Between her new preoccupations about her relationship to Joseph Krasnowsky, her concerns about her mother and Evelyn, and her own overwhelming passion for Philip, she had been grateful to let him do it all: make the contacts, the calls, the inquiries, the arrangements.

She, the investigative journalist who had once been so much in control of her life, was now glad to hand the reins over to her lover.

He released her at last and smiled down at her. "It's time for a drink. Want to go out?"

She shook her head. "I'm too tense. I keep thinking about what Lefkowitz said. Is it true all the treasure plundered from the Jews just disappeared?"

"It seems to be true." He nodded.

"But what happened to it all? I mean, all those Nazis were caught and tried, weren't they? Couldn't anyone get it back?"

"It wasn't that easy," he said. "They didn't leave the spoils lying around."

"So where did it go?"

"Like Lefkowitz said, mostly into Swiss banks. Some was destroyed during the war. A certain amount, maybe a few truckloads, was probably looted by Allied servicemen who stumbled over what was still in transit, or hidden in mines, or caves, or at the bottom of lakes in the occupied territories." He moved to the liquor cabinet and started making a small pitcher of martinis. "Immense sums may have been smuggled to Latin America in diplomatic bags and submarines by the top Nazis who got through the net, to finance their exile. It's hard to substantiate that kind of claim."

"But how could they have moved that kind of wealth around without being traced?" she demanded.

"Don't forget"—he shrugged—"the Nazis occupied most of Europe for years. The vast majority was simply moved to Switzerland and other neutral countries long before the war ended, and hidden in the banking system." He poured two martinis and passed her one. "The Swiss banks, in particular, were sacrosanct in those days. Cordell Hull, who was Secretary of State then, did his damnedest to get them to open their books. He never succeeded. The State Department couldn't even get back the half-billion dollars deposited by Jews who were later exterminated in the death camps. The Swiss simply kept it."

"You mean it's all still in Switzerland?" she asked incredulously.

Philip smiled dryly. "I doubt it. I think the people who put it there quietly went and got it back a couple of years after the war ended."

"That's disgusting!"

"Yes."

"So that's what Lefkowitz was talking about?"

"Presumably."

She was holding her martini glass, the cocktail untouched. Her eyes were fixed on Philip intently. "How do you know about all of this, Philip?"

"I'm interested. Like Lefkowitz."

"But you're not a Jew."

"No."

"So why are you so interested in the Nazis? How come you're so knowledgeable about the Holocaust?"

He did not answer, and she held the martini glass up to the light, studying the oily shimmer of the alcohol in the cone of glass. "Philip, you're hiding something from me," she said. She put the glass down and walked to him, her face very serious. "Please. Tell me the truth."

"I've told you the truth," he said quietly, the beautiful face as impassive as granite, his deep blue eyes holding hers unwaveringly.

"No," she said. "You've been lying to me. You've lied to me from the start."

"What have I lied about?"

"I don't know." She was as taut as a bow. "But I've sensed it. There's something off-kilter. Your interests are not the same as mine or my mother's. We're interested in missing Americans. You're obsessed with Nazis. You're looking for something else."

"I'm looking for the same thing, Anna."

"No. You've got your own agenda. Why don't you tell me what it is?"

Philip turned away from her and walked to a marble pedestal that supported a bronze woman's head, the eyes closed in sleep. Or death. He drew his fingertips down the bronze cheek, his back turned to Anna. She could almost sense him turning something over in his mind, as though he were debating telling her the truth.

Or another lie.

She waited, feeling as though a steel spring were coiled inside her.

But when he turned to face her again, his face was expressionless. "You're getting overwrought about this, Anna. You have no cause to suspect me."

Her eyes filled with tears, and she turned to leave the room.

"Anna!" He came after her and grasped her arm, pulling her round to face him. "Why don't you believe me?"

"Because I know you're lying," she said sharply. "I've been your lover for four months now, Philip. I can tell when you're hiding things from me."

He bent to kiss her. "No!" she exclaimed. She tried to fight away from him, but he was too strong. His lips silenced her. Then he picked her up in his arms and carried her to the bedroom.

They made love with curtains open on a pale New York sky, sex such as she had never known before, a desperate search for comfort that had nothing to do with desire or arousal. He understood exactly what she wanted and gave it to her. After her shuddering climax, she wept, temporarily released from the unbearable tension.

"I'm sorry," she said tearfully. "Sorry I doubted you, Philip. I don't know what's happening to me."

She Flew Down to Colorado the next day.

It was the height of the season in Vail. A glorious white bounty of snow had carpeted the slopes; Vail Mountain had turned into a gigantic snow tiger, flanks striped with ribbons of white among the trees. The village was crowded to capacity and in a festive mood. The spectacular Christmas tree at the top of Bridge Street was still decorated with fairy lights, and wreaths and garlands were strung prettily along the buildings.

Carr Memorial Hospital, too, greeted her with decorations and Christmas trees. Children of the Valley schools had made posters for the patients, bright splashes of color on the pale cream walls, and holly wreaths hung on many doors.

Her mother was sitting up in bed, music playing at her side, when Anna came into the room. Anna felt her heart contract as she saw the joy animate her mother's face. Kate lifted her arms clumsily, and Anna embraced her tightly, her eyes flooding with tears.

"Anna," she whispered. "Anna . . ."

"Did you miss me?" Anna asked thickly.

"Yes . . ."

She drew back at last, wiping her wet eyes. "I brought you some things," she said, rummaging in her bag. "A silver bracelet I bought in

Milan, a cashmere cardigan from London, a whole slew of books, and ... oh, masses of things." She laughed a little shakily. "Even this. A bottle of heather honey from Great Law."

She watched her mother take the bottle, her fingers still inexpert. It slipped, and she picked it up again, holding it to the light. A smile spread across her mouth. "Evelyn ... " She turned her eyes to Anna inquiringly.

Anna swallowed painfully. "She's not very well, Mama. She looks wonderful, and she's as formidable as ever. But she's sick." She touched her mother's hand. "She's dying, Mama."

Her mother's eyes were suddenly wet. "Must go ... to her," she whispered.

"Yes, Mama. As soon as you're up and about, we'll both go to her."

"Needs me."

"Yes. She needs you."

"Pain ... ?"

"Evelyn? They're giving her drugs. A nurse spends the nights with her. They promised me they wouldn't let her suffer."

"So sad. Evelyn sick ... me here."

"You'll be able to travel soon," Anna promised. "Then we'll go and be with her."

It was so wonderful to see her mother's face alive again, animated by emotions and intelligence after so long as a mask. Anna shuddered now as she remembered her mother, strapped to that motorized steel bed, hooked up to machines that looked as though they were preying on her body, rather than giving her life.

The short crop of dark hair that had now grown in gave her a girlish look, as though the attack had somehow given her back her youth. Her speech was still uncertain and seldom rose above a whisper, but Anna knew that the essence of her mother's mind had miraculously survived undamaged. With physiotherapy, her coordination was improving dramatically, too. Anna watched as she absently took the heavy silver bracelet Anna had given her and fitted it on her wrist. "Worried about you, Anna ... "

"Worried about *me*?" Anna smiled. "Why?"

"Take care."

"Don't worry about me. Just concentrate on yourself, Mama. You're getting so much better. Every day you get better."

Her mother held up her wrist, the silver bangle gleaming. She smiled a little sadly at Anna. "Beautiful. Thank you."

Anna poured a glass of orange juice from the jug on the nightstand and passed it to her mother. "Mama," she said seriously, "we might be very close to finding Joseph Krasnowsky."

"Joseph . . . ?" Anna saw the strange expression flit across her mother's face.

"You still don't remember?" she pressed, searching her mother's eyes.

"No."

"You spent so long looking for him. Don't you remember finding the diary? Going to Russia? All your research trips?"

Her mother shook her head, frowning unhappily. "Nothing . . . "

"It'll come back." She stroked her mother's hand soothingly. "Don't worry about it."

"Joseph . . . " She turned her face to the window, her large, dark eyes staring at the snowy mountain peaks. She repeated the name quietly several times more. Anna held her breath, praying. Ram Singh had warned her there might be substantial gaps—he called them lacunae—in her mother's memory, and he had been right.

Mercifully, she seemed to remember nothing of the attack itself. So far they had let her believe she was here because of a car crash. But she seemed also to have forgotten everything connected with her researches into the fate of Joseph. Ram Singh had asked her not to press her mother in any way, nor to make any sort of fuss about these gaps of memory. Anna had not shown her Lefkowitz's photograph or brought up any of the other information he had given them. When her mother turned to her again, shaking her head in bewilderment, Anna smiled reassuringly.

"Don't worry, Mama. It's not important."

"Can't remember anything . . . Russia . . . Joseph."

"Hush. It'll come back to you in time."

"I went . . . Russia?"

"Yes, Mama."

"Sure?"

"Sure."

"But *why*?"

She laughed. "Good question. Maybe you'll come up with the

answer yourself one of these days. There'll be plenty of time to fill in the gaps when you're stronger, I promise. Want to try on the cardigan?"

The cashmere cardigan had cost her almost three hundred English pounds in London, but it suited her mother beautifully. She snuggled into it blissfully, pulling the rolled collar around her throat. "Gorgeous."

"I'm glad you like it."

"Evelyn . . . loves cashmere."

"I know." She took the envelope out of her bag. "She gave me this letter for you. Would you like me to read it to you?"

She shook her head. "No thanks. Can read myself . . . slow, but prefer it." She took the letter in her hands. "Poor Evelyn. So much love. No way to show it."

Anna nodded. "I felt I got closer to her than I've ever been. She's always overawed me, you know. This time . . . she didn't hold back so much."

There was a tap at the door, and Constanze Graf stepped in. "Am I interrupting?"

"No." Anna smiled. "Come in, Connie."

Connie sat on the other side of Kate and took her hand. Kate smiled at her warmly. "Managing . . . without me?"

"No," Connie said. "Not managing without you."

"Back . . . soon as I can."

"I know you'll be back. You're the wonder kid."

The three women sat talking in the sunlit room for another hour until the physiotherapist arrived to supervise Kate's daily routine in the gymnasium.

"We'll go now," Anna said, standing up preparatory to leaving.

"No," her mother said. "Wait. Something to show you."

The physiotherapist, smiling, put a walking frame next to the bed and helped Kate to sit up and then stand. Grasping the handles of the frame in her fingers, Kate nodded. The physiotherapist stepped back. An expression of intense concentration appeared in Kate's face. Slowly, she moved one foot forward, shifted her weight, moved the other foot. Then she lifted the aluminum frame and swung it forward. She had taken a step.

Anna was astounded. "You can walk!"

"Not exactly . . . walk," her mother said ruefully. "Shuffle."

"But that's wonderful!" She turned to the physiotherapist. "It's a miracle."

"Mrs. Kelly is a very determined person." The young woman smiled. "The kind of patient we like best. She works her own miracles."

When her mother had gone to physiotherapy, Anna walked out with Constanze. The older woman looked splendid in a check suit, pearls setting off her naturally pale skin coloring.

"She's always worked her own miracles," she said to Anna. "Your mother is an extraordinary woman."

"I know." Anna smiled.

"Campbell Brinkman came to see her while you were away in Europe."

"Did he?" She glanced at Constanze. "How did she react?"

"Pleased to see him."

"No more than that?"

"I get the impression that her lapses of memory cover some of her relationship with Campbell."

"You mean she's forgotten him?"

"Not exactly. More like she remembers him as a friend, rather than as a lover."

"That must be hard for him to take," Anna said thoughtfully, remembering Campbell's dark misery.

"Poetic justice," Constanze said in her blunt way. "He had no faith she would ever recover from the coma. He turned his back on her then. She's turning her back on him now."

"Poor Campbell."

"He's a selfish playboy," Constanze said pitilessly. "He was no good for her. He underestimated her right from the start. She deserves better."

Anna winced at the judgment. But she recognized its truth. Her mother *did* deserve better than Campbell. "Poor guy."

"She deserved better from me, too," Constanze said quietly. "I also underestimated her. I thought she was crazy. I should have known better."

"It did sound crazy," Anna admitted. "And she was so secretive. You couldn't have known."

"I should have known better," Constanze repeated. "I won't let her down again. How close are you to finding this man?"

"We might be very close," Anna replied. She'd passed Constanze a copy of the translation of the diary before Christmas. Now she gave her a brief account of the search, leaving out the more personal details. "I just hope Joseph Krasnowsky is still alive," she concluded. "It's been so long."

"Why?"

"Why?" she echoed. "Well, for one thing, I hope finding him will do wonders for my mother. Help her put herself back together again."

"What if it has the opposite effect?"

"But she was looking for him for so long, Connie. An obsession that deep can't just have vanished. This is something she *needs* to know."

"And you? Do you need to know it, too?"

"Oh, Connie . . . "

They came to a stop near Gorsuch's, crowds of skiers moving around them. Constanze touched Anna's shoulder. "It's only a guess, you know—that this man might be her father. The tangled history, the family resemblances, all that could be no more than coincidence."

"Finding him is the only way to be sure." Anna smiled wryly. "He might even agree to a blood test."

"As you say." Constanze nodded, her cool gray eyes fixed on Anna's face. "If he's alive." She nodded toward Gorsuch's. "I need some new ski goggles."

❧

She Got The call from Drew McKenzie that afternoon, while she was reading through the diary again, her mind unquiet with shadowy, hazy images.

"Anna? Drew McKenzie here."

"Oh, hello, Mr. McKenzie. Any news?"

"More than we bargained for. Hear about Levêque?"

"No—what about him?"

"He killed himself in jail three days ago," he said heavily.

"Oh, no," she said in shock.

"Yeah. Hanged himself when nobody was looking. Got himself back on the front pages again."

Shocked, Anna had to sit down. She felt sick. "God, how horrible."

"It has nothing to do with you," he said forcefully. "Hear me? Nothing at all."

"If I hadn't done that interview—"

"Somebody else would have done it," he cut through brusquely. "I was the one who put you onto him, remember? If it hadn't been you, it would have been somebody else. The man was dead in the water, morally, ethically, and in every other sense. You just had the bad or good luck to be on the spot."

"It's not that simple, Mr. McKenzie—"

"Sure it is. And none of it would ever have happened if he hadn't murdered his patients, Anna. If he hadn't been a monster."

Suddenly she remembered his parting words to her. *See you in Purgatory.*

Levêque had been an evil man. And yet he had also been a great surgeon. He had saved lives. By his lights, he had even acted ethically.

What right had she had to judge him? He was the healer, not she. He was the man with the knife. He'd been able to justify what he did. The benefit of hundreds against the extinction of a few.

Extinction? He had murdered *children,* she told herself. He had been a child-killer. She'd told him to his face it was one of the foulest crimes she could think of.

But the ethics of the case were a dark tangle, and the deeper in she got, the more entangled in thorns she became. And no rationalizing could change the fact that until a short while ago, André Levêque had been *alive.* And now he was dead. And she was implicated in his death.

She said nothing, but a dark burden had descended on her.

"You still there?" McKenzie demanded.

"Yes," she said.

"Believe me," he said forcefully, "the world's a better place without him."

"Is it? What about his patients? What about his clinic in Haiti?"

"There are other doctors in the world."

"Not like Levêque."

"Oh, come on," McKenzie snorted.

"He was brilliant. And now he's gone, and we're to blame."

"Jesus, get your priorities straight, kid! You ever hear of the

Hippocratic oath? Either a man's a healer or he's a killer. He can't be both. Nobody can play God, sitting up there on some golden throne deciding who lives and who dies!"

"Isn't that exactly what we did?"

"We did our job, which was to tell the truth. Never forget that, Anna." The editor's voice was grim. "We don't have any other function in life. We're not crusaders, we're not avenging angels. We just tell the truth. We didn't kill Levêque. The truth killed him. Now, forget him. I got that other information you wanted."

"Yes?" she said numbly, staring out of the window.

"We've had the Casper city records checked, and the whole of Natrona County, too. No Philip Westward was born there in the last fifty years. In fact, the name isn't on the registers in any form. There's no family called Westward in those parts."

"Are you sure?" she gasped.

"No record of any Philip Westward in the Rangers, or any other Army outfit, either. Philip Westward Associates checks out okay. In fact, very healthy. They have a good reputation, and Westward himself is reputed to be a rich man. But prior to founding the firm in 1978, he doesn't seem to have existed. He arrived in New York fully fledged, but nobody knows where he came from. I can ask the researchers to dig deeper if you really want, but I'll need to know what this is all about."

"No," she said slowly. "It's all right. Thank you, Mr. McKenzie."

"Now that your mother's getting better, when can we expect to see you back in Miami?" Drew demanded. She closed her eyes, letting his tirade of demands and entreaties wash over her.

She sat by the telephone, immobile, for a long while after McKenzie had hung up. She felt numb all over, numb to her soul, as though two separate blows had slammed into her heart, one after the other.

A cry of anguish rose in her heart.

Philip.

He had lied to her about the place of his birth. On top of what she now recognized as weeks of half-formed doubts, that was enough to shake her to her foundations.

There were a hundred explanations. Maybe he'd changed his name because his mother had remarried. Maybe his mother had never been married to his father in the first place. Maybe there had been some computer error, maybe some careless clerk hadn't done his job properly, maybe . . .

There were a hundred maybes, a hundred explanations to convince her that everything Philip Westward had ever told her was not just a gigantic lie.

Philip Called From New York the next day, Friday, saying he would be flying down to Eagle that evening. He promised he was bringing her some interesting information.

Anna went to meet him. As she waited in the airport, she was shivering, but not from the cold.

She watched the bright landing lights of the Beechcraft approach over the mountains. She held her breath as the white plane came down on the illuminated runway. It swung round and taxied toward the building. Philip's tall figure emerged, and he waved to Paul the pilot as he taxied back toward the runway, evidently going back to New York for the weekend.

She was waiting for him at the door as he arrived, lugging a heavy bag. She turned her face aside as he bent to kiss her, so that his lips touched her cold cheek. Philip examined her closely. "What is it? Is something wrong?"

"Nothing." She forced a smile. "I'm just very cold."

"Well, let's get home then," he said in concern.

She was silent as she drove, concentrating on the road. Her knuckles were white on the wheel. She felt Philip's eyes on her and knew he was puzzled at her aloofness. "How's your mother?"

"Getting better."

"That's wonderful. I'm looking forward to seeing her."

"Yeah."

"What is it?" Philip asked again, his voice quiet. "What's happened? And don't tell me it's the cold. Out with it."

She forced herself to speak. "I got some bad news today."

"Oh?" His voice was even quieter. "What sort of bad news?"

"André Levêque. The surgeon I interviewed in Haiti."

"Yes?"

"He's dead. He committed suicide in prison."

Philip was silent. "I'm very sorry," he said at last. "Are you blaming yourself?"

"Yes," she said shortly.

Unlike McKenzie, Philip made no attempt to rationalize her part in Levêque's downfall. He spoke little after that.

The Potato Patch apartment was warm and cozy, and she had left a shoulder of lamb baking slowly in the oven, which made the place smell like home.

"I'm sorry about Levêque," Philip said. He reached for her again, wanting to embrace her, but she turned away, her face set.

"I'll get the dinner ready while you unpack," she said, and went to the kitchen before he could reply. She was as taut as a steel spring.

She busied herself with preparing the meal. Her mouth was a grim line. Once he had eaten, she intended to confront him with what Drew McKenzie had told her. She wanted an explanation. She wanted explanations not only about that, but about everything else, too. About who he was. About what he wanted from her.

About what he really felt.

Her falling in love with him had been carefully planned. She was sure of that now. It had happened because Philip Westward had intended it to happen. All those wonderful romantic moments. Buying her the diamonds. Making her his lover. It had all had a purpose. It had all been part of a coldly laid plan, and she had been too stupid and too emotional to see it.

She had walked into the trap, just as she had walked into Carl Beck's trap at Gypsum. Her eyes had been open, but she had seen nothing. Suspected nothing.

He had used sex to blind her. That hurt worst of all. Looking back, she could remember occasions when she'd started asking pointed questions and he'd used sex to distract her, taking her to bed, using his marvelous body to drug her into acquiescence.

She wanted explanations for all that. Damn him, she wanted the truth for once. She'd never loved anyone the way she'd loved Philip, and if he had betrayed her, she would never hate anyone as intensely, either.

Anna's hands were shaking as she hacked at the meat, cutting it into ragged lumps, not caring that she was ruining the meal she had so carefully prepared. Gobbets of fat and flesh spattered as she sawed.

"I've got something for you."

She turned to face Philip, clutching the knife. He was standing in the doorway, wearing a tartan shirt and denims. His chin was dark with a shadow of beard, his eyes serious. So beautiful it made her heart feel as though it would break. He was holding a slim book in his hands. He held it out to her. "Look."

Anna wiped her hands and took it. It was an expensive-looking production. She looked uncomprehendingly at the cover photograph, which showed a handsome red-black-and-white snake, coiled fatly on sand, the rattle on its tail lifted in warning. The title was *Rattlesnakes of the Sonoran Desert*, by James Kaplan.

"What is this?" she asked him, frowning.

He wore an odd smile, his eyes burning darkly. "It's Joseph Krasnowsky."

"What?" she asked sharply.

"Lefkowitz was right. There was a trail. It led straight to him."

She opened the book stupidly, staring at handsome color plates of snakes, the dense, scholarly text full of Latin words. "But this—?"

"It's him. Joseph Krasnowsky. He changed his name to James Kaplan in 1963."

She was suddenly weak, drums pounding in her ears, the room swaying. "Joseph?"

"Yes. Joseph."

"Where is he?"

Philip's strange smile widened. "New Mexico. He's been there for thirty years. Your mother went all the way to Moscow to find him, and the whole time he's been living in the next state, five hundred miles away." He looked into her blank face. "Do you understand what I'm saying? He's alive, Anna. We've found him."

Philip Left For New York again forty-eight hours later, on Sunday night. She drove him to Eagle, wondering when her feeling of being in a dream would ever lift. She could not seem to break out of this sense of unreality. The weekend had passed in a fog, almost without any kind of human contact between her and Philip. Only one thing had seemed real to her—that Joseph had been found.

They arrived at Eagle early and sat drinking coffee while they waited for the Beechcraft to arrive. Philip laid his warm hand over hers.

"I hope you snap out of this soon." He smiled. "You're starting to worry me."

"I'm fine," she said with a mechanical answering smile. "Don't worry about me."

"I am worrying. I've never seen you like this before."

"Maybe I'm in shock."

"You sure look like it."

He had been extraordinarily gentle with her all weekend, one of the very few periods they had spent together without making love. She hadn't even been able to bring herself to sleep in the same bed with him; pleading insomnia, she had slept in her mother's bed, leaving Philip alone. He'd accepted it with grace, though he must have been puzzled. She'd been glad. A lover's argument with Philip would have been more than she could have borne.

She'd never got around to confronting him with the lies he had told her. Suddenly, with Joseph found, the whole context had changed. For the first time since this whole thing had started, she could see her way forward. For the first time, she knew exactly what she had to do.

Philip had brought her Joseph Krasnowsky in a briefcase. He'd spent the weekend explaining all the complexities of the paper chase to her, as though it was some kind of intellectual puzzle he'd successfully solved.

She had listened with only a part of her mind. She'd already been burning to go. For months she had been hungry for information about Joseph Krasnowsky. But now, beside the knowledge that he had been found, everything else had become irrelevant. She no longer cared about what he had done in the long years gone by. She no longer cared about the past; it was the present that mattered to her, with a blazing intensity. The present, and seeing her grandfather in the flesh at last.

But she had forced herself to seem interested in the catalogue of information Philip so proudly laid before her.

Lefkowitz had pointed the way unerringly. Without his assistance, none of this would have been possible. Philip's lawyers had been able to use the information about the trust funds Alexander Krasnowsky had established to track down Joseph Krasnowsky's financial dealings over the years. It had been a winding trail, but it had never petered out, because just enough of it was on public record to tell them where *else* to look. It was the skeleton of a life.

They had been able to follow his move from New York to New

Mexico in the early 1960s. Thereafter, every major transaction had been registered somewhere, and it had simply been a matter of contacting enough data banks, of computers tapping into other computers.

Computers had tracked down an astonishing amount of data, from taxes paid to automobiles purchased. Other computers had ferreted out the change of name to James Kaplan, by deed poll, in 1963; his purchase of a large ranch called the San Andrés estate, near Alamogordo, in 1968; various acquisitions of neighboring land throughout the 1970s.

He had gone under his new name ever since; but not in complete silence. Over the years, as James Kaplan, he had published many articles in scientific journals, concentrating on desert reptiles. He had even contributed an article on antivenom to *Scientific American*. He had published two books on vipers in 1982 and 1987, and was considered an authority on the species *crotalus,* the rattlesnakes.

Yet other computers had revealed that Joseph Krasnowsky had never contacted the military authorities to change his status from Missing in Action. Like the change of name, it had been the action of a man who wanted isolation.

But they were going to interrupt that isolation.

"I'll make all the arrangements about New Mexico," he said. "Paul can fly us down to El Paso in the Beechcraft, and we can rent a car at the other end. I know a good hotel where we can make our headquarters. Okay?"

"Yes," she said, nodding.

"I'm sorry I can't be ready any sooner," he said apologetically. "I know how you must feel. You still look like a ghost. But I really do think we should do this together. You're going to need someone at your side, Anna."

"Yes," she said again. She eased her hand out from under his and drank the coffee, a thin and bitter brew.

"Just take it easy this week. Try and relax. Spend plenty of time with your mother. And," he added gently, "don't get your hopes up too high about him. He may not even agree to see us."

"I know."

"He changed his name, after all. That's a signal we should play this carefully."

"Yes."

He drained his cup. "Still upset about Levêque?"

She shrugged. "It's a horrible thing to have happened."

"Look," he said, speaking carefully, "I won't insult you by try-ing to talk you out of your feelings. Just remember that he was a bad man. He may have been a great surgeon once, but he had become corrupt. There's no corruption worse than a man playing God. You are not responsible for the evil in his soul, even if you were partly respon-sible for bringing him to justice. You understand what I'm saying?"

She heard the urgency in his voice and nodded.

"Remember, too, that you've probably saved the lives of other children he would have sacrificed. He would have gone on to commit even greater crimes. More innocent lives would have been lost."

She was staring through the plate glass at the heaps of snow that had been cleared off the runways. Philip didn't matter, she told herself. Not anymore. The pain would come, later, when the dreamlike feeling had lifted. For now, it was irrelevant. All the lies he had told her were irrelevant beside the single truth he had brought her this week-end. That Joseph was alive, at an address in New Mexico.

She had got where she was going to. Almost. There were just a few more steps on her journey, the journey her mother had started months ago and that fate had decreed she was to finish. Dealing with Philip came after that.

"I think this is Paul," she heard him say.

The bright lights came glowing in through the fog, unearthly for a while, like the arrival of some biblical heavenly chariot. Then the white Beechcraft materialized out of the clouds, prosaic and modern. They watched it as it made a perfect three-point touchdown, flaps lifting to slow it. It swung round, and the lights stabbed into her eyes blind-ingly as it started to taxi to the airport building.

They rose and went to the door. She was shivering again, as she had done waiting for him to arrive on Friday. He took her in his arms and held her so tight she felt crushed. She pressed her face to his shoulder, tears stealing from behind her shut lids.

"Please take care of yourself," he said urgently in her ear. "Don't brood on anything, okay?"

"I'll be fine."

He wiped the tears off her cheeks and kissed her mouth hard. "We'll be in New Mexico next weekend. Possess your soul in patience until then."

She nodded, speechless.

His fingers bit into her shoulders as he stared into her face. "Remember what I said—don't make any attempt to contact Joseph until we're down there together. No phone calls, no letters. No matter how tempted you are."

"I won't."

"Good."

He walked quickly out to the Beechcraft, carrying his bag. The plane was streaked with moisture from its descent through the clouds, the propellers still whirling. Paul had lowered the folding steps into the cabin and stood waiting for Philip, huddled into a mackinaw. The two men shook hands. Philip turned to look at Anna and waved. She waved back, her eyes blurred with tears.

You never said you loved me, she thought. *At least you spared me that.*

Then Philip was climbing up into the airplane. The pilot followed him. At the oval doorway he gave Anna a brief wave and pulled the steps up behind him. The door thumped shut.

She stood at the plate-glass window, immobile, and waited until the Beechcraft had accelerated down the runway and had lifted off over the mountains, its winking red and green lights glowing in the low cloud.

When it was gone, she turned and walked quickly to the AirAmerica ticket counter.

"But . . . Where Are you going?"

Anna took her mother's hand and stroked it gently. "There's something I have to do, Mama."

"What?"

"A man I have to see. When I've spoken to him, maybe I'll have some good news to bring you."

Her mother's dark eyes looked at her searchingly. "Good news?"

"I hope so. And I hope I won't be long. No more than a few days."

"Can't you tell me?"

Anna smiled tautly. "Not yet, Mama."

"Is it about . . . this man Joseph?"

"Yes, Mama."

She could see that her mother was troubled, grappling to form the words she wanted to say. "Anna . . . I'm worried about you."

"You keep saying that there's nothing to worry about."

Her mother's fingers tightened around her own. "Take care. Take care."

"I will, don't worry."

"Drive carefully."

"I always do."

"How far are you . . . going?"

"Not far. Just to the next state. New Mexico."

A slight smile crossed her face. "At least you'll be warmer than here."

Anna checked her watch, then leaned forward and embraced her mother. "Take care," she said, trying not to let her emotions dominate her. "I'll be back soon."

She turned at the door and looked back. Her mother was sitting in the chair by the window, watching her with a strange, intent, searching look on her face. Did she know? Somewhere, as yet inaccessible, were the memories still stored in her mind? Did she understand, in some unconscious way, what Anna had discovered and who she was going to see?

She smiled brightly, fighting down her tears, and hurried out.

Her car was parked outside the hospital main entrance. She got into it and checked her tickets one last time. Then she set off for Eagle Airport.

New Mexico

She parked the hired Chrysler outside the little tin-roofed adobe bar behind the filling station and walked in.

It was an arid place, as befitted its desert setting, bare of furniture or any other sign of comfort but for the bottles of alcohol ranged behind the bar. One wall was hung with tawdry Western paraphernalia—ancient saddlery, miner's lamps, some battered old license plates, a Winchester rifle with the action missing. On the facing wall, the skulls of various antelope had been mounted by ungifted amateurs.

A group of faded-looking men sat along the bar, all wearing sweat-stained hats and cowboy boots. She wondered where they had come from; hers was the only car parked outside. Their desultory conversation stopped as Anna came in. Heads turned. There was a low whistle of appreciation and a rough laugh.

The bartender, a scrawny middle-aged woman, looked Anna up and down without friendliness. "What'll it be?"

"A beer, please."

The woman uncapped a dewy Coors longneck and slid it in front of Anna. "There you go."

"May I have a glass, please?"

The scrawny woman picked a glass off the shelf, gave it a perfunctory wipe, and put it next to the bottle. Anna poured, feeling the men's eyes on her. She lifted her glass to them briefly. "Cheers."

They all nodded in return. They were grizzled-looking men, tanned dun as saddle leather, wiry arms sprawled out on the scarred counter, knotted fingers grasping the necks of bottles. Not a glass in sight.

Anna was wearing denims and a loose T-shirt, and they were all studying her backside with frank admiration. She drank gratefully, closing her eyes. The thirst had started as soon as she had left the populated banks of the Rio Grande and headed into the wilderness. On the long, straight drive across the Tularosa Valley, she'd found herself watching the temperature gauge of the rented car with anxious eyes, counting the miles in her head, one by one. It was winter, and the temperatures were equable, even some snow on the distant peaks, but she'd seldom seen so desolate a landscape.

Though it was an extraordinary irony that all this time Joseph Krasnowsky and her mother had been living in neighboring states, there could scarcely have been a greater difference between the wooded valleys of Vail and this baked desert. Even fenceposts and barbed wire had been a welcome touch of humanity in such an endless ocean of sand, thistle, and sage. For miles, the only sign that other cars passed this way had been the occasional dead javelina or rabbit on the road, a feast for crows that had scattered and settled again as she passed.

It was a landscape that had bleak historical associations, too, a land of old battlefields, new missile ranges, and military reservations. The next town was Alamogordo, and across the mountains lay Trinity, where almost fifty years ago the ingenuity of man had unleashed the first nuclear fireball, and the human condition had changed forever.

From where she now stood, the unearthly flash would have lighted up the sky, the rumble of the great thunder would have been easily audible.

She had wondered, again and again, what would draw a man into such an ominous and forsaken wilderness, and had found no answer.

She drained the glass, staring at the faded pennants behind the bar, advertising beer and tortilla chips. The cowboys had resumed their soft-voiced conversations, but one leaned over to her.

"Saw ya lookin' at the holes." He tapped the bar counter with a stubby finger. "In the old days a cowboy would sink a silver dollar into the wood. To keep his tab, know what I mean? When he'd drunk a dollar's worth, the barkeep 'ud dig out the coin."

She looked at the counter and saw that it was pocked with coin-shaped holes. A few tarnished Mexican pesos remained embedded in the wood, but almost all the holes were empty now.

"Turquoises, too," another man chipped in. He looked at the bartender wistfully. "You got a few turquoise nuggets from the old days, don't ya, Alice?"

Alice shrugged indifferently. "Used to have. Sold 'em to a collector. We don't give no credit these days," she added, looking at Anna with a touch of sharpness.

Anna glanced at the men. "I'm looking for the Kaplan ranch. I was told the entrance was along this road, but I couldn't find it."

"Kaplan?"

"James Kaplan. He has a ranch round here. I believe it's called the San Andrés."

The weathered faces were frowning. "Ain't no ranch of that name round here to my knowledge," a man with a Bill Cody mustachio said. "Nor no rancher named Kaplan."

"Never heard of no Kaplan herd," agreed another. "What cattle does he run? Longhorns? Herefords?"

"I don't know," she said helplessly. "He's an expert on reptiles."

There were blank expressions for a moment. Then a man laughed. "She means the feller with the critters. His name's Kaplan, ain't it?"

There were smiles. "Hell, that ain't no *ranch*," one man said. "Unless you could call it a dude ranch. More like a city park."

"He don't keep cattle," Alice the bartender put in. "Only snakes and such."

Anna nodded. "That sounds like him. Can you tell me how to get there?"

"Sure," the mustachioed man said, showing broken teeth in a grin. "If you don't mind rattlesnakes. You interested in critters?"

"I'm a journalist," she said. "I've come to interview Mr. Kaplan."

"Be the first goddamned interview he's given in thirty years, then," someone growled. "He's a solitary old booger."

"You wouldn't find the place because you're on the wrong road," the mustachioed man explained. "And even if you hit the right road, there ain't no sign to tell. Kaplan don't seem to encourage visitors. Come on. I'll show you."

Anna reached into her pocket. "How much do I owe you?" she asked the bartender.

Someone tossed some coins onto the counter. "Have one on me."

She thanked the man for his courtesy. They all tipped their hats. She followed the mustachioed man outside, feeling the weather-creased eyes watching her intently. Someone said something in an undertone, and there was more laughter as she reached the door.

The glare of the desert was cruel after the darkness of the bar. The ranch hand took her arm in one horny hand to point her toward the distant peaks. "You gotta take that road outta town. Keep following the barbed-wire fence about ten miles. You'll start seeing some trees. That's the Kaplan place. He's got him a fair spread, though he don't ranch it. Like Ferdy said, it's more like a park. The entrance is just a gap in the barbed wire, with some boulders piled up. The boulders used to be whitewashed, but the whitewash is probably gone by now. Turn in there. The house is around four miles along the track."

"Thank you so much," she said, smiling.

"What paper you with?"

She told him.

"You got an appointment with Kaplan?" he asked, watching her curiously as she got into the car.

"I've got an appointment of a sort," she said, holding the door open.

"Yeah? They say he's an educated man, but he sure don't get many visitors." He slapped the car as though it were a horse. "You take care, now. And mind the rattlesnakes, okay?"

She Drove Along the back road, dust piling up in the rearview mirror, following the endless trail of the barbed wire. Philip crossed her

mind, a dark and painful shadow. She had shelved any attempts to re-
solve her feelings for him until this was over. There would be time for
a reckoning with Philip, an accounting of the truth, but not yet. This
came first.

And she wanted to get to Joseph before he did. Whatever he
wanted with Joseph Krasnowsky, hers was the more important quest.
She had priority.

She was in a state of intense nervousness, her breathing fast and
shallow. She'd had few misgivings up to this point. Her actions had
been unthinking, each following logically on the last. Excitement and
dread were mingling in her now, a turmoil of hopes and fears that made
her unbearably restless. Over the past few hours, she'd been clenching
her jaw so tight that her whole face ached; she had to make a conscious
effort to relax, so she didn't grind her teeth or clench her fists.

She was coming to the end of the long trail.

She passed a signpost reading ALAMOGORDO 17 MILES. It
was a name with such ominous resonances. Why, out of all the beautiful
territories of the United States, had he chosen to come here? A kind of
self-punishment, Cain fleeing into the desert for the terrible crime of
having killed a brother? She could only guess how the killing of David
Godbold had haunted him over the decades, had driven him into this
wilderness under an assumed name.

Joseph. It was a name as beautiful as Alamogordo was ominous,
she thought. A beautiful story. Like his Old Testament namesake, this
Joseph, too, had been betrayed in his youth and cast into a pit. Like
that Joseph, he had passed into bondage in a strange land. And like
him, he had survived to triumph under a new incarnation.

A dust devil, whirled up by thermal currents, danced along the
road toward her. She slowed as it broke around the Chrysler, little
pebbles rattling on the windshield, buffeting the car.

When the dust cleared, she found she had breasted a slight rise.
Ahead of her, a line of trees broke the monotony of scrub and sand.
Her heart lurched. She was in sight of the Kaplan estate.

As she approached, she saw that the line of trees was in fact a
great plantation, an extraordinary sight in this dry wilderness. She recognized the trees as Australian ghost gums, tall white trunks supporting
long-leaved, aromatic foliage that could survive the harshest summer.
They were alien to this landscape, but their vigorous greenery was infinitely refreshing to the eye.

How many years, how much money and effort, must it have taken to plant this forest here? Bumping along the dirt road, she watched the regular lines of trees swing by, like an endless army of soldiers on parade.

The mustachioed cowboy had said, "He's got him a fair spread." In this land of cattle empires, the thousands of acres registered in the name of James Kaplan were not considered extraordinary. Anywhere else in the world, the Kaplan estate would be considered a kingdom. Had he wanted to ranch it, the land could have supported thousands of head of cattle. But he had turned the endless range into a paradise instead. The extraordinary character of the man she had traveled so far to see was already apparent.

She almost missed the entrance to the property, seeing the avenue between the gum trees just as she passed it. Backing up, she saw the pile of sandstone boulders, a few flakes of whitewash still adhering to their rounded surfaces. There was no signpost, no notice; but there was no gate, either. She swung the Chrysler around and set off down the road.

It seemed perceptibly cooler among the gum trees. They cast a dappled shadow that was delightful to the weary eye; and when she wound down the window, the air was richly scented with eucalyptus. It was a powerful, exotic smell in this land of creosote bush and sagebrush, but it seemed delicious to her.

After a couple of miles, other trees started to appear, cut into the eucalyptus plantation, groves of pistachio, fig, and a large, green-leafed tree that looked to her like carob. She could now see the thick galvanized pipes of an extensive irrigation system. Here and there the soil was wet from recent watering. There must be water here, water in abundance. She marveled at the expenditure of money and labor, the iron will that had ordained all these things; he had made the desert bloom.

Again, the parallel with the biblical Joseph struck her forcefully. That Joseph, too, had made the desert bloom, had made Egypt fruitful. Had that been a deliberate choice? Had he, too, felt the significance of his name, molded his life to follow the Old Testament story?

Suddenly, she had come to a gate that cut across the road. She stopped the car.

It was a formidable affair, clad in sheet metal, over ten feet high, and mounted on massive stonework pillars. Nothing could be seen past it. To either side of the gate, a tall chain-link fence stretched away through the ghost gums. There was a single notice on the gate, reading simply CAUTION—RATTLESNAKES. On one of the pillars was a stainless steel grille and a button. Nothing else, no name, no invitations.

She got out of the car and pressed the button for a few seconds, wondering if it rang anything at the other end. She stood waiting, listening to the dull thud of her own heart and the tinkle of cooling metal from the car. The wind out in the desert had been hot and arid. Here it was cool and scented, refreshing as a draft of water.

She was just about to press the button again when the grille clicked, and a female voice crackled, "Yes?"

She put her mouth to the grille. "I'd like to speak to Mr. Kaplan, please."

"Who are you?"

She hesitated. "My name is Anna Kelly." She could think of nothing else to say. Not, at least, to this impersonal grille among the gum trees.

She waited for some response, some further question, wondering what she would answer. There was none, but a long while later, the gate clanked loudly, and a yellow light on one of the pillars began to flash. With a rumble like thunder, the gate slid back on rails, revealing a long avenue lined with tall hedges stretching ahead.

She stood for a moment in puzzlement, staring down the avenue. Nobody was in sight. Then she got into the car and drove through the gates. In her rearview mirror, she saw the steel gates sliding closed again. There was something eerie about that mechanical entry.

The hedge continued for a while before suddenly falling away. Astonished, she found herself looking at a sheet of water that dazzled in the afternoon sun.

The lake was clearly manmade, sweeping gracefully around sandy beaches. Swans and other waterfowl drifted on the smooth surface. The banks were planted with hundreds of date palms, their feathery fronds reflected in the water.

The road had been shaped along the banks of the lake, taking advantage of a series of views across the water. To the other side of the road, orchards of fruit trees stood in orderly rows; working among them were the first human beings she'd seen since entering the estate, a man mounted on a tractor and two or three others working with hoes. They were dark-skinned, possibly Mexicans, and they stopped their work to stare fixedly at her car as it passed.

It was an astounding oasis in this desert plain, surrounded on all sides by olive-green belts of ghost gums. She thought of all the scenarios she'd envisaged: finding Joseph in some hospital, fading away in a shabby old-age home, living in the crowded streets of some city. Never in her wildest imaginings had she come even close to this magnificence, this manmade Eden in the desert.

So this was what had drawn Joseph out here. Not to live as a hermit, but to make himself a hidden and beautiful retreat. The ranch hand Ferdy had said the place was like a park. This was no park. This was Joseph's Egypt, a land of milk and honey.

When she had rounded the lake, she came in sight of the house. She'd expected a mansion, but it was a long, low, Western-style ranch with buttressed adobe walls and a tile roof. Down one side of the house the roof poles extended to form a shaded terrace. As she neared it, she realized it was impressive in a way that a mansion would have been ridiculous. It was of this place, fitting perfectly into this setting.

It was lent grandeur by being set on a rise of land, and by the expert landscape gardening that surrounded it. Tall palms towered over it, making an impressive backdrop. An extensive rock garden had been built in front of the house, planted with magnificent specimens of cactus: tall saguaro and even taller cardoon; prickly pear, its flat blades covered in brilliant flowers, and barrel cactus fat as hogsheads.

A group of cars and pickups was parked at the bottom of a long flight of stone steps that wound through the rock garden up to the house. She parked next to a new-looking Cadillac and took a deep breath. She was trembling all over, sweat breaking through her skin. She had arrived.

Journey's end.

She would have liked twenty minutes to compose herself, to get her emotions under control, but it was too late for that. She opened the door and got out. The vastness of the silence contained tiny sounds— the distant noise of the tractor, ducks calling on the lake. Staring up at the adobe walls of the house, she walked to the staircase, clutching her bag, in which she had the diary.

"Hold it right there, ma'am!"

The urgency in the voice stopped her. She looked around. A massive, dark man in overalls was walking toward her. His broad-cheeked face suggested Indian blood, and he carried a straw broom in his hands.

"Hello," she said. "I rang at the gate—"

"Didn't you see the sign?" he demanded.

She followed his pointing finger. A signpost at the foot of the stairs read STAY IN YOUR CAR—WAIT FOR AN ATTENDANT.

"I'm sorry, I wasn't looking—"

"Don't move."

He walked past her, pushing the straw broom ahead of him. She watched in perplexity. Then, ahead of the rustling broom, she saw a patch of rock unwind and slither forward. The fat, speckled flanks of the snake undulated as it moved, weaving its arrow-shaped head from side to side.

Suddenly she was cold all over.

The snake paused at the edge of the steps. The man in the overalls twitched the broom. The tip of the snake's tail cocked up in the air swiftly. It gave a little dry rattle. Anna saw the small black eyes staring, the tongue sliding in and out of the lipless mouth. The man made no further movement. She saw he was wearing knee-high rubber boots.

Then the snake started to move again, rolling over the boulders into the rock garden. The reptile's rattle, like a fat ear of wheat, disappeared between the stones.

"Problem ain't that they'll attack for no reason," the big man said, turning to her. "Problem is they look just like a piece a dirt until you step on 'em. In winter they won't always get out of your way. Accidents can happen."

She was not looking at him. She was staring in icy fascination at the rock garden. Among the spiny trunks of the cacti were other rocks that uncoiled, other speckled shadows that moved. As her perception changed, her eyes made out the shapes of serpents everywhere, looped into compact bunches, or slithering with slow deliberation over the stones. The rock garden was alive with vipers.

"Ma'am?"

She could not move. The sweat had become frost on her skin. She had never thought of herself as afraid of snakes before. She'd had none of the phobias some people suffered from. But she was standing a few feet away from hundreds of rattlesnakes, with nothing between them and her body. Deep in her brain, some primitive wisdom told her if she moved they would strike. Her muscles had locked into a kind of paralysis, even the muscles of her throat, so she was scarcely breathing.

"Ma'am?" He took her arm gently. "No need to be afraid. Nice and slow, now."

He pushed her forward, so she was forced to take a step to prevent herself from falling. Terror made her close her eyes, waiting for the fangs to strike. He did not let her stop.

"You hear all kinds'a foolishness 'bout rattlers," he said, his voice soothing. "Folks'll tell you how they'll chase a horse twenty miles. Or how if you kill a rattler, his mate will come lookin' for to kill you. It's mostly hogwash." He was steering her up the stairs, his hand still grasping her arm. Once he stopped her and gently nudged a snake out of their path with his broom.

She wanted urgently to empty her bladder. Her throat was tight and dry as a bone. She hardly dared turn her head to look at the rocks on either side of the staircase, but she could see them anyway; geometric patterns etched in glossy scales, diamonds and stripes and checks; little black eyes and flickering tongues; uplifted rattles quivering. Some of the snakes were huge, over two yards long and thick as a man's calf. If they had wanted to strike, nothing on earth could have stopped them from rearing up and sinking their fangs into her flesh. Now and then came the dry warning rattle, but there was no other sound.

She thought she could smell them now, a sharp zoo tang of urine and rotting meat. Her legs were strengthless, weak and yielding, but the massive man kept her moving.

"Pretty soon," he said, "you learn to see what a beautiful animal they are. Most people will kill a rattler soon as look at it. But they're a beautiful animal."

At last they had reached the top of the steps. A broad patio stretched to the house, crossed by a large ornamental pond. In the turquoise water, waterlilies bloomed white and cream, floating among glossy green pads. A series of wide stepping-stones crossed the pond, leading to the porch.

The Indian released her arm. "You're okay now, ma'am. Just go 'cross the stepping-stones. The snakes don't hardly ever go into water. Keeps 'em outta the house."

A long shudder loosened the paralysis. "Thank you," she said weakly, taking her first full breath. "I'm sorry."

"No need to be sorry."

"Do they have the run of the estate?" she asked, looking back in incredulous horror.

"The whole place is full of 'em."

"But those men, working in the orchards—"

He tapped his boots with the shank of his broom. "Everybody here wears these. And you learn how to deal with rattlers."

She shuddered again. "I don't think I've ever been so frightened in my life."

"First-time reaction." His face was impassive, unsmiling. "Next time you come, won't be so bad. Time after that, you'll be able to walk up on your own."

"Jesus," she said, shuddering.

"You just gotta learn to see 'em. Need to educate your eyes. Educate your mind." His Asiatic eyes were lined with a thousand dry wrinkles, and she realized that despite his huge frame, he was older than he looked. He pointed. "They waiting for you, ma'am."

The door of the porch had opened and an elderly woman was standing in the doorway. Feeling as though she had been disemboweled and the hole stuffed with cotton waste, Anna gathered herself and walked across the stepping-stones.

The White-Haired woman, who had introduced herself as a house-keeper, led her into a huge sitting room that was like a double-page spread out of *Architectural Digest,* beautifully but simply furnished with traditional wood furniture, handsome Mexican rugs spread on the clay-tiled floor. One wall of the room consisted of sliding glass doors that opened onto a stoop and gave a panoramic view of the grounds and the snow-tipped mountains in the far distance.

"Do you have a card?" the woman asked in a harsh voice, staring at Anna with grim eyes.

"A card? Oh yes, I see." She fumbled clumsily in her bag until she found one of her business cards and passed it to the woman.

She studied it briefly and looked up, her face even stiffer. "I have to warn you that Mr. Kaplan will not speak to journalists without an appointment, Miss Kelly. You've wasted your time."

"Oh, I'm not—this is not for an interview." She swallowed. "It's a personal matter."

The grim eyes looked her up and down with patent disbelief. "I see. Please wait here."

The woman left the room. Anna's heart was pounding so hard she could hear it in the silence.

She was in Joseph's house. Her eyes searched instinctively, hungrily, for information about the man she had hunted for so long. It was a pleasantly dark house, the temperature perfect. There were several large-scale paintings on the walls. Above the fieldstone fireplace hung the biggest of all, a triptych. Each of the three panels, which were almost six feet high, showed a naked woman. Drawn to it, she walked over to study it more closely. It was, to her eyes, a technically brilliant work. The exquisite details of the flesh and the background settings were of the sixteenth century, reminiscent of Albrecht Dürer; but she was certain it was modern, and at last found a signature: Sepp Hilz, 1941. The faces of the nudes were severely beautiful, golden hair braided and drawn back from marble brows, the details such as nipples, fingernails, and facial features done with loving realism.

Anna turned. Almost all the other paintings in the room were also figure studies, though none of the others were nudes. One showed a brawny, angular-jointed peasant sowing grain in a sunlit field. Others portrayed solemn-faced family groups, posed in oddly formal attitudes, or elderly people with severe, noble faces, reading or sitting with hands calmly folded. All were executed with the same detailed realism.

Something gave all the sitters a common bond, though it was hard at first to tell what it was. It was a certain massive quality, she decided at last. Perhaps it was because all of the artists had concentrated on giving their sitters an almost uncanny presence, a superhuman gravity. Perhaps that was why Joseph had chosen them, for the massive sense of personality that hung over the works. Perhaps they represented company to him. It touched her that Joseph, in his solitude, had surrounded himself with these human presences.

There was only one landscape, an oil painting of rolling European countryside, rich golden wheat under a heavily turbulent sky. It, too, possessed that supernatural presence. Mounted in a large frame beside it were the skins of five snakes, beautiful and strange designs in earth colors.

Her legs were too weak to stand any longer, and she sat. There was a long, low table in front of her, on which were arranged an extensive collection of clay artifacts. She reached out and picked up a modeled head. Age had made it as light as cardboard. The flat nose and thick-lipped mouth were by no means handsome, but it had a primitive splendor. The ornate headdress of writhing snakes proclaimed it as the head of a priest, or a god. Like all the other objects, it looked very old, possibly excavated from some pre-Columbian site, and possibly extremely valuable. She put it down gingerly.

"Miss Kelly?"

She had not heard him come in, and she rose with a violent start, turning to face him.

The old man was tall and erect. He stood watching her with his arms by his sides in an almost military bearing that was emphasized by the pressed khaki shirt and pants. A scarf of the same color was knotted at his throat. The mane of hair was completely white, combed back from a high forehead and reaching almost to his collar; but his eyebrows were disconcertingly black, descending heavily over glittering black eyes. There were also black streaks in the full beard that was clipped to reveal his lips.

She knew he was at least seventy-five, but it was hard to believe it. He looked sixty. His skin was darkly tanned, and though his face bore harsh lines, it was free of the smaller network of old-age wrinkles that would have made him seem elderly.

She could find no words. She was too intent on looking at him, searching that face for any trace of her mother's, of her own. Recognition was swift and potent. She knew his face, had known it for a long, long time. Its lineaments were new to her, yet something like them was profoundly familiar to her, etched indelibly into her mind.

Yes. This was the man.

And yet there was also something unexpected, something that disturbed her. She recognized the face, and yet it was somehow not the face she had been dreaming of for so long.

Instinctively, her eyes went to his jaw, looking for the scar. It was there, beneath the beard; she could see the misshapen bones beneath the concealing hair, the silvery tracks that reached to the pink skin of the mouth, pulling it into a permanent grimace, almost a sneer. As he spoke again, she saw his lower lip twist awkwardly.

"Miss Kelly?"

"Yes," she said, finding her voice at last. "I'm Anna Kelly."

He walked forward, and she saw he wore sandals on his feet, with khaki socks. He had her card in his hand.

"You're a journalist?" he asked, the pink lower lip twisting as he spoke. His voice was deep, older than the rest of him. Apart from a slight sibilance on the Ss, due to the scar, the accent was neutral and calm.

"Yes. But I hope the housekeeper told you this is—a—a—personal inquiry."

The black eyes met hers, and Anna felt a sense of shock that jolted her. She remembered what Evelyn had said. *Black wolf's eyes.* Candida, in the diary, had also spoken of a wolflike look. His gaze was almost frightening in its intensity. Here was the face Candida Cipriani had known and loved. Here lay her own roots. She stared at him in a kind of awe.

"A personal inquiry?"

She clutched her handbag, the diary feeling as heavy as a lump of lead in it. She had prepared speeches for this moment, but they had all gone now. She was bereft of words. "I'm so sorry if this is an intrusion," she said, her throat dry. "I could have called first. Maybe I should have. But I was so afraid you wouldn't see me—"

"What kind of personal inquiry?" The sibilance made the question harsh, though the voice stayed calm and deep.

She was helpless, staring at him as though hypnotized by those piercing black eyes. "I—I—don't know where to begin."

He simply stood there, staring at her, a straight-backed old man with silver hair and a twisted mouth. Evelyn had said the scar amounted almost to a mutilation. He must have had plastic surgery over the years; she thought she could see where the bone had been built up, where skin had been grafted over the wound. She suddenly felt the absurdity of her behavior, staring at him like a rabbit in a car's headlights.

"I'm sorry," she said. She felt her skin flush first hot, then cold. "You must think I'm some kind of madwoman. My name doesn't mean anything to you?"

"No," he said.

"I think—I think what I'm about to say is going to come as a shock to you." He said nothing. She went on, hearing her own voice shake. "My mother's name is Catherine Kelly. Her maiden name was Catherine Godbold. She was born Catarina Cipriani. Her mother—her mother was named Candida Cipriani."

She did not know what she had been expecting; that austere face did not look capable of expressing astonishment or wonder. Nor did the massive presence seem as though it would be easily shaken. But she had expected some reaction. There was none. He simply stood there, watching her, his expression unchanged.

Her emotions had been so wrought up that she herself was now close to tears. Only his impassivity stopped her from yielding to them.

"Mr. Kaplan," she faltered, "do *any* of those names mean anything to you?"

For a while longer he was silent. His stare was somehow awesome, as cold and emotionless as the stare of the snakes she had seen outside. "What have you come here for?" he asked at last.

She winced as though he had struck her across the face. "I'd hoped that wouldn't need explanation. Maybe I'm making some terrible mistake. But I don't think so." She took a deep breath. "Your real name isn't James Kaplan, is it? You were born Joseph Krasnowsky." She watched his face for some sign of emotion. There was none. "As Joseph Krasnowsky," she went on, "you knew a young woman named Candida Cipriani in Italy, during the war. She died in childbirth in 1945. The child, who was my mother, survived. Something else survived, too." She reached into her bag and took out the diary. She offered it to him. "This."

His eyes did not leave hers. "And what is that?" he asked.

"It's a diary. Candida Cipriani's diary."

At last she saw some movement in the old man's face. His lids slid down slightly, hooding his eyes. The expression was a strange one; it struck her that he had suddenly found the answer to something, and that the answer had aroused in him a weariness, even a kind of contempt.

"So," he said softly. "Candida kept a diary."

It was, at least, an acknowledgment of a sort, and it heartened her a little, though she was getting steadily more upset by the icy reception he was giving her. "Yes. She kept a diary. It was lost after her death. It turned up last year and someone sent it to my mother. She started looking for you."

He reached out his hand at last, but not in greeting. He wanted the diary. She gave it to him. He flipped it open and studied the neat, faded script. Anna was feeling that the whole scene was somehow unreal. After the first electric recognition between herself and this man, she'd expected powerful emotions to be unleashed. On her side, that had happened, with an intensity that had shaken her. On his side, there was apparently nothing but a dry suspicion. He was deliberately shutting her out.

What did you expect? she asked herself. That he would gather you, a stranger, into his arms?

She studied him, desperately wondering how she could break through that stone wall. He was far more striking than she could have imagined. His face was an extraordinary one. He had a formidable presence that was, in a way, not unlike Constanze Graf's. He bore the same aura of present authority and past suffering. But there was no softness about him. Nothing yielding. If anything, he projected something that almost frightened her.

He was also taller than she had anticipated. Age had not shrunk him. The sandals were odd in a place where everyone else wore boots, but the erect frame was impressive; his shoulders filled his khaki shirt, the knotty hands looked powerful. Without looking up from the pages, he asked, "How did you find me?"

"Through David Lefkowitz. Saul Lefkowitz's son."

"Ah, yes. Lefkowitz." Again she saw the slight hooding of the eyes, the weary contempt. "He knew where I was?"

"Not exactly. He gave us information which enabled us to trace you."

He looked up at her, the black eyes if anything even colder now. " 'Us'?" he repeated with that sharp hiss. "Who do you mean by 'us'? "

"My mother and I." She had instinctively decided not to mention Philip yet. "My mother is in the hospital right now, in Vail, Colorado. She suffered a serious attack last year, and she was in a coma until recently. That's why I'm here in her place." Again, she had expected some reaction, some show of concern. There was none. She licked her dry lips. "Mr. Kaplan, I came because I believe you may be my grandfather."

He closed the diary slowly. There was something speculative in his eyes now, a sense of intent appraisal. "That is a somewhat extraordinary claim," he said coldly.

Anna felt her face flush. "I don't think so. Not when you read the diary. And there's other evidence."

"Other evidence?"

She reached into her bag again and took out the photograph.

"David Lefkowitz gave this to me. He was struck by the resemblance. Can you see it now?" she asked quietly.

He examined the photograph in silence. If it affected him, there was little sign of it in his face. He looked up at Anna. "Yes. There is a resemblance."

She tried to smile, but her lips trembled. "You're not very pleased to see me, are you?" None of this was going remotely as she had anticipated. She felt that the whole interview had got derailed at the very start, that nothing was following in sequence, nothing was making complete sense. She had come here with her heart in her hands, and had found she was trespassing where she was not welcome. And she was about to trespass even further in one last attempt to break through to him. She braced herself. "There's something I want to get out of the way right now," she said. "It's important, though you may not like it."

"Yes?" he prompted with dry sibilance.

"I believe I know the reason you chose to change your name and came out here to live."

She felt, rather than saw, his whole body alter. It seemed to tense like a coiling spring. His face changed, too, took on savage lines of age and distrust. "Yes?" he said, even more quietly.

"We've managed to trace a part of your life. We think you escaped from the Soviet Union some time in 1959 or 1960." She faltered, daunted by that grim stare. "David Godbold was killed in 1960. My mother saw the man who killed him. I believe—I believe that if she had met you last year, she would have been able to identify you as that man."

"Last year," he repeated, eyes never leaving her. "And now?"

"Now she remembers nothing. The injuries she received have blotted out all her recent memories. They may never come back. Even if they did, I doubt whether she would blame you for what you did. I certainly don't. I'm not saying I condone the murder of David Godbold. Just that I understand it. And that it's not my intention you should ever suffer for what you did."

"How very kind," he said. The sudden, biting irony in his tone made tears start to her eyes.

"God, I'm handling this so terribly badly." She rubbed her temples with trembling fingers, where a sudden pressure was making her giddy. She was aware that she was too upset to keep going much longer. "I just don't know how else I could have done it." Accumulated stress and exhaustion were making her head throb. She should have rested today in Santa Fe. Rushing out here had been a stupid mistake. "I've intruded. I'm sorry."

He was flipping through the diary. He held a page up to the light, examining it with narrowed eyes as though to test its authenticity. "Where exactly did this document come from?" he demanded.

She drew an unsteady breath. "Apparently it was hidden in Candida's bedroom. Under a loose tile. The house is being modernized right now—one of the workmen found it. It was sent to my mother."

"Pretty," he said softly.

"I'm sorry?"

"A pretty story."

"Don't you *believe* me?" she asked in astonishment.

He ignored her. She saw him hold the pages to his nose, sniffing them.

It came to her in a sickening flash that he suspected she had been trying to deceive him. That he suspected she was a fraud, and the diary was some kind of cunning forgery. That was why he had treated her so coldly. He did not believe any of it.

Hurt to the bone, she opened her mouth but could find no words. There was only a sick feeling of despair in the pit of her stomach. Bitter tears flooded her eyes.

"Jesus," she said in a choked voice. "Do you think I'm *lying* to you? I've come all this way—you don't understand—you don't *under-stand*. My mother spent months looking for you. She even went to Russia. She practically destroyed herself to find you—and now I've reached you—and—and—" She broke off, unable to continue for the lump in her throat.

"Mrs. Berg!"

"Yes, Mr. Kaplan?"

Anna turned. The elderly housekeeper was now standing in the doorway. "Miss Kelly has upset herself," Kaplan said, still studying the diary. "She needs to recover her composure. Could you escort her to one of the bedrooms? See that she has anything she wants."

"Please," Anna said, trying to smile through her tears, "that won't be necessary. I'll just get in my car and drive back to my hotel—"

"You will feel better once you have washed and rested. Perhaps some refreshment. We can talk more rationally then. Yes?"

"Yes," she said quietly.

"Mrs. Berg, please."

The housekeeper came to Anna's side and took her arm. Her fingers were bony and cold. "Please come with me, Miss Kelly," she said in the peremptory tone of a governess.

Glad of the chance to recover a little, she followed the housekeeper. The man with the mane of silver hair did not look at her again as she left the room. He was absorbed in the diary.

The housekeeper marched ahead of her along the corridor. They passed the doorway to a large laundry room, where modern washing and drying machines gleamed. Then another, even larger room, lined with shelves on which were stacked rows upon rows of big glass jars. As if in a dream, Anna saw they were bottled fruits, jams, pickles, the harvest of those hundreds of fruit trees.

Then the housekeeper was opening a door at the end of the corridor.

"You'll be comfortable in here," she said brusquely. "There is a bathroom through there with fresh towels and soap. You may lie down on the bed if you choose."

Anna wandered into the suite. She stared at the bed, the pleasant-looking armchairs, the doorway to the bathroom. "This is very kind," she said numbly.

The housekeeper was standing in the doorway. "Mr. Kaplan has instructed me to give you anything you want. Tea? Coffee?"

"Some tea would be wonderful," she admitted.

The old woman inclined her head. "I will see that it is brought to you directly," she said. She left the room, closing the door behind herself.

Then Anna heard the key clatter in the lock.

She Sat In the darkness, taut and humiliated. It had been many hours since the housekeeper had locked her in here. She had never returned with the promised tea.

Anna had given up banging on the stoutly locked door long ago.

The windows, which were in any case heavily barred with

Spanish-style wrought iron, were sealed shut. They looked out onto a deserted brick courtyard, and though panic had risen in her many times, she had resisted the inclination to break the glass and shout. She was shut in here by order of the master of the house. Nobody would come to free her unless he gave the command.

Instinctively, her hand went out to the light switch again. It clicked under her finger, but there was still no answering light. The room had no electricity. There was not even water in the bathroom. Her throat was parched with thirst. The comfortable suite was a prison.

Anna had lain on the bed or paced restlessly around the room for hours, watching the light fade as the day died, her weary mind wrestling with questions that felt too heavy for it to move. Mental and emotional exhaustion were intensifying with each hour that passed. She had done this very badly. She had made some kind of terrible mistake. She knew only one thing, that she had found Joseph Krasnowsky, and that he had not believed her story.

That was a bitter irony. *That* was a scenario she had never envisaged in all her wild imaginings of this meeting.

He had taken her for an imposter. Some kind of gold-digging adventurer who had cooked up a story hoping to prize something out of him, money, property, an inheritance. Perhaps even to try and black-mail him; her reference to the murder of David Godbold had been stupid and inappropriate.

So he had shut her in here, as a gamekeeper might lock up a poacher. Leaving her to stew in shame and dread.

It was incomprehensible, but she had tried to see things through his eyes. After so much suffering and so many ordeals, he must be pathologically mistrustful. After a lifetime of living in the shadows, he must be a man of infinite caution.

He would be checking her story now. Examining the diary. Making inquiries. Comparing dates and places. She wondered how long it would be before he was convinced that she was who she said she was. Before he came and turned on the lights in this dark prison.

And then what would he do with her?

Beneath the humiliation and the anger, there was a darker undercurrent. She knew nothing about this man's character apart from what Candida had written in the diary, almost fifty years ago; and not even Candida had ever understood him fully. This was a man who, to the best of her knowledge, had shot David Godbold like a dog. It was not beyond the bounds of imagination that, in order to protect himself, he would be capable of further violence . . .

She fought down the fear, trying to be rational. She was his granddaughter, for God's sake. She believed that. But did he?

So many things were haunting her. The familiarity of that face, and yet the strangeness of it. The black, emotionless eyes, the sneering lip.

Those strangely massive paintings. About them, too, there was now something familiar. Some distant echo in her mind. They reminded her of something, but she could not think of what. Something somehow ominous, something else that was both familiar and yet unexpected. She wrestled with the vague ideas. But she was in the dark.

She was shivering more or less constantly now. As the sun had gone down, the room had become first chilly, then cold. There was no heat in the radiators, and the desert warmth had evaporated with nightfall. She was hugging herself. If it got any colder, she would have to wrap herself in the quilt.

Philip had warned her not to do it like this.

Philip had known that Joseph Krasnowsky would not welcome her with open arms. She had defied him.

But what else could she have done? She no longer trusted Philip. She had desperately wanted to get to Joseph before him; there had been no time for diplomacy or finessing.

She needed Philip right now with a painful urgency. Whatever his secrets were, she had never loved any man the way she loved him, and to be in this mess without him was an added torture. Her love for him rose up in her, yearning for his strength, his comfort. She needed him so much . . . She lay back on the bed, trying to imagine his arms around her, his warm breath in her hair.

Suddenly the world flared crimson. Her hands flew to her eyes to shut out the pain. The lights had been switched on. She heard the rumble of water rushing in the bathroom cistern.

She rose from the bed, squinting through dazzled eyes.

The key rattled in the lock, and the door opened. The light made a silver halo out of James Kaplan's white hair. He was still wearing his khaki shirt and pants, but he had now pulled on a soft leather jacket against the evening chill. The man who followed him in was massive. Anna recognized the Indian who had guided her up the steps, hours ago. He still wore his overalls and rubber boots. They closed the door behind them and locked it.

She faced them in an uncertain silence, all her indignant words fading on her lips. The old man's eyes were black as night, no light reflected in them.

"Where is Philip Westward?" he asked softly.

She was startled. "How do you know about Philip?" she asked.

The Indian stepped forward, his face impassive. Before she could register what he was doing, he thrust something into her midriff.

The convulsion of agony doubled her over, the oxygen seared from her lungs. She hit the floor with a bone-jarring crash, her head cracking on the tiles.

She heard the deep voice from above her, the Ss hissing softly. "Where is Philip Westward?"

She could not speak. Her diaphragm was still paralyzed.

This time the explosion ripped between her shoulder blades, arching her back like a bow as her muscles spasmed. The pain was terrible for a long moment. Then it faded slowly into a scorching heat and she flopped back.

She heard a thin keening wail and realized it was coming from herself.

A massive hand grasped her arm and dragged her upright. Her legs buckled under her. She was thrust onto the bed, held upright by a biting grip on her arm.

She looked up at the two men with dulled eyes, too stunned to comprehend. The Indian's face was as stolid as when he had first greeted her, calm Mongoloid eyes watchful. She saw that he held something in his right hand, something from which two steel prongs thrust outward. An electric cattle prod.

"Where is Philip Westward?" the old man repeated, his voice unchanged. She saw the electrodes move toward her again and screamed in panic.

"I don't know! I left him in New York!"

The cattle prod thrust into her stomach again. The convulsion curled her up. She doubled forward, her head between her knees.

They left her for a while, then pulled her upright again. Where the electrodes had shocked her the skin was burning.

"Please," she whispered, her whole body shaking, "please don't hurt me anymore—"

"Where is Philip Westward?"

"I don't know! I told you, I left him in New York! I didn't tell him I was coming!"

This time the cattle prod rammed into her abdomen. Huge claws sank into her bowels. When the pain turned to heat, she could no longer breathe. She arched her head back, transfixed by the terror she would die of suffocation. Through a red mist, she saw the two emotionless faces staring at her.

Then iron fingers grasped the back of her neck and rammed her head down to her knees. Her locked diaphragm broke, and air rushed into her lungs.

Kaplan stooped, the silver-bearded face coming close to hers. She saw the pink lower lip twist, heard the voice hiss quietly. "Where is Philip Westward?"

"I swear I don't know," she sobbed jerkily, still held in the Indian's grip, her bulging eyes fixed on the floor. "I left without telling him I was coming! He doesn't know I'm here."

"Why did you not tell him you were coming?"

"I wanted to see you first." She retched. "There's been some terrible mistake. I'm telling you the truth. I'm your granddaughter—"

The huge claws ripped at her kidneys. Her body convulsed backward. They watched her as the seizure slowed. The slow, searing heat spread into her, almost soothing. She crawled across the bed, away from them, arms upraised to try and defend herself.

"Can we talk?" Kaplan asked softly.

She nodded, her hair tangled in front of her eyes.

"Who is he?"

"I don't know," she whispered. Her eyes were fixed in dread on the twin probes of the cattle prod. "He was my lover. But I don't know who he is."

"How is that possible?"

"He lied to me. He helped me find you. I don't know why. I only found out he'd lied to me a few days ago. That's why I came on my own." She saw the Indian move and flattened herself against the wall. "Do you think I would *lie* to you?" she burst out. "Don't let him touch me!"

Kaplan was considering her, pinching his scarred lower lip reflectively. The dead black eyes were those of a snake, unemotional, watchful.

"Who did you tell you were coming here?"

"No one!"

The Indian grasped her ankle and dragged her forward. She was screaming as the cattle prod stabbed into her side. The terrible grip of thousands of volts cut off her voice, crippling her.

When it stopped, she was lying on the floor like a disjointed doll.

They dragged her back onto the bed. Kaplan leaned over her, peering into her eyes. He waited until she started to stir with slight, broken movements. "Can we talk?" he asked softly.

"I'm . . . telling . . . the truth." She could only form the words with her lips. There was no breath in her body.

"Who is he?"

"I . . . don't . . . know."

"Why is he involved?"

"I . . . don't . . . know."

"What does he want with me?"

"His . . . father . . ."

Kaplan's eyes narrowed. "His father—what?"

"Like you . . . his father . . . missing in action . . ."

Her whole body was burning, every joint feeling as though it had been wrenched out of its socket. If they hit her with the cattle prod again, she would die.

"Ramón. Water."

The Indian went to the bathroom and came back with a glass. He pulled Anna upright and held it to her lips. She drank, choking in her desperate thirst. The glass was small and soon empty. "More— *please.*"

"In a while." Kaplan folded his arms. "Tell me about Philip Westward's father."

"Like you," she whispered. "He was a soldier . . . disappeared at the end of the war . . . Philip thought he went . . . Russian prison camp . . . like you."

"Is that what he told you?"

Anna nodded. "Told me . . . he'd been looking . . . all his life. Wanted to help me find you . . . thought you could . . . help him."

"Help him?"

"Help him trace . . . his father."

"What has his father to do with me?"

"Thought you might have been . . . same camps . . . have information . . . "

"Do you believe his story?" Kaplan hissed.

"I don't . . . know . . . " she moaned.

"He is not what he says he is. Is he?"

"No . . . "

"Then what is he?"

"I don't know . . . "

She screamed as the Indian moved the electrodes toward her again.

"What is he?"

"*I don't know!*" Somewhere in her agony was a blazing rage against Philip. He was to blame. Because of him, she was enduring this agony. *"He used me!"* she screamed. "Can't you understand? He used me!"

They released her, and she rolled away. Kaplan considered that in silence for a long while. The apprehension of further pain was making her shake violently, her teeth rattling in her head. Her eyes, stretched wide, could not tear themselves away from the instrument of torture in the big, callused hand of the Indian.

"What do you think, Ramón?" Kaplan asked at last.

"Her clothes," the huge man said. "They give too much insulation. I gotta get the electrodes right into the muscle, Mr. Kaplan. We should strip her."

She shriveled away from them, whimpering in horror. "Please. Please. *Don't.*"

She saw a slight smile cross Kaplan's twisted mouth for a moment. "I think she may be telling the truth, Ramón."

"Please. I *am* telling the truth," she whispered.

"You won't know for sure 'less you go all the way," the Indian said. He checked the instrument briefly. "Plentya juice left."

Kaplan watched Anna's terrorized face for a while, black eyes thoughtful. Then the hissing reptile voice said, "I don't want this to get too messy. And we may not have too much time for your sort of games, my friend."

He sat on the bed beside Anna. She twisted away from him in terror, but he reached out and grasped her wrist. His fingers bit into her pulse, and he watched the steel Rolex on his wrist for a while, checking the fluttering beat. Then he grasped her shirt and jerked it out of her denims.

"*No!*" she screamed, flailing at him.

The Indian's vast grip pinioned her arms at her sides, immobilizing her.

"I won't hurt you," Kaplan said patiently. He lifted her shirt and examined the skin of her stomach. Then he pulled her around and checked her back. "There's some burning."

"Bodies get all kindsa marks," Ramón said imperturbably. "All kindsa blotches and signs. Could be insect bites."

"Could be," the old man said. They released her, and she crawled as far away from them as she could, drawing up her knees and hugging herself into a fetal ball so that only her huge, dark eyes showed through her tangled hair. Kaplan took the cattle prod from the Indian and moved it toward her. She could not help the spasm of terror that threw her back against the wall.

"It's an interesting phenomenon, isn't it?" Kaplan said calmly. "The burned child dreads fire. You're telling me the truth, aren't you, child?"

"Yes," she whispered. "I swear I am."

"You see, Ramón? It's important to assess when a subject is telling the truth. If you go beyond that point, the subject will enter a world of fantasy. It is partly encouraged by an instinctive desire to flee reality, partly by a desire to tell the interrogator anything that may end the suffering. Subjects invent quite freely under those conditions. The whole process becomes counterproductive."

The Indian's broad face was stolid. "Yes, Mr. Kaplan."

Kaplan rose. "I think we can leave Miss Kelly to rest awhile now. There may be a few more questions later on. But I'm sure we won't need to apply any further pressure. Will we, Miss Kelly?"

Anna shook her head infinitesimally.

"Good," the old man said seriously. "Unlock the door, please."

The Indian obeyed. Anna watched them preparing to leave. "Wait," she heard her own voice say hoarsely.

Kaplan turned to her incuriously. "Yes?"

"You're not Joseph Krasnowsky, are you?"

He smiled again, lower lip twisting. "Pretty little ingenue. I really believe that comes as a complete surprise to you."

"You're not Joseph."

"No."

She hugged her knees, her whole world one dark pain. "Who are you?"

"I am who I am."

"What happened to Joseph Krasnowsky?"

"Krasnowsky?" Again the twisted smile. "Isn't that obvious?"

She felt the hot tears spilling down her cheeks, blinding her, blotting out the evil face at the door. "What happened . . . to . . . him?"

"He returned to the elements. Joseph Krasnowsky has been dead for exactly forty-eight years."

She heard the door close, the key clatter in the lock.

The lights went out.

6

The dawn began with a dim blue glow.

She could hear noises beyond the door; the quiet murmur of voices, the occasional footfall. They would be coming for her soon.

She spent hours between waking and sleeping, in a kind of limbo. The savagery of the attack had stunned her mind and her body. Too brutalized to sleep, too dazed to be fully conscious, she had drifted on a sea of pain. She felt disjointed, her thoughts as fractured as the nerves that still shuddered and ached throughout her body. She was lost in the depths of a giant emptiness.

It had all been folly. All waste. Joseph Krasnowsky had been an illusion. A false light that had wrecked her mother on the rocks, and was now wrecking her, too.

She was too battered to try and comprehend the mystery now. But she knew the man with the scarred mouth had told her the truth. He was not Joseph. Joseph was dead. Joseph had died twenty years before she'd even been born. His place had been taken by some monstrous evil.

First her mother, and now she herself, had touched that evil. All the time they had been searching for Joseph, they had been inexorably approaching it. It had struck out at them, warding them off, but they had not been warned. With blind obstinacy, they had persevered, tracking it deep into its lair. Hoping to find the impossible: a father, a grandfather, lost since 1944.

But Joseph had not been there. Only his husk. Only his shell.

A parasitism had taken place.

Something potent and sinister had killed him and taken over what was his: his identity, his property, his life. That parasite had been living on his substance ever since.

Like the owl they had found in the Hunter's Tower, making a slaughterhouse of the room Joseph had once inhabited.

Like the wax moth that had invaded Evelyn's hives and fastened itself on the hard-won honeycomb.

As Anna looked back, she could see the signs and omens that had warned her about this, as though some dumb spirit had been trying to show her the truth. She'd been blind. And yet the omens had been there, had she had eyes to see.

André Levêque had been the strongest omen of all, a man as sinister in his way as the man who had tortured her last night. Another man who had played God with human lives, deciding who was fit to live and who was not, stripping organs from one child to give to another, taking life from those to whom it rightfully belonged and selling it to others.

She did not know who the man was who now inhabited Joseph Krasnowsky's husk. She only knew that such a transplant could not have taken place without great evil; and that great evil also meant great danger.

The horror of it haunted her in the darkness. There was no strength in her. It hurt too much to move, and she had been in the same position for hours, curled up in the corner, as in a womb, her mind filled with the terrifying images.

Only Philip could save her now.

If he guessed what she had done, if he somehow heard her silent screams to him, and followed her out here . . .

Philip, she called to him desperately, come for me. Come for me soon.

Toward five A.M., she heard the first hesitant calls of some bird outside, a sleepy whistle. A short while later, she heard the key in the lock. Instinctively, she shrank back into her corner. The places where they had burned her with the cattle prod last night were suddenly aflame. She could face death with courage. Further pain was more than she could endure.

The hulking shape of Ramón filled the doorframe. He wore his overalls and boots, a wool hat pulled down over his broad face. He was holding something in his hands, but it was not the electric prod. It was a leather thong with two loops, a kind of double dog collar. He stooped over her, fitting the loops around her wrists, jerking them tight so that her hands were fastened in front of her.

"Come," he said brusquely.

She moved with painful slowness, climbing off the bed like an old woman. Her stomach hurt. She had to walk hunched over.

The big man took her arm in one hand, pushing her ahead of him. She gasped in pain as the movements shook up the sediment of her pain. Getting up had made her head spin wildly, her ears roaring, and she stumbled more than once, feeling she would faint. Ramón jerked her to her feet each time.

They emerged from the house into a cavernous garage that smelled strongly of diesel fumes. Kaplan was waiting for them, sitting in a battered Land Rover with the engine running. He glanced at her briefly, black eyes incurious, his white mane of hair tucked back under a wool hat like Ramón's. As she shrank from him, the flash of recognition passed through her mind again, the familiarity she could not quite place.

Then Ramón was pushing her into the back of the Land Rover and getting in beside her. "Don't do anything stupid," he commanded. His fingers bit into her elbow, making her gasp with pain.

"No bruises, Ramón," Kaplan said sharply, glancing in the rear-view mirror.

"Yes, Mr. Kaplan," the huge man said. His fingers relaxed fractionally.

Kaplan reached a bony hand out of the window, pointing a remote-control transmitter at the door. It began lifting with a deep rumble, and he eased the Land Rover forward.

The sky was still dark overhead; in the east, the blue glow was taking on a first tint of rose-pink. As they emerged from the garage, a bitter cold wind blew through the open windows. She shuddered, hunching over the raw hurt inside her body. Both men were well-covered. She was still in her soiled T-shirt and denims.

"Miss Kelly is cold," Kaplan said over his shoulder. "Shut the window, Ramón."

The Indian obeyed. Kaplan rounded the house, driving through a courtyard, past stables and outbuildings. There were no lights in any of the windows. As they passed the front of the house, she looked at the group of parked cars by the rock garden. Her own rented Chrysler was not there. It had been moved in the night.

Rounding the lake, Kaplan accelerated onto a bumpy dirt track with a roar, heading out toward the dim glow, into the desert. The Land Rover was an unyielding vehicle, its hard springs jolting and jerking her until she almost cried out in pain.

Kaplan half-turned his head so he could talk to her. "It's a pleasant property, is it not? Quite a spread, as they say in these parts. It has taken me more than twenty years to build it up to what it is now." He had to raise his voice over the rumble of the Land Rover's diesel engine, and the hissing on the Ss was more pronounced. She saw a little spittle flecking his lips, catching in his beard. "Because of you, I will probably have to leave it behind me forever."

Anna sank back against the hard seat, closing her eyes, trying to brace her battered body against the cruel jolting.

"But you will be surprised to hear that I bear you no malice," Kaplan went on after a while. "We have simply been the victims of bad luck. You, your mother, and I. The irony is not without its symmetrical beauty. And in any case, I have been preparing for this day for many years. Many, many years."

She opened her eyes painfully. "It was you, wasn't it?" she said in a low voice. "You sent Carl Beck. To stop us from getting to you."

"Beck seems to have been a clumsy oaf," he said. "I asked some old comrades to do me a favor. I wanted neat work. To save money on a professional, they used a known criminal, a psychopath. That angered me."

"Beck almost killed my mother. He almost killed me."

"I spared your mother's life in England in 1960. It was a mistake. Had I killed her then, none of this would have happened. A moment of weakness."

"If you're not Joseph Krasnowsky," she said in a low voice, "why did you kill David Godbold?"

"That was incidental. A dress rehearsal for Lefkowitz."

"What do you mean?"

"I needed to see whether I could pass as Krasnowsky. Godbold was the ideal guinea pig. He believed me. His reaction convinced me I could deceive Lefkowitz, too." He peered up at the sky through the windshield. "I thought I had done with the Krasnowskys, root and branch. I did not calculate on a bastard daughter left in Italy. I certainly did not calculate on a diary. Until yesterday, I could not fathom why your mother should have begun this odyssey. I never understood. That fool Beck never found it. Another costly mistake."

She felt empty. "Will you tell me who you are?"

"No," he said calmly. "I am who I am. That is all."

The orange streaks were becoming more intense, lighting up the great black dome of the heavens.

"By the way," he said conversationally, "how was it the boy met such an unfortunate end? You don't strike me as resourceful enough to fight off a psychotic rapist."

"A truck came down the hill suddenly," she said wearily. "I got out of the way. He slipped. There was heavy snow. He couldn't get up. The truck couldn't stop."

Kaplan lifted his chin and laughed with genuine amusement. "Like a raccoon on the highway, yes?"

She remembered that dark, smashed shape in the snow, and was silent.

They were now some five miles from the ranch. It was getting light enough to see that they were heading toward a low clump of hills where a few spindly palo verde trees were silhouetted against the coming dawn.

"Where are you taking me?" she asked, hearing her voice shake.

"To conduct an experiment. A most interesting experiment."

"You're going to kill me."

"Don't be hysterical."

Silence fell. Anna looked vacantly out of the window at the lightening sky. The stars were fading, leaving the heavens as empty as the earth.

Kaplan pulled off the road, heading toward the rise of earth. She could see a long, low structure half-hidden among the palo verdes. The glowing sky was reflected in its dew-beaded tin roof.

Kaplan pulled up nearby and switched off the engine. The silence was absolute, vast and majestic. She tried to cling to the seat, resisting like a child, but Ramón grasped the leather thong that linked her wrists and dragged her out of the Land Rover with casual brutality, so that she sprawled on the earth. He hauled her to her feet and thrust her toward the building.

It was made of prefabricated, joined sections. Slit windows, covered with chicken-wire mesh, had been cut high up in the board walls. Pipes rose out of the corrugated tin roof at intervals. It appeared to be a series of pens in which some kind of animals, perhaps pigs, might be kept.

Ramón held her while Kaplan slotted a key into the padlock that secured the door. He pulled it open. A faint ammoniacal smell drifted out. Then she knew what kind of animals Kaplan kept in this place.

Blind terror made her try and break free of the huge Indian. She fought wildly for a moment, gasping. Then Ramón cuffed her across the head, a blow powerful enough to drop her to her knees, her senses reeling, her brain throbbing. He yanked her upright.

"Don't cut her wrists with the thongs, Ramón," Kaplan said warningly. "Bring her through."

In a nightmare daze, she was pushed into the shed. They passed through a small, neatly kept laboratory, steel benches covered with equipment and glass tubing. At the other end of the laboratory, Kaplan paused to start a compact generator. It purred into life, and fluorescent lights glimmered overhead for a moment before igniting.

A faint squeaking and rustling started up. Beyond, she saw cages filled with mice, hundreds of mice, their furry bodies scuttling among clean sawdust. Food for what he kept in the pens.

"Don't touch anything," Kaplan advised her calmly. "Don't make any foolish noises. Come and see my babies."

Ramón thrust Anna forward so that she was hemmed in, with Kaplan ahead of her and the Indian behind her. She saw that Kaplan wore a heavy hunting knife strapped to his belt.

Deeper into the shed, the air was warm and humid. They entered a narrow, dimly lit corridor. To either side were cages three feet deep, covered with sloping glass lids. She knew what she would see in the cages, but she could not tear her eyes away.

The cages were lined with gravel or sand. Some contained only one snake, coiled immobile or half-buried in the sand. Others contained two or three, some moving sluggishly, disturbed by their footsteps along the board floor.

Kaplan's head swiveled from side to side, peering into each cage. In the dim light, she saw there was a smile on his twisted mouth. "My babies," he crooned. "My beautiful babies."

Fear had done something to her spine: it seemed frozen, so she walked with the stiffness of a marionette, her jaw clamped shut, her arms pressed to her sides to avoid even touching the cages.

Kaplan stopped to lift a sheet of paper pinned to a clipboard, which hung over one of the cages. She saw that all the cages had similar clipboards hanging over them.

"This is a special friend." He said, turning to her. "*Crotalus tigris*. The tiger rattlesnake. One of the least-understood of rattlesnakes. I flatter myself that I have contributed more to the natural history of this species than any other scientist." He raised the glass lid gently. Anna shrank back as he reached in and lifted out the snake. It was banded buff and gray, the thick coils winding lazily around Kaplan's arm. He tilted the small, neat head up so he could look into the little black eyes. The snake's tongue flickered. "Yes," he whispered, with that strange sibilance. His expression was that of a lover. "My special friend. My special baby."

The tip of the tail lifted and quivered, giving out a soft rattle. Anna huddled against Ramón.

"Are you afraid?" Kaplan asked her. "No need to be. She is sleepy and content. And she does not belong to one of the excitable breeds. Touch her."

He reached the snake toward her face. She gripped the cloth of Ramón's overalls, as if she could bury herself in him. She squeezed her eyes shut in horror.

The snake's skin was cool. The scales were smooth, though their tips were sharp and scraped a little as Kaplan brushed her cheek with the coils. Frozen, Anna felt the roots of her hair stir, gooseflesh ripple across her body in panic. She heard the whirring rattle close by her ear, heard the rustle as its coils slithered together.

"She's a beautiful creature," he whispered. "Like you."

She waited for the curved fangs to pierce her flesh, her heart bursting. He withdrew the snake at last. Her eyelids fluttered open in time to see him lower it back into its pen and shut the lid. They moved on. Now her legs were wobbling with weakness, her stomach heaving.

"Look." He lifted another lid and drew out another handful of coils. "*Crotalus ruber*. The red diamond rattlesnake. Is she not handsome?" He held the reptile out for her to see. White speckles glimmered on brick-red flanks. The snake writhed irritably in Kaplan's hands, its rattle sounding in sharp bursts. The head reared up quickly, weaving in front of her face. Behind it, Kaplan smiled, the pink lower lip contorting. Adrenaline was rushing into her system again, driving her heart ever faster, so that her lungs were heaving to keep up with the wild drumming of her blood.

"Please take it away," she whispered.

He clicked his tongue. "You will offend her, and she is a guest here. Her range does not extend as far as New Mexico. She likes the fresh coastal zone. That is why we have to keep her dwelling cool and moist."

He put the snake back and it slithered into a corner, coiling up angrily.

"I have given my life to them," he said as he led the way deeper into the shed. "They were waiting for me here. At first, I am ashamed to say, I would kill them when I found them. I was their enemy. Then, one day, I underwent a conversion."

He paused, leaning on a frame to stare down through the glass. The cage contained three snakes, all active. She stared, transfixed, at the winding and unwinding spirals, the swaying heads and flickering tongues. The bold geometric patterns were in contrast to the sinuous movements, producing an almost hypnotic effect. "But you will not be interested in the details of my conversion," he went on. "Suffice it to say that since that day, I have made them my study and my vocation. Almost, were it not too whimsical a concept, my religion." He looked at her face. "Have you any idea how many ancient cults took the snake as their symbol?" He laughed softly. "Your expression shows only disgust and fear. You feel only negative emotions. You understand nothing."

"I'm terrified of snakes," she said in a low voice.

"You are ignorant," he said, harsh contempt in his voice. "This young lady is pregnant. See." He opened the lid and lifted out a large, banded snake. He held it over his head, peering up at the fat belly. "She's a live bearer. She has at least ten children. Look. You can see them moving inside her. Extraordinary, isn't it? Her venom is deadly.

It can kill a horse." He replaced the snake. "But this is the one we have come to see. The queen of this place."

He opened another cage and reached in. The snake he drew out was huge, five feet long and as thick as Kaplan's arm. It was spectacularly marked, dark diamonds stamped on a white background, vivid black and white stripes emphasizing the tapering rattle. As he lifted it, it began to move restlessly, the muscular body looping around his hands, the flat, blunt head bobbing. "She is heavy." He smiled, gathering the coils in his arms. "Few of her family reach such a size. This is *Crotalus atrox*. Do you understand Latin?"

"No," she mouthed, mesmerized by the fluid power of the huge snake.

"Of course not. You are a child of the modern era, ignorant of your roots. *Atrox* means 'the terrible one.' A compliment to the power of her venom." He stroked the snake's thick body lovingly before taking its neck in a firm grasp. The snake's head was spade-shaped, bigger than his fist, the long black tongue ribboning in and out of the lipless mouth. The rattle clattered so loudly that activity began in the other pens, hissing and rattling, the movement of sinuous bodies. Kaplan jerked his head at Ramón. "Move."

The huge man turned, pulling Anna after him as he led the way back out. Kaplan followed, lovingly cradling the rattlesnake in his arms.

Ramón stopped her in the laboratory. She was panting with fear. He unfastened the leather thong on one of her wrists and tied the loose end to a steel ring that had been bolted onto one of the workbenches. Then he pushed her into a chair.

Kaplan followed with the checkered snake. He was smiling dreamily. "Ready?" he asked Ramón.

Ramón grasped Anna's free arm and twisted it up between her shoulder blades. She gasped in agony, hearing the tendons crack. At the same time, he pulled the chair back swiftly. It slid on rollers, jerking to a halt as her left arm snapped flat across the bench. She could not move. Though she now knew what Kaplan was going to do, she could not quite believe it. She tried to scream, but her gullet was too dry for that.

He reached out and pressed his thumb into her throat, feeling for the pulse. "About a hundred and sixty," he said in his soft, serpent's voice. "Perfect."

He lifted the head of the snake, squeezing carefully with his finger and thumb until the jaws opened. The thick body jolted in protest, the rattle exploding in rage. He controlled it with strong arms.

Anna saw the fangs, two inches long, curving out of the mauve interior of the snake's mouth. An expression of intense concentration on his face, Kaplan brought the snake's head to the naked skin of her left forearm, struggling to keep the rest of the writhing body clamped under his arms.

Anna, too, was fighting for her life, kicking wildly. But she could not move her upper body. Ramón's lock on her right arm was agonizing, his strength monumental. With her other arm stretched flat on the bench, she was helpless. She jerked her head back, trying to butt his face, but only struck the mahogany solidity of his chest.

"No!" she screamed. *"No!"*

"This is probably the most toxic of the species," Kaplan said, intent on his task. "I have been milking her venom for two years now. I use it in my experiments. I believe that regular draining not only increases the volume secreted, but intensifies the toxicity. You will soon be in a position to confirm whether I am correct. Ah. There."

He had aligned the razor-tipped fangs with the blue veins that ran down the inside of her left forearm. There was a little bead of liquid at the tip of each point now. With a sudden snap of his wrist, he dug the fangs into her flesh.

A scream of horror and grief tore out of her lungs.

Carefully, working the snake's head from side to side, he forced the fangs deeper into the vein. A burning pain surged through her left arm, as though white-hot nails were in her flesh. When the fangs had penetrated half an inch, he shifted his grip. Placing his thumb on the back of the spade-shaped head, Kaplan began pressing rhythmically, eyes narrowed. She realized he was pumping the snake's venom into her. The burning intensified; her whole arm was on fire. A sudden wave of nausea swept through her. The fight went out of her, conquered by despair. She became faint, her muscles relaxing, her head sagging forward.

It all became unreal. As though watching something happening on a television screen, she saw Kaplan insert the tip of his little finger cautiously into the rattlesnake's mouth, probing. He nodded in satisfaction. "She has given all she had to give. The ducts are empty."

He pulled the fangs smoothly out of Anna's flesh and studied the snake's mouth intently. "Did I hurt you, my pretty?" he crooned, caressing the thick coils. "I apologize. You did well. You did wonderfully, my queen." Still stroking the snake, without looking at Anna, he went back into the pens.

She was sagging now, her mouth open, her cheeks wet with tears she had not known she was shedding. She was dazed. Two beads of dark blood had welled in the puncture marks. The beginnings of a yellow bruise had already appeared around them.

Ramón released her other arm at last, and it dropped limply by her side. He stood back, staring down at her with impassive eyes in which a little curiosity now dwelt.

She sat there, apathetic now, knowing it was too late to fight, too late to do anything that would save her. The raging heat was flowing up her arm into her shoulder, around her heart.

Kaplan came back from the pens, empty-handed. "You will not die immediately," he said, black eyes emotionless. "I am sorry, but I cannot be more specific than that. It varies so much from individual to individual. The amount of venom injected, the site of the wound, the species of snake—all have a bearing. It will be an interesting scientific experiment to see how long it takes you." He checked his watch. "We will deal with Westward as and when the necessity arrives. But you had to be dealt with first. You are the immediate enemy. I'm sure you understand that." He stooped to examine the bite, pressing his fingertips into the flesh, massaging the swelling that had started to appear. "You were very foolish, you see. Foolish and unlucky. You were driving at night. Your car ran out of gas on a quiet road. You decided to walk to town. You met with our terrible friend and were unlucky enough to receive a bite. Foolishly, in your panic, you began to run. That only pumped the venom more thoroughly around your system. It was not long before you were overcome. Deaths by snakebite are so tragic. They only increase the ignorant hostility of man." He smiled at her. "It is as well the rattlesnakes do not generally share man's habitat, is it not? *Atrox* is a desert dweller. She loves to lie among the Joshua trees, where man seldom ventures. Your car is already conveniently parked at just such a spot."

Anna was sobbing quietly, her mind a blur of terrors. She was confused, sometimes not knowing quite where she was or what had happened to her. Kaplan's sibilant voice drifted in and out of her consciousness gently, soothingly.

He reached out and unfastened the leather thong that had secured her left arm to the bench. "Let's go and watch the sunrise."

They led her out of the laboratory. The east was flushed angrily
with pink and orange. Long, unearthly shadows pooled and streaked
the desert. The sight of the dawn dispelled her apathy, making her lift
her head.

"Now," Kaplan said, releasing her. "Let us see how resourceful
you are."

She was free. She took a few stumbling steps away from them,
but found her legs were too weak to run. The bite was throbbing heavily
now, hammer blows that seemed to be knocking on the bones of her
arm.

Her mind cleared for a moment, and she clawed at her T-shirt,
pulling it clumsily up over her head. The two men watched her in silence
as she worked it off. She sank onto her knees, wearing only her denims
and brassiere, and tried to tear a strip off the T-shirt. The material only
stretched, and her wounded arm was starting to feel numb. There was
little strength in her fingers.

"Good," Kaplan said approvingly, nodding. "Very good, Miss
Kelly."

She tore at the material with her teeth, trying to rip a hole in it.
Her breath was rasping in her lungs. Finally, she felt the material shred.
Using her fingers, she worked the hole bigger, finally managing to tear off
the circular strip around the hem. A wave of weakness washed over her,
beating down her strength. She fought it with the wildness of panic.

She managed to loop the strip of material around her elbow.
Thrusting her finger into it, she twisted until it pulled tight over the
vein, making a rough tourniquet.

"Good," Kaplan said again. "The classic approach." He was
smiling, enjoying the show. The massive Indian watched with no display
of emotion, leaning against the shed with his arms folded across his
chest. She staggered to her feet and hunted around her for something
to push through the tourniquet and hold it in place. At last she found
a twig. She pushed it under the loop of material, twisting even tighter.

The hammer blows were heavier now, hurting badly as the
trapped blood beat against the veins she had closed. She lifted the puncture to her mouth and sucked on the bite as hard as she could.

"Excellent," Kaplan murmured.

A surprising amount of fluid, salty and bitter, rushed into her mouth. She choked and spat it out in a red spray, lifting her left arm to suck again, then again. The flow of liquid stopped. She had drained the wound, and nothing more was coming out.

Kaplan was laughing softly. "I think we can leave Miss Kelly to her own devices for a while, Ramón," he said. "Let's get everything ready."

"Yes, Mr. Kaplan."

They turned away from her, Kaplan going back into the shed, Ramón to the Land Rover. The purr of the generator died. The lights went out. Kaplan emerged from the shed and padlocked the door. The Indian returned from the Land Rover with a shotgun slung over his shoulder, his straw broom in his hands. They both ignored her.

Recovering from another wave of dizzy unreality, Anna turned and began to walk toward the little hillocks. She hardly knew what she was doing, only that she had to get away from the two men. But she had hardly made ten paces before a violent bout of nausea stopped her in her tracks and doubled her over. There was nothing left in her stomach. Though the vomiting was violent, she managed only to retch up a few strands of saliva. She could not walk any farther, and sank back onto her knees.

The orange rim of the sun had edged up over the distant horizon.

The Indian was meticulously sweeping away their tracks with the broom. Erasing any trace that she had ever been there. Backing away, sweeping behind him, he edged over to where Anna knelt. She looked up at him blindly. Something was wrong with her breathing now. Her lungs felt heavy. Her diaphragm was laboring to draw the air in.

"Come," he said. He reached for her. With some last vestige of energy, she twisted away from him and lurched to her feet. Muttering something under his breath, he grasped her arm and pulled her to his side. She was starting to gasp a little, the hammer blows beating into her breast. Carefully sweeping away their tracks as they went, the Indian forced her back toward the Land Rover.

"Ready, Mr. Kaplan."

"Wait." Kaplan was standing motionless. He had pulled off his wool hat, and his silver head was cocked to one side.

The Indian stopped at once and listened, too. "Jeep," he said quietly.

Unaware of the significance of what they were saying, she stood with her head hanging, laboring for breath. Rough hands seemed to be clutching her lungs, squeezing them. Her left arm and shoulder were numb. She could no longer move them.

"Did you bring another gun?" Kaplan asked.

"No. Just the one."

"Pass me the woman."

Ramón thrust Anna over to Kaplan. His fingers grasped her arm tightly. He reached to his side and pulled the hunting knife out of its sheath, the broad, razor-edged blade glinting in the cool light.

Ramón unslung the shotgun and worked the pump action with a clatter. "Here he comes," the Indian muttered.

There was a distant rumble. Anna lifted her head slowly. Something was coming along the dirt track toward them. The rising column of dust from its wheels glowed amethyst in the calm dawn air.

"Now," Kaplan said calmly, "what the hell is this?"

She had been too dazed to feel any hope, but as the Jeep approached, her heart lurched. There was a single occupant, silhouetted through the windshield.

The Jeep drew to a halt some twenty yards away. The door opened and a tall figure stepped out. Darkness rushed before Anna's eyes.

"Philip," she screamed.

Philip Walked Slowly toward them.

Ramón was standing with his legs spread, the shotgun at his shoulder, aimed at Philip's chest.

"Stop right there," Kaplan said softly. Philip obeyed. The sun was halfway above the horizon now, turning from crimson to orange. The world was infinitely silent but for her sobbing, a tiny voice in the wilderness. Philip had come for her. He had heard her silent screams in the night. But what could he do in the face of a shotgun?

"Why did you come without me?" he asked her gently.

She shook her head and lifted her left arm, showing him the tourniquet. There were dark streaks running up the veins now, and the flesh was badly swollen. Her hand looked like a rubber glove that had been inflated, fingers protruding stiffly from a bloated palm. She saw his expression change. "Rattle—snake—bit—me."

"Untie the tourniquet," he said quietly.

"No!" She fought for breath. "Poison—blood—"

"You'll lose the arm." His voice was still quiet. His dark blue eyes met hers, urging the command. "Untie it."

Her chest heaving, she obeyed, numbed fingers fumbling with the knots. Kaplan made no effort to stop her. He held the hunting knife in his free hand, slowly turning the blade from side to side. "So," he said softly. "Mr. Philip Westward puts in an appearance at last. How interesting."

"You may as well tell your man to put the gun down, Kaplan. The state police are following close behind me."

"I don't think so. You have not contacted the police. That is not what you would have done, Mr. Westward. Whoever you are, the police would only get in your way."

"He's not—Joseph—Krasnowsky," Anna gasped out.

"No," Philip said, his eyes turning to her for a moment. Their expression was intent. "He's not Joseph Krasnowsky."

"Who—is—he?"

"His name is Klaus von Jena." He turned his eyes back to Kaplan. "He was the son of a Weimar chicken farmer, but he had a distinguished war career. He led a special detachment within the SS *Totenkopfverbande*. The Death's Head Units. His special responsibility was rounding up and exterminating fleeing Jews in the Eastern Zone."

"A—Nazi!" she gasped.

"Yes. A senior Nazi. In 1943, he was made one of the youngest *Obersturmführers* in the SS. Even though the SS was short of officers by then, it was quite an achievement."

"Do go on," Kaplan said in his softly hissing voice. Ramón was motionless behind the shotgun, its twin muzzles pointed unwaveringly at Philip.

"He is personally responsible for the deaths of tens of thousands of people," Philip said in the dispassionate tones of a judge. "As an added distinction, von Jena is credited with such extraordinary brutality that even the SS were troubled. An investigation was launched against him early in 1944, and its findings were submitted to an SS court. Though you were never put on trial. Were you, Klaus?"

"However, I lost my promotion to *SS Oberführer*." Kaplan smiled.

"They made it up to him, Anna. They made him deputy com-

mandant of Varga concentration camp. You saw his picture there. He
was younger then, of course, and didn't have the scar."

Anna turned her head at last to look at the man who held her
arm. His mouth was twisted in a quiet smile, the mane of hair glowing
silver in the dawn light. The black eyes were hooded. The grip of his
fingers on her arm did not ease.

"If the Russians had caught him," Philip went on, his eyes never
leaving the old man's face, "he would have been hanged with the rest.
But he was too clever for that. He and some of his brother officers
formed an escape organization when the end was approaching. They
called it *Quecksilber*. Each man matched himself with a real identity,
taken from an American or British national held in their concentration
camps. Using those papers, posing as POWs in the chaos of the final
days, they knew they would be able to make their way through any but
the most scrupulous of checks. Von Jena chose Joseph Krasnowsky."

"The physical resemblance was close," Kaplan hissed through
his deformed lips. "That was a prerequisite."

Anna stared at the old man in an emotion beyond horror. She
had known there was a great evil here. She had simply been too stupid,
too innocent to guess at its name.

She thought suddenly of the paintings she had seen. She recognized that style, now. The sterile, inflated style of the Third Reich.
The style that marked everything this man had done.

Kaplan was hefting the heavy knife in his free hand. "You have
been very clever, Mr. Westward. Though I would never have dared to
take Krasnowsky's place so fully under more normal circumstances. The
identities were intended simply to get us through the Russian lines and
into Switzerland or to the Vatican. But I had bad luck."

"The Russians didn't believe your story. They suspected you
were not Joseph Krasnowsky. They'd heard about *Quecksilber*."

"They tortured me for months," Kaplan said quietly. "But they
could not break me."

"So they just held on to you. And then they forgot about you."

The black eyes narrowed. "The Russians forgot about me, as
you put it, for fifteen years. Fifteen years of hell, Mr. Westward. You
cannot imagine what that was like. Even I, in the darkest hours of the
night, cannot comprehend what I went through. It is beyond
comprehension."

"But you survived."

Ramón shifted from one foot to the other, the shotgun still pointed at Philip.

"Oh, yes. I was born to survive. But I got to Switzerland fifteen years too late. The funds we had stored in Zurich were gone. The others had given me up for dead years ago, and gone to new lives in South America. They took it all with them. The gold, the shares, everything. They left me a pistol and a handful of diamonds. Nothing else. There was only one course for me."

"To go to America and claim Joseph Krasnowsky's inheritance."

"*My* inheritance," he said with a touch of sharpness. "I believed I had earned it." He touched the knife to his scarred jaw. "The Russians gave me this before I escaped. It helped greatly. It distracted eyes that would otherwise have examined far too closely. A blessing in disguise. My life has been full of such blessings, Mr. Westward. I was singled out by fate. My father, though you contemptuously call him a mere chicken farmer, saw that, even when I was a boy. That was why I was put forward for the SS. In that vault in Zurich, I had to decide my own fate. It took no more than a moment. The groundwork for my move to America was already laid. The Krasnowsky parents had been eliminated. I had seen to that long before the war ended. Professionals from the American Nazi Party did the work. They were good comrades. Without them, the *Quecksilber* conduit could never have worked so well. The only real obstacle was convincing the administrators of the estate."

"Saul Lefkowitz."

"Exactly. The old Jew lawyer."

"A breathtaking achievement," Philip said softly. "That is what David Lefkowitz called it."

Kaplan inclined his silver head in grave acknowledgment of the compliment. "Bluffing my way through inefficient and chaotic bureaucracy was one thing. Deceiving people who had actually known Krasnowsky was quite another. I experimented on Miss Kelly's grandfather first, of course. That was vitally important. During interrogation, Krasnowsky had told me all about David Godbold. It was necessary to empty the man of every detail about his life, you see. Of course, much of it was painfully tedious. I'd thought Godbold merely another extraneous detail at the time. But I noted it. It was another of those special blessings. Godbold was the perfect person for me to approach before I saw Lefkowitz. I went to England to meet him. I introduced myself as Joseph

Krasnowsky. His reaction was gratifying. He had not the slightest suspicion I was not Krasnowsky. He burst into tears of remorse and shame. He even knelt before me to beg my forgiveness. It made shooting him much easier." He glanced at Anna. "By the way"—he smiled—"I shot Krasnowsky in the same way. One bullet to the back of the neck. He was grateful for the release."

Anna choked on bile. Her chest was laboring ever more heavily. Her diaphragm seemed to be freezing, each breath coming with more difficulty. The rattlesnake venom was paralyzing her lungs.

"And Saul Lefkowitz?"

"He, too, wept." Kaplan laughed softly. "I had gathered confidence by then. I knew that if I could deceive Krasnowsky's wartime comrade, I could deceive a doddering old Jew who had not set eyes on the man for twenty years. I gave a good performance. Oh, yes, the old Jew wept." He looked around the empty horizon. "Your friends the police are a little slow in arriving, Mr. Westward. I don't see them."

"You killed Saul Lefkowitz, too," Philip said. "Didn't you? After you'd persuaded him you were Joseph Krasnowsky, and got the money, you killed him just in case he should have second thoughts."

"The sun's getting high," Ramón said, cuddling his cheek into the stock of the shotgun. "We ought to be moving right along, Mr. Kaplan."

"In a while, Ramón. There is no hurry."

"They gonna find her car pretty soon. They gonna start looking for her."

"Time enough to deal with that. It will be necessary to arrange something for this new contingency." He studied Philip speculatively. "A great pity I no longer have the cyanide spray I used on Lefkowitz. But perhaps the best thing will be to simply shoot him now and leave for South America at once. I have already taken the precaution of transferring sufficient wealth there to make a second retirement comfortable, if not quite as splendid . . . But Mr. Westward has something to tell us first." He was having to hold Anna up now, her weight dragging on his arm. "It is evident why this poor child got herself into this mess. She was engaged in an ill-advised search for the poor defunct Krasnowsky. But you? What is your motivation, Mr. Westward?"

"I have been looking for you all my life," Philip said in a strange, dry voice.

"Indeed. And who sent you? Mossad? Simon Wiesenthal?"

"Nobody sent me."

"Then you are some kind of Jew vigilante?"

"No. I am your son."

The silence was absolute. Anna felt the iron fingers relax around her arm, and she slid to her knees. Heaving for breath, she stared blindly at Philip's taut face, uncomprehending. He was watching the old man.

"My *son*?" Kaplan laughed suddenly, a rough bark. "You're insane. You're a filthy Jew!"

Philip shook his head. His deep blue eyes were calm. "No. I'm a German. I was born Philip Mann in Berlin, in 1945. My mother's name was Lorelei Mann."

Kaplan seemed to shrink physically. "Lori," he whispered.

"Yes," Philip said. "Lori. You remember her, I am sure. She never forgot *you*. She told me all about you while I was a boy. Endless tales. All about the romantic love you and she shared under the shadow of war. That last summer before the end. The sunlight in the trees. The cold wind blowing from the east. You and she on a blanket in the grass. Her grief when you had to go back to the front. She told me all about your heroism. What a brave, gallant German soldier you had been." For the first time, a deep bitterness touched Philip's face. "My poor mother. How she wept for you! She never fully understood what you were. She was too innocent. Too good. Like so many Germans of her generation, she simply could not believe that an officer and a gentleman could do the things you did. She did not believe authority would lie to her. And you were very authoritative, weren't you, in your black uniform, with your medals and your campaign ribbons? You told her you were a hero, and she believed you until the day she died. She told me you had been killed in the war, of course. Later on, when I was older, I learned other things about you. I read all about your military career. Your *true* military career. I won't try and describe my feelings, Klaus. I leave you to imagine them. There was no shortage of information for a boy who wanted to find out what his daddy did in the war. You're in all the books about the SS. Most of the studies on the persecution of the Jews mention you. You even have your own entry in the *Encyclopedia of the Holocaust*. I know it by heart. Most important of all, I learned that you were not dead, after all."

Kaplan's face was now white and strained, the black eyes staring. "Lori's son," he said, speaking with difficulty, spittle flecking his lips.

"*Your* son."

"Lori? Is she alive?"

"She died when I was sixteen."

Kaplan made a guttural sound, his face creasing. *"Ach . . ."*

"I buried my mother in our little village in Germany and came to America. I wanted to leave the past behind me. Leave *you* behind me. Find a new life, out of the shadows. But you would not let me go. For years you came to me every night in terrible dreams. No matter what I did, no matter what success I achieved, you were there to pollute it, drench it all in blood." His face wore an expression Anna had seen on it once before, of icy coldness, of a vision into black interstellar space. "I am sure, Klaus, that you cannot have thought half so much of all the human beings you murdered than I have done. I sometimes think I have experienced the death of every one of them, the agony of every one, for your sake. You say you spent fifteen years in hell. But I have spent my whole life in a worse hell than you could ever imagine. Sharing your guilt. Knowing I was the son of a man as evil as you. Knowing I had your blood in my veins. Wondering whether the same evil had infected me, whether I, too, would become like you. When I could bear it no longer, I knew I had to find you."

Through the dark clouds that had started to billow through her mind, Anna saw it at last, saw the strange resemblance in Kaplan's features that had haunted her. Not her own face. *Philip's* face. Philip's high forehead. Philip's handsome mouth, twisted out of shape by the scar. Philip's body, too, broad-shouldered and tall, with quick, decisive movements.

Pity and horror filled her as she understood at last—saw the evil shadow that had haunted Philip's whole life. At last she saw why he had lied to her; at last she could understand the terrible wound that had impelled him to seek this man.

You don't share his guilt, she wanted to scream at him. *You are not responsible for that.* But she could not speak.

Philip's eyes met hers, and he nodded slowly. "I lied to you, Anna. I'm sorry. I don't know what else I could have done. It was a tragic situation. Your mother was looking for Krasnowsky, I was looking for von Jena. I knew about *Quecksilber,* and that von Jena had probably used that route to escape. But I could find no trace of him in South America or anywhere else. When the KGB files were finally opened, it started to dawn on me what might have happened: that he might never have reached the West at all, that the Russians might have kept him." He glanced back at the old man. "That was something else you didn't bargain on, wasn't it? You thought the Russians would be in awe of your American papers, your expertly rehearsed tale. It took me a few months to connect von Jena's name with Joseph Krasnowsky's. Last year, in Moscow, I finally spoke to Alexei Feodorev, who conducted the initial KGB interrogations in 1945 and 1946. Feodorev had always believed that 'Joseph Krasnowsky' was in reality a senior SS man, though he could never prove it. That was why the Russians never released him. He told me that your mother had spoken to him, too, a few weeks earlier. He had not confided his suspicions in her, though he had hinted at them. He gave her the name *Quecksilber,* hoping she would find her way to the truth. I went to your mother as quickly as I could. We needed to talk. She had to know the terrible possibility that hung over her. In my stupidity, I did not suspect that she could be in danger. But she was. And it was already too late." He gestured at the old man. "The spider had already sensed someone tugging on his web. The neo-Nazi organizations are very good at finding out when one of their cult heroes is in danger of exposure. They had warned him, and he had already used his contacts among those madmen to have her attacked, her papers ransacked. I had to continue the search at your side. I knew you, too, might be in the same danger, and that it was my duty to protect you. But I could not tell you the terrible truth until I was certain . . . "

Kaplan's lips shook as he interrupted. *"Ist das Gottes Wahrheit? Bist du Lori's Sohn?"*

Philip inclined his dark head slowly. *"Ja. Ich bin dein Sohn."*

Ramón had lowered the shotgun now and was staring with open mouth at the two men. Anna's lungs were burning, her breathing little more than choking gasps. She could hardly hold herself upright. She opened her mouth to call to Philip, but could not form the words. He moved forward instinctively, reaching out, but Kaplan spoke sharply.

"No."

Ramón shuffled a little, lifting the shotgun half-heartedly. Philip stopped, his face taut as he took in Anna's agony.

"Respiratory distress," Kaplan said, almost absently. "Characteristic of *crotalus* venom. Krasnowsky's granddaughter does not have long to live."

"You can't let her die like this," Philip rasped.

The old man looked up emptily. "Why not?"

"You must keep antivenom," Philip said harshly. "You're an expert. You can save her!"

"She is a Jewess. What does she matter?"

"I love her. And I am your son."

The two men stared at each other for a long while, eyes locked. The sun was over the horizon now, a scarlet ball of fire. In the red light, the man whose true name was Klaus von Jena looked suddenly old. The knife trembled in his hands. The harsh stare of the black eyes had grown blurred.

"My son," he whispered. "All these years. I never knew. And at last you have come to me in the guise of an accuser. Your mouth filled with Jew obscenities. Your eyes blinded to the truth."

"The truth?"

"The truth about National Socialism."

"There was never any truth in National Socialism," Philip said, his eyes flickering restlessly from his father to Anna. "I know. I studied it for twenty years, trying to make sense of it. At last I understood that there was no sense in it. Only evil."

Slowly, von Jena drew back his shoulders and lifted his chin. *"Es machts nichts,"* he said slowly. An implacable expression hardened his face. "It makes no difference. What are you to me?"

"Nothing," Philip said, almost wearily. "As you are nothing to me. That is what I came to find out."

Von Jena spoke in a slow hiss. "Kill him, Ramón."

Anna saw Philip suddenly reach behind his back, dropping to a crouch. His hands came forward again, grasping a heavy black revolver. She saw the blaze of yellow, heard the deep thuds through the thunder that was roaring in her ears.

Ramón, an expression of astonishment on his broad face, was now sitting on the ground, the shotgun slipping through his fingers, his overalls stained with dark splotches. He stared at his own chest for a moment. Then, blood spilling down his chin, he slumped sideways and lay still.

Von Jena uttered a harsh cry, like the shriek of an eagle. He grasped Anna's hair, jerking her head back. He laid the razor edge of the hunting knife across her throat, glaring up at Philip with wolf's eyes. "I'll kill her!" he screamed.

"No," Philip said urgently, the revolver lowering at once, *"don't!"*

"What did you come for?" There was torment in the old man's voice. The knife edge quivered against Anna's throat. "What did you come for, boy?"

"Don't hurt her!"

"Answer me," von Jena screamed.

"I came because I had to!"

"But what for? To kill me?"

"Put the knife down." Philip was trembling, the revolver pointing at the ground. "She's my life. Don't hurt her."

An incredulous expression crossed von Jena's face. "You give your life to a Jewess?"

"She's my life!" His voice shook. "Put the knife down."

With unexpected strength, von Jena began dragging Anna toward Ramón's corpse, the knife grazing her throat. "You should—not—have come," he panted. She could now hear the German consonants beneath the neutral accent. "You made—a bad—mistake."

"Stop," Philip commanded, moving forward.

"You—came—to kill me—for a Jewess." He grunted with the effort of dragging Anna. "Now—you will—pay."

"Stop!"

Von Jena released Anna suddenly and grasped at the shotgun that lay at Ramón's side. *"Bastard,"* he screamed in German.

He swung the shotgun up. The blast was ear-splitting, sparks exploding from the muzzle. Anna saw claws tear Philip's shirt open, saw him flung back with outspread arms. He stumbled to one knee, his head bowed. An instant flood of dark blood darkened his chest.

Von Jena stood pointing the shotgun at him, panting like a wolf. "Stand up," he gasped. *"Stand up!"*

Slowly, Philip lifted his head. His eyes were clouded, his face spattered with his own blood. He looked at von Jena. He lifted the revolver in a hand now wet and red and pulled the trigger.

Von Jena's body jerked and fell. The shotgun clattered on the rocks. The second barrel fired with a roar, the shot scattering among the rocks. The echo rolled around the hills like thunder, diminishing into silence.

Philip staggered forward, throwing the revolver aside. He crouched over Anna, cupping her face in his hands. "Anna," he said desperately. *"Anna!"*

She tried to speak, but could only form one word with her lips: "Philip . . ."

He ran over to von Jena, who was huddled on one side like a bundle of rags. He rolled the old man over onto his back. The black eyes were open, staring up at Philip.

"Antidote," Philip shouted at him. "Where do you keep it?"

Von Jena's chest heaved, his neck arching back. He twisted around to stare at Anna. Their eyes locked, each knowing the other was dying.

"Where?" Philip sobbed, grasping von Jena's shirt and lifting him up. *"Where do you keep the antidote?"*

The old man looked up into his face. His hand reached up and grasped Philip's hair, dragging his head forward. For a long while he stared into Philip's eyes, searching, devouring. Then his fingers released their grip on his son's hair and trailed down Philip's cheek, leaving a crimson track. His face twisted, the scarred mouth opening. *"Echt,"* he said in a guttural voice. *"Ganz echt . . ."*

"Father, please," Philip whispered. "Where is it?"

"In—the—laboratory," von Jena said. "Yellow box."

Von Jena's head dropped back into the sand as Philip leaped forward and ran to the door of the shed. The old man's legs began to quiver in the dance of death.

Anna turned her head away and then lay motionless, her chest unmoving. The sky overhead was a clear, pellucid blue. The color of purity. She felt the sun touch her skin, a warm caress.

She could hear Philip smashing the door with his heel. It was all over. All the tortuous paths of their lives had led to this point. The tangled threads had finally formed the pattern of the web. The truth was naked at last. There was nowhere else to go, no more roads to travel, no more shadows to flee.

There was no breath in her lungs, but her cheeks were wet.

She was crying silent, bottomless tears of sorrow; grieving for her mother, for Evelyn and David Godbold; for herself; for Philip Westward; and for Joseph Krasnowsky.

Epilogue:

"SOME OTHER PLACE"

1 9 9 3

NORTHUMBERLAND

"Yes," Kate said. "She's fine. Yes, I'll tell her. Thank you."

She put the telephone down and walked out onto the terrace where Evelyn sat in her rocking chair, enjoying the afternoon sunlight. Evelyn looked up at her.

"Who was it?"

"Anna's editor in Miami."

Evelyn smiled faintly, looking over at Philip and Anna, who sat holding hands at the edge of the parterre, lost in one another. "If he thinks she'll ever go back to work on his newspaper, he's in for a disappointment. That young man doesn't ever intend to let her go."

"No, I don't think McKenzie expects that anymore. He wanted me to pass on a piece of news to her about the Haitian surgeon."

"Levêque?"

Kate nodded. "He's apparently left his fortune to found a clinic for sick children in Pétionville. It's to be called the André Levêque Foundation."

Evelyn held a rosebud in her hands, cut for her by Anna. She lifted it to her lips. "Do you think she'll be pleased?"

"He thought it would help her round things off in her own mind. You know she was upset about the man's suicide."

"She's had more important things on her mind lately." Evelyn reached for Kate's hand. "We all have."

The two women smiled into one another's eyes as their fingers twined.

How close they had all come to destruction, Kate thought. How dreadfully close.

Her own body was still not fully healed, though it was strong again. She faltered sometimes as she walked or lifted objects, and sometimes she groped for words that should have sprung easily to her lips. Small things. Very small things. Despite Ram Singh's assurances that she would fully recover all her faculties in time, she still had no direct memories of anything that had happened between her mother's diary arriving in Vail and her own recovery in hospital; she only knew the full story because they had told her. Perhaps that was for the best. She had been unable to give evidence in the investigations that continued in Colorado, rounding up the savage old men who had paid Carl Beck to attack her and Anna.

The important thing was that she had survived. Thank God, they had all survived their separate and joint ordeals.

Evelyn continued to survive the illness that stalked her. With the grim strength of will that had characterized everything she had done, she was holding on. The summer had blossomed, and she was still in life. She would hold on until the end, whenever it came, their matriarch, their guide.

Anna had survived the horror in the desert. Philip Westward had arrived just in time to save her; after a few days in the hospital, close to the brink, she had pulled through. They had still not told Kate all the details of what had happened in New Mexico. Perhaps they never would. Perhaps that, too, was for the best. Now, seeing her daughter's beauty glowing in the golden sun of an English summer, seeing the happiness and life that radiated from her as never before, Kate knew that Anna had done more than survive. She had emerged from the shadows into the full glory of her womanhood, the full beauty of her promise.

Philip had survived, too. His darkness had perhaps been the deepest and most mysterious of all. He had killed his father, a strange and terrible fate for a man to meet. She knew it had taken him many months to cope with that knowledge; she also knew that without Anna, he might not have survived at all. He drew on her strength as she drew on his. They were in perfect symbiosis. Born for each other.

They were so much in love. Watching Anna now as she reached up to stroke Philip's cheek, Kate felt with a pang of distant sorrow that neither she nor Evelyn had ever known such love. It had not been their lot.

But they could experience it through the children. Fate had been kind to them in that. Their lives would be warmed by the bright heat of the love between Philip and Anna; and the love that their children, in turn, would bring.

"I'll go and tell her."

She started to move forward, but Evelyn's fingers tightened around her own, stopping her.

"Not yet," Evelyn said softly. "Let's just watch them without disturbing them. They are so beautiful."

Had She And David ever possessed that beauty? She could not remember, though she remembered with diamond clarity that day in 1945 when she had walked along this same terrace with David. So dashing, so romantic, he had seemed to her then. She had looked up into his eyes and known that she was his mate. That destiny had singled her out for him, and him for her.

Even then she had known his faults. They had been so glaringly obvious to her; she had always been able to look into his heart. Poor David. Poor, handsome, weak David.

Could she have done otherwise?

No. The answer was certain. She had loved him. Perhaps not as these bright two loved each other; they had passed through the fire together and emerged purified. She and David had not survived the fire. The clay had cracked, the urn had fallen apart.

But she had loved David in her way. Loved him still, for all his weaknesses, all his failings. They did not matter now.

She would be going to him soon. This reprieve was already over. She had felt the summons within. Soon, in some other place, she would be with him again, to offer him solace, reconciliation, the love he had never valued in life.

Kate was not David's daughter. She had suspected that for so long. Now she knew it for a fact. It did not matter. She had no regrets.

On the contrary. On the contrary. She had been a childless woman. Bringing Kate to England had worked a miracle in her life. By doing so she had given herself what she could never have otherwise had—a family. A life. A future. A posterity.

She was leaving Great Law to Anna. Philip had the money and the will to make the house great again, if that was what he and Anna wanted. If not, they could sell the place. It did not matter. It was their legacy, whatever the blood ties.

She turned her head slowly and glanced at Kate, who was watching Anna and Philip with soft eyes. It has taken me all this time, she thought, to tell my daughter I love her. But I have told her. She knows now. I have accomplished at least that before death.

The Depth Of his love frightened him.

He had never loved like this before. He had never been able. For most of his life, he had lived in the shadows. He still did not know whether those shadows had entirely gone from his life; he scarcely dared believe he could at last be free of them.

But he knew one thing: that the young woman who smiled up at him now would save him. She and no other.

When he had come to America, he had changed his name to Westward, because that was the direction in which he had moved. With the sun. Following its light and heat. It had led him to Anna. It had led him to his roots.

He had never quite known what he would do when he found his father. His imaginings had never gone beyond that. He had searched endlessly, not even knowing what it was he was searching for.

Lately he had come to believe, though he knew it might be no more than folly, that his father had deliberately forced his hand in that wild dawn. That his father had wanted it to end like that.

The shotgun blast had torn his shoulder open, damaging muscles, leaving him with a scar that he would bear until the day he died. But the old man had aimed wide, sparing the heart and lungs. And he had not fired the second barrel, not even when Philip had lifted his own revolver . . .

With his dying words, he had saved Anna's life.

Klaus von Jena had been evil. He had lived with evil, survived by evil, died in evil. Philip was not a religious man in the conventional sense, but he sometimes thought that in his last moments, his father had snatched a few sparks of salvation. Perhaps they had clung to his fingers as he entered the void, a tiny light in the immense darkness.

Perhaps it could have ended no other way than that. His father had stared into his eyes as he died, and said, *"Echt . . . Ganz echt."* Words of quiet approbation. Perhaps of thanks.

His death had been clean and quick. Not the shameful death he had escaped in 1945, kicking at the end of a murderer's rope. A soldier's death. A lucky death. None of the drawn-out humiliation of a trial. Klaus von Jena had never had to face the condemnation of a world in which his deeds had made him infinitely more loathsome than the bright and deadly reptiles he had chosen as his companions in the wilderness.

In the months since New Mexico, Philip's grief had faded. So, too, had the haunting. There were no more ghosts in his dreams. No more rivers of blood. Not anymore.

Only love.

At forty-seven, his life had changed. He was the possessor of a treasure so great he trembled when he looked on it, a treasure that made all the wealth he had accumulated up to now seem like dross.

She was what mattered. She and no other. The more he let her into his heart, the more she dispelled his darkness, brought him into the light, healed him.

He had made her his wife as soon as they had both recovered, terrified that she could somehow slip away from him again. Looking into her dark, glowing eyes now, he did not think there would be any more partings between them.

"I love you," he said softly. "You are my life, Anna."

"You Are Mine," she said.

She did not know how any of them had survived. She could only imagine it had been the strength of their love that had saved them. What else was there in life? Only love. The great redeemer, the great healer. The only future.

There were no scars on her heart, just as there were none on her body. Only love could have had the power to protect her from so much danger.

The profound attachment between them had been strengthened in the final fire, as steel is tempered. It could not break, she knew that now. It would hold them together until they were both old and gray. Their marriage vows had been no more than a formality, next to that knowledge.

She felt the stirring under her heart, the unfolding of a petal within her.

How much she loved him!

How he had suffered!

She would make it up to him. She had sworn that. She would make it up to him very soon, when she placed their first child in his arms, and saw the expression on his face.

Joseph was dead. He lay in a nameless grave in Latvia, unmarked. But not forgotten. And not entirely dead. He lived through her, and through the life she carried in her womb. The life that led from the dark past to the bright future.

"I love you," she said and smiled at him with the brilliant warmth of a woman who had attained redemption for herself and her beloved.

$\mathscr{A}$UTHOR'S $\mathscr{N}$OTE

Forty-five thousand Jews of Riga died, together with up to forty-two thousand others selected for extermination, in a camp at Salaspils, some twenty kilometers from the city of Riga. The camp commandant and other senior officers were captured by the Russians and put on trial for their crimes. They were convicted and hanged. A museum stands on the site of the camp.

To the best of my knowledge, no such organization as the one I have called *Quecksilber* existed, although the use of stolen identity papers by individual high-ranking Nazis, attempting to escape, is documented.